WHAT OTHERS ARE SAYING . . .

From Kirkus Discoveries

First installment of an ambitious sci-fi trilogy plays out global warfare in the not-too-distant future. The wieldy initial volume in Friar's complex and, thus far, engaging trilogy is epic not only in its breadth—weighing in at nearly 700 pages—but in the scope of its inventiveness.

The author tackles a mix of current environmental, social and economic trends, playing out how they might converge in the future. Friar's clairvoyant vision, however, isn't for the faint of heart: A new empire arises, with powerful tyrannical urges that lead to an all-consuming and almost gruesomely pro- phetic third World War. The year is 2039, and the wildly ambitious German ruler Geiseric and his henchmen, "the principles," have—in Hitlerian fash- ion—taken over Central Europe and threaten to parlay their successes into world domination. Friar uses the first two World Wars as the template for his fictional third and, in spite of its eerie familiarity; the plot remains rich with suspense. Book one of this series concerns itself with the efforts of a new group of Allied powers that attempt to drive Geiseric back and stymie his ruthless imperialism.

World War III is that rarest of sci-fi creations: a hugely innovative tale both smart and entertaining. Friar takes on a smorgasbord of arcane topics—from Platonic philosophy to the science of biomimicry—and makes them not only comprehensible but relevant. Such intellectual tangents might prove tedious fare in the hands of a less skilled author, but here supply the novel with depth and texture that will only enhance the reader's experience. Friar's characters are lavishly imagined and his painstakingly crafted observations of human relationships provide a nice balance to the book's scientific and military con- tent. Despite the wide compass of his novel, Friar has an eye for the intimate; he's as good at evoking artisan-like detail as he is at developing imaginative histories. Colossal effort and colossal fun!

From BookReview.com

The Keepers is an eerie, monumental novel. Friar skillfully blends history, and social theory with scientific imagining to portray the rise of the new republic, which has been planned down to the tiniest details. The most ingenious (and in some ways most disturbing) element of the book is the evolution and use of new classes of super weapons developed by the new regime. Geiseric's regime, the Apex, employs high tech bio-mimicry to create war chariots that hover like humming birds, ships that move like sea creatures and tanks that gallop on all fours. *The Keepers* is an impressive piece of speculative fiction—written plausibly, dramatically and comprehensively in prose that is better than one often finds in books of this kind.

From Dante D'Anthony, Contributor, Space Age Magazine Author, *Tales from the Pandoran Age*

Richard Friar's near future drama *The Keepers* reinvents the dynamics of fascism rising again in the world for a new generation. Tirelessly, he weaves historical and political background (often left out by the watered down educational systems of our current day) so even the most pop-culture fed of fans gets some grounding in political science. He manages to cover that ground, and the events of the near future without missing a beat.

His choice of Germany as the epicenter of the rise is ironic, since that in the present day it seems an unlikely candidate for such. Of course, when one writes a parable, one doesn't name the real target. A fine read for the young, and a refreshing review for us a little older, of some of the lessons of history in a clear, prosaic style reminiscent of classic 50s sci fi. At almost 600 pages, it is an ambitious work. Additionally, it's only the first in a continuing series.

From Midwest Book Review

The Keepers: Part I World War III is the first novel in The Keepers series telling of the Apex Empire and its desire to bring the entire world under a single banner, one that wishes to neutralize the chaos of the world through despotic control. Conflict remains all around as the few that could stand against the Apex are slow to do so. A gripping political SciFi thriller, *The Keepers* is a must have for any who enjoy that action and adventure in science fiction.

From Charles Horn, Author, *The Laugh Out Loud Guide*, Emmy-nominated Writer, *Robot Chicken : Star Wars*

The battles especially were top notch, on the order of *Ender's Game*—seriously, the battles were that good.

From Sci-Fi Lists (Top Science Fiction Online)

Set just over two decades from now the new Hitler is a messiah figure named Geiseric. He takes Germany down the path of a utopian dictatorship based on Plato's Republic, enslaving the conquered and keeping them in check with benevolence.

In the face of the high-tech superweapons of the Apex even the United States has little hope as World War III ravages the planet. As with conquered France in World War II, a small but highly-skilled underground resistance movement carries on the fight.

Friar dazzles readers with big battles and saucy science, all driven by an astute sense of history and human motivation. Given the pace of Geiseric's blitzkrieg one suspects that the chinks in his armor might begin to show in the next eagerly anticipated volume.

From B. Pearce, Military Analyst

Friar has an inventive alternate future for the planet. He capitalizes on historical social issues to develop a plausible reality, and populates it with intriguing characters. The necessity of combat drives exceptional blending of machines with animal characteristics. The technical leaps forward required to reach this future seem tantalizingly close.

THE KEEPERS

THE KEEPERS

PART ONE
WORLD WAR III

RICK FRIAR

The Keepers, Part One: World War III, by Richard Friar
Revised Second Edition, 2009

ISBN: 978–0–9796915–2–2

Library of Congress Control Number: 2009910868

A generation which ignores history has no past and no future.
ROBERT HEINLEIN

CONTENTS

Many are recognizing that the 00s has brought us an amazing talent pool of new science fiction writers. Richard Friar is an emerging author increasingly recognized within the sci-fi community. He is a visionary akin to Robert Heinlein, a comparison Friar has often received due to his ability to balance bold and challenging social themes with exciting action sequences and detailed descriptions of futuristic technology. Richard's Trilogy will help us to glimpse into the not-so-distant future and cause us as human's to pause . . . possibly for long enough to regain a new awareness regarding our place and importance in a civil world. That awareness may define our future.

J. A. Heinlein
Publishing Professional

— 1 —

HIDEAWAY

Winter 2039

The dawn light was breaking over a small tropical island and its creatures were stirring to life. The sea was calm, lapping placidly onto the white sand, which had yet to heat up in the sun. Where the dense jungle foliage met the beach, a lone tamarin squatted high up in a sago palm tree, banging a nut into the trunk. As the nut cracked, he triumphantly peeled the shell and used his fingers to dig out the meat. Suddenly, the tiny monkey halted and listened closely. With a disgruntled chatter, he threw his prize to the ground and scampered further up the tree, out of sight amongst the leathery leaves.

Birds scattered from the overhanging tropical foliage as a large group of teenagers sprinted past. Their military cadence, led by the instructor, cut through the humid jungle air in rhythmic unity. They looked a ragged bunch. Tank tops, T-shirts, and athletic shorts were torn to differing degrees and washed out from use. The physical condition of the youths, however, was exceptional. Lean bodies deftly navigated the slick terrain of loose soil and mossy rocks. Negotiating a slippery bed of boulders more cautiously, the group passed under a wide waterfall, using the tunnel created between the descending water and ivy-laden bedrock. The cool mist felt good on their hot skin, but quickly dried as they emerged into the warm air.

The instructor was a large, powerfully-built man in his thirties, with a thick red beard, giving him the semblance of an ancient barbarian. He yelled words of encouragement as he directed them toward a clearing. Still chanting, most of the group was barely winded from the run, though the instructor noticed a younger boy had fallen behind. He barked to the youths to help the boy finish. A lithe girl and well-built young man slowed to take the boy's arms. Placing his arms over their shoulders in support, the two continued at a brisk pace, while the boy's feet dragged limply in exhaustion. The group made their way across the clearing and out onto an expansive white beach. The instructor picked up the drained, red-faced boy, relieving the two youths who were acting as his crutches. Heaving the boy onto his back and pushing himself for pure sport, the instructor sprinted to beat the teens to the finish line.

He made shocking gains across the sand, bearing the boy on his back. His large frame moved with astonishing speed. Accepting the instructor's challenge, the older youths at the front of the group burst forth, running as fast as they could. The two who had helped the tired boy took the lead. They were breathing heavily, arms and legs pumping with exertion. The air on the beach was humid and thick with tropical pollens. Sweat poured off of everyone, but they were used to this type of drill.

With a remarkable final push of force, the instructor beat them to the destination: the jade water of a lagoon that sparkled invitingly in the peaking sun. They dove into its waters stirring up ripples. Within moments, the rest of the group reached the lagoon, everyone joining in with an exuberant splash.

"Good work, kids. We took three minutes off our previous best time. Don't forget to stretch and get the lactic acid out of your muscles," the man commanded with temperate authority, taking in the gorgeous surrounding landscape. A cloudless, azure sky hung like a vast canopy over the emerald jungle. The soft white sand, broken only by the emergence of an occasional crab, seemed to stretch forever, in either direction. The youths bathed in the sparkling morning light, absorbing the sun's warmth, feeding off its revitalizing power.

After about ten minutes, the drill instructor led everyone on a brisk walk through the dim jungle interior. Following a beaten dirt pathway, they passed many homes that were hidden under lush vegetation. There were over three dozen of them, painted different shades of sage, olive, and hunter green and strategically camouflaged with seemingly endless branches and vines. The homes were simple box-shaped structures, some being two stories. The taller ones were still protected from view by the immense foliage of the jungle's formidable ancient trees.

The pathway abruptly ended at a meeting hall about the size of a small church. Like the homes, it too was concealed by overhanging trees and crawling plants that had been planted atop the roof. The outside walls had a sloped façade, giving the appearance of a small hill overgrown with vegetation.

The instructor led his group through sturdy double doors into the simple, yet modernly equipped meeting hall. Unpainted walls and exposed ceiling beams gave it a Quaker starkness. A man in a long, loose, silky shirt and shorts stood at the back wall, warmly eyeing everyone as they came in. His clothes were noticeably less tattered than theirs. Although muscular and very fit, he was slightly shorter than the instructor. His cropped, jet black hair showed signs of gray and there was a mature angularity to his face. But his tanned skin and his general appearance were youthful; he could pass for a man in his late twenties. He had confidence and power in his stride as he slapped five to the instructor.

"Hey, John," he said with a half-hearted smile.

"How's it goin', Mark?" the instructor answered.

"It's going," Mark sighed, knowing his friend would understand the resignation in his tone.

The youths found seats on large sofa chairs and plush couches. Some returned to stretching or meditated quietly, while others lay or sat Indian-style on the carpet. Both adults seemed restless, as if tension loomed just beneath their pleasant exteriors. As they conversed, they kept their voices low and seemed hyper-aware of anyone wandering within earshot.

John exited with a nod in Mark's direction. Mark made his way to a table near the back wall, where he picked up a book titled *The Republic*.

After a moment of appearing lost in thought, Mark began his lecture. "Alright," Mark glanced around at each of his students. "So, does everyone remember what's going on in the book so far?"

Most of the kids replied by saying, "Yes sir," but a few pressed out a hesitant, "No, sir."

Mark smiled at those who shook their head. "It's OK. So, here's the deal," he said, drawing a crude illustration on the electronic display board suspended from the ceiling by thick metal cables. He barely touched the stylus to the board, which was actually a digital screen that registered his movements upon it, displaying the renderings.

"There's a bunch of people sitting in a cave, chained down, facing a wall," he explained, drawing stick figures for people. The kids laughed at his pathetic rendering. He chuckled a bit too.

"These people are watching shadows go by on the wall, but," he raised his pointer finger in emphasis, "they do not know that these are shadows. They think the shadows are real objects." Mark paused to see if his students were following. Content that the youths were engaged, he continued the lesson. "Now, what if these people were suddenly unchained?" He let that thought sink into his students' minds.

"The first person to get up and look around would see that there is a fire behind the people and objects moving in front of that fire. These objects create the shadows on the wall. The person who sees the fire and the objects becomes closer to the truth, but reality is not revealed to him quite yet."

Mark was pleased to see that most of the youths were intrigued by the story. "OK, let's read on," he said, flipping to the page he left off on the previous day.

"Logan," Mark said, "it's your turn to read. You'll be Socrates."

He passed the book to a young man sitting on a couch with two of his peers. Like most of the island's populace, Logan was sun-baked to a russet tan, which complemented the naturally bleached copper and gold streaks in his short, auburn hair. A sharp, penetrating gaze issued from his light brown eyes. He did his best to ignore his best friends, Megan and Adam, who were sitting next to him whispering into each other's ears. Megan's honey blonde hair was coming un-tucked from a ponytail. Strands dangled seductively, shadowing her wide, blue eyes. She conveyed a still anxiety, but her angst decreased palpably in response to Adam's continued whispers. She giggled softly as Adam caressed her thighs, revealed amply by her tiny shorts.

Mark shushed the young couple.

"Megan," he said, "you will read the part of Glaucon."

Logan held the book open on his leg, close to Megan so she could share.

"And suppose once more," Logan read aloud, "that this person is reluctantly dragged up out of the cave and held fast until he is forced into the presence of the sun himself, is he not likely to be pained and irritated? When he approaches the light, his eyes will be dazzled, and he will not be able to see anything at all of what are now called realities."

Megan read her part with detached apathy, her mind clearly brooding over something else. "Not all in a moment."

The rest of the class sat quietly as Logan resumed. "This person will grow accustomed to the sight of the upper world. First, he will see the shadows best. Then, he will gaze upon the light of the moon and the stars and the spangled heaven. And he will see the sky and the stars by night better than the sun or the light of the sun by day?"

"Certainly," Megan replied.

Logan's eyes squinted in concentration as he read. "Last of all he will be able to see the sun, and not mere reflections of it in the water, but he will see the sun in its own proper place."

"Certainly." Megan read in a hushed tone.

"He will then proceed," Logan continued, "to argue that it is the sun which gives the seasons and the years, and is the guardian of all that is in the visible world and the cause of all things."

"Clearly," Megan responded, edgily rolling her eyes, "he would first see the sun and then reason about it."

Logan focused on the words, trying to interpret their meaning. "And when this man remembered his old habitation, in the cave, and the lack of wisdom of his fellow-prisoners, would he not pity them?"

"Certainly, he would," Megan replied. She glanced over at Adam. He shrugged subtly, acknowledging Megan's unspoken concern.

Logan's eyebrows rose, as he began to understand what he was reading. "And if his companions in the cave were in the habit of conferring honors among themselves on those who were quickest to observe the passing shadows and to remark which of them went before, and which followed after, and which were together; and who were therefore best able to draw conclusions as to the future, do you think that the man who escaped would care for such honors and glories, or envy the possessors of them? Would he not say 'better to be the poor servant of a poor master and to endure anything, rather than think as they do and live after their manner?"

"Yes," Megan said, "I think that he would rather suffer anything than entertain these false notions and live in this miserable manner." Adam squeezed Megan's hand.

"Imagine once more," Logan read, "that the person coming suddenly out of the sun was to be replaced in his old situation. Would he not be certain to have his eyes full of darkness?"

"To be sure," Megan replied.

"And if there were a contest," Logan went on, "and he had to compete in measuring the shadows with the prisoners who had never moved out of the cave, while his sight was still weak and not adjusted to the darkness, would he not be ridiculous? Men would say of him that up he went and came back down without his eyes. They would say that it was better not even to think of ascending! And if he tried to loosen the others' chains and lead them up to the light, the people would put him to death."

"Now," Mark interjected, "as I've said before, this was written by Plato after Socrates died. Plato was the most creative and influential of Socrates' disciples. Here, Plato is summing up his views of an ignorant humanity. He sees humans as trapped in the depths and not aware of their own limited perspective. It's the rare individual who escapes the limitations of the cave." His eyebrows perked and he paused to let everyone think upon this. "Through a long, tortuous intellectual journey, he discovers a higher realm and becomes aware that goodness is the origin of everything that exists. Such a person is then the best equipped to govern in society, knowing what is ultimately most worthwhile in life, and not merely arbitrary rituals.

"However," Mark said with emphasis, "being that this enlightened person has seen the sun, when he goes back into the cave he can't see, because it's too dark there in the world of man. So, this enlightened person appears ignorant compared to those he left behind. He appears blind, even though it's he who has seen the truth."

Without warning, a short series of thunderous, crashing booms descended upon the room. The meeting hall rocked in its foundation. Rattled, the youths murmured with curiosity. The youngest kids were relatively calm, with a lot of the boys thinking the sounds were cool. A few of the ones in their late teens and early twenties were tense, though, and they stared at each other with stiff bodies, for they knew more than their younger peers. They flashed angst-ridden eyes at their teacher. Megan burst into tears.

"It's OK," Mark assured them. "How many times do we have to tell you guys, those are just transport planes. Nothing to be afraid of." He was not very convincing today, and he knew it. He wiped perspiration from his forehead and stalled to compose himself, while many of the students shifted nervously in their seats. The mood remained sheathed in tension.

The sonic booms emanating from the sky did not seem to bother Logan. He was still mesmerized by the story. "What's wrong with you two today?" he asked Adam and Megan. Megan wiped tears from her eyes and tried to get the words out, but failed.

"We'll tell you later," Adam whispered. Logan shrugged and turned his attention back to Mark.

"Plato's talking about why they killed Socrates, huh?" he asked.

Mark was happy to divert everyone's attention back to the lesson. "Yes!" he replied enthusiastically. "This is one of the travesties of justice that's gone down in history. The citizens of Athens accused Socrates of all sorts of contrived crimes. But, the reason they were angry with him is because he challenged them. He annoyed them so much with his endless questioning, they actually wanted to kill him. He referred to himself as a stinging fly sent to goad the horse into action with its bite. Unfortunately, the people were in no mood to be goaded."

Mark walked back to the electronic display board and once again touched the stylus to it, writing: Homework — 12/9/39 — What do you Question?

Turning to his students, he said, "What do you question? Tonight, take the time to really think about this . . ."

"I question the necessity of this class," remarked a tall, lean man with a thin, sharp face. He was standing in the back corner. Mark hadn't noticed him enter. The man stood with his right foot slightly forward, clasping his hands behind his back, defiantly staring down his nose at Mark, who glared right back at him.

"Excuse me?" Mark slightly cocked his head, seething with indignation.

"There are more important things to learn," the man retorted, standing strong and upright, pushing his chest out a bit.

Mark's eyes widened, his pupils dilated from anger. He struggled to keep his cool.

"Clint," Mark forced a mild tone through gritted teeth, "let's go in the other room and talk about this." Mark started toward the door, indicating with authority that the present conversation in front of the students was over.

"There's nothing more I need to say," Clint remarked flippantly, standing his ground.

Well, there's *plenty* I have to say." Mark glanced up at the streamlined chrome clock and saw he had a little class time left. He looked at his students, forcing himself to maintain a calm demeanor. "Class, you are dismissed early."

The relieved youths got up and the loud murmur of their talking filled the room. Mark walked through the door from whence Clint came and into a small room just outside the main hall. Clint followed and closed the door behind him. The kids could hear them arguing and quieted down to listen. As the adults' voices grew louder and louder, bits and pieces could be heard clearly.

"Who do you think you are?!" Mark shouted.

"You know damn well what I'm talking about!" Clint roared back. He caught himself and quieted his voice. The kids could not decipher what he said next.

Mark, unable to contain himself, shouted, "How dare you assume that just because I believe in the power of intellectual development . . ." He lowered his voice so the students could not hear the rest of the sentence. Clint said something inaudible behind the door and then Mark erupted.

"This *is* important! This is *all* part of the Formula! Just because primitives like you . . ." He quieted once more.

"You're an Isaianic sympathizer and you know it!" Clint spewed with rage.

"You goddam Neanderthal!"

Abruptly the voices ceased, replaced by a ruckus that was clearly the sound of fighting. Suddenly, the two adults burst through the thin door, splintering the wood by the lock.

Mark tackled Clint and they fell to the ground. They wrestled across the unforgiving wooden floor, punching each other in the face and gut. Neither one landed a serious blow, but not because they were weak. In fact, the opposite was true. They were both full of strength, energy, and ability. Clint put Mark in a choke hold, but Mark quickly grabbed at Clint's forearm to ease the pressure on his windpipe. He escaped from Clint's hold, turned to face him, and rushed Clint, throwing a barrage of punches. Clint kept his arms up to his face and took the punches on them, but that moment of blocked vision allowed Mark to get behind him. Mark wrestled Clint into a full nelson head and arm lock and tripped him to the ground, slamming his face into the floor. Clint was stunned, as were the students, as a line of blood trickled from his lip.

John, having heard the commotion, came running. John's presence snapped Mark back into reality and he separated from Clint, leaning against the wall and closing his eyes for a moment to disperse his rage. Clint was still too rattled to do anything but wobble as he stood, shifting his weight from one leg to the other.

"What the hell is going on here?!" John shouted with absolute disbelief. He looked around at the youths, their faces full of surprise and awe. "All right kids, get out of here," he sternly commanded. "Go outside and do something. Go on."

The kids did as he said, moved by the power of his bellowing voice. As they walked out the door, they heard John angrily chiding his peers.

"What the hell were you guys thinking?! This is the *last* damn thing we need."

The students exited the jungle pathway and strolled out onto the beach. The sun was now high and sea birds were swooping down on the tranquil water at a distance. Some teens played volleyball and soccer, others simply soaked up the sun. There were younger kids not old enough to attend the classes, and so they often spent their days out on the sand where the adults could better supervise them than in the forest. The little girls collected seashells while the young boys ran out and splashed them. For them, all seemed relaxed and carefree. The adults and older teens, however, were noticeably riddled with anxiety.

Adam, Megan, and Logan walked along the shore, letting the cool tide kiss their feet at even intervals. Unexpectedly, the loud series of sonic booms returned. Everyone looked up to see three jet streams that, within a split-second, had traversed from horizon to horizon.

"What the hell *are* those things?" Logan tilted his head back in wonder. "There are so many lately?"

Adam dug his foot into the wet sand as the tide pulled back. "There's something I wanted to tell you earlier, but I couldn't find time. Shit's not going too well, Logan."

Logan came to a full halt, as a chill ran up his spine. "What do you mean?"

"The Allies are getting their butts kicked," Adam said, his face adorned with utter solemnity.

Logan narrowed his eyes, his expression a mix of alarm and curiosity. "How do *you* know that?"

"I came home from playing hoops yesterday and I heard my mom crying inside. So, I went around the side of the house and listened through the wall." Adam breathed in deeply as he remembered what he heard.

"She was going crazy! I've never heard her that way. She'd gone nuts!" He looked at Logan with wide-eyes. "She was banging on the walls and throwin' a fit. She was like, 'what are we gonna do!' And my Dad was tryin' to calm her down. He didn't want me or my sister to hear what was goin' on, ya know?"

Logan nodded, stiff with fear. Adam gulped and looked down for a second, shaking his head slowly.

"And then, she was like . . ." He had to pause to summon up strength. "She said, 'what the hell does it all matter anyway! We can't hide from Geiseric!" Adam imitated the sound of his mom's disconcerting outbursts, pronouncing the name as if it were spelled "Guys-Eric."

Standing on the beach and staring blankly off to the horizon, Logan tried to put on a courageous facade, but his eyes betrayed his shock.

"So," Adam continued, "later, me and Megan snuck up to the roof to get a look at the TV in my parents' room."

Adam recalled what had happened. His parents, Patrick and Helen, came home later than usual, having had a few drinks at one of the neighbors' houses. Helen stumbled as Patrick held her up. She laughed with a hysteria that conveyed the terror underlying.

"Let's have some more shots of the stuff we made," she said with an inebriated stagger in her speech.

"I think we've had enough, sweetheart," Patrick replied with a caring tone.

Making it to their house, Helen summoned up her balance enough to walk on her own accord. She checked all over to see if her children were home. Seeing that they weren't, she looked for her small two-way radio, fumbling through the large carrying bag that hung at her shoulder.

"Patrick!" she called.

"Yes," he replied, undoing his tie in front of the hall bathroom mirror.

"I can't find my walkie-talkie," Helen said with a drunken inflection. "Give the kids a ring and see where they are."

"Ok, dear," he nodded. "I'll do it in just a sec."

Helen grabbed a key from her bag and unlocked her and Patrick's room door. She sat on the bed and picked up the remote control to the only television in the house, which was mounted on the wall across from her. There was a satellite dish on the roof that allowed them to get most television stations that were still broadcasting. Pressing some of the buttons on the remote, she entered in the four character password to switch on the TV. Up came the channel she was previously viewing, which was a news station.

"You shouldn't watch this stuff for a while," Patrick gently warned, looking to Helen with worried eyes. Helen laughed with a slight belligerence.

"You speak as if we had a while. We'll be lucky to live through next week."

Atop the roof, Megan had leaned over the edge while Adam held her tightly around her thighs. He lowered her until she could look through the window of Adam's parents' room. From her upside-down perspective, she could see what all of the parents on the island had attempted to hide for so long from their children. What she caught sight of was worse than she could have ever imagined. Now, standing on the beach trying to recall those horrible visuals once again, her throat constricted and dried, hindering her ability to speak.

"What'd you see?" Logan asked.

Megan tried to get the words out, but she kept heaving, as if she was going to vomit. She looked up, closed her eyes and breathed in deeply through her nose.

"It was terrible, like a horror movie. It was *so brutal!*" She buried her head in her hands and began to sob uncontrollably.

Logan was growing impatient. "What was it?!" He startled Megan with his volume and, feeling bad, he rubbed her shoulder. "I'm sorry Meggy," he cooed softly, "but please, one of you, tell me what you saw," he looked pleadingly to her and Adam.

Adam took a deep breath as he remembered what Megan had told him. "There was a massive pile of bodies, like, two hundred feet tall and hundreds of feet wide! A lot of the people were hacked into pieces!" Logan's eyes widened, not believing what he was hearing. Adam held Megan tightly, doing his best to console her and wishing he had been the one plagued by the visions now haunting her.

Logan paced back and forth. "We gotta get to the bottom of all this. I mean, we're eighteen! I'm tired of being lied to!"

Megan stared Logan in the eye. "If you saw what I saw, I don't think you'd say that."

Adam shook his head. "Let's just forget dealing with our parents and get to a TV. Megan saw my mom punch in the password. Guess what it is?"

"What?" Logan asked, raising his eyebrows.

Adam looked him dead in the eye. "Hell."

An hour later, Megan, Adam and Logan sat crouched behind the bushes by Adam's house, waiting for his parents to leave. The setting sun had left a light dusting of coral pink across the clear sky. Logan stared out at the sunset, and its beauty brought a moment of peace before the inevitable storm.

He was brought back to attention by the sound of voices, as Patrick and Helen finally left their house, walking down the darkening path toward the beach. The sun was quickly descending, giving way to night. The stars were becoming visible and the Moon drifted upwards on the horizon opposite the sun, shedding a soft glow across the seascape. Down the pathway, the youths could see Logan's parents, Tom and Bibi, meet up with Adam's parents. They chatted as they strolled out of sight.

The two boys immediately sprang into action, clambering up to the roof on a sloped, flora-covered lattice. Megan stayed hidden in the bushes to keep lookout. She froze as Helen's voice suddenly belted out of Adam's two-way radio.

"Adam!" she called out. Adam scrambled to pull the two-way out of his pocket.

"Yeah mom," he replied.

"I'm just making sure you're alright," Helen said. "Alright, I love ya."

"Love ya too ma," Adam replied. He then turned off the two-way and gave Logan the thumb's up to continue with their mission.

"Alright, let's do this," Logan commanded with resolve.

Logan held Adam's legs as he reached over the edge of the roof and popped the screen off his parents' second-floor window. Struggling at this awkward angle for a brief moment, the sliding half of the window finally shot to the side.

"OK, I got it," Adam said. "Pull me up!"

Logan pulled Adam up, then helped lower him again, this time legs first through the window. Logan then scrambled down from the roof. Looking nervously over his shoulders as he opened the front door, he ran in and up the stairs to join his friend. Adam had opened the door to his parents' room and turned on the TV.

Megan remained in the bushes to keep lookout. The light from the television emanated through the open window, catching her eyes where she sat hidden in the vegetation. She began shaking uncontrollably at the thought of the gruesome images her friends would shortly be inundated by. Sitting in an upright fetal position, she held her bent knees with one arm and, with the other hand, gently tugged leaves off the branches of the nearest bush, one after another, as if she was plucking away at the vile memories.

Inside, Adam and Logan stood beside each other, staring at the TV in disbelief. On the screen was the image of a long, fortified wall that had been camouflaged to match the surrounding desert terrain. It was five hundred meters long, twenty tall, nearly as thick, and armed with a vast array of weaponry, according to the specs described in a written display at the top corner of the screen. The most conspicuous of the armaments were the "drill bolt cannons," which were twenty meter long guns along the top of the wall. Ball turret machine guns lined the front and back of the wall, positioned so close together that they resembled a necklace of pearls.

The wall wasn't part of a greater fortress or compound. It stood independent of any other structures, out on the open terrain. Suddenly, it began to move, sending waves through its length, back and forth, gradually gaining speed.

"Whoa," both boys gasped breathlessly.

Aside from friction with the ground, this writhing behemoth didn't make any noise. There was no creaking, no sounds of powerful engines and

hydraulics. The silent power-source produced a wriggling motion that propelled it broadside first.

Adam couldn't take his eyes off the TV. "What the hell!"

"What *is that*?!" Logan asked, his voice shaky.

Adam shook his head. "Dude! I don't know."

An intense barrage of large, explosive mortars and shells struck the ground around the moving wall, which dodged the bombardment.

The program cut to another display of something called an Artillery Net. A diagram showed an aerial view of a battleground. Green dots displayed the location of underground systems across the territory that formed a deadly defensive line.

Next, the program featured two jets, identical except in color. The startlingly unique characteristic of these jets was that their wings could spin around the axis of the frame, which allowed the pilot to turn the craft just by rotating the wings, while the cockpit stayed level. A woman's soothing voice provided a narrative.

"This is the Allied Bald Eagle," she explained. A white-nosed jet appeared on the screen, displaying its unique wing ability.

"The Bald Eagle and Golden Eagle are the exact same design," the woman's steady voice continued. "But, the Allies far outnumber the Apex in Eagle jet planes, with a ratio of three to one."

The scene switched to a sky filled with long, thin, steam trails emitted by criss-crossing jets. Three streams seemed to suddenly appear in the sky. Traveling at nearly two kilometers per second, they streaked from east to west, leaving a loud, crashing series of booms to shake the ground far below.

"That must be what we're always hearing!" Logan realized. Adam just nodded, fixated on the screen.

A slow-motion replay of what had happened showed a Golden Eagle being chased down by two Bald Eagle jets. The Golden Eagle was struck by fire coming from the double-barreled laser cannons mounted on the front of the Bald Eagle jets in pursuit. The footage returned to real time, showing the Golden Eagle crashing to Earth with the speed and intensity of a meteorite. The explosion as it slammed into the ground was immense.

Logan changed the channel, finding a live feed of the British Prime Minister, Charles Dandau. He was delivering a speech to the United Parliament. All thirteen levels of the amphitheatre were filled, seated with three thousand delegates and leaders from the countries that constituted the Allied nations.

"Like a swarm of locusts," Prime Minister Dandau addressed the crowd with the charisma of a seasoned public speaker, "Geiseric's Kolibri have infested and devastated the great civilizations of Europe. The Juggernaut then pierced Allied North America's eastern and western coastlines. The Panzers and Scythians devastated the great New England cities and wrought havoc up and down the East Coast. Yet, I am unafraid. The Juggernaut is stayed and our interior Laser Net defense system will soon be impossible to puncture. We are cramped, but this will only serve to consecrate our sense of unity under this common adversity. I look out upon this mass of people, and I see endless power and resources. Geiseric, like every tyrant before him, has once more underestimated the power of a world united against him."

Logan grabbed his radio phone and called Megan. "Megan, you've got to come in here and see this . . . They won't be home for awhile. Just come check this out . . . OK . . . Yeah, it's open."

Adam turned to Logan with a look of frustration. "That was dumb, Logan. Why'd you do that? She shouldn't see this."

Logan was adamant. "We've all gotta know what's going on, Adam. I can't believe how in the dark we've been. This is crazy."

Moments later, Megan walked tentatively into the room. "What is it?"

Logan turned to her, ignoring Adam's annoyed glare. "It's the British prime minister."

Adam shook his head at Logan and, with a sigh of resignation, took Megan's hand in his. They all turned their attention to the TV.

". . . and our defenses are incredibly strong. When Napoleon sought to divide and conquer, we united and prevailed!" Dandau spoke with authority and conviction. "When Hitler's fearsome Blitzkrieg almost plunged the world into a second Dark Age, we pummeled Germany *back to* the Dark Age! Now, Geiseric, in his foolish arrogance, has made clear to the world his evil intentions — to subjugate the human race! But like those who had the same aspirations before him, Geiseric has made a fatal mistake. Yes, he is correct! The Spartans *were* the mightiest land army of ancient Greece. Everyone feared them, and they dominated ancient Greece for a brief period, but could Geiseric have really forgotten how the story ended?"

The prime minister gazed upon the audience with an austere dignity. "A Theban named Epaminondas resolved to end the tyranny. Epaminondas forced his soldiers to endure the grueling training the Spartans had undergone. When they met the Spartans on the battlefield, they were evenly matched.

"But the soldiers of Thebes had an ace in the hole. For those who fight to keep others down have far less strength and resolve than do a people chafing under the yoke of oppression. The Spartans were used to winning. Just like the Napoleonic soldier. Just like the Axis soldier. And just like the Apex soldier! Whereas we! *We* remain *determined* to throw off the shackles of this odious regime! Once again, Germany has unleashed chaos. Each world war has been ever more global. This one has enlisted the entire human race!" The camera intermittently panned to the delegates, who were listening attentively.

"This common threat has turned us into a united force that will prevail. We must be strong enough to do what Epaminondas did. We must push ourselves to the limit, to the very breaking point! We will overcome this tyranny. We will win!" he exclaimed, slamming his fist on the podium with each word. "The Allied leadership has initiated another draft that will be put into effect immediately, a draft of *all* persons of military age for compulsory service to the war effort. I realize that these measures may seem extreme, but to be afraid of making small mistakes in haste is to forget what the worst mistake would be — to let Geiseric own the planet, and all of us! Mark my words — the end of the Apex Empire is at hand!"

The Prime Minister stepped away from the podium in a triumphant exit, as the delegates rose to their feet and erupted in applause.

Logan looked to his friends. "So, they're drafting everyone," he said in a raspy whisper. "That's not a good sign."

On the television, another man stepped onto screen, standing tall and strong at the podium. The officiator introduced him as Kassian Van der Klute, the Allied Minister of Defense. His dirty-blonde hair fell to his ears, and his steely, blue eyes assessed the audience. Although probably in his forties or fifties, he looked young for his age, strong and vital.

He spoke with solemnity and determination. "People of the Allied nations, God knows how much the Allied citizens, *you*," he said, pointing towards the camera, "have sacrificed. But, we have mustered our forces and," he stared at the viewing audience with his steely eyes, "we *will* kill the immoral Apex invaders, who have slaughtered and raped the innocent, who have burned women and children alive! We will cut off their army and we will *annihilate it!* And then we will drive on towards Germania and the Apex Empire shall *know our wrath!*"

Logan, Adam, and Megan sat frozen in their positions, dumbfounded. They stared at the television screen with utter dread.

18

"All citizens need to participate in the Allied war effort," Kassian continued, resolute in his tone. "If we lose, the Apex will enslave all whom they don't kill! They wish to treat us like *animals!*"

The Allied Supreme Commander paused, breathing heavily in his fervor. "This is our Last Stand! We *all* have to fight! Our forces have been newly equipped with the latest weaponry and . . ." Suddenly, the television screen became static.

The reception returned with a different picture. It was a similar scene, with a commanding leader standing behind a podium. Only, this podium was a massive, sculptured piece of granite. And the man standing behind it was a far more imposing figure. Although he was not as tall as Kassian, he had broader shoulders and a generally daunting frame. Adam, Megan and Logan knew very little about what was going on beyond their tiny island, but they did know who this man was.

He had changed little in the five years since they had moved from the mainland. He was handsome, slightly rugged, a factor that helped in his ascendance to global fame and, eventually political power. The stage of celebrity had not been large enough for Geiseric.

His caustic blue eyes shined with menacing authority, contrasted by the shortly-cropped, dark brown, almost black hair on his head and framing his lips in a moustache and chinbeard. He spoke with a metallic voice in a cold, methodical manner.

"Citizens of the Allied nations, your leaders cannot protect you anymore. Resistance is futile, and surrender is necessary if you wish to save your lives. We will not tolerate any prolonging of our inevitable victory. This feeble last stand that your government has prepared is nothing more than the signature on your death certificates!" He pointed to the camera. "If you all fight, you will all die!"

He was facing a large crowd, which could be heard cheering him on. They hushed as he continued.

"Leave your guns, your posts, your crafts on land and sea, and go somewhere to wait. You can all leave without fear of reprisal, for there is nothing your government can do. We have killed or captured most of your army. They have nothing with which to compel you." His icy words bit at the three youths' psyches.

"Your citizen's army will stand no chance against my elite divisions. They have stood against your best forces time and time again and destroyed them! If you wish to be cannon fodder to hone my troops, then so be it!" He threw his fist up to emphasize his words. Pausing for a moment, he then stared into the camera sending his image across the world.

"But, don't say you weren't warned."

The screen went black. Megan shut off the TV. "I've seen enough!"

Logan quickly turned to his friends. "We've gotta talk to our parents." He looked at Adam and Megan for agreement.

Adam sat down on the floor and put his head in his hands. "Holy shit. I don't know, Logan. No, I don't think we should rock the boat. I think it's better just to pretend we never saw this."

Megan noticed that Logan seemed to be wincing in pain as he rubbed the back of his neck. "What's wrong, Logan?" she asked quietly, wiping tears from her eyes.

"I don't know," Logan answered, somewhat dazed. "Something strange is going on." Logan was blindsided by a tremendous pain at the base of his cranium. He arched his neck and the entirety of his spine, reaching his right hand back to grab the painful spot. His eyesight blurred and the room began spinning. He put both hands on the floor to ground himself.

Adam jumped to his feet and quickly moved over to help his friend. "What's happening, Logan? Are you OK?"

Logan shook his head, trying to clear it, and opened his eyes wide. He looked around the room as if trying to remember where he was. "I'm OK. It's all right."

Adam and Megan did not believe him, but right now there were more pressing issues.

The trio walked stridently to find Steve. Unlike Logan, Adam and Megan, who were only twelve when they left California more than five years ago, Steve had been sixteen when he moved to the island. They were sure that, now twenty-one, he would have some idea of what was happening. If he did know, he had not disclosed anything to them. That wasn't allowed. However, Logan didn't care about the rules set forth by the parents anymore. His resolve to find out the truth vastly outweighed his reluctance to rile the elders.

They found Steve hanging out in his usual spot, sitting cross-legged on a giant boulder overlooking the lagoon. Staring at the moonlit water, he strummed a guitar peacefully, composing melancholy lyrics.

"Steve-o!" Logan called out as they neared. Steve jumped a bit, startled. He turned around as they walked up beside him.

"What's up, guys?" he replied laconically.

Logan crept up on the boulder and sat beside Steve, facing out at the water, while Megan and Adam sat behind them, huddled closely together. Logan gathered his thoughts, deeply inhaling the invigorating ocean air.

"Steve-o."

"Yeah, buddy," he replied, looking at the strings, lightly plucking them.

Logan paused for a long moment. "You gotta tell us what's goin' on."

Steve continued to look down. "What are you talking about?"

"Don't play stupid. We got to a television," Logan admitted.

Steve paused his strumming. "Really?" he asked, intrigued.

Logan nodded.

Steve looked at them without saying a word, stone-faced for a moment. "What did you see?" His eyes gave away his deep curiosity.

"First," Logan demanded, "you tell us what *you* know."

Steve looked up and saw the desperation and anxiety in the group's eyes. He sighed and placed his guitar gently across his lap.

"You can't tell anyone," he sternly asserted. "Cause you know my dad will kick my ass if he finds out I told you guys anything."

The trio agreed and swore.

"OK," Steve began. "All I really know is, there was going to be a war," he paused as he drudged up the unpleasant information. "A big one. And Germany's the main enemy, only it's now called Germania. The Allies still called it Germany, when I left, and everything else was called the German occupied territories."

"Who are the Allies besides America?" Adam asked.

"They're the same as in the first world wars," Steve said. "America, Britain, Russia, and France."

Logan was perplexed. "Then we can't be in *that* much trouble."

Steve forcefully exhaled. "Yeah, well, I don't know. It scared our parents enough to evacuate us out here. Besides, it's not just Germany. India's on their side."

"India?" Megan asked.

"Yeah," Steve replied, "and there was this big Middle Eastern war and, like, that whole region got unified into an empire, or something. I don't know, exactly, but it involved Germany allying with Israel."

"*Israel* allied with *Germany?!*" Adam's voice conveyed his shock.

Steve nodded. "Yep."

Logan was confused. "But, from what little I've heard, Geiseric is like the new Hitler."

Steve shook his head. He looked up to the clear skies, with the countless stars and diaphanous celestial forms. "It's a trip. Geiseric's real slick. I pretty much told you all I know. So," he said, turning his lips to the side for a moment. He licked his teeth and stretched his back. "What did you guys see?"

The three started talking over each other, repeating one another and giving Steve confusing bits of information. Nonetheless, he discerned what they were saying.

He inhaled shakily. "If they're starting to draft everybody, then the Allies are on their last fuckin' legs." He looked around aimlessly, deep in thought.

"Shit," he remarked in a frighteningly subdued tone.

Later that night, as the adults poured out of the meeting hall, they were surprised to see their children silently waiting for them. Nearly a hundred youths were clustered there, staring at their parents and the other elders with questioning eyes. The parents looked at their children in shock, and then at one another in resignation.

Logan spoke for the group, making an effort to sound assured and confident. "We need to know what's going on."

They stood there, parents facing children, but before anyone could answer, an ice-cold sensation crept through their veins. An invasive force was inside of them, in their bodies and — worse — in their minds.

Everything went black.

Then, there was nothing.

— II —

DOMINION

Logan woke up in a daze.

He lifted his head a bit and looked around. He was on a low bunk bed in a seemingly endless white hallway. Bright sunlight poured in through large, square windows framed high along the walls. Hundreds of three-tiered bunks lined the bare walls. Confused, he wondered if he was in some sort of hospital or institution. His lips felt dry and cracked and he licked them groggily. He tried to lift his hand and noticed his mother was holding it.

Following her gaze, he noticed there were other people in the room. His mother was staring at a couple hugging their crying children. They were wearing sleeveless, knee-length tunics that looked somewhat like potato sacks with belts around the waists. At first, Logan thought he must be dreaming. But as his mind cleared of sleep, he realized he was also wearing a gown. The material felt good on his skin — silky and comfortable. He also felt clean and freshly showered.

Fully conscious now, he scanned the room. There were drink dispensers lining the walls between the bunks. All around him, people seemed to be waiting — waiting in line for water and something that looked like green juice. Waiting in line for the restrooms. Waiting for whatever was going to happen to them. Every face had an expression of frightened uncertainty, but they seemed healthy. No one looked bedraggled or hurt. People seemed to be standing in family groups, talking in hushed whispers, as if they weren't sure who else to trust. They were hesitant to wander far from each other, for fear of being separated.

Suddenly, a strange sight passed by overhead. It was something akin to a mythological creature — half man, half beast. It looked like an armored knight from the waist up, with his legs encased in a craft that had two wings on it that moved in the manner of a hummingbird, at blurring speed. The armored man was propped upright in the vehicle, in a standing position. He buzzed over slowly, bearing a bar-shaped implement, some sort of weapon.

Logan jerked up in his bunk. "Wait! What's going on?!"

His mother looked startled. "Oh, Logan!" She quickly embraced him, hard, as if she had not seen him in years.

"What's going on, Mom?" Logan whispered with terror.

"Everything's gonna be fine, sweetheart. Don't worry." She ran her fingers through his hair and pulled him closer.

Logan's father, Tom, walked down the hallway toward them carrying a cup of water. He seemed dazed and indifferent to his surroundings, until he noticed Bibi waving to him. He hurried over and crouched down next to Logan.

"Hey, pal," he consoled in the voice he used when Logan was a child, frightened by a shadow or closet monster. "How ya doing?"

"Fine, I guess. I just . . ."

Tom and Bibi exchanged a quick glance, then looked at their son.

"Logan, don't be afraid," his father said, matter-of-factly. "We were captured. It's OK though. They've treated us well."

Bibi did her best to smile reassuringly and continued patting Logan's hand.

Logan stared wide-eyed at his parents. "What?! The Apex won?! How?!"

Tom placed his hand on Logan's shoulder. "We don't know exactly what's going on yet. But, don't worry. Everything's gonna be fine."

"But, what happened to the Allies?" Logan asked fearfully. His chest constricted and he had difficulty breathing. He began to panic. Bibi embraced him while Tom rubbed his shoulders.

Tom breathed in deeply. "We're not sure where the Allies are . . . but, don't worry pal, we're . . ."

24

"How'd they find us?" Logan interrupted. "I thought no one knew where we were?"

Tom was frustrated that he didn't have more information for his son. "I don't know, Logan," he replied. "I don't know, but everything's . . . "

Logan jumped up. "Don't lie to me! It's not going to be OK!" he shouted at his parents, startling a nearby Chinese family that was conversing in their native language.

"I know what the Apex is capable of! I saw it all on TV!"

The Chinese family consoled their young ones who were upset by Logan's outburst. The elders looked angrily at Logan. Bibi stood up and quickly walked down the hallway. She returned with a ceramic cup filled with the green-tinted juice.

"Here, sweetie," she said offering it to Logan. "Drink some of this."

Logan ignored her. "We were on the beach and this horrible feeling came over me and . . ." Taking in the stark hall crowded with strangers, he again started to panic. He looked back and forth, from his mother to his father, desperately wanting an answer. "We're prisoners! Oh, my god . . ."

Bibi was heartbroken to see her son so frightened and not be able to help him. When he was a baby it was so easy. A reassuring hug could solve anything. But in these times . . .

She hugged him as tightly as she could anyways. "Logan, honey!"

A tear crept down Tom's cheek. He wanted to be brave for his family, so he faced away until his emotions were in check. He calmed himself and looked at his son.

"You need to hydrate yourself," he said definitively, putting the drink into Logan's hand.

Logan was shaking, making it difficult to hold the cup in one hand. Using both hands, he grasped the drink suspiciously.

"What is it?" he asked.

"Try it. It's good," his father replied in a soothing tone.

Logan took a tentative gulp of the strange liquid. "Wow . . . it is good." Suddenly realizing how parched he was, he quickly chugged the rest down.

His father stood up, relieved to have a task. "I'll get you some more." He took Logan's empty cup and walked down the hallway.

Logan looked at his mother with pleading eyes. "So what are we doing here? What happened, Mom?"

"I'm not sure." She tried to sound calm, unalarmed. "It seems that every-one was overtaken by that . . . that whatever it was at the same time."

Logan's eyes went blank as he recalled the bone-chilling, invasive presence that had crept through his body. "That horrible, cold feeling?"

"Yes." Bibi held her tears back and gathered her strength.

Logan stared into space, transported back to that moment. "It was the strangest feeling I've ever experienced . . . like I had become a puppet to some spirit, or something. I don't remember anything else."

Bibi sighed and rubbed Logan's back, as she rocked on the edge of the bed. "Dad and I woke up yesterday. Most of the adults did. Some of the adults and most of the kids woke up a couple days ago. They said they were brought to another area and cared for by the Apex until their parents woke up. We were all gathered in this hall yesterday. Most everyone was awake, but you . . . you were here . . . sleeping in bed." Bibi fought tears, trying to compose herself before continuing.

Gently rubbing Logan's cheek, she explained, "One of the Kolibri guardsmen, those are the guys flying in those chariots around here, he brought us to you. There were only a couple of other people still asleep and they were pretty old. We were so worried that you wouldn't . . ." she trailed off, taking a breath. "The guard told us you'd be fine. Still, I was worried after ten hours passed and you were still out cold."

She wrapped her arms around Logan and pulled him close to her. Tom returned with a full cup, handed it to Logan, and tried to lighten the mood. "We were wondering if you were gonna wet the bed, you were asleep so long."

His father's goofy grin was contagious. Logan couldn't help laughing a bit. He drank more of the strange, pleasant juice. "So, some people woke up two days ago? Maybe they were just captured before us?"

"No," his father explained. "They confirmed the same date we all got hit by that weird darkness."

"Were we asleep for that long?" asked Logan.

"I guess so," his mother said.

Logan's eyes grew wide. "I wonder what they were doing with us?"

"Don't worry," his father assured him. "The kids who woke up first said they got to see their parents sleeping. They said we were laying on hospital beds in some huge room. We were being fed intravenously. They were taking care of us."

"What are they gonna do with us now?" Logan asked, nervously.

Tom looked Logan straight in the eyes. "Well, they've gone out of their way to make sure we're healthy and comfortable. So, there's absolutely no reason to think they'll do anything bad. They're a little strict right now, but I think even that will settle down soon."

Logan remembered what he'd seen on television. "But, what about all the stuff about them wanting to kill us?"

Tom sat beside his son and put his arm around his shoulders. "That's not gonna happen, pal. That was just war hype. It's not like the Allied propaganda made it out to be."

Logan was confused. "How do you know?"

Tom smiled genuinely for the first time. "We've seen this drama playing out for fifteen years. Geiseric's goal was to take over the world, not to kill people. Things are gonna be OK now, son. It'll be a change," he shrugged, "but it's gonna be OK. How do you feel? Better?"

"A little bit," Logan admitted. "I don't know why."

Tom pointed to the empty cup next to Logan. "It's that drink. They call it ambrosia."

"What's in it?" asked Logan.

"I have no idea. It's some sort of fruit blend, and there's something, some drug or herb in there."

Logan stopped mid-sip and looked at his dad. Seeing his son's concern over the unknown ingredient, Tom again tried to lighten the mood. Mustering a little laugh, he said, "But drink up! This is no time to be a Puritan!"

Logan looked around at the sea of faces that filled the long dormitory hall. There were so many people, but he didn't recognize any of them. "So, where's everybody else? Where's everyone from the island?"

His mother's lip trembled a bit. "We're not sure . . ."

Once again, Logan was struck with a bolt of fear. "Are they OK?"

Tom and Bibi did their best to hide their concern.

"I'm sure they're fine, Logan," Tom said.

Suddenly, a voice came over the loudspeaker, startling everyone. A man sternly barked instructions. "Prepare for departure. Stand in two, single-file lines, parallel to the walls."

Chaotically, everyone began forming lines side by side near the opposing walls. Logan saw some of his captors for the first time. A group of ten soldiers walked down the isles, carrying large assault rifles held diagonally across their chests.

The soldiers wore full body armor, which more closely resembled a Medieval Knight than a modern warrior. They marched rapidly, raising their legs straight out and slamming them back down, heel first. The soldiers stepped in tandem, and the sound of their metallic boots hitting the ground simultaneously was loud and unnerving. They were inspecting the lines, making sure everyone had complied with the instructions. Logan gulped nervously as they passed his family and moved on down the hall.

Suddenly, the large double doors at the end of the hallway opened. Over the loudspeaker, they heard their next instructions. "Stay in your lines. Proceed out the doors in an orderly fashion."

Two by two, all of the people walked out the doors and found themselves in a lush, jungle rainforest. It was a beautiful, sunny morning and the air smelled sweet with tropical flowers. Everyone took a moment to adjust their eyes to the bright light. Prodded by the soldiers to keep walking, the crowd forged ahead toward a row of enormous transport craft, floating on the water a hundred meters ahead. A temporary harbor had been constructed, which kept the waves at bay.

The craft were serpentine in their appearance, like giant water snakes each at least as long as a football field. Their length consisted of multiple passenger cars attached by joints in a way that made them flexible, much like a train. What were particularly intriguing were the hundred pairs of wing-like appendages, each about ten meters long, which lined both sides of the craft. The wings had a teardrop shape, the wider end facing out like giant oars. With their long, segmented bodies, and the many small protruding appendages, the vehicles reminded Logan of giant centipedes. Thousands of people clamored into them, as groups of armored soldiers shuffled people into the different compartments, pushing them when necessary.

Bibi put her arms around her son and whispered, "Stay close, Logan. Hold on to me."

Logan's family kept tightly next to each other and were all sent towards the same transport. Suddenly, a commotion broke out ahead. Several people, scared and panicked, tried to resist getting on the transport. The guards rushed ahead to muscle the crowd forward and a stampede of people broke Logan away from his parents. Pushed by the tide, Bibi and Tom tried to resist.

"Please let us get our child!" Bibi begged the closest guard she could see.

"Don't worry," the guard replied without expression. "You're all going to the same place."

"And where's that?!" snapped Tom, his nerves completely shot.

"Just move." the guard answered, barely acknowledging him.

The guard pushed them to a different car of the same transport Logan was boarding. Looking around frantically, Logan spotted his parents as they walked up the stairs. Bibi and Tom looked at him with apprehension in their eyes that they tried to replace with confident expressions, to assure their child that all would be well. He managed to wave to them, and his mother blew him a kiss as they were herded onto the odd transport.

Inside, it very much resembled a train car. There were rows of booths with cushioned bench seats facing each other. Passengers were packed into the booths and many of the benches were already filled. Logan found a seat as people continued to file in. Finally, the doors were closed and sealed.

The cramped car reminded Logan of the subway train he used to ride as a boy in San Francisco. He found a strange comfort in this closeness. There were people of all cultures, speaking many languages. For the past five years, Logan had not been around anyone but the same few hundred or so people who inhabited the island. So, the scene in the transport was truly a bombardment to his senses. He found himself very stimulated by the sight of new faces. Oddly, the expressions of the people on board were not much different than the ones Logan used to see on the subway as a child. He vividly remembered how many of the subway passengers often seemed so lackluster. The people he was with now seemed vacant, as if looking but seeing nothing. There was no terror; they were merely turned completely inward. In fact, Logan himself felt peculiarly sedate for such a time.

Without warning, the craft began rumbling slightly. Gazing through the large windows, Logan watched as the craft came alive. Almost silently, the wings fired into full gear and the craft began to lift from the ground. The strange machine gently levitated upwards into the sky. Its take-off was so subtle, the passengers inside could barely feel any movement. It climbed to one thousand meters, or thirty-three hundred feet, which the captain of the transport announced over the speaker system. Leveling out, it made its way on a horizontal vector.

Sitting directly across from Logan in the booth, a middle-aged man spoke quietly to a young lady in her late twenties. The girl's naturally blonde hair was cropped very short and keenly framed her face. Her skin was pale, but she did not appear unhealthy. It had a natural sheen that, with the color of her hair, produced an angelic aura. Her companion's light brown hair was buzzed close, as if growing back from a completely shaved head. Both of them appeared to be extremely healthy and physically fit. While the young lady spoke English tinged with a Russian accent, the man's accent was clearly French. Logan could hear pieces of their conversation. She was anxious as she spoke.

"Jacques, I heard we're going to a forced labor camp!"

"I don't know, Sasha. Some sort of farms, I think," he replied, relatively nonchalant.

"Hold me, Jacques," she said, shrinking into his lap and broad shoulders. She kissed his neck a few times.

A teenage girl and young man who had been exploring the compartment joined Sasha and Jacques. They sat next to Logan, who slid over to the end of the bench to make room.

The young man appeared to be in his late twenties. He was handsomely mixed of race, with his African descent figuring prominently into his features. As he sat, he slumped down a bit, shrinking into his wrinkled gown. He seemed to be hiding his face behind the cup from which he was drinking, as if he didn't want to be recognized.

The teenage girl had a natural beauty, no make-up and a softness about her that comforted Logan. Her dark brown hair was cut in the same style as Sasha's, short and efficient, like the kind given in the military. Logan noticed that many women on the transport had similar haircuts, and most of the men had buzz cuts in various stages of regrowth. The girl and her companion were each holding two cups of ambrosia. She offered one to Jacques, but he declined gratefully. The young man offered a cup to Sasha, who happily accepted.

"Would you like to sit with me, Francesca?" Jacques asked with his soft French accent. Sasha's eyes opened wide, irate that her lover would displace her.

"That's OK, Papa," Francesca answered, with a similar but slightly different accent.

"How are you doing, *ma chère*?" he asked with deep concern.

"I'm doing well now, Papa," she answered with a soft smile.

She appeared to be about Logan's age. Her skin was lusciously tan, highlighting her emerald green eyes — eyes that seemed deeply sad, yet still full of life. Whatever tension Logan had felt disappeared at the sight of her.

She offered her extra cup of ambrosia to Logan. "Want a drink?"

"Sure," he happily replied. "Thank you."

"No problem." She handed the cup to him. As she did, their eyes met. Her hand quivered a bit and she spilled a little of the drink on her friend.

"Oh, sorry Ro ..." she gulped, putting her hand over her mouth, "Alistair."

Logan was preoccupied with the moment he just shared with her; the euphoric jolt he felt when their eyes locked. He stared out the window in feigned distraction, as he eavesdropped on the four people next to him.

"... lot of people died at the end ..."

"... when they were burning alive ... "

"... that son of a bitch ...."

"... Shhhh! ..."

"... slaughtered the whole civilian population ..."

"... Geiseric ..."

"... happened to Kassian ... "

The more Logan heard, the more distressed he became. Then, he heard a very clear string of words come out of Alistair's mouth.

"The last casualty count was almost a quarter billion."

Logan's heart raced upon hearing this horrible statistic. "I'm sorry, but did you say a quarter of a billion people died?!"

The group turned toward Logan in unison.

"They think maybe something like that." Jacques nodded with sadness in his eyes.

Logan stared at them wide-eyed and white with fear, the blood having drained from his face and extremities.

Jacques' eyes filled with sympathetic concern. "Are you OK?"

Logan looked at him with trepidation. Steadily, he mustered up the courage to ask the question to which he most feared the answer. "Where are the Allies?"

"Who knows?" Jacques replied with a sigh.

Logan rubbed his face in frustration. "How come no one knows what happened?" He looked back up at Jacques. "Did they lose? I mean, do you guys have *any* idea what's going on?"

Jacques shrugged. "No one's exactly sure what happened. We blacked out like everyone else."

"What *was* that?" Logan asked.

Jacques shook his head, inhaling slowly. "Who knows? It was probably some sort of Psychiclink device."

Completely perplexed, Logan's face crinkled up. "Huh?"

"You know," Jacques eyed Logan with subtle aggravation, "the technology that allowed us to operate the battlemachines."

Logan just stared at him blankly.

Alistair chimed in. "You know, the technology that interacts with our brains?" He gently poked Logan's temple. Logan just continued to stare as if they were speaking gibberish.

Alistair laughed. "This poor kid's gone nuts."

Francesca was concerned. "Are you OK?" She asked softly, touching his hand for a quick moment.

Gazing upon her lovely face, Logan came to his senses. He felt a warm pulse ripple up his spine, from his tailbone through his neck. "But . . . how?"

Francesca looked at him, confused. "How what?"

"How did all those people die?"

Sasha looked at Jacques with indignant bewilderment. "Who is this guy?" She then turned to Logan. "Have you been locked in a closet all your life?"

"Well," his eyes shot to and fro, looking at the others' faces to gauge their reactions, "actually, I was on an island in the South Pacific for the past five years."

Sasha crossed her arms in front of her. "So you're a draft-dodger, huh?"

"Relax, Sasha." Francesca stepped in, flashing her an angry glance.

Logan didn't know exactly what Sasha meant by her remark. "I have no idea."

Francesca studied Logan, trying to estimate his age. "How old are you?"

"Eighteen," Logan quietly answered.

Sasha rolled her eyes. "Most eighteen year olds I know had to actually fight."

"Yeah . . ." Logan didn't know what to say. He shifted nervously in his chair. "Our parents kept us pretty secluded. I mean, that's what I'm starting to realize," he offered feebly.

Sasha clucked her tongue disapprovingly. Logan noticed that Alistair was staring at him as if he had grown a second head or said something entirely out of the ordinary. Logan gazed around the compartment at his fellow prisoners. The loud, endless murmur of people consoling each other filled his ears.

"Do you know if we're gonna be okay?" Logan broke the awkward silence.

Alistair folded his arms across his chest as he leaned back on the booth seat. "We're gonna be fine. I mean, it's not going to be a cakewalk, but we're not going to be systematically murdered, if that's what you mean."

"It might seem overwhelming," Jacques interjected in a fatherly way, "but just have faith."

"Yeah," Alistair explained, putting his arm around Logan's shoulders. "Ya see, Geiseric and the Principles . . . you know who *they* are right?"

Logan shrugged. "Generally, yeah. I mean, I know they're the bad guys."

Alistair laughed. "Yep. They're just a bunch of elitist *arses* who want to rule a lot of people. And corpses make for bad subjects!"

Logan's fear was not assuaged. "Then why was the British prime minister saying that Geiseric was going to kill everyone?"

Alistair patted him on the back. "That was just to get the Allied citizenry riled up and scared enough to fight. Take it from me and, for the record, I'm a good source. We're not going to be killed. Geiseric and the Principles think they're so much more intelligent than the rest of the world that they deserve to rule us. In their minds, everyone is better off being ruled by them."

Alistair leaned his neck back into his palms and interlocked fingers. "The Principles Party started out as a pretty benign group of scientists, philosophers, artists, and politicians. I mean, remember, Geiseric himself was just a hippie rock star at first."

"*What?!*" Logan shook his head, clearing it, as if he had heard wrong.

"You didn't know that?" Alistair laughed. "Well, yeah, like Adolph Hitler and Ronald Reagan, this world-changing leader started out as a mere artist."

Logan sat there, mouth slightly agape, his mind taking in these bewildering details.

"The Principles Party motto," Alistair continued, "was 'Infinite Conception Phase,' a concept Geiseric himself came up with. It's reaching a point of mental transcendence where you never stop improving, like a perpetual state of evolution, which sounded real nice at first. They seemed legitimate. But, the party became more and more fanatical and they formed this Utopian ideology where they would be the keepers of the planet," he parted his hands out to show all that was around, pointing out to Logan the evident fact that that this mission was accomplished. "You know Plato?"

"Yeah," Logan replied, noticing Alistair's subtle British accent for the first time. "I was just studying Plato. A lot of the adults on the island were obsessed with him."

Alistair raised his eyebrows while taking a sip of his ambrosia drink. "Ha, that's interesting. Geiseric's actually a lot like him. Plato was a real totalitarian. He believed in aristocracy, which means the rule of the best. He hated democracy because he thought that the masses were ignorant. He thought only the intellectual elite could make the right decisions. That was his concept of Utopia, where the smart, the Guardians, would rule and the dumb, the masses, would be the labor force."

"Really?" Logan asked, perplexed. "Plato believed that? That seems so counterintuitive. Wasn't he trained by Socrates?"

Alistair was impressed. "Counterintuitive," he repeated. "Very good." Alistair smiled. "You're a smart kid. Plato *was* a student of Socrates and

Socrates was the ultimate democrat. When the citizens of Athens all voted to kill Socrates, he accepted his fate. But, this really soured Plato." Alistair's accent came through more prominently as he became engrossed in his own story.

"He wrote *The Republic*, which was a huge inspiration to most of the absolutist regimes that have ruled Europe for the past two thousand years."

He paused for a moment to let everything sink in. Logan held his chin in his hand, processing the information.

"Plato," Alistair continued, "thought the average person was too ignorant to rule as equals with the Guardians. Of course, the problem with such an elitist society is that not all smart people are good and not all good people are smart. For instance, Socrates was an intelligent and good person. However, while Geiseric is brilliant, he's not a good person."

Sasha rolled her eyes. "That's the understatement of the century.".

"Still," Alistair assured Logan, "he's not going to harm us. Utopia can't exist without its ignorant lower class. Geiseric's goal was never a mass genocide. It was to rule us and force us to live by his law. His followers think that ruling the world is their God-ordained right. This war, and all the horrors the Apex perpetrated during it, were done to attain that goal, to win, which Geiseric sees as altruistic. The Principles think the world would be better with a Kind King, a 'Philosopher King,' as Plato idealized."

Logan felt his chest tighten from a minor anxiety attack. The situation he now found himself in was infinitely bizarre. Such larger-than-life characters like Geiseric were a phenomenon that were supposed to be relegated to the past. "How the hell did this guy come to power?"

Alistair could see by Logan's expression that the young man was getting overwhelmed. He looked Logan squarely in the eye. "Chug the rest of that ambrosia, man."

Logan placed the glass to his lips and tipped it up. Relaxed by the drink, his eyelids drooped a bit, though he felt quite lucid.

"What's in this stuff?"

Alistair laughed. "Don't worry about it, man. It's not bad for you." He looked at his friends. "Somebody get this guy another ambrosia."

"I'll do it," Francesca volunteered, walking off towards a dispensing fountain at the end of their compartment. She returned with a full cup for Logan. As he took it, he gazed upon her face once more and, for a moment, his fear vanished. He took a sip of the ambrosia, but Alistair reached over and lifted the bottom of the cup, so that Logan would have more.

34

"Drink up, man. You're gonna need this," he chuckled, leaning back in his chair. "So, you wanna know how Geiseric, the king of Krautrock, came to power?

"Well," Alistair began, "the Principles didn't come right out with their full agenda. Just like Hitler wasn't elected based on his wish for another world war or to kill Jews. Most Germans had no idea what they were voting in with either man," his eyes drifted up and to the side as he contemplated the long road that had brought the world to its present circumstances. "When Geiseric came to power almost thirteen years ago, back in '27, most people around the world didn't see him as a threat. He masked his intentions with well-worded justifications. And his charisma pacified the citizens of all the future Allied countries. Oratory was truly his gift . . ."

III

THE FUROR

Winter 2027

On the morning of February 10, 2027, Berlin was experiencing crisp, cool weather with intermittent drizzle. Geiseric was going over his speech in his head one last time. He kept checking his watch impatiently. 10:05. Why couldn't everything run on schedule? He glanced out the window and could see an enormous crowd had gathered in the *Gendarmenmarkt* to watch his State of the Republic address. Technically, he wasn't supposed to call this speech a State of the Republic address, for it was required in the rules which speak of such formalities that he serve a year as chancellor first. Thus, his speech today was officially called a Speech to the Republic, but he still referred to it as a State of the Republic address, casting light onto his perpetually iconoclastic nature.

The square was packed with German citizens — the people that wanted *him* to lead them. The Principles had won a majority in parliament the previous fall and Geiseric was the newly-elected chancellor of Germany. A temporary wooden platform had been constructed just in front of the *Konzerthaus*, "Concert House," which was the main performance venue in the German capitol. Atop the platform in front of the building, was a sleek, metal, voice-enhancement podium, so that all could clearly hear their new leader. News cameras were everywhere, vying for the best angles. Journalists from all over the world rapidly spoke into their microphones, facing the cameras, giving preliminary reports to their viewers as they awaited the main event.

Finally, Geiseric got his cue to go on and the crowd in front of him erupted in wild cheer as he emerged, waving and smiling. He wore a sleek, Italian-cut suit jacket, coupled with a white silk shirt, and pleated pants. His dark hair was cropped short, and he appeared polished and collected as he took his place behind the podium.

For the first half minute or so, Geiseric continued to wave as he waited for the applause to subside. This gave him a chance to carefully survey the audience. Acting on a hunch, he subtly nodded to his security chief and pointed out a curly blond-haired man near the front of the crowd, whom he felt was behaving strangely. The chief spoke briefly into his two-way radio and three agents approached the man to escort him away. He threw a fit as they dragged him off, but the cheering crowd was oblivious to the commotion.

Geiseric chuckled. Gazing before him, he saw tens of thousands of his ardent supporters in the square and lining the perimeter streets. They carried home-made Pro-Principles signs with German phrases like *Wissen ist Macht*—Knowledge is Power. Others proudly displayed nationalistic statements, such as *Nieder mit der E.U.* (Down with the E.U.) and *Lässt Deutschland Alleine Scheinen!* (Let Germany Shine Alone!).

A perimeter of law enforcement agents, strategically stationed around the square, barricaded protesters from the audience. The protesters had also come in great numbers and bore signs reading, *Nieder mit dem Neuen Hitler!* — Down with the New Hitler! Caricatures of Hitler and Geiseric, their arms around each other's shoulders and smiling widely, decorated their posters and T-shirts. Angry voices, competing with the cheers, hurled charges against Geiseric and the Principles. Though the dissidents were much farther from the platform, Geiseric could clearly hear their agitated hisses and shouts. He merely smiled at their jeers. After letting the crowd expend its energy for a while, Geiseric brought out his hands and lowered them in a gesture that silence was needed. The journalists quieted and focused their cameras on the new chancellor.

"*Hallo, meine Leute!*" Geiseric called out warmly into the microphone.

"*Hallo!*" the audience called back. A few protesters spat vulgarities at him, but Geiseric laughed it off and straightened himself, taking in a deep breath.

"It is good to see such a vibrant crowd before me today," he began, speaking German in his more colloquial, Bavarian manner, while still enunciating enough for the rest of Germany to understand him.

"Even though it is threatening to rain any moment, you have still come out here. Thank you for your support."

Geiseric pointed to the protesters at the back. "And it is good to see such passion in Germans, even if it is against me. That is the beauty of democracy, which I do not want to destroy. Hitler, on the other hand, would have had them all sent to Buchenwald."

The audience laughed, but the demonstrators gasped, as if hearing a veiled threat. They shouted unrestrained retorts. Geiseric smirked and pulled on the hem of his suit jacket a bit.

"I know there are some people who are convinced I'm going to become a tyrant," he shouted, looking directly at the group of agitators, "but, I'm not pushing my will upon you. Have you forgotten that Germany democratically voted the Principles in? I was elected by the people, and as long as that continues to be, I will be your chancellor." Geiseric cleared his throat, pausing for a moment as the protesters got in another round of shouts. Police began discreetly escorting away those who were causing too much ruckus. Raindrops began to fall in the *Gendarmenmarkt*. An assistant tried to cover Geiseric with an umbrella, but he waved him off.

"That being said," Geiseric continued, "I hope these next four years prove to be unifying for the German people, rather than so divisive. However," Geiseric leaned forward, placing his hands on the podium, "I will not shy away from conflict, if that's what is necessary.

"Germany is at a crossroads. Without decisive action, the European Union will bring about the degradation of our ancient and great nation." His nostrils flared with vehemence. "Our neighbors need to be set in place. We can remain a part of the Union only if it is finally recognized that Germany is the *crux* and that, without us, there is no E.U.!" He gazed into the many eyes staring at him.

"Why must this be done?!" Geiseric threw his arms up in an exaggerated stage shrug. "Because we are constantly made to be the bad guys of Europe! This reputation has its roots in the first and second World Wars and, to this day, we feel the constraints of our history. Are we to be forever punished for actions taken by our ancestors a century ago? Germany has bent over backwards for the E.U. since its inception. We gave up our dominant Mark in 2002, unlike the Brits who cannot shake their Pound. We have opened our doors to

Eastern European immigrants who experience a higher unemployment rate than the Germans, violating E.U. standards. Yet, it is those Eastern European nations who hold us most strictly to the immigration rules of the E.U.! The E.U. does not acknowledge or enforce Germany's minimum environmental or animal welfare standards in other countries! So it is the Germans that must work around everyone else!" He was shouting now, bringing his left hand up in a tight fist.

The drizzle became steadier, yet Geiseric still did not summon for an umbrella. Since he did not read from a piece of paper, or from a prompter, the rain did not hinder him. He had the core of his message memorized and the rest was created spontaneously by his zeal. Wiping the water from his brow, he continued.

"France is jealous of Germany's economic strength! But they remain content by considering us to be a happy, suppliant E.U. work horse, ridden by a French jockey."

Geiseric slammed his hand down. "All I have to say is," he shouted to the cameras, "*horse shit!*"

His supporters roared with laughter and approval. It was refreshing to hear such straightforward sentiment from a politician. That type of talk had won their hearts and the election. Journalists from around the globe were feverishly writing down the quote, pleased to have such controversial fodder for their programs. Geiseric barely noticed the reaction. Absorbed with rage, his jaw muscle tensed and he clenched his teeth together as he mulled over his words.

"We will not be a slave to inferior nations!" he roared and his audience cheered once again, drowning out the protests of the demonstrators.

"For over twenty years, in our position as a donor state, we have forgiven unpaid loans. We have given ten times more to Europe than what they have given to us! The only things they have given us ten times more of are immigrants, which we have welcomed with open arms into one of the best social welfare states in the E.U."

He paused to let the facts sink in, before unleashing his next tirade. "*Yet,* do these immigrants want to accustom to *our* culture?"

"No!" his supporters shouted back.

Geiseric leaned over the podium, as if speaking intimately to a group of friends. "Who are *we* to ask that *they* should conform to *our* culture?" He asked sarcastically, placing his hands on his chest in a feigned gesture of meekness. "They think we should accustom to theirs! But it is the economy that our culture provides which draws these immigrants to Germany. They want to have their cake and eat it too!" He shook his head in disgust and straightened himself back up to his full height.

"No, no, no. This simply will not do. As I said, we are at a crossroads." He held his hands out in a manner imitating measuring scales, first tottering right. "On the one hand, we can let Europe tear Germany down, which will only destroy the Union, or," tottering left, "we can seize control of the situation and stave off a disaster for everyone. What is good for Germany is good for Europe! We *must* take the reigns!"

A heavy rain was now falling, and a sea of umbrellas decorated the *Gendarmenmarkt*. But the audience, completely absorbed in the rhetoric, did not disperse. Geiseric, focused on his speech, seemed completely unaware of the weather.

"We can and will attain the sense of pride and motivation that occurs when a country's citizens are unified. All immigrants who come here should want to be German first. They must want to learn the language. And they must want to learn the social norms. We have been engaged in a twenty-five year struggle with the Muslim community of Germany because they insist on wearing their desert garb. Well, you are no longer in the desert, I assure you," he laughed, and his audience accompanied him.

Geiseric smirked. "But, there is plenty of brutal sunlight in your native land. We will be happy to send you back to the desert, if that is the weather you wish to dress for."

His supporters vigorously applauded his comments with the fervor of people feeling their views have been well-expressed.

"And this acculturation does not end with immigrants," Geiseric pointed his forefinger towards the cameras, to those at home who he was about to speak of. "All those who have grown lazy and accustomed to living off others will be made to work. I dare say it . . . forced! And forced to learn!" The chancellor took on a calmer, more serious tone.

"From now on, to get their welfare checks people *must* go to school and get passing grades. We will push the spoiled out of their comfort zone. Modern economies are based on educated people, not ignorant, low-cost labor. Our previous reforms mandated that we create trivial tasks for people to earn their welfare. No more! We have reached the time where machines have almost completely taken over the mindless tasks that once belonged to the lower class. We need our unemployed to become skilled in something that is necessary and vital to the economy. Inability to learn is no longer a viable excuse. You *will* learn and you *will* like it!"

Uproarious approval came from the audience. Resounding cheers and joyful praises, even prayers of blessing upon their leader echoed across the square. Riding on the wave of enthusiasm, Geiseric continued.

"This message is particularly aimed at the disaffected German youth. Selfish attitudes are in abundance amongst the younger generation. They think everything is owed to them, yet think little, if at all, of what they could give back to their society. I propose that we reform the education system to include social education. In order to graduate, students will serve at least ten times the present number of mandatory community service hours — compulsory volunteer work."

Acidic shouts and booing from the protesters could be heard in faint increments over the noise, but they did not work to deter Geiseric from making his proposals. In fact, they spurred him on. His confrontational personality thrived off such emotions. The more his enemies hated him and wanted to quell his words and his agenda, the more he was empowered to fight.

"Many in the upcoming generation," he began again in a lucid tone, "are acquiring ambiguous degrees in majors like sociology, business, economics, and communications. These are fun things to learn, and everyone knows that I believe learning *anything* is of use. However, when it comes to professions, we need our children to be more specialized and, as such, productive. We especially need engineers, physicists, scientists, and the like." He rolled his hand about his wrist in front of him as he spoke, emphasizing his points. "People to invent new technologies. Therefore, this needs to be the focus of our education system. Creating people who create things. I propose that we also get our youth motivated with government-funded extra-curricular science and engineering clubs, much like the ones that sprouted up in the nineteen-twenties. We can have rocket and jet societies, where kids get hands-on experience. Let the youth meet with top people in the field and be inspired by them," he squeezed his hand into a fist and squinted his eyes a bit, to stress this vital endeavor.

"And that brings me to my plans for the space program." Geiseric gazed symbolically up to the sky.

"There is no country that deserves more accolades for space exploration than Germany!" The chancellor looked out at his people, pausing to make sure he had their attention for this key point. "It was German minds that built the Russian and American rockets. It was Werner Von Braun who designed and engineered the rocket that brought the Americans to the Moon. Von Braun was working for the United States by then, but as many of you know, during World War II he was still working for his home country. He designed the first ballistic missile in history, called the V2. Thousands of V2s rained down on Britain and other Allied countries during World War II.

"Of course," Geiseric chuckled, "that was all water under the bridge when the war was over and the U.S. needed Von Braun's brilliant mind. One of the main objectives of the Russians, Americans, and British was to attain as much German technology as possible and those German scientists who did not go with the Americans were forced to work for the Soviets. For the Allies knew that a new war was brewing amongst themselves — a war waged with *our* inventions!" he roared indignantly.

"The jet plane, the cruise missile, the stealth bomber, all were created in Germany! Of course, some of the best physicists were Germans of Jewish ancestry, Einstein being the most prominent. These scientists were kicked out of Central Europe by Hitler's insane racism, a demonstration of his complete irrationality. These were the irreplaceable minds who conceived the American nuclear bombs, both the fission and fusion bomb."

Geiseric bobbed his head from side to side a few times, stretching his neck. "Of course, Hitler was not a proponent for knowledge." He waggled his finger at the screen. "We are not Nazis, and you will not find any Principles burning books. *Knowledge is power!* It is that simple. The German people were powerful *in spite* of the Nazis, not because of them!"

Geiseric was now sopping wet, rainwater dripping from his chin and nose. The unique sight of this quieted the masses, even the demonstrators. All were transfixed on their leader.

"Hitler broke Germany's back for a century. But, we have paid our dues! We lost millions along with everyone else! We lost our strapping youths and our brilliant minds! We were divided in two and the front-line of nuclear Armageddon was on our doorstep!" He looked out upon his audience, contemplating the momentous things he spoke of.

"Then, we were united and we were so joyful that we did anything we could to please our neighbors. But now, they hold us back!"

His remarks diffused through the square. As he hoped, the audience was leaning in anticipation of his next words. Geiseric knew that even those watching his address on televisions in Germany and indeed around the world, listening to a myriad of simultaneous translations, were on the edges of their seats. His rhetoric found favor in the hearts and minds of many people inside Germany. His nationalism was also creating many enemies at home and abroad. However, as angry as he made many people, there were many more who did not know what to make of him. His every word and action was saturated with

42

charisma and authority, captivating the average person of the world. While most disagreed with him and his movement in general, they found it hard not admire him on some level.

There was, though, a vocal and powerful opposition to the Principles that had sprung up around the globe, fueled by a fear of the newly elected German chancellor. But, as he stood in the square, his supporters riveted before him, Geiseric felt that the force of his movement was unstoppable. He pressed on.

"Let us all consider the European space program for a moment. We have not met our deadlines for the Martian project. It is now 2027 and it is unlikely we will get to Mars in five years. Why? *Because*," he blasted, "other *unmotivated* nations in the E.U. think exploration of Mars is 'a waste of time'," he imitated them with a mockingly whiney voice.

"Yes, the whole continent was excited about the project at the turn of the twenty-first century, but over the following two decades, many of our neighbors lost their conviction. They have attention deficit disorder! The Germans remain committed to this endeavor. Yet, in the E.U., the German voice is considered equal to Poland's or Slovakia's. We are being instructed on what we can and cannot do by such nations. Well, I hate to sound base, but a lioness will not bend over and take it from a housecat!"

The crowd burst into uproarious laughter and cheered at the fact that he would use one of the vulgar idioms of the time. Even a few of the protesters stifled a laugh and were instantly met with angry glances from their comrades.

Geiseric chuckled. "Man needs to press forward with space exploration and Germany must lead the way. This is a fundamental mission of the Principles Party. If other countries do not want to commit, then we will seize the reins."

The chancellor looked right into the cameras that were on a raised platform thirty meters in front of him.

"Therefore, I propose that we immediately nationalize the European Space Agency's infrastructure in Germany . . ."

Gasps rang out in the square. The phones began ringing in the offices of every major world leader. The journalists were stunned into speechlessness. Even the wild protesters were so stunned that the entire mass of them momentarily ceased their catcalls. Geiseric's own supporters were startled by this unexpected and drastic revelation. They worried that such a pronouncement might antagonize or alienate potential allies.

But, Geiseric had a grand plan not apparent to most. He was further drawing in Germany's conservatives, who were opposed to much of the Principles' ideological stances, but enjoyed the party's love for their country.

The chancellor could not contain a wide, close-lipped smile. His eyes shone and his voice boomed louder.

"The Americans triumphed with the first Moon landing. They won the Space Race of the twentieth century. But it will be the Germans who first set foot on Mars! We will be the pioneers of the *new* Space Race!" He threw his fist into the air. "*Not* the Americans. *Not* the European Space Agency's "politically correct" choices. The Germans will have reason to be proud again. *You!*" he exclaimed, pointing a finger at the audience. "The inventors, the technologists, the engineers — *you* will lead again! Through your accomplishments, you will give us the spiritual capital to lead all of humanity for many generations to come! We deserve to be the first nation to put a man on Mars and we expect no less!" He slammed his fist down on the podium.

Again the square erupted in the applause of wild fanaticism.

"The European Union will be compensated," Geiseric assured, in a condescendingly placating tone. "We will pay a more than fair price for whatever we nationalize, and the E.U. has every right to compete alongside us," he said, pausing and looking from side to side, "but good luck!" He laughed and his supporters joined in.

All that could be heard throughout the square was the extraordinarily loud and overwhelming sound of tens of thousands of people cheering at once, with the mad intensity of spectators after the winning point is scored at a sports game.

Even Geiseric was moved by the immediate outpouring of approval. As he took in the scene, confidence and faith swelled inside him. His address being over, he put his hand to his lips and cast it up to the crowd, walking triumphantly off the stage.

Backstage, Geiseric went straight over to his main political advisor, the parliamentarian Helmut von Ribbentrop. He took off his soaked jacket and threw it over a rack, flinging water everywhere as he did. Combing his drenched hair back a few times with his fingers, he glanced at the tall mirror on the wall for a moment. He looked to Helmut in the mirror and smirked.

"This is going to be far too easy."

Helmut had a wide, toothy grin. "I know."

The Principles encountered little resistance to their proposals from the opposition parties in parliament. Geiseric's agendas were steadily gaining ground in the hearts and minds of the people. Polls established that the Principles had made a favorable impression upon seventy-five percent of the country. By June, only four months after his inauguration, all of the ground-breaking legislation that Geiseric had proposed at his address was passed.

ESA, the European Space Agency, evacuated all of their non-German scientists and officers at the operations center in Darmstadt. EAC, the astronaut university in Cologne, was also purged of foreign workers. It was a dismal day for many of these people. Through decades of teamwork, they had formed a community of sorts, with ties that bound far deeper than nationalism. In fact, many of these scientists, the Germans as much as any others, had come to think of themselves as Europeans first.

German scientists hugged their comrades and tears were shed as their teams were forced apart. A similar mood prevailed over the continent's entire European Space Agency infrastructure. For, as the foreign staff left Germany, the German staff left their posts in other countries. Many Germans working in other countries had lived in those countries for half of their lives. Packing and moving back to their homeland, they were emotionally torn and heavy-hearted. Many wondered how this divisive attitude sprung out of the German masses, who had once been the greatest proponents of a United Europe.

There was, however, a noticeable sect of German ESA employees who were undeniably joyful, even ecstatic at the new direction Geiseric was taking them in. Some truly believed the division would speed up the race to Mars; others had a renewed sense of nationalism previously suppressed by the yolk of the European Union.

Overall, though, the transition was proceeding relatively smoothly. Then, a storm of controversy broke when an ESA investigation found that German scientists and engineers working in the Netherlands had stolen designs and prototypes from ESTEC, the research and technology center.

The moment the accusations were lodged, Geiseric held a press conference. It was a beautiful, warm day in Berlin. So, he removed his suit jacket before exiting the Reichstag Building, home of the *Bundestag*—the German parliament. He took his place at the podium, set up in front of the massive pillars. Hundreds of journalists were seated before him, television cameras poised to once more feed his comments live to the world. Every few seconds, a flash went off.

Before taking questions, Geiseric made a statement:

"The European Union has made allegations that German employees of ESTEC have stolen property that belongs to the European Space Agency. This, however, is a misrepresentation of the truth. Property has indeed been taken. I *personally authorized* the taking of files, equipment, designs, proto-types and the like, which ESA claims belongs to them. However, it was German scientists and engineers at the core of the inspiration for and creation of these effects. Therefore, they belong to Germany."

He made eye contact with each of the cameras. "The European Union will be compensated fairly for the acquisitions Germany has made. I submitted a bill to our legislature that will authorize the remittance of twenty five billion euros to the E.U. Money is intrinsically worth *nothing*. We," he said, nodding at the closest camera, "have the irreplaceable minds."

His statement was perfunctory and once he was done, he was immediately barraged with questions and waving hands from the reporters.

✦ ✦ ✦

Fall 2027

School began on a Thursday. Summer vacation had ended and German teenagers returned to *Gymnasium*, which was semi-equivalent to high school in the United States' education system. Things had vastly changed and the students were shocked upon return. Two and a half months earlier, they had left their schools for summer break. When they came back, everything was completely different.

One of the more spectacular school renovations was in Garching, a small town north of Munich. News cameras were gathered at the awesome new institution to watch its christening—the first day of classes. The former music school had been transformed into a groundbreaking learning institution, fit for many useful pursuits.

The flat front lawn where the students used to spend their lunchtime talking, soaking up sun, and practicing their instruments was replaced by a large, open-air amphitheatre. It was a semi-circular set of bleachers, with no empty spaces between the raised benches. The students were ushered through the rows by thirty strapping men and women. They each had badges pinned on their shirts that read "Instructor," with their respective names printed below. Their hair was uniformly cropped—a close buzz cut for the men and ear-length bobs for the women. Each wore beige shorts and crewneck T-shirts, and silver whistles dangled around their necks.

Blaring their whistles, the Instructors motioned the crowd of oncoming youths into the amphitheatre seats. Startled by this new approach, the students looked at each other for confirmation. But they caught on quickly and, within ten minutes, four thousand teenagers were almost all quietly seated in the amphitheatre bleachers.

Several Instructors patrolled the aisles, silencing the chit-chatters. Finally, the largest man of the Instructor crew stood at the front of the stage to address the students. He had a deep bellowing voice which, although jovial in tone, was a bit intimidating. The news cameras were rolling, airing everything live around Germany and other corners of the world.

"Hallo studenten, ich bin Herr Corbitt," the man said. Some students said hello back, though most didn't. The man was perturbed.

"Wann ich hallo sage, sagen sie hallo Herr Corbitt!" he roared. The kids, frightened out of their lethargy, did as they were told.

"Hallo Herr Corbitt!" they all replied in near unison. *Herr* was the German word for "Mister," and was the polite way to address an elder male.

Herr Corbitt smiled. *"Gut."* He went on, speaking German in the local Bavarian dialect of the Munich area.

"Today, you begin a new journey in your lives," Herr Corbitt stridently began, the acoustics of the theatre carrying his voice to every ear. "Today, you enter into a school unlike *any* other. *Today,* you enter into the Formula education system."

He paced from either end of the stage, looking over all of the students. "One of the fundamental differences between a Formula education and the old education system is our focus on the body, as well as the mind. Fifty percent of the time will be spent towards physical activities and fifty percent will be spent towards the mind *and* the spirit," he said, pointing his burly finger in the air to enunciate his words. He began to smile widely with excitement, looking almost silly, like a father enthusiastic about something at which his cynical children simply scoffed.

"The activities will be interspersed many times throughout a school day, so we require that all students wear a uniform that will allow for exercise. Those will be given to you. Also, you must wear socks and athletic sneakers to school every day. Girls, or any of you gothic boys for that matter, are not allowed to wear make-up to school. No one wears that stuff here." He waved his hands out horizontally. "Neither will anyone have any products in their hair. Hair length is regulated in boys and girls. Piercings, necklaces, bracelets, watches and the like are also prohibited at school."

Some students yelled out in rebellion to these rules. They were immediately spotted by the Instructors walking the aisles. One girl stood and booed loudly. She was grabbed strongly by the shoulder from behind. She turned to see a powerful-looking female Instructor whose face and firm grip conveyed a silent ferocity. Shocked, the girl and her friends became silent.

A young man and his friends, all wearing dark, moody clothing, with dyed black hair, facial piercings, and chains dangling from their pants, interrupted Herr Corbitt with their outbursts. The ringleader was immediately grabbed by two beefy Instructors and was escorted to the front of the amphitheatre, onto the stage. Corbitt picked up a bucket of ice cold water, which was placed at the back of the stage, and dowsed the young agitator while he was restrained.

"Cool down!" Corbitt shouted, laughing at the boy who was wide-eyed with shock. All the students were surprised, although many of them laughed also. Everything was caught by the all-seeing lenses of the news cameras, which were streaming live around the world.

The students were herded towards a hallway, where they waited to enter a large room for quick physicals. Blood pressure, body fat ratio, and other health markers were recorded as they passed through the room. Finally, their sizes were measured for their school uniforms, distributed as they were ushered out the door on the opposite side. Both girls and boys were issued brown shorts and crewneck shirts, and swim suits with matching hair caps. The sneakers that were provided looked funny, but were amazingly comfortable and easy to run in. Equally comfortable sandals were also distributed, which were part of the required apparel to be worn during all non-physical classes.

During this entire activity, the students were kept from becoming too rowdy by the Instructors, who sometimes shouted in the students' faces to keep them from being insubordinate. The Instructors never shouted directly into a student's ear, in order to not damage the kids' hearing. They shouted at the face, which was perpendicular to the ear, having the most intimidating effect without harm. The majority of the kids had grown up in extraordinarily tolerant households, with parents who did not use even the most remote of disciplinarian tactics. The menacing squeezes from the Instructors' commanding hands were frightening to even the most tough and street-wise students.

The visiting journalists were amazed how a little old-fashioned fearmongering whipped the obstinate teenagers into shape. And the students were quick to learn how to avoid correction — absolutely no attitude was tolerated. As the morning wore on, the students' outbursts became ever fewer.

All four thousand students gathered outside on a wide, grassy field. They sat cross-legged on the ground, which was slightly wet, yet none of the kids grumbled or even talked to each other. Their eyes were fixed forward on Herr Corbitt, who was standing on a raised oak platform before them. He held a cordless microphone and spoke more calmly than in the morning session. Ten students were chosen from the audience to stand at specified points in the crowd and hold small cordless speakers, which projected Corbitt's words out to the assembly.

"What can you expect this semester as a student of the Formula system?" he asked rhetorically. "As I said this morning, this is a school like no other. For one thing, all students who graduate from here will have attained a certain level in math, science, and the liberal arts. If you are a senior and you have not met these requirements by graduation, you will be held back."

This was received poorly by many seniors in the crowd. Their resentful groans were met with buckets of icy water. As it struck them, their bodies stiffened and their necks cramped. It felt like thousands of small needles piercing their skin. But, no towels were distributed to most of them. The punished were left wet and shivering until the sun warmed them, which took hardly any time at all, due to the dry heat of the day. Some who appeared to be too cold were given towels and brought out of the crowd to be heated by lamps. Though these students were cared for after, this unique form of discipline was still unpleasant enough that none of the other students wished to have it done to them. The Instructors aimed to soak the sources of most agitation, but the people sitting around them usually got wet too. Thus, the agitators were also subjected to the wrath of their peers, which quickly hushed the crowd into a manageable and obedient group.

"Don't worry about how old you are when you graduate," Herr Corbitt explained. "You won't be here forever. Anyone who isn't mentally retarded can graduate from this school in five years."

Many of the students laughed at Herr Corbitt's politically incorrect remark.

"What's an extra year?" he went on. "It's better to leave here equal in knowledge to your fellow classmates, than for us to allow you to go on only to boost your self-esteem. As my mother always said, 'tears now or blood later.'"

Herr Corbitt strode in a determined and energetic manner from one end of the platform to the other as he spoke. "Don't think that these rules and methods are meant to be punitive. On the contrary, they are meant to be inclusive and inspiring. But, the best way to understand something new is to partake in it. Today is the start of Homecoming month. To celebrate the month, all four grades will compete in activities together throughout the day. The theme of Homecoming month is Ancient Greece.

"The Ancient Greeks," Herr Corbitt explained, his voice belting out powerfully, "were the founders of Western Culture. Greek culture had a tremendous influence on the Romans, who created an empire the likes of which few have managed to equal in power and grandeur. Through the Roman Empire, Ancient Greek civilization spread to Western Europe, particularly Spain, France, Germany and Britain, who would become the major players of the next one and a half millenia. The United States is but a continuation of Western cultural and military dominance."

Herr Corbitt looked out upon the quiet mass of students and smiled, for here began the first step in a grand agenda so large it even made him uncertain at times. But, not today.

"The Greeks were a collective of culturally and ethnically similar peoples whose standard of excellence began with the Minoan civilization on the tiny island of Crete five thousand years ago. Lead by Alexander the Great, the mightiest conqueror ever known, their ways spread over the entire known world." Corbitt's enthusiasm was contagious and most of the students remained gripped. "The Greek Scholars set out to learn about and put order to their universe. Scientists like Euclid, Pythagoras and Archimedes advanced the study of mathematics, and historians such as Herodotus and Thucydides brought accuracy and reason to the recording of events. The word philosophy itself," Corbitt threw his pointer finger up in emphasis and once again grinned, "is a Greek word meaning love of wisdom."

Many of the students chuckled to themselves, amused by the Instructor's paternal zeal, for it was a softer side of this intimidatingly strong and gruff man.

"The Greeks investigated the metaphysical as well as the physical worlds. Thus, they already understood the Formula system. The mind, body, and spirit, activated and acting in concert, can produce incredible leaps in evolution of the human being."

Herr Corbitt took on a powerful demeanor, speaking with the vigor of a military officer.

"It was this Formula that produced the man who would successfully take over most of the powerful civilizations of the ancient world. Alexander the Great was a Macedonian prince, but his heart and his mind were Greek. He was educated by Aristotle who is considered by many to be the founding father of modern science. Aristotle was a student of Plato, the great philosopher who himself was an apprentice of Socrates, the founder of philosophy in the Golden Age of Greece." Corbitt gazed out upon the collective of endless human resources — four thousand youths out of the generation who would soon be the powerbase of Germany.

"What Aristotle saw in the young prince Alexander was a person with an unending thirst for knowledge. Aristotle bequeathed upon him the great knowledge and power of Golden Age Greece. But Alexander was not just a scholar, or a geek as you might have called him," the students laughed. "He was the son of a warrior king!" Corbitt boomed. "King Phillip of Macedon was a mighty general and had brought up his son in the fashion of a warrior. Alexander was therefore tough, strong, and incredibly smart. He also had another very important dimension. He believed that he could do anything, as *you all must!*" Corbitt pointed out into the crowd.

"Alexander's mother had convinced him that he was descended from Achilles and Zeus! He believed this and acted accordingly. He led his military from the front lines, charging into the enemy before anyone else and, for whatever reason, it seemed as though he couldn't be killed in battle. He was brilliant, strong, and confident, and this combination, this simple *formula*, produced Alexander the Great!" Herr Corbitt threw up his fist to give potency.

"Today, our knowledge is that much more, so the Formula can bring us to *even greater heights!*"

At this, all of the students were intrigued. Most of them were actually inspired and excited by this pep talk, but they were still reluctant to admit it to their friends.

For the rest of the day, the students were made to exercise. They were divided into arbitrary groups of fifty. Led by the Instructors, the groups were taken around the school on different routes, running two by two. They were taught songs and sang in tandem on the slow jogs. While these workouts were not too challenging for most of the students, the weakest were allowed to walk around the school in designated groups.

The completely revamped campus was like a gorgeous park, with flowers and trees, fields of cut grass, unusual buildings interspersed and well-blended amongst the landscape.

After running, the students stretched in various yoga-like positions. Next, they went through repetitious drills of slow push-ups and abdominal exercises, loudly calling out the number of their repetitions.

Numerous drinking fountains were interspersed amongst the school grounds and water breaks were constantly insisted upon. Food was also handed out to the youths twice in the day. For the first meal, everyone was given an apple, an assortment of nuts, and a strange smoothie concoction that tasted good, though it was green and a bit chunky. It restored their energies well. At the second meal, they were given healthy sandwiches made with a meat substitute packed with protein, iron, and other nutrients. The students noticed that the meat substitute did not weigh them down. It actually restored them faster than their home diets, so that they could get back to physical activity.

The day ended with mandatory showers in the giant locker room buildings. Both the girls and boys sections had a hundred shower spigots, which they waited in line to use. The students were given special shower sandals and a choice of open showers or private stalls. Used to more modesty, many of the students waited their turns to use a curtained stall.

After school the students were boarded onto buses to ride home. Parents were discouraged from picking their children up from school. Those who insisted on driving their children were relegated to waiting at a designated pick up area that did not block the roads used by the buses. A burly traffic guard patrolled the area to ensure compliance.

The buses were designed to help the students feel calm and relaxed at the school day's end. Tranquil melodies played over the speakers. The drivers, all men, were dressed exactly the same as the rest of the Instructors. They were also the strongest, for they were in charge of their buses and often had their backs turned. Just looking at the drivers' broad, rippling shoulders, made students think twice about becoming too rowdy. At every stop, the bus drivers instructed those students staying on the bus to clap for those getting off, until the last one was out. This final act of camaraderie gave closure to the day.

There was no homework assigned from the new school. The students needed only to get enough rest and nutrition to prepare them for the next day.

The students came to school the next day dressed in their fitted brown uniforms. They were again divided into random groups of fifty, mingling students from different grades. Today, the students met *die Professoren*, the professors.

The professors wore white togas akin to those worn in the days of Ancient Greece, which the students thought was incredibly eccentric. Most, though not all, were silver-haired women, noticeably older than the Instructors. They looked very healthy for their age though, with lean, strong bodies and vibrant skin. But, to the students, their most likeable attribute was a warmer, calmer manner than the Instructors.

The professors brought their groups out to several nooks in the park-like setting of the school. They had the students walk for a few minutes, to get out some excess energy. Then, when they found somewhere pleasant to sit, *die Professoren* began their lessons for the day.

With the sunlight warming the students' skin, and the fragrant air from the lush landscape wafting into their lungs, all the students were attentive to their lessons. Each professor had a unique approach to their particular subject.

Professor Grunwald, who was quite old and seemed particularly wise, sat on a thick, low-hanging tree branch, while his students sat on the grass before him. The class was intrigued by the diminutive, elderly man, who had a bit of a protruding stomach. He had a full head of silvery-gray hair, grown past his ears, and although almost elf-like in stature, he spoke with a clear and brawny voice.

"You kids are so lucky. I wish I could have gone to a school like this. I wish I could attend this school right now! But, I have to settle for teaching here. So, consider yourselves blessed that you may come to this public gift for your minds, bodies, and souls, paid for by your parents' taxes." He adjusted his position on the branch to get more comfortable.

"Now, the brain does not like to learn things in a vacuum. Memory is based on making connections to other things, which have more resonance in the mind. This is how mnemonic memory devices work. When you know the bigger picture, it's easier to remember the many details. You will be learning Western Civilization in my class. My lessons during this next month shall focus on and give you a full perspective of the Greek peoples."

Professor Grunwald had a very jovial manner about him that the students loved. He was not at all like the teachers they had had in previous years. Professor Grunwald actually seemed to enjoy his job and really got excited about sharing his wisdom with them. He took in a deep breath of fresh air and encouraged his students to do so as well. All of them inhaled and exhaled deeply a few times.

"Good, you have to get oxygen to your brains." He waved his hands around his head and closed his eyes, doing a few last inhalations. The students laughed at his eccentric behavior. He reopened his eyes.

"So, how did the Ancient Greeks become so magnificent?" He shrugged. "Well, one reason might be that they pursued the art of theoretical knowledge. That is, they pursued knowledge for the sake of knowledge and they were the first to do so!" he exclaimed, pausing for effect and looking his students in the eyes. Many were already intrigued by the brief lecture, though some were noticably bored.

Grunwald pushed himself off the tree-branch and stood in front of the youths.

"Come along," he waved and began walking away. The students did not lag behind. They immediately rose and followed him. Though, no Instructors could be seen in the vicinity, their effect on the students remained, instilling enough fear to make them behave in a disciplined manner.

Professor Grunwald took them on a brisk stroll through the beautiful gardens on the perimeter of the school. He stopped at a thick and sturdy, wooden fence that blocked off the school from the open farmland behind.

The fence stood nearly two meters high, much taller than the professor, yet he grabbed the top and jumped over in one maneuver. He was far stronger and more flexible than the students imagined. Excited at this interesting turn of events, the students scrambled to stand on the boards running along the length of the fence, to peer over it. They were startled to see the professor walking towards a bull. The animal did not look happy about the intruder in his pasture.

The bull was huffing and trotting around in circles, about twenty meters from the professor. Its horns were cut down slightly, lacking the pointed tips. But it was still a very intimidating sight; its neck was thicker than the widest point of Grunwald's torso. Not knowing what they should do, the students just stared in amazement.

Suddenly, the bull began to charge, running full bore at the professor. The students held their breath. As the bull neared Grunwald, everyone's hearts pounded in frightened anticipation. When the massive beast was within just a couple meters of him, the professor grabbed it by the horns. The bull jerked its head up violently, as its instincts told it to do when attacking, and vaulted Grunwald's tiny frame high into the air. The professor did a somersault and gracefully landed on his feet behind the bull.

The students were awestruck. Not only did the feat seem amazing in and of itself, but coupled with Grunwald's age it seemed superhuman. The class fell silent for a moment. The bull didn't know what had happened and, not noticing Grunwald now at his rear, simply walked off. The professor walked back over to the youths. He was breathing a bit heavily, having engaged all his faculties in those few, high-performance seconds.

"Now," he said, smoothing his hair, "have I gotten your attention?"

The students wanted to learn how to do Grunwald's cool trick. He assured them that they would do it one day. They just needed a lot of practice with spring devices and other training mechanisms before taking on a real charging bull. He told the students about extra-curricular classes now offered at the school to learn the technique of bull-jumping.

He led them over to a scenic place to sit, in a cove of grass surrounded by delicate pink and gold flower blooms. The late morning sun cast a warm glow upon the foliage. The kids sat cross-legged in concentric circles, and the professor stood in the middle. To look at everyone, he turned slowly as he spoke.

"Now, I have to tell you," he laughed, "I am not a handsome man . . . "

Some of the girls stopped him and said he was very handsome. They enjoyed tickling the self-esteem of the adorable old man. He laughed and waved his hand in front of them in a gesture of humility.

"No, no, no," he said, "you don't have to lie to me. I know the truth. However, when I was younger, there were plenty of wonderful ladies who liked me just because I could do that." He pointed back to the pasture. "And I always liked to do it because it pitted me against the beast, without having to harm it."

He shook his head slightly. "However, you have to be very serious about learning such a dangerous skill. When *I* learned, I was a stupid kid raised by an ignorant family that didn't think about the dangers. Now I know how to do it by second nature. But if you are seriously interested in learning it, then we have safe methods of training. You can do *anything*, if you put your mind to it," he looked out to his class. They were smiling at his confidence in them.

"So, let's get to *why* I did that," he laughed. "I didn't do that *just* to wake you up. The sport of bull jumping was first done by the Minoans, who were the founders of Greek civilization, and, thus, the ultimate root of Western Civilization." His students silently contemplated this connection.

"The Minoans were a sports-centered society," Grunwald stated happily. "They were unlike the great cultures of their time, in that they enjoyed sports for the sake of the *sport*. The ancient cultures of the Middle East and Egypt only played sports for religious and political purposes. The Minoans represented a completely new phenomenon in the ancient world!" He emphatically crossed his hands in front of him and tossed them upwards.

"The Minoans also created art for the simple sake of its beauty. This was a concept previously unbeknownst to the ancient world — a love of something for the sake of it. It parallels the great contributions that came later from the Golden Age of Greece."

He looked at his students. Their eyes had not yet glossed over. He could continue to feed their minds.

"As I said earlier, one of the greatest contributions from the Ancient Greeks was their love of knowledge for the sake of knowledge. The love of knowledge for the sake of it did not exist until the Greeks *invented* that concept," he articulated every word with force. "Think about that."

After the lecture, Grunwald allowed his class to enjoy the new recreational park. A group of friends, all freshmen, sauntered around the beautiful site. One of the boys had unfilled piercing holes in his face. He looked completely different without his facial jewelry.

"Man, he went on forever at the end," the boy said, trying to gauge his friends' reactions. "But, you know what . . . it was actually kinda interesting. And that bull jumping stunt was fucking nuts!" He laughed with astonishment.

His friends agreed as they recalled the stunt.

Twenty minutes later, a bell rang for the students to switch classes. Professor Grunwald led his class over to a large, flat building that blended into the surrounding landscape. Once inside, the students gasped with excitement.

Spread out over a rectangular, cement floor the size of a football field, were dozens of simulator machines. They resembled the front of a jet and moved using large hydraulic pumps attached to the sides and bottom. The students were instructed to find a machine of their own and sit in the cockpit. Everyone ran to find a place, like kids boarding a ride at a theme park.

Inside, the simulators were identical to a real jet cockpit. It was equipped with a video game version of jet training, which the kids found tremendously fun. For twenty minutes, they played on their own against the computer simulators. Next, the students went against one another, in a giant royal rumble. After thirty minutes, the games ended and the hydraulics shut off automatically. On the front screens of all the simulators, the image of a young woman appeared. She was pretty, but spoke in a very cold and stern manner.

"Achtung!" she blared, startling the kids out of their leisurely mood. "This is not just funtime!" she asserted with vehemence. "I am Professor Austerlitz and in this class you are going to learn how to be a fighter pilot!"

Most of the students cheered, finding this to be the coolest class they could have imagined.

"*Achtung!*" she shouted again. The students fell silent within their cockpits. They realized that she must be monitoring them from the inside of their machines. Some of the kids glanced around their cockpits trying to spy a camera.

"We are going to get right to it then," she smiled. The screen cleared and three German words appeared on their screens. In large, bold letters it read: "Basic Flying Maneuvers."

"You are flying the EF-2015 Korbinian," Professor Austerlitz explained proudly. "The Korbinian was hypothetically built by a European consortium. However, Germany's MBB and Dornier put in the bulk of the money and manpower."

Some of the kids rolled their eyes. They did not care about all the Principles' nationalistic talking points.

"The Korbinian is a jet that is matched by no other power, not even the U.S. It was designed to gain air superiority. The Korbinian is meant for dog-fighting!"

All of the students, boys *and* girls, were really excited to hear this. In fact, the more they heard about this class, the more they loved it. Their machines were turned off and the cockpit tops and sides came down, allowing the students to see around them. The kids finally saw their professor in person, as she walked by on a raised platform that weaved among the simulators. She was a tall, slender woman who had a feminine grace while nonetheless being obviously muscled beneath her one-piece, gray flight suit. As she walked by, she looked down on them with a menacing sneer.

Austerlitz continued in her military manner of speaking. "Extensive aerodynamic refinements to the jet during the demonstration and validation process have increased maneuvering capabilities. It also has the highest thrust to weight ratio of all other fighter jets in the world." Her voice echoed in the large, uncarpeted room that had many metal structures within to resonate off, bestowing upon Austerlitz an even more commanding sound.

"The Korbinian has true 'hands on throttle and stick control,' which means that all important switches are mounted on the throttle or stick." After she had toured the class briefly, Austerlitz returned to the front of the classroom and her image came back on the students' screens.

"You have a helmet-mounted sight for aiming ASRAAM missiles," she said, and on the screen came: ASRAAM — Advanced Short-Range Air-to-Air

Missile. It was written in English for its type was first created in the United States and all other countries broadly referred to such missiles, whoever they were made by, as "ASRAAMs." Below on the screen, it was translated into German.

"The ASRAAM is the dogfight missile. It is highly maneuverable and combat effective. The Korbinian also has a thirty millimeter Gatling gun which, because of its rotating barrels, is capable of firing five thousand rounds a minute without melting." She barked the specifications to the students loudly, as if they were truly in cadet school.

"The Korbinian has 13 different types of rockets, totaling 300 altogether. As the pilots in this fighter jet, you are the deadliest in the air!" she shouted enthusiastically.

"Today, you will receive an overview of Basic Flying Maneuvers, which is the art of exchanging energy for aircraft position. When I speak of energy, I am talking about the fighter speed and altitude. 'Pulling Gs' and turning will cause all aircraft to slow down, or lose altitude, or both. Gs, or G-force, refers to the synthetic gravitational force exerted on the craft and pilot during acceleration. The jet accelerates when it increases *or* decreases in speed, or when it turns. All these things can exert many times the force of gravity on the craft and the pilot."

A computer graphic enactment of jet fighting maneuvers appeared on the simulator screens, as Professor Austerlitz described them.

"The goal of offensive maneuvering is to remain behind your adversary and to get in a position to shoot your weapons. In defensive maneuvering, you turn your jet and move out of your enemy's sights. In head-on maneuvering, you get behind the bandit from a neutral position. When you execute maneuvers to accomplish any of these objectives, you use and lose energy. In this lesson, you will learn the geometry of the flight and the specific maneuvers needed to be a successful air-to-air Korbinian pilot."

Words in bold came up on the screens and Austerlitz read them out loud as they did. "*A pilot flies in the future, not the present!*

"The fighter pilots of World War II," she went on with a greater calm, "engaged in aerial battle as if they were chess pieces playing in a sequential game of move and countermove. Modern aerial warfare, however, is more comparable to a wrestling match. It is a fluid contest of quick reactions with both opponents executing their maneuvers in a blur.

"A pilot is *always* flying in the future and not in the present," she sternly enunciated once again. "You must constantly predict the enemy fighter's future position. You must know where the bandit will be a few seconds from the time you observe him. Then, you must fly your jet based on this prediction!" Professor Austerlitz whipped the pointer stick onto the iron railings of the platform she stood upon. The snapping sound startled the students.

Professor Austerlitz taught them the two characteristics of a turning aircraft one had to understand — turn radius and turn rate. Turn radius was a measure of how tight the jet made a turn. Turn rate measured the speed of the turn, or how fast an aircraft could get its nose on the enemy. Since the air-to-air weapons systems of the jet required pointing the nose on the target, turn rate was vital. The students also learned the basics of keeping a balance between too much and too little speed. The speed of their maneuvering was dependent on the Gs a fighter was willing to pull. Finally, the students learned the turn rate equation — K G/V, where K was a constant, G was for G-force, and V was for velocity.

In just one afternoon, the students had been instructed on both the physics and algebra of flying. But, they never felt the information was being crammed down their throats. Just as kids could remember all the statistics of their favorite sports players, or could learn all the inane realities of video games, the students had received functional knowledge in a way that engaged their minds.

When the simulator lesson was over, the students were escorted across the campus to a very bizarre-looking building. It was circular, with a coned roof and made entirely of large, pole-like bamboo shoots. As they entered, the students were hit with a wave of refreshing fragrances. Inside, was a large, circular room, dimly lit and painted in many relaxing hues. Calm music filled the space with the sounds of harps and other meditative instruments, and the subtler sounds of the ocean and nature.

In the middle of the room stood a woman who appeared to be the youngest professor they had seen so far. She looked twenty-five, though she was ten years older. Beautiful orange hair curled down past her waist and she wore a silky, full-body outfit. It was form-fitted, but plenty loose enough for movement.

In a soothing voice, she invited the students to sit down. She had the quality of a person that had achieved complete satiation. The class was guided to sit in concentric circles going out from her to the wall. She introduced herself as *Fräulein Kinski*, a *Lehrerin*, or teacher.

She began her lesson by telling them about the peculiar bamboo building.

"Bamboo is a giant grass, but it can grow as tall as trees and it's a very sturdy material for building. It's even sturdier than wood in some cases. It grows very fast, some as fast as a meter a day. Most bamboo reaches full height within two months. When it's harvested, the root system is left unharmed and ready to produce more shoots, just like a grass lawn. So, it's also far more ecologically sound than using trees.

"So you see," Fräulein Kinski explained, rolling her neck to stretch it out, "this building is both efficient and in harmony with nature. Being resourceful is one of the highest forms of intellect," she blissfully remarked, looking around at the inquisitive faces.

She taught a few mild yoga positions, while making sure that everyone was breathing correctly. The room was well-ventilated with oxygen and, though it was dim, the students felt the perfect medium between awake and relaxed. After the stretching, she began to teach the students about visualization.

"Visualization transports your mind to a calm and peaceful place," she explained in her mellow tone. She breathed in and out deeply, while the students followed her lead.

"I will now escort you through a visualization meant to refresh your eyes. Those simulators produce eye strain, as does television, video games, and computers. The color green helps to bring the nerves and muscles that control the movement of the eyes back into proper alignment."

Most of the kids were cynical about this proposition. It sounded like incredible nonsense.

"Now," Fraulein Kinski continued, "close your eyes and take slow, relaxed breaths. Visualize an emerald green pool, right in front of your eyes. Now, imagine that this color is flowing gently into your eyes . . . then into the muscles surrounding your eyes. See your eyes and their muscles filling up with the pool of green."

Most of the youths were visualizing green, whether they wanted to or not, because of her prompting.

"Inhale," she mildly commanded, "visualize the green pool flowing from the back of your eyes into the optic nerve. Exhale, and let your mind's eye watch as the green energy flows through the optic nerve, to the back of your head. Let it flow down into your neck and through your entire body. Now, inhale, and watch it flow out of your hands and feet."

She stood slowly and gracefully. All the students did so as well. They followed her example, shaking their hands and one foot at a time. By the end of the exercises with Fraulein Kinski, the students felt much less agitated and more at peace than they had in a long time.

✦ ✦ ✦

As the month wore on, the students learned everything about the Classical world, from 1500 B.C. to the Roman Empire, up to the Roman conqueror Julius Caesar and Cleopatra.

They also learned some basics of the ancient Greek and Persian languages. *Die Professoren* explained that learning other languages expanded the mind. It forced a person to think in a completely different way. Music was like another language, the most fundamental in many ways. Like the youths of ancient Athens, the students in Germany during Homecoming Month learned a song on the lyre. They also experimented with Ancient Greek war flutes, imagining what it would have been like to have walked into a phalanx of spearmen to the tune of these instruments.

Numerous artistic activities kept the youths perpetually entertained. There was pottery, sculpting, painting, and drama. The students performed the great works of Sophocles and other ancient plays. Historical scenes were reenacted. The metallurgy of the time was also learned and the students worked with iron using a safer version of the ancient techniques.

The students were becoming in ever greater shape. Physical activity was simply slipped into the day with the lesson or as a game. They would take strolls across the premises while the professors spoke idly to them. They were engaged in games of the ancient world, as well as more popular sports, like dodge-ball and flag football. They were taught to march in step in a phalanx formation, learning how hard it was to do simple choreography on a large scale. By the end of the month, they could maneuver in formations a thousand strong, wearing outfits representing their team's classical city-state. Teams were segregated by class, the eldest getting to be the Spartans, which they savored. The Juniors were the Athenians, the Sophomores were Thebans, and the Freshmen were Corinthians.

The month ended with almost two weeks off from school, which the Instructors did not announce until the day before the vacation's start. On the last day of Homecoming Month, everyone gathered in the large field at the middle of the school, dressed in their replica panoplies, standing upright in their formations, and carrying the large hoplon shields and dull-tipped iron spears they had crafted in metallurgy class. The students were made to bear their gear, standing for a half hour, while they listened to Herr Corbitt go on endlessly about the link between the Ancient Greeks, Europe, and then the modern world. He rambled on about how they understood the Formula, which was to stimulate the mind, body, and spirit.

It was cold outside and the students were getting agitated, though they had toughened over the past month. Not one of them knew when Corbitt was going to finish. Yet none misbehaved, not even the youngest, for they now knew the repercussions. They all just stood upright with their chests pushed out, bearing their panoplies.

Then, just as it seemed Herr Corbitt's speech would never end, he suddenly, casually, announced a twelve-day vacation for the whole school. Most of the kids were not paying attention by then, focusing only on their sore shoulders, arms, and legs. A student called out, asking Herr Corbitt if he had heard right. Corbitt looked out on the crowd and shouted into the microphone.

"I will see you all in twelve days. Now get the hell out of here!"

For a moment there was only silence. Then, an outburst of euphoria cascaded through the classes. They shouted and some slapped the person next to them on the shoulder, but they did not break formation. They knew this would anger Herr Corbitt. Calmly and methodically they funneled out, as ordered, line by line, safely exiting the field and stowing their panoplies. Herr Corbitt gazed out upon the order.

"*Gut. Sehr Gut,*" he said to himself.

All of Germany was experiencing the radical changes of the Principles' new system. Every citizen was entitled to a free, one-hour massage each week. The masseuses and masseurs were the best in the world, for the art of massage was such a highly respected trade in the new Germany, they were paid twice as much as they earned in other European countries and the United States. Many of the massage therapists were not even Principles sympathizers. Coming to Germany was an act of pure economic rationale. Almost all of them were, by no coincidence, attractive as well. The Principles' government and bureaucracy had no qualms about setting politically incorrect guidelines.

Everyone had their place in the new Germany though, and everyone was given equal fundamental benefits, such as universal healthcare. Healthcare meant something far more vigorous than was applied anywhere else on the planet. The citizens were given the best nutritionists in the world, again because of the regime's respect for the profession. Respect was demonstrated by compensation and stature equal to a surgeon's. Nutritionists monitored and prescribed vitamins, minerals, and every kind of herbal supplement, which the patients could attain for free at the local pharmacy.

The nutritionists focused on holistic preventive care, rather than waiting until the patients became ill and then seeking a cure, or simply masking the symptoms. They were sure that almost all physical illnesses, and even most psychological illnesses, were derivative of a simple lack of nutrition, exercise, and proper rest. It was plain to the nutritionists that putting poor materials into the body led to sickness and fragility. Living off an unhealthy diet, like fried or fast foods, was like building a car out of Styrofoam. And withholding the proper vitamins and minerals from the body was like expecting a car to run without oil or coolant.

True to the Principles' spirit, patients who were unhealthy because of lifestyle and personal habits were criticized heavily by their nutritionists. Brutally honest, they told their patients when they were too fat, too lazy, or too gluttonous concerning some other unhealthy habit. Patients were often berated for being drains on the economy because of all the preventive medical care they would need, which would be given free of charge but paid for by taxpayers.

The medical doctors and surgeons had the same attitude. They would not be cruel to their patients in times of healing or weakness, but the moment the patient recovered, the doctors would berate them. The biggest criticism, by far, was obesity. The doctors also criticized people who abused free healthcare by clogging up appointment times with minor ailments and illusionary problems. The German physicians called such people "parasites."

At the introduction of the Principles' Universal Healthcare Plan there were incidents of nutritionists and doctors being attacked by angered patients, so guards were put in the hospitals and professional offices. Soon, however, many of the patients who were berated either changed their behavior accordingly, or stopped coming to the hospital, eliminating most of the problem.

Overall, though, the Principles' healthcare plan was adored by the people. The main problem with universal healthcare systems around the globe was abuse by healthy people with nothing better to do. Abuse attributed to huge amounts of wasted time and money. Geiseric had come up with a fundamentally socialist system and streamlined it to the efficiency of a capitalist program. People worldwide were filled with awe and admiration.

With the Universal Healthcare Plan successfully in place, the Principles set about centralizing the food industry. They wanted to produce the best products without relying on the private sector and the devices of capitalism to improve standards. Geiseric argued that, in some cases, capitalism worked to purge out the weak and substandard and, therefore, improve society. However, in many cases, this capitalist machine also drove people in a race towards the bottom.

The Principles Advocacy Group created ad campaigns that targeted cereals, a common breakfast for children and many adults. Breakfast was touted by the new German regime as the most important meal of the day. This was a common nutritional belief, because it started the body off strongly in the morning, shoring it up the entire day. The Principles argued that too much sugar and carbohydrates in the morning wreaked havoc on a person's insulin balance. The blood sugar would go up, giving an immediate surge of energy, but later the insulin level crashed, leaving a person fatigued for the rest of the day, until they could get back into balance with the rejuvenating powers of sleep.

The German state took control of the cereal industry, a very controversial move in the eyes of big-business. To gain support for this legislation, the Principles argued that the private sector had proven incapable of providing for the proper needs of the citizens, especially children. They said that in this case capitalism had favored those who took money away from taste and nutrition and poured the funds into advertising. Those companies got more exposure than the morally upright companies who provided healthy food, which inevitably cost more to produce than corn-syrup and depleted grains.

This argument struck a chord in the hearts of almost all Germans over thirty who, like their parents and grandparents, had grown up on healthier cereals. But the increase of American-made and American-like cereals, all artificially colored and flavored, and full of sugar, were steadily crowding out the older German brands. The commercials for these "candy brands," as Geiseric called them, pandered to children, so that they would goad their parents incessantly for the product. Geiseric compared the executives and advertisers of these companies to drug dealers who peddled to children knowing that the kids were not aware of the dangers of the enticing substance.

The healthy cereals provided by the new centralized system cost less, because there was no advertising. People were expected to go to the store, read the nutritional information on the cereal boxes, and decide what was best for their families.

The cereal campaign was just one example of the many sectors of the food industry taken under the control of the Principles administration. Most of the German citizens were feeling better, in general. Incidents of depression, suicide, and other psychological ailments decreased evermore below their record lows every month, especially in the teenage demographic. The risk of cancer and heart disease was lessening to the vast majority of those who previously seemed to be in danger. Senior citizens were dancing in the woods at the *Volksfesten* until long into the night. There was an aura of youth and vitality filling the country, seen upon the happy faces and in the sparkling eyes of all the German citizens.

—— IV ——

PROJECT FOR A
NEW GERMANY

Logan was captivated and at the same time terrified by the information Alistair
shared with him. Geiseric was like some insane character out of a dream — or
nightmare. This was a feeling Logan often experienced when learning history
at school or on television. When he watched historical documentary shows, he
often viewed the grainy film images as if they were a fictional movie. It was all
too surreal to believe.

Now, Logan realized that he was experiencing one of the most surreal eras
in history. He was surprised by how little he knew about recent world events.
Before he moved to the island, he didn't even know that Geiseric was such an
incredible threat. He had heard others talk about the "German dictator," or the
"New Hitler," and he had heard about new nations and other political entities
being created, but his parents sheltered him from the truth and he didn't think
to ask too many questions. Most of his friends in San Francisco were quite
naïve as well. Some seemed to know more than others, but most didn't talk
about what was going on in the world, nor did they seem concerned. They
were just twelve at the time, after all.

The adults on the island had deluded the kids into believing that things were going well for the Allies. Logan knew his parents just wanted to protect him, but it was incredibly traumatizing to learn the truth all at once.

Suddenly, the certainty of the situation resonated fully with Logan — he was the captive of the enemy regime. It hit him with a wave of panic so boundless that not even the calming drugs in the ambrosia could stay it. He was completely unaware that Alistair was in the midst of telling him more. His head throbbed and he pressed his temple onto the cool window glass for comfort. As he looked out, he saw three other strange aircraft, identical to the one he was riding in. How strangely the transports undulated through the air, subtly waving up and down as they flew, like long serpentine dragons. They almost seemed to be alive.

The windows of all the aircraft were tinted so that the passengers could look out, but it was difficult to discern more than shadowy shapes when peering in from the outside. When the transport Logan was riding in made a subtle change in vector to the left, it would curve slightly, allowing him to get a good look at the riding cars behind his. He thought he saw the one into which his parents were pushed and he tried in vain to identify his parents' forms through the opaque glass.

Logan felt a gentle, feminine hand on his shoulder. Lost in thought, he had almost forgotten his present company. Francesca sat close to Logan and looked out the window with him. He couldn't help but smile slightly as he looked at her.

"Don't worry," she said. Her melodic accent calmed Logan's nerves. "Your parents will be fine . . . and so will you." She massaged Logan's stiff neck a bit. He was soothed by her words, but her touch stiffened his muscles with nervous excitement. He hoped she wouldn't notice his reaction. His mind soon came back to everything he had been told by his companions so far during the flight.

"Why did the world just let Geiseric do anything he wanted?" he asked. Francesca leaned her face in, close to his.

"Like what?"

Logan turned and looked at the other occupants in the compartment. "Why did the European Union let him just snatch up what he wanted?"

"Pretext," Jacques answered, leaning back and throwing his right leg across his left. "Geiseric gave a very rational line of reasoning for everything he did. It was hard for most people to see how dangerous he was, at first. Geiseric knew how to strike when the iron was hot and he was always three steps ahead of the public." Jacques became obviously frustrated as he thought about it, but he brushed it out of his mind with a deep breath and shake of the head.

"Certain leaders in the world," he continued, emotions in check, "were completely against him from the very beginning. But, they couldn't rally their citizens until it was too late. A lot hinged on the Americans, like in the first two world wars. But in the first two, the U.S. got in just in time." Jacques sighed and looked out of the window, into the distance.

"Geiseric was not stupid enough to perpetrate another Lusitania, or Pearl Harbor, or 9-11. So, the most powerful country in the world stood impotent as the beast grew in the heart of Europe . . ."

✦ ✦ ✦

Fall 2027

Geiseric was prepping himself for yet another important speech. He looked in the mirror and smiled, as he smoothed a dab of mousse in his hair. The Germans were prospering and Geiseric's administration was polling increasingly well, gaining an eighty percent approval rating with his nation's voting populous. So, he wasn't surprised when his political opponents, at home and abroad, began to launch a major diplomatic offensive. The first salvo came from the neighboring country of Poland.

A week earlier, the German government and four of Germany's top ten companies were served with a highly-publicized class-action lawsuit. Over six thousand Poles, mostly of Slavic ethnicity, filed the suit to recoup damages for the havoc the Nazis rained upon their country — their grandparents — in those years between 1939 and 1945.

They sought one of the largest awards ever demanded by World War II victims of the German government. They had an ulterior motive, far more important than any monetary gain. They wanted the opportunity to remind the German populace, and the entire world, about the horrors the Nazis perpetrated upon the Slavs. Using the publicity of the lawsuit, they hoped to open Germany's eyes to a possible disaster that could come with the acceptance of Geiseric's Hitlerian tendencies.

Unfortunately for the Polish, Geiseric intended to use this lawsuit to his advantage.

Since the day the lawsuit was filed, Geiseric and the Principles had employed their propaganda attack dogs, working the German people into a frenzy. As a result, the Germans became infuriated with Poland and experienced a renaissance of nationalism. Yet, there was still a vocal minority of the country adamantly opposed to the Principles' push for Germanic hegemony in Europe.

Geiseric knew today's press conference to address the lawsuit was an opportune moment to get the remainder of the country behind him. He exuded confidence, as he took his place in front of the Reichstag, its giant transparent dome behind him. Tens of thousands of people crowded the large, cropped grass field before the Parliament building, spanning at least a half-kilometer into the distance. Many were singing Das Deutschlandlied, the German national anthem, while carrying signs that read, *"Deutschland Uber Alles!"* This was the opening line to the anthem and it meant, "Germany, before all others." Though it was a song written about uniting the German states and people at a time when they felt more Prussian or Bavarian than German, it inevitably took on the connotation of being a nationalistic chant for militaristic expansion. These words were so frightening to the World War II Allies who occupied the nation, they outlawed the first paragraph of the song and it was *verboten* until Geiseric officially reinstituted the anthem in its original form.

The vast majority of people in the streets were jubilant when Geiseric appeared on the stage, waving and smiling. The event was once again televised live and being watched not only in Germany, but in every other nation of the world. The political analysts at home and abroad had predicted a pivotal speech, and Geiseric didn't plan to disappoint them.

He stood at the large podium, which was carved from cobalt blue marble. It was a sunny day and he wore a sleek pair of shades, the lenses casting many different colors as they reflected the light. His hair had been cropped to look more presidential, but he still combed it in a youthful style. He had chosen a casual ribbed, silk crewneck T-shirt, pleated khaki pants, and black boots.

As at past speeches, there was a loud minority of people booing. This time the dissenters had anti-Nazi signs — swastikas circled and slashed through. Others had signs that read "Germany must always remember its past," and "Not Another Hitler!" or, "Pay the Polish!" Still, they were the minority. Geiseric removed his glasses and surveyed the crowd for a good minute, eyeballing different people, taking in the cheers and boos. He smirked and began.

"Guten Tag meine Leute," he greeted calmly, his voice echoing over the loudspeakers all the way down the streets. Many of his supporters clapped

and shouted back *"Guten Tag!"* Many dissidents shouted back other things. Geiseric smiled, pretending to hear only the good.

"Ah, dankeschön," he thanked his audience. He stood up straight and breathed in deeply. "As you know, Germany has been sued by some citizens of Poland. The action is endorsed by the Polish government itself."

He spoke using the more presidential northern dialect. "They are seeking reimbursement for damaged property and infrastructure, and confiscated property, including paintings, jewelry and other personal belongings. They are also seeking compensation for atrocities committed on the Polish during Hitler's quest to purge out Slavic peoples. The total amount they are seeking is over thirty billion euros."

Many in the audience hissed, indignant at such a request.

But the voice of a protester roared out, "We could never pay them enough for what Hitler did!"

Geiseric nodded. "It's good that you feel that way," he remarked, with a tinge of sarcasm. "We do not want to be like Hitler. For one thing, Hitler lost!"

Many in the crowd laughed, yet not as many as before. Geiseric made a mental note to refrain from pushing the limits too far with his off-the-cuff humor. He quickly continued with his prepared speech.

"However, the Germans of today are *not* Hitler or the Nazis. There is no one alive today that was alive during those atrocities, except for a handful of those who were toddlers. Yet, there are some who would say that two-year-olds of the Third Reich *do* share in the responsibility?!"

This received a howl of laughter from most of the crowd. Others hurled irate remarks with vehement contempt for his lack of solemnity. Geiseric chuckled.

"Some of you can't take a joke," he wryly remarked. "But, we did not come for jokes. It is no joke for Poland to claim that we are responsible for our nation's war on Poland nearly a hundred years ago. So, we are not going to wait to see how Brussels rules on the issue of its legality," he asserted with a cold, underlying rage. "I am putting an end to this nonsense right now. We are *not paying!*"

The crowd sent up an intense cheer that completely overwhelmed the opposition voices for a moment. Geiseric waited for them to calm before continuing.

"As I've said before, major changes must be made for Germany to continue as part of the European Union. We have been ridden like mules, that grateful workhorse whom everyone takes for granted. Since the E.U. began taxation, Germany has received seventy-five percent of every Euro we give. As compared to France, which gets eighty-five percent, or Britain which receives ninety percent. Poland, of course, is a charity case and receives one-hundred and fourteen percent of every Euro they put in. So, they do not put in anything, basically. They just take!" he asserted, pounding his fist into his other palm.

"Germany's economy is one and a half times the size of Britain's, so we are giving four times as much to the Union as they are. The same applies to France, the next highest donor state, which ends up giving *one half* of what Germany does."

Geiseric raised his hands and shrugged. "And for what? So that we may build up Poland?"

Geiseric leaned forward, holding the sides of the podium, and faced into the camera as he spoke his next words. "Why don't you give Germany a little land in return?" he asked, cocking one eyebrow up. "After all, the second largest immigrant bloc coming to Germany for the past ten years has been Polish immigrants. And we welcome all who come. But, don't you think it's getting a little crowded here?" he asked, in a pseudo-demure manner. "After all, both countries have the *same* land area, but Germany has three times the population. Why not let *us* take administrative control of Polish land, instead of having the immigrants come to our already overburdened space?"

Geiseric turned his direct gaze away from the camera and surveyed the quiet crowd. They seemed somewhat in shock. Then, frenetic cheers began picking up throughout the audience. Simultaneously, angry dissidents rang aloud. The chancellor smirked and breathed in deeply again, as if inhaling the invigorating fragrance of the intense emotion coming at him.

"Today, I go to Brussels to state some of the demands that must be met in order for Germany to stay in the European Union. Germany can walk away from the E.U. and be the better for it. However, there are many things which can be accomplished with the Union, if they are finally willing to compromise. It is their turn to go along with Germany, instead of Germany always having to placate them!"

Once again, the cheers of the crowd dominated. Banners from both sides were waved vehemently. Geiseric waved triumphantly and nodded at the cameras once more, as he stepped down and walked back into the Reichstag.

Prime Minister Charles Dandau thoughtfully puffed on one of his favorite cigars. He had just watched Geiseric's speech on a flat-screen television that was built into the backseat area of his armored limousine. He was dressed for his destination in a black, pin-striped suit, well-tailored to his lean but sturdy frame. His gray hair was trimmed short and parted down the middle.

A security detail of six agents rode along with Dandau; two in the front passenger seat, one being the driver, and the rest in the back. The officer in charge of the security force, a tall middle-eastern man with a curly, but neatly-trimmed black beard and mustache, sat in the back with the British prime minister. The agent had piercing, cat-like, green eyes.

Dandau picked up the microphone beside him, untangling the cord that ran from its base to a compartment on the interior wall nearby. He then pressed the small recording button on the microphone and spoke into it.

"In 1918 . . . ." he pressed the button to stop it. He carefully thought over the message he was going to deliver. Oratory was the prime minister's passion and he savored this moment. Collecting his thoughts, he pushed the recording button again and began once more.

"World War I was to be the war to end all wars . . ."

Three hours later, the leaders of the nations in the European Union were gathered at the Justus Lipsius Building in Brussels, Belgium. All the chancellors, prime ministers, and presidents of the thirty-three E.U. nations sat in their seats facing the podium on the front stage. Prime Minister Charles Dandau shuffled his notes, preparing to address the consulate. Cameras focused on both Geiseric and Dandau, with live feeds airing around the world. Geiseric sat quietly in the audience, breaking a subtle smile.

"World War I," Dandau began, looking out to his peers, "was to be the war to end all wars. It was dubbed the 'Great War,' for it killed more than any before it. It threw the entire world into tumult, unlike any conflict had ever done. It was then that our predecessors tried to develop a Union of European Nations to stop the slaughter. Europe was to unite under a common umbrella, so that our disputes would be settled in congresses and courtrooms — not on the battlefield."

Dandau took a deep breath and glanced at his notes before continuing his address. "Then, there came Hitler — the Great Tyrant! His lust for world domination tore apart all hopes for a peaceful Europe and brought the world to the brink of cataclysm. World War II killed more people than all wars before it in total. And the offspring of World War II — the Cold War –almost brought doomsday itself," he remarked with dramatized stoicism.

"Of the fifty-six million people killed in the Second World War, the majority were civilians. After that vile bloodbath, that grand orgy of violence, the European people were left disgusted by war. European leaders, led by Winston Churchill, fought hard to never let it happen again."

Dandau outstretched his arms, sweeping them around to indicate each of his colleagues.

"And look at what has been accomplished! We went from unified coal and steel industries to a federal government, here in Brussels. Yet, Geiseric wants to throw away all those hard-fought years towards unity."

The prime minister pointed directly at Geiseric, who was still smiling pleasantly. "He wishes to also gain German Lebensraum in Poland!" Dandau slammed his fist down on the podium. "Am I the only one seeing a pattern?!"

He calmed himself and straightened his suit jacket a bit, ready to drive his point home.

"So, before Geiseric comes up here and works his charisma and intellect on you and the world, I plead to the citizens of Europe and to Germany in particular — please, do not forget what one man like Hitler can do. And do not underestimate the potential of Geiseric! He has a grand plan and his cause will not stop in Germany!"

Many of the leaders sitting before him clapped profusely, but Geiseric was the first to stand in ovation, perturbing Dandau and many of his most ardent supporters in the audience. They rose up quickly after Geiseric to take the focus of the cameras from him, which then led the entire room in a standing ovation.

Geiseric, still clapping, stood and walked briskly down the main aisle. He jumped onto the stage before the prime minister was off. Guards moved in to protect Dandau, but he waved them off. He was not about to let Geiseric intimidate him in front of the entire world. Hands pushed securely into his pants pockets, Dandau stared down his nose at Geiseric. The cameras focused in, eagerly awaiting a confrontation. But Geiseric simply walked by Dandau, glaring him in the eye as he passed. Geiseric's lips were sealed into a plastic smile that hid an obvious rage beneath, as he continued clapping all the way up to the podium.

Dandau, eager to show the room that Geiseric's little game was not working on him, returned to his seat in a leisurely manner. Geiseric stopped his applause, and waited patiently before beginning his rebuttal.

"Great speech, Charles." Geiseric pointed to the prime minister, gazing at him coolly. He spoke English in a neutral, western United States dialect. Seven years spent in California during his youth came in handy, for his German accent hardly came through, which would ingratiate him to the Western media.

"You are a very talented orator. Unfortunately, I must dispute your facts." Geiseric stood up tall and took in a few deep breaths. As he did, his smirk vanished, replaced by a look of bitter fury.

"Germany will no longer be forced to stomach your versions of history. It was *Lloyd George* and *Woodrow Wilson* who caused World Wars I and II! It was their desire to do whatever it took to destroy an economic competitor in World War I that brought about the great evil of World War II! And it was the Versailles Treaty that brought Hitler into power more than *anything else!*"

Gasps could be heard around the room in response to Geiseric's aggressive manner. He looked them all in the eyes and grinned. He was satisfied at getting a rise out of them, but knew he needed to appear calmer. With greater deference, he continued.

"But, I did not come here to argue about the past. I came here to state terms for the future. I do not wish to unsettle the world, as Prime Minister Dandau would have you believe. I am completely content with ruling Germany by the Principles' code. I have no desire to gain more power, or to convert others. It is out of simple logic that I ask for more land.

"Everyone is flocking to Germany!" he shouted, startling many of the leaders and making them jump in their seats. "There are more immigrants coming there than to the top three E.U. countries combined. Yet, Germany is half the size of France. And *why* do the immigrants come to Germany? Not for the scenery," he answered himself sarcastically. "They come there because of the German state," he counted off on his fingers, "the jobs, the education, the healthcare system. These are a function of the culture! These are why people have come to such a cramped little country. So, why not let that country grow — grow to accommodate those who wish to live there. Grow into the land which the most sizable immigrant group comes from. That's what makes sense!"

Geiseric looked around the room. The tension was palpable, with all the European leaders in the room summoning up the sourest expressions possible, in order to show how indignant they were. As usual, this did not serve to repress the chancellor.

"Of course there will always be a natural, selfish inclination to keep land that you are less deserving of, just because it was yours first. But, the facts are facts — the Germans could use the land better than the government which administers Poland now. It *is* that simple. Germany needs to grow. At the current rate, even if we cut off immigration, our population will reach a hundred and fifty million in twenty years. The point is, why stifle a good thing?" He shrugged. "Germany needs to grow into the east. There are vast tracks of land occupied by few people, most of whom are still living in substandard conditions compared to Western Europe. With a land annex, these people will get a better system without having to immigrate." Geiseric held out his arms. "It will be good for everybody."

"Here are the facts," he asserted boldly, focusing his eyes briefly upon the prominent politicians in the room. He then looked into the main television camera, to make his point to those watching across the globe.

"The American empire was built off the blood and deaths of an entire race of people — the Native Americans. They were the first humans in the Americas. The Anglo-Americans committed genocide in their manifestation of destiny to the Pacific, based on the idea that their population was expanding. They believed they were more advanced than the natives, and so they deserved it more. If that was done today, American leaders would be tried for war crimes. In fact, it *was* done by Hitler only a hundred years after Andrew Jackson's infamous 'Trail of Tears.' Do the leaders of the world constantly deluge the U.S. with guilt for successfully erasing an entire native nation? No! But, the *Germans* are *ever* the evil ones for their history!" He shook his head and took a few deep breaths before continuing.

"The policies of the United States towards the Native Americans were an inspiration to Hitler, who was unsuccessful in his ruthless bid to manifest *Germany's* destiny in the east. Yet, it was only the Nazis who were tried for their war crimes. The world does not think a hundred years is so distant now. Why should it have felt that way to Hitler?"

Geiseric carefully observed the audience before him. The European leaders were not as furious with him as they were moments before, for many were in agreement with some of his points concerning the war crimes of the United States throughout its history. However, they ultimately saw the issue as irrelevant concerning what they would do in Europe.

Gazing back into the television camera, the German chancellor addressed the audience to which he truly wished to communicate his message — the citizens of the United States. The Americans were the people whom almost everything hinged upon and they needed to stay out of European affairs for Geiseric's agenda to roll into motion. As long as the United States did not become immersed in the political conflict, Germany had the power to stay its neighboring opponents.

In this light, the chancellor's attacks upon the U.S. might have seemed counterintuitive. However, Geiseric had closely studied the "American animal," as he called it. He assessed that the nation was a gentle beast, which was self-deprecating and, by its very nature, isolationist. Liberals and conservatives alike were against intermingling in world affairs for the most part, though for far different reasons. Conservatives tended to not care about anything going on outside of their nation, seeing such issues as being "not their problem." Liberals tended to "blame America first," as many of their opponents would say. Geiseric was giving them fodder to do so.

The German chancellor pointed into the camera.

"Either the U.S. should give the land back to the Native Americans, or Germany should be allowed to expand. And don't worry! We Germans won't be so brutal as the Americans like we were under Hitler. For, I am *no* Hitler! I hate racism. I despise the ignorance that causes people to look past a person's soul because of his race. Hitler professed many reasons to hate the Jews, not the least of which was that they were bankers and lawyers. He argued that they were rich while everyone else was poor. But in reality only the *wealthiest five percent* of Jews made up these professions. These five percent made up only fifty percent of the bankers and lawyers in Germany. The other fifty percent were largely Germans. Many Jews were suffering in the German depression along with everyone else. Hitler targeted the Jewish race out of ignorance.

"As for me, I *am* with Shakespeare when he said 'first thing we do, let's kill *all* the lawyers,' and bankers for that matter." Geiseric chuckled. No one in the room seemed amused.

"It was a bad joke. I'm sorry," he sighed and went on with a calm but assertive voice. "My point is, I am not insane and I do not wish to take over the world. However, Germany does deserve more land. If Poland wishes to hold onto theirs, let her fight for it!"

The room stirred with the frenetic murmur of horrified politicians. Geiseric threw his hands up in deference.

"Wait, I know what you all are thinking," he said, rolling his eyes. "You're thinking, is he endorsing a war of expansion, a war of aggression? I'll answer that for you." Geiseric leaned over the podium slightly and put his hands on its sides. "Yes."

Everyone in the room gasped with shock, their mouths agape.

"Yes!" The chancellor slammed his hand on the podium, shouting over their murmur. "By *your* standards, that is a war of aggression. But, war *by its very nature* is aggressive! The term 'aggressive war' is a redundancy. Some of you seem to think that no nation can ever expand again. The borders set now are set for eternity. That must be nice for empires such as the United States who possess thirty times the amount of land as Germany. And Britain who knows that they will never again be conquerors, only conquered. It is nice for everyone but Germany, who lately does nothing but prop up the E.U. Well we want some room to live, or more aptly, some room to breathe!"

He stared calmly into the cameras facing him. "I have no will to take over the world in the name of the Principles' doctrine. Germany is the size of California, and all we want is some land. Land the size equivalent to Nevada. We will not harm the people. If we are forced to wage war, we will wage an extremely merciful war. We will take extreme caution towards civilians, monuments, and infrastructure."

No one at the European Summit could believe what they were hearing. Those viewing the summit via the live satellite feed to their televisions, were simply stunned, not the least of which being the German citizens watching from home.

The leaders of Europe sat wide-eyed and silent. Some were trying to figure out how to respond. Others simply waited for someone else to respond. Taking advantage of the unexpected silence, Geiseric continued with his pronouncements.

"Yes, we would wage a very clean war with minor damages. Polish citizens will be treated with the utmost respect and given all benefits granted to German citizens. Both economies will end up better when merged as one. Germany *needs* their land and Poland will *shine* with our administration!"

The E.U. leaders were still slack-jawed and dumbfounded. Suddenly, a tirade of angry shouts and jeers of vulgarity came at Geiseric from the crowd. Order was lost in the assembly as, one by one, egged on by their fellow leaders, the members reacted. Fists were slammed down on the tables. Shouting and bickering echoed throughout the chamber.

Geiseric smirked, standing at the podium tall and unfazed.

The German chancellor was not so ignorant as to actually invade Poland. He had rocked the boat simply to test the waters. He would now see how the citizens of the world would react, especially those in the United States. To his delight, the average American was not riled by his speech. In fact, they were placated by it. They didn't understand complex politics and most just took Geiseric's speech at face value. They thought that he only wanted to expand Germany's borders like the United States had once done, except without the genocide this time and, then, that would be it. No quest for world domination. Ultimately, the people of the United States just saw one little European nation squabbling with another. On the other hand, their president, John Hollier, was well aware of the threat posed by the new German dynamo and he did his best to inform the public, with little success.

Of course, Geiseric did not want to rock the boat too much. It might have shaken the American citizens out of their complacency. A military incursion into Poland would rile Germany's European neighbors to such a degree that the United States would have to take notice. Geiseric had learned what he wanted to know. He had confirmed that the average person of the world was apathetic, even in the face of brazen militant-expansionist rhetoric. No doubt they would be even more indifferent if he used less conspicuous tactics.

The crafty chancellor didn't mention Poland again for a while. He lessened his general intensity, not giving any raucous speeches or press conferences. Everything about his administration became placid. His ambassadors pursued a congenial, even subordinate, relationship with the United States, France, Russia, and China. And with his administration adopting a more compliant role at the meetings in Brussels, the German chancellor seemed to be coming back towards the Union.

An entire year passed with Geiseric's administration maintaining a demure posture. As the 2028 Olympics came up, most people had forgotten about the tumultuous previous year. They were excited, gearing up for the World Games.

The Summer Olympics were being held in Iraq this year. A massive public relations campaign by the Iraqi government touted the area as the Mesopotamian Olympics in the "Cradle of Civilization." Iraq had become quite rich since Saddam Hussein's Ba'athist dictatorship was toppled by the United States' invasion in 2003. In the twenty-five years since, Iraq had cultivated a close relationship with Iran through Shi'a Islam, the majority religion in both countries.

After the United States troops pulled out of Iraq, not only did the Shi'a majority begin to dominate Iraq politically and economically, but Iranian ex-patriots controlled key segments of the Iraqi infrastructure. Many of the Imams and Ayatollahs, revered by the Shi'ite Muslims as messengers of God, were citizens of Iran, still living in Iran.

However, this was not a bad thing for anybody except, maybe, the Sunnis. They lived in the middle of Iraq and, though they were the minority, had maintained control before 2003 through vicious force. Some Sunnis still held resentments, because they were no longer the power base. But the majority of Sunni Arabs were happy with the current climate; they weren't being oppressed in any way. In fact, even though Iraq was somewhat of a puppet government for a Greater Iran, they had an even more liberal judicial system than Iran. Indeed, many thought it was more liberal than that of the United States, for Iraq outlawed the death penalty.

The Iraqi government was under the microscope of the world. Everything they did sent out large ripples, necessitating complete political transparency in order to appease the world. Because of this, the Kurds, who had been given progressively more independence, were eventually given complete emancipation from Iraq to form their own nation. This angered the Turkish government, because it gave rise to a rebellion from the Kurds living in Turkey, on the border of the newly formed Kurdish nation. Still, it was a move that the world viewed as liberal. Especially, since the massacre of the Kurds by gas attacks was one of the key reasons the Americans went to war to topple the Ba'athist regime in 2003.

Under Shi'ite bureaucratic and political domination, Iraq flourished, and all her people became richer. The economic upturn had a lot to do with the dropping of trade borders between Iran and Iraq, which proved mutually beneficial to both countries and served to further unite them.

Thus, it was announced in 2020 that Iraq would host the 2028 summer games in the southern part of the Tigris-Euphrates area, in the city of Babylon. It was a daring move to hold the Olympics in Babylon, due to its biblical prophecies concerning the rise of Babylon and the end of the world. Yet, many were tickled with its audacity. The Babylonian Olympics sounded mystical and romantic. Tickets were bought years in advance. The Iraqi government immediately realized they had to increase the size of their developing infrastructure, based on the amount of people predicted to come.

Worries soon sprang up among those who wished to attend the games. Summer in Iraq was sweltering. The glaring sun and waves of heat would brutalize the athletes and the spectators. The Iraqi government was quick to assure the world that this would all be taken into consideration when designing the new Olympic complex.

Seven years passed and, while Iraq was making its preparations, the Olympic Committee was being wooed by the leading nations of the world who wished to host the 2036 Games. In 2026, Germany was in the lead in its bid, but when Geiseric came to power the next year, many in the Olympic Committee questioned if they should have the games there. Doubt increased when Prime Minister Dandau personally began petitioning intensely for the Games to be held in London for the fourth time. London was unique in having hosted the Olympics three times previously, the last time being only 15 years earlier.

Things were up in the air.

By the December of '27, it was becoming apparent that Iraq was struggling in the face of the overwhelming logistics for the Games. Although they had reached the economic status of a mid-range European country and were being helped by Iran, they were nonetheless unable to complete the infrastructure necessary to protect the athletes and spectators from the extreme summer heat.

The Olympic Committee was panicked. Summer in Babylon could reach 54 degrees Celsius, 130 degrees Fahrenheit. The track stadium was covered with an ugly dark material and lit on its interior with large fluorescent lights. More crude approaches were implemented in other sections of the Olympic village, and in some sections no work had even begun. As the media broadcast the lack of progress, the world became less enthusiastic by the day.

Geiseric was ecstatic to hear of this, knowing that this was Germany's chance to be a hero to the entire world. He rallied the German people behind him, promising that his bold plan would make Germany shine. With the country's support, the Principles passed a bill allotting twenty billion euros to save the Babylonian Olympics. Germany also committed technology, designers, and engineers to complete the work.

Shamed by Germany's generosity, most nations wished to contribute to some degree. However, in doing so, they also wanted control in the overall design. But, the Iraqis liked Germany's plans so much, they declined charity from anyone else.

Within six months, the Olympic Village was finished — ahead of schedule. The entire complex was kept under intense secrecy. All the structures were hidden under giant cloth tarps, with designs of gold, black, and azure. The complex looked like a sea of giant wrapped gifts.

The press estimated that, over the course of the Games, ten million people would attend. To accommodate the first night's projection of two-hundred thousand attendees, a gigantic coliseum had been built for the opening ceremonies. Revealed to the public before all the other structures, the spectacular stadium was a sight to behold. Immense replications of ancient Sumerian,

Akkadian, Assyrian and Persian stone carvings covered every wall. The expansive inner hallways had similar carvings, with brilliant gold-plated artwork, and were lined with numerous, scaled-down versions of the ancient Babylonian step structures called ziggurats.

The problem of heat had been solved by constructing transparent, polarized ceiling domes. They kept the sun at bay, but gave the audience a feeling of openness. Plus, the stadium and all the buildings were incredibly well ventilated. Cool breezes wafted about everywhere. The ceilings doubled as solar collectors. Numerous small cells in the domes, which could not be seen by the spectators, powered the wind generators and air conditioning.

On opening day, nearly a quarter of a million roaring fans sat in the coliseum. Tens of thousands more wished to attend, but there were no tickets left. The opening show was a fantastic spectacle, leaving no one disappointed. On the wide field of the coliseum, thousands of actors interpreted the long history of Babylon through dance and acrobatics. Mock battles, with incredible imagery and stunts, demonstrated history from the time the Akkadians conquered the Sumerians of Mesopotamia to the many great empires that followed. The audience was completely captivated during the entire three hours of the ceremony.

The marathon was the second-most viewed event. It took the runners, and the spectators there or watching on television, through a recreation of ancient Babylon. Much of it was replicated in full size, with modern materials, but made to look as authentic as the actual cities of antiquity. The competitors ran through the Ishtar Gate, toward the Street of Processions, and past the Stepped Tower. Much of the marathon took the runners through wide, well-cooled tunnels designed like streets from the Sumerian to the Roman empires. The spectators were truly in awe, and the athletes were likewise. Inspired by their run through the Cradle of Civilization, most of them beat their previous record times.

After the '28 Olympics, Geiseric could do no wrong. Beyond the fact that he saved this important event for the world, he also won a Nobel Peace Prize for his campaign to clean-up the irradiated areas of Iraq.

Much of Iraq's environment had been poisoned by debris left over from the U.N. and U.S. invasions. Uranium was an oft-used material in creating projectiles, for it was extremely dense and heavy and, so, had greater force upon impact than other metals. The United States in particular had used millions of tons of depleted uranium in its conventional weapons, such as millions of armor-piercing bullets and tank shells. As a result, depleted uranium shells, bullets, and microscopic dust was trapped deep in the sand and water systems, periodically surfacing.

Geiseric brought this problem to the world's attention. It was radiation sickness, he claimed, that lay behind the syndrome many American veterans returned with from the wars in the Gulf. The U.S. government unequivocally denied this, but the Iraqi public and the fans who were going to attend the Games were frightened. Geiseric sent in a huge contingent of technicians to purge Iraq of the contaminants before the Olympics were held, at another hefty expense to Germany.

The chancellor and the Principles shined in the eyes of the world.

Out of the public eye, however, Geiseric had never halted in his quest for expansion of power in Central Europe. He had known for a long time, before he was even elected, that the most likely line of attack was first through Austria.

Otto Volkenheim, the Austrian chancellor, arrived in Munich that September under heavy security. Great care was taken to keep the two chancellors safe, for there was the omnipresent threat of assassins. Before he took office, Geiseric had survived three well-orchestrated assassination attempts and managed to come out of them unscathed. Superficially, these failed attacks seemed to be launched by random political factions. Geiseric had many enemies, many of whom were drawn down religious lines. There were Jews who thought Geiseric was the new Hitler. They thought his pro-Semitic speech was a clever ruse. There were Muslims who thought he was the new Barbarossa, the German crusader who nearly conquered the Middle East. There were Christians who thought that Geiseric was the Antichrist, because there had been prophecies since the fall of the Third Reich that in the ashes there would rise a Fourth Reich, which would be led by Satan's apostle. Geiseric could not prove it, but he believed that one or more of the attempts on his life were funded and orchestrated by the CIA and/or Britain's MI6. So, great care was taken in protecting the German chancellor and those close to him.

Aided by helicopters with cameras that could detect body heat, hundreds of camouflaged German special forces units fanned out into the woods and hills around the city. They searched for possible terrorists who would be using high-powered and caliber rifles, or shoulder-launched missiles to take a plane down.

Though Geiseric did his best to keep the meeting between him and the Austrian president low profile, everything he did was closely watched by his opponents and thousands of people came out to protest. They were kept at a safe distance from the airport and thousands of police officers, wearing black, domed helmets and full body armor kept watch for anything or anyone suspicious. On every rooftop, a sniper team surveyed the perimeter with binoculars. There were even hundreds of plain-clothed agents milling around with the crowds of people.

Geiseric's cell-fueled, armored limousines arrived on the airport runway as Volkenheim's private plane touched down. Geiseric was surrounded by a cavalcade of defensive vehicles, mostly black Mercedes SUV's. As was his habit, there were three limousines: one in which he rode and two each containing a squad of his personal guards. The public never knew which limo the German chancellor was in; only his guards and the drivers were privy to that information. Geiseric made the choice at the last minute, so no one could plan ahead.

This time, he was in the middle limousine. The door opened and Chancellor Volkenheim entered, sitting next to Geiseric on the back seat. Geiseric, his friend and comrade, smiled and offered up a bottle of champagne. He popped the cork, nearly hitting one of his guards in the face.

"Es tut mir leid," Geiseric apologized to the guard, who just smiled. Three of Geiseric's personal guards sat in the car. They all wore black, metal body armor and headgear somewhat akin to a knight. The armor was well-tailored to their bodies and highly flexible around the joints, so their movement wasn't hindered. Their face masks, now up, could swing down for protection.

Champagne foamed out of the bottle all over the limousine floor. Geiseric laughed and poured a glass for himself and the Austrian chancellor. Holding them up, they clinked their glasses together in toast.

"Have you heard the good news?" Geiseric asked, taking a sip.

"Of course," Otto replied.

"The '36 Olympics will be held in Munich!" Geiseric raised his glass again and both jubilantly cheered and took a celebratory drink. The limousine sped off the runway and onto an autobahn ramp, which was cordoned off momentarily, until the defensive caravan passed.

Otto finished his champagne, waggled his head a bit and held out his glass for more. "How did you manage to convince the Committee to keep it here?"

Geiseric poured more champagne for his friend. "Let's face it, Otto. They love me!" He laughed confidently and poured himself more to drink. "They know that there's no person more receptive than I, and no nation more capable than Germany, to embrace the Olympics. I will put on a show the likes of which has never been seen. It shall make the Babylonian Games pale in comparison. That's what the Olympic Committee wants. That's what the people want. And it's what *I* need. Besides, a lot of the Committee members are closet Principles, and a lot of the rest . . . I paid off!" He chuckled.

"But, it's worth it, because it will allow the Germans to see their abilities. I have many things to do between now and 2036," he explained, gazing inward as he thought of his future strategy. "By then, we will be ready to enact the final phase of our plans. The Munich Games will allow the entire world to see the power of the Formula. It will give the Germans and our allies a priceless burst of spiritual capital," he said, pausing, and then remarked nonchalantly, "to go on into the inevitably tumultuous years to come."

Otto patted Geiseric's back and looked at him in awe. "You have incredible foresight."

"Well," Geiseric shrugged, "I just have to stay in power until then." He smirked and laughed again, as if there were no real doubt that he would be re-elected.

Otto smiled. "Yes, well, your people adore you. So, I don't think you will have too much of a problem, if you stay the present course. You have done well in motivating the Germans." He shook his head and sighed. "I wish I was half as good at doing the same with my people. It's amazing what the masses do when they have such strong morale."

Geiseric slapped Volkenheim on the shoulder. "You haven't seen anything yet."

The two finished their glasses and opened another bottle. Otto swirled the champagne in the crystal wineglass for a moment, pondering something.

"I can't believe that the world hasn't been paying attention to what I've been doing in Austria," he remarked with a sly smile on his lips.

"It's no surprise to me," Geiseric shrugged. "Dandau and Hollier were so busy trying to see what I was up to in Iraq that they didn't even pay attention to your subtle propaganda. And you've been doing brilliantly by the way, without any help from me." He once again clinked his champagne glass upon Otto's.

Chancellor Volkenheim took another sip and smacked his lips. "You are too kind, but the people we're going up against are fools. How can they not see this coming? I am the only other leader of a nation who is a Principle."

"Yes," Geiseric nodded, "but our enemies don't see the historical bond between our countries. They only see the polls reported in the media. Austria may have the strongest Principles Party demographic outside Germany, but only 10 percent of Austrians support annexation to Germany. And *who would* want to be *annexed*?" Geiseric asked rhetorically, smacking the back of his hand lightly on Volkenheim's shoulder. "We must make the Austrians feel that we are all benefiting, and that the sum shall be greater than the parts."

Chancellor Volkenheim went home two days later with a well-orchestrated plot in his mind. His propaganda campaign intensified, disguised as an attempt to win some of the tourism that had been flooding into Germany. Most of the tourists were Principles party supporters from around the globe, but many others visited Germany simply because they were fascinated with the interesting new culture developing there.

Volkenheim commissioned a worldwide public relations campaign, with the thrust being in America and Europe. The campaign played on the commonality between Germany and Austria, not only as the major Principle nations, but also in many other ways throughout history. The ad blitz showed how Austria was part of Germany in the Medieval period, when it was known as the Holy Roman Empire, or Germania. It showcased that Austria was the ruling nation in the Empire, during most of its history. Austria was home to the Habsburgs, the mightiest familial dynasty in Europe, providing monarchs for many of the leading nations.

The campaign also aired at home. It appeared to be targeting Austrians that chose to vacation in Germany. However, a study commissioned by Volkenheim's political opponents proved that the ads worked to accomplish the opposite: increasing Austrian tourism to Germany. The opposition, however, could tell that this campaign never had anything to do with tourism. It was propaganda intended to strengthen the ties between Austria and Germany. Of course, Volkenheim publicly questioned the validity of the study his opponents had commissioned. Everything was in place.

Germany's nationalization of the European Space Agency's infrastructure led to sanctions from the European Union. But for the first time in two decades, most of the nations did not support the ruling of the centralized government. Germany was the strongest economic power in Europe. Europeans felt too economically dependent on, or at least too much of a symbiotic relationship with Germany, to just sever the ties. Due to pressure from European leaders, Brussels quickly toned down the sanctions.

However, all the E.U. countries, except for Austria, did agree to place tariffs on German goods. The Principles in Austria worked towards opening their borders completely with Germany. Volkenheim knew that defiance of the E.U. would likely result in tariffs on Austrian goods. To mitigate the damage, he began subtly slanting his domestic propaganda campaign against the E.U.

Again, it was all done under the pretext of keeping tourism at home. With clever advertising manipulation, the Principles reinforced the already pervasive Austrian distrust and dislike for the E.U. Much of the dissent had to do with the environment. The Austrians were particularly environmentally-minded. Austria was a beautiful country and they wished to preserve it. The magnificent Alpine mountains and foothills stretched across the land, providing breathtaking views, ski slopes, and hiking trails. Part of the Danube River gently flowed through Upper Austria, enjoyed by both locals and tourists for recreation and leisure. And a diverse mix of plants and animals, butterflies and birds called the forested woodlands and gently sloping pastures home.

The domestic ads showed that many E.U. countries, especially to the east and south, were still big polluters. Coal and oil-fueled power plants, agricultural runoff, and truck shipping transits that used Austria's roads as a throughway were all partially to blame. And, unfortunately, pollution moved through the air and water, which could not be contained within a country's borders. Pollution was breaching Austria's natural resources. So, while they tried to lead the way as a positive example for environmental preservation in Europe, they had to simultaneously combat contamination from their neighboring countries.

Despite the E.U. tariffs, Germany was still doing well economically. Geiseric simply increased trade with India and Japan, and kept things going steadily with China, Russia and the United States. To even things out, he established tariffs on imported goods to Germany from the E.U. countries. Many Europeans questioned punishing Germany with tariffs after everything that had transpired through the beginning of 2028. France wavered, enacting then taking away the tariffs multiple times.

When Austria opened its borders to Germany, most of the E.U. did stick to its guns and enacted tariffs on Austria. However, now that Austria was the only E.U. member with open borders to Germany, the Austrians experienced a major economic upturn. Germany and Austria became even more closely bonded.

✦ ✦ ✦

While the tariff battles raged, Geiseric announced that he was national-izing another E.U. program. The European Union had made it a goal to be a HydroCell-based economy by 2050. HydroCells were a non-polluting alter-native to gas fuel; its exhaust being simply water. However, many European countries were not only missing the deadlines, they were dragging their feet to even begin. Being that the Germans were as environmentally-minded as the Austrians, they had taken the reigns of the HydroCell fuel project long before Geiseric came to power, but now he planned to speed up the project on his own terms. The E.U. HydroCell project had been based in Germany and a number of nations had long since pulled out by the time Geiseric came to power. By the end of 2028, Geiseric claimed the HydroCell technology for Germany, rationalizing that the Germans had bore the brunt of the project.

This turned out to be another key economic turning point that was extremely beneficial for the country. Mercedes-Benz, Bavarian Motor Works, and Volkswagen all came out with the first mass-produced HydroCell cars. They were sleek, stylish, and well-designed, and quickly became the new "it" cars to own. Simultaneously, the German and Austrian parliaments passed laws that required all cars on their nations' roads to run on HydroCell fuel within ten years.

Geiseric also subsidized the creation of HydroCell stations internationally. Starting in Britain and California, hundreds of these stations were installed. Outside of Germany and Austria, it was Britain and the coasts of the United States' that had the strongest environmentalist lobbies in the world. HydroCell cars were in high demand and the American companies had nothing similar to offer. The market was rapidly cornered by German auto-makers, since they possessed the only competitive HydroCell infrastructure in the world.

Soon, HydroCell stations opened up all over North America and Europe, and then in Japan, India and China. The cars were on backorder, being bought faster than they could be built. To help keep up with demand, the German Parliament offered subsidies to hundreds of upstart car companies and manufacturers within their country. The technology was provided to these companies free of charge, provided they stayed in Germany and paid a high tax. Dozens of the new companies came out with their own unique lines of cars, providing ample variety and filling most of the voids that would otherwise have been filled by the U.S., Japanese, and other major automobile-manufacturing nations.

The demand for designers, engineers, machinists, and specialized repair and sales associates skyrocketed. Millions of jobs were created in Germany and

Austria. And the taxes the governments were collecting provided for higher-end job creation and the expansion of a variety of cradle-to-grave benefits for citizens.

Geiseric wished to show Europe that, despite the E.U. tariffs, Germany's economy could not, and would not, be held back. And to drive the point home, Geiseric announced the commissioning of another bold new project. It was an idea that had circulated within Austrian environmental groups for decades, but was deemed too costly. The Brenner Pass, the trade route through the Alps, brought millions of trucks through every year. It was the primary trade route for goods traveling from the Mediterranean region into Central Europe. The Alpine regions through which much of this traffic passed were especially vulnerable to ecological damage. The narrow valleys were not conducive to noise and pollutants from motor vehicles. The E.U. had promised to address the problem. But, as with the slow conversion to a HydroCell fuel economy, the Austrians felt the E.U. was bowing to other countries and tolerating their slow progress. Their beautiful country was being sacrificed to appease less efficient nations.

So, the German Parliament passed a bill to fund a tunnel, to be built predominantly under the ground, stretching from Garmisch-Partenkirchen in southern Germany to Bolzano in northern Italy. It was for both trains and automobile traffic, each with its own interior tunnel. It was built so that the Alps could be free of commercial traffic. Even though pollutants could be eliminated with HydroCell cars, the negative effect of the constant and intense vibrations caused by large trucks and the heat from so much traffic was inevitably devastating to the pristine, snowy environment.

Many in Europe applauded Geiseric for helping to preserve the Alps, which was of worth not just to the Austrians, but to many in Europe and around the world. It was something that many politicians and businessmen throughout the E.U. had been promising to fund for several years, to contain the pollution and speed up trade.

The tunnel was designed primarily to use bullet trains for large cargo, which would dramatically decrease the transportation time. An underground tunnel was also a much safer alternative to crossing the Alps. Many independent investors, particularly Principles Party sympathizers in Europe, America, and Asia were anxious to help fund the project.

Within a few months, the pro-annexation movement had gained incredible momentum. Seventy percent of Austrians were in favor of joining their

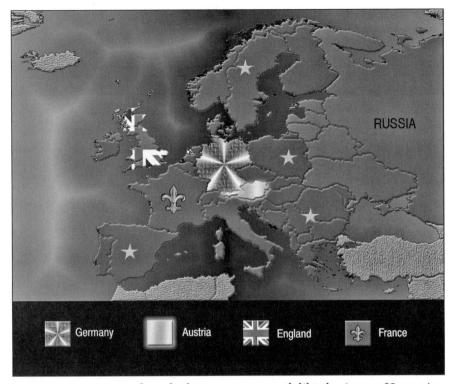

nation to Germany under a dual state system, much like the Austro-Hungarian Empire that existed in the nineteenth century until the end of World War I. That empire was a dual monarchy, with different laws, but under the overlordship of Austria.

The German and Austrian governments passed legislation to unite their countries. In Germany, there was only jubilation over this unification. While most Austrians were also pleased, there was a strong dissident movement of people who did not want to lose their nation's individuality.

When the new tunnel opened, Geiseric was the first to break it in. There were actually four tunnels, though they were all encased together within an outer layer of concrete and steel protection, like wires within a sheath. Two of the tunnels were used by the cargo trains. One was designed purely for the driving of commercial trucks and had a lower speed limit. The thoroughfare meant for normal civilian use allowed the driver to go up to 180 km/hr, roughly 110 miles per hour.

Geiseric jumped into the driver's seat of his HydroCell-fueled Porsche and, true to his puckish character, he sped through the wide-lane, underground highway at just above the speed limit. Following were the vehicles of his large security force caravan and a handful of news vehicles with their cameras rolling. The German chancellor got off the highway and emerged from the underground tunnel system at one of the exits in Austria. An even larger Austrian security escort met him at the planned stop. Hundreds of police officers on motorcycles and in heavily armored cars formed a perimeter and guarded the front and rear of Geiseric's own security team. The massive caravan quickly made its way to Salzburg, near the Austrian border with Bavaria. It was here that Geiseric was scheduled to give a speech.

Word came over his guards' two-way radios that a large protest rally in Salzburg had gotten out of control. However, it was tamed quickly by well-coordinated police units. Geiseric proceeded as scheduled.

Chancellor Volkenheim gave a short introductory speech for Geiseric. He then allowed the German chancellor to deliver this historic address, which would inevitably place Geiseric in a superior position. Volkenheim not only understood that this was a necessary part of the grand plan, but his reverence for the leader of the Principles Party made him happy to defer to Geiseric.

Another grandiose stone podium had been created just for this speech. Behind, the Romanesque walls of the Festung and the Hohensalzburg Fortress created a dramatic backdrop. The largest fully-preserved European fortress was the chief landmark of Mozart's city, and the only place Geiseric considered fitting for his official introduction to the Austrians. More than one hundred thousand supporters were crammed into the square in front of Geiseric, awaiting his words.

"*Hallo, meine Leute!*" he greeted warmly.

"*Hallo, Herr Kanzler!*" they shouted back.

"Ah," he deeply inhaled the clean Austrian air and looked up at the clear, sunlit sky. "It's good to be in Salzburg!"

The audience cheered happily, slowly quieting as Geiseric went on.

"The genius Mozart was born here. You know, listening to Mozart's music actually increases your intellect. Because of its complexity, classical music is one of the few arts that actually exercises your brain. And it is Austria that has provided so many of these musical prodigies." The German chancellor gazed upon the tens of thousands of Austrian citizens who turned out for his speech, in full support of his movement. Never before had he felt so confident that his ultimate agenda was going to become a reality. He continued with his unabashed praise.

"Austria is a nation with a long history of intellectual leadership and prestige. From the fifteenth to the nineteenth centuries, it was the leading nation of the Holy Roman Empire, of Germania. We are one and the same! In fact, Bavarians and Austrians have more in common, both ethnically and culturally, than do Bavarians and Prussians!" As usual, Geiseric did not have a teleprompter to read off of or any cards on his podium. He had practiced his speech but a few times and this was all he needed, for these were arguments long ago conceived by him.

"No one thought of Austria as separate from Germany until the mid-nineteenth century," he waggled his finger in scorn of the modern attitude towards the subject. "This began when the Prussians moved to push Austria out of the newly forming German Empire, in the wake of Napoleon. The Prussians, though being leaders themselves in the academic and military fields, had good reason to fear Austrian dominance when looking at history."

Geiseric paused and briefly surveyed the audience. They were hanging on his every word, waiting to hear more praise for their country. Their approval animated him as he continued.

"Prussia officially took control in the eighteen-seventies and Germany went on to be quite powerful in every way. But Austria formed her own empire, which had a flowering of scientific activity based in Vienna. Sigmund Freud was not the least of these great minds." While every Austrian knew this, Geiseric's speech was also intended to enlighten the people who were watching in Germany and all over the world.

"Still, though the two nations had officially split, many people could only vaguely distinguish the difference between an Austrian and a German, beyond political boundaries. Then," he became more solemn, "the world wars formed this contrived need for everyone to disassociate from Germany. The anti-German attitude that was rampant in the world since the First World War became that much more commonplace after World War II. Who could blame the Austrians for not wanting to be associated with Germany? But, lest we forget," he smirked, "I must remind everyone that Hitler . . . was Austrian." Many in the audience laughed mildly, for they knew that it was absurd to run from Nazi Germany's legacy.

"My point is," Geiseric concluded, "Germany and Austria *are the same!* Just as we suffered together, just as we were both shamed in the World Wars, so shall we attain glory together in the future! We have been united far longer than we have been separated. Take pride in our common culture and goals!"

The audience roared their approval. Geiseric smiled broadly, waiting for the accolades to quiet.

"So, I hereby announce the unification of our nations," he declared in a firm and proud voice, building in intensity, "into one greater Germanic state — the state of Germania!" He clenched his fists, raising his arms up into the air to give emphasis to his words. "And let the easternmost Reich become the *bulwark of Germania!*"

The people in the crowd were wildly jubilant, many throwing their hats up into the air with joy. The pro-Principles demographic cut through a wide cross-section of the Austrian populous and the young and old, the wealthy and those with modest incomes, all danced together in the streets.

Once again, the citizens of the world and, thus, their leaders, quietly acquiesced. Some even applauded the maneuver. Most Americans and even Europeans simply felt that the unification of the countries was inconsequential. Now, instead of Austria and Germany, there was just Germania. No big deal; Germany was now the size of two states of the fifty in the United States. But, many of the leaders of the world were a bit more cautious than their people. They recognized the danger. Geiseric was now in direct control of more people, more land and ultimately had . . . more power.

The E.U. leadership in Brussels decided to punish Germania. They declared that all of Austria's individual political power within the union's central government was null and void. Therefore, Germany and Austria no longer each had seats in the E.U. legislature. If they wanted to be one with Germany, then Germania would be treated as one country in the union.

Geiseric, Otto, and most of their constituency expected this type of reaction. The Principles launched a domestic ad blitz glorifying the new, better Germania. The ads showed how Germania's new potential far outweighed the downsides of losing certain "dubious" privileges in the European Union.

Brussels did not bother sanctioning Germania, for it only hurt Europe economically. Germania could survive on its own, as it was the top trading partner with Russia, China, India, Japan, the United States, and sometimes France. Every time the E.U. tried to control Germania with sanctions, Geiseric retaliated in a number of ways, including cutting down his nation's substantial payments of taxes to the E.U. Geiseric had been diligent about making sure his country paid their tithes, knowing that it would keep Brussels beholden to him somewhat. In this, they would not be unable to act against him in a meaningful and decisive way. If Germania was sanctioned, the payment of taxes slowed. But, Geiseric never authorized the payment of less than half of the expected dues, for that was enough to punish the E.U., without making them desperate enough to retaliate. He had illuminated the impotence of the European Union's government at this young stage, still in its infancy. Geiseric lay in wait for the right time to pounce again. It did not take long.

China and Taiwan had long been at odds. Taiwan, a small island off the mainland, was part of China. It had declared itself to be a democratic state, opposed to the more dictatorial state of the mainland. Taiwan was independent in almost every way, yet if the island ever declared its independence, mainland China claimed a right to invade. This militant stance was carved into law when the Chinese government passed an anti-secession bill in 2005. This bill was a promise to use nuclear force if the tiny island seceded.

Soon after the bill was passed, tensions began to slowly simmer between China and the United States. The U.S. had supported Taiwan's independence as a democratic country. Europe had taken a shifty position with China, but France and Germany had whole-heartedly supported the "Two Systems, One China" stance of the mainland for over two decades.

While Geiseric worked towards a unification of historically German provinces, the Chinese premier, Lo Hung, studied the dynamic new chancellor and was inspired. Geiseric was communicating with the premier, through secret channels. He assured Hung that, if China took a harder line towards Taiwan's increasing independence, Germania would back it. That promise kept economic lines flowing freely between Germania and China during the times when the leaders of other powerful nations, namely the United States and Britain, were threatening to put sanctions on Germany. But, with China refusing to back them, the sanctions were not a viable punishment. China had a one and a half billion strong population that inhaled German products.

In exchange for sticking with Germania during the hard times, the Chinese Premier expected staunch support from Geiseric when he acted to unite Taiwan and the mainland. Taiwan was of benefit to China for a number of reasons. One was that it was disproportionately rich. Another was that the United States military had bases in Taiwan, and American warships patrolled the area. They were there to defend the Taiwanese, but they were an affront to Chinese sovereignty.

Even more importantly, Taiwan to the Chinese was a point of pride and they were never going to give it up. Gaining back dominion over the relatively prosperous island nation would be a boon economically, but it would have even higher returns in terms of the nation's morale. Premier Hung intended to fully integrate Taiwan into the rest of China, by hook or by crook. He deployed a huge invasion force on the mainland eastern coast, in the Fujian province, right across the Taiwan Strait. The United States, in response, deployed more battle cruisers and an aircraft carrier. President Hollier pushed for more U.S. troops to be stationed in Taiwan, to stave off an assault. The isolationist American people and Congress, however, were strongly against this.

Prime Minister Dandau immediately saw that a united Chinese and German front was far too much of a threat to the worldwide balance of power. Outside of the United States, Germania and China were the most powerful nations and they were, coincidentally, highly aggressive and nationalistic in terms of their foreign policies. Therefore, the prime minister determined that the Anglo-American front, the main Allies since the First World War, should drive a wedge between the newly developing enemy front.

Dandau convinced Hollier to let Taiwan go. Hollier agreed with his politically savvy compatriot and made a 180 degree turn about in his stance towards China. Not only did Hollier back off from his requests to send more troops into Taiwan, he began to sway the American Congress to pull out *all* defenses in the region. He knew that wouldn't be hard, since it was the exact opposite of the president's previously unsupported stance. Meanwhile, Dandau easily did the same with a similarly isolationist British parliament and people.

Dandau and Hollier arranged a meeting with the Chinese premier, in Beijing, to discuss the plans for pulling away from the area. When they arrived, they informed Hung that he had nothing to worry about, in terms of reprisals from their countries, telling the premier that they wished to be on good terms with China.

After showering Premier Hung and his country with relentless compliments, Prime Minister Dandau led the way towards shattering the Sino-German front. He debriefed the premier on the latest intelligence reports from the CIA and MI6, as evidence that Geiseric was developing close ties with India and Japan, and that China was nothing more than a transitional ally to get through the present times. The Chinese premier was shown facts and suppositional data, largely conjecture, about what Geiseric would probably do, based on his modus operandi and general world order viewpoint.

Dandau and Hollier claimed that the CIA and MI6 had been able to tap one of Geiseric's supposedly secure underground communication lines running to India. Some of the questionable transcripts of the chancellor's dialogue with the Indian prime minister were quite incriminating and stated blatantly what the Western allies were telling Hung. One of the transcripts included Geiseric telling the Indian leader that he was pushing China to be more belligerent, to take the heat off Germania for a while. There were also a number of other documents which all pointed towards Geiseric eventually double-crossing China.

Dandau and Hollier reminded Hung that Geiseric did little to come to China's aid when the premier was facing off against the American president over Taiwan. They showed Hung more documents illustrating how Geiseric had been doing nothing more than plotting to take over most of Central Europe to incorporate into Germania. The Germanian chancellor was only using the Chinese premier for a distraction.

Hung felt deeply disturbed by these transcripts, for many reasons. He knew that he could not completely trust these findings. They could all be false — a ploy. He had little information from his foreign intelligence agency to back them up. Hung recalled countless times throughout history in which intelligence had been falsified, and the British were masters of the art of deception. A good leader knew what to trust, and when to be suspicious.

However, the Chinese premier did know about the optical fiber line to India. Chinese operatives had not been able to tap into the line and surveil whatever was being communicated, but they knew it was there. This made him suspicious. Geiseric also had ground lines installed going from his two main headquarters in Munich and Berlin, to Hung's main headquarters in Beijing. This was created so that the two leaders could converse over the great distances in supposed "secrecy," and it was an obvious commitment to alliance-building. Hung also saw what was going on in public view. The leaders and parliaments of the Czech Republic, Slovakia and Poland all seemed to be closet Principles; they were hiding their agendas from their people and running for office on false platforms. The Czech Prime Minister, Oldrich Novotny, was elected for his second term largely based on his promise to disallow annexation to Germania. But, in reality, he seemed to be moving his country subtly towards that very thing.

Prime Minister Novotny used many of the same methods of propaganda that Chancellor Volkenheim had, creating an ad blitz that was touted as an attempt to gain some of the tourism going into Germania. Tourism, being the number one money-making industry in the world, was worth fighting for and there was no doubt that every year Germany and, now, Germania received more tourists, the majority being those who were tantalized by the spirited and vibrant culture rising there. Geiseric and his movement also had followers worldwide, who flocked to the revolutionary nation annually, as if it were a pilgrimage. Many others came to Germania out of almost a morbid curiosity for a culture born out of such brazen and controversial ideology.

The Principles were passionate patrons of the arts. They hammered a multitude of bills through legislation that gave billions of euros to artistic and musical learning institutions. Wealthy Principles Party members individually funded the burgeoning renaissance in Germania and thousands of artisans, musicians and craftsmen immigrated to the country just for this reason. They set about renovating the Medieval cities of Germany, many of which had been bombed out by the Second World War and had yet to be rebuilt. Many were tastefully recreated with a new spin. Most Germanians and those tourists who visited the country were awestruck with the beauty of what had been created. Plus, the administration's pro-environmental policies created the natural grandeur of more pristine wilderness than most humans had seen in the area for hundreds of years.

With all of these factors working together, Germania received a three hundred percent increase in tourists from 2027 to 2029. The Czech prime minister pushed his ad blitz saying that he wished to gain some of this tourism for his nation. The ads once again emphasized the historical bond between the two nations, with the Czech Republic having once been called Bohemia, which was a state of Medieval Germania. Like what had occurred in Austria, the campaign turned out to be pro-German propaganda that increased Czech tourism to Germania.

Those opposed to annexation within the Czech Republic were paralyzed by the fear of military repercussion. With the uneasy state of things in Europe and the world's indifference, they could not be sure anyone would come to their aid if Germania invaded their country. Geiseric could possibly get away with a takeover and, then, Czech sovereignty would completely vanish. If the opposition gave in, the republic could retain semi-independence within Germania, almost like a confederacy. Outside of these countries, Geiseric's opponents in Europe were overwhelmed and stunned by the speed and efficacy of the Germanian chancellor and his cohorts.

Premier Hung contemplated all of these facts. He knew that Geiseric would not stop with Central Europe in his plans for a new world order. The Chinese

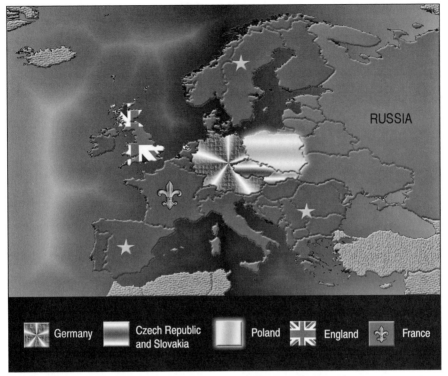

Germany		Czech Republic and Slovakia		Poland		England		France

premier was himself using Geiseric as a temporary ally for Chinese expansion. But, while Geiseric was gaining substantial swaths of land in Europe, Premier Hung had gotten a little island.

The Chinese premier needed time to decide who was more dangerous to China's long term interests . . . the Anglo-American front, or Germania.

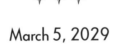

March 5, 2029

President John Hollier sat in the Oval Office reading the latest edition of *The New York Times*. He threw it down in frustration.

"God damn liberal media!" he bellowed in his rich Texan drawl, looking to Defense Secretary Brian Tierney, who was also sitting in the office.

"I don't get it Brian!" the president spouted with exasperation. "The bleeding heart libs are always cryin' about things, but they never want to do somethin' about it." In agitation, he got up and paced around the room.

"Doin' nothing to stop evil is as bad as helpin' it. There's that great quote ... what is it?" he said to himself, snapping his fingers as he tried to remember. "Somethin' like, the worst evil is the righteous man who does not act, or somethin' to that extent. Anyway," he faced a table with a white, marble bust of Winston Churchill on it, "we can't let Geiseric get away with this. I can't believe that he's doing *exactly* what Hitler did and the world doesn't see it! He's annexed Austria. He's leaning on the Czechs. He's got the Poles scared as shit." Hollier turned and looked straight at Tierney. "Well, we damn well know that Glinski and Novotny are closet Principles. The Czechs are already all but absorbed into Germania. We can't let Glinski give Poland away too!"

"Sir, the problem is," Tierney paused for a second and shook his head. He was strongly built, rugged and tall, yet had surprisingly intuitive eyes. "It's not just liberals. It's most conservatives too. Geiseric's speech about the justified war of expansion was highly effective. And in the year and a half since then, he's done a good job assuring the average citizen of the world that he doesn't want anything more than a little more living space in Eastern Europe. Eighty percent of the American people wouldn't want to go to war, even if Germania invaded Poland." He rolled his eyes and angrily sighed as he read the statistics. "In fact, if Germania *did* invade Poland militarily, most Americans say they would only be willing to put in place economic sanctions." Tierney threw his hands up in exasperation. "France and Russia are on Geiseric's side for now. Both are looking to get a piece of the pie. China's still wavering."

Hollier kicked one of the chairs across the room. "God damn it!" he shouted. He then paused, looking at the upside down chair with its leg now broken.

"I hope that wasn't an important chair," he said, looking to Tierney.

"What d'you mean?" Tierney asked.

The president shrugged. "You know how some of this furniture is from former presidents. I mean, I hope it wasn't Reagan's chair or somethin'."

"Doubtful," Tierney replied. "Besides, do they do that in this room? I thought people just left stuff in other parts of the White House."

"I wonder," Hollier commented.

"Ah don't worry," Tierney assured him. "It was probably Clinton's chair. I think I saw a protein stain on the pad."

The two men broke out in belly-shaking laughter. But, quickly, they came back to grave reality. The Defense Secretary grabbed a remote on the desk.

"Anyway, I did have a purpose to my meeting with you. There's a show on TV right now . . ." When he pressed a button on the remote, a wide flatscreen television came up out of the desk.

"Oh good, what do we have? Austin versus Dallas?" the president laughed.

"No, this is important. I wanted to make sure you caught it . . ." Tierney pressed another button and a program came on. It was a FIX News show called "Your Country." People were being interviewed on the streets all over America. A blonde lady came on the screen who was attractive, though she had an unusual mouth that seemed slightly turned to the right side. She wore a trench coat, holding it closed because of the cold.

"Hello, I'm Kitty Long reporting to you presently from Des Moines, Iowa. I've been all over America this week, getting reactions from average Americans on the recent developments in Central Europe. With Austria now annexed to Germany, and the Czech and Polish leaders close to caving, here's what some of your everyday Americans had to say."

Kitty poked the microphone at a man wearing a parka and beanie cap. "What do you think should be done about Germany's annexing of Austria?"

The man shrugged and made a face of indifference. "I think that there are bigger problems for us," he replied in his Midwestern twang.

Kitty pressed him. "Do you consider Geiseric to be a threat?"

The man shrugged again. "Nah, it's Geiseric, the weirdo rock and roll star," he laughed.

"Did you know that Hitler was an artist before he became a dictator?" Kitty asked.

The man lifted his eyebrows in surprise. "I didn't know that. But, I mean, a lot of people think he's gonna try to push his Principles ideals and stuff on everyone, by any means necessary. But, I don't believe that. He's got his thing going on in Germany, or Germania, or whatever it's called." He laughed again.

Kitty pressed him further. "He's already threatened to take Poland by force. Do you think he will stop there?"

"Yeah, but that's a different thing," the man replied. "I mean, I can understand wanting to make a country that's so small and tightly packed a little bigger. That's why he's doing that. And, besides," he said, looking away and waving his hand downward in a gesture to show how inconsequential the hysteria was, "that Poland thing was a bluff. He's totally backed off from that."

The camera panned out to the public street Kitty was stationed on. This time a college-aged, red-haired woman, bundled up in warm clothing, stopped for an interview.

"Do you consider Geiseric to be a threat to the world?

The woman looked up in contemplation. "Ummmm. I really think that Geiseric is frightening in a lot of ways. But, I just don't see a real threat to the United States at all. I mean, I'm always hearing on the news that if Germany acquires the Austrian, Czech, and Polish land, it will be larger than Texas. And, I'm always thinking, like, so what? I mean, they will be bigger than *one* of our *fifty* states. If that scares the U.S., then I don't know what to think."

A tall, elegant woman appeared next. She had glasses and wore a suit underneath her black trench coat. She carried a briefcase and seemed in a hurry to get somewhere. This time, the clip began with the young woman's reaction.

"You know, it's never good when people take. But, Geiseric did back off from his invasion threat on Poland and he seems like he got the hint that it's not the way to go." She shook her head a bit to give emphasis. "But, I think we have no right to stand in the way of a peaceful, diplomatic unification.

Next, a man in his forties was interviewed from his truck. He had a cowboy hat and sunglasses on.

"What really makes me upset," the man said, brow furrowed in agitation, "is that no one sees the patterns!" He paused to calm himself. "This is exactly what Hitler did. We can't let the Germans get powerful. You know, I just don't understand the Democrats these days. What happened to the Roosevelts and the Kennedys? I mean, they're trying to make President Hollier look like a war-monger because he threatens to attack Germania if Geiseric ever attacks Poland. Sometimes you have to put your foot down with people like that! This has nothing to do with living space. Geiseric wants to make Germany strong enough so he can push his Isaianic Principles crap on all of us!"

The television show next cut to a teenage boy of voting age. Kitty asked her question.

"Hypothetically, do you think Geiseric's argument for a legal war of aggression makes sense?"

The boy thought about it for a moment. "That's hard to figure out. It seems kinda logical. It's just hard to wage a war without killing innocents. But, if you could somehow, hypothetically, wage a war against just a military force to take some land when you're cramped," he shrugged, "I mean, that sounds oddly rational."

"Do you think that this may open Pandora's Box?" Kitty asked. "People have said that such thinking would allow America to conquer the world, because our military is stronger than all of the next ten strongest nations combined."

The young man thought about it some more. "Well, I guess, if the U.S was becoming incredibly overcrowded and everyone was immigrating here," he raised his eyebrows and nodded, "yeah, I would agree with taking some land if people don't want to share. But, what's really important here is making sure that it's only against the military. You can't target civilians at all. And, I've heard that a lot of America's military power comes from its 'strategic' nuclear capability," he made quote marks with his fingers, "which, and you can correct me on this if I'm wrong, but 'strategic' means bombing cities and killing civilians."

"That's not *exactly* what it means," Kitty interjected, "but go on with your argument."

The young man continued. "Like, you couldn't use any weapons of mass destruction. Everything would have to be smart bombs and cruise missiles and stuff. You couldn't commit any atrocities when you occupy the people and try to bring them into the new government." He looked up and to the side in contemplation. "It would be hard."

Kitty asked him one final question. "So, if America had a population density equal to Germania's, we could let's say, take over Canada, or even Europe, as long as we use smart bombs and cruise missiles and stuff?" she asked, subtly making fun of his simplistic argument.

The guy smiled. "I don't know about that. I mean, we're not talking about all of Europe or even Canada. We're talkin' about a little piece of farmland. I mean, it's Poland! Who cares?"

The camera returned to Kitty. "There you have it. These interviews represent the general mood of America. According to the latest FIX News polls, only one in five Americans believe that strong measures should be used against Germania if Poland is annexed. These five people gave the typical arguments I've heard nationwide. An especially common sentiment is, as you just heard, 'it's Poland, who cares?'

Tierney switched the television off. "You see what we're dealing with?"

The president stood by the window for a moment, silent. When he turned back to Tierney, he appeared a man who was just struck by an immense realization. His face was like a blank slate, neither angry nor pleased. He laughed slightly, merely by exhaling quickly through the nose, an expression of his disbelief at what was transpiring.

"Geiseric's gonna take most of Central Europe, and the world's just gonna let him. He isn't even going to have to use force." Hollier rubbed his lip with his thumb and forefinger and clenched his jaw repetitively in between talking.

"And all those who would normally oppose him in those countries are too afraid."

The president walked over to a globe sitting in its gilded stand in the corner. He spun it around to Europe and traced out the new borders with his fingers. "That's all gonna be Germany, or Germania, as he likes to call it." Hollier turned back towards Tierney.

"He's won this round Brian," the president resigned. Focusing his fury, he became resolute. "But, this is where it ends. Geiseric won't be able to get everything he wants so easily, through this veil of diplomacy." Hollier sneered with contempt for his enemy's deception.

He plucked the globe from its stand and threw it down on the floor, startling the defense secretary. The globe cracked and rolled lopsided into a wall. The president looked directly into the eyes of his top military man.

"From now on, we don't let him have anything without a fight!"

—— V ——

RESISTANCE IS FUTILE

Logan stared wide-eyed at Alistair, Jacques, Francesca and Sasha. Overwhelmed once more with the information coming at him, he gazed off into the distance, zoning out to the hum of the wings that powered the strange aircraft transporting them.

Suddenly, a large explosion came from the ground below. The shock wave from the blast did not shake the craft much, but everyone crammed to look out the windows. They were closer to the ground than before, flying under the puffy white clouds. Down below, the passengers could make out a pentagonal industrial complex. It was in the middle of a forest, and stretched several square kilometers in all directions. A large cloud of gray smoke emanated from a crater in the ground just outside the complex. Logan estimated that it was at least the size of a football field. Another explosion sent fire and smoke shooting up into the sky. The passengers gasped as the debris careened toward the aircraft, seeming to come nearer than it was.

The second explosion demolished a bunker. The passengers could only see the roof, a cement dome about a hundred meters from the crater on the perimeter of the complex. As it imploded and collapsed, dust and small particles spewed out, leaving another jagged basin on the pockmarked ground. Smoke poured into the air, blighting the view below.

Alistair looked out in the sky. There were almost a dozen other transports within his vision.

"They're showing this to us," he realized.

Francesca leaned over Alistair and Logan to look out the window. "Is that the main bauxite facility?" she asked, looking at the demolition on the ground.

"Yeah," Alistair sighed.

Francesca's head drooped. "All those people who died defending it was for nothing."

Sasha shook her head and rolled her eyes. "*All* of the Allies died for nothing."

As the smoke dissipated, Alistair studied the ground. "That's why they're doing this." He pressed his forehead against the window. "The bauxite plant was one of the most tightly defended pieces of land in the world. They're showing us that resistance is futile."

"Yes," Jacques added. "They want us to see our fortifications demolished. They only did a couple of demolitions. They will save the rest to humble others."

"But, God," Alistair remarked with awe, "look at all those Panzers that were trashed trying to take the plant." He referred to a graveyard of burnt and broken vehicles that lay in heaps around the plant's perimeter. It was impossible for Logan to distinguish what they must have looked like before being destroyed.

Alistair turned away from the window and observed Logan as he looked out beside him. Logan wasn't looking at the ground, but was, once again, trying to spot his parents through the tinted windows of the aircraft. Eyes squinted in concentration, he searched through the windows for some distinguishing characteristic he may have missed.

Shaking his head slightly in pity, Alistair tried to distract Logan and pointed to the other aircraft in the sky, which were gliding through the air in the same, undulant motion.

"Do you know why they move like that?"

It took a moment for Logan to realize Alistair was speaking to him. "What?" he replied breathlessly, with a dry throat.

Alistair turned to Francesca. "Why don't you grab us some more ambrosia," he suggested softly.

"No problem," Francesca replied as she patted Alistair's leg. "You want some too, Papa?" she asked, looking at Jacques.

"Why not?" Jacques answered with a shrug.

"Come on, Sasha," Francesca said, her eyes making it clear she would not take no for an answer. "Come help me."

Sasha stood up, saying to no one in particular, "I wouldn't mind a break from this conversation." She and Francesca walked off toward the line at the drink counter.

Logan, not wanting to be obvious about watching Francesca saunter away, quickly turned his glance back to the window.

Alistair pointed to one of the closer transport aircrafts.

"You know why they move like that?" he asked again.

Logan stared at the almost hypnotic motion of the long sky trains drifting in their fluid, wave-like motion. "Why?"

Alistair rubbed the tip of his nose a bit with his left thumb and forefinger. "They move with the air turbulence and transfer it gracefully over the length."

Logan had noticed that there was no turbulence during the flight. The undulations of the aircraft were so slow and subtle that they did not make the passengers sick or nervous.

"Cool," Logan remarked placidly. He had no energy for excitement, and he wasn't in the mood to admire his captors' technology.

Then, something peculiar caught his eye. About three hundred meters in the distance, popping up above the clouds, were long cables that reached up into space, to some distant point that Logan couldn't see. They were flat and wide, more like a long ribbon of tape. Large, ovular containers traveled on the cables, up from the ground and through the sky.

"What are those?" Logan asked, pointing out the window. Alistair's eyes followed Logan's finger.

"Space elevators," Alistair answered nonchalantly, as if it was common to see such a sight. Upon noting Logan's amazement he exclaimed, "You've never seen . . . nevermind. The cables are made of nanocarbon tubes, which make a far stronger cable than steel."

"But what are they?" Logan couldn't take his eyes from the strange elevators.

"Literally, elevators into space!" Alistair was glad that Logan was temporarily distracted from their situation. "The cables are tied to some point on Earth," he explained, "preferably near or over the equator. The other end attaches to a large space station more than a thousand kilometers above the Earth, in space. The cables are kept taut by the rotation of the earth and the space station, as if you were holding a rope with an anchor on the end and spinning with it."

Logan stared quizzically at the space elevators. "I can't believe those cables are that long. Why make something like that? It seems inefficient."

"Not at all," Jacques replied, smiling. "What was inefficient was blasting everything up into space by rockets. Space elevators are hard to make, but they are highly efficient. They require just a tiny fraction of the resources and energy of rockets to function. Plus, flying up to space and back is far more dangerous, especially when entering our atmosphere."

Logan watched the elevator cars move. They looked like normal elevator cars, except that instead of climbing up a building, they vanished into the blue abyss of the sky. It was quite fantastic and surreal, watching the elevators move up and up, until they became so small they disappeared.

"What are they transporting?" Logan asked.

"Who knows?" Alistair answered, thinking about it. "Mmm, maybe supplies, maybe people?" A thought crossed his mind and he turned and looked at Jacques. "It may be that there's still some fighting going on up there," he smirked.

Jacques nodded and looked out the window. He studied the space elevators, trying to discern any information he could. But, the elevator freight wasn't visible.

It took a moment for Alistair's words to sink into Logan's mind. "You mean, the Allies might still be fighting?"

"Yeah," Alistair nodded. "There still might be some Allied holdouts in space." He noticed that this seemed to raise Logan's spirits.

"Like what?" Logan persisted impatiently. "Like, is there still a chance of them winning? Could they rescue us?!" He was nearly jumping out of his seat, looking up into space.

Alistair hooked his right arm around Logan's neck and shoulders.

"For all I know, the war is still raging in full on the Moon or Mars."

Sasha and Francesca returned with the drinks and handed them out to everyone. Francesca carried three cups and handed one to Logan.

"Thank you," Logan gazed at her eyes.

"Um hmm," Francesca replied, flashing him a flirtatious glance. She caught him off guard and a wave of euphoria radiated out from the base of his spine, up through his neck and head, arms and fingers, legs and toes.

Each of them gulped down the drinks and sat in silence for a few minutes. Logan could feel the liquid's relaxing elements circulating throughout his bloodstream and body. Finally, he returned to the moment. He felt refreshed, though there was one particular question that hung in his mind. It was a word he had heard many times while growing up, before he went to the island. It was mentioned by his newfound companions quite a few times as they recalled the past to him, but they never explained its meaning, assuming Logan would know.

"What's Isaiism?" he asked.

Sasha glared at Logan with a look of contempt. "That's his religion! You *do* know about Geiseric's religion? Don't you?!" She badgered him. Her Russian accent came through stronger in her disgust for Logan's naiveté.

Logan shifted slighty with uncomfortability. "Oh, yeah." he lied. "That's right. What was I thinking?" He was embarrassed to ask any more about that for a moment. Sasha's glare really bothered Logan. She was a beautiful, yet shockingly cold girl, capable of making him feel quite small. Her stare completely sapped his courage. She was so unlike Francesca, whose gaze warmed and comforted him.

He quickly glanced over to Francesca—her eyes, her gentle appearance—and then stared into his cup. He spoke quietly, avoiding eye contact with Sasha.

"How could the Americans not see this coming?"

Jacques, sitting on the bench seat across from Logan, Alistair and Francesca, uprighted himself from his slightly hunched position. He repositioned Sasha, who was lying across his lap.

"Well," he said, stroking his fingers through Sasha's hair to content her. "I was living right nextdoor to Germany during Geiseric's expansion into Eastern Europe. And the average European was not afraid enough. They had forgotten history and, so, we were doomed to repeat it."

As Jacques spoke, Sasha nuzzled her nose as far as possible into his chest. She looked like she wanted to crawl into the safety of his clothing. Logan noticed that, for someone so cool and critical, she was very needy of comfort and love from Jacques, who had a soothing quality.

"The thing is," he continued, "people all over the world actually thought Geiseric *would* stop after getting just a little *lebensraum* for Germany."

"He really is Hitler incarnate," Logan coldly remarked.

"Geiseric is no Hitler." Jacques corrected him. "He is far more intelligent. He gave far better arguments for everything he did and people thought that, if he can sound lucid, then he's probably not crazy enough to try and take over the world. But, Geiseric's ideology and the very nature of the Principles Party and Isaiism necessarily pushed them towards world dominance." Jacques had a hard time speaking these words without becoming riled. He nearly growled as he spoke.

Alistair, noticing Jacques's rising agitation, continued where he left off. "Right after Poland was annexed into Germania in 2029, I mean, *right after*," he repeated to give affirmation, "Geiseric began to stretch his tentacles into countries beyond those on Germany's borders. And, he found that his best route was through Greece."

Logan was puzzled. "Greece?"

"Yeah, this was one of Geiseric's greatest publicity coups," Alistair expounded, becoming more animated as he relived the past. His face and tone betrayed a range of emotions, with even a hint of admiration coming through. Of course, the most predominant sentiment he expressed through his attitude was subtle, persistent frustration.

"The Greek people were strongly against some of the core values of the Principles Party. But, Geiseric won them over with all of his pro-Greek rhetoric. He realized that the Greeks are romantics, and he wooed them like a slick man looking to get laid."

This comment made everyone laugh, especially Jacques, who was particularly amused. Alistair smiled, happy to see Jacques lighten up for a moment. "Geiseric realized that all people, especially those with such a rich history as the Greeks, tended to want a rebirth of their former glory to some degree. It's a vice shared by all former empires. So, Geiseric conjured up memories of Athenian or Byzantine greatness." Alistair made gestures, as if he were plucking invisible objects from the air, to give metaphor to what happened. "He connected their history with that of Germania's, creating a sense of common destiny."

Alistair leaned back, lifting his arms up and interlocking his hands to cradle his head. "One tactic Geiseric used *does* invoke memories of Hitler. He united a lot of his empire with hate. And it so happened that a lot of Greeks didn't like Muslims. Their hatred came from the Ottoman Turkish occupation, which lasted some four hundred years and ended in the 1800s. The Greeks are also very committed to their religion, the Orthodox Church. So, they had a policy that tried to force Muslims to convert. The Muslims retaliated with suicide bombings. It started getting really bad after the turn of the century, with all the terrorist activity going on around the world. Geiseric came at a perfect time."

"Chaos breeds the will for radical change," Francesca spoke quietly, glancing furtively at Logan. Logan was impressed by her astute comment. He did not realize she was so insightful, being that she had remained rather silent when discussing these larger issues up until now.

Jacques nodded in agreement. "Geiseric warmed the Greeks over to him with his propaganda. Then, he used the ultimate tool of building an alliance," he took a sip of ambrosia. "War."

VI

SPIRITUAL CAPITAL

March 25, 2029

The Greek Prime Minister, Constantine Metaxas, clapped upon introducing his friend, the Germanian chancellor, to the people of Athens. The two leaders shook hands and hugged with their left arms, smacking each other's backs a couple times. Geiseric took to the podium, standing with a view of the Parthenon behind him. In front of him was an audience of joyful Greek citizens. As usual, they were ringed by a police barricade. Thousands of protesters circled the outside perimeter of the barricade. Television crews from every nation staked out the best spots to film the chancellor.

Soft pinks and yellows streaked the sky. Geiseric had chosen to speak just as the sun set, casting a myriad of colorful shades upon the ancient ruins.

"Good evening," he spoke in Greek.

"Good evening," most of the audience replied.

"Isn't it a beautiful evening in Athens?" he fluently articulated in their native language, much to the pleasure of the crowd. True to his modus operandi, he began with a shower of compliments. He held out his arms to indicate the surrounding scenery.

"God wanted the world to gaze upon the splendor of this historic and breathtaking city. Athens was the epicenter of the Golden Age, where the arts of knowledge have their roots. Throughout history, your nation has shown a deep yearning and respect for wisdom, a pursuit with which I can identify. Of course, the Principles as a whole are great admirers of the Ancient Greeks." He nodded. Smiling at the audience, he took in a deep breath.

"My mind and spirit are inspired beyond my imagination, standing here in the city where Socrates and Plato gathered and argued. You Greeks," he pointed to the audience, "and your country, have tremendous spiritual capital. Your history has a priceless, empowering and invigorating quality. Ancient Greece was, in my opinion, the birthplace of the Principles. It is the birthplace of the line of thought that shaped the growth of civilization in world history." He looked to the sky, which was full of what appeared to large waterfalls consisting of smoke and heat, remnants of the celebratory fireworks that preceded his introduction. Looking back upon the audience, he was filled with an energetic zeal.

"As modern Greece celebrates its independence, won two-hundred years ago, you can be proud that its vibrant culture continues based upon the beliefs in intellectual pursuits, first forged in classical Greece over 2500 years ago!" he passionately shouted, throwing his hands up for emphasis.

The people applauded vigorously. Many threw bunches of wild poppies at his feet. Geiseric mouthed a thank you into the noise, but let the audience continue their accolades. Taking a step back from the podium, he clapped with the crowd. When they quieted, he stepped back up and began again.

"On March 25, 1821, Bishop Germanos of Patras boldly raised the Greek flag at the monastery of Agia Lavras, inciting the Peloponnesians to rise against the Turkish oppressors. On this day of the Orthodox calendar, the archangel Gabriel appeared to the maiden Mary and announced the news." He took on the tone and demeanor of a father telling a story. "She was pregnant with the divine child," he continued. "Bishop Germanos chose this day to deliver a different but not unrelated message. A new spirit was about to be born in Greece. In 1829, after many years of brutal warfare, the Greeks finally won their independence!" Geiseric paused for effect.

"I come to you this day," he announced with fervor, "two-hundred years after Greece gained its independence from the Ottoman Empire!"

There were more cheers of equal ferocity, but Geiseric roared on over the shouts and applause.

"Vigorous Greek fighters rose up and defeated the Muslim forces on land and sea!" Geiseric stood upright and took on a sinister, rage-filled glare.

"Yet, *to this day*, the Greek people are being oppressed by Muslims!" He looked out upon the sympathetic crowd. "For fifteen years, the fanatics of modern Islam have been murdering innocent people in this country." The riotous distaste of the protesters could be heard. His words sent them into a frenzy that was hard for the police and soldiers lining the barricade to contain. The protesters were primarily Turkish, but also included many Arabs from a multitude of countries, Albanians and even many ethnic Greeks.

"They come from within and from abroad," Geiseric continued. "Their backwards interpretations of a strong religion have resulted in the decline of their civilizations. Now, they want to come into the West and bring down our cultures as well. Since the Niqab, the face veils for Muslim women," he covered his face with his hands to show what he was talking about, "since these odious adornments were first outlawed in Germany, they have fought it. Why do the women fight to maintain traditions which oppress them? The Muslims fight too hard for things that hold themselves down!"

The protestors became ever more riled, chanting, "Allah Akbar! Death to Geiseric!"

Geiseric chuckled. "Now, they want to bring *our* cultures under their insidious grip, with their Sharia law! And listen to these primitives who are so angered with me. Listen to how they threaten me. They always resort to violence while we bend over and take it! We faced this same problem in Germany and now Germania. Germany outlawed animal sacrifice over two decades ago. Yet they spat in the face of my nation's laws and continue to do so! They assassinate our politicians, as they have done all over Europe! They just kill whoever criticizes or challenges them! And we took it! *But, no more!*"

Geiseric slammed a heavy fist down on the podium. The protesters had become so angered that they began fighting with the police and soldiers. Flailing arms and kicking legs could be seen over the crowd as dozens of young men were hauled away, shouting.

Geiseric pointed at them, his eyes aflame, matching their rage with his own. "It's time they see that every action has a reaction. We need to put *them* on the defense! We must see them as what they are — a nation unto themselves! All Muslims are responsible for the way their fanatical brethren behave, for they all share in creating the mood which tolerates, condones, and *even hails* this behavior!"

The supportive audience rallied behind Geiseric's words with cheers. He barely drew a breath before raging on, lifting his left fist before him. "The firm majority of Muslims identify so much more with other Muslims than with the country they have been welcomed to, that they *enjoy it* when terrorists strike us! It is time they choose a side. They are either *with us,* or *against us!*"

His supporters applauded and whistled, shouting gleeful praises for Geiseric and his homeland. Some profusely blew kisses to the Germanian chancellor with both hands.

Suddenly flames shot up over the crowd. A store had been set on fire behind the barricade. The dissidents had broken into a full-scale riot. People near the perimeter began screaming and fleeing as the police shot tear gas canisters into the angry mob. The canisters landed far enough away from the audience that the gas would not reach them. Still, the supportive crowd was visibly frightened, not sure whether to disperse.

"Do not be afraid of *them!*" Geiseric commanded over the noise. "Face them now!" Then, he shouted to the demonstrators. "We are not afraid of you!"

Taking his cue, the audience turned and began hissing angrily at the protesters. They shouted curses in Greek and made lewd gestures. This only added fuel to the fire of emotions and the protesters rushed the audience, who stood their ground. The scene devolved into immense chaos, however it was Geiseric's supporters who far outnumbered the dissidents and, having stood their ground, they brutally beat many of the rioters in the streets. The police rushed into the ferocious mob to stop them from killing the agitators.

Geiseric knew the entire world was watching this live. He smirked and nodded.

Hera was hot, smoky, and packed to the brim. The second most popular nightclub in Athens had never seen a larger crowd. It had only been a month since the chancellor of Germania visited the city, and already people flocked from all over the world to Greece, much as they had to Germania, seeking the cultural vibrancy that came with the Principles and their allies.

The pulsing club was as crammed with European and American foreigners as it was with Greeks. Four Greek soldiers acted as club security, patting people down and making them pass through metal detectors. It was a warm night in late April, which meant that those arriving in heavy apparel were especially targeted and searched. Two of the soldiers had bomb-sniffing German Shepherds that monitored everyone who passed through. Suspicious clientele were taken out of line and made to pass through a bomb-detection device.

One man was wearing a large coat and the dogs started to bark upon catching a scent of something on him. He was pulled out of line and went peacefully. It turned out that the dogs had picked up on a chemical within the coat, which was appropriate for them to identify as a possible dangerous agent. However, it was also used in the production of this particular line of clothing and it was found in miniscule, non-threatening amounts on the coat.

When it was determined that he was not carrying a bomb or anything else, the guards began to let the line of people go into the club again. A young couple was next in line. The young man was clean-shaven and wore pungent cologne. His short, ruddy-brown hair and light-skinned face appeared to be of a European phenotype. The guards quickly patted him down and let him proceed. After all, suicide bombers were almost always alone, or would come as a group of men. They had never come disguised as a man/woman couple, both in such secular apparel, being that most terrorists were fundamentalist Muslims who usually could not dress in such a way. The couple also did not fit the ethnic profile that sparked suspicion. With so many trying to enter the club, quick decisions had to be made to let people in or turn them away. The young lady passed her purse through a metal detector and, being that her outfit was so tight and revealing, she was waved through without a pat down.

The couple walked casually through the densely packed room. Their heads began to bob with the dance music. Soon, their entire bodies were moving with the pounding bass. The man bent down and scratched his right ankle, right above his shoe, and then took his girlfriend's hand. They pushed through the throngs of people, making their way out onto the dance floor. People were so close, strangers rubbed and bumped up against each other. The body heat was stifling, but no one seemed to mind.

The young man and his date danced for a moment, moving their feet and hips. They looked relaxed, like they were having as much fun as anybody else. The young lady leaned in and gently kissed her man on the lips. He embraced her and, for just a moment, they both closed their eyes, swaying together. A single tear slipped from her eye. Then, he let her go and she disappeared into the crowd. As he watched her walk away, his face showed no emotion. He waited until she was out the door.

He fell on his back and put his feet up, as if break-dancing. He slapped his palms on his knees and the soles of his shoes exploded powerfully, firing out dozens of tiny, spherical projectiles. They shot out horizontally, ripping through the flesh on the torsos and faces of everyone around him. Some were killed instantly; others were critically injured and maimed. Blood spattered all over the dance floor. In an instant, the only noises that could be heard were the screams of people trying to escape. They slipped and fell in the crimson puddles as they rushed for the exits. The painful cries of the injured and the wild stampeding of the frightened echoed through the room, overwhelming the music blaring over the speakers.

Within fifteen minutes of the attack, Geiseric received a call from the Greek prime minister on his personal line in the chancellor's office in Berlin. Constantine did not greet Geiseric.

"Did you hear the news?"

"I'm watching it right now. How did he get in?"

Constantine sighed. "This has the fingerprint of a nation-state on it. It was a high-profile job. The preliminary conclusions are that he had a bomb in the sole of each shoe. The explosives that were used would have been picked up by the dogs, however they were made up of three chemicals which, separately, did not alert the dogs. The bombs must have been unmixed when he walked in. Somehow, he was able to mix them upon entering. The shrapnel was made of boron carbide ceramic, so that it wasn't caught by the metal detector. The detonator switch was some sort of fiberglass device, with optical fibers and chemical electricity. I mean, we're talking about some tricky stuff."

"What about the bomber?" Geiseric asked.

"He didn't die right away," Constantine explained. "His legs were blown to bits, but his upper body and head were relatively unscathed. But, he died of blood loss before we could extract any information from him."

"Where do you think he's from?"

"He looks Turkish," Constantine replied.

Geiseric spun in his chair with jubilance. "This is perfect!"

Constantine was startled by Geiseric's reaction. "No Geiseric, this is not good. We have been attacked by many Saudi Arabians, Moroccans, Syrians, Lebanese and even Iranians, but not many Turks. If they are becoming more fanaticized, they will be hard to spot."

Geiseric laughed. "I'm sorry, Constantine. I realize I have not yet informed you of all the grand plans I have for Greece."

"Then tell me now," Constantine invited.

"All in good time," the chancellor puckishly replied. "We need to have a meeting. Come to Germania next weekend. Until then, hype the Turkish connection to the terrorism in Greece. Make it look like the Turkish government was behind this attack . . ."

"We don't know that," Constantine interrupted.

"So what?!" Geiseric retorted, raising his voice. He quickly calmed himself. "Constantine, my friend, who's looking out for you, eh? You're a good man and you're honest. I like that. But, sometimes you have to play the game. God has blessed us with a Turkish face to slap on the television and internet. That's the man who murdered all those kids. We *know* a government has to be behind it. Who's next door to you? Turkey! You follow me?"

"Got it," Constantine said, cracking a smile.

"Good."

Prime Minister Metaxas came to Geiseric's Bavarian Alpine retreat in the picturesque resort city of Berchtesgaden. They met at the Berghof, formerly the fortress retreat of Adolf Hitler. This building was bombed during World War II and nearly completely demolished by the German government in 1952, so that it wouldn't become a cult focal point. Geiseric hated to see historical markers go by the way, so he had the resort-like mountain fortress restored to its former splendor, stone for stone, tile for tile. It was a grand mountain chalet of white stone, topped by a sloped roof that easily shed the winter snow. Much of the cliff-side wall was made of glass, so Geiseric and his guests could constantly behold the heavenly valleys, forest, and the sparkling *Konigssee*, King's Lake, below. He and Constantine sat at a small mahogany tea table near the window and drank beer from oversized steins. Upon arriving, they had chatted mostly about the incredible success of the Greek prime minister's campaign to demonize Turkey. Although they were quite jubilant for this, Constantine felt a bit uneasy.

"There is the minor problem with the terrorism," he remarked. "It's gotten far worse. In the past two months, more people have died than in the past five years."

Geiseric took on a solemn face. "But, don't you see, this is playing right into our hands?"

Constantine cast a confused and indignant glance at him. Geiseric laughed and placed his right arm around the Greek prime minister's neck.

"Constantine, buddy," he said, "don't you understand that the world is sympathizing with the Greeks right now? These terrorists are going to allow us to act decisively," he smacked his palm on the table. He took a large gulp of beer, wiping the froth from his lip with a broad stroke of his forearm. "Because of the terrorists, we are going to be able to give the Greeks what they want, but would *never* expect," the Germanian chancellor paused, knowing his remark would be tantalizing.

Constantine leaned in a bit, as if someone were around to listen. "What do you mean by acting decisively?"

"I mean," Geiseric began, taking another swig of the rich, dark beer, "what would make the Greek people love you and I more than anything else right now?"

Constantine shrugged and shook his head. Geiseric flashed a toothy smile and poked his comrade's shoulder with his index finger as he spoke each word.

"If we kicked out the Muslims . . . and took back *Byzantium!*"

Constantine stared at Geiseric in shock, chewing the side of his lip in thought for a moment. Slowly, a smile began to warm up his face.

"You are crazy, Geiseric," he laughed, finishing off another stein-full. "But, if anyone can do it, you can."

Geiseric laughed and smacked Constantine on the back. "Now that's what I like to hear!"

The Greek prime minister considered what Geiseric had just said. Byzantium was a city that had gone by many names. It was founded by Greek colonists more than 2500 years ago and called Byzantion. In the fourth century AD, the city was made the capital of the New Roman Empire and was dubbed Constantinople after the emperor who had given the city this prestigious role. Such was why the name Constantine was a common name in Greece. The city was located on both sides of the Bosphorus strait, a small channel of water that separated Asia from Europe. Thus, it was the only metropolis to lie on two continents. When the Western Roman Empire collapsed in the fifth century, the eastern part continued to flourish and became known as the Byzantine Empire, an extremely prosperous and glorious era in the history of Greece. In the fifteenth century, the Ottoman Turks conquered Constantinople, renaming it Istanbul, which it continued to be called to this day. It was now the richest and most populous city in the country that was all that remained of the former Ottoman Empire — Turkey.

While Geiseric fixed two shots of schnapps, Constantine studied the inhabitants of a gigantic saltwater aquarium that was the centerpiece of the great room's left wall. Constantine casually sauntered over to the large, aquatic spectacle. Numerous small, colorful fish darted around playfully. Starfish clung to the interior walls and urchins drifted in the sand.

There were at least a dozen crabs, some crawling along in the sand and on the coral, others hiding in their shells. Suddenly, an octopus appeared right before Constantine's eyes, on a piece of coral. It came out of camouflage, turning a ghost white. Constantine was surprised and intrigued.

"That octopus is amazing!" he marveled.

Geiseric handed Constantine a shot. "Her name is Helena."

Constantine pointed. "I couldn't even see her and then, out of nowhere, she became completely white."

Geiseric clinked his shotglass against Constantine's and led them in cheers. Taking down the shot, Geiseric smacked his lips a bit and admired the cephalopod, each of its arms about a meter long. The metamorphosis began again like many clouds of color billowing over the skin, until it had entirely changed, this time to a deep purple-black.

Geiseric smiled. "She's nervous. Isn't she beautiful?"

Constantine took down his shot, wincing a bit from the mild burn of the hard alcohol. He was normally a wine-drinker. "What is she nervous about?"

"She's not used to seeing other humans besides me," the chancellor explained.

Constantine felt the warming and loosening effects of the schnapps radiating throughout his body. "How does she change like that?"

Geiseric was happy to edify the Greek prime minister. "It's interesting you should ask that. The octopus is the ultimate chameleon, so to speak. *Not only* can it change color, but its skin can also bunch up and what not, to create textures resembling that of rock and coral."

"That's a handy trick," Constantine remarked, nodding in amazement.

Geiseric smiled reverently as he gazed upon the astonishing creature. "It is indeed."

The two leaders stood in silence for a moment, taking in the mesmerizing creature. "What does she eat?" the Greek prime minister asked. "The crabs?"

Geiseric waved at the octopus through the glass. Constantine half expected Helena to raise a tentacle and wave back. "I wouldn't allow such primitive activities to occur in my aquarium," Geiseric remarked with jovial indignation. "Helena is a vegetarian."

Constantine smacked Geiseric's shoulder. "Only you would have a vegetarian octopus!" He laughed. "So, she just leaves the crabs alone?"

"Yes," Geiseric nodded. "I have taught her good manners. Octopi are incredibly intelligent. Some say they are the most intelligent animal besides man. If the world were covered in water, intelligent life would have evolved from them, rather than monkeys."

Constantine tilted his head in curiosity. "Fascinating . . . ," he raised his eyebrows. "But, aren't they carnivores? How do you feed her anything but meat?"

Geiseric shrugged. "It's no different than what they do in factory farms, where they feed herbivores, like cows, pellets made from the meat of other *sick* cows," he shuddered. "I, however, prefer to modify my animals' diets by feeding them wholesome foods."

The chancellor pressed a button, which released a small brick of food into the water. "Watch."

Helena moved toward it, crawling over crabs that she left unscathed. She ravenously devoured the meal provided to her, grappling at it with her tentacles before bringing it to her beak on her middle-underside.

Geiseric smiled. "Like all things, you need to package something in a way that is palatable to the consumer."

He made them each another drink. They walked outside onto the balcony and stood looking at the splendid green valleys, lit by the crisp afternoon rays.

Constantine breathed in a full chest of air and exhaled slowly. "So, Geiseric, how can we possibly accomplish these big plans for Greece?"

Geiseric surveyed his beautiful Alpine view before carefully answering. "Well, not everything is under our control. Like most things, it takes two to tango. We are going to need the Turks and Muslims to dance with us. They need to play into our trap, which we can almost guarantee they will do." He snickered and shook his head, relishing in his opponents' predictability.

"The Hera bombing was a terrible event, but it was the best thing that could have happened to us. A lot of French, British and Russian citizens died, or were seriously maimed. A couple of Americans were hurt. Basically, this *one* act has mobilized the world. Everyone pities Greece." He assertively looked Constantine in the eye.

"So, we must act now, before emotions simmer down. What you need to do is *really* provoke the Muslims. Spout off things that you know will rile them up, like how oppressive they are to women. Hell, you can even say, 'Islam holds its people down!' Geiseric shouted, lifting his fist, pretending to be giving a speech. "You have every right to your opinion. The Americans, Brits, French and everyone else will let you get away with such rhetoric right now. Tell the world how we must work together to stop future attacks. Say things like, 'This is a crusade against evil!' Of course, the Western World will interpret 'crusade," he raised his fingers up to make quotes, "as meaning against terrorism.

But, the Middle-East, as I'm sure you know, will be stirred up like a swarm of hornets."

Constantine's eyes widened and he shook his head a bit. *"That's for sure."*

Geiseric leaned back. "You must start doing this the moment you get back to Greece. And, I mean the *instant* you get back. It cannot wait any longer. Start kicking out all known Muslim radicals, suspected radicals, and their entire families. You must do this before global public opinion cools down. Now, by default, you'll be kicking out a lot of Muslims who have nothing to do with *outright* radicalism or terrorism. But they are all radicals to some degree." Geiseric's eyes flashed red, reflecting the bright autumnal sun. "If we kick a fourth of their community out of Greece, much of the remainder will no doubt start to aid terrorism, or even become terrorists." Geiseric tilted his head side to side, as he considered the many variables.

"What's most likely to happen is that the Muslims will bring radicals from other countries into Greece, maybe with the help of Turkey or Iran. That will only help us. After a suicide bombing or two, you cut off all tourism and immigration of Muslims into Greece. You also prevent any Greek Muslims who visit the Middle East from coming back.

"Now, here's the beauty of it," the chancellor smiled, becoming animated as he often did when he strategized. "If they just calmed down and didn't do anything aggressive, this plan would fail. However, you know that the Muslims who remain in Greece, cut off, feeling under siege, fed by their extremist propaganda, riled up by your antagonism — you know they're going to go on the offense! There will be a few coordinated suicide attacks and . . . *bam!*" He slammed his fist into his other palm. "You kick them *all* out! You kick every single practicing Muslim out of Greece. You don't take any of their belongings. Anything that's tied down, you pay them well for and send them on their way. Germania will help with your deportation fund."

Constantine was slightly overwhelmed, but he trusted Geiseric's reasoning enough to feel confident that the plan could work. "We will let them give us a Pearl Harbor, so we can give them Hiroshima."

Geiseric pointed to him with a wide grin. "Exactly!"

"OK," Constantine shrugged, "where, then, does Istanbul come into all of this?"

"Well," Geiseric explained, "we basically use the same tactic. We have to constantly make them look like the aggressor, but that's not going to be too hard. I already have a few ideas based on the intelligence I've been receiving from inside Turkey."

"What's going on?" Constantine asked.

"Right now, I can't talk about it. But all in good time, comrade. Before you know it, Istanbul will no longer be." He turned to Constantine, with a devilish glint in his eye. "And *Byzantium* will once again be in the rightful hands of the Greeks."

Over the next three weeks, Constantine stoked the fires within his people. He had learned well from his mentor. His skillful oratory drove the populace into a frenzy. Upon his return to Greece, he ordered the deportation of all "suspected" Muslim radicals. This directive single-handedly removed a fifth of the Muslim population in Greece. Other Muslims were expelled from Greece on Constantine's personal authority, merely as provocation. Two Muslim parliamentarians and all Muslim judges in Greece were included in his purge.

Constantine accused all of the suspects with connections to terrorism or radical nations. The intelligence community did nothing to substantiate the deportations, for as Prime Minister Metaxas claimed, it would endanger operatives who were presently spying on the enemy and could be exposed, if the evidence they gained was made public. The people were assured by their prime minister that he had all the proof necessary to take the actions he took. After the furor over the Hera bombing, the Greek masses and, indeed the world, simply were not as scrupulous in their monitoring of Constantine's decisions.

There was still a thriving Muslim community left in Greece. As their friends and family members were escorted out of the country by air, rail, and ship, they became angry. And just as Geiseric had foretold, most who were not extremists before the purge, became extremists in the wake of these provocations.

Islamic radicalism had found a new arch-nemesis and battleground to call their suicide soldiers to arms. Fatwas, issued by Imams against Geiseric, Constantine and the Greek people, became the daily routine. The Muslim clerics proclaimed that all Greeks were infidels and should be killed on the spot. Terrorists filtered secretly into Greece, from the Middle-East and Muslim communities in Europe, including Germania. Most were caught at the borders, but a few slipped through. Three more suicide bombings rocked Greece, one in Thebes and two just outside Athens. The Greeks felt under attack, from the inside and out. They became desperate for quick, decisive action.

Constantine proclaimed that the terrorist cells were based in Eastern Thrace, the tiny piece of Turkey that extended into Europe. Considering that he provided no substantiating facts, this was a very controversial accusation. However, Constantine insisted that whether they were coming out of the Middle-East or Europe, the bombers were coalescing and forming their leadership in this part of Thrace, which lied on Greece's border. During a television interview, Constantine proclaimed that the Turkish government was aware of and compliant with the terrorist cells. He accused the Turks of helping the terrorists get over the border.

The Greeks supported their leader and the average citizen of the western world also believed him, or were angered enough to not heavily question the facts presented to them.

On a beautiful June morning, a peaceful Sunday service in Athens ended in blood and tears. Just as Father Antony was reminding the parish of the promise in John 3:16, that "whoever believes in Him shall not perish but have eternal life," four young men stormed his Orthodox church. They pulled out automatic side arms, gunned down the two guards stationed at the door and, rushing inside, they opened fire on the unsuspecting congregants. Making no distinction between young and old, Greek families screamed in anguish and horror as bullets pierced their loved ones. In a final hurrah, the attackers screamed "Allah Akbar!" just before detonating the bombs taped to their torsos, underneath their clothing. The shrapnel decimated its wearers and everyone surrounding them.

Word of the attack, soon dubbed by the media as the "Sunday Slaughter," terrified the Greeks and disgusted the entire world. There were some skeptics who believed Geiseric or Constantine were behind these latest terrorist attacks, for after all, this hostility did serve to help the broadly apparent agendas of the Greek and Germanian leaders. But, like true politicians, Geiseric and Constantine waved away the accusations like pesky mosquitoes, and appeared indignant that such horrifying supposition was even being entertained by their political opponents.

Constantine struck when the iron was hot. Before the horror of the Sunday Slaughter waned he had, by authorization of Parliament and with the support of the Greek people, ordered the internment of all practicing Muslims until deportation could be arranged. All immigration of Muslims into Greece was suspended. Greece was now almost one hundred percent Greek Orthodox, united in their faith and, no less, their hatred for Islam.

Then, came the provocation that would allow Constantine and his German overlord to go on the offensive.

Four tour buses riding through the outskirts of Istanbul were simultaneously commandeered by well-armed terrorist squads in a brilliantly coordinated attack. The buses were filled with Greeks and a few other foreign tourists. The hijackers allowed citizens from any country besides Germania and Greece to leave the buses unharmed. They then forced two male tourists to the front of the bus and executed each with a single bullet to the skull. The victims were two of the richest men in the world: one a wealthy Greek who owned the largest fishing fleet in the Mediterranean and Caribbean; the other, a CEO of a pork company in Germania.

When the deed was done, the remaining tourists were quickly herded into five vans, which sped away to parts unknown. Word of the hijacking reached Constantine and he immediately called the Germanian chancellor.

Geiseric was enjoying a walk through the evergreen forest that surrounded his Berghof mountain retreat. He whistled, holding his hands casually behind his back. But his peace was suddenly interrupted when one of his personal guards, in metallic, full-body armor ran up to him with a thick telephone. Its long cord was attached to a ground line.

"*Mein Führer! Es ist Constantine,*" the guard announced, handing Geiseric the phone.

"*Dankeschön,*" Geiseric said as he took the receiver. "*Hallo Constantine!*" he warmly greeted his friend.

Constantine's mixture of excitement and a mild state of panic came clearly over the line. "Geiseric, terrorists have taken hostage almost a hundred Greek citizens who were vacationing in the Istanbul area."

Geiseric smiled widely, but feigned shock. "No!"

"I know," Constantine replied. "How could they be so stupid!"

Geiseric licked his bottom lip. "What are their demands?"

Constantine laughed with a quick exhale through the nose and mocked the demand with an overdramatic whimper. "They want the persecution of Muslims in Greece to stop."

"So, they *have to* be somewhere in Eastern Thrace. I mean, it would be hard to get all those people away on boats."

"I can hear the wheels spinning in your mind, Geiseric."

Two days later, the world watched in sickened fury as the terrorists posted video on the internet, showing the hijacking of the tourists and later executions. Ten hostages were decapitated with a bowie knife, in a torturous, drawn out sawing action. Some of the killings took nearly half a minute. The video, picked up by every news program, only served to consolidate the power of Constantine in Greece. The television news channels obviously couldn't show the actual murders. They cut the video right after the terrorists were done chanting prayers in Arabic, when the blade touched their victim's skin. For those who wished to see it in full, the internet provided ample sites to view it. The Greek legislature voted to give their leader near war-time powers, allowing him to dispatch a small army without alerting parliament.

Though most civilians around the globe didn't feel that this was acting outside rationale, the majority of the political and military leaders in the European Union and the United States believed this was a very dangerous situation. Geiseric was about to make a power grab through Constantine, and most political elites, no matter what country they were in, knew this.

True to his word, President Hollier refused to just *let* it happen.

He took a vacation with his family to a publicly undisclosed location. Coincidentally, Prime Minister Dandau was doing a similar thing. No one but their top advisors were in the know. Representatives in the British Parliament and the United States' Congress were outraged. Clearly, their leaders were being deceptive and a secret meeting was taking place.

In San Juan, Puerto Rico, Hollier and Dandau met in a bunker-like, one-story building on a secured compound. It was guarded by dozens of both men's top security agents, working in tandem with the squads of Special Forces commandos who were based on the compound. The leaders were left to speak alone in the single, large room of the building. A thick-paned window overlooked the tropical landscape. The interior was lined in dark mahogany, and by the window there was a wooden table skirted by a few matching chairs. Otherwise the room was sparse. Hollier poured his protégé a gin on the rocks. He also offered Dandau a Cuban cigar, which the prime minister happily accepted.

The two thought quietly for a moment, lighting up their cigars, taking a few starting puffs, and savoring the taste. They stood in front of the window and sipped their drinks.

Hollier broke the silence. "My God, what will the next years bring us, I wonder?"

Dandau took a long set of puffs from the cigar. "Indeed."

"So," Hollier looked to Dandau, "what's the news on your side?"

Dandau flicked his ashes into a small, glass tray. "Our guy on the inside says that a large Greek military contingent is being trained by Germanian intelligence agents. They are going through what's called, 'military-grade Formula training.' It seems that this is the ultimate use of the Formula — to create 'super-soldiers.'"

Hollier rubbed his chin. "Military-grade, huh?"

"Correct," Dandau ominously replied.

"I've talked to our generals," Hollier said, "and they say that the *basic* Formula training is really somethin'. I know some people who've gone through the public version in Germania. It does seem to really get people in shape and more alert."

Dandau shrugged and took a gulp of his drink. "People see it as so mystical," he rolled his eyes. "But it's a very basic, instinctual process. Good nutrition, balanced physical and mental activities and what not. A lot of it is based on good trainers, who can identify people's weaknesses and shore them up, while honing their strengths. I'm sure this military-grade Formula doesn't deviate far from the basic principles. It's just far more intense."

"Yep," Hollier laconically replied, "interesting."

The prime minister took another large swig of gin and puckered his lips. "MI6 has gained enough intelligence on their methods for us to begin training our own soldiers. I recommend you begin doing the same."

Hollier looked out the window on the well-armed British and American security detail. "How much more effective do you think a Formula-trained commando is than, let's say, the SEALs?"

Dandau made an analytical frown and quickly cocked his head to the side as he considered this. "That's really hard to gauge until we test it. What I recommend is that you begin Formula training for your special ops. That's what we're doing. That way parliament or congress won't find out. Not for a while, at least."

Hollier took in a long breath, assessing the situation. "Do you really think they're gonna try and take Istanbul?"

Dandau looked out the window, up at the sky. "There's no doubt about that, my friend." He inhaled deeply and let out his breath with a slow hissing sound. "We need to start training Turkish troops. There's no way the British or American people will let us get many of our forces involved."

Hollier shook his head. "They think it's just between Greece and Turkey."

"My, how the people are dim," Dandau sighed. "I've already authorized the SAS to send agents over to consult the Turks."

"Right." Hollier finished his whiskey on the rocks and wiped his lips. "Thank God I've got Ericson heading the CIA. Otherwise, we'd be up shit creek."

Germanian Special Forces operative, Martin Schneider, marched briskly across the interior hallway of the Greek Parliament Building to the prime minister's office. This building was once dubbed the King's Palace, for it was built by Otto of Bavaria, who ruled as king of Greece in the wake of the nation's liberation from the Turks two hundred years ago.

The Bavarians were back. Besides Geiseric being from this area, Sergeant Schneider was as well, along with half of the one hundred Germanian military advisors who were sent down to Greece over the past two weeks. This was no coincidence. Germany's strongest Principle demographic was in Bavaria and, as passionate supporters of the cause, they could be trusted not to leak information, more than an operative who was beholden only by a commitment of duty.

Schneider passed through security and entered Constantine's elaborately decorated office. The Greek-key patterns along the top of the walls and the velvet drapes gave the room a warm, Victorian feel. The sergeant stood at attention while the prime minister finished a call. Constantine was talking on a secure ground line with Geiseric's director of foreign intelligence based out of Munich.

"... and we have confirmed that Turkey was given F/A-22 Raptors," the director told Constantine. "And the CIA, MI6 and SAS sent teams over to train Turkish pilots and soldiers. But, don't worry. With the training we're giving to your men, they will run circles around them."

"Alright, good," Constantine said in impeccable German.

"We have it covered," the director assured him.

"Dankeschön. Auf wiedersehen." Constantine hung up the phone and looked up to the sergeant. "What is the news, Sergeant Schneider?"

"Omega Force is ready to go on your orders, sir," Schneider replied gruffly.

Constantine paused and thought for a moment, then fixed his gaze straight ahead at the wall. "Send them in."

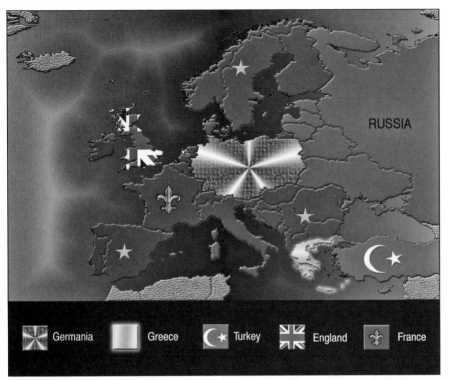

| Germania | Greece | Turkey | England | France |

Thirty six Greek commandos funneled into Eastern Thrace. Shadowed by a hazy night, they slipped past the Turkish soldiers guarding the border with Greece and crossed the Evros River, which divided Western from Eastern Thrace.

The commandos moved out in four black inflatable rafts, in teams of nine. They were camouflaged with green and black outfits and face paint. All were heavily-armed with the latest in weaponry, and a few were electronic surveillance specialists, carrying a myriad of high-technology devices required to track down the terrorists and hostages. One of the Omega Force squads carried the rations of food and water — enough for the commandos to be in Turkish Thrace for weeks.

The first order of business for all the commandos was to make hidden base camps in the luscious forests. The rich, wetland vegetation allowed a comfortable cover from sight.

Radio communication between squads was kept highly coded and at a minimum. Electronic surveillance and other intelligence gathering equipment was set up under camouflaged tents amongst the trees and tall bushes. The commandos used these devices to intercept all transmissions in the area, with the hopes that their voice analyzing equipment would identify the people they were after. A few of the terrorists had spoken on the videos they sent out to the world via the internet. Their voices could now be found if they used a cell phone or some other transmission device to communicate with their superiors over the airwaves. The commandos could then triangulate the calls to locate the person talking. It wasn't new technology, but it was the best ever put into use.

Omega Force was on a dedicated mission to save the hijacked tourists, of which there were less every day. The commandos were highly motivated, sickened by the videos of Greek citizens having their heads sawed off with knives. The fires of vengeance coursed through their veins, and only the blood of the hijackers would quench it.

Within two days, they had identified their targets and narrowed down their enemies' location to within a three kilometer radius. All of the commando squads moved out and encircled the target vicinity, an area in the mountains about seventy-five kilometers east of the Greek border. They awaited darkness.

Just as the last rays skirted the trees, scouts warily crawled on their stomachs across the ground. Their uniforms were outfitted with grass and other loose brush, so they melted into the landscape with the fading light. There were a few small sheep ranches on the hills, but the commandos easily slid past without alarming the animals. They switched their goggles from infrared mode to extricate mode, which allowed them to see through walls made from normal building materials, up to half of a meter thick. Most walls were fairly transparent to radar or radio frequencies. The goggles used an ultra-wide-band, short-pulse radar system that worked by scattering microwave energy signals, which bounced off objects to calculate distances. Sending out millions of pulses per second, the goggles in extricate mode could screen out the still objects and provide 3-D images of moving objects. They could even detect the minute motions of a person attempting to stand still.

All that the scouts had yet observed during their surveillance, besides animals, were large families having dinner or settling down to sleep. Some farmers were still outside, up late shearing the sheep or slaughtering the lambs, whose baleful cries echoed through the hills. None of these homes held the cutthroats the Greek commandos were after.

Then, the find came.

A scout surveilling a hillock to the southeast spied through the walls of a larger farm's slaughterhouse. The extricate goggles revealed dozens of human figures. He could clearly distinguish their shapes. The hostages were cramped on the ground, their hands bound behind their backs. The scout swung his head toward the small residential house near the slaughterhouse. It looked like more hostages were lined up on the wall as the gunmen sat around a square wooden table.

Looking back towards the slaughterhouse, the scout discerned several figures standing amongst the bulk of seated hostages. Some were holding long objects, probably machine guns. No doubt these terrorists had bombs, either on their bodies or somewhere in the slaughterhouse. If the rescue wasn't executed fast enough, they would blow themselves up with the hostages.

The scout carefully examined the grounds around the building, assessing the situation. Six terrorists guarded the farm outside, seemingly innocuous as they sheared sheep in normal farmers' clothing. The Greek commando switched his goggles to thermal mode, so that he could see the terrorists' body heat emanating from under their clothes. They were packing machine guns, hidden under their loose garb, and each wore a suicide-bomb jacket, both of which blocked the body heat more than the clothes.

Knowing a call over the airwaves might alert the terrorists, if they also had equipment to intercept frequencies, the scout retreated slowly to notify his comrades.

Upon hearing this report, the man in charge of the operation in the field, Stephanos Nicos, gave orders for more Omega Force commandos to gather intelligence on the terrorist hideout. They came back with confirmation of what the first scout had seen.

Lieutenant Nicos analyzed the defensive posturing of the terrorists. It was a typical suicide contingent — the base force for such a hostage taking. Without a quick victory for the commandos, the mission would be a failure.

The lieutenant paced in his tent, looking down at his high-laced boots as he walked. He knew it would not be too hard, as long as every last one of the terrorists was known, but he needed another day's surveillance to be completely sure of the situation. That was a problem, however, for an average of three hostages were decapitated daily. Nicos sat heavily on his cot as he weighed his options.

Suddenly, there was no question in his mind. He would rather be responsible for a failed early strike, where dozens of hostages were killed by bombs and guns, than to be responsible for even one more person beheaded in such a cruel and inhumane way.

The strike was simple and well-coordinated. The Omega Force commandos surrounded the sheep ranch. They surveyed the grounds with extricate and thermoscan goggles, clearly pinpointing their enemies.

The commandos readied seven, fifty-caliber automatic rifles — weaponry that could tear through far more than the thin walls the terrorists were hidden behind.

Sounds of humming insects filled the night air. Unrecognizable to an untrained ear, some of the insect chirps were coded communications. The commandos were equipped with tiny microchip devices that imitated the winged clicks of several different insect species.

Positioning themselves within a fifty meter radius of the targets, the commandos began to assemble their guns. To avoid detection, the assemblage had to be done slowly. With the guns in place, the commandos readied to strike the terrorists surrounding the hostages. Lieutenant Nicos' final communication was clicked to the soldiers: on his word, everyone fire at their mark.

Suddenly, a shout ripped through the natural night cacophony.

"Fire!" Nicos cried out, and fifty caliber guns lit up in fully automatic mode, rumbling the ground.

Torsos and heads exploded, spraying debris and entrails over the horrified Greek hostages. Not knowing what was happening, they thought their kidnappers were detonating their suicide bombs. The hostages cried out in fear, and ducked their heads and faces into their laps. But, in moments they realized no shrapnel was hitting them. It was just shredded body matter. Luck was with the commandos. The bullets did not detonate any of the bombs, as was predicted, considering the types of materials often used by terrorists.

Within seconds, the terrorists inside the slaughterhouse and farmhouse were dead, unrecognizable. Using precise, semi-automatic bursts, the commandos turned their rage on those outside, who were running around, trying to assemble or find cover. But none could hide from the scopes of Omega Force. Within another few seconds, every last hostage-taker was obliterated.

The commandos stormed forward to secure the premises, holding submachine guns in both hands, raised up to their shoulders in the firing position. Two squads moved to secure the slaughterhouse and farmhouse. Another squad checked the rest of the ranch.

Bursting into the twenty-by-twenty meter room where the vast majority of hostages were being held, the commandos' eyes met a terrible sight. The people there had not been allowed to walk, not even to go to the bathroom. They were soaked in urine and the floor soiled with fecal matter. They had open sores and many appeared to be ravaged with sickness. The commandos covered their noses and gagged, for the room's vile reek was difficult to bear. The terrorists had all worn surgical masks over their mouths and noses, but the poor hostages had not been given anything and they had not become used to the smell. Vomit covered their clothing.

Immediately, the commandos worked to cut the bindings on the ankles and wrists of the people. As they ripped the gags off their mouths, the rescued hostages screamed out for their children. Where were their children?!

Inside the farm house, fifteen youngsters were found, untied and clean. They had been allowed to move about and use the restroom and appeared well-fed. Before the hostages were allowed to leave their prison, the soldiers secured the area, and installed a perimeter. While they waited, the hostages were cleaned and their wounds tended to by the Omega Force field medical team.

"All clear," Nicos shouted. The children immediately ran through the door seeking their parents and tearful reunions moved the soldiers.

In a smaller room at the other end of the slaughterhouse, opposite from where the adult hostages had been held, the Omega Force commandos discovered a sight more despicable and atrocious than anything prior. The room had been used as a *human* slaughterhouse. The smell of death permeated the still air. Mattresses were propped up along the walls to make it sound proof. Corpses lay decomposing on the floor in the back corner. Two dozen bodies lay beside two dozen heads, the faces still in a wretched, gaping state of terror.

One commando could not and did not want to internalize the immense negativity building inside of him by being exposed to such horror. Rage and bitterness consumed him and he marched out of the room, disgusted and hoping to find one live terrorist. The Omega Forces had done a good job of blowing the hijackers to pieces with the fifty-caliber guns, but the commando was in luck. He found one terrorist outside, lying on the ground, gurgling as death closed in. His arm was blown off at the socket, and blood pooled in a gaping hole in his chest. The commando pulled his knife from his belt, and sliced the man from waist to sternum. The terrorist let out only a slight shriek.

Lieutenant Nicos called for escape transports the moment the ranch was secured. Three large jets were dispatched from the east of Greece, rapidly moving over the Turkish border to pick up the commandos and hostages. The large transport jets, along with ten fighter-bomber jet escorts, represented the top technology of the Germanian Air Force, though they were flown by Formula-trained Greek pilots.

Before these jets even crossed the border, the Greek pilots sent messages out to the Turks, telling them that they were not coming in for an offensive strike. They had a recording playing over and over again, in Turkish, explaining their mission to quickly pick up the rescued hostages.

Constantine knew what he was doing when he sent out such a large contingent of airpower to accompany the transports. The Turks could not know the motive of the Greeks and certainly would not take their word that they weren't launching a pre-emptive strike. And using fighter-bombers, as opposed to just fighters, alluded more to an assault force than a defense to a rescue operation. The transport planes themselves could possibly be super-bombers, capable of devastating a city with nuclear weapons and the like. Constantine was fully aware that crossing into Turkey's sovereign area with such a threatening force could only result in a defensive strike by the Turkish military. He and Geiseric were counting on it.

President Hollier had authorized selling Turkey one hundred of the USA's top-of-the-line anti-aircraft missiles. They were hidden along the entire border of Eastern Thrace and Greece, ready to launch. However, intelligence gathered by Germanian agents and passed to Constantine showed the locations of each installation.

A much larger wave of Omega Force commandos had invaded Turkey right before the air rescue contingent took off. Ten squads of commandos took down a group of installations and, by puncturing a hole in the defense, they allowed the Greek rescue planes to move through. The commandos were ordered not to kill any Turkish soldiers in the first assault. Each missile launcher was guarded by three Turkish soldiers equipped with 30-06 caliber assault rifles, but little body armor. The Greek commandos easily shot fast-acting tranquilizer darts into the unaware soldiers, slapping high-fives as each guard slumped to the ground unconscious.

The Turks prepared to send out their fighter jets, also sold to them by the CIA. Fourteen F/A-22 Raptors, the top U.S. jets for more than twenty years, had been secreted to Turkey. The Turkish pilots were trained by the best officers in the United States, under the supervision and administration of the CIA. MI6 had managed to gather much information on the military-grade Formula training of Germania and Greece and they prepared the Turkish pilots as much as possible for a skirmish against their Greek protégés.

The fighter–bomber used by the invaders was the *Flededermaus* — the Bat — and they had the same capabilities as the Raptors. The Turks had a slight numerical advantage in fighter jets, so they felt they were going to blow the Greeks out of the skies. The Raptors took off from an airbase just inside the Turkish border and flew off at over Mach 2 towards the invading jets. Simultaneously, the Bats pulled off from near the transports and moved toward the incoming Raptors, engaging the Turks outside of range of the rescue planes. When they broke the sound barrier, the booms shook the air and ground below like many small tremors preceding an earthquake. The fight was on.

Coming at each other at a collective speed of nearly five thousand kilometers per hour, the Bats and Raptors reached firing distance within seconds. Both sides armed their air-to-air missiles and let them away. The missiles took off at nearly twice the speed of the jets.

Using the tactics they were shown in their training, the Raptor pilots arched off downward and sideways to evade the oncoming explosives. The Bats, however, flew right at the oncoming barrage. In a remarkable display of reflex and skill, the Greek pilots deftly turned a split-second before impact and the oncoming missiles rocketed past them in the opposite direction. Quickly, the Bats were out of range of the missiles' tracking systems, causing the missiles to lose their target locks.

The Turkish pilots barely avoided the air-to-air barrage sent at them by the Greeks. They arched off as a group, to the right and down, dropping dozens of flares and chaff to repel or jam the heat-seeking and radar-guided missiles. But, their decoys and missile-debilitating systems were not as effective as expected and the Raptor pilots had to release nearly everything they had to get the last of the first round of enemy missiles to lose their target.

Before the Turkish pilots could breathe a sigh of relief, the Bats were hot on their tails. Alerts flashed red on the screens inside the Raptor cockpit. The enemy had them locked on radar! Away went the second round of missiles from the Bats. Having only a small number of flares and chaff at their disposal, the Turkish pilots were left with few alternatives. The missiles were upon them faster than some could react and three F/A-22's exploded in mighty orange plumes of fire, pieces flying to the ground aflame.

The Greeks now had the numerical superiority and they proved to be unstoppable. They hunted down the remaining Raptors, who maneuvered erratically across the sky trying to evade their pursuers. The Greek pilots laughed with each other over their radios as the dual Gatling guns on their Bats fired thousands of rounds in seconds, tearing through the Raptors, slicing off wings, and blowing up the engines.

Within a minute, the air battle was over. At the end of the dog-fight, most of the Turkish pilots were no more than ashes scattered in wind and fire.

Only three Bats were destroyed and the pilots of these jets had ejected and landed safely. There were no Greek casualties and the hostage rescue mission was proceeding better than envisioned.

The jet convoy moved to the pick-up location. The large planes hovered vertically to the ground by swiveling their huge jet engines downward. This provided for a gentle descent. Their fighter-bomber escorts remained circling in the air above.

Crying with relief and hugging the Omega Force commandos, the freed hostages clamored onto the three transport planes. Not one of them turned around for a last look at their wretched prison. Although all the hostages could have fit in one plane, the soldiers divided them up between the three planes so, if one was shot down, not everyone would die. Within minutes, the transports began a hovering ascent and, with the Bats leading the way, they headed back towards the border.

It hadn't taken long for the Turkish forces to figure out that their surface-to-air defenses had been breached. When the unconscious soldiers failed to answer over their two-way radios, an alert for replacements was immediately issued. The Turks' fast action cost Omega Force their first two casualties. The rest of the Omega Force commandos in the ten squads that had secured passage through the missile defense, retreated under vastly overwhelming enemy manpower. This hole in the Turkish missile defense was quickly sealed.

Now, the only way left for the rescue planes to cross back over the border was through a hole in the Turkish missile defense on the far north of the Thracian border. It would take five minutes for the transport planes to get to this spot, five minutes longer over Turkey. A lot could happen in that amount of time. The rest of the Turkish Air Force could be scrambled. With the Raptors decimated, Turkey's air power consisted of totally obsolete planes. However, with overwhelming numbers, some could get through and shoot down the transport jets. The hostages were, right now, at their most vulnerable.

One of the Greek fighter pilots realized that the fate of the mission hung in the balance. He selflessly burst out ahead of the pack, informing the rest of his squadron that he was going to puncture a hole directly through the Turkish defenses. They knew he would be shot down, but they also knew it had to be done.

The pilot moved ahead ten kilometers and arched high into the air. He took on a horizontal vector at twelve thousand meters. Pushing the throttle to the fullest, his jet accelerated to nearly three thousand kilometers per hour. He neared the border and the Bat's warning system picked up on seven missile installations within range of tracking him. Suddenly, he was radar-locked and two surface-to-air missiles were bearing at him. He deployed his four guided bombs at installations that had not yet fired. Then, knowing that it was impossible to avoid the high end U.S. missiles coming at him, he ejected.

Striking their target, the missiles destroyed the Bat in a deafening blast. The smart bombs deployed by the pilot were equipped with rudders on the back, which steered them through the air, careening them forward in a diagonal path to the ground. The guided bombs landed two kilometers ahead of where they had been deployed in the air, reaching their targets, leaving four gaping craters where four missile installations and their Turkish crews had stood milliseconds before.

The heroic Greek pilot, sweating and his heart racing, fell to the Earth in a sky dive. At five hundred meters, he ripped the cord and released a small parachute that slowed him down enough to land safely, but also let him fall fast enough to the ground to avoid detection by the enemy.

Two other Bats flew to the forefront to see if they could spot their comrade's parachute. The last ground-based missile in the area was deployed at them. The two jets parted, arching up and down to confuse it. The surface-to-air missile went after the Bat that arched high. The pilot deployed his chaff and flares to confuse the missile, but to no avail.

The pilot ejected, and his jet was struck while he dove to the ground. He laughed with joy as he released his parachute, knowing that he had been the final part of a breakthrough to save his fellow citizens, who had been so evilly brutalized. He made a hard landing in a small clearing in the trees, and worked quickly to shed and bury his parachute. When he looked up, the transport caravan appeared overhead. He laughed and waved his hands to let them know he was alright. His fellow pilots spotted him on the ground and were relieved to see that he was not harmed, but they could do nothing to help their downed comrades, for they had to continue on.

Immediately, a special bulletin aired on television and radio channels all over Greece and, soon, across the entire globe: the remaining Greek hostages were rescued unharmed!

The Omega Force commandos were the new heroes of the Western World and, in the minds of most European and American citizens, their actions were completely justified. Their daring and courageous rescue of people whom the world had come to pity through media coverage, made them above contempt.

Even Constantine and Geiseric became near irreproachable heroes, most prominently to the Greeks. After all, they had orchestrated the entire rescue endeavor. The world media pegged them up as the "Decisive Duo," in adoration. They could do no wrong.

President Hollier, Prime Minister Dandau, and the leaders of other countries in the West and Asia did not dare speak out against the rescue mission. Although it had obvious hostile overtones and was sure to be the beginning of more aggression from Geiseric, by way of the Greeks, the average citizen of the world did not see that. They saw people rescued who otherwise would have been cruelly butchered. For now, the leaders of the world who were opposed to Geiseric's growing power had to act supportive of the hostage recovery operation and leave the underlying issues for future resolution.

The CIA was stunned that the training they gave to the Turks was so inferior to that given to the Greeks by the Germanian military advisors. U.S. Intelligence had a lot to learn.

Constantine knew that this was the key time to act. The day after the rescue, he demanded that Turkey allow Greek planes to fly in and locate their, altogether, five downed pilots. The Turkish Prime Minister, Mustafa Bayar, assured Constantine that when his soldiers found the Greek pilots, they would be treated well. However, the pilots would, naturally, be detained for interrogation. In the meantime, if any more Greek forces came over onto his land or into his airspace, it would be considered an act of war.

Prime Minister Bayar had not read the global emotional tide well. Dandau and Hollier each called him and demanded he let a small contingent of Greek commandos into Turkish Thrace to find the pilots. There was so much sympathy for the heroes, that the Western leaders could not do much to help Turkey if a war broke out with Greece, even if the Greeks invaded. But, Mustafa was too agitated to heed the warnings. He would not let Constantine do whatever he wished on and over Turkish land.

Three nights after the hostage-rescue operation, fifteen hundred Omega Force commandos poured across the Thracian border into Turkish territory. It was a new moon, and the blackness was lit by only a few particularly bright stars. The Greek warriors, donned in solid black, took no mercy. Using lethal force, they knocked out all the remaining American-made missile installations. Dozens of unsuspecting Turkish soldiers fell, often with their throats slit or shot through the skull. Over a hundred more Turks were captured, destined for interrogation. The rest fled in the face of the overwhelming invasion.

The way was open and ten Germanian helicopter gunships flown by Greek pilots moved in. Though they stretched over ten meters long, they were designed not to be picked up by radar and had specially designed propellers that were incredibly silent. The gunships were specially equipped for the mission. They carried numerous small explosive-warhead rockets to target the anti-aircraft weapons in the second line of defenses.

Thousands of Chinese-made missiles and anti-aircraft guns, placed only six kilometers behind the front, composed the interior line of air defense, ordered into creation by Mustafa after the Greek rescue planes had punctured his first line three nights earlier. However, the second line was nowhere near as advanced as the first. Sheer numbers were useless, when the missiles could not detect the enemy.

The helicopters parted and, flying at speeds of four to five hundred kilometers per hour, they spaced themselves along the line and came in fast. Aided by electronic imaging equipment, the pilots easily spotted the camouflaged defenses under the grassy facades. Simultaneously, they all opened fire. Tiny missiles rained down mercilessly upon the targets and their human defenders.

The Turkish soldiers couldn't see what was coming at them. The anti-aircraft gun crews caught glimpses of the helicopters with their spotlights, but could do nothing because of the copters' amazing speed. Ironically, the spotlights made it easier for the Greek pilots to spot their enemy, allowing them to trace the streamers of light to the source and unleash their fury upon the beleaguered Turks.

When the gunships had spent their air-to-ground missiles, they opened up with seemingly endless Gatling-gun fire, each spewing out dozens of rounds per second, laying waste to the Turkish anti-aircraft weapons and crews who stood their ground with futility. In the aftermath of the final barrage, an eerie silence hung over the Turkish camp. The majority of their installations lay decimated, burning, and abandoned. Omega ground forces moved in to secure the interior line.

The missing Greek pilots were found and brought back home to heroes' accolades. They were paraded through the streets of Athens and the media ran wild with their stories of survival in the Turkish wilderness. Without question, the victory reinforced the world-wide adoration for the commandos and the Greek leader who led so decisively against terrorism.

The next night, Constantine visited Germania to express his gratitude to Geiseric and the Germanian people at a press conference in Berlin. The two leaders shook hands and smiled widely for the cameras.

Afterward, they retired to the chancellor's office in the parliament house.

"What do we do now?" Constantine asked directly. He was antsy and paced the room in an erratic line.

Geiseric sat comfortably back in his plush, swivel chair and lit a cigarette, which he did on the rare celebratory occasion.

"Well," he replied, "for one thing, you must leave Omega Forces in Eastern Thrace, on the edge of the interior defensive line."

Constantine furled his eyeline in a perplexed expression. "We cannot leave our forces in Turkey without reason."

"Of course not," Geiseric shrugged. "You need a pretext. So, say that those anti-aircraft guns that weren't destroyed could be used for offensive purposes, which they can. Loaded with different shells, they have the range to launch an attack on Greek border towns from where they were."

"But, we didn't find any artillery shells," Constantine replied with confusion.

Geiseric closed his eyes, looking slightly pained and frustrated. He rubbed the top of his nose, by his brow, with his thumb and forefinger. "Constantine, you're killing me. Would you get with the program?"

For a moment, Constantine looked like an insecure youth being chided by his father. Geiseric laughed and eased up on his comrade.

"We have enough to delay the pullout for a couple of weeks. In the meantime, you have to piss off Mustafa. Get him to do something stupid."

"What if he doesn't?" Constantine asked, his nerves immediately apparent. "I'm just playing Devil's advocate."

Geiseric took a drag off his cigarette. "You've met Mustafa."

"Of, course."

"And isn't he an arrogant prick?"

Constantine laughed. "Yes."

Geiseric leaned towards Constantine. "And is he not the dumbest son-of-a-bitch you have ever met?"

"Yes."

"Well," Geiseric smiled and tossed his hands up, "that's *exactly* what we need!" He pointed to Constantine. "You just play on his pride and the pride of Turkey. Insult him and, more than anything, be pushy. Say things like, 'we'll leave when I am sure there is no threat and not a moment before!' Oh!" Geiseric stood excitedly, "or something like, 'no matter what Bayar says, my forces will leave when *I* deem it is ok!"

Constantine rubbed his chin, grinning widely. "Oh, that *will* piss him off."

Constantine returned to Greece and immediately began to provoke the Turkish prime minister. Hollier and Dandau sent envoys to Mustafa and personally called him a number of times, warning him not to fall into this obvious trap. But the Turkish prime minister, the government, and all the Turkish people were united in their hatred for the rude and treacherous Greeks. Doing nothing was out of the question. Letting the Greeks do as they pleased on Turkish land was an insult that had to be met in kind. Bayar refused to let Turkey appear weak.

President Hollier and Prime Minister Dandau were frantic. They knew Geiseric and Constantine were just waiting for something to justify an offensive — some clever pretext. If a full-scale war broke out between Greece and Turkey, they knew Greece would win. The citizens of the United States and Britain would not support involvement, and there was only so much contraband that could be provided to the Turks under intense secrecy.

Despite the pleadings of Hollier, Dandau, and other major leaders secretly allying with Turkey, Mustafa was obstinate. He demanded something be done to force the Greeks out of his country. Crafting a plan to end the situation on his terms, he called upon Hollier and Dandau for assistance. Bayar's plan horrified the two Western leaders, but they could not dissuade him. So, they agreed to do all they could to help him and hoped things would not go as they feared.

Seventeen days passed and the Greek commandos showed no sign of a pull-out from Turkey. Bats patrolled the air over the occupation zone. They even drifted past the zone, penetrating into Turkish airspace by as much as eighty kilometers, a provocation personally authorized by Constantine under the guise of patrolling for a build-up of forces.

World public opinion was still in favor of the Greeks, but the passionate support of their temporary occupation had softened. Even the Greek populace began to question what reason there was to stay. Still, the political channels were moving too slowly for Mustafa. So, he called a press conference and made a startling declaration. He announced that his country intended to destroy the Church of the Hagia Sophia, unless the Greeks left immediately.

Built in the sixth century, the church was considered to be an ancient wonder. It was revered as one of the holiest structures by the Greek Orthodox people. So large in size and scope, and graced with beautiful mosaics, it was originally deemed The Great Church and was the pride of Byzantium and the Byzantine Empire. But it now lay under the dominion of Turkey, in the city now known as Istanbul.

Mustafa, Hollier and Dandau knew that Constantine and Geiseric were probably not trying to capture all of Turkey. The Germanian and Greek leaders wished to take back Eastern Thrace and, most importantly, Byzantium. The move would be a public relations victory for Geiseric and Constantine in the eyes of the Greeks, and would win the peoples' hearts over to an Imperial Alliance.

In addition to the destruction of the church, if the Greeks didn't remove their presence from Turkish soil, Mustafa announced that everything from Greek and Byzantine antiquity within the borders of Istanbul and Turkish Thrace, would be destroyed. Pressed by journalists, Mustafa remained vague as to how he planned to carry out his threat, but he assured them he had the ability to do so at a moment's notice.

Geiseric and Constantine patted themselves on the back. It could not have played out more beautifully. The Turks now looked like the aggressors, and the Hagia Sophia was yet another innocent hostage being held by the militant Turkish government.

Seeing the cyclone of fury he had roused in the Greek citizens, Mustafa realized his mistake and back-pedaled, announcing he would only destroy the Hagia Sophia if Greek forces tried to push farther into Eastern Thrace. But the damage was already done.

TAKE BACK THE HAGIA SOPHIA

Prime Minister Metaxas came to the Berghof to meet with the Germanian chancellor. They sat beside one another on comfortable, cushioned chairs, facing the Germanian Intelligence Director, Edwin Riedl. Using a red laser, the director pointed at a screen that displayed an overhead shot of Istanbul. The

Greece   Thrace   Turkey   Istanbul

debriefing map was dotted with multi-colored markings and labels, showing the precise location of the Turkish defenses.

"Alright," Riedl began, "the Turks have hunkered down in Istanbul, leaving most of Eastern Thrace largely undefended. They are doing this for a number of reasons. First, they are concentrating their forces, because they know they are facing a stronger foe. Second, we have to be more careful when taking defenses in the city, because of all the ancient architecture. So, of course, they have put a large amount of their defenses in places like the Wall of Theodosius. They have at least one hundred and fifty artillery pieces lining the wall. They know we won't just bomb it."

Riedl tossed the laser pointer to his other hand. "Third, they are holding the Hagia Sophia hostage and the entire defense of Istanbul is based on making sure that we know, if we try to invade, the Greeks' beloved church is kaput!" He lifted his closed fist up to his face and blew into it, opening it quickly to represent the explosive destruction that would ensue.

"All the mortar and artillery pieces ringing the perimeter of the city are informed on the coordinates to shell the Hagia Sophia, which they *will* do immediately upon an attack. The entire church is also covered with explosives." Riedl's red laser highlighted the location in a circling motion. "Inside, there is enough plastique to destroy it many times over. The building is lined in strategic places for a clean demolition. There are two squads of twelve Turkish soldiers who are in direct charge of two detonators with lines to the explosives to blow the church to hell, and any one of them can throw the switch. These squads are located outside of the Hagia Sophia, within a block of it." Riedl glanced at the two politicians to see if they had any questions so far. Geiseric motioned for him to continue.

"If these two squads are taken out, there is a final layer of insurance," the director explained, with an ominous tone. "There is a suicide squad inside the Hagia Sophia, ready to blow themselves up with it. Their detonator is right in the middle of the church, in the nave. There are always six suicide-squad members in the nave, right beside the detonator. The other six patrol the galleries and narthexes. All of the windows have been walled up with cement and the doors were blockaded or welded shut. The suicide squad members have enough food, water and other facilities inside the church to last for at least twelve months."

Riedl laughed slightly, in awe of the challenge before them.

"As if that were not enough, the United States has provided three hundred Navy SEALs to patrol the waters around Istanbul. They did not provide land forces, because that would have been too high-profile."

Riedl pointed his laser on the map to the side of the peninsular city of Istanbul that faced land. "And finally, every meter of the western end is covered with Turkish troops. All of the exterior defensive forces check in over radio intercoms with a base on a ten-minute rotation. Meaning, if a man is taken out on the outer ring, like one of the SEALs let's say, we have at the most ten minutes before it will definitely be discovered. The interior defenses check in on a slower rotation of every twenty minutes. The base has high-end, British-made voice-analyzing equipment. So, we cannot just imitate someone's voice."

Director Riedl exhaled deeply and switched off the laser. "And, I think that's about it."

Geiseric clapped vigorously. "Bravo! Bravo! Great work Riedl!" He got up, smacked the director on the back, and shook his hand. Geiseric looked at the Greek prime minister. "Don't I have the best intelligence operatives in the world?"

"Yes," Constantine walked over to Riedl, nodding his head. "But, I think he just assured us of the futility of trying to take Istanbul without losing the Hagia Sophia."

Geiseric feigned that he was shocked. "What are you talking about?"

Constantine was puzzled and a bit aggravated. "Did you not hear what I just heard? How are we to get through all of that?"

Geiseric walked slowly over to his comrade, hooking his arm around the Greek leader's neck. "Constantine," he grinned, "how are they going to stop us?" The chancellor began to guide his compatriot towards a place to sit again.

"The hard part is over," he elucidated. "Intelligence gathering is ninety percent of a Special Forces operation. We know the whole plan. We know where every man is. Believe me, this will be a walk in the park for Omega Force. This will make them the most respected Special Force in the whole world. There will be action figures made of them!" The Germanian leader laughed gleefully.

Constantine's curiosity was piqued. "How did you get this intelligence anyway?"

"I'm glad you asked, my friend." Geiseric's face lit up as he readied to amaze the Greek leader. "Have you ever heard of the field of biomimicry?"

Constantine nodded. "Of course," he said, once more taking a seat in the plush armchair, "it is using the natural world to inspire the many fields of engineering."

Geiseric was impressed. "Well-worded, Constantine," he remarked, his eyebrows raising in surprise. "That's exactly what it is. Of course, many things we use in every day life were inspired by nature. Like Velcro, which a Swiss man came up with while dealing with the annoying Alpine burs that clung to his socks." Geiseric looked out through the large window at the Bavarian Alps before him, standing where Hitler had once contemplated his momentous decisions made during World War II.

"Ships and aircraft have become more aerodynamic based on the natural designs of whales and birds. But, the field of biomimicry has tilted evermore towards the outright *imitation* of nature, namely animals!" His eyes shined as he contemplated the technological possibilities. "It's been going strong for decades, but no one has been smart enough to embrace it to its full potential." Geiseric smiled and looked Constantine in the eye. "Except for the Principles, of course."

A small housefly descended from the air and landed on Constantine's lapel. He blew on it and shook his suit, but the fly would not go away. Constantine blew as hard as he could on the bug, to no avail. The tiny insect would not release its grasp. Constantine looked at it with admiration.

"That is one mighty fly," he remarked with humor. The chancellor merely smirked, cocking his head a bit to the side and down, looking up at his comrade with eyes that prodded Constantine to think. The Greek prime minister looked at the fly and began to make the connection. Startled, he looked to Geiseric.

"Is this a machine?" Constantine demanded incredulously.

"Of course!" Geiseric shouted, a bit frustrated that it took so long for his protégé to put it all together.

He grabbed a remote and turned on the television screen on the wall beside them. They saw Constantine's chin and neck, from the perspective of the fly. It detached from Constantine's lapel and buzzed around his head, moving exactly like a real fly. On the screen, they could see the Greek prime minister in high resolution footage transmitted from the fake insect by tiny cameras on its body.

"My God," Constantine remarked.

Geiseric turned up the volume and they could hear themselves talking.

"The tiny microphone on the bug is also replicated from the incredibly accurate hearing mechanism of a rare fly called the Ormia ochracea. Flies are pretty handy in this field." He waggled the remote at the screen as he explained. "But essentially, all living things are instructive to biomimicry. That's the beauty of it! Humans are so arrogant. They want to be better than nature. But one *cannot* be better than nature! God has been using evolution to experiment with forms on this planet for over three billion years! The animal kingdom is like a giant war zone, always spawning the latest and greatest machines. We should derive our military technology and tactics from nature and, still," he gazed off through the window, filled with humility, "we pale in comparison."

Constantine was duly impressed. He studied the small, mock fly hovering before his face.

Again, Geiseric commended Riedl and then told him to summon one of his officers. The dutiful director saluted his commander-in-chief and marched out of the room. Geiseric looked to Constantine. "Wait until you see this."

A minute later, Riedl returned accompanied by a tall officer wearing a full-body suit. Geiseric ordered the officer to take off his mask, which he did. The man was hard-faced, which was only amplified by his shaved head.

"Show us a couple sand variations," Geiseric commanded.

Right before their eyes, the man's suit began to transform into a golden, sandy color, with the texture of small grains. Next, the suit transitioned to a grayish silt color with black streaks.

"Show us the corals," Geiseric barked.

The man took on the expression of someone deep in concentration. The suit began to turn color and also imitated the texture of coral, with craggy pieces emerging a few centimeters all over.

"My God." Constantine's mouth hung agape. "How does this work?"

"It's based on the octopus," Geiseric explained. "Feel it," he said, touching the suit.

Constantine did so as well and realized that, though the suit appeared to be sharp and hard, it was made of a soft, pliable material. Geiseric smacked his comrade's shoulder.

"This is how we will get past the SEALS and the Turkish forces watching the Hagia Sophia! Streicher and his team of scientists have managed to create a synthetic muscle. This suit is covered with hundreds of thousands of cells, which you can see if you look closely. They each contain five pigments and each cell has a synthetic muscle surrounding it, similar to the muscle which contracts the iris in our eyes." He poked a finger toward Constantine's eye, making him blink.

"The tiny muscles inside the cells can cover some of the pigments, letting one or more show through. With these five colors, every color in the spectrum can be blended onto the suit. And the cells are connected to each other by synthetic muscle, which can contract to make the suit bunch up in ways that makes it appear like coral, rock and pebbles, or even more advanced things, like bark and bush. Show him those," he commanded the officer.

The man concentrated and his suit changed texture to have a craggy and layered appearance like a tree trunk, also becoming many shades of brown. Next, the suit changed coloration to varied hues of green, accompanied by a texture metamorphosis that was the most dramatic yet. Parts of the suit raised farther than Constantine had yet seen, leafing out several centimeters. Concealed within foliage, the officer would disappear.

Constantine was amazed and had many questions. "It seems as if . . ." he stammered, fearing that he might sound ridiculous, "as if he is . . . willing the suit to change with his mind."

Geiseric nodded. With a simple gesture, he commanded the man in the suit to turn around. There was a three centimeter-thick cable coming out of the suit, which split into numerous smaller strands that inserted into pin-prick-sized holes in the officer's spine and rear cranium.

"This," the chancellor announced grandly, "is Psychiclink technology. It reads brain waves, chemicals, and nerve messages."

Despite a failed effort to remain composed, Constantine was enthralled by the suit like a child who had just seen a cool toy. He stumbled forward to get a closer look.

Geiseric scoffed mildly at his comrade's emotional state. "Don't be too awestruck. This technology is also nothing new. The United States was actually leading the way in this field since 2004. They called it the year of the cyborg. But recently, the Americans have fallen far behind us," Geiseric snorted out a laugh, gazing lovingly upon the technological marvel.

Constantine stood with his arms crossed. "That is truly amazing," he remarked, taking a moment to absorb it all in, like a tourist observing a spectacular view. "Ok," he said, "now, suppose we get past all the defenses up to the Hagia Sophia. How do we get past the suicide squadron before one of them can detonate the explosives?"

Geiseric went over to the bar and grabbed four bottles of beer, placing them on the counter. "You know the sweating column?" he asked, flipping a bottle-opener in the air and catching it.

"Of course," Constantine replied.

"Well," Geiseric smirked, popping the lids off and pouring the beer into pre-chilled glass mugs, "you know that the column 'sweats,'" he said, using his fingers to make quotation marks in the air, "because of the water coming up from below the church, in the Basilica Cistern."

Constantine walked over to Geiseric at the bar. "Um hmm."

Geiseric handed him a frosty mug of dark beer. "Explain, Director Riedl," the chancellor commanded, handing Riedl a mug of brew as well. He gave the fourth mug to the officer in the camouflage suit.

The director gratefully accepted his drink and took a gulp, getting the froth on his nose. Geiseric laughed heartily at the sight. Riedl wiped it off and turned to the Greek prime minister.

"Well," he began, "the last place they expect to be attacked is from the cistern. So, they have not gone to great lengths to secure it. They do not see its strategic importance for their defense."

Geiseric looked to Constantine. "There is always a weak link, even when dealing with a worthy foe, and *thank God* we are not."

The Greek prime minister nodded. "Yes, but there is quite a bit of rock and dirt between the cistern and the nave of the Hagia Sophia, not to mention the base of the church. Are you just going to drill through it?"

Geiseric took a gulp of brew and slammed down the glass, wiping his lip with the top of his wrist. "That is exactly what we are going to do."

"But, that will take forever, will it not?" Constantine asked, knowing full well Geiseric had another trick up his sleeve.

The Germanian chancellor led his comrade over to a decorated wall. A Corinthian column was the centerpiece, upon which a life-size, white marble bust of Otto von Bismark was propped at eye level. Geiseric stared at the uncannily incarnate statue of Bismark. Constantine noticed that there were two miniscule holes in the eyes of the sculpture. Through these holes, a machine within the bust scanned Geiseric's retinas. Suddenly, the wall behind the sculpture began to ascend into the ceiling, revealing a secret chamber. Fascinating and strange devices hung on the walls at the front of the chamber. Constantine recognized a few of the strange camouflage suits, but there were many other mysterious gadgets.

Geiseric grabbed a large device with handle grips on two opposite sides, giving it the semblance of a jack-hammer.

"Help me with this, Constantine."

They hoisted it up off the hooks and Geiseric was then able to bear the heavy device alone. He had a proud look upon his face, like a young man showing off his muscle car, as he stood there with the machine in his hands.

"What is it?" Constantine asked.

"*This*, my friend, is a solid-state, optically-pumped, laser drill."

Constantine studied the drill and nodded in admiration.

Geiseric reveled in his friend's reaction to the new technology. "Do you love it?"

"I love it." Constantine grinned.

The chancellor was not too refined to contain his excitement. "This thing will cut through rock a hundred times faster than a conventional, rotating drill!" He gloated. "It can do this, not just because it is a high-powered laser, but also because it targets the facets of the rock or stone, or whatever, and therefore cleaves it using less energy. The laser pulsates to prevent secondary effects, such as melting the substance being drilled."

Constantine was temporarily speechless. He shook his head, amazed at the profound actualization of such devices. "Where did you get all these wonderful things?"

Geiseric shrugged modestly. "We Germans are brilliant." He kept a straight face for a moment, then cracked a playful smile. "But, like everything else, this stuff is nothing new. It's forty-year-old U.S. technology that was never utilized to its full potential. The whole laser drill idea came out of Reagan's Strategic Defense Initiative."

"Ahh, yes," Constantine recalled. "That's right."

"Well, there you go." Geiseric motioned with his head for Constantine to help him put the laser drill back up on the wall. "They wanted to use gigantic lasers to shoot missiles out of the sky and space. But then, of course, big American oil and gas corporations like Halliburton explored its use for drilling into the ground."

The two placed the laser on its hangers and Geiseric leaned against the wall, stretching his arm. "Way back in 2001, NASA and Japan's space program started on a joint project with the European Space Agency to design these lasers for use on other planets. And, voila! Germania now has a lot of this technology. Of course these drills were extremely large in size. It is *my* engineers," he said, pointing his thumb at his chest, "who have recently designed this mighty little sonofabitch!"

October 13, 2029

As the dusk light cast down upon Istanbul, dark clouds loomed on the horizon, heading towards the city. It had been like this all day — short bursts of heavy rain and gusty thunderstorms releasing their fury every hour or so. The clouds moved in fast, pouring a dark sheet of water into the tumultuous ocean below. The black waves thrashed and foamed, as if the brief flashes of lightning were electrocuting the sea. Deep distant rumbles thundered across the endless gray.

Under the water's surface, surrounding the European section of Istanbul, the Navy SEALs patrolled their vicinities. They moved in sixteen-man platoons, surveying the shallow coastal waters. In each platoon, two of the SEALs guided a self-propelled, sonar-tracking device near the ocean floor. The readings revealed anything tunneling a few meters underneath the ocean floor. Other sonar specialists rode in three-man groups in open-top, mini-submarines with dual, thirty-five millimeter cannons on each side. They took readings of the surrounding environment, detecting anything swimming around in the sea, including small fish.

Each platoon reported back to base every ten minutes on the dot. So far, the sonar readings had only detected schools of fish and dolphins. As the 9th platoon prepared to check in, they moved through a large school of mackerels. The platoon leader, Commander Pershing, spoke into the microphone in his facemask. Using their codenames, he called out over the earpieces to his six subordinates, who were each in charge of their smaller 2 to 3-man group. They each replied back with their assigned coded response.

"Redneck!" the rough-throated commander called out. The transmission sounded slightly muffled from speaking inside his facemask.

"Oblong," Lieutenant Benachi, who was patrolling in a two man group called back. Each SEALs commander was equipped with voice analyzing equipment to make sure their subordinates were who they said they were. Benachi's voice was accepted by the device.

"Cardinal!" Pershing continued gruffly. Having done this almost non-stop for a day and a half straight, the monotony was beginning to wear on him.

"Antique," answered the lieutenant in charge of guiding the subterranean detection module.

"Critic!" Pershing called out.

"Rose," Lieutenant Miller called back. Miller was in charge of a mini-sub group and, just then, he picked up a blip on sonar. It did not concern him much, but he was under orders to report everything he saw to the commander. "Looks like we got a school of fish coming in a few hundred yards off." He focused on the image he was receiving. "They're about two feet long. I'm guessing mackerel."

"Keep tabs with me until you identify," Pershing answered, then continued with the roll call. "Aries!"

Miller watched his sonar reading carefully. As the sub got in close and shone its lights, the lieutenant could see a few dozen of the gold-tinted mackerels swimming toward him and his crew. The school dispersed, startled by the sudden light and strange gadgets, and regrouped on the other side of the SEAL team.

"All clear," Miller reported over the earpiece. "Like I thought, just mackerel . . . wait a minute. We got another grouping of larger objects coming' in. I'm guessin' dolphins."

Sure enough, approximately twenty bottle-nosed dolphins swam out of the darkness and into the high beam lights of the sub. The mass of dolphins and fish cast hundreds of shadows on the sea floor. The mackerels' golden scales reflected the moonlight, making the water seem filled with thousands of twinkling stars. The dolphins were chasing the mackerel, herding the fish into a cluster before devouring them.

"Yep, just dolphins," Miller confirmed.

Pershing finished off his roll call a few seconds before the scheduled check in to base. "This is Static 9, Architect," he reported in.

The dolphins passed right over six Greek commandos, slowly belly-crawling across the ocean floor. They were weighted down by small cylinders of Tungsten, heavier than lead, which were strapped onto their waists.

The commandos blended in well with the rock, sand and coral, their suits imitating the texture and color of everything they moved over. As they crept along from one groundcover to another, their suits became many different textures at once. At times the legs of their suits were coral, while their torsos were sand.

Several SEAL commandos swam above the Greeks, stopping the Omega team for a moment. The SEALs wore thermal output detection goggles, but the Omega Force suits concealed body heat with an internal cooling system and imitated the heat signature of whatever substance they were on. The SEAL team passed overhead, oblivious of the well-disguised enemies in their wake.

Making their way past the patrol of U.S. commandos, the small Omega Force squadron crept through increasingly shallow water, until they were nearly cresting over the surface. This was one of the trickiest parts of their mission: they needed to breach the ocean and crawl onto shore, which could create disturbances in the water that might be spotted. The Greek commandos had practiced this part numerous times while training for the assault. It wouldn't be easy. There were dozens of guards watching this particular stretch of beach just north of the ancient Wall of Theodosius. The disadvantage now lay with the Omega Force commandos, who were fully aware of the situation.

It was now in the hands of God.

They timed the tide. When the cycle brought a large swell towards shore, they belly-crawled onto the beach along with it, going as far as they could. Stirring up the sand in front of them, they tried to bury themselves enough so that when the tide retreated, it pulled the sand over them. They hoped this would create a more hydrodynamic surface that would allow the water to rescind without bubbling and splashing around their forms. They executed the maneuver well. As the ocean wave ebbed, the water moved smoothly over their semi-buried bodies.

But, danger lay just fifty meters off. Four Turkish soldiers were making their rounds, heading straight towards the commandos. The patrol handled two dogs trained to smell for anything unusual. The guards sauntered along, talking and laughing loudly, completely unaware of what lay in their path.

The commandos had to act fast. One of them tested the wind and took out a pistol-like mechanism, pointing it at a forty-degree angle toward the patrol. He fired two silent bursts, shooting two small projectiles right over the Turks' heads. They landed about ten meters behind the soldiers and their dogs, on the edge of the tide. Perfect execution! The projectiles were capsules that quickly dissolved in the salt water, seeping out a clear liquid.

The Turks had picked up their pace a bit, as the commander chided them over their earpieces for talking too much. The dogs were getting excited, sniffing here and there erratically, but they did not catch a scent. They did, however, seem to notice that something was on the beach that didn't belong. The Greeks' suits were made to keep the smell of their bodies in, and the suits themselves had the odor of seaweed. But, despite these technological advantages, it was evident by the dog's erratic behavior that they operated on unknown instincts that could sense the intruders.

Now, only thirty meters away, the buried commandos could only sit as still as possible and wait for the liquid in the capsules to do its job. The dogs barked and started pulling forward, catching their handlers' attention. Panning the beach ahead of them with their infrared goggles, the guards could not spot anything unusual.

Suddenly the dogs' noses went crazy and, stopping dead in their tracks, they turned around and ran back the way they came, wrapping their leashes around their handlers' legs. They frantically pulled the soldiers toward the patch of beach where the pellets had landed. The dogs sniffed the sand intensely while the men surveyed the area, firing machine gun bursts into the wet ground and shoveling up parts with their hands. When they found nothing, they called in another unit.

With the Turks distracted, the Omega Force commandos made their way across the sandy beach and into a cluster of bushes, where they were perfectly concealed. They had done the best job they could of covering the paths they made when crawling across the sand. They watched from the bushes as more Turkish soldiers and dogs joined the disconcerted patrol on the beach. In their hurry, the reinforcements ran over the commandos' only slightly visible tracks, scattering what little evidence remained of the enemy invasion. The Omega Force squad breathed a silent sigh of relief.

The liquid in the pellets was intended to dissipate after a couple minutes and did exactly that. The dogs no longer smelled anything and they lost interest in the patch of sand, trying and failing to pick up the scent in other places. The soldiers radioed in to the watchtower guards, who were scanning the whole vicinity with four spotlights, informing them that the stir was over nothing. As a matter of protocol, the guards in the towers kept on high alert for the next fifteen minutes, as the Omega Forces expected. The Greek commandos just sat, still concealed in the bushes, calmly waiting until the hubbub quieted.

Soon, the lights went off and the alert came down. Waiting to make sure no one was around, the commandos crept out of the bushes and ran swiftly, but lightly, across a concrete pathway, ducking low, their padded shoes muffling any sound. They stealthily made their way through a shopping plaza and numerous small parks that ran parallel with the Wall of Theodosius. One at a time, each commando moved, at most in twenty meter increments, making their way past the Topkapi Palace, the largest building in Istanbul. It was from this palace that the Sultan of the Ottoman Empire had ruled. Some of the Greek commandos quickly made vulgar gestures to it as they ran by.

The leader of the team ran from a bush to a wide cypress tree, his suit changing color and texture to imitate the bark. Seeing enemy soldiers coming his way, he pressed his back up against the tree and flattened himself as much as possible. The Turkish soldiers walked within ten meters of him and looked in his direction, but they did not spot their well-camouflaged enemy. The Omega Force leader was exultant to see how well the suit worked. He carefully signaled to the rest of the team, giving the all clear. This began the second phase of their operation and, without saying a word, the six commandos divided into groups of two, heading in three different directions.

The first group moved toward the entrance to the Basilica Cistern. Crawling on their stomachs, they crossed a small weedy field and made their way into another patch of bushes. Here, they began assembling part of their gear while monitoring the guards at the entrance.

Also making their way towards the cistern, the two commandos of the second group parted to strategic vantage points overlooking the entrance. They made their way slowly and cautiously, acutely aware of the enemy patrols and all the sharpshooters watching the area from rooftops and windows. This whole area of the city, from the Wall of Theodosius in the East, to five hundred meters west of the Hagia Sophia, had been evacuated of civilians. It was, however, infested with trigger-itchy Turkish soldiers on strict orders to destroy anything that moved.

The positions taken by the commando groups were planned for them using the information provided by Germanian intelligence. Crouching in bushes and amongst trees, the second group set about assembling their thirty-six caliber machine guns.

Finally, the third group of commandos split, each one moving solo in different directions. Their positions were both within three hundred meters of the Hagia Sophia, on near opposite sides, within view of the two detonator squadrons that were outside of the church. One of these squadrons lay inside of a clothing store. The Omega Force commando scoping the area pushed a button on his goggles, switching them to extricate mode. They allowed him to see most of what was moving inside the second floor rooms of the store. He could see the forms of six soldiers holding what looked like large automatic guns. They appeared to be guarding an interior room, but the Greek commando's scope could not penetrate into it. Director Riedl had warned that there would be a thick metal barrier on the interior room, which gave cover from the prying eyes of extricate goggles, while also acting as a shield on the inner walls. This was definitely the mark and, according to Germanian Intelligence, inside the room were six more heavily-armed Turkish soldiers. The commando began to assemble his fifty-caliber gun.

The other commando of his group was monitoring a detonator squad on the first floor of another shop, just west of the church of the Hagia Sophia. He also spotted an interior room with armored walls impenetrable to short-pulse radar. This was his mark and he prepared his gun. The many pieces were built up into a large fifty-caliber automatic rifle. It was smaller than was typical, specially designed for this operation. When the two commandos of the third group finished assembling their weapons, they quietly unrolled the chain of bullets they had folded in soft material. They each had two hundred rounds, which would be expended in ten seconds of firing.

The bullets had armor-piercing, depleted uranium tips that could easily rip through the metal armor coating the walls, ceilings, and floors of the interior rooms. The objective for these two Omega Force gunmen was similar to those in the hostage rescue. However, this time, the commandos could not see through the walls and spot the enemy. The twelve soldiers of each detonation squadron had to be killed before one of them could throw the switch and level the Hagia Sophia forever.

Watching for the rotation of Turkish soldiers patrolling the perimeter of the cistern, the first and second group of commandos awaited their time to pounce. Every ten minutes, a patrol of soldiers made their rounds by the cemented-up entrance to the Basilica. Two guards also stood permanent watch here. They were bored and somewhat unmotivated — lethargically slumping on the Cistern's entrance with their fingers off the triggers.

Every twenty minutes, the defensive forces within the city of Istanbul went through their rotation of checking into base over hand-held communication devices. The check-in coincided with one of the ten-minute routine patrols that came by the cistern. Every other time this patrol of soldiers made their rounds, they would visually confirm the identity of the guards at the entrance, while the two Turks' voices were analyzed over the radio back at the base. The four Omega Force commandos watching the cistern checked their timepieces — it was only ten seconds until one of these "roll-call" patrols came around again.

The patrol was not as lackadaisical as the guards, and their shadows rounded the corner right on time. Using their flashlights, the patrolling soldiers flashed the guards in the face quickly, to visually identify them.

Just as the patrol passed out of sight, the two Greek commandos of the second group simultaneously fired their silent but lethal thirty-six caliber rifles. They had sighted the two guards and took them out quickly with precision sniping. It all happened so fast, the guards could not fire a round, not even by reflex.

Omega Force groups one and two swiftly bolted out of their hiding places towards the entrance to the cistern. They carried with them thin pieces of explosive tubing, which the commandos taped to the concrete blocking the entrance, making a one-meter wide square. Ripping a fuse, they ignited the explosive incendiary and jumped out of the way. The tubing shot out an immensely hot, blue and white flame. As it sliced through the concrete, the flames made a sharp, crackling sound, which had a low enough volume so as not to alert the patrol that had just passed by.

The extreme heat cut a square perimeter into the concrete five centimeters deep. The commandos repeated the exercise. On the second try, they were able to place the tubing into the concrete, which confined the explosion, so the flame cut nearly a half meter deep this time. The commandos kicked the center of the square a few times to knock it in, sending the chunk of concrete into the cistern's water with a loud splash. It careened off the submerged stone stairs inside, which was painfully noisy to the commandos, who froze and listened for just a second, but the sound did not echo far and went unnoticed by their enemy.

The commandos of group one jumped into the underground reservoir. Group two stood watch outside, taking off their octopus suits and throwing them through the hole in the cement, along with the two dead Turks. Underneath their suits, the commandos of the second group wore Turkish soldier uniforms, including the beret-like caps. They were chosen for this mission because their faces resembled the men they had killed, enough so that the patrolling soldiers would not likely notice the difference in their typical, quick glance with the flashlight. The two commandos concealed their high-powered rifles behind them and held the machine guns of the dead guards. Germanian Intelligence had secreted numerous voice recordings of the Turkish guards and analyzed their particular manner of speaking. The commandos practiced this with a speech coach and, though their ability was not exact enough to get by the main defensive base's voice analyzing equipment, it should have been sufficient to convince the patrol.

Placing swim fins on their feet, the two commandos inside the cistern plunged into the water, which was filled to nearly the top stair leading into the subterranean reservoir. The two men switched on their flashlights and swam down the stairway into the vast monument.

Like the Hagia Sophia, the Basilica Cistern was built by the Roman Emperor Justinian in the sixth century. Used as the reservoir for the imperial palace and for the city in case of siege, it was 140 by 70 meters wide and held more than 15 million gallons of water. There were 336 columns, each over three stories tall, which rose from the floor and supported the vaulted brick domes that comprised the ceiling.

Inside the Basilica Cistern, it was incredibly dark, but the commandos swam with flashlights designed to illuminate long distances. They swiftly kicked towards the other end of the cistern, swimming under numerous archways, past many columns, most of which were unique relics from even more ancient buildings, reused in the creation of the reservoir to save time and money. A few carp and other ornamental fish occasionally flitted past the commandos, reminding them that this eerie chamber was recently a shallowly filled tourist attraction. The two Greeks swam past the Column of Tears, with its many drop-shaped carvings that seemed to glide down onto the ominously tipped, stone Medusa-head the column was perched upon.

The commandos finally located the spot in the ceiling from where they planned to pierce into the Hagia Sophia. They had assembled the many segments of the laser drill into two large pieces, which each commando had hauled through the water. Snapping together these two pieces, both men held the machine by the four provided handle grips, manipulating it with relative ease in the buoyancy of the water. Treading to keep afloat, the commandos pointed the drill up against the ceiling and fired.

As if a thunderstorm had erupted in the watery darkness, a greenish-white beam resembling a welding bolt arched out of the tip of the drill. The beam illuminated a large volume of space with a supernatural aura and emulated the frazzled, tearing sound of violent lightning. It immediately began puncturing a ten-centimeter wide hole into the stone.

As pieces of rock fell away, the commandos pushed the tapered tip of the laser drill up into the hole. The laser did not have the capability to cleave material from a distance. The drill had to be within close proximity of the substance and travel up the small tunnel it was making. And so, much like an oil drill puncturing down into the Earth, the head of the machine, the actual laser, was self-propelled. It was thinner than the rest of the device, only five centimeters wide, with expanding tracks on its sides, so that it could detach from the body of the cylinder and go up the tunnel it was drilling.

The main body of the device generated the power and the commandos held it in place with its top up against the hole in the ceiling. Two cables fed out to the head from the body of the machine; one consisting of optical fiber tubing, which carried energy to the drill. The other was a one centimeter thick cable that contained a type of synthesized muscle, which pushed the drill head up into the thin tunnel, like a snake pushing something with its nose.

Now, the six Omega Force commandos had to just wait for the break-through. It could take anywhere from eight to ten minutes to drill from the ceiling of the cistern, through the ground and rock, up to the base of the Hagia Sophia. And it would take approximately five to six more minutes to puncture through the base into the middle of the church, the nave.

As the two commandos kept themselves suspended in the water, they were completely calm, breathing at an even pace. Only their silent prayers to God, asking that they might be victorious in this Holy Crusade, stirred in their minds.

Ten minutes passed since the commandos had taken out the guards in front of the cistern. Inside, the drill was taking longer than predicted, for there was more bedrock than expected. Still, the commandos were not alarmed — yet. Their nerves were just being tested, for they knew that an enemy patrol was about to make their rounds by the entrance.

As the patrol neared, the commandos who were pretending to be guards spoke to each other in Turkish. Four of the patrollers passed without even bothering to flash their lights at the guards. They unsuspectingly greeted the two impostors, joking with them a bit as they walked by.

However, a straggler came up from behind and flashed his light quickly at the faces of the imposters. Keeping their cool, the commandos let him perform his check. He nodded and continued moving on a few steps, before stopping again. He did a sudden double take. Again, he shined the light on them, moving the beam, from face to face, back and forth. He was not sure until . . . the hole in the cement! Before saying a word, the Turkish soldier went for his gun, but the commandos were quicker. One of the Greeks pulled his gun and shot the soldier right in the face, blowing a hole out the back of his neck. The other commando quickly grabbed his thirty-caliber, setting it on automatic fire, and wasted the other four soldiers before they could turn around. His partner helped finish them off.

They moved in quickly, not breaking a step, to survey the area and see if any other defenders had noticed, or possibly had heard the slight sound the Turks made just before their execution. But no one came. The commandos' silencers had reduced the noise of their gunfire to the decibel-level of a cricket. They gathered the torn bodies of the Turkish patrollers and shoved them in the cistern.

Although this contingency was planned for, it could diminish the amount of time they had to get the job done before other patrols noticed some of their own were missing.

The commandos of group two were the only ones who knew about the present situation. They could break radio silence to tell their partners inside, but there was no doubt that the drillers were going as fast as they could. Besides, it was too risky to break the silence and possibly have their message intercepted by the enemy defenders. Commando group two kept their cool and prayed silently.

Meanwhile, group one had broken through the foundations of the church and had only thirty-centimeters of stone to go before puncturing through the bottom floor. They pressed a button on the drill device that pulled the laser back down, and quickly checked their watches. Taking off the laser drill head of the device and detaching the optical fiber tubing, they attached a small package to the end of the long, serpentine cable that was made of synthetic muscle. The commandos fed the cable up the tunnel again, this time pushing up the small package. When the cable detached to descend out of the tunnel, a time fuse was activated in the package, which would ignite another incredibly hot-burning incendiary.

After ten seconds, it lit up, creating an intense heat with near complete silence. Some of the heat came down the thin drilled tunnel, creating steam from the water at the mouth. The drill was now only a hindrance to the mission, so the two commandos dropped it, letting it fall through the water to the bottom of the cistern. One of them used a much smaller device to feed a tiny camera at the end of a thinner serpentine cable up the hole in the ceiling.

The explosive had burned out a sphere in the rock at the end of the tunnel. Looking through the camera, the commando saw it had not yet burned through the floor, as they wanted. There were probably only a few centimeters left, by their calculations. At the end of the cable, near the camera, was a small gun specially designed to squirt a thin stream of highly corrosive acid. The commando aimed the camera and gun towards where he believed the thinnest part should be. He pressed the button, which began to squirt the acid out, taking care not to get any of the substance on the cable and camera.

Outside, a tower watchman noticed that he had not seen one of the patrols in awhile. He got on the radio and called out for all of the patrolling soldiers to check in. The orders came through on all the earpieces of the interior ring of defenders in Istanbul, including the ones taken from the dead guards by the Greek commandos at the cistern's entrance. As the Turkish patrols began checking in, group two nervously gripped their weapons.

When the missing patrol did not check in, the watchman immediately put the area on high alert. All of the alarms went up, filling the air with disconcerting, ascending sirens blasting from speakers all over the vicinity.

The two Omega Force commandos of group three had been patiently waiting and watching the two detonator squads outside of the Hagia Sophia, just a block away from the church. They were startled by the sudden alarms. It was their first realization that things were no longer going as planned. They maintained their calm as much as possible, but cold, fearful sweat draped their skin as their breathing quickened. They watched with clenched jaws as the Turkish soldiers outside of the armored rooms manned the spotlights and checked their assigned areas.

Group two did their best not to panic. They knew that their enemy would be scouring for any unusual communications now. If the invaders broke radio silence too early, it could mean the end of the mission. So they made the decision not to alert their comrades swimming in the underground reservoir.

Group one had nearly accomplished their task in the cistern. The commando operating the camera and acid gun device finally managed to dissolve through the floor of the Hagia Sophia, silently creating a small hole. He protracted the small camera slowly up into the church, swiveling it about to look around. He had punctured into the exact point as planned, off to the side of the nave, in a gallery right beside a column so that the camera would be slightly hidden and go unnoticed by the suicide guards inside.

The commando maneuvered the camera around to locate the positions of the guards inside the Hagia Sophia. He could see six of them in the nave, standing around the detonator. They wore warm clothing, but no face-masks. The camera's miniscule microphone clearly picked up the guards' voices that the operating commando heard through his earpiece. He was alarmed to hear five of the suicide squadron members praying, their Arabic calls spoken loudly in tandem, while one of the squad members was arming the explosives, preparing to activate the detonator.

The other six suicide squad members were running about checking the whole of the church, armed with powerful automatic weapons. They yelled to each other, confirming that each place was clear. When the suicide-bombers around the detonator finished praying, the groups swapped places. Now, those who were running gathered to pray and those who were praying ran around checking the church. Meanwhile, the squad member who was arming the explosives stayed in his place to complete his task.

Using sign language, the Greek commando monitoring all of this quickly communicated to his partner everything he saw going on inside. They had to act quickly. A glowing red button on the camera was pressed and out of another small nozzle attached to the camera came one of the most deadly neurotoxins known to mankind. The commando attached the controls of the device to the ceiling of the cistern, while it dispensed the clear, odorless gas through the long tube going up into the nave of the Hagia Sophia.

Finally breaking their radio silence, group one gave groups two and three the long awaited order to begin the final assault.

"Omega!" they called over the radio intercoms.

Group two heard the message and one of them immediately repeated it to be sure that their comrades in group three heard it. As soon as the two commandos watching the detonator squads in the shops received the order, they opened fire with their fifty-caliber guns, raking the shielded rooms with armor-piercing bullets. The uranium-tipped rounds careened through the metal protection of the interior room, making something of a screen out of the walls and floors. Now, the two commandos could partially see inside the detonator rooms. Everyone seemed to be dead, but it was difficult to tell.

Before going in to check, they went about sniping with single shots any soldiers patrolling outside the rooms. In less than ten seconds, all the Turkish soldiers in the vicinity were down, most eviscerated into unrecognizable pieces, torn by the heavy projectiles bursting through their bodies at tremendous speed.

The two commandos of group three lifted their large guns, switched their goggles to thermal output mode, and stormed towards the detonator rooms, executing anyone outside who survived the first salvo. As they approached the rooms, which were sealed by thick metal doors, the commandos fired a few short bursts with their large guns to shoot out the locks. Kicking the door open with a grunt, they jumped into the detonator rooms and rolled behind anything they could find for cover. With their guns held up at their shoulders, they whipped around in all directions looking for any sign of life. But all the two Greeks saw were the bodies of dead Turkish soldiers. Blood and pieces of flesh floated around the floor, paying tribute to the commandos' potent weaponry.

The two commandos began the next part of their mission: dismantling the two detonators and tying down any enemy forces that tried to retake the rooms. They would stand their ground and wait for the second wave of Omega forces.

Group one made their way out of the cistern and took off their swim fins, throwing them into the water. They joined up with group two, who led the sprint. Group one, still wearing their camouflage suits, acted as rear guard, blending in from bush to bush, tree to tree.

Group two, posing as their enemy, ran through the streets as if they were bringing a message to their fellow defenders, yelling in Turkish. When one of the patrols told them to stop, they did and that's when group one would snipe the Turks from their hidden positions. The imposters dropped to the ground and started firing as well, making quick work of the patrols with their silent weapons.

As the commandos approached the squads of soldiers guarding the western entrance to the Hagia Sophia, the same tactic was used. However, these guards were far more skilled than the others. They quickly dispersed and launched an immediate counter-strike, pinning down the two imposters in the crossfire. Out in the open and unable to get to cover, one of these commandos was shot through the head and killed. His partner was shot in the leg and shoulder.

Hiding at the rear, the commandos of group one laid down an intense covering fire and hastily moved forward to protect their injured team member. The Turks were amazed and startled as they saw two commandos run out of the bushes and drop onto the grass, suddenly blending into the new terrain. Some of the guards were filled with such fear of the two "ghosts" attacking them that they just ran away. The remaining soldiers noticed one of the "ghost" commandos spring up from the grass and sprint to the right of their line, away from the church, disappearing into some bushes.

The guards fired at the bushes, letting loose a dense barrage into the vegetation. Meanwhile, the other commando went unnoticed as he crawled in the opposite direction of his comrade. The guards heard something behind them and they swiftly turned. Their hands shook and the sweat dripping down their face glistened in the moonlight. They strained their eyes to spot whatever they heard. Suddenly, the bark of a cypress tree right in front of them began moving and a gun seemed to poke out of the trunk. Before they could react, the guards were shot dead.

The commando who was camouflaged against the tree ran over to the massive doors at the main entrance to the Hagia Sophia. Amazingly, his suit metamorphosized to blend into the coloring and markings of the carved iron doors. He set about placing incendiary tubing on the middle of the doors, along the line where they were welded shut. Pulling the fuse, the fire lit up brightly and white flames shot out, as if some luminescent spiritual force inside the church was bursting through the doorway.

A diligent Turkish sniper on a rooftop managed to pull the commando into view of his scope and shot him through the back of the head. The dead Greek fell limp to the ground in front of the iron doors. Shouting with a furious rage, the injured commando of group two began firing into the rooftop where the sniper shot came from, pounding the spot relentlessly until he saw two dead bodies topple over the edge. He crawled over to his partner who had been killed moments earlier and pried the thirty-six caliber gun from his teamate's cold, stiff hand. He propped the dead body of his comrade in front of him as a shield.

"Sorry about this, brother," he whispered, as he opened fire with both guns on the closest watchtower. The snipers in the tower ducked, but quickly realized the Greek's aim was way off. However, the Turks' hesitation was just enough time for the surviving commando of group one to run out of the bushes and charge the Hagia Sophia. Putting on his gas mask, he ran towards the Iron Gate, threw it open and stormed inside.

He was immediately met with gunfire, but with quick reflexes he jumped to the side and targeted the man firing at him. The defending suicide squad member seemed weak and incoherent. No doubt the neurotoxin had seeped into the exonarthex, the outer vestibule of the church.

Five gateways led into the inner vestibule, the esonarthex, where only the baptized, the "saved," were privy to enter before the Ottoman takeover. The Omega Force commando stepped on the dead suicide squad member in his way and entered the esonarthex through the Imperial Entrance, the tallest archway at the middle of the five. The mosaic panel above the door depicted Christ the Pantocrator, the Almighty, sitting upon his throne with an Earthly emperor pleading to him for divine mercy. All of the commandos on this mission had, of course, been baptized in the Greek Orthodox Church, so there was no higher glory to this Greek man than to run through into the nave, no longer as a foreigner, but as one of the owners who had taken back his national inheritance.

As he passed through into the center of the Hagia Sophia, he saw eleven dead Arabic men lying on the ground, four of them around the arming device for the detonator. The process of arming the explosives was not that difficult, but the nerve gas had clearly taken effect, creating confusion before death. For a split-second, the overwhelming magnificence of the voluminous central room knocked the breath from the commando. The vast, thirty meter-wide dome towered nearly eighteen stories off the ground. It gave the impression of being suspended in the air and its imminence covered the entire space. The walls and the ceilings were adorned with marble and mosaics. Altogether, thirty million gold tiles glittered in the church's interior, especially within the dome.

The commando was in such awe that he immediately bowed on one knee, closing his eyes in a mandatory gesture of humility. He quickly rose to his feet and began dismantling the detonator and explosives.

When the task was complete, he looked to the sweating column in the northern corner of the church. A bronze belt encircled the lower section of the column, where there was a small hole. Over the centuries, people had created this divot in the column by rubbing the area with their fingers to feel the "miraculous" moisture, which they saw as a divine omen. The commando went over and placed his finger inside. Even knowing that it was the moisture from the underground reservoir that permeated into the column, he still felt that it had God's blessing.

Artillery began to sporadically shower the area, dangerously close to the church. The Turkish defenders along the outside of Istanbul were trying to take out the Hagia Sophia, getting their bearings despite the wind. They were not off target by much.

Suddenly, coming in fast from the sky, twenty large missiles rained down upon the artillery. Though American interceptor missiles were secreted to the Turks and were encircling the city, they were not fast or agile enough and were only able to take down twelve of the incoming missiles. Eight rushed down towards Istanbul, pulling up and racing along horizontally, parallel to the ground over their targets. They were fired from Germanian fighter-bombers called *Guntrams*, which was old German for "War Ravens." The pilots guided the missiles with special controls. The missiles then acted as mini-bombers, deploying small bay doors on their underside and dropping dozens of bomblets onto the lines of defensive artillery, including those on the Wall of Theodosius.

But, while the steel shrapnel within the bomblets was perfectly designed to wreak havoc on the soft bodies of the Turkish artillery crewmen, it was relatively harmless to the ancient wall, compared to a normal bomb. The Wall of Theodosius escaped heavy scarring from the shrapnel, which just left tiny holes in the ancient ruins. Most of the crewmen, on the other hand, were utterly obliterated. Looking from above, the gray landscape was suddenly brightened by splashes of scarlet.

Some of the artillery crews remained functional and they quickly tried to determine the correct coordinates for inflicting a direct strike on the Hagia Sophia. A powerful and fickle gust was blowing in all directions in the city, making it hard to target the building from far away. The winds were with the invaders.

The commando who was in the nave heard and felt an explosion coming from above. An artillery shell blasted a one meter-wide hole into the church's gigantic dome. Small pieces of stone sprayed down onto him and he jumped out of the way just in time to avoid a much larger piece. The church shook again as another shell struck somewhere on its exterior wall, and then another.

Moving in fast over the water of the Dardanelles, twenty-five mini assault helicopters raced forward toward Istanbul. The small, one-man helicopter gunships had an advanced stealth design. Their propellers could not be heard outside of a hundred meters and they came in low, at five hundred kilometers per hour. By the time the Turks heard the helicopters, they were already upon them. The defenders looked up in horror as the gunships swooped down, easily wiping out the rest of the artillery crews with hundreds of rapid-fire missiles, burning and melting the soldiers and artillery guns with a napalm-like substance.

A second and much larger wave of invasion forces arrived by air in dozens of Germanian transport planes, all of which were escorted by War Raven fighter-bombers. The Greeks of this second wave were euphoric to receive the transmission that the operation to take the church was successful. Now, it was time to take the city.

With elation, five hundred Omega Force commandos jumped from the transport planes, releasing parachutes that were purposefully small, designed to minimize their descent time and, therefore, their vulnerability. They hit the ground going fast, but they buckled and rolled gracefully to diffuse the impact.

Within an hour, the Greeks had secured the city. The Turks were so over-whelmed that the new round of commandos barely needed to fire a shot. The

SEALs were prepared for this worst-case scenario. They summoned for help and retreated by way of a nuclear-powered submarine.

The world was in awe of the Omega Force operation. The Greek and Germanian governments did not reveal the classified technology used to win back the church. It was the result of highly trained and motivated military personnel, and a little bit of luck, the administrations claimed.

In the aftermath of the skirmish, Istanbul and all of Eastern Thrace was wrested from the Turks and occupied by Greece. The occupation was kept ambiguous, and neither Constantine nor Geiseric would reveal if it was temporary or permanent.

The two leaders met once again in Germania, just outside Munich. A huge caravan of security vehicles met Constantine at the airport. Once more, three black limousines were among the vehicles on the tarmac awaiting the plane. Constantine was escorted by a Germanian secret serviceman to the limo with Geiseric inside. They drove off surrounded by their security caravan, passing ten minutes with pleasant small talk, reveling in their accomplishments. Noting that they were almost to their destination, Geiseric opened the sunroof to the limousine and poked out his head.

"Check this out!" he shouted to Constantine, who stood up and looked out with him. A colossal stadium stood on a wide and flat, grassy field, towards which the limousine was driving. It was only slightly bigger than the largest stadiums presently in the world, but what was particularly striking was its beauty. It was a gigantic version of the Roman Coliseum, before it was run down by the ages. Constantine marveled at the architectural feat.

Like the Roman Coliseum, this coliseum was built primarily of concrete, but unlike its ancient predecessor, it had to be reinforced with steel, due to its tremendous size. Scaffolding netted the entire exterior, from the bottom to the top, ten stories high. Construction workers were placing white marble over as a skin to the structure.

Only a small percentage of the outer walls were yet covered, but Constantine imagined how it would look when finished, when the gold and silver inlay and the statues were added. He saw the hundreds of giant, concave ports where the sculptures would be placed and there were craftsmen working on a dozen of them already, out on the field. The mammoth stone creations were all ten meters tall, three stories, and were of different historical figures, from scientists to politicians to warriors. Constantine recognized the likeness of Abraham Lincoln, with his awkward, lanky build and top hat. He also recognized Friedrich the Great, Julius Caesar, Albert Einstein, Galileo and others, all carved from large boulders of white marble.

As the limousine drove nearer, the coliseum grew ever larger in view. A small group of reporters, who had been carefully selected to unveil the secret project to the masses, awaited the two leaders at the massive stadium. Geiseric and Constantine posed for photographs. The Germanian chancellor then prepared to give a speech.

He stood at an optimum angle behind the podium, so the immense coliseum could be seen in all its grandeur. The reporters hushed and began rolling a live feed. In Germania, Greece and in fact most of the world, special reports interrupted regular programming on the network stations and cable news channels. The chancellor spoke in English, being that it was the *Lingua Franca* of the planet.

He began with brief salutations and then swept his arm upwards, gesturing at the momentous coliseum standing at his back.

"Many of you watching out there are probably wondering, what is this magnificent structure behind me? This will be," he paused for effect, "the main stadium for the 2036 Olympic Games! Which, as you all know, will be held here in Munich!"

Almost everyone watching the speech on television was very excited about this. The world had seen what Germania was able to do for the Iraq Olympics. With what they were being shown now, they could imagine how incredible the Olympics in the heart of Geiseric's beloved homeland was going to be.

"However," Geiseric said, "before I go on about that, I must congratulate the Greeks and the Omega Force commandos for their stunning victory. And God bless Prime Minister Metaxas." He pointed to Constantine with an open hand. "For without his decisive leadership, Greece would still be another hostage of Islamic fascism!"

The cameras focused in on Constantine for a moment, as Geiseric shook his hand.

"For so many reasons, Prime Minister Metaxas is one of the greatest Greek leaders of all time," Geiseric remarked with gravity. "He has given the Hagia Sophia back to his people!" He cheered, raising Constantine's hand like a triumphant athlete.

"Hagia Sophia," Geiseric worded slowly, grinning, "means 'Divine Wisdom.' We have wrested back the church of the Divine Wisdom!" he roared.

He looked into the camera and every hair stood up on his body, as he was overwhelmed with a sense of power and ecstasy.

"The Greeks have always placed knowledge on a pedestal. The friendship between Germania and Greece thrives based upon this common cultural bond and our shared national values. As we celebrate the Greeks taking back what was rightfully theirs, we should remember the history of this ancient and mighty nation. We Germanians value our continuing partnership with the government and people of Greece, and we commit to work together to provide greater opportunities to our peoples, and to the world!"

Geiseric placed both his hands on the podium and flashed an evocative smile into the camera. "And so, I have come before you today to announce that the Greek and Germanian people shall unite under the same banner, in a confederacy where rationale is the highest order! And let the 2036 Games show the world what this partnership can do!"

After posing for additional photographs — standing side by side, adorned with congenial expressions, shaking hands — the leaders retired to Geiseric's lavish and regal office on the top floor of the stadium. As they walked down the elegant hallway, they passed by ten of Geiseric's elite secret servicemen, all wearing metallic body armor, helmets and face masks.

The two leaders entered the office through a huge, carved wooden door. They crossed the room and stood facing a wall-sized window that framed a gorgeous view overlooking the amphitheater and the abundantly green foothills beyond. Perched on spherical, marble pedestals, two large golden statues of nude female angels framed each side of the window. There was no desk, just a large, semi-circular couch facing the window, winged by two sofa chairs. The furniture, patterned in hues of gold, scarlet and royal blue, matched the elegant carpeting and drapery.

Geiseric led a toast. "To politics, science, and all the arts of the mind!" he cheered merrily, raising his glass.

"To God!" Constantine added.

Geiseric took on a more solemn face and sipped from his glass. "Aye . . ." he remarked stoically, "to God."

At Omega Force headquarters in Greece, Commander Apostolos was interrupted from his officer's card-game by one of his subordinates — Lieutenant

Nicos. The lieutenant asked Apostolos if he could speak with him privately. Obligingly, the commander brought Nicos into his office.

Nicos looked uneasy and he spoke in a whisper. "There is something really strange going on."

Apostolos looked worried. "What?"

The lieutenant rubbed his nose and looked out the office window to see if anyone was around.

"Well," he explained to the commander, "those hostages ... who were supposedly decapitated by the terrorists at the sheep slaughterhouse," Nicos leaned in, "they appear to have been dead for weeks. They were already dead prior to their decapitations. It appears they died from natural causes, like heart attacks and other congenital problems and were artificially preserved. They were never on those tour buses and they were not murdered!"

"That's ridiculous! Where did you come up with this information?" Apostolos demanded. "None of our doctors confirmed any of this."

The lieutenant nodded. "They must be in on it."

Apostolos seemed angered by the lieutenant's audacity. "In on *what?!*"

"I don't know," Nicos retorted in an agitated voice. "I realized that there was something wrong when I found the bodies in the slaughterhouse. They looked different than the people I saw being decapitated on the video. It was hard to tell, because they were badly decomposing by then. So, I brought in someone from outside to do autopsies on the bodies."

The commander's expression of anger was replaced by that of nervousness. "So, what do you think is going on?"

Nicos walked towards the desk and slammed his palms onto it. "Come on, sir! Isn't it obvious? There were *no decapitations!* It was all a trick!"

"Then what did we see on the video?" Apostolos inquired with a perplexed expression.

The lieutenant was growing impatient with his superior's poor extrapolative capability.

"Sir," he looked Apostolos straight in the eye, "with the technology nowadays, they can create almost anything on video and make it look real. But, like I said, I noticed something was different about the bodies."

Apostolos shook his head. "And what about the terrorists we killed?'

"I don't know." Nicos thought for a moment on the issue. "Pawns, I guess. They probably didn't know that their part in the plan was to die." He speculated. "Or, they could have been a suicide contingent who knew they had to be killed off to fulfill the plan. All *I know* is that those people who were supposedly decapitated had already died of natural causes before the hijacking even took place. Probably the bodies of John and Jane Does that were stolen from a morgue or a hospital somewhere. Now, Sir . . ." Nicos took a deep breath before pressing his conclusion further.

"This plot has to go all the way up the ladder." He gulped a bit as it fully dawned upon him what he was about to say.

"I believe Geiseric and Metaxas orchestrated the entire thing."

Apostolos appeared physically pained by the information the lieutenant was relating, as if his illusion of a genuinely good regime had just been shattered. "Why would they do that?"

Nicos was perplexed by his superior's inability, or unwillingness, to grasp what was happening. "Sir! The taking of the Greek hostages was what ignited us to go into Turkish Thrace! Bayar would have *never* been so stupid as to allow Greek civilians to be decapitated on his soil. But, it served *Geiseric's* interests and it allowed him to take *our* country under his dominion!"

Apostolos cringed, as if he had been struck in the gut. Closing his eyes and exhaling through his nose, he turned away from the frustrated lieutenant. Nicos took this time to look out the office door window, checking for eavesdroppers. "You are the only one I can trust, sir."

With a sigh, Apostolos turned back towards the lieutenant, quietly pulled a handgun out of a holster under his arm and rapidly crept up behind Nicos. With a quick pull of the trigger, he shot the lieutenant in the back of the head.

Apostolos' gun had a silencer and the lieutenant noiselessly slumped to the ground, his mouth opening and closing, perhaps trying to express his confusion. His grey eyes were fixed up at the commander, the man he had come to think of as a paternal figure. Apostolos again pointed the gun at Nicos, his bottom lip quivering.

"In many ways, you were like a son to me." He breathed in deeply, trying to stay his nausea. "But, you never embraced the cause. You just never understood its importance. But, I want you to know," Apostolos brought the muzzle of the gun closer to Nicos' forehead, "this will be the hardest thing I have ever done and, hopefully, will ever have to do."

Nicos' eyes widened. Apostolos swiftly pulled the trigger again. Blood and bone fragments sprayed out onto the carpet. He stepped backwards. Walking slowly over to the window behind his desk, which faced outside, the commander gazed solemnly up to the night sky.

"God, help me."

— VII —

ISAIISM

Logan stared out of the aircraft window at the luscious, green rainforest below. Alistair had gone to use the restroom at the back of the riding car. Sasha and Jacques sat in silence, wandering off in their minds.

Francesca rubbed Logan's back with her left hand. "Are you okay?"

Logan nodded. "Yeah, yeah, I'm cool," he lied, gazing at her gentle face. Her soft touch once more sent a tingling sensation throughout his body, from the place where her hand made contact to his spine, radiating out to all his limbs and up his neck. He breathed in deeply and his eyes relaxed a bit.

But his euphoria didn't last long. Suddenly, Logan was overwhelmed with a sense of panic. A dark, cold sensation crept over him, as a horrifying thought burdened his exhausted and overloaded mind. He felt as though he might vomit.

"Excuse me," he smiled at Francesca, got up and walked to the bathroom on the other side of the compartment. It was a unisex restroom with three stalls and two urinals. Relieved to find a stall open, Logan rushed in and collapsed to his knees. He leaned forward, placing his hands on the seat as his mind spun. Soon, though, the cool tiles and air began to alleviate his wooziness. The stalls were self-cleaning and a soothing lavender fragrance wafted into his nostrils.

Composing himself, Logan walked out and, upon closing the door, he heard the steam hoses in the vacant stall turn on, firing out hot sheets of water on every surface within. Next, he heard the quick and fast inundation by the heating fans. Alistair happened to be washing his hands as he came over to the sink. Alistair slapped him on the back.

"You okay, man?"

"Yeah," Logan nodded. He pulled in his lips a bit as he thought about what was on his mind. Tilting his head from side to side, he finally burst out with it. "Are you *sure* we're not just being shipped to some death camp?"

The people waiting to use the sinks looked at Logan with alarm. Alistair empathetically hugged Logan with his right arm.

"No!" He laughed, trying to lighten up the situation. "It just wouldn't make sense. They would've just put a bullet in our heads and left our bodies for the predators. That would be the most efficient way. Why would they go through all the trouble of imprisoning and transporting us as harmlessly as possible, just to turn around and kill us? Believe me, they wouldn't."

This did seem logical to Logan. He was placated and returned to his seat in a remarkably better mood, helping Alistair bring some more ambrosia for everybody. The five of them chatted and sipped on the drinks. Soon enough, the conversation came back to the pressing issue of what events had led to the present reality. Alistair continued where he had left off, right after Greece came into Geiseric's fold.

"Of course," Alistair said, taking a gulp of ambrosia, "everything Geiseric was doing was infuriating the Muslims living in Germania. There were a couple of suicide attacks and assassinations. A few Principles parliamentarians were killed and mutilated by random Muslim fanatics." Alistair shook his head and rolled his eyes.

"They played right into Geiseric's hands. He kicked all the Muslims out of Germania. Whether or not they actually participated in the attacks didn't concern him. If they were a practicing Muslim, they were out," he said, pointing his thumb behind him in a metaphorical gesture.

"It was the fastest deportation ever. Geiseric made sure that, like in Greece, the Germanian government didn't confiscate any property that wasn't fixed in the country and when the Germanian government confiscated land or buildings, they paid the deportees generously. That way, to the rest of the world,

Geiseric looked decisive instead of authoritarian." He imitated the motion of hammering down.

"Geiseric's a smart man," Alistair expressed with a tinge of admiration, "and he had a plan for the Middle East for which Greece was just a springboard."

Logan leaned back, as memories from his youth flooded back. "I remember all those wars going on in the Middle East. I didn't realize they had anything to do with Geiseric."

"Well, the Middle East had been a hotbed of violence for the past hundred years," Jacques chimed in. "Truth is, it's been a focal point for hostilities for two thousand years, especially the last thousand. That's why it was hard for most people to see that Geiseric was behind the new turbulence. Of course, Dandau and Hollier were going nuts, but no one really listened to them. Geiseric was skilled at pitting long time enemies against each other in a way that was beneficial to him, so he could stay out of the political hot seat." Jacques shook his head and laughed just slightly, amazed at this skillful deception perpetrated on the world.

"Geiseric built most of his empire on alliances against Islam. That was one of the reasons India joined. India had been warring with Pakistan since the nineteen-forties, when the British left and the Muslims in India rebelled and founded Pakistan. The only thing is, the Pakistanis took the Indus River Valley, which is a holy place to Indians and was where India got its name. This was at the root of the conflict. Both sides also claimed Kashmir, which was right between the two countries. Geiseric took India's side. Not only did he say that India deserved all of Kashmir, instead of just the half they owned then. He also said that Germania didn't officially recognize Pakistan as sovereign from India. He preached that Islam had no place in the Indus River Valley, which was the birthplace of Hinduism, one of Geiseric's favorite religions."

Logan was struck by this fact. "Why was Hinduism one of his favorite religions?"

"*Hello!*" Alistair raised his eyebrows and looked at Logan with an expression that implied the answer was obvious. "Hinduism and Buddhism," he counted off on his fingers, "and Jainism and *all* those Indian religions were the most animal-loving religions in the world."

Logan digested the information, not quite sure what it meant. "So?

Sasha snorted out a laugh, burying her face in her hands. She shook her head in disbelief. "You didn't know that Geiseric and the Isaianics are animal rights militants?"

"No way!" Logan exclaimed.

"Of course!" Sasha snapped. "How can you know so little?! I mean, you were only on that island for five years, right? All of this has been big news since Geiseric took power in Germany thirteen years ago!"

She was starting to get on Logan's nerves. "My parents sheltered me even before the island. I didn't really pay attention to shit like this then, and I didn't really care what was going on in the world when I was *twelve!* And when Geiseric took power, I was only five!"

He thought about his parents and how they always cautioned him to be good to animals. When he was just a kid they told him of the gargoyles who protected the animals. As he grew, his parents instilled a sense of fear of harming animals. Logan's mother told him about karma. She told him that whatever he did to another living being would be done to him tenfold. His parents taught him that it was inherently wrong to purposely harm a living creature, even an insect. They never ate meat on the island, maybe more out of fear than of ethics, though there was the underlying notion that meat was not right. This was truer for Logan's parents than for most of the others on the island. The other adults seemed like they abstained from meat because of some ambiguous phobia, which Logan now understood. The adults would often get mad at Logan's parents when they would remark that it was better for everyone's souls to be without meat. Logan understood the context of all that now.

"What does being an animal rights activist have to do with the Principles thinking they're smarter than everyone?"

Alistair's eyebrows lifted. "Everything," he took a hefty swig of ambrosia. "You see, Geiseric and all Isaianics believe, as Plato did, that ignorance leads to immorality. They believe that truly intelligent people can see what is right and wrong. Of course, they think that they are right and so those who don't agree with them must be inferior of mind. Plato and Socrates both favored a vegetarian diet and looked down upon animal cruelty. Plato, of course, was the architect of this elitist concept of Utopia, where the intelligent rule, while the supposedly stupid and immoral do as they are told. Now, twenty-five hundred years later, Geiseric is trying to create this Utopia."

Logan put his forehead into his hand and ran his fingers through his hair. He felt like he was in some bizarre dream that he couldn't wake from. "Whoa."

— VIII —

UTOPIA

December 2030

Germania's Gross Domestic Product had doubled over the previous year. One of the major reasons for this was that tourism, the largest grossing industry of the world, had been exponentially increasing in Germania. A multitude of travelers came to the new superpower of Central Europe out of curiosity and fascination. However, there was a steady stream of wealthy tourists who visited due to their sympathies with the animal rights and/or environmentalist movement. They came to Germania to give support to the new culture thriving there, under an administration that took pride in protecting the environment and had already eliminated such things as fur and leather products. The Principles Party had many rich and powerful supporters internationally, both in the public and private sectors, making it more wealthy and influential than the Catholic Church, for the animal rights activists and environmentalists of the world had come to see the party as their only hope.

The animal rights movement had been really heating up since the turn of the millennium. Soon, though, there came an international backlash, a sort of counter-reformation, launched primarily by large corporations attempting to turn back the environmental and animal cruelty laws put in place since the 1970s. All of the meat producers, animal testing labs, furriers and the like banded together to form the "Advocates for Consumer Freedom."

With billions of dollars at their disposal, the Advocates for Consumer Freedom were able to get candidates elected to do their bidding. They managed to get the largest and most respected animal rights organization in the world put on the domestic terrorism watch list in the U.S., despite the fact that the organization had never harmed a single person. Destruction of property, such as when the members of the organization threw fake blood on the fur coats of runway models during a fashion show, was considered terrorism. The legislators working for the ACF claimed that terrorism could also be "anything which impeded the flow of business."

Thus, almost all forms of civil disobedience became terrorism, for like the sit-ins launched during the civil rights movement, most forms of activist disobedience disrupted the "flow of business." That definition even irritated a lot of people who hated the animal rights and environmental movements, because it diminished the significance of true terrorist attacks. But, the pro-corporate lobbyists got their way and being placed on the terrorism watch list meant that the government could freeze incoming private donations to activist groups and could harry them and their donors, as if they were terrorists.

Riding a wave of success, the Advocates for Consumer Freedom crushed the infrastructure of every major animal rights and environmentalist organization in the United States and Britain. In these countries resided the strongest antithetical movement against that of the progressives. What the ACF did not realize was that these organizations actually tamed the animal rights activists, channeling their anger into legitimate campaigns. By criminalizing animal protection groups, there was a void left for extremists like Geiseric to fill.

The Advocates for Consumer Freedom began gaining power in all of the first-world countries with very little grassroots support. Most people had never even heard of the Advocates for Consumer Freedom. The coalition consisted of wealthy elites and, while they espoused humanist motivations, it appeared as if they were fighting for their pocketbooks. Such was why, it seemed, many corporate polluters did not improve their standards, even though more people were getting cancer and heart disease from these pollutants every year. And why many animal products were not inspected thoroughly, allowing for contamination. Such was why Geiseric's Formula was later to be vilified by the pharmaceutical companies, for the new craze cut dramatically into their profit margin.

The Formula was not a single magic bullet. It relieved and even cured a person's ailments through exercise, learning, doing new things and getting the necessary nutrients. The pharmaceutical companies couldn't patent and control these holistic activities and so they couldn't make money off of them. Money also appeared to be the reason why the vivisectionists chose to perform torturous medical experiments on animals. There were plenty of alternative methods to live animal dissection, such as interactive computer simulations, data mining, diagnostic imaging, laser holograms, DNA chip technology, acoustic microscopy, and a multitude of others. But, the businessmen behind these laboratories argued to their stockholders that to do it any other way would have cut into their company's profits, even though these losses would have only occurred during the transition period.

The inability of the large corporations to bend with the tide pushed a lot of activists into a corner, making those sympathetic to the progressive movement more vulnerable to becoming radicalized by a charismatic leader. Germany was the only place where the ACF could not gain a powerful lobby. Hundreds of thousands of environmentalists and animal rights activists were already flocking there from the U.S. and U.K., starting more than a decade before Geiseric came to power. After he was elected chancellor, millions more immigrated to the land. Many of the people who left were the most dynamic of their countries, like the British producer of the hit television show *Who Wants to be a Teen Idol,* and the U.S. Democratic presidential candidate of 2016.

This restless mob of intellectuals was burning with zeal and fear of being run off the Earth by the ACF. Geiseric came with his passion and way with words. He was able to claim precedence for his animal rights crusade by quoting the Bible, mainly the Old Testament, becoming yet another person to start a spin-off religion of the Jewish faith, like Jesus or Mohammed. Geiseric occasionally referred to his followers as "True Jews." Officially, he dubbed his religion to be Isaiism and, naturally, *he* was the leader of the Isaianic movement.

Isaiah was one of the most important prophets of the Old Testament. His writings preached that the savior of the world would end all predation on Earth, all carnivorism, in his eleventh chapter stating,

"The spirit of the Lord shall rest upon him, the spirit of wisdom and understanding, the spirit of counsel and might, the spirit of knowledge of and fear of the Lord. And he shall not judge after the sight of his eyes, neither reprove after the hearing of his ears. But with righteousness shall he judge the poor, and reprove with equity for the meek of the earth. He shall smite the world with the rod of his mouth and with the breath of his lips shall he slay the wicked. Righteousness shall be the girdle of his loins and faithfulness the girdle of his reins. In that day, the wolf shall dwell with the lamb and the leopard shall lie with the young goat; so shall the calf and the lion. And the cow and the bear shall feed; their young ones shall lie down together: and the lion shall eat straw like the ox. A young child shall lead all of them. They shall not hurt nor destroy in all my Holy Mountain, for the earth shall be full of the knowledge of the Lord, as the waters cover the sea."

Most Judeo-Christian scholars saw these verses as a metaphor for world peace. However, many took the passage literally and this was where Geiseric found affirmation for his animal-rights views. He used Isaiah to give biblical precedence to his ideologies and, upon founding the political wing of his movement, the Principles Party, he personally wrote a manifesto titled the "Isaianic Constitution." The beginning line read: "*We hold these truths to be self-evident, that the Earth and all its inhabitants are to be treated with respect and kindness.*"

It should have come as no surprise to the ACF that the Isaianic movement gained a foothold in Germany. In 2002, Germany became the first nation in history to recognize animals within their constitution as living beings with basic rights. As ironic as it was, even Nazi Germany was unparalleled in its compassion towards animals. Notably, the Third Reich outlawed vivisection and many German elites during this time, including Hitler, were practicing vegetarians.

Nazi propaganda used Jewish ritual slaughter practices to justify anti-Semitism, even though it was originally derived more than two thousand years ago from one of the most humane ways to slaughter an animal for its time. A Kosher slaughter was supposed to be done quickly with an extremely sharp knife without imperfections, so that the slice was not more painful than needed. The arteries to the brain were to be quickly severed so that the animal became immediately unconscious. However, many Jews believed that this procedure was not for the animal's benefit, but was intended to prevent the poisonous toxins, which an animal in pain produced, from getting into the meat. Most Jews put the laws of keeping Kosher into the category of chukkim, which literally meant, "laws for which there is no reason." Like many of the religiously observant, they did as their sacred book told them and faith alone alleviated their need to make sense of the ritual. However, while Kosher slaughter was a humane practice when it was established two thousand years ago, in the modern world the practice seemed antiquated and cruel when compared to new alternatives.

While the majority of Jews did not see Kosher slaughter as being for the benefit of the animal, there was a significant minority who did believe that showing compassion towards *all* living beings was core to Judaism and was interwoven throughout its prophecies and rituals.

It was well-known among the Jewish community that prominent Jews during Hitler's time and in his country, like Einstein, were animal rights activists. Rav Kook, who was the first chief rabbi of the reborn state of Israel, was a fervent animal rights activist and vegetarian. Yet, Hitler branded the Jews as cruel to animals in order to rally the Germans against them. He found any possible reason to hate them, even where reason did not exist.

Geiseric, however, loved *anyone* who had compassion for animals, no matter race or culture. And he had an undying hatred, no matter what their ethnicity or nationality, for those who did not feel as he did.

Thus, most analysts working for the United States and Britain had predicted that Geiseric would try to maneuver India into his fold. The Indians were the creators of the "Great Ahimsa Religions," as Geiseric called them. By this, he was referring to Hinduism, Buddhism and Jainism, all of which pre-dated the birth of Christianity. Hinduism, being the oldest, pre-dated all of the world's existing religions. Ahimsa was the ancient Indian word for "respecting all life." The base of these religions was the fundamental belief in karma, which taught that what people did upon others, including animals, would come back upon themselves.

Within three years as chancellor, Geiseric had expanded his nation's borders, creating a new political entity in the heart of Europe that had an economy three quarters the size of the United States, but with a little under half of the people. This meant that the average Germanian was earning fifty percent more income as the average American worker.

So, Geiseric made a political tour of India, surveying the state of the people, particularly the poor — their living conditions, the disease and the starvation. While the nation had been rapidly rising amongst nations in output of scientists, doctors and other such professions, there was still much poverty in the billion plus population. Geiseric announced that, over a five-year process, Germania would contribute 180 billion euros in aid and infrastructure development for India. On top of that, the international Principles Party pledged more than 60 billion euros of humanitarian aid to India.

India was usually averse to taking charity, for reasons of pride, a paradigm they first set when they refused such help after the 2004 tsunami disaster. However, they were not only being offered money, but the time and insight of the top architects, designers and engineers in the world. These were the minds who had made Germania the model of efficiency and quality of life. With this gift of human capital, plus the money to put their ideas into motion, Geiseric to some degree bought off the Indians.

Of course, the United Nations didn't believe that it was all for charity. Many Indians were suspicious too — but in the end the money fed and educated a lot of poor people and that was hard to ignore. Geiseric told India that it was not a loan, but a gift. One of the first major projects he commissioned was the clean up of the Ganges, the Indian holy river. The Indians bathed in it for religious reasons, but they also used it as a toilet, to brush their teeth, and many other things. There were millions of people doing this all the time, so it was full of disease and pollution, and the people were getting sick and dying.

Geiseric told them, "When the British were here, they ran you all like your country was a business venture to be exploited! Their intention was to *take!* Germania's intention is to *give!*"

By the end of 2030, India had renounced all attachments to its former Imperial mother. The Indian Prime Minister, Priya Divakaruni, announced that her nation would be leaving the Commonwealth of Nations, which was led by Britain and made up of the former subject nations of the British Empire. Instead, she declared with the overwhelming support of the people, India would be joining Greece in becoming a member of the Germanian Commonwealth. The new "commonwealth" differed greatly from its British counterpart, in that far more political power was deferred to the leader nation. In fact, the Germanian Commonwealth was little short of a Germanic Empire, which was how President Hollier and Prime Minister Dandau chose to refer to it.

Shortly after this shocking news was announced to the world, the Indian government passed radical legislation:

"This new legislation is necessary," Prime Minister Divakaruni declared in a television address to the people of India. "It is necessary to ensure that all the people of India have enough food. Meat is expensive and inefficient," she argued. "Far more agricultural products can be grown on the same amount of land it takes to feed livestock."

While this was true, most politically savvy people knew this drastic change had nothing to do with food supply and was a direct result of the Principles' Isaianic agenda. The legislation officially eliminated meat from the Indian diet.

The most extreme ahimsa religion in India was Jainism. Demonstrative of their ascetic nature, some Jains would wear a cloth over their mouths so as to not swallow a bug. The Jains only made up a half of a percent of the Indian population, but they were among the wealthiest of the Indians and were the single largest donor group to the Principles Party. They alone accounted for fifty billion euros in donations to India's new infrastructure. Geiseric made sure that the Jains received credit for everything they were doing for their country and he even gave accolades to them for many changes that were actually funded by Germanian taxpayers. The Jains became ever more popular within India and, soon, the Indian government was completely controlled by them. They, in turn, were all beholden to Geiseric. All political opposition to the Germanian Commonwealth and the Isaianic agenda was, thus, completely removed from power.

With so many religious values based on ahimsa, the Indians were more prepared for a transition to a meatless diet than any other society on Earth. Most Indians were just happy that their families had any food at all, especially in such great abundance. The new vegetarian food was also healthy and delicious. That was all the average Indian cared about, and their Hindu or Buddhist non-violent beliefs only served to make the dietary change easier.

But the radical legislation did meet with a relatively small, but potent domestic backlash from a significant minority. The Indian Muslims formed the core of the resistance, because the new law also had a bill attached to it prohibiting *any* acts of animal cruelty, such as sacrifice, which the Muslims regularly practiced. The Jainist government wasted no time in quashing the political dissidence. All leaders of the opposition, predominantly Muslim religious leaders, were rounded up and indefinitely detained at military bases all over India. Tens of thousands were imprisoned. The detainees were treated well and their detainment was made transparent to the world. Foreign journalists were welcomed inside the bases to film the treatment of the political prisoners. News programs showed well-fed people who were interrogated politely and never treated in any sort of cruel way. They were allowed to see their friends and families, but the Indian government did not hide the fact that all visitors were constantly under intense surveillance.

Geiseric was worried. He did not want to project a negative image of the Germanian Commonwealth to the rest of the world. So, in a strategic effort to boost their image, he sent his *Staatsminister,* or Minister of State, Karl Heinz Teller, on a highly publicized tour of the major industrialized nations of the world. Acting as a "good-will" ambassador, Teller first visited France, Spain, and Italy, where he received a warm welcome from the political leaders. A significant minority of people within these countries were Principles Party supporters and Isaianic-sympathizers. Inevitably, though, wherever Teller went in his tours through the Western European nations, he was met by protesters fuming with indignation, roaring at him and into the media cameras. However, it was nothing that the charismatic Germanian ambassador couldn't handle.

Teller spoke with a very humble tone to those who angrily brought forth their arguments. Whether they were reporters, politicians, or even random people off the street who had yelled curses at the *Staatsminister*, Teller would walk over and engage those people in debate, always speaking in a respectful manner that soothed the masses. He was very unlike Geiseric in that he was always calm and, when someone spoke to him, he appeared to be sincerely listening, with a look of deep concentration on his face.

After getting his tour off to a good start in the Western nations of continental Europe, Teller moved on to Britain, where he was met by an incredibly divided nation. Prime Minister Charles Dandau was Geiseric's most vocal opponent, and he was supported by just over half of the people in his country. Within the other half of Britain was a large pro-Isaianic demographic. The Principles Party of Britain had received nearly thirty percent of the vote in the last election, which thoroughly petrified Dandau and his nationalist-conservative base.

The Prime Minister did not officially invite Teller to come to his country, as the chiefs of state of France, Spain, and Italy had. But the parliamentarian leader of the British Principle's Party, John Clarke, held a press conference in which he formally invited the Germanian *Staatsminister* to Britain. It was a move that helped to legitimize the ambassador's visit to the island nation in the eyes of its inhabitants.

Wherever Teller went, he was struck by a deluge of scornful comments from a country rife with his antagonists. Many in the British media and political spectrum berated him with interrogatory questions, ranging from the Germanian Commonwealth's treatment of Muslim prisoners to Geiseric's seeming quest for world domination. Teller continued to speak in a deferential manner to those who were infuriated and rude to him. He avoided replying with simplistic, packaged answers. Instead, he went into great detail about everything he discussed. Whether he was lying or not was difficult for his enemies to discern, but Teller was not so naïve as to think that he could just make a blanket statement that everyone would believe unquestioningly. One opinion letter printed in a London newspaper remarked that, "Teller does not astound people with logic. He baffles them with bullshit!"

Whichever it was, his unwavering tact had a favorable effect on the British people, and he was able to move confidently on to Russia. President Kurtkin had personally invited Teller and warmly received him, holding a large parade in Red Square. Russia did not have a particularly strong Isaianic movement, and Teller's colorful reception was not a symbol that Germania's power was encroaching into its immense neighbor. Rather, the parade was a symbol of Germania's and Russia's alliance based on the common goal of attaining land. Kurtkin had signed a pact with Geiseric in which the leaders agreed that Russia would not attack Germania, if Poland was annexed. In return, Geiseric guaranteed that Germania would politically support Russia's seizure of all the rest of Eastern Europe. This bartering tactic was nothing new.

On August 23, 1939, Hitler and Stalin had their foreign ministers sign a non-aggression pact ensuring that neither country would attack the other, even though the fascist Nazis were avowed enemies of the Communists. The pact was, in truth, a bargain between the two dictators to take back land that had once belonged to their countries' former empires in the nineteenth century. Back then, Eastern Europe was divided into German and Russian spheres of influence. On September 17, 1939, only two weeks after the Germans invaded Poland from the west, the Soviet Union invaded from the east and the country was divided in two. But the British and French saw who the true threat was, in terms of power, and so only attacked Germany.

The political flavor of Russia in 2030 was very similar to that of a hundred years earlier. Russia had, once again, degraded into a semi-dictatorship. The drift away from democracy began soon after the fall of the Soviet Union, with the coming to power of President Vladimir Putin. Putin unabashedly glorified Russia's totalitarian past. Incidences like the Beslan massacre in September 2004, in which a school full of children were taken hostage and executed by Chechen militants, only served to help Putin consolidate his grip over Russia. The Russian people were frightened and looking for a strong leader.

The two Russian presidents who followed Putin further stemmed the tide of democracy. Ivan Kurtkin took power in 2024 and carried the torch, essentially gaining dictatorial control over Russia. Now, he wished to regain the former Russian Federation and Soviet states that had fallen into the European Union, such as the Ukraine and Baltic States. To do that, he needed a major

Germanian Commonwealth (Germania and India)

continental power to acquiesce. So, a German and Russian leader once more signed a mutually beneficial pact of non-aggression, though they were not ideologically aligned.

Overall, there were many aspects of the 2020s and 30s that preceded in much the same fashion as a century earlier. But, there were some fundamental differences that favored Geiseric. For one, Geiseric's takeover of Poland had been accomplished without war. Hitler's invasion of the neighboring nation gave a pretext for Britain and France to declare war on Germany and, thus, began World War II. Geiseric also made sure to placate the French. Though he seemed hostile to his European neighbors sometimes, Geiseric knew exactly which countries he had to appease and how to do so. He doted on the French as the only competitors to Germania within the European Union.

The EU assemblage had been pushed aside, relegated to little more than a formality, and it was every nation for itself in Europe. From the moment Geiseric came to power in Germany, he worked to accomplish this task, for if the European Union stood united against him, it would have been hard to accomplish any part of his agenda. Thus, the German chancellor worked hard to keep France split from the union, by playing on French nationalism.

After taking over the European Space Agency's infrastructure in Germany, Geiseric worked with the French and Russian governments on the Martian project. On January 21st, 2030, the feat was accomplished — man stepped foot on Mars. This boosted the self-esteem of the Germanian, French and Russian people, much like the Moon-landing did for the citizens of the United States. Germany, and later Germania, provided most of the technology for the project. In return, France held out from uniting with the EU central government in Brussels. Geiseric needed to win over the two major powers of Europe outside of his country, and he managed to do so.

After the Germanian *Staatsminister* had concluded the remarkably successful European phase of his tour, he moved on to Asia. As instructed by Geiseric, he made the strategic decision not to go to China, though he had been publicly invited.

Premier Hung had invited Minister Teller to China for two reasons. Though he had already decided to align China with the United States and Britain, Hung had not yet informed Hollier or Dandau of this. The Chinese premier wished to extract as much as he could from them before he officially came to their side. He had already used the threat of a potential Sino-German alliance to scare the British and American leaders into ceding Taiwan to China. Now, Premier Hung wished to annex most of Indochina, including Vietnam, Cambodia and Laos.

The other reason for inviting Teller was that the *Staatsminister's* tour had been publicized as a trip through *all* of the major industrialized nations outside of the Germanian Commonwealth. Hung knew that Teller planned to visit Japan, for it was obvious that Geiseric was beginning to ally himself with the Japanese Prime Minister Hidekio Honomura. Hung wished to put a wedge in this alliance for as long as possible. Equally important, he didn't want the world to think his nation wasn't good enough to be visited by the Germanian ambassador.

China and Japan had long been at odds, their animosity fueled by the events that both preceded and occurred during World War II. The Japanese, much like the Germans in their approach towards the Slavs and Jews, thought they were superior to the Chinese. The tiny island of Japan was becoming overcrowded and the Japanese used their self-stated superiority as an excuse to take over their continental neighbors and massacre the inhabitants. Millions of Chinese civilians were killed in the takeover and hundreds of thousands were tortured during hideous human experiments. Ever since the Second World War, China and Japan had thus been engaged in a subtle, yet omnipresent competition with each other, to prove who was the superior Asian race.

Geiseric snubbed the Chinese premier and, so, practically handed the large and powerful nation to Hollier and Dandau's growing web of alliances. However, Geiseric had never considered China to be anything more than a temporary ally, a stepping stone in order to cross a muddy path. He knew that the China of modernity was diametrically opposed to his ideological movement. Historically, China had a strong history of vegetarianism, stemming from its Taoist roots that began more than two and a half millennia earlier. However, it also had a history of the strongest counter-movement to Taoism. At the end of the Third Century BCE, Emperor Chin became the first leader of a united China. Where the monks and scholars believed that all humans were good and, thus, a good king with moral behavior was best for a nation, Chin believed that humans were innately evil and had to be ruled through fear. And so, he buried the dissenting pacifists alive. Naturally, their vegetarian culture was buried with them, and it forever had to battle with the violent counterculture established by Chin. Now, among the Chinese masses, the elites and the leaders, Geiseric found very little sympathy for his cause. Plus, the ideals of Isaiism, like those of Christianity, were forbidden by the Chinese government to be expressed in public.

Though Japan was the leading whaling and fishing nation in the world, the Japanese had a history of pesco-vegetarianism that led them to this. A unique feature of Japanese dietary history was its taboos on meat consumption. In 675 CE, Emperor Temmu gave the first recorded decree prohibiting the eating of cattle, horses, dogs, monkeys, and chicken. Evermore decrees were made by emperors during the following centuries, their arguments based on the Buddhist prohibition on killing and Shinto respect for nature. All mammals were banned from being hunted, except whales, which were categorized as fish. Believers in Shinto did not eat fowl, for they believed roosters were God's sacred messengers, sent to announce the dawn.

While meat-eating wound its way into Japanese culture evermore intensely in the twentieth century, along with Westernization, the Japanese continued their pesco-vegetarian traditions. They were still the least consumers of mammalian flesh per capita out of any industrialized nation. Japan was also one of the world's most environmentally-conscious nations, stemming once again from their Shinto and Buddhist heritage, which preached both deference to nature and harmony with the living world as virtues. Because of this deep undercurrent of Isaianic virtues, a strong majority of the Japanese intellectual elite were Isaianic sympathizers and Principles Party members. Prime Minister Honomura was not in the Principles Party of Japan, nor was he a professed Isaianic. However, President Hollier, Prime Minister Dandau and Premier Hung all suspected that, secretly, he was.

Minister Teller was personally greeted by Honomura on the tarmac at the Haneda airport in Tokyo, symbolizing to all the leaders of the world, and to all those who were politically-savvy, that there was a new and powerful alliance developing between Japan and Germania, right under the noses of a largely unsuspecting Japanese populace.

Teller concluded his global tour in North America, first visiting Canada, where once again he had not been invited by the leader of the nation, but by a parliamentary subordinate in the Canadian Principles Party. Teller arrived to a very lukewarm reception by the Canadian people. While Canada did have a thriving animal rights and environmentalist movement and even many Isaianic-sympathizers, many of them were a breed apart from those in Germania, or most of the world for that matter. The Canadian activists did not like Geiseric's militant approach towards the issue, considering it to be self-defeating and, more importantly, hypocritical. Therefore, many Canadians who were sympathetic to the cause were almost as opposed to the Principles Party as those who could not care less about animals or nature.

Teller's grand finale was a visit to the United States. His reception there was most similar to that which he received in Britain. He met another strongly divided country, but for far different reasons. The United States had the weakest animal rights and environmentalist scene, proportional to its population size, out of all the major Western nations except Spain. President Hollier was a vocal opponent of Geiseric's ideologies and a fervent advocate for "consumer freedom."

However, while the extreme right of America, representing about a quarter of the population, was rabidly anti-Isaianic, anti-German, and anti-Geiseric, the rest of America was not sure about anything, except that they did not want any problems. The citizens of the United States tended to be extremely isolationist. They only entered into war when they felt it was brought to their doorstep, as with Pearl Harbor and 9-11. The events leading up to those attacks had foreshadowed what would happen, yet the American people maintained a blind eye until the eleventh hour, when they were rudely awakened by their enemies.

The Germanian minister's tour through the U.S.A. got off to a good start and, though President Hollier snubbed him by refusing to meet with him,

Teller made a favorable impression upon a majority of the people and politicians. Ever-humble, yet admirably intelligent and well-spoken, Teller managed to bring a small portion of the moderates over to the Principles' Isaianic cause. Even many of those who absolutely did not agree with him felt that he was still likable and trustworthy.

He traveled up the New England coastline, flew over to the West Coast, moving up from Los Angeles to Seattle, and back down to San Francisco. By the time he had flown back to New York, it seemed as though he would leave the United States on a good note, just as he had done in the other countries.

Confidently, he made the rounds of news programs based in New York City, some of which were ultra-conservative. Teller was harangued by all of the right-wing hosts, but he managed to keep his composure. That is, until he was invited to speak with Shepherd Savidge on FIX News.

From the start of the show, Shepherd did not attempt to hide his disdain for the Germanian *Staatsminister*. Coming back from a quick commercial break, the cameras focused in on the cantankerous host's head and upper body.

"Welcome back to *Shepherd of the Flock*, on FIX News, the cable news channel where people go to find real journalism that's most trusted," he said, reiterating the station's tagline. Since FIX News was in perpetual competition with other cable news stations that had coined more graceful and memorable phrases, FIX executives took an amalgam of other taglines and clumsily slapped together their own.

Shepherd introduced his guest again and started right back into his arguments.

"Now, Minister Teller, have you and Geiseric considered toning down your rhetoric a bit? Your beliefs tend to be inflammatory, wouldn't you say?"

The cameras focused in on Teller who, sitting opposite his host at an irregular-shaped, elliptical table, kept a congenial smile and answered calmly. Though, one could tell that the interviewer's belligerent approach was finally starting to wear on him.

"Listen, what we say is our truth. You here at FIX News all unabashedly espouse your viewpoints, because the platforms you defend have been indoctrinated into you. Some of the ideologies you espouse on a daily basis are intolerable to a person of my sensibilities. But, it is your right to say what you believe and when I, or my colleagues, say that those who defend the slaughter and torture of animals are no better than the Nazis, we really believe that! The Nazis have come to represent the embodiment of evil to much of the world.

So, I use them as a general *metaphor* for atrocity. I could maybe compare you better with slave-owners, but that does not pack the same punch. People hate being called Nazis." Teller stared back at the host with a challenging smile, and laughed a bit. Shepherd glared back at him.

"Calling someone a Nazi," Teller continued, slightly building in volume, "is very appropriate in another way. Ignorance is the cause of all evil and people like you, Mr. Savidge, do **Not-See . . .**" he paused, his eyes sparkling with mischief, "the evil of your ways."

Savidge gritted his teeth and squinted his eyes in anger.

"You know," Savidge replied venomously, looking down his nose at the minister, "I've spoken with many Apex politicians and businessmen. None of you respond with any sort of rational argument!" He enunciated his words by jabbing his finger towards Teller's face.

"I mean," Shepherd continued, "some people *might* even have some sympathy for your views, but you turn them off with your outrageous rhetoric!"

Maybe, it was because the *Staatsminister* had not been able to sleep or rest well during the last leg of his tour, flying over so many time zones in such a short duration; or maybe it was because he had been deferential to people he did not agree with for too long . . . but Teller finally snapped.

"Listen!" Teller roared back at his host, pointing his forefinger at Shepherd's ribcage as if he were going to gut him. His true personality reared up, crunching his polite façade under its cloven hooves. Shepherd, startled by the outburst, sat back wide-eyed.

"I'm not here to *turn you on!*" Teller seethed with rage. "If you want that, you can go *fuck yourself!*"

Realizing what he had just done, he closed his eyes for half a second and then decided to cut his losses. He ripped the microphone off his collar and stood up, looking down at his shocked and frightened host. As Teller fixed his collar and straightened his tie, the news station's security walked in. He held up a palm to assure them that there was no need for them to forcibly remove him from the building. Posturing himself upright, Teller walked calmly and proudly out the exit, escorted only by his own bodyguards.

Geiseric was infuriated by the hostile treatment his ambassador had received. The interview was at eight o'clock in the evening on the East Coast of the United States. In Germania, it was the middle of the night and most people were asleep. Within an hour, Geiseric held a brief and impromptu press conference specifically aimed at the people of the United States, in which he announced that he would be giving a groundbreaking address to his people at four o'clock p.m. German time, ten o'clock a.m. East Coast time.

All over Germania, friends and families gathered in their homes to watch the chancellor's address on television. People all around the world were once more tuned in to hear the speech, for almost all the major news programs were broadcasting it live. It was rumored that Geiseric would address what happened with his "good-will" ambassador during the trip, particularly in the United States. The media was happy to feed the gossip train.

Naturally, the FIX News staff was euphoric that Shepherd had been able to rile Teller up to such a degree, and they aired the short clip and sound bite of the *Staatsminister's* remarks constantly that morning. FIX was able to take credit and assert to their audience that they were the most "Powerful Name in News on Television." This was achieved mostly through self-aggrandizement, for those who ran the FIX News station believed that, "if you don't toot your own horn, who else will do it for you?" They also realized that *any* publicity was good publicity. Therefore, they interrupted their regularly scheduled programming to air the full length of Geiseric's speech.

The chancellor appeared on screen in a controversial setting. He was standing atop an Alpine mountain in the Obersalzburg, the former site of a massive Nazi complex on the Bavarian-Austrian border. His backdrop was the stunning snow-laden mountain peaks glistening in the descending sun. Fingers of light cascaded through the clouds on the horizon, blanketing the infinite splendor of the pristine wilderness.

Geiseric was dressed in a most unusual fashion, attired with merely a white toga, draped across one shoulder. The chancellor, though in his forties, was still in the prime of his life, in peak shape and the ancient apparel exposed his sculpted abdomen, shoulders and arms. Only a single gray streak shot through his dark hair from the top of his forehead. It had appeared two years ago, the only hint of his true age.

This time there was no fancy new podium adorning a stage or platform. Instead, Geiseric stood barefoot on the moist dirt. He intended the humble uniform and setting to send a message before he spoke — and it did . . .

He was about to kick off the next phase of the Isaianic movement.

The television audience was captivated by the scene, and their eyes were glued to the screens in anticipation and curiosity, as the Germanian chancellor began his address.

"In the beginning . . ." he pronounced, stoically gazing into the camera,

"God created the heavens," he pointed his hand upward, "and the Earth." He brought his hand down and gestured toward the ground with an open palm.

"And the Earth was without form," he continued, putting more inflection in his tone. "It was void . . . and darkness was upon the face of the deep."

"And *God said*: Let there *be light!*" he paused for dramatic tension. "And there was light."

He gathered more passion from within. "And *God said!* Let the waters under the heavens be gathered unto one place, and let the dry land appear . . ." He stopped and looked into the cameras, then said softly, "and it was so."

Geiseric rubbed his chin and looked down in contemplation.

"And God called the dry land Earth, and the gathering of the waters he called the Seas. And God saw," he halted again for effect and looked up to the camera, nodding, "that it was good."

Becoming more exuberant, his voice rose. "And God said, let the Earth bring forth grass, and *herb yielding seed! And the *tree yielding fruit!*"

He used his hands to motion to what was all around him; the awesome, green environment.

"And God saw!" he asserted fervently, "*that . . . it . . . was . . . good!*"

The chancellor stopped and took a few deep breaths of the clean mountain air, closing his eyes to savor the moment.

"And God said," he began again, with hyperbolic animation. "Let the waters bring forth abundantly the moving creature that *hath life!*"

He raised his right hand up beside him, and then his left, as if he were summoning up the creatures he spoke of. "And God created the great whales, and every living thing which the waters brought forth, and he created birds, which fly over the Earth in the open expanse of the heavens! *And God saw!*" He threw his fist triumphantly into the air. "That it was good," he finished calmly.

"And God said let the *Earth* bring forth the living creature! Let it bring forth the cattle and *every thing that creepeth upon the Earth and God saw* . . . that *it . . . was . . . good!*" The chancellor bowed his head again for a moment.

"And God said," he calmly looked back up, "let us make man in our image, after our likeness . . ." Geiseric brought his two hands up and clenched them, his tone gathering fervor. "And let them have *dominion* over the fish of the sea, and the birds of the air," he pointed to a bird of prey, a large Alpine Golden Eagle, that happened to be flying by, "and over the cattle."

He gazed out upon the overwhelming natural splendor.

"And let them have dominion over *all the Earth* and *every living thing* that creepeth upon it!" Geiseric flung his arms out as if to embrace the view and take it under his control.

He turned back and faced the viewing audience. His eyes were ablaze with vim and vigor.

"And God *blessed them* and said unto them, *be fruitful*," he smiled as he waved about emphatically, "*and multiply! And replenish the Earth, and subdue it!*"

He paused for a while this time, inhaling and exhaling with tempered fury, his eyes closed. He slowly opened them and spoke with a deep tone that could not conceal the rage boiling right beneath the surface.

"**And God said, Behold!**" Geiseric held an opened hand out towards the camera. "*I have given you every* **herb bearing seed**, which *is* upon the face of *all the Earth,* and every tree, in which there *is* the fruit of a tree-yielding seed . . ." the chancellor's nostrils flared with fervor. "**To you**," he roared, "**it shall be for meat!**"

He went on with a ferocity that had only just begun to display itself through the speech. "And to *every beast* of the Earth, and to *every fowl* of the air, and to *every thing* that creepeth upon the Earth, wherein *there is life* . . ." he belted out, "*I have given every* **green herb for meat!**"

Geiseric looked up, as if he was suddenly reminiscing about this paradise.

"And God saw every thing that he had made, and behold . . . it was . . . very . . . good."

The chancellor closed his eyes and lowered his head, taking a moment for the audience to digest the words. He raised his head very slowly and stared back into the camera, looking almost like a different person. His lips quivered in an uncontrollable sneer of passion and fury. His caustic blue eyes pierced into the souls of those glued to their television screens. He pulled himself upright to begin his oral manifesto.

"I come before all who are watching today to testify, to *bear witness*," he declared with conviction and authority, "to the fact that we live in *hell!* And *we*," he beat his palms upon his chest, "*we are its keepers!*"

An energy of sorts was noticeably overtaking Geiseric. He seemed to be almost growing in height and stature while speaking, as if this energy was becoming mass within him. His face muscles pulled tight and his eyes dilated, making him appear entranced, as if he were no longer speaking, but something was speaking through him.

"Many of you are surely wondering, 'what do I mean?'" He imitated an expression of consternation, as if empathizing with his audience. But quickly it morphed into a look of bitter condescension.

"What do I *mean*?!" he repeated in an acid tone. "Of course, many of you are content," he said, choosing not to answer his question right away. "Even though most of the world suffers, those people in power are content with their lives and would like to keep things as they are."

He walked briskly over to an Alpine fir tree. "Look here at nature's splendor," he smiled, running his fingers through a fluffy bough of needles. He then became solemn. "Look at what man destroys for toilet paper and junk mail. And do not think that those in power give a damn about their fellow man either! The corporate giants who rule the world through their greedy political puppets care nothing for the Earth or *any* of its inhabitants." He poked his finger at the camera to amplify the points he was making. His other hand still gently held the fir bough.

By this point, the producers at FIX News realized that he was not addressing what happened to his ambassador. Not wishing to give him a platform to espouse his talking points, the FIX producers were trying to figure out how to cut from Geiseric without looking like they were afraid of what he was saying.

"They poison our water, our air, our land and our food," the chancellor pounded, "with their pollutants and cheap additives. Yet, the majority of humankind refuses to acknowledge this." He shook his head sadly and looked incredulously at the camera.

"Most of the world has gone *mad!* They view those who care about the environment and animals as oppressive radicals. *We* are the oppressors!" he blared with indignant rage.

"How dare they!" he roared. "I *will not* deal with these fools, these ingrates," he remarked with disgust. "Their critical thinking skills are inferior and, therefore, there is no point in even arguing with them. If those selfish few in power had their way," he added, chin pointed up at a defiant angle, "the whole world would be consumed by factories and refineries . . . except for the neighborhoods where they themselves live, of course! And they would sell expensive pharmaceuticals to the sickly and depressed masses so that they won't notice what is happening right under their noses!" In a dramatic display, Geiseric took some imaginary pills with a chaser of imaginary water and feigned sedation. But within seconds, his wrathful glare returned.

"But, wait!" he shouted, feigning shock. "We already *are* at that point!"

THE KEEPERS: WORLD WAR III

Geiseric fumed with anger, his nostrils flaring in and out. "This cannot be allowed to go on any further!" He threw his fist into the air with a punch. "It *cannot* be tolerated. It *will not* be tolerated!"

He thrust forth into an unstoppable tirade. "*No longer* will we destroy this beautiful planet to line the pockets of oil billionaires and the like! *No longer* will these inconsiderate bastards be allowed to buy off governments around the world!

"There is a *new* world order on the horizon," he vehemently declared, staring down the camera, "and not everybody's going to like it."

Geiseric shook his head, as if clearing it, and took a moment to lower his pulse rate. It was not healthy for his mind or body to summon up so much negative emotion.

"Such is the way with all change. Therefore," he asserted calmly, "Germania will undergo a vast overhaul of its entire economic infrastructure, so that the world may gaze upon a sustainable economy and see that it is possible to do business, acquire resources, and engage in all the gratifying aspects of capitalism, without raping our environment."

He shrugged and nodded as if everything was obvious. "The restructuring will involve every aspect of public and private life, but," he raised his forefinger, "do not think that the life of the average Germanian will be affected in a negative way. If anything, your lives will be better." He flashed a wide, toothy smile.

"It's all very simple. Instead of paper made from trees, we will use hemp. It's stronger, more efficient, and will also be valuable for the production of many other basic necessities."

He held his palms upwards, imitating a scale. First he tipped slightly to his right. "Instead of giving out plastic dispensable cups and utensils at Americanesque fast food and coffee franchises," he tipped slightly to his left, "there will be only reusable or biodegradable containers and utensils."

Geiseric let his hands fall to his side. "Where there is a will, there is a way. Or, as Thomas Jefferson once said: 'Principle will, in *most* cases, open the way for us to correct conclusion.'"

The chancellor shrugged. "There will be some major changes and not everyone will come out unscathed. *However*," he pointed into the air, "there is no reason that everyone cannot adjust and come out better off."

He took on a determined, confident stance angled toward the camera and his television audience. "Two years ago, our government declared that Germany and Austria's economies would be hydrocell-based within ten years.

This commitment is now shared by all of Germania, but the timeline is not good enough. The world, the atmosphere, does not have much time. We must lead!" He chopped his hand down, pointing it forward.

"I now declare, that we shall be a hydrocell economy by *next year!* No more of this procrastination of our *destiny!*"

Geiseric looked toward the horizon, as if gazing into the future. No matter from which country they were watching, the audience was not very shocked by Geiseric's speech, so far. Although what he was saying was quite controversial, the general population of the world had become somewhat desensitized to his radical pronouncements. Even those Germanian citizens who were not Principles sympathizers were used to Geiseric's style by now and remained unshaken by this relatively minor proposal.

But, they also knew that Geiseric's plans were usually grandiose. Whether they were sympathizers or not, everyone knew that the chancellor was just getting started.

Geiseric rolled his neck, his eyes closed, breathing slowly and deeply. He lifted his head and faced the camera once more, slowly opening his eyes.

"Now to an even greater matter concerning sustainability," the chancellor began, in a low, solemn voice. He paced slowly and, with a hypnotic stare, he kept his eyes locked on the camera. The audience felt as though he was looking right at them through the television screen. It was as if his eyes were following them, an optical illusion that gave many the chills.

The chancellor now spoke calmly and methodically.

"Albert Einstein once said that 'nothing will benefit human health and increase the chances for survival of life on earth as much as the evolution to a vegetarian diet.'"

Geiseric halted mid-step. "Now, I think most people would agree that Einstein's opinion is of *some* worth," he sarcastically understated.

Moving his toga out of the way of his feet, he continued walking back and forth, facing partially towards the camera, but looking towards the ground much of the time, as if he had not rehearsed the speech and instead was letting it free-flow in a stream of consciousness. In fact, this was the case. He did not need index cards or a teleprompter for this speech. This was his passion — what he thought about everyday.

He brought his hand up to his heart. "I feel an obvious kinship with a man such as Einstein. He proves Plato's theory that the most intelligent will choose the moral path. Einstein was a genius and so he saw what World War II really was.

"World War II . . . was one of the *finest* examples . . ." he took a deep breath and sighed, "of humans treating humans like animals."

Geiseric let this statement sink in before continuing.

"Every analogy to the Holocaust has to do with animals! They packed them together for transportation *like cattle!* They exterminated them like *vermin!* In fact, experimentation was done on humans instead of animals in Nazi Germany. A lot of people do not realize that the Japanese were doing far worse over in Manchuria. They were dissecting Chinese people, *while conscious,* by the thousands! Why did this all happen?" he asked rhetorically. "Because a world that justifies the torture and slaughter of tens of billions of living beings a year, will soon bring those who justify the same towards other forms of life, including humans!" He slammed his fist into his other palm, with an audible smack.

"As Charles Darwin so eloquently put it, 'there is no fundamental difference between man and the higher mammals in their mental faculties. The lower animals, like man, manifestly feel pleasure and pain, happiness and misery.'"

He looked up into the sky, as if seeking a power to fill him up and carry his voice.

"Do we need to perpetrate these crimes in the labs? We torture the very same animals that we give to our children and invite into our families as pets. We break the legs of beagles! We spray acid in the eyes of bunnies! We dissect Guinea pigs while they are alive and conscious!" Geiseric began to sweat from his zealous oratory, but the gentle mountain breeze kept his antique garb from sticking to his skin. He ran his hand thoughtfully through his hair.

"And even the most evolved of animals are not spared. Our cousins, the chimpanzees, are dealt the same cruel and unusual punishments as any other creature. Humans and chimpanzees are practically identical genetically. We have similar brain structures and show near-identical behavior in the first three years of life. All five hominids are unique in sharing human-like characteristics that scientists group under the labels of self-awareness, theory of mind, and incipient moral awareness."

Geiseric grabbed at his stomach like he was about to be sick. "It's the same as if we were performing these horrendous experiments on *human toddlers!* Billions of innocent creatures are condemned to endure burns, mutilation, induced psychological trauma, and countless other indescribable tortures!"

The chancellor stood there in the cool mountain air, his hot breath misting before his face with his powerful exhalations.

"Now, undoubtedly, many of you out there watching me right now are unnerved by my display of human emotion. If someone took *your* dog, *your* pet, and tortured it, everyone would understand your anger. However, these atrocities are committed daily in the name of scientific research, so it is *okay?!*" he shouted ferociously.

"This was the same argument that Imperial Japan and Nazi Germany used to justify performing experiments on the Chinese and Jews! It is always the same goddamn argument! So long as we treat animals horrifically, there will be humans whom are treated like animals!" Spit sprayed out of the chancellor's mouth as he vocalized his frustration. He wiped his lip with his left thumb and forefinger.

"And those who offer an alternative are ignored!" He definitively smacked his left fist into his right palm and then clenched his hand over it. When he released it, it was reddened from his own grip.

"For a prime example of society's reluctance to change, one need only think about history and all the horrors of slavery that were committed less than two hundred years ago." Geiseric imitated the motion of cracking a whip. "When human beings were beaten and sold on the block. When they were *bred* for slavery, so it was *okay*?" he asked, shrugging. "Just as animals are bred for meat or fur, so it is okay?!"

Geiseric shook his head like a parent considering how to deal with a petulant child.

"Look back through the ages. Slavery was the norm for the vast majority of history. Everyone's ancestors were enslaved at some point. Those who fought against it met *bitter* resistance from the conservative forces of their times! The Southern United States was absolutely convinced that their economy would collapse without slavery. And they were even more convinced that it was *nobody's* business to say they could not hold slaves!" He imitated the indignant finger waggle and eye-stare of a person who felt this way.

"They *actually* thought men like Abraham Lincoln were tyrants! Tyrants because they dared to push their abolitionist beliefs on others! And *now*, many say that the *Principles* are the tyrants for so aggressively pushing our interests. But it is our duty. Let *history* judge us!"

Geiseric looked momentarily worn, as if he had just left battle. "Those who fight the status quo, those who fight for something better, are *tyrants*?" He sighed audibly.

"If that is a tyrant," he said coldly, "I do not want to be otherwise."

This remark, more than any other, struck a fearful chord in Geiseric's opponents. However, his supporters in Germania and abroad were stirred into a jubilant frenzy.

"And that brings me to slaughter," he spat with disgust, "the basis of all evil. The word itself is atrocious," he glared into the camera, and used his hand as if to highlight the imaginary letters displayed before him, *slaughter*.

"This world is a giant slaughterhouse. Billions of living beings are . . . *slaughtered . . . every year*," he enunciated clearly and slowly.

"Do you know how your food is prepared? How those nicely packaged little steaks got to your local market? The animals' necks are sliced open and their blood is spilled in a torrent upon the ground as they cough and gasp for air. It's not only inhumane. This is *inhuman!*" Whether they agreed with him or not, the audience was locked onto every motion he made and every word he spoke.

"The lucky ones have their throats cut," the chancellor fumed with disgust, making the motion with his finger across his neck, as if it were a knife. "Many sadistic farmers would prefer to disembowel the poor creatures!"

Geiseric was trembling with rage, the animosity in his eyes and facial expression utterly terrifying anyone watching who was opposed to his words. His hair had begun to unglue from its combed position, and strings of it fell over his forehead.

"Those who *sow evil* shall *reap hell!* Call it karma! Call it an eye for an eye! *Woe to those* who *revel* in disrespecting life," he warned, glaring at the audience with a sinister gaze.

"*Woe to you* who fight for death," he pointed menacingly at the camera, "*for death will come to you!*"

From their living rooms all across the globe, most of those watching gasped and wondered what he meant by his strong words.

"It is *God* who will punish your souls," he clarified, nervously shooting glances from side to side, realizing his prior statement was a bit too inflammatory. He cleared his throat and prepared to wrap up his address.

"So, I come before you today, to declare that Germania's soul has been saved! Today, I announce the birth of a state which respects *all life!* Today . . ." he proclaimed unflinchingly into the camera, "I announce the birth of a country founded on principles! When the United States was born, it was the first government of its kind. It was a nation founded on values, where all *humans* are respected. Even then, it took them a while to see who was human. Well, we shall not make the same mistake by living in a state of hypocrisy. I am here before the people of Germania to tell you that, starting today, your nation is based on values. In Germania, we respect *all life!*" He raised his arms up in a metaphorical embrace of all that was around him.

"We hold these truths to be self-evident, that *all* living beings should be treated with dignity! And we *shall not* destroy this gift from God called Earth! We shall not destroy the planet simply to feed our consumerist desires. We *shall not* leave our children a concrete jungle, where the air is synthetic and all of Noah's animals are trapped two by two in zoos, labs, and slaughterhouses!

"I will not allow it to go on any further!" He pronounced, revealing once again his dictatorial tendencies.

"*It* can not be allowed!" He corrected himself.

Making a concerted effort, he calmed himself and took a long, deep breath. He wanted to finish off in a more reserved voice, to leave the audience with as little agitation as possible.

"I would like to thank my constituency in Germania for their continuous support. Thank you for caring enough about animals and nature to put it at the forefront of your agenda. Today, following India's fine example, parliament has voted to make Germania a vegetarian state!"

Geiseric knew his audience would be shocked. He paused to let the viewers make their exclamations to their friends and family. Even Principles supporters never thought Geiseric would institute such a sudden, daring change. They were happy, of course. But, no transition period? There would certainly be a backlash. Already, in their living rooms, families were thrown into heated debates. Children challenged their parents' values and siblings were set against each other.

But, as Geiseric spoke once more, everyone quieted to listen.

"Now, you may think it is fascist to push the Principles agenda upon the whole of Germania," he said, smiling pleasantly, "but that's how things work in a democracy. Laws are enacted based on what the majority of the country considers to be appropriate."

He mentally prepared for his congenial finale, appearing at peace. His face was subdued and welcoming, which was not typical for Geiseric. No matter how jovial he was, he usually remained slightly intimidating. For the first time, people saw a completely non-threatening, almost child-like expression upon the mighty Germanian leader.

"I want to take this opportunity to announce that Germania shall open her borders to anyone who wishes to become part of our new state, born of idealism!

"Just as the United States started a new paradigm by opening her arms to those fleeing injustice, so shall Germania embrace all those brave and intelligent enough to seek justice for all. Come to your new homeland, all of you who will no longer tolerate the injustices of this world!"

He looked into the camera, his eyes almost pleading.

"This invitation is particularly pertinent to animal rights activists and environmentalists living in Britain and the United States. Your countries have forsaken you! Your governments have cheated you out of a voice by labeling you terrorists! If *you* are terrorists, then *Gandhi* was a terrorist! Then Henry David Thorough was a terrorist! Their definition of terrorism is any civil disobedience that results in big business losing money!" Geiseric cried out.

"Well, we know where their hearts lie. The conservative administrations of Britain and the United States are nothing more than puppets to the oil companies, the pharmaceutical industry, and other consumerist ventures, whose only goal is to attain the *great Satan*," he rubbed his thumb, forefinger, and middle finger together, up in front of his face, **"money!"**

A vein, which ran from Geiseric's hairline to his eyebrow, began to bulge out as the anger rose inside him once more. So very quickly, like a possessed man, he reached his boiling point again.

"Then let them all *choke* on their Mammon! Let those who live for money be *damned!* And for those who care about the planet God gave them, and the creatures under our dominion, come to Germania! Make your statement! Bring your intellectual and spiritual capital here!"

Geiseric tried to stifle shouting his last words, attempting to end on a pleasant note. With a warm smile, he held out his arms invitingly.

"Any U.S. or British citizen who wishes to immigrate to Germania shall be given immediate citizenship, tax breaks, and free permanent housing. There are plenty of government-funded luxury housing developments, which can provide homes for millions of families. If more people come, more shall be built, always in harmony with nature of course. So, come one and come all to Germania, the land of intellect, beauty, compassion and prosperity!"

Within two years of Geiseric's groundbreaking speech, ten million expatriots of the United States had immigrated to Germania. As large as the influx of Americans was, nothing compared to the mass influx of British émigrés. In the first year alone, more than fifteen million British citizens had left their homeland forever. Together with the immigrants who came from other countries, the population of Germania swelled to nearly two hundred million. Those flocking to Germania were disproportionately rich and talented, giving far more to the state than they took.

There were also millions of Isaianic sympathizers who chose to immigrate to Greece or India. India, though, was also experiencing a mass outflow of its citizens, predominantly Muslims, who had accounted for thirteen percent of the nation's inhabitants before the Principles came to power. Still, India was left with a billion plus populace.

Having seduced this incredible reservoir of human resources, Geiseric now had dominion over a fifth of the world's population.

IX

THE UNDERCLASS

Out of the window of his air transport, Logan saw a giant spire jutting out over the horizon. It was at least 300 meters tall, more than one hundred stories, and had nearly one thousand leaf-like platforms stemming from it, some larger than others.

"Look at that!" He exclaimed, pointing to it. Countless Kolibri darted around the incredible obelisk as the convoy of aircraft headed towards it.

"That's a Rose," said Jacques. "It's where the Kolibri go to refuel. You see, their wings are driven by Vasculosynth, which is synthetic muscle fiber. That's how all these machines work. Vasculosynth, like muscle, runs off sugars," he explained. "The Rose is a giant solar energy collector, just like a real plant. It captures the sun's energy off of the 'leaves," he said making air quotes with his fingers, "which are solar panels. Then, using water and carbon dioxide, it synthesizes a type of sugar that fuels the synthetic muscle."

The air transports carrying the prisoners began descending from the sky, moving closer to each other as they neared the docking areas by the Rose. Their downward slope was gentle and their deceleration subtle. As each craft came in, they hovered ten meters above the ground and waited to be waved through into the disembarking terminal.

Crackling back to life, the loudspeaker projected a man's voice that ordered the passengers to exit the aircraft in an orderly fashion. Throngs of people pushed forward, moving between Logan and his new companions as they headed for the exit and whatever lay beyond. A hand grabbed out for Logan's and held tight. He looked back to see Francesca's wide green eyes. Her face revealed concern for their situation, but even in her anxious state she looked beautiful. The crowd moved quickly as Kolibri guards just outside the front exit of the aircraft siphoned people into two lines.

Once outside, Logan and Francesca watched in awe as the swarm of Kolibri came up to the many filling stations on the Rose. They took only a brief moment to refuel, before jetting off in the blink of an eye.

Suddenly, Logan was grabbed from behind and trapped in a bear hug.

"Oh, Logan!" his mother exclaimed. "I was so worried!"

While Bibi hugged Logan, Jacques grabbed Francesca. He held Sasha with his other hand.

"Let's not lose each other. OK, *ma cherie.*" he said to his daughter.

Kolibri guards hovered above crowds of people flooding out of the many centipede-like aircraft all around the vicinity. Their wings generated small gusts that frequently caressed the people being herded toward a mammoth terminal building. Although the entrance was staggering, about twenty-five meters wide and tall, the sheer size of the building made it look small in comparison.

Logan and his parents moved with the rest of the crowd into a large hallway. Jacques, Francesca and Sasha followed behind, but Alistair was nowhere to be found. Everyone was ordered to face an immense television screen on the right wall. Soon, a twenty meter tall image of a Germanian officer appeared in his black and gray, squared-off uniform with the similarly-colored Iron Cross medal hanging on his breast pocket.

"Greetings citizens of the Allied nations!" He spoke in English, the common language of the prisoners. "Do not be afraid. None of you will be harmed. You will be treated humanely," he asserted. "You will get all the food and drink you need, and we will try to make your lives as comfortable as possible. We will also ensure that you are not separated from loved ones, and we will do everything possible to reunite you with those loved ones who are not with you now." He smiled briefly, then, became sterner in appearance.

"The Apex does not want to cause you unnecessary stress, but it is important that you understand that you are now a part of the underclass. You forsook your right to be treated as equal citizens in this new world order when you chose to side with evil. Now, you will atone for your transgressions through labor. Do not worry. We will not overwork you. But, by the sweat of your brow, you will contribute to the Apex world state!"

The message abruptly ended and the murmuring crowd of people was guided through a doorway into an enormous room, where there were thousands more captured Allied civilians already waiting in dozens of lines. Each line diverged into more lines, and Kolibri guards helped keep everyone organized. Things were not rushed and, as promised, families were not separated. Each of the lines ended at a different kiosk, where Apex personnel stationed behind protective windows helped the new arrivals.

The Kolibri guards directed Logan and his family into a different line from Jacques, Francesca, and Sasha. Logan looked back at them as their lines parted.

"Don't worry." Francesca called uneasily. "We will see each other again."

Logan wished he knew what to say to her. He hoped she was right, but anything could happen now.

Bibi looked at her son curiously. "Who was that?"

"Just someone I met on the transport-thingie," Logan answered, slightly forlorn. He gazed around at the masses of people as the room buzzed with speculation about what exactly would become of them. The Apex personnel helping in the kiosks wore one-piece, collared, grey uniforms, with small, pill-box hats.

Tom, Bibi and Logan were directed to step up to the Plexiglas window. A uniformed woman sat on a stool at a counter, a computer and keyboard before her. She spoke to them in a firm voice through an intercom.

She directed her attention to Logan's father. "Hello, is this your son and wife?"

"Yes," Tom replied, leaning forward toward the separation glass.

"Do you have any other children?" she asked, looking to both Tom and Bibi.

They shook their heads, both saying, "No."

The woman typed for a few seconds. "Is there any extended family you wish to be reunited with?"

"Yes," Tom replied anxiously. "My father and mother, and my wife's father."

"Also my brother and sister!" Bibi interjected. "I don't know what happened. We were all together!"

"Hold on," ordered the woman. She asked for the names of the relatives, finished typing, and then stamped the backs of the family's hands with an invisible ink.

"You will be assigned a counselor," she explained perfunctorily. She had obviously given the same spiel hundreds of times. "Until then, you will stay here. Your room is 1342. You will leave through that door," she pointed to an exit on the opposite end of the room. "The arrows will take you to the elevators. To get into your room, just wave the top of your hand across the sensor," she demonstrated the motion. "You'll see the sensor in front of the door. The stamp on your hand is a chemical tracer that will allow you to get in your room and other places you need to go. It does not wash or rub off. It is usable for three days, at which point it deteriorates and fades away with no damage to your body. Upon entering your room, make sure that you turn on the television and listen carefully to everything. You'll see the screen on the wall across from your beds. Press the button next to it to turn it on. If you have any problems, press the large red button on the outside of the room door. Someone should come and help within a few minutes. If nobody arrives to assist you, go here." She handed them a photocopy on recycled paper, which had a simple map clearly indicating a place within the building.

"Do you understand?" she asked gruffly.

"Yes," Tom answered. Bibi and Logan nodded.

"Good," the lady looked them in the eyes and her face took on a warmer expression. "Concerning your family and friends, I'm sure they are all fine. People got mixed around in the shuffle. We try our best to keep familial units together. But, this is a large job. You will be reunited with them as soon as possible."

She once again directed Logan and his parents to the door that would take them from the checkpoint area to a walkway tunnel with clear, fiberglass walls. Inside the tunnel, the family could see that there was a gorgeous shoreline outside, waves crashing against the beach and frothing backward into the sea once more. They noticed that the buildings they were walking towards looked like luxury hotels, some of which were still being erected on open pieces of land a few hundred meters off the beach. However, they were aesthetically engineered to complement the environment, rather than to demolish it. Thousands of construction workers in orange hats scurried around the sites, motioning as they yelled orders at each other. Kolibri guards were hovering outside the tunnel, posted every ten meters or so, like ever-present watchdogs.

Logan was startled by a tap on his shoulder. He turned around and looked into those lovely eyes. "Hey, all right!" Logan exclaimed excitedly. "I thought that might be you."

"Yeah," Francesca smiled. "I knew I would see you again. Just had a good feeling, you know?"

"Well, I would have come looking for you if we didn't run into each other," Logan admitted. Francesca blushed ever so slightly.

Logan looked back and saw Jacques and Sasha.

"Hey guys! Have you found Alistair yet?"

"No," Jacques replied, seeming relatively unconcerned. "We'll find him. So, what room number are you?"

Logan had to think for a second. "Uh . . . 1342."

"Cool!" Francesca jumped a bit on her toes. "I'm 1368, and my dad and *Sasha*," she remarked, with some venom, "are in 1369. Anyway," she looked to Logan, "so, we're close, I bet."

They all exited the tunnel and entered a small lobby of elevators with a multitude of other people, who were talking amongst themselves. Some were clearly frantic, but most seemed resigned to their capture already. The hum of their talking soothed Logan. He found that observing them kept his mind distracted and serene.

Logan's father looked at the signs above the elevators and pressed the button designated "Elevator 6 — Rooms 1250-1400." While they waited, Logan introduced his new companions to his parents. When the door opened, they all crammed into the elevator car with some other people. Logan and Francesca were pressed up against each other and they exchanged a glance as the doors began closing slowly. Suddenly, they heard a voice yelling frantically from the hall outside.

"Hold that door!"

Logan pressed the button to reopen the doors and Alistair sprinted into the lift.

"Alright!" Alistair said, reaching back to slap Logan five.

"This is Alistair," Logan explained to his parents.

"Nice to meet you, Alistair," Tom reached across Logan to shake Alistair's hand. Bibi said hello, but not feeling in a congenial mood, she kept her arms wrapped snuggly around her husband's arm and wandered off in her mind.

The elevator began moving upward so gently that it was barely noticeable. The other passengers in the large elevator car all seemed part of the same family. They were huddled close and speaking rapidly in a Slavic tongue. None of them seemed too angst-ridden. The grandfather hugged his grandchildren and daughters, surrounded by his wife and son-in law, and comforted everyone in a deep, soothing voice.

"I wonder what our rooms are like?" Alistair blurted out, inhaling through clenched teeth in semi-excited anticipation. Sasha rolled her eyes.

The doors opened without warning. No one had even noticed the elevator car slowing to a stop. The group piled out of the elevator and stared at the rows of numbers and arrows pointing down the three different hallways. The walls and ceilings were beige, with blue crown-molding. Oriental carpets with tan and blue artistry lined the floors, while generic still art pictures adorned the walls. It wasn't a far stretch to imagine they were in a hotel on a family vacation.

Tom pointed out where to go, directing his family down the middle hall. Alistair, Jacques and Francesca's rooms were down a different hall.

"Come visit me . . . us . . . in a little bit," Francesca said to Logan.

"Will do," he smiled and watched until they disappeared around the corner.

As they headed down the hall, Tom, Bibi and Logan passed by many rooms, some with open doors. They saw several people apparently having nervous breakdowns, screaming and sobbing on the hotel beds, their loved ones trying to comfort them. Most of the people were relatively calm though.

"Here it is," Bibi stopped at the door. A light on the wall beside their door began blinking. Tom waved his hand in front of the light.

All three were startled as a female voice coming from the speaker above the door said, "Thank you," and the door flew open.

"Hmm, good thing there was no one with a gun behind it!" Tom joked, trying to lighten the mood. Bibi looked incredulously at him, her mouth agape, shocked that he would say such a thing. Tom gulped, and looked down at his feet.

"Now is not the time," Bibi remarked, brushing past her husband and entering the room.

Completing the façade of normality, their quarters looked like a typical hotel room — queen size beds, sparse furniture, a basic closet, all decorated in muted pastel colors. A large, flat television screen was built into the wall opposite the beds.

Logan checked out the bathroom. It seemed relatively normal, except that there was what looked like a second toilet bowl. Logan pushed the button on it and water squirted upwards from inside the bowl. He had seen things like this in his younger days, back in California. It was a bidet, meant to clean a person after using the toilet, instead of using paper.

"Hmm," he muttered.

Bibi surveyed the whole room thoroughly, checking to see if it was to her satisfaction — as if she had the choice to object. She opened the sliding glass doors and walked out onto the spacious balcony. Tom joined her and they stood in silence, feeling the warm wind envelop them, taking in the expansive ocean view. They surveyed the scene around them. Below was a gorgeous tropical beach that stretched on endlessly in both directions. They were staying in one of many hotel-like dormitory facilities that went on into the horizon. Though they were numerous, the buildings blended well into the rainforest, and it was obvious that the designers had preserved as much of the natural environment as possible. The wild vegetation grew right up to the windows on the bottom floors, and large trees had been left unharmed, the buildings having been cleverly built around them.

Tom and Bibi came back inside and went over to their beds, where there were two covered platters on two trays, one tray on each bed. They raised the lids to see twenty finger-sized, egg-salad sandwiches and twenty small sandwiches that appeared to be made with a white meat in cold-cut form.

As Logan came out of the bathroom and sat next to Bibi on one of the beds, he was delighted to see the egg-salad sandwiches.

"Alright!" he exclaimed, wolfing down a sandwich with one bite, and doing so twice more.

Bibi furrowed her brow in concern. "Slow down, Logan. You're gonna get a stomach ache."

Logan smiled at her with egg on his lips and mumbled over the sandwich still in his throat. "I was just *so* craving eggs. And this did just the trick! Better than an omelet or anything!"

Bibi thought about that for a moment, squinting as she did, slowly taking manageable bites. "You know," she said, "I was really craving eggs too, or anything with lots of protein in it."

"Well, I was having cravings for a good turkey sandwich," Tom added, ravenously stuffing a sandwich into his mouth as he spoke. "And this stuff tastes remarkably like turkey. I mean, I know it's not. But, it sure tastes real. The same texture and everything. It's been a long time since I've tasted this." A satiated expression dawned upon his face.

Logan frowned in concentration as he poked at one of the imitation turkey sandwiches, and raised his eyebrows, his curiosity piqued. "Are you *sure* it's not real turkey?"

Tom shook his head profusely. "Yeah, there's no way in hell they would give us meat. Now," Tom worked to swallow his last bite, "it's time you knew what our captors' fundamental beliefs are. They . . ."

"I know about Isaiism," Logan cut his father short. "I had a long conversation with those people you met. But," Logan replied, "for argument's sake, what if they are adjusting us all, since a lot of Allied citizens were probably used to eating meat. And he's giving us eggs."

Bibi shook her head. "No, there would be no way Geiseric or the Apex would give anyone meat," she daintily picked a piece of food from her teeth before continuing. "But eggs and milk are not outlawed by Isaiism. It preaches vegetarianism, not veganism. You just have to treat the chickens and cows well, like pets that you love."

Logan didn't really care about the logic at this moment. He was just grateful for the delicious sandwiches.

Suddenly, a beeping sound started emanating from the direction of the television screen embedded in the wall, and it got progressively louder. The button beside the screen flashed red in rhythm with the beeping.

"Whoops, guess we forgot to turn it on." Tom walked over, pressed the button and stood back next to his family.

A beautiful woman, whom all of them recognized, appeared on the screen. Else Dietrich, the world-renowned German actress, became famous in the later 2020s, and she was still at the peak of her youth and beauty. She looked well-meaning, even innocent, in a white, silky gown. She warmly smiled.

"Hello, I am Else Dietrich," she greeted cordially, "and I am going to explain to you some of the rules you will now be living by. These are few and they should be easy to remember because they should come from your own personal intuition. Think of them as your 'New Commandments.' There are only two really important ones to remember.

"Thou shalt not kill," she stated assertively. "That applies to everything. You cannot purposely kill humans or any other animals. And, thou shalt not harm. That means that you can not *purposely* hurt any humans or animals. Now, we understand that there are different levels of sadism and, believe it or not," she tilted her head towards the camera slightly, "we do recognize that some orders of life are higher than others. We like to think of it in the same way people regard each other. If they had to choose, most people would rather kill anyone other than a family member or friend. And similarly, most people would prefer that harm come upon people they don't know, rather than their acquaintances. And finally, most people react with more sympathy when someone from their own nation dies, than when someone from across the globe dies. But, in the end, most humans would prefer that no one died at the hands of another person." Dietrich concluded with poised serenity.

"So, let me give you some examples of how we apply this to animals, so that you may better gauge our laws."

On the screen, footage appeared showing a myriad of types of insects, in all their many forms. They were all incredibly unique and often bizarre, but the footage showed how truly amazing they were. Whether alone, or in massive colonies creating amazing structures, the footage impressed upon the viewer a sense of respect for these tiny creatures and the feats they could accomplish despite the size of their brains and bodies.

"If you kill insects on a regular occasion, for no other reason but that it titillates you, then there is something wrong with you. And, if this behavior is witnessed by your Imperial Supervisors, it will be taken into account and we may force you to undergo psychological rehabilitation. But, you would not be corporally punished, unless the behavior continued for an extended period of time after psychological rehabilitation. Even then, the punishment would be limited to paddling, which the Apex Supervising Staff administers with a paddle like this."

Dietrich came on the screen holding up one of the paddles. It was flat, about thirty centimeters long and was not very wide. She showed that it was made out of a rubbery substance that bent easily when she flexed it with her hands.

"As you can see," she went on, "the paddles are not hard. They are specially-designed with a near-frictionless padded surface to avoid abrasions and to inflict pain without long-lasting injury."

As strange as everything had been up to this point, Logan and his family felt this quick tutorial on their new paradigm to be most bizarre. Maybe it was because it was now, as they sat comfortably in a bed, eating finger foods away from the prior chaos, that everything was finally setting into their minds. The ironic juxtaposition between their relatively luxurious surroundings and their present circumstances as prisoners of war was also perfectly embodied by the warm and beautiful woman on screen who was speaking of the reasons they would be paddled.

"Now, for animals of a higher class, such as mammals, the penalties become far more severe. The Apex takes the murder of mammals very seriously. But, let me once again make clear that we are only talking about the purposeful kill-ing of a mammal. We do not punish people for accidentally killing or harming another living creature. You may ask yourself, how are they going to know?

I assure you that the Apex judicial system has all the technology of modern forensics at its disposal. We also have the ultimate lie-detection equipment."

The image on the screen cut to a man sitting in a chair with six wires suction-cupped to his shaved scalp. The wires connected to a machine placed next to him.

"This is a Psychiclink device," Dietrich said, narrating as the screen demonstrated her lecture. "As many of you already know, Psychiclink is a broad word for any technology which allows a computer to interface directly with the brain. A relatively simple application of the technology is to create a lie-detector that is far more accurate than the polygraph test. So, the Apex will *always* know when you are lying."

Else's image came back on the screen. "But, don't worry. The Apex will not abuse its power. Believe it or not, your supervisors do not wish to oppress the Allied civilians or make you uncomfortable in any unnecessary way. There is a new world order that needs to be established. That is all." She waved her hands across horizontally, in a gesture to emphasize her sincerity.

"The rules of the Isaianic Creed are not hard to live by. Driving accidents aside, how many times have people accidentally killed *anything* but an insect? And you no longer have to worry about killing a human or animal on the road, because the underclass does not have cars!" She remarked with droll humor. "Those who purposefully kill higher-classed animals will generally be punished with solitary confinement for eight to twelve months. Repeat offenders will receive harsher penalties. But, and you must listen very carefully to what I am about to say," Else straightened herself, taking on the look of a military officer glaring down at her subordinates. "There is always the possibility that the penalty may be death."

Logan gulped, Bibi felt her stomach turn, and Tom just sighed and stared at the television screen. They did not fear that they would ever purposely kill an animal; however, there was the immediate reaction of paranoia based on instinctual and arbitrary feelings of guilt and retribution.

"Death is the punishment when the offender is too cruel to live!" Else railed loudly, displaying for the first time the radical tone that was the very essence of the Isaianic movement.

"If a person *tortures* an animal, even a frog, that person should rightly fear the ultimate punishment. If you are the type of person who laughs at the sight of a small creature suffering, then you should dread living under the authority of the Apex Empire!" She quickly calmed. "Otherwise, you have absolutely nothing to fear. Naturally, the Apex rules also apply to humans. Cruelty to and murder of humans is, of course, punished just as severely. Under the Apex though, the circle of compassion has widened to embrace *all* living beings!" Her eyes sparkled as she spoke this Apex slogan.

"We will be able to distinguish the good from the evil. But we mean no harm to the innocent. Just as you did not live in perpetual fear under the administration of your prior governments, neither should you fear the Apex."

A picture of the resort-like detainment facility that the Allies were now relegated to came up on the screen. The footage appeared to be shot from a flying craft, which could also hover, most likely a Kolibri of some kind. Logan, Tom and Bibi watched carefully as the camera surveyed the magnificent land-scape and architecture. Dietrich continued her narration.

"For those willing to adapt and become part of our new global standard, you will find comfort and peace in the underclass. Most of you will live more satisfying lives than before. As you can see, we are doing our best to keep you comfortable."

On the screen, a slideshow of images appeared, one after the other, dis-playing the gorgeous and luxurious dormitories. The picturesque structural designs varied depending on the landscape. Equally fascinating and wide-ranging were the interiors. Some had lobbies with large trees allowed to grow through the floors, with glass ceilings for sunlight to nourish the trees inside. The ceilings had holes allowing the tallest trees to grow upward and rainwater poured into the lobby from these open sections. A wide patch of the floor was missing at the base of the trees, and dirt and small vegetation of the rainforest surrounded the protruding roots. As the water fell to the natural floor, it was simply soaked up without flooding the rest of the lobby.

After many dazzling images of the facility complexes, the screen once again displayed footage shot from outside. The view started right above the waterline, near the shore. The camera slowly ascended into the sky, zoom-ing out to film the facility below. As it rose higher, it became obvious that the resort-like detainment facility was completely isolated from civilization, sur-rounded by jungle and ocean.

"One final thing," Dietrich remarked in a cautionary tone, "do not bother trying to escape. This is for your own benefit. The Apex security personnel are equipped with state-of-the-art surveillance and detection equipment. So there is little chance of a successful escape. When you are caught, you will be brought back and detained. We in the Apex understand that there are natural inclinations to try and getaway, but," she waggled her finger assertively at the camera, "do not try our patience or you will be paddled. Paddling does not injure someone permanently, but it sure is a pain in the *ass!*" She laughed a bit, tossing her hair.

"However," she said, more solemnly. "If you *were* able to slip past our border security, you would quickly find you have nowhere to go. There is nothing but hundreds of kilometers of ocean in one direction and hundreds of kilometers of jungle in the other, with numerous carnivorous animals that would surely make a meal of you within hours, if not minutes. And wouldn't that be terrible, to be vulnerable to the food chain like that?" She snidely remarked. Footage came on the screen of sharks swimming in schools, blood still in the water and on their snouts from a recent kill. This image was followed by a shot of a panther in the jungle eating what was left of an animal carcass.

"Do not worry about these predators coming onto the detainment facility's premises. We have special instruments and guards to keep these types of animals at a certain distance, but please, when we allow you out to stroll the premises, do not stray beyond the marked areas."

Up on the screen flashed a picture of a boundary line in the rainforest; it was an immense, glowing, holographic projection, which looked like a large wall. The pink and green boundary line encircled the entire complex. On the holographic wall, in many different languages, the words "Stop! Boundary Line! Go Back!" were clearly written. The screen then cut to the same type of hologram wall a few hundred meters off shore. The projection went under and above the water, so it could be seen by all.

"Look at what lengths the Apex goes for its captives," Else commented. "We want this adjustment to be as easy as possible, but again, do not try our patience."

The screen displayed a shot of the detainment facility from nearly a kilometer above. The shot panned away to show most of what was called Colombia, then South and North America, with the Caribbean, Atlantic and Gulf of Mexico. Finally, the shot zoomed out until the whole Earth could be seen floating in space. Time-lapse photography showed the Earth spinning faster than normal, so that all the land, continents and oceans were visible, intermittently covered by white and gray weather systems, lightning flashes strewn throughout.

"The Apex now has dominion over Earth," Dietrich stated authoritatively. "The Allied Forces have been crushed and exiled from the planet."

Bibi covered her mouth in horror of this realization. Tom leaned over and put his arm around her shoulders.

"There is no escape from the new world order. For those who are willing to live under the Isaianic Creed and embrace all living beings within their circle of compassion, good things await you. There is always the possibility to rise in the ranks of the new order. But, for those of you who are embittered, who accuse us of forcing our ways upon you," she began with ominous intonation, "learn to cope now, for you no longer have the choice of returning to your former evil ways."

The program ended and cut to a slideshow of nature pictures, with relaxing harp music accompanying the images. Logan yawned with exhaustion, both physical and emotional. "What do you think she meant," he asked his parents while he was still yawning, "when she said that the Allied forces were *exiled* from the world?"

Bibi closed her eyes. "Just an expression, to confirm that they've been beaten."

Tom, however, thought about it a little more. "That *is* an interesting way to say it, though. I mean, it could mean, I suppose, that the Allied Forces are on the Moon, or Mars. You know, with all the space exploration that's been going on."

Bibi didn't seem so sure, but she relaxed a little under her husband's embrace. Logan smiled and laid down on his bed. "That's kind of what Jacques and Alistair were saying."

"Really?" Tom prodded.

The bed was amazingly comfortable and Logan passed out before they could speak any longer on the issue. His parents gently tucked him into the covers and followed soon after, falling asleep above the covers of the other bed.

Francesca came to their room later that night and softly knocked on the door, but no one heard her.

Logan awoke and drowsily looked around the room. His parents were still asleep on the other bed. He noticed that his father was not snoring, which he almost always did. The walls back in their modular living units on the island were thin enough that Logan sometimes felt like he was sleeping in the same room with his parents. Bibi used to complain about her husband's snoring every morning, saying he sounded like a truck down-shifting. Eventually, Tom had to spend at least four nights of the week on the couch and, for most of the other days, Bibi just suffered through it. Tom had noticed that the only time he did not snore was when he was in a particularly good and relaxed mood, but that was rare on the island because of the dire global situation. Logan thought it was strange that, at a time like now, Tom could be relaxed into a silent slumber.

Getting up, Logan walked over to what looked like a water cooler and dispenser. He pressed the button above the nozzle protruding from the box, and liquid squirted onto the floor below.

"Oops," he mumbled. He went into the bathroom for a towel and saw that there were only small ones meant for drying hands. He wondered why there were no larger ones. Grabbing a hand towel and also one of the glasses that was on the sink counter, he wiped up the mess and, trying the nozzle again, he filled the glass with what looked like a multi-colored ambrosia smoothie. Sniffing the concoction, he shrugged and swallowed it down. The smoothie was incredibly invigorating and tasted like a blend of tropical fruits.

Since there was nothing else to do, Logan decided to take a shower. He stepped into the gigantic tub, which was surrounded by transparent fiberglass walls, with altogether six nozzles mounted on them. Two were down below his knees, pointed up; a horizontal pair was at his navel and the final two were above his head, facing down in a conventional manner. He turned the shower knob to a happy medium between hot and cold and pressed the "on" button next to it. He watched as water rushed through small tunnels within the transparent walls. The nozzles all came to life at once, diffusing a mild spray across his body. Logan pressed a dispenser on a wall and pine-scented shampoo poured into his open palm. After applying and rinsing the shampoo, he grabbed the unwrapped soap, which smelled refreshingly natural.

When he finished his shower, he was about to open the door to grab one of the small towels, but before he could do so, dozens of small holes slid open in the ceiling and the floor of the shower, and warm air began shooting out. Within seconds, Logan was completely dry. He found a silky robe folded in a cabinet by the sink and quickly wrapped himself up before he lost the wonderful warmth.

When he emerged from the bathroom, his parents were awake, enjoying the view of the sunrise from the balcony. He walked over to the television screen and pressed the button next to it. The screen displayed fifteen yellow-framed boxes with channel choices. The choices included various types of music and informational channels, but no movie channels or the like.

Since he was able to access an endless amount of music stations, he selected the light Classical station as the best for the morning, turned up the volume, and brought cups of ambrosia out to his parents on the terrace. The three drank to the strains of Vivaldi's *Sonata in C Minor*.

"So, what are we going to do?" Logan asked his parents.

"Son," Tom wrapped his right arm around Logan's shoulders, "I'm afraid there's nothing we can do. But we're gonna be fine. You heard everything last night. We'll just take it day by day. All right, pal?"

"I can handle that," Logan shrugged nonchalantly, taking a sip of his ambrosia and gazing out at the sun rising pink over the beach.

Bibi hugged Logan and smiled warmly. "Things won't be bad. They just won't be the same."

Before they could dwell on the issue any further, the room doorbell rang. All at once, they turned and looked towards the door. Bibi cupped her hands together at her chest in an anxious reflex. Logan rubbed his mother's back, his eyes protectively following his father, who tentatively walked towards the door. Tom placed his cup of ambrosia on the coffee table. He looked through the peephole to see a large green eye staring back at him. He smirked and began to unlock the door.

"Who is it?" Bibi asked.

"It's Francesca," Tom replied.

"Can't she give us some time alone?" Bibi whispered.

"Mom!" Logan whined, irritated, but trying not to let Francesca overhear. He ran to the door and opened it to see Francesca's smiling face.

"You wanna go check out the pool?" She asked.

"Yeah!" Logan looked back towards his parents. "Is that OK?"

Bibi obviously wanted to say no, but looked to Tom. Tom smiled a bit. "Of course, son. Have fun. Just check in with us here and there, so we don't get worried. And remember the Isaianic rules," he remarked with austerity. "You heard them. They take it seriously. These people don't fool around when it comes to animal abuse."

"Dad, what makes you think I would randomly go out and hurt an animal?"

"Well," Tom shrugged, "I know you wouldn't son, but don't even joke about it or anything, okay?"

Logan gave his parents a thumbs-up.

Bibi remained on the porch, pouting. "Don't be too long."

"I won't. Thanks guys," Logan called, as he ran out the door with Francesca, still in his robe.

Bibi turned to her husband. "But Tom . . ."

"Sweetheart," Tom interjected, looking her in the eyes. "Let him have his fun. He needs this now."

Francesca and Logan walked briskly down the hall with each other.

"Oh crap," Logan stopped and tossed his arms up a bit. "I just realized I'm wearing my robe."

Francesca grinned mischievously. "That's OK."

Logan was confused. "Do they give swimsuits out there, or something? Because, I don't have any underwear or anything on under this that I could use as a suit."

Francesca walked up to him, grabbing the collar of his robe and pushing it together a bit, looking down. "I checked and . . . they don't give us swimsuits here," she raised her head, glancing coyly into his eyes. "It's European style . . . we go in the nude."

"Really?" Logan suppressed a smile.

"Yeah," Francesca looked downwards again, feigning modesty. "I know that's strange to an American, but I lived in Italy and France. So, to me it's nothing. But you know, if you're not cool with it, we can . . ."

"Francesca," he interrupted, "you don't need to convince me." His voice deepened with elated relaxation as he gazed playfully back into her eyes. "I definitely want to go. Lead the way."

Francesca smiled, put her arm around his elbow and escorted him down the hall.

As they walked through the back doors of the hotel, Logan saw hundreds of naked people of all nationalities around the pool. The "pool" was as large as a small lake and was surrounded by sandy beaches. As they neared the water, Logan noticed its slightly green color.

"What's up with this pool?" He asked, wrinkling his nose.

"It's an organic pool," Francesca explained. "It's kept clean and fresh by maintaining a homeostasis with algae and plants."

Throwing off her tunic and exposing her entire naked body, she ran to the water and dove in. Logan, not even thinking twice, shed his robe and quickly followed. She was a good swimmer and he did not catch her until they were behind a large rock, hidden by thick trees and bushes. There they halted, lightly treading the water to keep afloat.

"You swim fast," he complimented.

"Yeah, well I went through low-level Formula training," Francesca replied shyly. "It was *really* low-level. All of the Allied citizens had to at the end, because Allied High Command was preparing a Citizens' Army."

Logan was startled and intrigued. "No way! They were preparing you to fight in the war?!"

Francesca nodded and looked up at the sky. "Yeah, they were preparing everyone that was eighteen and over to fight." She paused and breathed in deeply. "But, how are *you* in such good shape?" She vivaciously squeezed his bicep. "I'm impressed. Are you just a naturally good swimmer?"

"Well," Logan looked down, humbly, "come to think of it, I think my parents and the other parents on the island were kind of putting us kids through some kind of Formula training of their own. They got us all up in the morning and made us run the beach and swim in the lagoon. It was filled up by the tide and rain. I used to wonder why they cared so much about fitness. But, I guess I understand now."

"Yep, sounds like the Formula," Francesca paused. "Wow, your parents were smart to have done that," she swam closer to Logan and draped her arms around his neck.

Logan was stunned by the touch of her warm body against his and he inhaled the wonderful scent of her skin. "So, you lived in France and Italy, huh?"

"Um hmm," she purred.

"You have a real cool way of talking." His eyelids drooped slightly in euphoric contentment.

"Thanks," she smiled.

"Which country did you stay longer in?"

"Well," she cast her gaze up and to the side, "my father moved to my mother's hometown in Italy when they married. That's where I lived most of my life. Then, I went to France for a few years, until we were evacuated to the States."

"So . . ." Logan began, not knowing if he should ask the next question, "what happened to your mom?"

Francesca took a pained breath. "My mother is dead. She was murdered right before the war."

"God . . . Francesca," his mouth fell agape. He could find no words, so he merely hugged her tightly for a moment.

A blank stare adorned her face. "The hooligans cut her throat," she gulped, looking on the verge of tears.

"What?" Logan took on an expression of disbelief and revulsion. Francesca broke down and pressed her face into Logan's chest. She sniffled and wiped her eyes with the back of her hand.

"My mother was walking back from the butcher shop, having just bought some pork, when two hooded men came out of nowhere and slit her throat, leaving her there to bleed to death in the street. That band murdered thirty people in one night, and left the butcher hanging upside down gutted."

The thought made Logan's stomach turn. "That's *horrible*." He held her even tighter in his arms, periodically stroking her head. "*Who* did this?"

"The hooligans," she replied with a congested voice. "They were this huge animal rights terrorist organization. What's ironic is that they were founded the day that the ACF started declaring all animal rights groups to be terrorists. They were condemned by most of the major animal rights groups. But the major groups didn't have any power anymore. So, the way I see it, the *Advocates for Consumer Freedom*," she spat with venomous disdain for the euphemism, "are as responsible for my mother's death as those terrorists. The ACF did more to turn the activists into extremists than Geiseric ever could have."

Logan shook his head, disgusted at the thought. He gently pushed back the wet hair plastered to her forehead. They held each other in silence for a while, treading the water. Logan felt alive with her in his arms and, with him holding her, Francesca was at peace.

He spoke in a low, soft voice. "You are a very strong girl. You've been through more than I can imagine."

She laid her head on his left shoulder. "That was almost three years ago. A lot of people had to go through what I did."

Logan did not know what to say, so they were both quiet for another moment. Suddenly, she lifted her head up and brushed his lips with a light kiss. He took in her full lips, every hair on his body standing on end.

"So," she laid her ear upon his chest and was comforted by the rhythmic sound of his powerful heartbeat, "what did your parents do before they went to the island?"

"Well ..." Stupefied with ecstasy, he attempted to regain his senses. "My mom was a journalist and my dad was actually a pretty famous film producer."

"Really?" She lifted her head, her interest piqued. "What movies did he produce?"

Logan shrugged. "You know *The Ark*?"

Francesca was noticeably excited to hear this. "Yeah! That was the one about the meteor that turned out to be an alien craft or something?"

"Yeah," he nodded, "and they began changing Earth to resemble their own planet."

"I love that movie!" She exclaimed with wide eyes. "Wow, that's *so cool!* You're a celebrity!" They turned slowly, as if they were dancing as they bobbed shoulder-deep in the water.

"Yeah, well I *met* a lot of celebrities," he divulged, trying to say it as humbly as possible. "A few of them were on the island with us."

"Like who?"

"Like Art Sadalbari and Kelly Reynolds."

"No way!" Francesca exclaimed, her mouth agape. "I had a big crush on Art Sadalbari. Wow!"

"Yeah, my favorite thing to do back in California was watch movies with my father," Logan said with a reminiscent tone and expression. "He had a big room with a huge movie screen. We used to screen movies there, or just watch old movies for fun. We especially loved stuff from the last century."

"What era is your favorite?" Francesca asked.

Logan was glad for a chance to talk about one of his passions. "I loved the black and whites of the thirties — their romance and starkness. And I loved the old color films, with the cartoonish, Technicolor quality. The sixties and seventies had some classics. The eighties going into the early nineties was probably my favorite era of all. Though, there were some really good ones around the turn of the century too. I mean, they're all really good." He laughed.

Francesca leaned closer to his ear and, as she spoke, her breath caressed him. "So, Logan, have you ever had a girlfriend?" She looked away, up to the sky. "Oh, what am I talking about? I'm sure you've had many."

"Well, not really," he shook his head a bit with shyness. "I didn't really have the chance to find the right one for me," he looked into her eyes, "trapped on a little island with the same people for more than five years. I've had flings here and there, but that's it."

"Are you a virgin?" Francesca boldly asked.

He was taken aback by her directness and at first didn't know if he should lie. "Yep," he admitted, blushing slightly.

"That's cool," she remarked.

He smirked. "So, what about you?"

She smiled, took her arms from around his neck, and propelled backwards away from him with a splash.

"That's for me to know and you to find out!"

They played in the water for another hour, chasing and wrestling each other. Though he did not exert his full energy when they tussled, she was a remarkably better opponent than he would have imagined. She was amazingly strong for her size and feminine build. Most of the time he let her get him in a head and arm grip. She would laugh as she dunked his face in the water, clenching the powerful arms she knew full-well could escape her. After a few dunks, Logan picked her up on his shoulders and tossed her back into the water. Later, they joined in on a beach volleyball game with a few other underclassmen. After, they just relaxed beside each other in the sand, soaking up the sun's energizing rays. Underclass vendors came by, distributing a wide assortment of nutritional foods and relatively healthy desserts. Drinking water faucets could be found every fifty yards around the outer perimeter of the beach. Dusk soon began to set in and finally the darkness descended completely, the stars shining brightly in their nightly constellations. Logan and Francesca found a lone piece of beach away from the crowds. They reveled in each other's company, quietly gazing at the heavenly lights that were innumerable in the clear night sky.

Reluctantly, they headed back and put on their apparel they had left in the sand earlier. Logan realized that, with Francesca leading the way, he hadn't really felt shy about his nakedness at all and, furthermore, he no longer found it unusual that there were so many naked bodies around him. Logan and Francesca dressed and walked back into the dormitory. He put his left arm around her waist as they entered through the sliding doors.

"You know," he looked into her eyes, "I've never felt so comfortable with another person so quickly."

"Me neither," Francesca replied, dreamily gazing back at him.

A wave of euphoria washed over Logan. "Really? You're not just saying that?"

"Not at all."

That night, they went for an ambrosia smoothie at the snug diner in the hotel lobby. There were hot meals of almost every sort, but they did not have big appetites, for they had grazed on food from the vendors all throughout the day. When they headed upstairs, they held hands and she pecked him on the cheek before strolling away to her own room.

After Francesca turned the corner, Logan knocked on his door and Bibi opened it, obviously relieved to see him. Though he had checked in a few times earlier in the day, he had forgotten to do so for a few hours. He hugged his mother and headed straight for bed. Bibi kissed Logan on the forehead and climbed into the other bed with Tom, able to relax now that her son was near.

— X —

HAVE NO FEAR

Tom awoke early the next morning to the familiar sound of sloshing tides and squawking seagulls. For one glorious moment, he thought he was back on the island. He quickly sat up, in a dreamy state, between unconsciousness and consciousness, but was disappointed when he realized the beach sounds were not the same ones he had been listening to for the past five years. The balcony doors were open and he heard the sounds of the Caribbean waters tumbling rapidly onto shore.

Something was slid under the door of their suite. Before Tom could get out of bed to investigate, an odd ringing, like a throbbing whistle, emanated from the TV screen, slowly increasing in volume.

Tom gently nudged his wife. "Bibi, wake up, honey. It's time to get up."

Bibi woke with a start and sat up quickly. "What's going on? Is there a fire?"

"It's OK," Tom assured her. "I just think it's telling us we need to get up now."

"What is it?" Logan slurred, turning over groggily. "Huh . . . what's that noise?"

Tom laughed at his son's comical incoherence. "It's time to get up, Logan."

"What's *that*?" Logan asked, sitting up against the headboard and pointing to a flashing green glow on the television screen.

Tom got out of bed and pressed the image of a button on the screen that read, "Press Here to Receive Message." The flashing stopped, and a neon green message faded slowly into focus on the black screen.

You are scheduled to meet with Counselor Dorner in two hours. Please clean yourselves and put on the clothes provided for you. Then report here.

A map came up on the screen, displaying a simple schematic of the facility, which was divided into three main areas: the dormitory buildings, where the underclass stayed; the customs area, where they were processed upon arrival; and the school buildings, which were adjacent to the hotel-like dormitories. Arrows pointed a path to the designated location, which was marked with a flashing neon green star. After a few minutes, the map faded and the words, "Have you received your clothes?" appeared on the screen, followed by, "Press if received." The image of a circular button blinked on the screen next to the words.

Tom looked at the thin packages that had been slid through the large gap under the door. He unzipped the one with his name on it and pulled out a silky shirt and pair of pants — both were loose and slightly oversized. Raising his eyebrows, he looked to his family. "I guess they're one size fits all."

He went over to the screen and pressed the button acknowledging that he received the clothes. Next, came up the words, "Have you received the instructions within the envelope?" Tom picked up the brown envelope that had also been slid under the door. Inside, printed on beige, recycled paper, was another map of the facility, along with the instructions on when to report to the counselor. Tom pressed the "yes" button on the screen. Next, on screen came a digital clock counting down from two hours.

Two hours later, Logan and his parents, dressed in identical silky apparel, sat across the desk from a woman with a friendly face and inviting smile. Though her silvery hair and shallow wrinkles suggested that she was older, she retained a youthful glow and had the trim body and upright posture of a woman in her twenties.

"I am Andrea Dorner," she began, "and I will be your primary counselor." She switched on the holographic computer monitor on her desk. Up came the hologram of a computer screen, on which she could press buttons that were merely illusions of light. In fact, her "touching" of the buttons was registered by a proximity sensor within the desk. She scanned over some of the information and then looked up at the family. "I'm here to guide you through this transition. There's no need to be afraid. Your quality of life will undoubtedly improve. My job is to find a place for you in this new world order, so that you may contribute and also be happy. There is much to do, believe me, and many choices of occupation." She smiled and again set about punching some of the buttons on the hologram monitor.

"First, you'll need to know proper etiquette, because this new state highly values good manners. You will address all of your Supervisors, from here on out, as 'Herr' or 'Frau,' which means 'Mr.' and 'Mrs.' in German. So, I am Frau Dorner. *German* is the first language of the Apex and your first priority is to learn the language. Do any of you know German at all?"

Tom spoke for his family. "No, Frau Dorner."

"OK," she said, plugging away at the screen. "I have signed you up for lessons."

Next Frau Dorner interrogated them, in a relatively gentle way, and recorded their answers in a file. Tom, Bibi and Logan told the truth. They had left California the moment the world seemed on an irreversible course for war. They had been living with family and friends ever since. Frau Dorner seemed suspicious of some of their answers. She arched her eyebrows and frowned a lot, as she scribbled in the file. She reminded Logan of a school principal putting demerits on a student's permanent record.

Frau Dorner designated them as non-combatants. She then handed each of them a long list of rules.

She stood up to indicate that their meeting was over. "To get a hold of me, just inquire at the front desk. We wish to work closely with you to ensure your comfort and by no means do we want our underclass to feel alienated. You will find that your jobs will be no more difficult than the average career most people had before, and you will have far more leisure time. We give sufficient vacations to the whole of the underclass." She pointed her open hand towards the door.

"You will please return to your room now, where you will find a meal waiting for you."

They all recited, "Goodbye, Frau Dorner," and left her office.

As they walked back into their room, the aroma of hot chocolate greeted their noses. They had not realized how hungry they were until they inhaled the delicious smell of warm food. The cocoa sat in a pitcher atop a food cart, next to a large bowl of exotic mixed fruits and three plates of a meat-like substance drenched in a thick, creamy mushroom sauce. A large, round platter hosted steamed broccoli, carrots, squash, and spinach.

Logan threw his original gown out across his bed when he changed, and now it was gone. He opened the closet to see if maids or the like had tidied up in their absence, and found that the top drawer in the closet had been labeled *Schulkleidung*. He opened the drawer and found three loose, beige, silky tunics, all neatly folded.

"Here we go again," Tom's voice complained from the living room. Logan emerged from the closet to see the screen on the front wall was blinking again. Tom pressed the "on" button and a women's voice came out of its speakers. "Hello, this is an important message concerning underclass apparel. Please press 'continue.'"

As instructed, Tom pressed the touch activated button on the screen. A picture of two different outfits faded into focus. One was the beige tunic in the closet drawer. The other was the white shirt and pants they were presently wearing. There was also a picture of the unisex, boxer short underwear on the screen. After ten seconds, the narrator began her monologue.

"These are the uniforms of the Apex underclass for our warm, tropical climate here in Colombia. The tunics are your school clothes, or *Schulkleidung*, as you will find them labeled for your convenience, in the closet. Make sure you wear them to class, or you will be reprimanded by your teacher. Your clothes must always be clean, both in look and smell. Don't hesitate to wash them every night. In fact, this is what we recommend. Simply place your clothes outside your door in the evening and they will be collected and clean by morning. That is all. Please press 'repeat,' if you would like to hear this again."

Tom pressed the "Done" button and the screen flickered off.

They all took their plates out onto the balcony to enjoy the view while eating. The family barely spoke to each other, focusing their attention on feeding their voracious appetites. Logan noticed that all the food, although just as healthy if not healthier than what he was used to eating, also tasted better. Even the vegetables were delicious, subtly flavored. As he dined on the savory meal, his mind ruminated on what the counselor had said. "Do you think Frau Dorner was telling the truth, about wanting to make things easy on us?"

Tom wiped his mouth with his napkin and sat back in his chair. "Of course, son."

"You're not lying to me, are you?" Logan asked skeptically. "I don't need to be sheltered. I'm not a kid, anymore."

Bibi laughed a bit at this comment.

"What mom?! I'm not!" Logan whined, revealing he still had some room to mature.

"I'm not lying to you, pal," Tom insisted, rubbing his forehead as if warding off a headache. "The Apex is an empire with a very complicated personality. You know, there was a time when your mom and I considered moving to Germania."

"*Really*?" Logan asked incredulously.

Bibi nodded and finished a bite of food. "Yep," she confirmed. "The Apex nations were rich and progressive. But, in the end, Geiseric was a warmonger and we wanted no part of that. All we wanted to do was keep our family safe. But," Bibi shrugged, "beyond his wanting to push his rules on everyone, there wasn't anything intrinsically frightening about Geiseric, like there was about Hitler. He's not on a mission to kill entire races like Hitler wanted to do to the Slavs and Jews. He just wants to make this world obey the Isaianic Creed, by any means necessary. In the end, Geiseric doesn't want to hurt us. He wants to accomplish something," she paused, "and war helped him do it. This caste system that we're in is just a result of the war. This is just a transitional period. It might be a long one, but it won't be permanent." She tried to assure Logan, though her intonation betrayed that she was not sure about this herself.

"But he did such horrible things!" Logan protested.

"Yes, yes, he did," Tom acknowledged. "But that was *during* the war. That's why your mother and I hate war. War is horrible and a crime to all mankind. In every war, on both sides, there are always incredible atrocities."

"So, you're saying there was a good reason for what they did during the war?" Logan was shocked that his father could be dismissive of so much death.

"Not at all," Tom shook his head, talking over a mouthful of food. "But as they say, all's fair in love and war."

Logan swallowed the mashed potatoes he had been gorging himself on. "How about what the Apex did *before* the war?"

Tom lifted his open hand, tilting it from side-to-side. "Mmm, that's a gray area," He said, inhaling another bite of imitation meat.

"To Geiseric, the war began in his mind when he determined that he could not make the whole world respect animals, so he had to take it over. Everything the animal rights terrorists and Apex forces did was done to break our will to fight, which is not uncommon in wars of such magnitude. We did it to the Germans and the Japanese in World War II. Geiseric had an agenda, which has been accomplished. The world is governed by Isaianic law."

Logan still wasn't convinced. "So, why has he enslaved all of us? Even those who didn't do anything to animals?!"

"You have to look at it from a different perspective," Tom reflected optimistically. "We're no more slaves than we were before, really. I mean, we'll be forced to work, but that's nothing new. And I believe them when they say it won't be any harder than most of our jobs before."

Tom paused to gulp down a glass of fresh squeezed orange juice. "That's good," he commented, licking his lips. He looked at his son again. "Your mother and I have been watching this drama unfold for twenty years. We're going to be a lower class because we did not become Isaianics and move to the Apex. They don't know what our ethical beliefs are, so they can't completely trust us. We won't get to have full citizenship rights for now. It won't be forever." Tom smiled and hung his arm around his son's neck and shoulders.

"But, I believe them when they say we'll have free time. They have this ethic called Kraft zu Freude, which loosely translated means 'strength through joy'. They believe that people are much more productive when they are happy and not overworked. So, I mean, it may be strict and even harsh sometimes, but it won't be any more terrible than living in the world before. Trust me, son." And for the first time in days, Logan did.

Alistair and Logan sat at the beachside cabana bar that night. The full moon illuminated the waves breaking offshore. A myriad of constellations sparkled in the clear night sky. Out on the sand, a steel drum band played melodic rhythms. Some underclassmen had been assigned the job of providing music all around the facility. Guitars, flutes, or violins — even harps and xylophones — were often heard all around. Tonight, bongo drums accentuated the tropical flair of the beach music.

Logan and Alistair thanked the bartender as he handed them each a frosty glass of dark beer. Logan took a big gulp, wiping the froth from his upper lip.

"What do you think they're going to do to us?"

Alistair's nostrils flared as he breathed in deep through his nose. "All empires need an underclass, Logan. They're the ones that do everything from agriculture, to engineering and craftwork. When the Babylonians conquered Israel, they took many of the Jewish craftsmen back to their land as slaves to help all their other slaves build up the great city of Babylon. Geiseric has big plans like that, I'm sure." His eyes sparkled faintly as he considered what was in store for the world. Though he would never admit it, the idea of Geiseric's creativity being let loose on reality was tantalizing. "He loves building beautiful, environmentally-sound cities. He admires fantastic architecture and sculptures." Alistair imagined the possibilities and took a swig of beer.

"He also wants to clear the oceans and skies of pollution, and stuff like that. That's a huge task, so he needs lots of labor. Beyond that, any good ruler knows that he can't inflame his subjects too much." Alistair wiped the foam from his upper lip.

"They know as long as we're treated well, we won't obsess about escape. But, if we do keep our minds on freedom and study our captor's methods and habits, we could possibly outwit them." Alistair and Logan exchanged quick glances. Logan arched his eyebrows, intrigued.

"See, they will keep us as content as possible. They'll give us good food, plenty of ambrosia and beer to keep us feeling good, so that we forget that we are slaves," Alistair held up his drink as an example. "They'll keep us around our families, people that make us feel safe. We'll even be able to have fun after work. Geiseric thinks he's won," Alistair remarked with an entranced expression upon his face. "He may be right. And generation after generation will eventually forget the past, or think of it as almost like a mythological world. People will eventually come to accept their existence. And acceptance is the mother of all tyranny." Alistair's expression turned to consternation, realizing that this was a real potentiality.

Logan shook his head. "People will never stop wanting their freedom."

Alistair laughed, very slightly. It was more of a quick exhalation through the nose, coupled with a smirk. "Ah, Logan," he smacked the young man lightly on the shoulder, keeping it there. "I wish you were right. But, history disagrees with you. Those who don't know any better accept their situation. They are like domesticated animals. But, *we* are like animals caught in the wild and caged. We know what it's like to be free." He paused and looked up at the stars, letting out a long sigh.

"The truth is, the longer people live under this regime, the less of a chance there is for rebellion. The history of the world is on the shoulders of all the people alive today!" Alistair slammed his beer mug onto the wooden bar. He suddenly realized that he was being too loud with his rhetoric. He became paranoid and looked around, over his shoulder and down the length of the bar. There could be undercover agents, or listening devices, to spy on the underclass. But, it seemed that no one around him had heard what he said over the loud din of their own conversations and the band playing marimba music in the background. Regardless, Alistair decided he better cool off.

"I have to take a piss," he announced suddenly, as he swiveled off his barstool. "I'll be right back."

"I'm not going anywhere," Logan answered, taking a chug of beer. He looked out at the southern end of the beach. Dozens of bonfires blazed orange in the night, and hundreds of underclass youths in their early twenties gathered around them. Most were wearing their tunics, but many were nude or in their underwear, throwing Frisbees, talking and lounging in the cool sand.

Logan felt a finger poke his shoulder and a warm shiver travel up his spine. He instinctively knew it was her before she spoke.

"Hey," Francesca said softly, brushing her fingers across the back of his neck.

Logan sat up straight and turned casually around. Upon seeing her, he grabbed his tunic by his chest and waved it a bit to cool himself.

Francesca giggled and sat down next to him. "Are you okay?"

"Yeah," Logan smiled "it just got a little hotter around here." His senses suddenly felt sharpened; colors looked brighter and sounds seemed louder. Her presence gave him a sensual clarity. He focused on the drums in the background and fell into a meditative mood. Gazing upon Francesca, she seemed more beautiful than ever. Though she was currently clothed, now that Logan had seen her completely naked figure, the sight of her in a drab tunic could easily stimulate his primal instincts.

Francesca snapped in his face to alleviate his apparent trance. He flashed a goofy smile. She waved at the bartender and asked for a beer. He came over right away and winked at her flirtatiously. She thanked him and flit her eyelashes. An intense feeling of jealousy rose up inside Logan. He was filled with a lust to do something violent to the man. He locked eyes with the bartender, eyeing him menacingly. For a moment, they stared each other down, but the bartender, though taller and exceedingly muscular, backed down. He seemed intimidated, and turned quickly to help some new customers at the opposite counter. Logan leaned back a little, somewhat relieved, his pulse pounding heavily.

Francesca, quietly watching the whole exchange, loved it. There was something about Logan, some inexplicable power she was drawn to. She got up from her stool and sat on Logan's lap, whispering in his ear. "Once you grow into your spirit, you will be unstoppable." Her warm breath in his ear made every hair on his body stand up. His heart pounded even harder and faster.

"I'm not sure what that means," he said, wrapping his arms around her lithe waist.

She did not answer, but moved her leg across to straddle his lap, facing him. They both stared into the others' eyes, happy to be enjoying each other in silence.

— XI —

FIRST DAY OF CLASS

Logan rose early the next morning with only a trace of a hangover, even though he drank too much beer the night before. He was slightly groggy and dehydrated, which was cured as he gulped down a few cups of ambrosia. The family's underwear and clothing, cleaned and neatly pressed, had been pushed under the door. He and his parents rushed to get ready, afraid of the repercussions of arriving late to class.

They found the voluminous, Ionic-columned hallway that they had been directed to by a map provided to them. The hall was nearly sixty meters tall, with four floors of walkways spaced exactly fifteen meters above or below one another. Doors on each side opened to dozens of spacious classrooms of a multitude of sizes. Between the columns, Logan could see out onto a beautiful courtyard with hundreds of different plants and several ornate, stone fountains. Dawn sunlight cascaded into the hallway between the columns like ghostly sheets.

Logan's classroom was on the ground floor. Tom and Bibi paused before leaving their son and heading off to their own class, which was for adults over thirty. Bibi kissed him on the cheek and tried to hide the anxiety she felt any time she was separated from her son recently. Tom gently put his arm on Bibi's back and guided her away.

Stopping in front of the wide, open doorway, Logan took a deep breath. As he walked inside, two things immediately caught his eye. The classroom was an auditorium, with at least thirty seating levels and hundreds of chairs. The top level was three stories high and over twenty-five meters wide; the bottom level was only slightly narrower. Logan was already used to the expansiveness of Apex architecture, having toured many of the detainment facility's buildings. What really caught his attention was the *style* of the architecture. He felt like he was entering an ancient church. The classroom was Gothic, built of stone of varying gray and black shades, with flying buttresses and a vaulted ceiling that soared twelve meters higher than the top level of chairs, coming to a steep peak in the middle of the room. Stained glass windows covered the ceiling and the wall opposite the entrance. The sun's rays filtered across the classroom, dappling the floor with a full spectrum of colors. In the corners of the room, there were huge flaming torches hanging five meters above the heads of those students on the top row. All around Logan, people filed into the auditorium. Once again, he suddenly felt a hand touch his shoulder and a flash of warm exhilaration shot through his entire being.

"Alright!" She cheered, bouncing up and down with endearing femininity. "We have the same class!"

"*Sweet*," Logan exclaimed with the trill of a young child.

"But there's no way I am going to sit up front," Francesca grabbed his hand and led the way up the stairs to the back of the auditorium. Logan followed, hypnotized by her strong stride. He noticed that she never seemed remotely strained by any movement, as most people did, if only just slightly, when ascending a flight of stairs. In the grace of her gait, Francesca almost seemed to be carried by some unseen energy. She was the perfect combination of strength and grace. Logan found himself staring at the back of her exposed legs, which showed below her tunic. When they were almost at the top level, she stopped and turned. Logan quickly looked up to her eyes. She smiled and made her way into an empty aisle, sliding into the farthest seat to make room for him.

"You sure we aren't going to get a nose bleed up here?" Logan laughed.

"You can go sit in the front like a dork if you must," Francesca frowned playfully.

"I'm not leaving you to be harassed by these fools," Logan gestured to a group of guys ogling Francesca from a few rows down. He did not care that he had spoken loudly enough for them to hear. They made bitter expressions, but said nothing back.

As they waited for class to begin, Logan looked around at some of the students. A man with a tattoo across the back of his bald scalp sat in front of them. The tattoo was black, nondescript, and tribal in design.

As the last stragglers walked into the auditorium and found seats, the doors were pulled shut. At the front of the room, a gray marble platform towered two stories above ground level. On the wall behind it was a projection screen about five meters wide and four meters tall. The final bell tolled at the language school and a commanding figure burst onto the platform at the front through an open doorway high on the wall. The class quieted; only a few whispers could be heard.

A powerfully built German officer stood before them. He strode confidently down the few steps from his door to the platform. He wore a neatly-pressed officer's uniform: black pants and a black, collared shirt with the Iron Cross medal on his left shoulder. A long, silky cape, black with a red and gold tapering Greek key pattern, was draped over his shoulders and hung down to his knees. It was fastened by a thick gold chain hung across his neck and chest. As he moved onto the platform, he removed his robe with dramatic flourish, unhooking one side of the chain and tossing it forcefully to an underclass servant, who smoothed it out and walked out the door, closing it behind him. The man swiped his hand across his forehead, removing the bit of his blonde hair that hung into his face. He stared out at the students with steely blue eyes.

There were hundreds of students of all ages in the auditorium, but there was barely a sound. Logan and Francesca exchanged puzzled glances, and others in the room did so as well, but no one dared speak.

"*Achtung!*" He blared in a powerful voice. All eyes shot forward onto him. The man smiled. "*Gut, sehr gut.* For those of you who do not yet know, *achtung* means attention." He did not use a microphone, for the acoustics dispersed his booming voice clearly throughout the auditorium. He opened the book he was carrying. It was quite large and had a strange spine and cover made of what appeared to be a thin sheet of solid wood, with bark still on the edges. He placed it on the podium with a loud thunk.

"Now," he said sharply, in his upper-German accent, crisp and enunciated, "I am Herr Kraus. I am your teacher, your *Lehrer*. You will not refer to me as Herr Kraus, for you are not worthy of speaking my name! You will refer to me as *Herr Lehrer!* When I say '*hallo klass*,' you say '*Hallo Herr Lehrer!*'"

He paused for a moment, and then boomed out, "*Hallo Klass!*"

Everyone was startled, but quickly responded, "*Hallo Herr Lehrer!*"

"Everyone stand," he commanded tersely, raising his arms in emphasis. Everyone scrambled to their feet. "When I tell you something or call on you, you stand and answer, "*Jawohl Herr Lehrer! Class!*" He prodded.

"*Jawohl Herr Lehrer!*" Some in the class answered right away. The rest followed their lead and responded as commanded. Most got the words slightly wrong and the whole class was out of unison. Kraus shook his head disapprovingly and looked at his book.

"Terrible, terrible," he remarked quietly. He looked up again and quickly surveyed the standing class. "You!" he said, pointing up to the barren corner with Francesca, Logan, and the tattooed man. "You three in the corner!" he shouted. "You get down here and find a seat in the front. I hate people who sit so far back when there's room closer. *Macht schnell!*"

The tattooed man muttered something that sounded like, "You're already killing my ears from here." Kraus exploded.

"*Wechterrr!*" He shouted, rolling the 'r.' Suddenly, guards burst in from doors on either side of the front wall at the ground level, and from both sides of the back wall on the top level. They wore silver uniforms with protective padding, and bright silver and red helmets with facemasks. They each wielded a flat paddle that wobbled slightly as they ran.

"*Halt den Mann!*" Kraus shouted at the top of his lungs, pointing at the tattooed man who was running out into the stairs, searching frantically for an escape route. The man scrambled across the aisle and hurdled over the seats in the middle section. It was a display of incredible athleticism, but the guards were too well trained and skilled, and chased him like lions after an antelope. One of the guards caught up to him and subdued the tattooed man with a swift kick to the gut, sending him into the seats below. Quickly, two guards tackled him and held his arms from behind while he struggled and kicked.

"*Raus mit ihm!*" Kraus exclaimed, and the guards escorted the man out of the auditorium, closing the doors behind them. The crowd could hear him shouting and struggling as he was pushed harshly down the hallway. Kraus looked at Francesca and Logan, standing near the edge of the aisle, unmoved since the commotion began.

"*Bringen sie hier,*" Kraus said, pointing to them. "*Der Jungen und das Mädchen.*" The two guards who were still in the room came at Logan and Francesca from above and below. They grabbed the two youths and pulled them out into the stairway.

"Come with us," one of the guards said.

"What have we done?" Logan asked, acquiescing and walking down the stairs with them, Francesca right behind. The guards brought them to the ground level where Kraus stared down at them from above.

"Next time, when I say *move*, you *run!*" He bellowed at them. "*Jeder zehn schlaege*," he commanded the guards. They turned Francesca and Logan toward the front wall, so their backs were toward the seats.

"Hands against the wall!" The guards commanded. "Feet a meter apart and a half meter away from the wall!"

Francesca and Logan did as they were told. As the guards paddled them, the slaps echoed across the auditorium. The other students shuddered. Francesca let out a gasping sound with each painful hit. Logan's knees felt like they might buckle. Both their cheeks were already red at the first smack.

"Sieben!" Kraus counted aloud. He continued counting, and the guards smacked them again. Logan looked to Francesca as a pillar of strength and took his punishment like a man. She held up, but her legs quivered. Their behinds became ever more numb with each hit, so much so that the tenth strike did not feel as bad as the first. Doing as Kraus commanded, they turned about to face the class, wincing from the burn. The class stared at them, frightened into silence. Kraus gazed back at everyone contentedly.

"Now," he shouted, "you should all know that I could do this to all of you every day for *whatever* reason! It is my prerogative! You should consider yourselves lucky for every day you are not beaten. *Do you hear me?!*"

The class immediately stood, shouting. "*Jawohl Herr Lehrer!*"

He surveyed the room for anyone who exuded the slightest tinge of rebellion. "If I ever get any attitude, you will be whipped senseless! Now," he looked down at Logan and Francesca standing stiffly and lopsided, "I do not expect that you two can sit. So, you will be allowed to stand for this period. Go back up to where you were seated and stand up there so you do not block anyone's view. Go! *Macht schnell!*" He shouted, startling them. Logan and Francesca ran back up to their seats, holding the backs of their tunics as they did to stop the material from chafing their sensitive, reddened skin.

Later that day, as the sun still hung high enough in the air to warm the many naked bodies in and around the organic pool, Alistair and Logan had a beer together at one of the multitude of cabana bars lining the sand. There were no hard liquor drinks, nor was there wine in the underclass bars. Some of the ambrosia drinks had some sort of alcohol in them, but it was difficult to detect what kind. The light green smoothie tasted like tequila and Spirulina, a micro-algae containing mostly vegetable protein and a striking amount of vitamins, minerals, and phytonutrients. This explained why few people awoke feeling nauseous or achy the morning after drinking large quantities of alcoholic ambrosia, even if they also drank beer.

Alistair perched on a stool at the bar sipping his beer, while Logan stood by him, still unable to sit. Logan looked around and laughed at the sight of some of the younger kids having the alcoholic ambrosia.

"They let anyone drink who looks like they're not under twelve," he remarked.

"First rule." said Alistair. "Like I said, try to keep the subjects happy. Now, a lot of people, including plenty of hot-tempered kids like those over there," he said, pointing at a boy and his friends, all in their early teens, "got their asses beaten raw today by those fascists. In fact, that kid looks like he's walking funny. Oh, and he's sitting funny too!" He snickered. "That boy got his ass whooped!"

"I know how he feels," Logan laughed along.

"Now see," Alistair expounded, "the *least* they can do is give them alcohol. You can do a lot of things to people if you also give them the simple pleasures. But, I doubt they'll let those kids drink *too* much."

Right on cue, one of the boys waved at the bartender, trying to get a refill, but the bartender just shook his head no.

"See," Alistair said, "he cut him off. I'm sure he's been told not to let the kids, and people in general, get plastered. Let everyone drink, but don't let anyone get out of hand."

"Hey, you guys!" Francesca greeted. She smiled and slowly lifted her leg, wincing as she sat gently down on the stool next to Logan. He sympathetically made an expression of pain as he watched her sit.

"Bartender!" Logan called out. It was the same underclassman that had ogled Francesca the night before. He looked over, a bit timidly, which was not lost on Logan. "Can we get a green ambrosia for the lady?" Logan asked in a powerful voice. The man nodded and quickly filled a mug for Francesca. He slid it down the countertop to her, careful not to spill any.

"Thank you," she said, stopping it with her hand and taking a long sip.

The three of them took their drinks and walked over to sit on the soft sand. Out of the cacophony of voices, they heard Sasha and Jacques calling to them. They turned to see the two walking toward them along the edge of the water.

"*Bonsoir*," said Jacques with a wave.

"Hey, Papa," Francesca happily replied. "What are you guys up to?"

"We were about to jump in the water," Jacques answered.

"I'll hop in with you," Alistair said as he stood up and started toward the immense natural pool. Jacques looked to his daughter. "Do you want to have a swim race? Come on," he waved her towards him, "like we used to."

Francesca smiled, but shook her head. "I can't, Papa. I'm too tired from all the swimming I did yesterday. Later," she assured him.

"You're such a little baby, Francesca," Sasha laughed while stripping off her clothes and running naked out into the ocean water. Francesca stuck up her middle finger while Sasha's back was turned. Sasha dove into the water, and disappeared for a moment before resurfacing a little further out. Alistair followed, also in his birthday suit. Slightly more reserved in front of his daughter, Jacques waded into the water before taking off his tunic and throwing it on the sand. There were naked men all over the beach, which used to make Logan uncomfortable, but he rarely even noticed anymore. However, the sight of nude females, most of whom were in good shape, was still quite pleasing. But, he now admired them more like a female face, as a thing of beauty and attraction, but not intrinsically sexually arousing. Francesca on the other hand, was a constant source of stimulus, whether she was naked or fully clothed.

She looked contemptuously out at Sasha, who had jumped onto Jacques's back and had him swim her around in the water. Francesca's eyes thinned and her soft beautiful face sharpened with anger as she watched.

"*Puttana!*" She mumbled under her breath. Logan did not know what it meant, but he had a general idea.

Francesca casually took off her shirt and sat confidently with only her bra on. This excited Logan far more than all the fully nude young women around him.

Just as Logan was starting to feel relaxed and the pain in his backside was subsiding, out of the crowd came two shirtless men who looked to be in their late twenties. They both had strapping physiques with some scars from what looked like shrapnel wounds that were now healing on their chests. One of the men walked toward Francesca and kneeled next to her.

"You are the finest thing I've seen here," he remarked with a southern United States drawl. His friend stood beside him, smiling and nodding in agreement.

"Out of all the women here, you are the hottest for sure," he went on, clearly thinking he was quite smooth. "What's your name?"

Francesca glanced sideways at Logan. He seemed to not be paying attention. He was staring off at the water. So, she decided to play along, just to see what Logan would do.

"Francesca," she finally answered in a sensuous manner. The man smiled and repeated her name, looking up at his friend, who just drank his beer and smiled.

"Now, Francesca . . ." the man began to flirt with her unabashedly. He looked at Logan, knowing full well that he was infringing upon something, but he just laughed and kept talking to Francesca.

Logan was trying to keep his cool, but was not doing a very good job. He began stretching and cracking his knuckles in aggravation, casting angry glares at the man and his friend. They smugly grinned back at him.

Suddenly, he lost it and flung himself upon the interloper with tremendous speed and vigor. They fell to the ground grappling violently. The man was bigger and appeared much stronger, but Logan's adrenaline was pumping hard. He wrestled his larger opponent flat on the ground, gaining the top position, and shoved the man's face into the sand. Just as suddenly, Logan jumped off and brushed clean his hands. He stared challengingly at the friend, who just looked away. The humbled intruder got up, sand all over his face and in his mouth. Neither one of the two guys were smiling now.

The three stared at each other, two against one. Logan's pupils were completely dilated, he was breathing heavily, and his nostrils flared. Francesca, still seated, studied his face. She began to worry that he was really going to hurt them now, and there was a darker side of her that wished to see it. Logan had a distinguishable aura that was not visible to the eye, but she sensed it on a deeper level. He exuded an omnipresent power and, right now, it was at its most potent level. Some part of Francesca knew it was wrong to toy with his emotions, and the safety of his opponents, but she found it too enticing to see Logan riled.

The man spit some sand out of his mouth and he and his friend walked away, looking back to make sure Logan wasn't following.

Logan stood there, still trembling slightly with rage. He didn't exactly know what came over him. He had felt possessed, driven by some unseen force to attack the guy. Francesca could barely hide her sheer arousal, as she watched Logan breathing in and out, steam pouring off of his body. She stood up and began massaging his shoulders, fingering her hands through his hair, across his scalp. As she rubbed his arms, she reached around to massage his pectoral muscles, inhaling the scent pouring from his neck. It was impossible for her to contain a slight moan. Logan calmed with her touch and closed his eyes.

236

Both felt no need to discuss what had just happened, for they knew the other's motivations. They had a way of communicating with each other that was deeper than words.

As the sun set, a half moon lit the landscape fairly well, casting a shimmering silver aura on everything. The alcohol and excitement had coupled to make the two feel quite tipsy in the warm, tropical air. He studied the translucent cup in his hand. It was hard and clinked like glass when it knocked on something, but it was as light as plastic.

"I wonder what these cups are made of," Logan thought aloud. "They're practically indestructible from what I've seen. I've even slammed it on a hard post just to test it, but it doesn't break or even bounce back that hard. It's really weird."

"Yeah," Francesca said," I don't know."

Logan shrugged and finished off his drink with a large gulp. They both laid down looking up at the stars, Francesca resting on her side, pressing herself up against Logan, placing a hand gently on his chest. He wrapped his arm around her, allowing her head to relax in the firm nook of his shoulder, as he embraced her tightly.

Logan laughed, as he thought of something funny to him. "So, what kind of name is Geiseric anyway?"

Francesca giggled. "What made you think of that?!"

"I don't know, but I mean *seriously*, who names their kid Geiseric in this day and age. It sounds like a Viking or something."

"Well, it *is* something like that," Francesca explained. "Geiseric's mom supposedly named him after the king of the Vandals, who was around sometime during the time of Attila the Hun and the fall of the Roman Empire."

"What?" Logan said in semi-disbelief. "So, *you're* a historian *too*?"

Francesca cutely flit her eyelashes, tickled by his compliment on her knowledge. "Well," she blushed slightly, "Geiseric being named after the leader of the Vandals was common knowledge. But, I did a little Formula training, like I said. And part of Formula training is being educated on more cranial stuff."

Logan gazed up at the brilliant stars, recalling the past. "My parents seemed to really want to educate us on the island. They made us go to classes, do homework and learn, as if everything was normal. There were a lot of really smart adults there. My friend Adam's dad knew everything about astronomy. We would sit outside and look up at the night sky, like we are now, and he would explain things. Like, he pointed to the orangey-red ones in the sky and told us they were red giants, which happens when the star is almost dead."

"Um hmm," Francesca nodded. She stared at Logan's profile, while he focused on the heavens and spoke.

"I was so fascinated by the birth and death cycle of a star. They fuse hydrogen into helium. They expand until they burn out their hydrogen, becoming red giants. Then, they collapse on themselves again until the pressures and speeds reach a boiling point where helium can fuse into a heavier atom. A star does this over and over again until it creates every element in the periodic table. Stars create the elements necessary for life. So, life is created out of stardust, you know." He flashed a lopsided smile at her.

"Yep," Francesca nodded, and they locked eyes for a moment. Logan's nervousness took over and he looked shyly away from her wonderful face and back up at the stars, which with all their majesty, didn't compare to Francesca. He took a sip of ambrosia.

"It's weird that they didn't teach us much history on the island."

"Well," Francesca lifted her eyebrows and swayed her head side to side a bit as she thought about this, "history is full of war, violence, and oppression. Things that your parents were probably trying to shelter you from."

Logan fell silent for a while, as he mulled this over. He watched Alistair, Jacques and Sasha run up to the towel stand, soaked from head to toe. Each grabbed a fresh towel and dried and covered themselves as they walked over to Logan and Francesca, sitting down next to them.

"Do you want some ambrosia?" Sasha asked Jacques.

"Sure," Alistair replied coyly.

"I wasn't talking to you," Sasha laughed, but as usual, annoyed. "Do you want some?" She asked Jacques again.

"Yes, please," he smiled.

"Come on," Alistair whined, with his British accent coming through more evidently, "you're going up there, already."

"I'm not going to carry three cups, Rod!" She retorted angrily. Then, her eyes opened wide and her lips closed.

"All right then," he nervously laughed it off, "I'll come with you. Do you guys want some?" he asked Logan and Francesca.

"Sure," Logan replied, "thanks."

"No problem," Alistair waved his hand down in a gesture of self-deprecation.

"How 'bout you, Francesca?"

"I'm fine," she said, holding up her still half-full glass of green ambrosia. Alistair and Sasha headed off toward the bar.

"Why'd she call him Rod?" Logan asked.

"It's just a way of making fun of someone," Francesca replied, nonchalantly. She laughed and punched him playfully on the shoulder. "You Rod!"

Logan did not buy it. He knew that they were hiding something. Francesca deftly changed the subject. "So, what were you saying about stars creating life? I didn't quite get the connection."

Logan smiled and subtly laughed at her obvious attempt to deter him from prying any further. However, he didn't really care to dig anymore, for he didn't want to risk ruining the moment with her.

— XII —

THE ANIMALIAN
PROJECTS

The next morning, the message on the television screen announced that there was no school for the day. Logan's parents took advantage of this surprise holiday by going out first thing in the morning to play their favorite sport: tennis.

Logan lounged in bed for a while longer, and finally dragged himself up. He took a quick shower, cleaned up the room, and walked over to visit Francesca. He knocked on the door and waited until, finally, she groggily opened the door.

"Oh," Logan said, feeling a bit uncomfortable now. He did not want to look desperate or clingy. "I'm sorry. I didn't want to wake you."

She opened the door just enough for Logan to see that she was not clothed. It rekindled in his mind what he had seen at the pool. In his mind's eye, he could perfectly see the parts of her hidden behind the door. It was obvious from her expression that she was happily surprised by his presence.

"One second." She smiled and shut the door quietly.

Moment's later, she emerged fully clothed. They walked around the entire, resort-like complex. There were more vendors around than usual, giving out all sorts of different food items. But, what was different was the amount of sweets being offered, from ice cream to churros, which were long, fried pastries with crunchy, ridged exteriors. Logan realized he hadn't seen such unhealthy food since he left California. He was surprised that he hadn't even really missed them. But, the churros looked really tempting and the vendors were everywhere. To Logan and Francesca, it felt like a holiday in an amusement park. Even the beach musicians were playing particularly jovial music. Most of the underclassmen walked outside in the sun, looking carefree and exuberant.

As the sun passed its peak and began its subtle descent towards the western horizon, the young couple sunbathed in the milder, mid-afternoon sun. Alistair, Jacques and Sasha walked by and Jacques spotted his daughter.

Alistair snuck up behind Francesca and startled her by pinching the sides of her waist. He laughed as she playfully rebuked his antics by slapping his shoulder and arm. Just then, a Kolibri guard quickly flew by overhead, with its characteristic hum. Logan watched the strange, hummingbird-like vehicle, which zoomed the pilot around with startling speed, just like the real bird. A realization popped into Logan's mind.

"So, did Geiseric have these machines look like animals because of his ideology?"

Alistair chuckled a bit, lying back in the sand, resting his neck and head in his hands.

"No. That's one of the more bizarre aspects in a war that already unbelievable."

Logan was confused. "So, you mean to tell me, there's no connection between the Isaianic ideology and these animal-like machines."

Jacques chimed in. "Well, Geiseric was more responsive to this new technology than most because of his respect for the animal kingdom. But, this technology was eventually used by both sides because it was the best."

Logan noticed how Jacques never seemed uptight. His voice was smooth and clear and his French accent made it that much more calming.

"Military technology had been heading in that direction long before Geiseric and Isaiism," Jacques expounded. "In fact, Thomas Edison said more than a hundred years ago that an aircraft won't be worth anything until it can move like a hummingbird, up and down, back and forth, in every direction."

Logan had no idea how far back this concept went. "Wow."

Jacques sat down in the soft bed of fine rock grains. "The U.S. Air Force had been toying with the idea of hummingbird-like flying crafts since the 1990s. Of course, it was all on a basic level, just models and theories. They were having an extremely difficult time creating a synthetic muscle." Jacques rubbed his chin in contemplation.

"If you really think about it, it makes perfect sense to design battlemachines after animals. The animal kingdom is in a perpetual state of war and the planet is the battleground. It is like one ongoing, chaotic melee," he spun his hands around each other in a tornado-like motion, "between biological mechanisms, living machines. Animals have been battle-tested and refined by billions of years of evolution. Since the beginning, when all life was single-celled organisms, there were carnivores," he raked his hand through the sand and slowly let it seep through his fingers, as if it were the countless cells he spoke of. "And since the beginning, all creatures have been developing bodies to either destroy, or avoid being destroyed."

Jacques pursed his lips for a moment and stared off at the horizon. "Of course, Geiseric believed this coincidence between his ideology and the Animalian Projects was an all-too-powerful omen."

It was 2026, and Berlin was experiencing the peak of yet another roaring twenties, just as it had a century earlier. Wealth had poured in from Isaianic-sympathizers all over the world, who wished to help Geiseric come to power in Germany. They poured much of their money into German art and science institutions, which while supporting the Principles' love for these endeavors, also served to improve the overall economy and morale of the German people, who then equated their good feelings with the charismatic and world-renowned leader of the Principles Party. Germany was having a renaissance of sorts, centered on Berlin. It all served the Principles' agenda, which was coming to a head. 2026 was an election year, and the new party intended to gain a majority in the German parliament.

Billions of dollars had been donated to key political cities — Munich, Cologne, Dresden, Berlin.

The capitol was the most spoiled — full of new and ancient art. Sculptures lined the streets and boulevards in a borderline gaudy fashion. It was a breeding ground for a very experimental, cultural revival. New-agers, rock stars, rebels, poets, and other artistic types flocked from all over to the world's hippest city. Many were not even Isaianic sympathizers. They were there because it was new and exciting, or because it was scandalous and many drugs were now legalized and offered at the local grocery store. The drugs were government regulated and provided optimum pleasure with as few harmful side effects as possible. They had fewer side effects than cigarettes, alcohol, prescription drugs, or even fast food did at the turn of the century. Not to mention the food and housing was cheap, a legacy of Berlin that actually had its roots in the aftermath of World War I. There had been many reasons for this over the course of the past century, but now, wealthy patrons had purposely built many cheap, but attractive apartment complexes to draw poor artists from all over the world.

Berlin was once more referred to as "New Babylon," or "the Babylon on the Spree," named after the river that flows by the city. The city was alive with sex, music and plenty of dynamism. At night, music pulsed from the newest clubs while droves of young people drank, danced, and got high. A new drink, with a slight green tint, was all the rage.

While the renaissance boomed, the Principles created a variety of think-tanks to best figure out how to strengthen Germany and their grip on it. The federal elections were now only two months away. Had they accomplished the miracle they needed? They waited anxiously to find out if they had persuaded a German majority within only three years of founding the party.

A structure resembling the Parthenon sat regally on the top of an Alpine foothill in southern Bavaria. Large torches lit the extensive staircase that led to the ornate front entrance. Hundreds of men and women of all ages sat on marble benches. Hundreds of others stood as they conversed with each other, sometimes forming circles so a main speaker could be heard by his surrounding group. As they debated, they drank beer from hefty glass mugs and inhaled tobacco or marijuana smoke off long tubes attached to large communal hookah pipes.

Geiseric ambled happily from group to group, taking in the many prominent personalities in the crowd. There was Tara O'Reilly, lead singer of an extremely popular Irish rock band. Reinhardt Gottlieb, Germany's top general, was surrounded by intent listeners as he spoke with his medaled jacket tossed over his shoulder, intermittently smoking a cigar. Manfred Heydrich, one of Germany's top bankers, sat amongst an impressive group of financiers. Phil Mayer, an American comedian and intellect who hosted his own controversial talk show, conversed with Helmut von Ribbentrop, the hot-headed German parliamentarian who waved his hands about as he vehemently argued a theory.

Geiseric brought a beer over to Johann Schroeder, the owner of DDU News, the second most watched news show in Germany, aired on a nationalist, right-wing learning channel. Geiseric chummily hooked his arm around Schroeder's neck and took a chug of the beer in his other hand.

"Johann! *Wie geht's!*" he shouted with drunken friendliness and excitement, asking his friend how it was going.

"*Ja, Es Geht,*" Johann replied in his peculiar Swabian dialect, laughing a bit.

"*Komm herein,*" Geiseric led him over to Helmut and the few dozen Principle Party politicians who had assembled there. They all clapped for their top propagandist.

Helmut held up his beer. **"Zum** *Johann!"*

"*Prost!*" the group cheered, lifting their beers and taking a swig. Parliamentarian Carl Katz walked over to Schroeder.

"You have done much for our cause," Katz's Saxon German was clearly enunciated, though he was well past drunk.

"Thank you," Johann replied, taking an encouraging swig. "Listen, I'll be honest with you. I don't know if I agree with everything your party stands for. But, as long as it involves reinstating Germany as the glorious power it deserves to be, we at the DDU are behind you all the way." He raised his glass of beer. "We are sick and tired of being a donor state to Europe. They all fought to press us into this tiny plot of land. The Germans work to make countries like Poland strong. Poland should not even exist! Gdansk should be Danzig! Let the better people be in charge of the land for God's sake!" Everyone cheered at Schroeder's salute to the homeland.

"And for that matter," Johann yelled over them, "Kaliningrad should be Konigsberg!" Everyone raised his or her glasses again.

"Europe should *finally* be recognized as *Greater Germany!*" Schroeder roared. Geiseric led a rousing toast to that.

"*Prost!*"

Much to Geiseric's delight, Germany's leading scientist, Richard Streicher, showed up. Streicher was slightly shorter than Geiseric, and completely bald. As the most popular and world-renowned scientist since Einstein, Streicher's pale blue eyes and long, curled mustache were familiar to most Germans. He motioned to Geiseric and General Gottlieb for them to come over. They excused themselves from the groups they were speaking with.

Geiseric held out his right hand, palm facing up to Streicher. "Wie gehts!" He smiled drunkenly.

Streicher slapped him five. The Germanian scientist just laughed at his inebriated friend.

"The results from our latest research regarding Vasculosynth are in," Streicher replied.

Geiseric's eyebrows lifted with interest. "Already!" Though drunk, he had no problem understanding Streicher's coarse, southern German verbiage, as Geiseric was a fellow Bavarian. Gottlieb, though, was from Northern Germany, and had to lean over to better hear and understand.

"Now," Streicher said, clearing his throat, "I cannot be completely sure what the Brits, Americans, French, Russians and Japanese are doing in their top secret military labs. But, they are only remotely considering it for future military applications." Streicher paused and thoughtfully stroked his mustache. "I am quite convinced that no one, except us, is making this field a priority. The United States, I believe, is the furthest ahead. However, they are still not committing the necessary resources." He smiled while rubbing his hands together in a somewhat mischievous manner.

"Based on recent intelligence, it appears no country has made any major breakthroughs. As excited as the world was when they first learned of this, no one has devoted the funds and scientific brain power needed for the research and development of synthetic muscle. All of the major governments of the world are controlled by corporate special interests, who don't want to push ahead because there's no immediate profit in accomplishing such a project. They are likely never going to change," he resolved, laughing with joy and relief at their complacency.

"Now, I am confident that I can synthesize a muscle strong enough to make a weapon that I have been envisioning. I was inspired by the U.S.'s inept attempt to create those hummingbird-like flying machines that you told me about," Streicher said, pointing to General Gottlieb, who nodded.

"A hummingbird can flap its wings more than thirty times a second. Its wings are specially articulated so that it can fly rapidly in any given direction, or simply hover," Streicher explained, moving his hands through the air to give a visual accompaniment to his words. Geiseric and Gottlieb both nodded in a way that expressed that they knew how a hummingbird moved. Streicher had a way of over-explaining things sometimes.

"So, it *does* seem wise to start by trying to imitate such a creature. I believe it will completely transform the sky cavalry. Helicopters will prove to be quite inferior to a hummingbird craft." The scientist took a gulp of his beer and looked at Gottlieb.

"You, Reinhardt," Streicher poked the general on the chest, "need to start developing strategies and tactics for what I am sure will be an awesome revolution in warfare. We just need *this* man to be voted in," he remarked, nodding his chin at Geiseric.

"Give me the details," Gottlieb said, smiling and puffing his cigar.

Streicher was about to begin when Geiseric held up his hand to stop him for a moment.

"God . . . I love you Streicher!" He proudly stated, in drunken revelry for one of his most capable people. Gottlieb laughed in his deep tone and smacked his cohorts on their backs.

The miracle happened. The German people had spoken at the ballot box and Geiseric's popularity, coupled with that of his party's generous donations to Germany's infrastructure, led the Principles to a majority in the parliament. Geiseric, as leader of the party, was elected to the office of chancellor of Germany. To avoid suspicion, Geiseric did not immediately begin a military-science build-up. He waited until 2028 before sending a flow of money and other resources into endeavors such as the Vasculosynth program.

The public did not know anything about most of these particular classified projects. They were told only about Streicher's plasma engine and laser drill programs, which were touted as indispensable for space and planetary exploration, especially on Mars. The laser drills, Geiseric told the media, were needed for geological and archaeological purposes, to cut through ground and rock for scientific viewing. Perhaps small fossils of tiny organisms that once lived on Mars, when water covered the surface, would be found. The quest to find possible life on Mars excited people all over the world and no one, except the political and military leaders, saw the inherent danger of Germania's laser drill program.

The laser drill program was made public only because it was already suspected by media investigators that Germania was pursuing this field. The German scientists had, after all, taken all the research and designs concerning this field from ESTEC, the technology arm of the European Space Agency.

However, the Vasculosynth and related projects were kept under wraps. More than nine hundred scientists were working on this research at a military base in northern Germany, near *Peenemünde*, where Werner Von Braun created the world's first rocket during World War II. The scientists working in this historic place were forced to live at the laboratory base and had to cut off all connections with the outside world until the project was finished. Their immediate families could live on the base with them, but were not privy to most of what their spouses or parents did in the labs. Housing, food, the children's education, and medical care were all provided for on the huge top secret base, so there was no reason for anyone to leave. They were compensated for their mild sense of confinement with salaries that were three times the average for their professions, while also having free room and board and a myriad of other benefits.

In 2030, nineteen months after they began, Germania's star scientist and his brilliant team perfected their breakthrough technology. They created the first heavy-duty synthetic muscle that could be easily mass-produced.

The Principles were re-elected in a landslide victory, keeping Geiseric in the chancellor's seat. They immediately pushed through legislation to fund a top secret Biomimicry Program. The bill described the program as the creation of technology for civilian transportation, such as rescue crafts and more efficient forms of shipping and so on. It was a façade used to cajole the minority opposition in Parliament, and prevent them from igniting public opinion. Almost twenty percent of Germania's annual budget was allocated to this one program, matching the financial resources that the United States had committed for its entire military over the same period.

A single facility was constructed for the project, on the western edge of the Bohemian Forest near the small German town of Weiden in der OberPfalz. In order to maintain the necessary secrecy, ninety percent of the facility was built underground. The most top secret areas of the facility were built as far as twelve hundred meters deep. Enormous tunnels, sixty meters wide and tall, and several kilometers long, were constructed for a gigantic factory-line production operation. Immense, subterranean tanks were bored out of the rock and filled with hundreds of millions of cubic meters of water, so that the newly designed aquatic crafts could be tested. Massive caverns were carved out to test the flying machines. There were long, flat rooms to test ground force technology.

Nearly a quarter of the entire facility was devoted to producing the key materials needed for the projects. Large, underground factories constantly pumped out the synthetic muscle and metal alloys that would power and create the cutting edge military machines. The metallurgy factory took up the most space and required thousands of workers.

A substantial amount of time and resources was used in the creation of revolutionary new alloys. Germanian facility staff experimented with every kind of specialized blending: metal with metal, metal with ceramic, metal and almost anything else. The new alloys were lighter, or stronger, or both, and had greater elasticity, which allowed them to return to form after being forcefully misshapen. There were an endless amount of possible atomic combinations, resulting in vastly different structural properties and outcomes. Then, the Germanian scientists gained an edge in metallurgy when the Japanese government began supplying research and technology to them, under the utmost of secrecy of course. The information included major advances made by the Toyota Central Research and Development Laboratories, which were granted government funding at the behest of the Japanese prime minister.

Prime Minister Hidekio Honomura was what was called a "closet Principle," for he secretly held sympathies for the Principles Party and the Isaianic movement. Hidekio was not alone. Numerous closet Principles held top positions in the Japanese political, intelligence and military communities, and other elite circles. Although it had cost Japanese taxpayers and Toyota billions of dollars to gain an edge in metallurgy, the closet Principles worked together to funnel most of the research and technology to Germania. The Japanese had been leaders in this area for thirty years, a legacy of research scientist Takashi Saito and his colleagues at the Toyota labs. They had shattered the glass ceiling on metal-alloy development limitations in 2003.

The Saito group jettisoned the traditional "trial and error" approach, or "discovery by accident," which had been employed since the Bronze Age when humans first began creating alloys by mixing copper and tin. With the ancient methods, the process of alloying more than three elements became extremely complicated and difficult to track. Precise calculations as to what elements to add and take out were necessary, and minute miscalculations could be costly. Instead, Saito turned to pure science, using quantum mechanics and high-powered supercomputers.

Since the program began, Japanese researchers worked to bring alloys up to what were thought to be "magic numbers" in terms of elemental properties. At first, the Saito research team worked with the supercomputers to develop an ultra-strong, titanium-based alloy. They had similarly phenomenal results with iron, aluminum, and other key metals as bases. As time went on, the new methods allowed for the scientists to punch the numbers into the computer programs and output an alloy with the exact properties and results they required. The process was far from instant, but a seemingly unbreakable boundary had indeed been broken.

In the underground facility, every state-of-the-art piece of machinery and equipment was being used. There were six, gigantic plasma furnaces, powered by helium and argon and able to generate temperatures higher than 10,000 degrees Celsius, which could melt any metal and just about anything else. More and more amazing new mixtures of metal were pumped en masse out of the Weiden facility's metallurgy lab and incorporated into the many new technology projects.

There were a number of other incredible materials coming out of the industrial-manufacturing area, most prominently the carbon nanotubes, which were hollow, cigar-shaped molecules, only nanometers thick (or a billionth of a meter), with wall atoms connected in a hexagonal, mesh wire. Japan had also been a leader in the area of carbon nanotubes since the turn of the century, and Prime Minister Honomura happily provided Germania with information on Japanese advances in this field.

Regular carbon fibers had long been used to create hard composites that were lightweight and durable, such as golf clubs, tennis rackets, and other everyday consumer products. Diamonds, the hardest substance on Earth, consisted of carbon. This basic element was alloyed with iron to create steel. Carbon was an extremely hard substance and carbon nanotube fibers, many times stronger than conventional carbon fibers, could be bonded with epoxy and then heated to create lightweight materials with unprecedented strength and hardness. Carbon nanotubes could also create fibers up to one hundred times the tensile strength of steel, for their weight. Tensile strength referred to the strength that a rope or wire had when pulled.

The enormity of the Weiden facility was also necessary to house the tens of thousands of engineers, scientists, and the manufacturing labor force. Since the work force was so large, and the overall program so lengthy, they could not be quarantined from society. However, only Geiseric and the top military man in the country, General Gottlieb, understood the big picture. Not even Streicher knew about every aspect of what was going on at the facility. The managing scientists and engineers below them only knew about their particular projects, and those farther down the ladder still believed their work was to aid advances in civilian rescue craft and transportation.

After two years of dedicated work, the Biomimicry Program and in particular the hummingbird craft designs were well ahead of schedule. Numerous prototypes had already been initiated. The designation for all of the hummingbird vehicles was *Kolibri* — which was the German name for the bird. Gottlieb, working with the top *Luftwaffe* commanders, supervised the creation of many large Kolibri crafts, which would take the place of helicopters in almost every way. One was ten meters long, egg-shaped, and had four hummingbird-like wings, one pair on each side, that moved at invisible speed just like the wings of the real bird. The Kolibri vehicle could move swiftly with an instant acceleration in any direction that a helicopter could never achieve.

On the side, Gottlieb also worked on a project with Captain Jan Von Edeco, the rabidly Isaianic German fighter pilot who became a hero when his Raven stealth jet was shot down over Eastern Thrace in the Greco-Turkish War. He had ejected out of his exploding jet and landed behind enemy lines. Because he attended the Berlin Formula Institution before joining the air force, he had studied many kinds of martial arts that were not yet part of the Germanian Air Force training.

So, when a squad of six heavily armed Turkish soldiers confronted him on the ground, Von Edeco amazingly killed or incapacitated all of them without sustaining a single injury. With almost super-human movements, he dodged those firing at him, moving out of the way right before his enemies pulled their triggers. He grabbed one of the bewildered soldiers from behind and, using him as a shield, Von Edeco shot five quick, well-aimed bursts from his attacker's gun, taking out the others. Then, to top it off, the Germanian fighter pilot saved two Greek commandos who had been captured by the Turks.

Formerly, just the Special Forces commandos had been trained to fight like Von Edeco. But, after word spread about his amazing feats, officers in all branches of the Germanian military were required to go through Elite Formula Training. It was the longest and most intensive regimen, also called the apprenticeship program, and relied on substantial interaction between the trainees and their elite instructors, called sensei.

Captain Von Edeco's diverse training and natural fighting ability made him well-suited to help in the brainstorming phase of what General Gottlieb called the "Kolibri Sky Infantry Project." Gottlieb had a broad idea for a "soldier with wings," and only a vague notion of how this airborne infantry flyer would stay aloft.

It was Von Edeco who came up with the Kolibri chariot. The chariot was akin to the body of a real hummingbird in shape. Its armored exterior was called the encasement and it encased the soft, inner synthetic muscle. The chariot was only a bit thicker than the shoulder's of the person riding in and piloting the machine, who was called the flyer. With his legs planted within the chariot, the flyer's upper body from the waist up was free to move about. The vehicle then tapered from halfway down to the bottom, leaving room for the wings to flap. A prototype was developed, but when the flyer stood inside the chariot, the apparatus became unstable due to the low placement of the wings. On the next prototype, the inventive duo had tungsten counterweights installed at the bottom of the chariot to maintain the center of gravity on the wings' axis.

Von Edeco shared Gottlieb's fervor for the sky infantry, because of its interesting blend of modern technology and ancient design. However, the few top *Luftwaffe* commanders that knew about the sky infantry project thought it was silly, inefficient, and a waste of resources. Nevertheless, they did not seek to end this pet project of Germania's top military commander, as he was one of Geiseric's closest friends.

So, like two extreme auto enthusiasts, Von Edeco and Gottlieb spent all of their free time with engineers, helping to find the perfect materials and cutting-edge weaponry. The two also shared a passion for Medieval and Classical armor. To them, it represented everything grand about the Utopian existence, particularly the Medieval Era, the age of valor, when those brought up on the aristocratic theories of Classical Greece dominated Europe on horseback.

Gottlieb and Von Edeco both had nationalistic reasons for their obsession with the knight. The ascension of the Western knight came during a time when Western Europe faced a number of threats. Viking raiders traveled down the Rhine on their amazingly swift boats, launching lightning assaults on German towns and looting everything within. To the east, yet another terrible threat roared off the Asian steppe, just as the Huns had done before and the Mongols were to do later. On the cusp of the second millennium, the threat was the Magyars. On the tenth of August, 955 AD, German forces led by Otto the Great faced off against a Magyar threat five times their size.

Coming five hundred years after Attila and the Huns brought about the collapse of the Roman Empire, the next breed of steppe riders swept in with shocking speed atop their small, fast horses. The Magyars, like all the hunters of the north Eurasian plains, were great horsemen and amazing archers who could annihilate infantry or light cavalry with a torrent of arrows. Such was usually the fate of all who dared oppose the horsemen.

However, Otto and his Germanic forces had brought with them a weapon new to this region: heavily armored men atop large, strong horses. This was where the European heavy cavalry first became the crux of the battle and, though they were outnumbered five to one, they shattered the Magyar forces. The once powerful marauders were never again a threat to Europe, and they lived on peacefully near Germany in the Carpathian Basin, to become the Hungarians.

On the battlefield, the German knights raised Otto on their shields and proclaimed him their Emperor. Thus, Otto became the first German ruler of the area once known as Eastern France. The Bavarians, Saxons, Swabians, and a number of other German tribes had been conquered by the Frankish kings, such as Charlemagne, over a hundred years earlier. Now, the newly re-empowered tribes declared their independence. It was the birth of Germany. It was the ascendance of the knight.

General Gottlieb and Captain Von Edeco knew that their sky infantry-men were going to need body protection, primarily from the waist up, since their lower torsos and legs were concealed in the Kolibri chariot. So, the two designers went to work on creating an astonishing array of armor prototypes. They enlisted the help of a few men and women who were descendents of the great Medieval armor-makers of southern Germany and had continued in the trade of their ancestors. The modern craftsmen had been relegated to designing armor strictly for display in the homes of the wealthy. Now, they had the chance to use their trade in a way that might be purposeful and vital to Germania's military success in the modern world. Each one of them was honored and thrilled.

Captain Von Edeco nicknamed them team Suessenhoeffer, after the German master craftsman who created the armor for Emperor Maximillian and other European royalty, such as Henry VIII. Team Suessenhoeffer began designing the modern knight armor like it was their life's mission, which most of them believed it was.

The weight of the armor would not be an issue. The sky infantry could bear a much heavier load than any of their predecessors for two reasons: they were being carried by Kolibri chariots, which were far stronger than horses, and synthetic muscle was used inside the suits, which enhanced the wearer's strength ten-fold.

Team Suessenhoeffer, Gottlieb and Von Edeco concentrated on designing a modern equivalent to the fifteenth and sixteenth century full, steel plate, body armor. This design originated when Suessenhoeffer was at the zenith of his craft, and before the matchlock gun put an end to armor's use on the battlefield.

With all the advances in the metallurgy lab, the team had many elaborate materials to choose from, but since weight was not a concern, a steel-based alloy was chosen as the main material, for it would still be the most effec-tive. Other materials were incredibly strong for their light weight, but steel was incredibly dense and heavy and so was still the strongest material, per volume.

Steel was a simple iron and carbon alloy, and was the strongest thing known to man for the past twenty-five hundred years, from the time when the Celts discovered it. Since then, it had been used as the fundamental armor for heavy cavalry from the knight to the tank. Now, at the Weiden facility, steel alloys had been brought to near ideal strengths, two or three times as strong as could ever be made before. Because of their lack of microscopic defects, the advanced alloys were incredibly hard, yet if enough force was applied, they would bend or stretch instead of breaking or shattering.

Gottlieb and Von Edeco each wanted to have their own specially designed armor. Von Edeco was working with some engineers to create a smaller Kolibri chariot with increased agility and speed. He had to sacrifice weight for that; yet his armor was still quite formidable. The cuirass, the armor that protected his torso, was made of advanced steel-alloy chest and abdomen plates, nine centimeters thick. To make the plates even harder, Von Edeco ordered his crew to perfect an advanced titanium-carbide alloy casing. The torso armor had pectoral muscles molded into it in the style of *all'antica,* which imitated the armor used by the warriors of ancient Greece and Rome. The shoulder pieces, full arm guards, gauntlets, neck guard, helmet and face mask were made of the identical materials as the cuirass.

It was not enough. Von Edeco wanted to ensure that his flyers would be unstoppable against small arms fire. So, Von Edeco commissioned a protective vest made out of carbon nanotube fibers to lie underneath the hard armor, instead of the Kevlar traditionally used. Bulletproof vests were designed to catch a round and displace its kinetic energy over a larger area, unlike hard armor, which was intended to stop the round. Due to the tensile strength of carbon nanotube fibers, this flak vest was fifty times stronger than those being used by most militaries, at half the weight. Any small arms rounds that made it through the exterior steel armor would be slowed down and caught by the interior carbon fiber vest.

But, Von Edeco was still not satisfied.

He ordered that a small layer of extremely hard, carbon nanotube fiber composite, with aerogel sandwiched in between, be placed on the exterior of the metal armor to help stop uranium-tipped bullets as large as fifty-caliber. Since uranium was pyrophoric, it became hot upon hitting most armor, causing the tip to partially liquefy and shave off like the sharpening of a pencil, keeping it pointed as it penetrated through. The carbon fiber composite and aerogel were both extremely resistant to heat. So now, the uranium would first strike this outer layer, causing it to slow before hitting the steel armor.

There would be less speed and friction when the bullet struck the metal and, therefore, it would not become sharpened and would hopefully not completely pierce the armor.

Only uranium-tipped bullets *larger* than fifty caliber, or other more powerful weapons, could do consistent damage to the armor. The wearer of the armor would be invulnerable to almost all small arms fire. Von Edeco was quite pleased.

As formidable as Von Edeco's machine and armor were, General Gottlieb had even grander ideas. He put his engineers in charge of creating a larger, much more powerful Kolibri chariot for himself, built for a much hardier defense. His armor resembled that of the Medieval German knight, emphasizing symmetry and vertical lines. He smiled enthusiastically as he tried on the prototype, like a child who had been handed the long-awaited Christmas present. A pronounced ridge ran down the center of the front torso armor, with reinforcing lines fanning out in either direction. At its thickest points, it was fifteen centimeters of advanced steel alloy with titanium-carbide casing.

Underneath, he wore a bulletproof vest made of forty layers of carbon nanotube fiber, as opposed to Edeco's thinner twenty-five. Gottlieb's exterior and interior armor would be able to stop some of the larger ammunition shot from the world's most powerful anti-aircraft guns. There was only one accessory missing. Gottlieb commissioned the design of a mighty shield that could stop a barrage of large, explosive shells. The shield was made of steel and ceramic-boride alloy and stood a meter and a half tall, a meter wide and weighed nearly one hundred kilos. The shield and armor together could stop almost anything. Three straps on the back would go around the fore and upper arm, so that the shield could be braced against the shoulder. Gottlieb's armor had to have ultra-strong Vasculosynth in it, to help the flyer inside lift the incredibly heavy armor and shield, which put together weighed about a metric ton. The synthetic muscle, particularly in the arms and shoulders, would also act as shock absorbers to withstand the impact of artillery shells upon the shield. He was extraordinarily pleased with the revision to his prototype, and congratulated himself with a shot of schnapps.

As General Gottlieb and Captain Von Edeco celebrated their accomplishments, they had no idea they had just created what would become one of the most vital weapons of the next World War.

As the final designs came fresh off the molding block, the two men set forth to prove that their revolutionary weapons were viable. First, they had to find a method for operating the vehicle. The Kolibri chariot could not be flown using conventional methods, such as a steering wheel or stick. If the Kolibri flyer's hands were occupied while maneuvering himself around, he could not fight. Plus, the incredible speeds and mobility that the chariot was capable of would be near impossible to guide by hand. They needed a technology that would allow the flyer's mind to interact directly with the vehicle. Fortunately, this technology was not only on the horizon, but sailing into grasp.

Rapid advances were being made in the field of Cybernetics, the study of the communication and regulatory feedback between living beings and machines. Cybernetics passed a groundbreaking milestone in 2004, the year many scientists described as "the year of the cyborg." For the first time, medical breakthroughs had allowed a person to interact with electronic equipment using just his brain. It began in the United States with a Bostonian man who had been rendered completely paralyzed by a knife attack. Medical scientists performed an experiment on him, probing into his brain with wires that could read neurochemical messages. The messages were then sent to a computer, which deciphered them and reacted accordingly. In the first experiment, the paralyzed man was connected to a simple video game. He was not only able to play the game by controlling it directly with his mind, but he was incredibly responsive to the technology, able to do increasingly difficult tasks at a rapid pace far beyond the medical community's expectations. In the thirty years since then, the research had progressed greatly, mainly in its military applications.

When Geiseric came to power, the technology was still far from the eventual dream of allowing a person to maneuver the agile Kolibri chariot with just their minds. But, the Principles were not ones to ignore fantastic scientific possibilities. Developing the still rudimentary Cybernetics program in Germany, and later Germania, was at the top of Geiseric's list and was yet another field of science that received extensive funding. Hundreds of scientists and engineers worked only on this particular field in the underground facility.

Gottlieb and Von Edeco diverted just a few of the creative staff from other mental interface projects, to create a sound method for the Kolibri chariot to be manipulated by the flyer. The general and captain were adamant that the interface technology would not involve deep connections into the brain. They did not want the soldiers to protest using the new technology. So, the scientific team came up with a helmet that could read the electrochemical messages firing inside a person's brain without actually inserting a connection through the cranium. The helmet, placed snugly onto a person's head, could monitor

the brain's impulses through the skull bone. However, the person using the helmet had to maintain a higher state of focus and clarity, a meditative calm, so that the technology could distinguish his mental directions.

This was not hard for Von Edeco, who in his passion for the martial arts and Isaiism had been well-acquainted with the culture of meditation. He immediately took to his specially designed machine like a fish to water — or perhaps, more precisely, like a bird to air.

For his weaponry, he commissioned two special handguns that were more akin to shotguns, with their barrels measuring almost as long as his arm from the shoulder to his fingertips. They weighed in at twenty kilograms each. To make sure they were the toughest handguns ever made, Von Edeco wanted the ammunition to be able to pierce his own armor. He ordered up special rounds called penetrators, designed to puncture through tanks. Penetrators were not bullets. Rather, they were pencil-sized rods with sharpened tips. They were made entirely out of an extremely dense element, such as tungsten or uranium, giving them incredible weight and, thus, when fired at high velocity, a tremendous amount of kinetic energy to pierce through armor. And so, the penetrators were classified as kinetic energy rounds. They had been widely used by the United States since the 1980s and were far more effective at destroying heavy armor than almost all explosive shells.

Uranium or tungsten penetrators were both highly effective on the armor Von Edeco had designed. Although uranium was the better choice, for it had greater pyrophoric capabilities, Von Edeco used tungsten. Tungsten was not radioactive and, therefore, not environmentally destructive. While Geiseric had previously allowed uranium tips to be used for small Special Forces operations, he would not permit his military to become uranium-based as the United States military was. All weaponry now had very specific environmental parameters, set by the Germanian government.

The cartridges housed powerful explosives that fired the penetrators at over one-thousand meters per second. As he tested the guns wearing his armor, Von Edeco realized how well the strength enhancing Vasculosynth not only allowed him to hold the guns, but to withstand the incredibly powerful kickback generated with each blast.

The captain decided to try out his new craft and weapons in one of the underground facility's "demolition zones," where prototype ammunitions and weapons were tested. Von Edeco flew his amazing winged chariot around the wide, long area, zooming by numerous practice targets, including old tanks and boats. He zipped about with unprecedented dexterity, able to accelerate from zero to one hundred kilometers per hour within a quarter-second. The top speed for the Kolibri chariot was seven hundred km/h, and Von Edeco did not hesitate to accelerate to full capacity. He flew rapidly from end to end of the underground demolition zone, firing his two huge handcannons, which each carried two large rounds and sixteen smaller caliber bullets. He could switch the gun modes from larger to smaller caliber by using his mental interface technology. Connections running from his brain to his gloves to the handles of the guns allowed him to accomplish this. To reload, he holstered his weapons in two compartments in the chariot on either side of him. A robotic mechanism inside the chariot instantaneously replaced all the ammunition, so that he could immediately draw again.

He sped about in the air, firing with amazing accuracy at the stationary targets. The captain was flawlessly ambidextrous, able to shoot with equal skill and precision with both his right and left hands, simultaneously. Von Edeco reveled in his new toys.

Gottlieb did not adjust to the mental interface technology as quickly. He was older and had received less Formula training than Von Edeco. The general first had to learn simply how to fly his Kolibri chariot with his mind. As he practiced, he stiffened like a zombie, his face and entire body tensing up as he focused all his mental energy on flying the machine. He could hardly speak or move his body, or it would break his concentration and the chariot would fall clumsily back to the ground.

But, he kept at it and, to the amazement of everyone on the project, Gottlieb's persistence paid off. He was soon flying it as easily as riding a bike. Pleased with his abilities, he joked to the team, "Not bad for an old guy." Now he was ready to move on to his weaponry, which he like Von Edeco was also going to specially design.

General Gottlieb envisioned having a multitude of different gunnery choices available to his heavy sky infantryman. Like the heavy infantry or heavy cavalry on the ground, the heavy sky infantry was given its title based on their heavier armament. The first gun that Gottlieb commissioned was a fully automatic, tungsten-penetrator machine-gun, which fired the same kinetic energy rounds as Von Edeco had chosen to use. However, the general had one thousand rounds at his unhalted disposal. It was a Gatling gun, which rotated six long barrels, spinning the barrels as the gun fired to keep them from melting under the intense heat generated by the rounds firing out. The large machine gun weighed in at nearly a hundred and fifty kilos, but with Gottlieb's strength enhancing Vasculosynth armor, it was easily whipped around and fired. The idea was for the heavy sky infantrymen to hold the large gun in both hands, standing somewhat oblique to the direction of flight. Also, in this position, the shield that was strapped around the shoulder and arm at the fore would provide cover to the heavy sky infantrymen. The cartridges were stored in the chariot and a long chain of rounds ran from the holding box within the chariot to the gun.

The tungsten penetrators, although plenty powerful enough to take down Von Edeco's lighter armor, were not good enough to penetrate Gottlieb's armor. The only penetrators that would be effective against a heavy sky infantryman would be those made out of uranium. Though Gottlieb had a special exterior designed to squelch the ability for uranium to ignite and sharpen, this was only applicable to smaller rounds. Size did matter when it came to projectiles, along with speed. In terms of devastating capability, no bullet could match the penetrators, and neither could most explosive artillery shells. But, depleted uranium penetrators were not a choice at his disposal. Lacking pyrophorism, tungsten became misshapen and the tip blunted like a mushroom, making it less effective.

The second weapon Gottlieb commissioned was a handheld plasma cannon. There were hundreds of physicists within the Weiden complex working on many different projects involving the plasma state of matter. As more and more heat was applied to a substance, it changed from solid, to liquid, to gas, and finally to plasma, which was an energetic fluid made of ions and free-wheeling electrons.

Plasma was being integrated into a number of special projects. For instance, work had begun on a super-fast jet that used magneto-hydrodynamics, the most cutting edge science in propulsion technology. And this was different than the plasma engine project, where scientists were designing a rocket to propel humans efficiently through space. Plasma could also be used as a weapon, and there were a number of projects in the works to create plasma cannons.

All the cannons used a similar process of magnetically binding the plasma so that it could be shot out in a focused stream, which at ten thousand degrees Celsius would melt through almost anything. The largest cannons were ten meters long and could fire a stream that kept its integrity for hundreds of meters, before dissipating into the air

But, the general envisioned a plasma cannon that was small enough to be held by a Kolibri flyer. The cannon would serve the function that flame-throwers once did, by blanketing the enemy in a searing hot substance. Gottlieb immediately diverted a significant portion of the staff working on other plasma cannons to work on his idea. The engineers manipulated the ammunitions box within the Kolibri chariot so that it could rapidly convert to store the plasma generator. A thick tube attached from the generator to Gottlieb's hand-held, plasma gun, weighing nearly a hundred kilos due to the heavy magnets that funneled the plasma into a stream. Like most flame-throwers, the stream lasted only fifty meters before fully dissipating. It would nonetheless be effective at annihilating enemy ground troops and opponent sky infantrymen.

To make what General Gottlieb conceived as the ultimate weapon for his heavy sky infantryman, he went to the laser development laboratories, where more scientists and engineers were working than in any other single part of the underground complex. Some of the most powerful weapons in the world were being developed there, including the laser drills.

Like the plasma cannon projects, the majority of time and resources for the laser drill projects was spent creating the immensely large capital guns that would, most likely, one day be mounted on large naval craft. A distant second in importance were the smaller guns, possibly to be loaded on the heavy cavalry machines. Almost no resources were approved by the government to develop smaller guns for use by the "bizarre" Kolibri flyers, which is what most of the government officials thought of the sky infantry project, even Geiseric, the self-proclaimed iconoclast.

But, the general was beginning to realize the potential of the Kolibri vehicles and predicted that they would be central to the Apex strategy in the inevitable conflict to come. His next assessment was that the greatest enemy to his heavy sky infantrymen would be other heavy sky infantrymen. If Apex enemies recovered a fallen Kolibri heavy during battle, they could mimic its design. Such was the way war often played out. A savvy general prepared for the enemy's counter-strike with a counter-strike of his own.

So, Gottlieb *needed* a weapon that could quickly take down a heavy sky infantryman wearing the same armor he had designed, and the laser drills certainly had this type of firepower. The laser drill had one major drawback, however. Because the solid-state laser was so hot and energetic, the gun barrel and generator would quickly overheat. A cooling process needed to be engaged after every shot, which would take a second or two. The ability to fire once every second seemed efficient, until one went up against Gottlieb's penetrator machine gun, which fired nearly one hundred rounds a second. However, the general insisted that the drill bolt gun be created and set broad design specifications that the weapon must weigh around one hundred kilos, had to be easy to wield about, and had to be able to fire a laser that was effective at one hundred meters.

Meanwhile, he and Von Edeco used the weapons they already had to show the Germanian military and political elite just how devastating their fanciful new vehicles could be. They demonstrated the unparalleled speed and agility of the Kolibri chariots. Because both vehicles were relatively small compared to the helicopter-sized hummingbird machines that were being created, the chariots could move faster than anything else the audience had seen. Von Edeco, in his typical daring fashion, demanded that one of his subordinate officers in the room fire on him with the assault rifle he was carrying. He ordered the officer to use up his clip.

The officer was tentative, but Edeco assured him that the bullets would not pierce his armor; he just wanted to make a point. The officer nodded, swallowed hard, and did as the captain commanded. Von Edeco dodged backwards, forwards, up, down and every which way. Whether the officer used aimed bursts, or relentlessly sprayed bullets, he could not hit Von Edeco. He tried his best to strike the captain's armor with just one round, but was only frustrated. When the clip ran out, there was silence as the audience sat momentarily awestruck, followed by a tremendous roar of approval.

Naturally, Geiseric was there and, upon seeing this fantastic new creation, he felt chills run up his spine. He now realized the strategic importance of this modern charioteer. The chancellor could not contain his excitement and smiled widely from ear to ear.

Von Edeco took off his armor and dismounted from the chariot to greet his leader. The captain, like many Isaianic and Principles officers, gave his leader, his *Führer,* the hand salute from his heart forward saying *"Sieg Heil!"* Although this salute was adopted by the Nazis, it actually went back to the days of the Romans. The cheer, however, was made up by the Nazis and broadly meant "Hail Victory!"

Geiseric and his most extreme followers loved this form of saluting, for it had a dramatic power that all others lacked. The Principles were not uneasy about Germany's history and they executed their salute just as swiftly and mechanistically as the Nazis had, and the Romans before them. But, unlike Hitler, Geiseric saluted back to his subordinates in a manner that made him their equal, repeating *"Sieg Heil!"*

Gottlieb slapped Geiseric on the back and started right into his explanation of the sky infantry's potential.

"I see the Kolibri chariot as being the pivotal war machine in the next stage of Blitzkrieg. One of the most important aspects of Blitzkrieg, as you know, is near-to-ground support. To serve this function, in my opinion," he said, jerking his thumb to point towards the craft, "our sky infantry is as good as it gets. Helicopters are simply not agile enough and jets fly over too quickly. The Kolibri chariot can easily dodge shoulder-launched missiles, which as I am sure you know are the bane of helicopters, tanks, and slow jets. There is *nothing* that moves like this."

The general pulled out three cigars and handed one to Geiseric and Von Edeco. He took from his breast pocket a German military issued lighter that had been given to him by his great grandfather, an officer in the First World War.

"Believe me," he smiled with satisfaction, taking a puff to light the cigar, "this will be the fundamental revolution. Out of all the Animalian designs, this one will change the way we approach warfare the most."

Geiseric nodded as he savored the aroma of the expensive cigar he had been given. "This, I can tell, is going to be that real edge we were looking for. With these vehicles, our Formula-trained fighters can fully utilize their capabilities. They will be unstoppable. In this war," he pointed to Gottlieb, holding the smoking implement between his thumb and forefinger, "we Germans will be fighting for the right cause and, mark my words," he took a puff and paused, "the third time will be the charm."

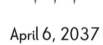

April 6, 2037

The leaders of the "Big 6" Allied nations arrived in New England for a meeting in a top-secret bunker in the White Mountains. They touched down in state-of-the-art, fully decked-out jumbo jets at a military airport hidden in the nearby New Hampshire foothills. The airport runway was protected by a steel fence ten meters high and camouflaged by the dense trees and bushes of the surrounding forest. Encircling the airport were elite groups of American soldiers, who had fanned out establishing a perimeter.

On the runway, many heavily-armored, black Cadillac limousines idled, in wait of the arriving leaders. British Prime Minister Charles Dandau was the first to touch down. He arrived with a large entourage, including much of his cabinet, advisors and military officials, including his top general, Rodney

Ackleworth. Dandau wore a black, pin-striped suit tailored to his tall, wiry body. His gray hair was cut short and combed down the middle. He stood in the jet doorway, smoking a cigar and smiling, looking out onto the beautifully bright, clear day. With his bodyguards both leading and trailing him, he strode down the staircase to the runway.

President Hollier waited on the runway, standing in an elegant, dark blue suit, laughing and joking with General Brian Tierney. Dandau walked confidently toward his friend and ally. They met each other half way and shook hands strongly, giving each other a quick hug with their left arms. Hollier placed his hand on Dandau's shoulder and guided him to one of the limousines. They stepped inside with their generals, and the remainder of Dandau's entourage piled into two other armored vehicles. The three limousines drove off into a thick-walled tunnel rising out of the ground that gently sloped down into the Earth.

Dandau and Hollier sat next to each other on the spacious, black leather bench seat in the back of the limousine. They chatted casually with Tierney and Ackleworth, who sat in the longer seat to their left. Sitting opposite of Hollier and Dandau with his back facing the direction of travel, was Germania's top scientist, Richard Streicher, twisting his dirty-blonde mustache with his right thumb and forefinger, glaring at the British prime minister.

2037 was a tumultuous year for Geiseric. He had many blessings come his way, but equally as many crises. Richard Streicher, the world-renowned German scientist, fled his homeland and the Principles Party that year. He secreted away to the United States and immediately began to expose his former leader and friend's agenda to the world.

At one point in time, decades ago, Richard Streicher was a peace activist. In his twenties, he was the ultimate liberal, "hippy," anti-war activist. During this time, he took up many platforms to be active for and against, including environmentalism and animal rights. These beliefs eventually pushed to the forefront of his mind, as he came to acknowledge the concepts espoused by many scientists whom he idolized, from Pythagoras to Einstein — "Until mankind widens their circle of compassion to embrace all living beings, we shall never find peace."

During this time, the Advocates for Consumer Freedom began their campaign to wipe out the environmental and animal rights activist organizations of the world. When they succeeded in the United States and Britain, Streicher was consumed with fear that the ACF may do so in Germany. He declared himself to be with the growing mass of radicals calling their belief system

Isaiism, which was centralized around the charismatic and brilliant young dynamo whom everyone knew simply as Geiseric.

Streicher had become a celebrity in his own right, having won a Nobel Prize for his research to synthesize organs and other biological systems, both for surgical implantation into a human and for experimentation, to replace the use of animals. Though it was effective, much of his research was banned in the United States and Britain by corporate advocates with vested interests in maintaining the status quo, which only further fueled Streicher's push towards radicalism.

Geiseric quickly recognized Streicher as his single most important ally at the time, and the scientist became the cultural icon's right hand man. Streicher brought much credibility to the movement, as he was well-respected by much of the world. With Streicher, far more of the intellectual elite came into Isaiism's fold. Soon, they founded the Principles party, based on Isaiism but interlaced with an extremist-twinge of superiority, underpinned by their conviction that true intellectualism led to morality.

Streicher reached the peak of his radical mindset right around Geiseric's ascension to political power. He had come to believe that military prowess and the threat of war was likely the only way to achieve victory for Isaiism — "threat" being the key word. It may have been naïve, but Streicher was ninety-nine percent sure that the situation would never escalate to war. He envisioned it as a *Cold* War scenario, where the "evil ideologies" would fail because of their inherent weakness. However, it soon became clear that Geiseric was more than willing to heat things up.

Regardless, Streicher still held out hope, against his better judgment, that Geiseric would never wish to go to war if there were another way to accomplish the Isaianic mission. When the Germanian Commonwealth was successfully formed, and later expanded into the Apex Empire, Streicher felt that there was no reason for war. The Apex was sufficiently threatening to hold its own against the world. All they needed to do was sit tight and wait for the Apex economy to out-compete the enemy and let the Isaianic ideology take over the world through legitimate diplomacy and illegitimate diplomacy — such as a closet Principle running under the guise of an anti-Principle campaign — either of which worked and both of which were peaceful.

There were many reasons for Streicher to be optimistic about his proposal, for things were already heading down that path. Many in the world were becoming so frightened of the Apex that they seemed willing to increase humane standards for animals and the environment, just to avoid war. However, the chancellor had become aloof to Streicher and his "diplomatic end-game scenario." Geiseric increasingly ignored the scientist who was once a best friend, choosing to side with the hawks, such as General Gottlieb, who saw the creation of the Apex Empire as little more than a build-up of human and natural resources, in preparation for *their* end-game scenario — World War III.

This shift of the dynamic in the top Apex cabinet meetings was accompanied by a noticeable onset of totalitarianism in the Apex Emperor's mindset. The military officers, much like their single-minded drive towards war and much like the regimented order of the military, were happy to feed into the concept of a new world order with, "One Empire, One Emperor. As God reigns alone in heaven, so shall the chosen leader rule on Earth." Such concepts were around far longer than democracy, but Streicher knew that, "Absolute power, corrupts absolutely." He was seeing it right before his very eyes.

So, Streicher defected to the United States, his former foe, thus allying himself also with Britain and all the regimes he once despised . . . and still did. However, Streicher had come to believe that nothing was more dangerous to ultimate peace than totalitarianism. Still, sitting now in the vehicle with his once avowed enemies, there was a palpable, icy chill of bitterness and anger in the air. Dandau tried to be congenial.

"Why, hello Streicher," he greeted with a lukewarm tone and expression.

"I know you tried to kill me," Streicher replied coldly. "MI7 tried to kill all the founding Principles and Isaianics."

"I won't lie," Dandau replied. "You were too much of a threat. Based on the intelligence we had then, I would make the same decision today."

"You're no better than Geiseric," Streicher venomously retorted. "You're just weaker. Geiseric is too singularly powerful. He is too good at what he does. Whereas you, you are just a reactionary thug who can only make a name for himself in reference to others, like all your types. Churchillite scum," he spat in scornful rebuke. "I want you all to know," Streicher looked at the two leaders and their generals, "that is the only reason I am here. Because you are the lesser of two evils . . ." he shrugged and cocked his chin up defiantly, "at least for now."

Dandau turned to Hollier. "Can we trust this man?"

Hollier rubbed his eyes, frustrated with their bickering. He looked at Dandau and shrugged. "Would he act this way if we couldn't?"

A few minutes later, the first military jet of the French Empire arrived at the secret airbase, carrying the French Imperial President Rene Sinclair, the

Russian Federation President Ivan Kurtkin and the Italian Prime Minister Romano Bonnicelli. Armored bodyguards poured out of the plane and down the stairs. They scoped out the perimeter and then gave the "all clear" for the leaders to disembark. The three chiefs of state emerged similarly outfitted in pin-striped suits and fedoras with cropped edges, comparable to their 1930s counterpart. Sinclair's outfit was tan, Kurtkin's hues of silver, and Bonnicelli's was black and red. The three men stepped into one of the limousines accompanied by their top officers. The remainder of their entourage jumped in the three armored vehicles waiting off to the side, and they all sped into the tunnel.

The Chinese Premier Lo Hung was the last to arrive. He made an impressive exit from the plane in a much flashier outfit than the other dignitaries. His apparel enhanced the fact that he was unusually tall for his culture, with a strapping frame that was hard to miss, especially in a canary yellow suit and wide-brimmed fedora with a feather in it. Hung's flamboyant outfit could not have reflected his personality any better.

When his security team gave him the signal that it was safe, Hung strutted smoothly over to the fancy armored automobiles. He and his group fit into the two remaining limousines and sped off into the tunnel. After only ten minutes of driving, the car slowed to a rather abrupt stop.

The end of the tunnel was blocked off by massive steel-alloy doors. As the men emerged from their vehicles, a camera fastened just above the doors turned to look at them. In a moment, the doors opened and Hung, with his entourage and personal security, walked through into a wide room with vaulted ceilings. At the opposite end of the room, the other five leaders were already seated at a large, round table, with their highest-ranking generals beside them. Streicher also sat at the table, next to Hollier. Everyone rose to greet Premier Hung, and gestured for him and his entourage to find seats.

"OK," said Hollier, "Let's not waste any time with formalities. Streicher, why don't you begin?"

Streicher waited just a moment too long, as if in defiance, and then stood slowly to speak.

"As you all now know, from what I've already said publicly, Geiseric has commissioned the building of a fortress of lasers around the perimeter of the Apex nations, called the Laser Net."

He pressed a button on the remote control he was holding and a diagram of the Apex Laser Net appeared on the large screen on the wall behind him. He moved so that everyone could see it as he pointed to certain parts.

"The main goal of the Laser Net is to take out aircraft, missiles and any sort of ballistic projectiles that might be sent over by the enemy. The Laser Net also defends the land from invasion and can be effectively used to take out ground forces. In addition, there are a variety of anti-aircraft interceptor missiles hidden along the border of the Apex nations, but those will not be needed once the Net is fully operational."

On the screen, a computer graphic showed missiles being targeted and vaporized by the Laser Net. "Eighty percent of the lasers are relatively small," Streicher explained, "but they are still powerful enough to take down something the size and armory of a typical ballistic missile. However, Geiseric was not content with that. The largest lasers are a hundred times more powerful, meant to take down anything the Allies could possibly put in the air. You see, if you wanted to get a nuclear bomb over Germania, or even near it, by missile or aircraft, that missile or craft would need to be so heavily armored that it would be nearly impossible to get it in the air. Of course, to create such a missile or bombing aircraft would be a ludicrous waste of resources. Even if it was produced, it would not be able to penetrate the Net." Streicher shrugged and then looked all of the leaders in the eye, before proceeding further.

"Basically, once the Net is fully operational, absolutely nothing of use will be able to make it through over land or by air. There are possible ways to get through it from space, but only the Apex has developed the technology to accomplish this. Clearly this is another area in which the Allied forces simply must be brought up to speed."

Streicher shook his head, frustrated with this infant stage of scientific development. He knew that it was, in large part, because of him that the Apex Empire was so powerful and threatening. But, he wasn't sure the leaders before him were prepared to accept that which he could offer. He held up the remote and pressed another button. This time in the middle of the table a hologram about two meters high popped up. The leaders readjusted themselves in their seats to face the center of the table where the image floated just above the table's surface. A holographic, three-dimensional diagram of a laser net bunker spun slowly before them, so that everyone could see all its sides. The roof of the bunker was level with the surface of the ground, with the structure extending eight stories underground.

"The walls are made of twenty solid meters of reinforced concrete." Streicher gravely declared.

Suddenly, the roof opened, with two gigantic doors quickly pulling away from each other. A laser cannon, nearly ten meters long, protracted out. It could twist and turn with amazing speed, indicating how rapidly the giant lasers could deploy, target, and fire on an incoming missile. Then, the cannon retracted back into the bunker and the roof doors slid shut.

The holographic diagram changed to show the interior schematic of the laser and the bunker. The laser cannon itself took up much of the room in the middle-top interior of the bunker. Most of the lower floors housed a huge energy generator. The rest of the bunker supported the synthetic muscle lift system that so speedily moved the cannon around. The holographic display showed a few dozen operators monitoring the different screens and stations throughout.

"This is a bunker containing a Kreuz Laser," Streicher continued, "the backbone of the Laser Net. For those of you who may not know, Kreuz is German for cross. It's fittingly named because it works by crossing two laser beams. There are two types of lasers. To avoid confusion, we shall simply refer to them as red and blue."

Streicher pressed another button on the remote and the hologram changed again. Realistic three-dimensional computer graphics displayed how the Laser Net worked. There were two bunkers, placed a good distance away from one another on flat ground. They suddenly opened. The hologram display pulled up in perspective, from near the ground to high in the sky to show twenty ballistic missiles coming in. Each bunker fired their lasers; one red and one blue. They crossed at the point where some of the missiles were. The missiles were capable of incredible maneuverability and they began moving erratically through the sky to evade the high-energy beams, but to no avail. The lasers struck all of the targets within a split-second. Once the two beams converged on them, the missiles were vaporized.

The German scientist gazed at the holographic display in restrained admiration for the powerful defensive weapons system. "Either laser is pretty much harmless by itself. If a plane . . . ach," he made the phonetic sound similar to clearing his throat, as Germans did for exclamatory emphasis, "if a bird was struck by one of these lasers, they would just warm its feathers a bit. But when these lasers touch, they create a burst of energy that is extraordinarily destructive. At the point where they cross, it is the equivalent energetic force and heat of being hit at ground zero by a one megaton bomb." Streicher looked up to casually observe the expressions of worried awe around the table.

"Such force leaves nothing left of even the strongest air weaponry. The lasers are devastating at a range of up to five thousand kilometers, except in water. The range drops dramatically in water to a maximum of a few hundred meters, because the wavelengths become scattered."

Streicher pressed a button on the remote and the large screen on the wall behind him came back on. As the hologram dissipated, everyone turned away from the table and back towards the screen, which displayed a map of Eurasia, showing the concentration of Kreuz Pods around the perimeter of the Apex Empire.

"This is the way it works," Streicher explained, standing beside the screen with a pointer stick.

"Two laser bunkers, one of each kind, are placed together in a Kreuz Pod, like two peas in a pod," he smiled. No one else did. "The lasers are placed within a certain distance of each other, depending on the geography. The same goes for the distribution of the pods. At present, Kreuz Pods are placed approximately every fifty kilometers around the borders of the Apex nations. They are particularly dense in Germania," he said, pressing another button on the remote to zoom in on the display.

The most powerful leaders of the Allied nations were fixed on Streicher's every word. Their reactions, evident by their faces, varied only slightly from extreme consternation to constrained fear. To further compound their stress and add to the humility of the situation, all of the leaders were having somewhat of a hard time understanding Streicher's English through his thick Bavarian accent. They were getting the gist however.

Streicher zoomed onto India, the Middle East and Japan consecutively, using his pointer stick to show the weak spots. Most of the Middle East was not defended by a Laser Net. Japan was the most heavily defended country in the empire outside of Germania.

"Currently," Streicher continued, "the Apex Laser Net is still quite porous. Aircraft can't get through, but an invasion by land forces is possible. It's much more difficult to guard land than the skies. Because of the curvature of the Earth, it is easier on land to get out of the line of sight of the laser cannons." The next holographic display showed a hemisphere, a dome, representative of a portion of the surface of the Earth. The Kreuz lasers were prohibited from connecting past a certain point horizontally, for they were hindered by the land itself. Thus, an enemy lying over the horizon possibly only a few kilometers away, could be beyond the "line-of-sight" of the lasers. A laser could only be fired in a straight beam and, therefore, could not be arched over the horizon.

Streicher cleared his throat and took a sip of water from his glass at the table. "In Germania," he went on, "many pods are placed on high ground to defend certain areas that land invasion forces would most obviously come in through. Still, there are many places on the ground defended only by smaller lasers, which can pack a wallop, but a large and overwhelming force could get through with minimal casualties. Geiseric plans on doubling the Apex Empire's Laser Net density over the next three years, which would make Germania in particular near impervious to invasion." Gazing once more at the facts, Streicher assessed the strategic capabilities of his former homeland and was ever surer of his conclusion. "We must attack the Apex Empire and defeat them before their defenses make them invulnerable."

Hollier looked around the table at the disconcerted faces. He took their silence to mean that they were taking seriously Streicher's unbelievably terrifying report.

"What line of attack would you best advise, Streicher?" Hollier asked.

Streicher nodded to the president and explained. "First, we must create a Laser Net of our own that is equal to that of Geiseric's. Otherwise we will be slaughtered. Then, we can think offensively. There *are* things going in our favor." This was music to the ears of all the leaders in the room. "As you all know, we have far more natural resources than the Apex. Also, it took the Apex significantly longer to develop the lasers since they did all the research and experimentation. I bring all of this knowledge, fully developed, with me." Streicher leaned forward and put his hands on the table. "Gentlemen, we must act quickly. Mark my words, this will be more complex and consuming than ten Manhattan Projects."

Hollier felt his eyebrow start to twitch, revealing his anxiety. Dandau held his chin with his thumb and the side of his forefinger in a relaxed manner, attempting to portray calmness, though his eyes gave his true emotions away. Kurtkin glared at the screen in contemplation. Hung looked much the same. Sinclair and Bonnicelli, however, had expressions of mild skepticism. Streicher clicked the remote again and a hypothetical scenario for an Allied defensive posturing appeared on the screen.

"In my opinion, there is a choice between only two strategies, considering the finite amount of time we have. We could try to box in the crux of the Apex — Germania. To do this, we would need to put up a Laser Net defense around France, Italy, the western Russian Federation, Denmark and southern Scandinavia, Britain, Romania, Turkey, and so on. So, basically, all the countries around Germania. Then, we would still have to install a laser net system around Germania's shores, to box in its forces. But, this is a real long shot. Beyond a space assault, the biggest weakness of the Laser Net is that you can tunnel under it through the ground. However," he held up his pointer finger, "that is only feasible, as far as I can see, if we are fighting an enemy right next door. We must remember that we are on the defense, because we are so far behind. So we do not want to be anywhere near Germania or the Apex Empire. If we were on the offense, I would recommend the opposite. He once again looked at all of the leaders, gauging their expressions.

"If we cannot box in Germania, we have to box ourselves in. But, time dictates how many of these pods we can create."

Streicher brought up a display showing a hypothetical defensive system of the United States and parts of Canada. "First, we must condense the amount of space to be protected to a single continent. Taking everything into consideration, North America would be best."

Dandau was captivated and overwhelmed by the extremity of the situation. Clearly *even he* had not realized how powerful Geiseric's empire had become, and in such a short period of time. At no time in history had so much been accomplished with such speed and efficiency. He would have had unending admiration for the Apex Emperor, had he not been part of the Allied leadership. But now, for the first time ever Charles Dandau, the steely-eyed, no-nonsense, take-charge British leader, and many of his compatriots, were genuinely afraid.

"So," Streicher expounded, "everything outside of the Apex we must consider to be resources for the Allied war effort. I'm speaking primarily about countries that have not aligned with either side, like the majority of Africa and South America. They will be," he paused, and then said euphemistically, "*encouraged . . .*" he snickered, "to give their land and resources to the cause. We cannot fool around with small nations or third world countries. They will not be asked twice to go along with us. We don't have time for that!" He shouted, smacking his right fist into his left palm.

"Every single resource must be pooled toward the war effort if we are to defeat Geiseric. We must be ready to take what we need." He placed his hands on the table again and leaned in confidently. "The world will thank us for it later, *believe me,*" he remarked ominously.

Hollier sat back in his seat and interlocked his fingers across his abdomen, resting his elbows on the chair arms. "We're with you loud and clear, Streicher."

"Aye!" Proclaimed Dandau, raising his fist in solidarity.

Streicher smiled for the first time that afternoon. He looked at Dandau, sitting across from him, puffing on his cigar. He could not believe that he and the British prime minister, who were so ideologically dichotomous, were now allies. "My, how war makes for strange bedfellows," Streicher muttered, shaking his head in disbelief of the horrible, yet comedic irony.

"Of course," he continued, "this is the far more daring decision of the two," he pointed to the diagram of a hypothetical North American Laser Net, "for we will have to move the whole of the world's population, all the nations outside of the Apex Empire, into North America, mainly the U.S."

Everyone in the room appeared shocked, as if they had not even contemplated that part. But, all of the leaders kept their cool, not wanting to show too much apprehension in the face of the others.

"The brilliance of this," Streicher explained with animation, "is that Geiseric will most likely expect us *not* to use this approach, because it is so daring. He will expect the boxing of Germania, which seems far more pragmatic." He looked at all the leaders in the room, and they seemed to be with him. "I am very happy with your show of solidarity. I thought this part would be much more difficult."

Just as he was speaking those words, however, Prime Minister Bonnicelli of Italy stood up.

"Now wait a minute," he spat indignantly. "You cannot assume that President Hollier and Prime Minister Dandau speak for us all."

"Yes," Sinclair arose, equally offended, "we are not their suppliants, who move on their decision." His contempt was made even more caustic by his French accent.

"Yes, I find it incredibly rude," Kurtkin, rising, said in his deep and serious Russian tone, "that you would assume we have spoken, when we have said nothing."

"Well then," came a man's voice from behind, "do speak."

Everyone turned to see who it was. Standing tall and completely unshaken by the political clout in the room was a man whom everyone recognized. He had been a celebrity on the international stage for almost three decades. He still had a full head of healthy blonde hair, with only a hint of gray showing through. His body had become more squared off and his baby face more chiseled, since they had last seen him. But it would still be difficult for a stranger to guess his age. As he faced the table, his crystal blue eyes shone with vigor and vitality, showing absolutely no fear.

Streicher was bewildered. "What is *he* doing here?"

Hollier stood up from his seat, put one hand nonchalantly in his pocket, and with the other waved the man closer to the table.

"Naturally, you all know Kassian Van der Klute," he said by way of introduction. "I'm sure that everyone here is aware that Kassian was Geiseric's bandmate in *Set Ablaze*. You are probably also aware of the fact that Kassian was a co-creator of the Formula with Geiseric. Kassian here was best friends with Geiseric during some of his most formative years and can provide much psychological analysis of our enemy." The leaders and their officials nodded. Hollier took in a deep breath and turned his mouth to the side in a nervous tick.

"In fact, though, he may be able to provide far more," the president began somewhat tentatively. "You're all well aware of Geiseric's supposed heightened," he bobbed his head a bit and waggled his hand by his temple as he found the words, "powers. Like his ability to spot any traitors in his midst, even without the help of Psychiclink technology," the president remarked, a tad skeptical himself. Sinclair, Bonnicelli and Hung all adorned faces of anger and cynicism. But, Kurtkin was intrigued and Hollier noticed.

"You see," he pointed to the Russian president, "Ivan knows what I'm talkin' about. The KGB did more psychic research than any of us has since World War II. I'm sure if we knew half of what he knows, we would not be tempted to doubt Kassian's talents." Kurtkin said nothing, but merely cracked a minute smile

"It's hard for me," Hollier put his hand on his chest in emphasis, "and my Intelligence Director tells me that the CIA has done a number of tests since the nineteen-fifties that proved beyond a 'statistical probability,'" he held his fingers up in symbolic quotations marks, imitating the technical jargon of his subordinates, "that telepathy is real. Telekinesis may also be possible. It's just that a lot of this research got shut down during the Clinton administration and no one has put the necessary capital towards it since." He pointed to Kassian. "All I know is that I've seen him identify people time and time again who are later proven to be spies."

Dandau frowned a bit as he looked at Sinclair's expression. "Why are you so doubtful Rene?" He eyed the French president with agitation. "It's as if you didn't know all of this, at least to a degree. You know all the research the French and British did during World War II. Those psychics were able to find Nazi subs just by holding pendulums over maps."

"Yes, well," Rene glared back at his British compatriot, "the percentage of success was not enough for me to say it must be that they had psychic powers. Maybe they just had a good intuition."

Dandau made a face of incredulity, tossing his hands up. "Exactly! What is intuition?!"

Sinclair indignantly pursed his lips. "I'm not going to mince words here with you, Charles."

Hollier, sensing things were getting too overheated, stepped in. "I get it Rene," he said in as supplicate a tone he could muster. "Like I said, it's hard for me to believe and I've seen *first hand* what Kassian can do." He pointed to the ex-rock star. "He has single-handedly almost completely cut off the flow of intelligence going to Geiseric." He shrugged, not being able to fully get his mind around the absolutely surreal nature of the issue.

Dandau stood up, still puffing off his cigar. "He's tried and tested," he said, looking to Kassian in awe of his capabilities. "He found three Apex agents at the top of mine and President Hollier's intelligence agencies. These people were eventually confirmed, beyond a doubt, to be spies and saboteurs. They had all gotten past our top watchdogs." He roguishly glanced to everyone, as he came to his point.

"So, we brought in Kassian to look over all of our agencies and everyone in the top government positions, and of course," Dandau said jauntily, "all of you. Just as a precaution."

The leaders of France, China, Russia and Italy were outraged.

"You dare bring in a watchdog on all of us!" Sinclair fumed with ire. "Without our knowledge! *Merde!* How are we to know he is not obligated to you and Hollier!"

Kurtkin's hostility came through loud and clear with the biting cold inflection in his voice. "You two have poisoned the banquet," he said, standing and staring Hollier and then Dandau in the eye.

"Don't worry," Hollier assured, walking over to Kurtkin, attempting to placate him. "Kassian is not beholden to any of us. He came to Charles first because he knew Charles was definitely not an Apex sympathizer. Charles put him to the test, and he did the same thing to me that we just did to you. So, let's all just sit down and relax. No one is trying anything funny."

He managed to calm the room and everyone sat back down, adjusting their suits and cracking knuckles to work out the tension. President Kurtkin looked at Kassian. "So what is your verdict?"

Kassian did not answer. He looked around the room and stared into the eyes of all the leaders. All of them looked back at him, some with indignity at having to be cleared by this ex-rock star whose only credentials seemed to be that he was once close friends with Geiseric. Kassian walked slowly and deliberately around the room. He tapped the Chinese Premier's shoulder saying, "Duck."

Premier Hung's face wretched up in perplexity, wondering what Kassian meant. For a brief moment he thought he was being accused, so he scowled at Kassian. But, Kassian just walked on to Sinclair.

"Duck," Kassian tapped Sinclair's shoulder just as he did to the Chinese Premier. Kassian then did the same to President Kurtkin.

When he came to Prime Minister Bonnicelli, Kassian calmly said, "Goose," knocking the Italian's fedora off with a flick. Bonnicelli abruptly rose, throwing his seat out with his legs as he did. Kassian deftly dodged the seat and retained his placid composure, as the Italian prime minister tried in vein to stare him down.

"You dare call me a traitor!" Bonnicelli roared.

"I dare," Kassian replied, undeterred. "I concede you are not a traitor in your own mind." The longer Kassian spoke, the more his Prussian accent rang through. "You have betrayed nothing, for you are not beholden to us, you are beholden to Geiseric."

"You lying dog!" Bonnicelli roared.

Kassian exhaled sharply, and slowly walked over to Hollier and Dandau.

"There is no doubt in my mind that Prime Minister Bonnicelli is an Isaianic. In fact, he has met with Geiseric himself recently. Geiseric's stink is upon him."

Suddenly, Kassian sensed that Bonnicelli was about to do something. He turned and rushed the Italian leader just as Bonnicelli reached into his inside jacket pocket. Bonnicelli pulled out a pen and pointed the top at Dandau, but Kassian quickly knocked Bonnicelli's arm upwards. The pen fired out a projectile, which barely missed Dandau, and lodged itself in the wall behind him.

Bonnicelli, though in his fifties, was a very strong and highly trained fighter, and Kassian struggled to subdue him. In the chaotic brawl to gain possession of the pen, it went off again. Another small, poison-tipped dart fired into Bonnicelli's arm, right through his suit. He was dead instantly.

Kassian stood above the Italian prime minister's lifeless body as the leaders, all on their feet, stared aghast at the fatal scene. Eight guards rushed into the room, summoned by the push of a button by Hollier. Hollier ordered them to hold their weapons.

Walking over to the wall, Kassian removed the dart that was meant for Dandau. He handed it and the deadly pen gun to a guard. "Get this out of here. We don't know what else it will do." The guard rushed out of the room.

The leaders of France, Russia and China stood near each other, looking down at Bonnicelli cautiously, as if he might still pop back up and attack.

"So," Kassian turned to them, "do you believe me now?"

Sinclair looked at Bonnicelli, then to Kassian, wide-eyed. He shook himself alert and pulled himself into an upright posture. He fixed his jacket and righted his hat before he spoke.

"This proves nothing."

Though he kept a noble exterior, Kurtkin looked bewildered, like his mind was rebooting. He stared speechless at Bonnicelli's stiff and sallow body.

Dandau was perturbed. He summoned the guards to take the Italian prime minister's body away. Bonnicelli's top general was also hauled off, shouting that he had no idea about his leader's duplicity before now. Kassian nodded in confirmation of this.

"He was not in on it."

"Yes, well," Dandau shrugged. "We can sort all of that out later. We have far more pressing issues to deal with at present." He gathered Kassian and Hollier near him for a private conversation.

"I'll have you know, Kassian, that President Hollier and I are obviously convinced about Bonnicelli, but what about Sinclair and Kurtkin?"

Sinclair, overhearing his name, was yet again incredibly offended. Kurtkin was still too shocked over Bonnicelli's sudden demise to mind such airs.

Kassian shook his head and said matter-of-factly and loud enough for all to hear, "No, they are okay. Kurtkin is just stubborn and Sinclair . . ." Kassian laughed slightly, "well, he's just an asshole."

Hollier looked down and tried to stifle his laughter. He took his seat again and waited for the others to do the same. Sinclair, who was taller than Kassian, walked over to and glared down at the man who dared be so rude to him. Kassian stared back, nonchalantly. Hollier shook his head and sighed.

"Alright," he said, his Texan dialect becoming more prominent, "we can act like a bunch of cowboys here, or we can be men, leaders."

Sinclair did not break his glare at Kassian as he spoke to Hollier. "You suggest I should just let this man insult me?"

Hollier threw his hands up, shrugging. "Hell! He insults me too . . . *and* Charles. What can we do?"

The French president broke his stare at Kassian and looked haughtily at Hollier, who just sighed.

"Listen," Hollier explained calmly, "we need him. There are bigger things than subordination and our pride at stake."

Sinclair closed his eyes, inhaled deeply, and tightened his lips. He looked like he was going to explode, but when he opened his eyes he simply went to his seat, giving no further acknowledgement to Kassian. Kurtkin and Hung quietly followed Sinclair to the table. Kassian took Bonnicelli's seat, between Dandau and Sinclair, but the French president made no displays of disapproval. He just focused his attention on Streicher, who was preparing to continue his presentation.

"I assume I am to begin?" Streicher waited for approval from the shaken up bunch, then continued. "There are two main things we must focus on, militarily. First, we must achieve Laser Net density equal to that of the Apex presently. I have estimated from a broad assessment of Allied potential that this will take us a year and a half to two years. We won't be invulnerable then, but we will be well protected. As I said, Geiseric will most likely wait two to three years to attack, because that's when his defenses will be impervious to almost any sort of viable assault. He wants his Net equipped to destroy tens of thousands of high-speed projectiles simultaneously." Once again, Streicher pressed a button on his remote control and a holographic diagram came up on the war table, displaying what the scientist spoke of.

"For instance, let's say we made numerous superguns like the ones the Germans used during the first two World Wars. Such cannons today could fire massive conventional, nuclear and chemical shells at thirty-thousand kilometers per hour deep into Germania. Geiseric wants his lasers ready to intercept a large scale bombardment of this kind, or any kind, anywhere on Apex borders, but most especially Germania." Streicher turned the holographic projector off, to have the full attention of those in the room.

"Until that time, we can feel somewhat safe from a full-scale Apex attack. However, once Geiseric achieves maximum density, he *will* attack. We can not hope to bring *our own* Laser Net to maximum density and strength in that amount of time, and certainly not before it. Thus, our Laser Net will be porous. We can only hope that the lasers wreak havoc on the Apex invasion forces to such a degree that we will be able to deliver the coup de grace with our forces." He slammed his fist on the table, bringing it down like a hammer.

"But, if we are to repulse the attack, we must also revamp all of your nations' military infrastructures. The machines of war have changed, my friends. You all have come to know about the Kolibri and Panzer by now, but they are just the beginning. Geiseric's ahead of us. However, we have an ace up our sleeves."

Streicher turned the hologram projector back on and it displayed an image of an immensely long, serpentine battlemachine.

"Geiseric's best line of attack would be an amphibious assault using overwhelming numbers. This is what they'll confront — what I call the Sidewinder."

The hologram of the machine writhed slowly over the table. "The Sidewinder is a theoretical model I designed, but never showed to Geiseric. I came up with it when trying to conceive of a machine that acts, essentially, like a moving fortress wall. And that's really what the Sidewinder is." He took a moment to marvel at his design.

"You see, Hitler's Atlantic wall was strong in many aspects, but its weakness was that it was stationary. So, it was only a matter of hitting it with a constant barrage from a battleship armada's large caliber guns, or two-ton bombs dropped from ten thousand meters high, before the Atlantic Wall smashed apart. But, the Sidewinder can easily dodge such large scale attacks." The holographic image of the machine slithered into action, demonstrating its capabilities for the duly impressed leaders.

"This moving fortress is only conceivable with the advent of Vasculosynth." The military officers in the room nodded, for they were aware of the tremendous logistics that such a colossal piece of machinery would entail. Streicher, ever the scientist and engineer, could not help but smile as he gazed upon his concept in action, though it went against the very grain of his peaceful nature.

"As you already know, I created Vasculosynth, and Geiseric and I both immediately saw its military possibilities. The machines he's commissioning are, more than anything else, agile. I was personally leading the design and creation of the Panzer. I don't know every machine he's commissioned, because Geiseric kept all military production disjointed. But, I can extrapolate that he will have some amazing things to throw at us. Let us first take a look at the Panzer."

The uncanny machine appeared on the wall screen with internal and external schematics diagrammed in detail. Another slide showed its various movement positions. Modeled prominently after the cheetah, the Panzer was lean and had long legs. When it stood on all fours, it was five meters tall from the head to the ground, and eight meters long.

A short video captured the Panzer deftly dodging attackers, during a training exercise. Streicher was once again pleased by the sight of his invention. "Panzer is German for armor," he explained. "And the Panzer quadrupedal battlemachine is what will take the place of the tracked armor vehicles of yester-year. This is the new generation of heavy cavalry. It is interesting how everything comes around. The Panzer, with its four animalian legs, resembles the original horse-based cavalry much more than the tank. It's much lighter than it looks, because of the particular alloys used. Not to mention the special

techniques I used in the design," he added mysteriously. After all, if he shared everything they would not need him anymore, which could be dangerous for a man amongst former foes.

Another moving hologram appeared over the table displaying footage of a Panzer battalion demonstrating their prowess in a war game at an Indian testing range. The battlemachines' legs moved so swiftly that it was hard to see them. The Panzers stormed across the hard ground at speeds over one hundred and fifty kilometers per hour. They were fired upon with non-lethal rounds by tanks coming over the horizon, but the battlemachines leapt from side to side with the agility of a feline, revolving around sideways and backward. The Panzers' movements were so swift that their enemies' shells consistently hit the earth where the Panzers had been a split-second prior, merely striking and dusting up the ground.

The hologram showed how the quadrupedal battlemachines had two large, thirty-caliber machine guns placed on their chests that could only fire in the general direction the vehicle was facing. The head of the machine served as the cockpit for the driver.

All of those in the bunker room watched the holographic display of the deadly machines as they bore down on the tracked vehicles, coming into killing range. "The Panzer is a close-quarters destroyer," Streicher elaborated. "Basically, it's a machine designed for thrusts of speed, like a predator. Vasculosynth allows it to move like an animal. Hydraulics, motors and similar types of powering technology could never produce these results. At least not with the mass-producability that can be achieved with synthetic muscle." He took another sip of water. The holographic projection showed the Panzer battalion rush in among the tank brigade.

"The Panzers are designed to engage the enemy from within its lines, sending the opponent into chaos. It's incredibly effective and explains why it doesn't require a cannon." A close-up picture of the Panzer's weaponry flashed onto the wall screen. "The chest guns fire kinetic energy rounds, which are meant more for killing the men inside, but will also do severe damage to the enemy vehicle as well. The Panzer does not rely heavily on its guns, though, because the Apex has prohibited the use of depleted uranium shells. And in close-quarters fighting, it's dangerous to be firing guns all over the place. So when the Panzers come upon the enemy, they fight like a true cat, which though admittedly bizarre, is quite effective I assure you."

The military and political leaders in the room fervently studied the fascinating weapon's method of attack. Although the Panzers were about thirty percent taller, the tanks were overall more massive, yet the Panzers were able to easily pounce on and smack their enemy between their two "paws," violently bending or breaking the tanks' main guns. Firing at close range, the Panzer's bullets tore through the armor towards where the crew would have been. Though it was a demonstration, with these particular tanks piloted by computers, there was no doubt to the military personnel watching that these new creations would be effective.

The Panzers ripped and swiped at the tank exteriors with five, thick, twenty-five centimeter long steel-alloy claws, which trashed the exterior faculties of the tanks, rendering them useless. Within seconds, the entire tank force was incapacitated. Then, like a cat teasing its prey, the Panzers pushed the tanks onto their sides and set about further dismantling and gutting the vehicles.

Looking upon the lethal battlemachines as they did their dirty work, Streicher was now humbled and felt a bit sick. The presentation made it all too real how destructive his creations would be in true battle, and how many people would thus die by them. He took a deep breath and pushed these thoughts far back in his mind. "Not only is the Panzer effective, but it's efficient," he explained with a mixture of dread and loathing. "It does not waste endless shells, which need to be made of harmful metals like uranium, to be most effective. A tank is a relatively easy thing to debilitate. If a tank's cannon is bent, or its track broken, it is rendered useless. The Panzers' arms are strong enough to break a main tank gun with one good swipe. They can then move on to other enemies and later come back to finish off their crippled victims."

Streicher turned off the projector and made a final appeal to those leaders in the room who may still have had lingering doubts about coming on board.

"Gentlemen," he slowly turned his head, fixing his eyes momentarily upon every person as he did. "I leave you with this. We must totally revamp your military-industrial complexes, because your weapons systems are obsolete," he stood and leaned forward, placing his hands on the table in an authoritative manner. "And we *must* begin Formula training for every single soldier in your militaries. As I said before, we have a small edge in that Geiseric will most likely assume that we are going with the more conservative approach of boxing Germania in. This could serve us well. We will deceive them, and while they are strategizing on how to break out of the box, we will be building our defenses in North America. But," he gazed upon the men who would decide the fate of the world, "there is *no* time to waste. Even though Geiseric's defenses are not complete, I'm still a bit surprised that he hasn't invaded yet. The world must understand that the moment Geiseric feels it is right — he *will* attack. Right now, he is not willing to risk the destruction of his empire to defeat us. But, who knows?" Streicher shrugged. "Perhaps tomorrow, he'll feel differently."

— XIII —

TRUTH IS STRANGER THAN FICTION

With Francesca by his side, Logan found that the days passed quickly in the Underclass Language School. Each day, they went to class for five hours, with two half-hour breaks. Their homework was simply to remember what was learned during class. There were no books. Herr Ribbentropp displayed everything up on the board and the students repeated their lessons over and over again.

But each day, Herr Ribbentropp singled out students that he decided were not giving their undivided attention to the lesson. They were brought in front of the class and made to recite words and spell them aloud from memory. If the students failed this test, they received one lash to the behind, just enough to motivate them to pay attention. One lash was painful, but it was more embarrassing.

Logan and Francesca managed to avoid flogging during the next week of school. They tested each other every day before and after class, determined to avoid another painful corporal punishment. The young couple didn't mind studying, because when they were around each other, they were on a perpetual emotional high. It didn't matter if they were racing each other in the pool, lying on the beach looking up at the sky, or cramming their heads full of German verbs.

Logan had not seen Jacques, Sasha, or Alistair at all during the entire week. He only asked Francesca once where they were, and she said that her father was resting a lot and Sasha was with him. Alistair was spending a lot of time with the counselors trying to find his family. Frankly, Logan did not really care what everyone else was up to. He just appreciated the alone time with Francesca.

Friday afternoon came and the duo once again raced to the organic pool. They swam until their arms and legs were exhausted, and then grabbed some ambrosia at the refreshment stand before heading out to the beach. It was a bright day, and a powerful, cool breeze invigorated everyone who was out enjoying the weekend's start. A number of volleyball nets were set up along the beach, and groups of young people played. Often they were not in the nude, for the girls wore sports bras so that they could move about with greater ease, and both men and women wore lower garments to prevent sand from going where it could be uncomfortable.

As Logan and Francesca lounged on the white sand, a familiar sight passed overhead. Two Kolibri guardsmen, their body armor and chariots gleaming in the sun, zipped along the length of the beach, about fifteen meters off the ground. The wind generated by their hummingbird-like wings was felt by those below them. The turbulence knocked one of the volleyballs in play off course.

But, the effect their presence had on the underclassmen was nothing like a week prior. Just eight or nine days ago, the sight of the Kolibri guards paralyzed almost everyone on the beach. Now, the reaction was much more subtle.

Logan laughed to himself and took a gulp of ambrosia. "That's so bizarre!"

Francesca, startled by the break in the silence, waited for him to explain. When he did not continue, she finally asked, "What?"

Logan shook his head, incredulously. "That these Animalian Projects came with an animal rights agenda."

"Yeah," Francesca nodded, staring off at the luminescent line where the sky met the ocean, "that is a weird coincidence. There were a lot of coincidences and ironies, like the fact that Israel allied with Germania."

Logan's eyebrows shot up in surprise. "That's right! I heard that. Why would Israel, of *all* places, ally with Germany?"

Francesca pointed to a boulder in the surf she wanted to go sit on. They waded through the shallow tide. "I know, it's so strange. Only a hundred years earlier, Hitler wanted to exterminate the Jews. Then, Geiseric comes around and declares that the Jews and Germans should be the best of friends."

Logan thought about this. "That *is* ironic."

Francesca nodded. "He saw something about World War II that a lot of people didn't, which is really interesting, because it seems so obvious now."

Logan took another gulp of his drink. "And what's that?"

Francesca smiled and clutched Logan's hand under the water. They continued to wade toward the boulder as she spoke.

"Albert Einstein," she explained, "who was, like, the biggest genius ever, was a Jewish-German. He was a Bavarian, from the same area where Geiseric was born. Bavaria and Austria are basically the same. Freud was from Austria, along with Hitler."

When they arrived at their destination, Logan climbed up the boulder and held his hand down to help Francesca up. They got comfortable, and sipped their drinks while enjoying the view of the endless horizon.

"If Hitler were not such an idiot," Francesca continued, "if he had recognized Jewish-German accomplishments, these brilliant minds would have worked for him and he would have had the nuclear bomb way before anyone else." She chuckled cynically. "The irony wasn't lost on Geiseric."

Only a small portion of Israel was won over by Geiseric's praise for the brilliance of the Jews and his conclusion that Jews and Germans were natural allies. However, Geiseric had made a good case for his Isaianic agenda by using the Jewish scriptures. Regardless, when Prime Minister Leon was elected in 2030, less than twenty-five percent of the Israeli population had converted to Isaiism, and only half of the Isaianic Jews were willing to cede their sovereignty to join an empire under another country's leadership, let alone Germania.

Solomon Leon came out of nowhere in the Israeli Parliament's Likhud Party. The Likhud Party formed the strongest opposition to the Isaianic movement in Israel. Though he was only forty, which made him the "baby" of the party, he was so polished, confident and daring that he quickly rose to a position of leadership. Little did his peers know that Leon was an Isaianic, something of which only Geiseric and a few top people in the Germanian chancellor's inner circle were aware. Even the Principles Party members in the Israeli Parliament never suspected Leon's affiliation. Geiseric stressed to Leon to keep this secret, so that the Isaianic parliamentarians would keep their behavior towards Leon completely real and, in that, they had to despise him. Being that the Israeli Principles were deceived into believing that Leon was their enemy, they did everything within their power to take him down, and Leon's fellow Likhud Party members were thus convinced that he was not an agent of Geiseric's.

The Germanian chancellor's tactic of training people and helping them to attain a leadership position, in order to change their government from within, was nothing new. It had been done before by the German government. During World War I, the German Army fought the Russians, the French and the British, on two fronts. The Germans were anxious to get the Russians out of the war so that they could focus on just the western front. So, the Germans trained Vladimir Lenin to be the leader of the communist movement and eventual dictator of Russia. Lenin had been exiled from his homeland, so the Germans secreted him back into Russia, where he stirred up the discontented lower classes who were suffering, starving, and dying more than those of any of the other warring powers. In 1917, Lenin and the communists toppled the Czarist government and murdered the entire royal family. The Bolshevik communists immediately pulled the Russians out of the war.

However, this method of manipulation was not simple. The government in charge of a state is always looking for traitors in their midst. The Germans in World War I got lucky, in this respect. The communist movement was already flourishing in Russia because of the harsh life that the average Russian peasant endured. Lenin had started his mission long before the war began. The Germans just helped him along and gave him what he needed.

Geiseric was truly a man of ethical conviction, and was not *just* hungry for wealth or power. The elites or lower classes of other countries would never sign their sovereignty over to Germany just because Germany wanted more power. The fact that Isaiism was a belief not constricted by any particular nationalism was its gift. Like communism or democracy, the concepts were deeper than a nation-state.

And so, the Germanian chancellor found a strong ally in the Israeli film star, Solomon Leon, who had his eyes on politics as ambitious men often did. Leon was a rabid follower of the Isaianic creed, but he had been very careful to conceal that fact from the Israeli populace and politicians. The tabloids had revealed that he followed a vegan diet, but he had done so for twenty years and, at first, it was truly only for health, which is what he claimed was still the reason. Leon was smart and he managed to keep his private life away from the paparazzi. Even as his mind began to turn toward Isaiism in the 2020s, he never revealed his personal beliefs to anyone except the leader of the Isaianic movement, his fellow celebrity, who he met through traveling the famous elite circles. Geiseric took the young actor under his wing and, in the utmost secrecy, trained him to be a political dynamo.

Seeing that the Principles Party could not win in Israel in the near future, Geiseric told Leon to run for the Likhud Party. As if it were his greatest role, Leon took up the antithetical position to Isaiism in the public eye. He furiously debated against the Principles and appeared to hate the new party more than any person in Israel. He rose up through the ranks and, when the Likhud Party won, Solomon Leon became the next prime minister of Israel. On this day, the Israeli Isaianics were greatly saddened and the conservatives were overjoyed. Soon, though, it became increasingly evident that things were not as they seemed.

Leon was careful not to immediately reverse his stance. He made slow, incremental changes. And, as the new Israeli prime minister subtly changed his nation into an Isaianic state from within, Geiseric was simultaneously doing and saying anything to get the Israeli people on the side of this movement. Geiseric asserted that the Jews were definitely a chosen people, and was often seen on television reciting his new favorite quote: *"From Genesis to Jesus, the Israelites have been purveyors of the Isaianic ideal."*

To show their uniqueness among the many nations, the Germanian chancellor reminded the world that Jesus was a Jewish man whom much of the world had considered to be a God for two thousand years. Geiseric proclaimed that Jesus preached Isaianic philosophies. There was one fact, in particular, that Geiseric loved to opine on, and which many around the world found interesting. Human sacrifice was out of style by the time of Christ for the most part, but animal sacrifice was in full effect. Christianity preached that Jesus was the last sacrifice, so wherever his religion went the practice of animal sacrifice ended, along with any remaining human sacrifice.

Germania paid homage to that legacy by adopting the iron cross as their flag's symbol. The squared-off, silver and black cross had been a German military symbol since the Prussians used it in the Napoleonic wars. Now, for the Isaianics, it had new meaning.

Most Jews did not believe that Jesus was *the* Messiah. If anything, they believed he was a good prophet. The Jewish Messiah, as opposed to the Christian one, was supposed to take political power, instead of be abused by it.

This was why Judas betrayed Jesus. He wanted Jesus to prove to be the Messiah. He thought Jesus would be forced to summon down the angels and the wrath of God upon the Roman soldiers and Pontius Pilate. Jesus, instead, as the story goes, allowed himself to be crucified. The point being, the Jews believed in a Messiah who would not take no for an answer. He would rule. It would be the return of *the* King.

As Geiseric was making headway with more and more Israelis and Jews all around the world, Solomon Leon subtly espoused the Isaianic interpretations of the Torah—the Old Testament. Isaiah's writings were easy to reference for they were numerable and consumed the largest portion of the Torah, by far, out of all the prophets.

The majority of Jews gave credence to Isaiah as one of the Biblical prophets who predicted the coming of the Messiah or the Messianic Age. Therefore, the Isaianics intended to show that Geiseric was the Messiah and that an "end to carnivorism," as they called it, was the correct interpretation of Isaiah's prophecies. Many non-Jewish Isaianics believed Geiseric was the savior of the world. Yet, the Jews were more suspicious of a beguiling leader than any other people in the world. They were cynical of a helpful outsider in general, let alone a German revamping their faith. There were many Israeli Jews who were sympathetic to Isaiism, but did not vote for the Principles Party. Even the Chief Rabbi of Israel, Shraga Somayach, who endorsed the Isaianic Creed, did not believe that Geiseric was the Messiah and was against the notion of Israel joining the Germanic Empire.

Somayach was much like Rav Kook, the first Chief Rabbi of Israel in the 1920s and 30s, during the nation's transitional period into becoming a state. Kook was adored worldwide by people of all faiths and there was a resurgence of interest in his teachings as the Isaianic movement built. His beliefs were a point of contention between those who believed in and those who were vehemently against Isaiism. Rav Kook endorsed vegetarianism as the natural ideal and believed that all living beings on Earth would be vegetarian in the times of the Messiah, when heaven was brought to Earth. However, he believed that his time was certainly not the time of the Messiah, for he was living during the rule of Hitler and Stalin. So, naturally, he thought it to be somewhat pretentious to fervently insist that humans must be vegetarian, when they themselves were being treated like farm animals.

Rabbi Somayach was slightly more radical than Rav Kook because he believed that most people in the world, especially those in poor nations, should be vegetarian. He argued that it would increase their food supply, since it took far more land to feed livestock and create meat, than to use that same land to produce other forms of food and nourishment. He argued that it was sinfully wasteful to use land for meat when people were starving. However, like Rav Kook, Rabbi Somayach did not believe he was living in the messianic times. Somayach thought that those times were very near, but he did not know what to make of Geiseric. So, he played the safer hand and became an opponent of the Israeli Principles Party and their advocacy for joining the Germanian Commonwealth.

Geiseric needed to enact more drastic measures in order to bring Shraga Somayach and the majority of Israelis into his movement. It just so happened that he had the perfect scheme.

Israel had been racked by terrorism for sixty years. What was becoming particularly disturbing to the Israeli Jews was that, in the past three decades, there was a noticeable upswing of radicalism amongst the Arabs living within Israel. Israel and the occupied territories were at one time all called Palestine. It was divided up to give the Jews a homeland after World War II. During that war, no country, not even Britain or America, was willing to give refuge to those fleeing Hitler's extermination camps.

From the moment Israel was established, the surrounding Muslim countries tried to drive the Jews into the sea. Many Arabs endorsed Hitler's genocidal agenda and wanted to pick up where he had left off by going to war with Israel.

However, each time the Muslim countries attacked Israel, they lost, and the Jews ended up with a little more land — a very little bit. Israel, altogether, was smaller than New Jersey. Over time, the tiny nation began giving back the miniscule territories they had gained from the wars, but it was not enough for their neighbors. In 2005, Israel gave up the Gaza Strip and pulled out all of its settlers. Later, the Jewish settlers were pulled out of parts of the West Bank, within which lay historic cities such as Jericho and other places of tremendous religious importance to the Jews. The Israeli government even gave up half of Jerusalem to the Palestinian state being created. But, it was not enough.

Radical Islamist groups such as Hamas still called for the destruction of Israel and they called for Muslims to kill as many Jews as possible. The majority of unrest had usually always come from outside of Israel, from the

Palestinians in the "occupied territories" of the West Bank and Gaza Strip. There were also over two million Arabs living within Israel, who were the descendents of former Palestinians living there since before Israel was created. These Arab-Israelis made up one-fifth of the population. They enjoyed far more economic success than most of their neighboring Arabic brethren in the West Bank, Jordan, or Egypt, and as a result were far less radicalized than most other Muslims in the Middle-East. However, this started changing around the turn of the millennium.

No one knows exactly why the Arabs within Israel were becoming more extreme, in spite of the fact that the Israeli government was doing much to include them into society and government. But, many people thought that it was inevitable; Muslims and Jews could simply never get along.

The Arab-Israelis complained of feeling ostracized within their state and that the Jews weren't doing enough to bring Muslims into the fold. On the other hand, Israel was doing a lot more for Muslims than Saudi Arabia, for instance, was doing for its Jewish population.

In the early twenty-twenties, the Arab-Israelis increasingly demanded that the "Palestinians of the Diaspora" be allowed to return to the homeland. This demand was posed in counterargument to the Jewish assertion that Jews had the right to reclaim Israel, after being ousted by the Romans nearly two thousand years prior. The Muslims of the Middle-East claimed that the Jews had forcibly deported most of the native Arab-Palestinian population when Israel was re-established in 1948. However, those native Arabs who chose to stay and live in the new state of Israel were given the right to vote and every other aspect of citizenship.

Most Palestinians left on their own accord. Perhaps they did not trust the Jews. Or, perhaps they wanted to avoid the inevitable attacks from Egypt, Jordan and Syria that would send the Jews back into the sea. Whatever the reason, three-quarters of the native Arab-Palestinians left Israel for their own reasons. Nearly one hundred years later, five million Arabs claimed the right to come back to their homeland from supposed exile. Most of them could not even prove that their ancestry came from Palestine.

However, the Arab-Israelis jumped on the reclamation bandwagon. They knew that if five million Arabs moved in, Israel would have a Muslim majority, and that would spell the end of the Jewish homeland. The Jews would be driven into the sea through democracy. At first the Arab-Israelis used labor strikes and the like to accomplish their goals. Since they made up such a large part of the country, it often brought the economic infrastructure to a standstill.

The Israeli government fired a huge portion of the strikers and replaced them with Jews who came to Israel for the new jobs. This gravely offended the Arabs and the terrorist attacks began soon after.

The Israeli government had its hands tied. They could not act decisively against the movement within their country, because the majority of Europe sympathized with the Palestinians and thought that the Jewish-Israelis were the oppressors. But, all that changed with Geiseric.

Geiseric threw in his lot with the Jews and brought the weight of Germania with him. The Germanians were won over by Geiseric's propaganda campaign, which put the Jews in a very good light. Within years, the Germans were the most pro-Semitic people in the world, besides the Jews of course.

Geiseric then endorsed the idea to expel all Arabs and Muslims from Israel, which set the Middle East ablaze more than anything had for a thousand years. Geiseric was seen as the new Barbarossa, the most feared of the great crusaders. Eight hundred years prior, the emperor of Germania, also called the Holy Roman Empire at this time, was Friedrich I, known as Babarossa — Red Beard.

The Third Crusade began as Barbarossa led a grand German Army that threatened to invade and reclaim most of the Middle East for Christendom. He was by far the greatest threat the Muslim world had ever faced, and he was victorious in his first two major battles, brushing the powerful Turks aside. But, the great terror to the Muslims and the great hero to the Christians came to a non-climactic end, when he fell from his horse while crossing a river. The shock of the cold water gave the older warrior a mild heart attack, which made him too weak to rise with all the weight of his armor. He drowned and his army, stunned and demoralized, disbanded and went home. The Third Crusade then became famous for the exploits of Richard the Lionhearted, who led a far weaker force and accomplished little compared to what Barbarossa did and, especially, could have done had he lived. The Islamic world was given a reprieve by Allah then, and the Muslims were now hoping for another miracle.

The sky sweltered from the endless heat of the summer of 2033. A young man walked into a Jerusalem café after submitting to a search by the guards posted at the doors. He passed through the entrance and, suddenly, a powerful blast rocked the café and fire ripped through the building.

That night, Prime Minister Solomon Leon spoke to a large mass of Israelis gathered on the terraced lawn in front of the Knesset, the Israeli Parliament building. As usual, a huge crowd of protesters pestered the audience from behind barricades. All of these protesters were Jews who either thought the deportation of the Arab-Israelis was unfair, or even illegal, or they were against the inevitable alliance with Germania.

Leon's voice was amplified through speakers behind him that were angled out toward the audience.

"Do not fret, my fellow Israelis. We have the might of Germania behind us, and Geiseric will not betray us! Some of you think my decision to pull out of the West Bank is nothing more than giving in to the terrorists. Others think that *I'm* the terrorist, because of the deportation of Muslims from what is left of Israel. But, we *must* pull out of these territories. The present conditions have gone on too long." Solomon looked out upon the crowd and was filled with an incredible energy that seemed to possess him. In his mind, he was standing at the brink of the ultimate redemption of his people. Chills ran up his spine and the words bellowed from his chest with tremendous power and confidence.

"We must be decisive! And, since we cannot go to war with nor subdue the entire Muslim world, we must back off. On the other hand, we will not let the Muslim world think that we are scared away by their terrorism, for that only justifies such behavior. So, I have had to be decisive in my approach. We will evacuate Muslim territory and, in turn, because of those few who commit heinous acts like today's tragedy in the cafe, we will force the Muslims out of our territory. Make no mistake, Israel is ours and it will *never* be a Muslim state!" he furiously asserted to the uproarious approval of his supporters.

"Many Palestinians, and I dare say others, would love to see us driven out of the Middle East, preferably into the Mediterranean where they could watch us drown like rats. At the very least, they yearn to once again overthrow us and rule all Israeli territory." His delivery built in ever greater rage and fervor. "They will never give up on that dream! That is why Joshua massacred the Canaanites! That is why the white Americans wiped out the Native Americans! One day, you realize that the natives will never accept that this is your land now. Back then, the weaker died. But, now there are rules that prohibit us from simply purging peoples from our land. Good! That is a good thing," he remarked, somewhat unconvincingly.

"I am no murderer or criminal. In fact, I am saving the lives of our people by deporting these terrorists. Many Muslim leaders have compared me to Hitler. But, Hitler certainly did not stop with the deportation of the Jews. So, this is a foolish remark. I wish my peoples were *just* deported! The Muslim peoples of the Middle East are lucky that this is a more refined time, for Israel has the might to defeat them again and again, especially with Germania on our side. We have done it before and, if they ever attempt to attack us, we will do it again!"

FLIGHT OF THE KOLIBRI

November 1, 2033

Prime Minister Leon reclined thoughtfully in his large plush chair in his office. He sat with his elbows propped up on the arms of the chair, head resting atop his interlocked fingers. In the two months that had passed since his controversial deportation of the Muslims, things had been quiet — almost too quiet. A knock on the door startled him out of his reverie, and his defense minister and two top generals walked in.

The shorter of the two generals spoke first. His voice was deep and he made liberal use of the jugular sounds of the Hebrew language. "The Palestinians are not holding to their side of the deal, Sir."

Leon smiled at the stocky man. "Who really thought they would, General Hakkak? Let me guess, the Palestinians of the West Bank are allowing a large Arab army to cross the river and assemble in their territory."

"Yes, Sir," replied Hakkak, raising his eyebrows, a bit surprised that Leon was so nonchalant about the situation. "They are, in fact, allowing huge Iraqi, Iranian, Afghani, and Jordanian contingents to cross the Jordan River. There are about half a million troops in the West Bank already. They are keeping their forces camouflaged, but there appears to be thousands of light-armor vehicles and at least two hundred tanks. Most likely they'll attempt to drive west and cut Israel in half. Then they will split, heading both north and south, where they will box us in between the Syrian, Saudi Arabian and Egyptian armies. Divide and conquer," the general reflected with trepidation. "They have the force to do it this time."

"Yes, well," Leon waved his hand in the air as if shooing an imaginary fly, "they have wanted to do this for some time. We would have been fools not to see this coming. This is a larger force than I would have expected," he clenched his jaw in contemplation, "but don't be afraid." He looked General Hakkak straight in the eye. "While they seem powerful enough to defeat Israel, they pale in comparison to Germania's forces."

Hakkak considered the possible consequences if Solomon was wrong. "Well, sir, I have only been given a vague idea of what Germania has. You, on the other hand, have seen what their military capabilities are and I will trust your assessment, but," the general raised the corner of his right eyebrow, "our intelligence reports say that the Muslim armies are technologically advanced and extremely organized. Who is helping *them*, I wonder?"

Leon shook his head, not wanting to even hear what the general was insinuating. "You must trust me," he demanded. "Geiseric is our ally. Whoever is helping our enemies, if they are being helped, it is not Germania."

"Well then," the defense minister implored, "what do we do?"

"We wait," Leon replied matter-of-factly. He stood and walked over to the large window behind his desk. He was silent for a moment, as he stared out at the lawn below. Suddenly, he whipped back around with a look of determined faith.

"There is no doubt that Geiseric knows everything we know and more. I'm sure that he is presently analyzing the threat and planning out the strategy to defeat their forces." He rubbed his chin with his left thumb and forefinger as he thought.

"We will prepare our troops for now, but Geiseric has personally assured me that, if our neighbors should ever try to invade, Germanic forces would bear the full brunt of the fighting." Leon's conviction was enough to momentarily assuage the fear of his top generals.

"Trust me, we need only watch and wait until it is over."

The armies of Iraq, Jordan, Iran and Afghanistan began preparing for battle. They were the first prong of the invasion. The leaders of these Muslim countries had secretly united their military forces, along with those of Syria, Lebanon and Egypt, who would take part in the second phase of the invasion. They were an Islamic Confederation specifically designed to drive the Jews out of the Middle East, once and for all. The Islamic Confederation infantry was equipped with the most technologically advanced military gear available to the United States and Britain. Underneath their desert-camouflaged uniforms, light body armor covered their bodies from head to foot. Their heads were topped with typical, Western-style helmets and night-vision goggles. The goggles were equipped with a mode that improved their visual range by twenty times, allowing the soldiers to see clearly for many kilometers across the desert at night. The soldiers loaded their semi-automatic and automatic guns, which even though they were slightly longer than most of their arms, were extraordinarily light.

The CIA and MI6, in their largest black operation in history, had secreted two-hundred fighter jets, two-hundred-and-eighty of the latest American and British tanks, one-hundred armored helicopter gunships and hundreds of thousands of machine guns, sidearms, nightvision goggles and other such equipment to the Muslim troops. China also made a tremendous contribution, covertly providing a startling ten-thousand, armored personnel carriers capable of transporting fifty men each.

As the troops outside prepared for action, the leaders met in a large war room at a nearby command post. There were two men in charge of the entire operation: General Javani of Iran and General Faysal of Iraq. They came from the two most powerful nations in the Islamic Confederation. In many ways, they were from the same nation, since Iraq was little more than a province in a Greater Iran. Though Iraq had been helped by Germania in the 2028 Olympics, much had changed in the five years since. The Iraqis had come to hate and fear Germania because of Geiseric's anti-Muslim stance and links to Israel.

General Faysal had a large, bulging scar traced across his cheek. He related the news to Javani in Arabic, the common language of the Middle Eastern coalition.

"They have pulled their troops back, far away from the border of the West Bank. They have deployed numerous anti-aircraft installations around all cities. It seems that they are using their army to defend the cities from bombing or shelling."

Javani was tall, light-skinned, and had emerald green eyes. "Why would the Israelis not face our armies? They cannot win this way," he wondered aloud. "They must know we are going to *pummel* them into the ground. They obviously did not expect us to be this powerful."

Faysal shook his head. "They are pulling back to let Germania's forces blunt our sword."

"Those cowards!" Javani smashed his fist into his palm, but quickly collected himself and spoke again calmly. "Oh well, no matter. I suppose I knew they would do something like this. But we have a mighty army at our disposal!

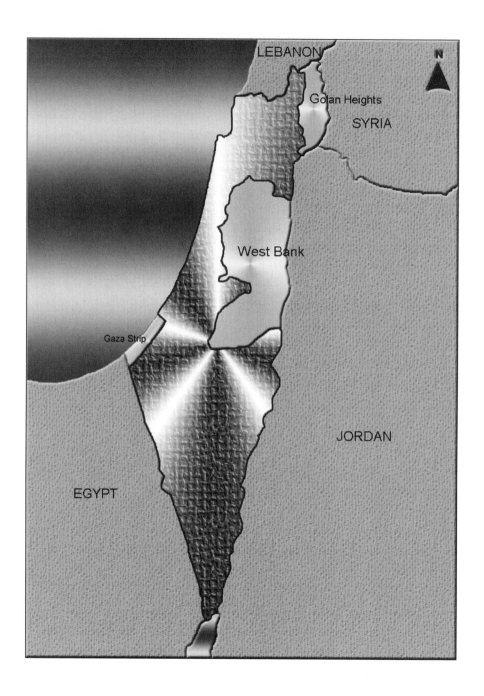

This is not even a quarter of it. We have the best equipment and the best training. If we pull out all the stops, we will *crush* whatever Germania sends at us. Then we will crush Israel!"

"Let us crush them right now!" the Iraqi general roared.

The Islamic Confederation troops were loaded into the personnel carriers and all the vehicles were fired up. At midnight, they poured out from the West bank into Israel. The tanks and helicopter gunships represented the climax of the United States' technology from an era that began in the first two World Wars. It was then that the cavalry became mechanized and propeller-driven crafts, such as planes and helicopters, gave rise to an air force and sky cavalry. The sky cavalry helicopters often worked alongside the ground cavalry tanks and carrier vehicles in leading the charge, and such was how the Islamic Confederation began their invasion.

The helicopter gunships and tanks spearheaded the invasion into Israel, with the personnel carriers only a few kilometers behind. As the army raced west toward the Mediterranean, divisions began breaking off, heading southwest and northwest. In perfect choreography, the Islamic forces in Syria, Saudi Arabia and Egypt received the signal to begin their invasion.

Initially, there was no resistance to the Confederation Army, and they were able to move through Israel completely undeterred. Then, the formations' lead helicopters picked up something on radar.

Hundreds of small aircraft were bearing down from the north, south and west, encircling the invasion forces. Their incredible acceleration and erratic maneuvering stunned the lead gunship commander. He quickly radioed his forces with the initial readings.

"I've got a mass of small craft coming in from all around, low and fast, at about seven hundred kilometers per hour."

The invading gunships fired their arsenals of small missiles towards the incoming mystery aircraft. Over four-thousand missiles, which homed in on radar-tracked points, were launched in all directions, but the small blips on the radar dodged everything that came at them! The gunship commanders were stupefied by the agility of these unidentified craft. As they looked out on the horizon through night-vision telescopes, they saw creatures that looked part bird, part insect, and part human.

It was the Kolibri flyers.

For a moment, the lead gunship commander was unable to think, his jaw dropping open in bewilderment. The creatures looked almost beautiful when the moonlight peeked through the clouds to shimmer off their armor.

But these graceful and bizarre forces were something to be feared and, within seconds, they were upon the invaders.

The heavy sky infantry, which General Gottlieb had designed, flew in first. With their thick and weighty armor, the "heavies," as Gottlieb called them in German, lacked the dexterity of Von Edeco's design. Nonetheless, they were still far more agile than the helicopter gunships. Thus, the mission was better served by the well-armored design. Once more, the Islamic Confederation gunships opened up on the incoming battlemachines, this time with everything they had. Laying down a seemingly impenetrable wall of machine gun fire and missiles, the invaders were unable to destroy a single one of the Kolibri.

Three flyers at a time took hold of the helicopters with grappling hooks, or just with their armored hands. Grabbing from different points and using the powerful strength-enhancers within their armor, the Germanian heavy sky infantrymen pulled the helicopters down from the air. They spun the gunships to make the soldiers inside dizzy and slammed the obsolete flying machines into the sand. When the choppers were on the ground, the Kolibri flyers used their guns to blow off all the rotor blades. They threw canisters of sleeping gas inside the helicopters, knocking out the soldiers. Those troops who scampered to put their gas masks on in time were knocked out by swift punches from the Kolibri flyers. Within twenty minutes, the entire invading sky cavalry had been taken out without a single Islamic Confederation soldier or officer killed. The Kolibri sky infantry was completely unscathed.

Once the Confederation's near-to-ground air power was fully subdued, the Kolibri flyers turned their attention toward the tanks. The invaders could not even assess what they were fighting with, let alone how to mount a counter-attack. The heavy sky infantrymen methodically set about incapacitating the enemy tanks, taking care to avoid harming the soldiers inside. Instructions had come in from the very top that this was going to be as bloodless a war as possible. They wanted to avoid global scrutiny at all costs.

The Kolibri swooped down on the tanks. If the tank commanders were looking out of the top of the tank, the flyers had no problem ripping them and the rest of the tank personnel out of their vehicles. But, if the top hatch was closed, the Kolibri could not get in despite their armor's muscle-enhancing strength. In these cases, they threw small bombs on the tank tracks, momentarily disabling the ground vehicles. The Kolibri then flew out of sight, pretending to have moved on to another fight. As the tank crews got out to fix their vehicles, they would suddenly find themselves swarmed by the winged charioteers, buzzing around them like harpies, firing on the bewildered Muslim soldiers with tranquilizer dart guns. Within another fifteen minutes, the Confederation's entire tank force lay shattered and disabled in the dunes.

The regular sky infantry brigade, led by Captain Von Edeco himself, was the next to descend upon the unwitting Confederation. "The Captain," being the designer of this type of Kolibri, was the natural leader of this force. He would have had it no other way. Von Edeco was in his element when in battle and, armed with his amazing new creations, he zealously stormed into the fray. He led a division of one-thousand sky infantry "regulars," as they were called, over the battlefield to put the enemy's half-million strong ground infantry force out of action.

Captain Von Edeco and his band of marauding charioteers systematically disabled all ten-thousand armored personnel carriers, shooting or breaking off the exterior defensive machine guns with such speed that the gunners could not even see them — let alone hit them. Three or four Kolibri at a time flew at the armored carriers, which looked like large Earthmover trucks. Using similar methods to those used against the tanks, the Kolibri regulars placed bombs on the metal tracks on the back half of the vehicle, or the large, thick tires at the front. The carriers were abruptly paralyzed as their tracks and tires exploded into shards of metal and rubber. Some of them toppled over onto their sides, sending their occupants scurrying out to safety.

The soldiers exited their carriers, weapons in hand and prepared to fight to the death, but the Kolibri simply ripped their guns away and either hogtied the invaders together, or if time would not allow this, the flyers knocked the enemy out with a swift, well-placed punch across the chin. Before the dawn was even near its approach, nearly five hundred thousand Islamic Confederation troops were stripped of their weapons and left prostrate before the Germanian sky infantry, leaving only pockets of resistance. The Muslim soldiers were stunned and confused, but went almost entirely uninjured. Only a few had been killed in the tumult, most by friendly fire.

The Islamic Confederation leaders back at the West Bank command post were bewildered and shaken by the unexpected turn of events. Only hours before, they had confidently sent out their troops to conquer all of Israel. Now, their army was in shambles.

All across Israel, people in their homes danced and hugged and cried with joy, as word broke of the night's battle. Most Israeli Jews had stayed up late, fraught with anxiety, terrified that this was the Islamic Army that would finally make good on the decades of genocidal threats to "drive them into the sea." The Jews of Israel were praying in their homes, keeping glued to the television to get the latest news. Suddenly, Prime Minister Leon appeared on the screen to proudly address his nation.

"I have just gotten word," he cracked an easy smile, "that the Muslim *invasion* forces have been defeated and we have suffered *zero casualties!*"

A cheer went up across Israel like none before in the land. People jubilantly tossed their hands up, slapping their brethren on the back in camaraderie.

"However," he continued, "our intelligence shows that the Islamic Confederation Army still has much of their military strength. Most of their force was not deployed in this initial invasion, and they now intend to use it. So," he declared authoritatively, "Israel will be embarking on an expeditionary mission with the forces of Germania, to all the countries known to have attacked Israel tonight. It would be foolhardy to not destroy our enemy's military strength now, before they re-organize and attack us again. You do not wait until wasps have left the nest to kill them!" He roared, purposefully making a non-Isaianic analogy in order to divert the scrutiny of critics who may have deemed this counter-strike to be an Isaianic mission.

"You smash them inside of their hive! We will take the fight to our enemies, so that they may know how *we* feel!"

As the morning sunlight rose upon the desert, the Israeli-Germanic front stormed across the Egyptian, Syrian, Lebanese, Jordanian and Saudi Arabian borders. The Israeli forces hung to the rear and allowed the Germanic forces to shoulder the brunt of the fighting, using their unstoppable weaponry. By the afternoon, all of Israel's immediate neighbors were subdued. The counter-offensive next moved into tougher countries like Iraq and Iran. Because of staunch resistance, it took a couple of days to subdue these countries, but it was done as thoroughly and cleanly as before. The Kolibri flyers mopped the floor with everyone from Afghanistan to Egypt. Panzers were also used to bust through the largest and strongest tank divisions.

The American, British and Chinese leaders had no idea what had happened. The Muslim Armies were overwhelmed so fast that few soldiers were able to escape and tell the rest of the world about the unbelievable creations they faced. A handful of Muslim fighters escaped becoming prisoners of war and babbled on to the CIA and MI6 about demonic spirits that had clawed, beaten and burned the Confederation forces with their uncanny, supernatural speed and abilities.

The world was in awe. In only three days, the Israeli-Germanic front had secured control over nearly the entire Middle East. The Israelis took administrative control over the conquered territories and put the captured soldiers in hospitable POW camps, where they were well fed and cared for. The Islamic Confederation soldiers were surprised by the decent treatment afforded them by their captors and considered that perhaps they had misjudged the Jews. Perhaps the other side was simply not the heartless, evil group portrayed in the Muslim propaganda.

The United Nations was furious at Israel and Germania for supposedly manipulating the Muslim countries. They alleged that Geiseric had tricked the Islamic Confederation into attacking Israel to serve as pretext for taking over their land. The American and British ambassadors alleged that Germania was secretly supplying the Islamic Confederation advanced technology to stroke their confidence, but not as advanced as that of Israel's. But, when the media investigated and found that the Confederation vehicles, though unmarked, appeared to be British and American-made, the world became suspicious of President Hollier and Prime Minister Dandau for first lodging the accusations.

Solomon Leon pulled out his troops and left the Islamic Confederation's military bureaucracy intact. Thus, the Muslim Middle East was now united under a single government for the first time since the Ottoman Turkish Empire of the early nineteenth century. The industry and economy of the nations within the united territory improved and became stronger than they had been before the occupation.

The newly united area was named Mesopotamia. Solomon set up a puppet government led by someone Geiseric chose personally. Abu Al-Alammeine, the new brawn behind Geiseric's brain, was given the title of caliph, an old Arab term for the leader of all the Muslims. Al-Alammeine forced the Middle-Eastern Arabs to do whatever Geiseric instructed. Although there was no base for Isaiism in most of these countries, Al-Alammeine forced the people to convert to Isaianic practices by the sword, much like their ancestors had been converted to Islam by Mohammed and his followers in the seventh and eighth centuries. The Muslims could still worship Allah, though, and perform any rituals that didn't involve killing or torturing animals. Unfortunately for them, many of their rituals did.

The caliph ruled from Iran, the only country in Mesopotamia with a vague history of animal rights. To the Greeks, the Iranians were known as the Persians. The ancient Persian Empire was founded on their native belief of Zoroastrianism, which preached respect for animals and nature. Zoroastrians believed that an end time would come when the forces of good conquered evil. This had a huge effect on the surrounding religions, especially Judaism and Christianity.

After the war, Israel laid claim to three times the amount of land that the nation had before. Prime Minister Leon insisted on keeping parts of Lebanon, Jordan, and Syria. The disapproving U.N. threatened war. In response, Geiseric made an announcement that scared the entire world like never before. He declared with angry rhetoric that, "If the powers that be chose to stand against the Germanian Commonwealth and its allies, there would be hell to pay."

The Germanian chancellor made it clear that the latest battle was just a *taste* of his military's technological power.

Less attention was paid to the Indian land grab of Pakistan, which was going on simultaneously as the Israeli-Germanic forces were storming through the Middle East, wreaking havoc on the Islamic forces. Pakistan remained neutral during that conflict and kept their eyes on the Indians, who the Pakistanis knew were trying to annex the Indus River Valley back into their fold. But, Pakistan had also been secreted weapons from the United States, Great Britain and China, and more importantly, Pakistan had "the bomb" — the nuclear bomb — thirteen hundred and forty-six of them to be exact. They were either shells that could be fired from artillery and strike Indian border towns, or they were warheads loaded atop hypersonic intermediate-range missiles that could be launched and strike anywhere in India in minutes.

Pakistan had become a nuclear power at the turn of the millennium, in order to stave off India, which had nukes of its own. They had been in conflict since their separation right after Ghandi won India's freedom from Britain. The divisions were drawn primarily down religious lines. The Muslim majority of the Indus River Valley, India's namesake, declared themselves to be the new independent nation of Pakistan. Almost ever since, the two nations had seen perpetual skirmishes with one another.

Small arms fire and artillery shelling over each other's borders into nearby towns and cities was a nightly occurrence, meant to terrorize the other side. The predominance of bombardment was done by Pakistan. One night, the Pakistani artillery crews situated along the border of India fired a few salvos over the line, in their routine manner. They were met with a return fire unlike that ever seen in history.

India sent twenty thousand cruise missiles over the Pakistani border. The missiles traveled far faster than any other in their class, almost eight thousand kilometers per hour. A quarter of them were aimed at the primary targets — the nuclear missile silos and nuclear artillery bunkers — which had been uncovered by Germanian Intelligence.

The cruise missiles sent over from India had redundant targets, with ten missiles aimed at every nuclear weapons bunker, silo and mobile unit, to ensure they were all knocked out. The missiles were specially designed to fly under the radar. By the time they were picked up by Pakistani control rooms, it was too late.

Explosions rocked the entire country of Pakistan, as thousands of the Indian projectiles hit their targets simultaneously, allowing not a single ballistic missile to get off the ground. Even the smallest nuclear weapons were targeted and destroyed. The cruise missiles that were not aimed at nuclear weapons instead targeted the Pakistani radar installations and military communications infrastructure.

While the last of the cruise missiles were still falling to the ground, the Indian military invaded Pakistan. They used Indian-made weapons and machines, since the economy of India was thriving and the country graduated more engineers than anywhere else. The only thing in the Indian expeditionary force that was made in Germania was the General. General Von Sanders led a mighty army that was powerfully motivated to take back their namesake. Giving a new meaning to Blitzkrieg, the Indian forces defeated Pakistan within three hours.

The next day, the Indian people awoke to wonderful news: not only was the Pakistani nuclear threat removed, but the Indians had taken back that which they believed was rightfully theirs. On that day, they threw celebrations and sang Geiseric's praises. Furthermore, to show their allegiance, nearly 750 million Indians converted to Isaiism, making India more than ninety-percent Isaianic. Many had already agreed with Isaiism's ethical values before, but never fully converted in name. It was the single greatest mass conversion in history by far. Isaiism now outranked Islam and trailed only Christianity in size.

✝ ✝ ✝

Solomon Leon and Abu Al-Alammeine announced that Israel and Mesopotamia were joining the Germanian Commonwealth. The new political entity was dubbed the Triax Empire by opponents such as President Hollier and Prime Minister Dandau, for it was divided into three main segments: the European sector (Germania and Greece), the Middle Eastern sector, and India. The United Nations did not know how to react, and the leaders plunged into heated debates. They knew that the Mesopotamian government was nothing more than a puppet state for Geiseric. The multitude of crimes perpetrated by Geiseric's regime from the moment he came to power, not the least of which being the disappearances of many animal vivisectionists and slaughterhouse owners in the Triax nations, could not be ignored. A lot of people were emigrating from their homelands in the Triax to safer harbors, and many more were disallowed from leaving. Some of these managed to escape and defect. Some who petitioned to leave were never seen again.

However, while the UN made threats, war could never be declared because the French and Russian governments both had veto power. At this point in time, early 2034, the French and Russian presidents were still using Geiseric to accomplish their own objectives.

Germania's, Russia's and France's alliance to colonize Mars resulted in their having control of the entire Red Planet. Each nation administered a third of the planet's surface and any resources beneath. The three mighty European nations were the first to establish empires in space. The leaders of France and Russia had attained for their countries the prominence and illustriousness that their people thrived upon. Plus, Sinclair and Kurtkin truly thought they had the upper-hand. For instance, Geiseric had made another deal with the Russian president upon seizing the Middle East, conceding that Kurtkin could extend the Russian Federation into Kazakhstan, Uzbekistan, Turkmenistan and the other Muslim nations of Central Asia. Geiseric's allies thought they were gaining far more for their nations and empires than he was, so they didn't fear him, nor did they fear the growing power of Germania and the Triax.

However, Sinclair and Kurtkin had not foreseen that Geiseric could establish dominion over a mighty nation whose technological and industrial modernity was near to that of Germania's and had superseded the United States in terms of innovation.

Japan, unlike the U.S.A, was a small country with few natural resources. Yet, Japan had become a super-power that out-competed the Americans in many fields of science and engineering. It was not hard to understand, considering that by 2020 Japan graduated five times as many scientists and engineers

as the United States, while having half the population. There was a simple reason for this as well — the Japanese cared about these important fields. The culture promoted interest for intellectual discovery.

Geiseric enticed Japan to join his empire using many different avenues, including the fact that Germany and Japan were allies in World War II, when both nations were attempting the takeovers of giant neighbors. The Japanese shared a sense of camaraderie with the Germans, and even had an admiration for them. Now, Geiseric was endorsing Japan's right to expand again, primarily into Korea and Indochina.

Modern Japan was inclined to be Isaianic only in the vaguest sense. It was Geiseric's endorsement for expansion that was greatly welcomed by the Japanese population. The Triax emperor even went so far as to mention California as a possible annexation to Japan, an idea once entertained by World War II Imperialist Japan.

There were a hundred and fifty million people living on the tiny island chain of Japan, an area about the size of California. The Japanese could do nothing but immigrate to other countries, namely the United States, to escape the overcrowding. Japan was constantly hemorrhaging some of its best citizens across the Pacific to California. The immigrants were industrious and thriving in America. Japan was also the single largest private investor in Californian business. The wheels were already in motion. Geiseric simply sped things up.

By 2036, there were sixty-million people in California, twelve million of whom were Japanese ex-patriots or first generation Americans whose parents had emigrated from Japan. The majority of these were tantalized by the idea of California being brought under Japan's wing. Pro-Isaianic native Californians wished to secede from the United States to be allied with the Triax. This was the only part of the United States where there could be found large numbers of people who seriously embraced the Isaianic movement. And so, the Isaianic and Japanese factions united and the Principles Party looked like it was going to gain a majority in the State Congress.

When Geiseric proposed the annexation of California to a new Japanese Empire, the present and more conservative majority in the California legislature became alarmed and eventually, with the backing of the Supreme Court, disallowed any Japanese ex-patriot to vote.

A constituency that managed to bulk up the anti-Isaianic and anti-Apex movement in California was the Aztlani movement. Twenty million Mexicans lived in the western state. They were the single largest racial population, even outnumbering those of European ancestry. The majority were those who had been coming to California since the Federal government had declared "closed borders" to be racist in 2015.

Ninety percent of those coming over from Mexico were believers in Aztlanism, which was an ideology based on the legend of the Aztec homeland. The Aztecs had an empire based in Southern Mexico when the Spanish came upon them in the early sixteenth century. Mexico comes from Mejica, the native name of the Aztec people. The Aztec Empire did not stretch far past southern Mexico, and certainly never had dominion over the land that became the United States. However, the Spanish Empire in the Americas did.

California, Nevada, Utah, Arizona, Texas and Mexico were first claimed as a single unit by the Spanish. When the Mexicans gained independence, they maintained power over the land based on the fact that it was part of the former Spanish Empire. However, many Aztlanis had a very anti-European stance, so to lay claim to land based on their inheritance from the Spanish was somewhat convoluted. To give credence to their claim, the Aztlan legend was created, which said that the Aztecs originated in the Southwest United States and immigrated long ago to Mexico before starting their empire. Thus, in the minds of those who bought into the fabrication, the Spanish Empire was nothing more than a continuation of the Aztec Empire.

And so, when the United States annexed the southwest in 1848, after crushing the Mexican forces, it was not seen as merely a European peoples taking land from a former European empire, but once again a raping of the natives by the "white man."

Aztlanis disassociated themselves from their own Spanish heritage, claiming to have mainly the blood of the Native Americans. They also neglected to focus on the natives' own brutality. The Aztecs, and many of the Native American empires that preceded them, practiced human sacrifice. During the few decades of their empire's peak, the Aztecs murdered somewhere in the order of fifty million of their Native American neighbors. The sacrifice involved cutting open the stomach of a live person, reaching up to the heart, and ripping it out still beating. Often children were used as sacrifices, even infants, for they were considered to be pure.

This was given little attention. Aztlanis claimed that they had more right to the Western United States than did the "evil Europeans." They declared California and the other southwestern states to be theirs. Thus, they were natural foes to the Japanese. Mexican gangs of every stripe merged their forces and formed numerous bands of terror squads known as the Mexican Militia. Their most effective means of obstructing their enemy was to attack pro-annexation demonstrations by the Japanese and Isaianic factions. It was expected that all the Mexican Militia need do was beat a few hundred pro-Apex agitators in the streets and they would send their opponent running.

But, the Japanese and Isaianics did not cower in the face of terror tactics. They formed security teams to protect the demonstrators that were highly successful at thrashing any would-be assaulters. When the Mexican Militia turned more violent, using knives and guns, the pro-Apex faction responded in kind. Arming themselves with weapons stealthily supplied to them from Apex nations, the security teams grew into a secessionist army two million strong.

Contemporary Japanese culture did not have a very strong animal-rights theme, in the conventional sense. The Japanese had an eye for the aesthetic and a love of nature's beauty. But, they were one of the few remaining nations with a whaling industry and they were doing it en masse to boot. They also had the most detrimental fishing industry in the world. Often, Japanese cuisine had an abusive side. For instance, fish were many times served so raw that they were, literally, still alive. Chefs would just slice open the fish's gut and put the creature on a plate, ready to eat as it lay gasping its last breaths.

What they did have was an environmental culture. Due to their over-population, the Japanese were forced to adapt a higher understanding of the problems of air and water pollution to protect the health of their populace. And then, there was Shintoism, a religion deeply rooted in Japan. It went back at least sixty-five hundred years to the original hunter-gatherer tribes of the island. Similar to some Native American beliefs, the Shinto worshipped nature gods, gods of the trees, the rocks, the air and the rivers, thus, not so indirectly worshipping nature. East Asians were systematic thinkers and, in general, had a concept of harmonious existence, which could be achieved through environmental practices among other things. This was especially true in Japan, where there was also a powerful intellectual elite. Yet, it was still a leap for the average Japanese citizen to become an Isaianic. Japan had the smallest Isaianic following of all the nations allying with Germania, but without that following, Japan never would have come on board.

It took some ego-stroking from Geiseric. He gave speeches about how the Japanese culture stood as one of the superior influences towards the civilization of mankind. Though the essence of this message was similar to that which he delivered to all nations he wished to curry favor with, Geiseric had a keen talent for customizing his words and making it sound fresh every time. He said that Japan had every right to invade China in the 1930s, and that the land would have been used a lot better if they had. Geiseric claimed the Americans were hypocritical imperialists. The Japanese media became fond of replaying one of Geiseric's speech snippets: "The Americans take a whole continent and eradicate a native people, but we Germans and Japanese, *we* are the bad guys?"

That quote really got the Japanese populace fired up, and helped to give Geiseric legitimacy in their eyes. They thought, why are we sitting on this little island? Why aren't we allowed to expand? Geiseric's speeches justifying wars of aggression for expansion rang true in the ears of the Japanese. Geiseric gave them permission to grow and this seduced enough of them that their president, Hidekio Honomura, a closet Isaianic, was able to cede his peoples' sovereignty to the Germanian chancellor.

The 2036 Munich Olympic Games were coming to a close. The main stadium was packed with an international crowd of spectators. Altogether, more than a quarter of a million people filled the seats. The competitors from every country stood on the floor of the arena, waving to the crowd. Fireworks filled the sky and, as the spectacle ended, the crowd erupted in applause for the athletes.

It had been a remarkable Olympics. Despite the incredible tumult building between Germania and most of the industrialized nations, everyone sent larger delegations of athletes to Munich than any Olympics prior. Competitive countries like the United States were not going to look like they were afraid of being outdone by the Triax's training system.

All of the powerful nations performed far better than they had four years prior, when the Formula training process was still in its infancy. In every game, records were broken and left far behind. Such gains had never been made in all of Olympic history. Every track and field star beat their best times and scores, making progress that usually took the world decades to match. Even more amazing was the fact that Germania, Russia, the United States, Romania, China and France all had gymnasts that received at least one perfect ten. This, also, had never been done.

What perhaps was the most outstanding aspect of the 2036 Olympic Games was the fact that not a single athlete from any of the industrialized nations tested positive for performance enhancing drugs or hormones. But, no one was surprised, because everyone knew that the Formula training system was behind the startling athletic progress.

Much had occurred since it was announced seven years ago that the '36 Olympics would be held in Munich. All of the powerful countries outside of the Triax had enacted a training system similar to the one designed by Geiseric. The most unique aspect of the Formula system of athletic training was that the trainees learned things that seemed completely unrelated to the game they were competing in. The athletes learned the basics of playing the piano, foreign languages, and physics. One of the primary tenets of the Formula system was that the human brain and body helped to develop each other, and specific exercises and studies worked well together, a contention backed by tried and true science. There were some subjects that strengthened specific skills. For instance, learning dance improved speaking skills and learning music improved math ability. One of the most unexpected results was that learning algebra seemed to really help athletic performance, especially in the track and field runners.

The fundamental difference between the Triax Formula training system and that of the rest of the industrialized nations was that the Triax prohibited their athletes from ingesting meat and dairy products. Dairy products were not prohibited to the average person in the Triax, because the creation of them was not inherently cruel to animals. Rather, the Isaianics believed that drinking a mother cow's or goat's milk was unnatural and perverted because no animal, human or otherwise, was meant to drink milk past infancy. The Isaianics argued that, if most humans felt it was so strange to drink a woman's breast milk as an adult, why was it not even stranger to drink the breast milk of a female cow or goat. They also felt it wasn't a good source of nutrition for an adult human, which is why it was prohibited to the Olympic athletes.

But the Triax did not outlaw dairy products in the empire, as long as the milk animals were treated kindly, kept well and never killed. Inevitably, because the factory farm process of milk-production was outlawed within the Triax, along with an embargo on goods produced in such a manner, the cost of milk products skyrocketed. Soon, they were considered quite a delicacy. Thus, dairy products became highly appreciated and not taken for granted as before, which fit with the Isaianic Creed.

The Isaianics preached that eggs were the only food produced by an animal that was ideal to eat. Chickens produced eggs all the time, without impregnation. Cows and goats, on the other hand, needed to be kept impregnated to produce milk. So, the Isaianics did not have criticisms with egg consumption, and they promoted it as a superior source of nutrition for vegetarians, as long as they were from chickens raised in a cruelty-free manner and who were, of course, never killed. Eggs contained B12, an extremely important vitamin found in animal products. Vegans had to take B12 in supplements in order to stay healthy. Eggs also had a tremendous amount of protein and iron that easily assimilated into the body, as well as vitamins A, D, E, and lecithin, which strengthened all the vital organs, including the brain, heart, and liver.

One of the main meals provided to the Triax athletes during their training was eggs with broccoli. The addition of the dark green vegetable nourished the competitors' bodies with all the calcium they needed—far more than milk could ever provide. Of course, this was a fact bitterly contested by the milk producers of nations outside of the Triax, the United States in particular, and most people outside of the Triax did not believe that an ova-vegetarian diet was healthier than one allowing meat and dairy products.

Therefore, it shocked the world when Germania attained gold in nearly half the competitions. The entire Triax team had an outstanding performance. Of course, the other countries denied this had anything to do with the Triax athletes' diets.

+ + +

Inside the gigantic Munich coliseum, the Olympic torch was extinguished and Geiseric walked to the podium in the center of the arena floor wearing a purple robe and a crown of olive branches, the attire of the Roman Caesars. He addressed the enormous crowd in German, the official language of the Triax Empire. His words were translated into English and a dozen other languages on an enormous video screen above and behind him.

"Today, something momentous has occurred." Geiseric raised both arms up and out. "I am very proud of all the athletes who came and tested their powers against the world," he gestured toward the competitors with a fatherly look of pride spread across his face. "Those who are champions, I salute you. I salute a person's will to be the best, to embrace challenges. That is why I love the Olympics.

"I wish to salute the whole world. Everyone has displayed dynamism these past weeks. Everyone deserves applause." Geiseric waited patiently as the crowd erupted into accolades for the athletes.

"There is no denying, however, how well the Triax athletes performed. I implore the world to embrace *our* Formula, the Isaianic Formula, and you too will have such results." A smattering of praiseful cheers from the Isaianic supporters in the audience commended Geiseric's words, but a large portion of the audience howled with disapproval at the Triax emperor's arrogance.

"I believe it is only appropriate that I announce something else that has transpired today," Geiseric began mysteriously. "There is no better venue for this auspicious announcement. My fellow people, today the Japanese Parliament signed an accord that will fuse Japan to the Germanian Commonwealth!"

Many of the Japanese athletes on the field applauded and cheered, but others stood stunned and reserved. A small number of them started cursing, while making obscene gestures and flailing their arms with outrage.

"Japan is the final component," Geiseric declared. "Our empire now has no match! So, from this moment forward, we shall be known as the *Apex Empire!*"

Most of the crowd cheered fanatically, throwing up their hats, chanting victory songs. But, many shouted angrily with equal ferocity. Arguments turned to scuffling and brawls soon broke out on the field and in the stands, erupting in every corner of the arena. Security guards and policemen moved in and quickly calmed the masses. Geiseric quietly watched his handiwork from the podium, smiling unabashedly.

"This is the most dominating empire that the world has ever seen!" he roared loudly. "To those of you outside the Apex, do not fear us. On the contrary, I invite you to *join us!* To the citizens of the Apex Empire, I *urge* you, let us use our power, the power we have so amply demonstrated during these Olympic Games, to expand the horizons of human accomplishment!"

Greater Japan encompassed a far larger swath of land than the nation previously had. With Geiseric's permission, the Japanese conquered and took the Indochinese nations of Vietnam, Cambodia and Laos. Next, came Korea under Japanese rule and all was ultimately Geiseric's dominion. In the wake of the creation of the Apex Empire, France and Russia immediately turned sides, allying with the United States, Britain and China. Now, the United Nations could act decisively together, except that, they did not know what to do. They felt helpless in the face of the Apex goliath.

Indochina went down without a fight, but the Koreans, with nuclear weapons of their own, believed they had a sizable enough force to intimidate the Japanese. They were bitterly mistaken. Just as in Pakistan, the Korean nuclear weapons were taken out before they could be deployed. The Chinese had threatened with great ferocity that they would go to war with Japan if Korea was invaded, but President Honomura did not even think twice about going through with the invasion, when Geiseric backed him up with an implied counter-threat to China.

Geiseric announced in a world-televised media interview that Germania, Israel, and India had far more nuclear weapons than was needed to exterminate every person in China. The Imperial Chancellor, as he was officially called, declared that, "With intercontinental ballistic missiles, and other delivery means, the Apex Empire could easily emerge victorious from a nuclear war!"

But at what cost?

When asked by reporters about the environmental results of a nuclear war, Geiseric admitted that it ran counter to Isaiism to destroy all life on Earth. However, he argued that nuclear Armageddon was also antithetical to the humanistic concepts professed by western governments during the Cold War. Geiseric asserted that war itself ran counter to any peoples' agendas, for almost all people wished to live. It was precisely because war was so terrible that it worked. He said that he would not cow down just because he had more compassion for the Earth than his enemies, for it would only empower them to continue destroying the world.

Geiseric was not truly willing to start a nuclear war. He had accomplished what he wanted with the interview: to let the entire world know that he was packing the big guns. He never outright admitted that he would authorize a nuclear attack on China, if China launched a strike on Japan. It did not need to be said, to be heard.

The people of the Apex Empire were terrified of nuclear war, especially the Isaianics, who were concerned about the health of the planet and all of its inhabitants. The nuclear threat was tremendously unpopular in Germania and it was the first time that Geiseric's base turned on him. The truth was, Geiseric was more alarmed than anyone by the prospect of nuclear Armageddon. He would have never made good on the threat. There would have been no need.

Japan was armed to the teeth with tens of thousands of the latest Germanian Spaatz missiles, which would blow down anything the Chinese could have sent over. Not only did China have the most primitive missiles of all the superpowers of the world, and the one thing the U.S., Britain, France and Russia wouldn't provide an ally with was nuclear weapons, but the Chinese government would only have launched a small percentage of their stockpile of ballistic missiles. They would not have wanted to throw away much of their nuclear arsenal over this. Otherwise, they might not have been able to deter an invasion of their homeland by one or all of the Apex nations. China's nukes also provided a bargaining chip to use against that country's Allies, so that they could convince the United States and Britain that China didn't *need* any allies. In this, agreements favorable to Chinese interests could be exacted.

Geiseric let the threat hang in the air for a few days, just long enough for the Japanese to invade Korea. The bluff had worked.

The Apex Emperor, as he was known by his enemies, found it imperative to back Japan in this relatively minor excursion, because he needed the Japanese fully behind and immersed in the Apex Empire and, eventually, all of his agendas. It was the only way he could guarantee that they would return the favor and fully back him when the time came for an even greater war.

The idea of getting California to secede from the United States was never truly entertained by the Apex elites. They tossed it out there to set the Americans off balance and to seduce Japan. Geiseric knew full well that, if California seceded and joined the Apex Empire underneath the wing of Greater Japan, the United States and other powers in the United Nations would declare war on the Apex. The emperor was not prepared for that . . . yet.

— XIV —

THE GREAT DIASPORA

Logan sat with his parents in Frau Dorner's office. She spoke to them almost entirely in German and they were able to understand most of it, even replying back in broken but understandable sentences. Those words that they didn't fully understand, the Frau would explain in English.

"Congratulations," she said. "Your two months of intensive language training are over and you have passed your courses. Because of your success, we are sending you on a month-long vacation."

Tom, Bibi and Logan stared at their counselor, unsure of what to say.

She tilted her head and smiled, the wrinkles in the corner of her eyes giving even greater warmth to her expression. "You're surprised? Remember, even though you are non-citizens, I told you before that if you fulfill your roles without argument, you will partake in the splendor of the Apex Empire. Go prepare. You will leave in one hour."

Frau Dorner handed them each simplistic maps printed on recycled paper. The maps showed where to go from their hotel room to the departure terminals, where they would embark on the strange, centipede-like aircrafts that had transported them to this detainment facility. The counselor then stamped Tom, Bibi and Logan on the top of their left hands with an invisible ink and abruptly sent them on their way.

On the way back to the room, Tom and Bibi both ruminated over the horrific thought that the stay at the hotel and everything else might be a grand charade meant to ease the minds of the Allied civilians so that they would not put up too much of a fight. Those who died in the Nazis' gas chambers were often told that they were going to the showers, and the chambers looked the part. The people going in were told to remember the number of the hook they left their clothes on, so that they may return to them. It must have been terrifying for them to have let their guards down and to let hope in, only to hear the gas instead of water seeping into the chamber.

Tom and Bibi hid their doubt from their son. There was no point in scaring him and they did not really believe that they were going to their deaths. They knew there were so many differences between the Apex and the Axis, Geiseric and Hitler. It was just hard not to let such terrible thoughts into their heads, now that they were prisoners under an enemy regime. So, Tom and Bibi did their best to keep their minds focused on the facts that shored up their faith. They found that, when the initial knee-jerk reaction of fear passed, they became evermore confident that everything would be fine and were even excited at the thought of their vacation.

All Logan could think about was whether he was going to see Francesca again. His heart was beating rapidly and he was nervously sweating. When he and his parents returned to their room, he ran over to Francesca's door and knocked on it, over and over again, but no one answered. He tried Jacques's and Sasha's room door, but they were gone as well, as was Alistair.

A half hour passed and none of them returned. Seeing how desperate their son was to find Francesca, Tom and Bibi waited as long as they could. But, the time to leave arrived and they pried Logan away, practically dragging him to the departure terminals. At the entrance to the station, the family swiped their hands under scanners, which identified the stamps on their hands and automatically opened the doors. Tom held his wife's and son's hands on either side of him, making sure he would not lose them as they entered.

The first thing to strike their eyes was a gigantic *Luftzug*, or "Air-Train," which looked just as strange and amazing as the first time they saw one. It appeared even bigger when the bottom was not partially submerged in the water, like the one they had boarded previously. The long, tear-drop shaped wings that resembled those of a dragonfly, were now easier to see and were especially fascinating as they ran along the sides of the whole length of the *Luftzug*.

Hundreds of people clambered into the cars and Tom pulled gently on his wife's and son's arms, urging them to go faster. Hopefully, they could get a booth for all of them to sit together, so that they wouldn't have to split up in different seats on the packed aircraft.

They ran to the least crowded door and found that their chosen car was hardly filled. With relief, they occupied a booth and stretched out in it, to deter others from sitting next to them. According to the instructions on the door, the opposing booth seats were each meant to fit three or more people. Fortunately, not many entered the car, as it was at the tail end of the *Luftzug*. It reminded Logan of riding subway trains in his youth. There was always a tendency for people to cluster into the nearest car, instead of just walking a few yards to a less crowded one.

He laid down, taking up the cushioned bench opposite his parents in the booth. He closed his eyes and thought of Francesca. He had looked for her in the depot, as his father had pulled him towards the *Luftzug*, but to no avail. The thought of not seeing her again was incredibly depressing to Logan, but there was nothing he could do about it now. He tried to cling to the hope that he would see her at their vacation destination, but his mind struggled with the "what ifs," and as it did, he became more and more tired, drifting into sleep.

Suddenly, his dozing was halted by someone sitting down on his legs. It startled him out of his grogginess and before he opened his eyes he was agitated, thinking some rude person had wanted to sit down and had chosen this way to communicate it to him. But, as his eyes lazily opened, he was ecstatically surprised to see Francesca sitting on his shins, talking to Tom and Bibi. She looked down at Logan, all snuggled up on the bench.

"Hello, there!" she greeted, cheerfully. Logan smiled widely.

"Hey you, cutie pie!" He wrapped her in his arms. "Ah, there's nothing better than waking up to the sight of a beautiful woman." He winked at her, laughing a bit. Bibi and Tom exchanged looks. Just then, Alistair looked over from the booth behind Logan.

"Hey!" Logan slapped him five. He leaned over into the other booth and saw that Jacques and Sasha were there as well. He smiled at them and looked back to Francesca. "I didn't know if I was gonna see you guys again."

Alistair nodded. "Yeah, well," he pointed to Francesca, "this girl was going nuts thinking she wasn't gonna see *you* again." He sucked in his lips and lifted the middle of his eyebrows in a playfully mocking, forlorn expression.

Francesca slapped Alistair's shoulder. "I was not! You're such a liar!" For the first time, Logan saw her intensely blush.

Alistair laughed. "We all heard a rumor that those who were doing well in the German language classes were going away on vacation, so she stopped by and knocked on your door earlier, but you guys were probably at your counselor's. But, then, *we* were summoned to the counselor's office and put on this transport." Alistair jerked his thumb toward Francesca. "Trouble here, managed to spot you in the station right before you went in, and she was freaking out because she didn't know if it was actually you. She made us rush through the crowds and she was knocking people over." Alistair laughed wholeheartedly as Francesca scowled at him.

"*Shut up!*" She slapped his shoulder again and looked down, folding her arms around her chest. Logan lifted her chin with the side of his forefinger.

"I was far worse, I'm sure." He gazed into her eyes.

Alistair smirked and shook his head, turning to Tom and Bibi. "These impetuous youths," he remarked sarcastically, in the voice of a reserved, elderly man. Tom laughed and nodded, but Bibi was a little more disapproving. Her son's relationship with the girl seemed to be growing too passionate, too quickly. Bibi worried about what would happen if he and Francesca were separated by their captors at some point? But, though she didn't want to admit it, Bibi was also upset to see that her "little boy" was a young man now. She supposed that she should be glad there was someone to make Logan happy, to take his mind off the stress of the present conditions, but it was hard to watch an attractive young lady steal her baby away.

Logan fell asleep again a few minutes later, exhausted from the overwhelming emotions brought on by returned infatuation. He drifted pleasantly off into the world of dreams, as did Francesca, who spooned in front of him as they lay in the wide, cushioned bench.

Logan was again startled from his slumber, only unlike before, this time by something extremely unsettling. The sounds and rumbling of explosions had carried into his dreams, and he did not wake right away. Then, as he came into consciousness, he realized that the sounds were real. Fear immediately sank in. He jumped up, eyes wide open, worried that there might be something wrong with the air-train.

"What's going on?!" he shouted, still disoriented in half-consciousness.

"It's OK, sweetheart." Bibi soothed him, reaching over and rubbing his shoulder. "There's something going on, on the ground down there." She pointed out the large, ovular window next to their booth.

Tom and Alistair were also staring out, so Logan rushed over to see what was causing the ruckus. At first he could not see much.

The aircraft made a subtle descent through the thin clouds hanging up in the atmosphere. As the Luftzug broke through, they had an unhampered view of the endless sky and the ground far below.

The land, like most of Central and South America, was covered with dense tropical forests. Many small, abandoned villages, mainly along the coastline, were interspersed through the foliage. The Luftzug made its way over a coastal city with several tall buildings of metal and glass that shone brilliantly in the sun. Some were bombed and tattered, and crews were working on demolition. Logan watched as a large, broken skyscraper was evenly leveled by controlled explosions.

As the air-train came over the horizon, the lush forest below suddenly disappeared. Even from so far up, the ground looked ripped apart and charred. Huge swaths of jungle were thrashed and the scene quickly degenerated from ravaged into nothing more than a moon landscape.

They flew over a thin isthmus of land that was devastated from war. It was sandwiched between two endless bodies of water and the formerly green and living terrain was debased to a thick layer of gray ash. The charred earth was pockmarked with an infinite amount of craters that seemed small from high in the air, but Logan knew they would be quite large up close. He was interested in all the destroyed war machines littering the ground below. However, it was hard to distinguish what most of them looked like because they lay in pieces and were so burnt out that they were well-camouflaged against the apocalyptic environment.

Logan thought he could make out the concentrations of bodies, thousands of them strewn across the land. Like everything else, their skeletons and body armor were charred black. Gazing down at the scene, Logan could only think of the terrifying Biblical prophecies about the Apocalypse.

Alistair swallowed back some stomach acid that made its way up his throat, a minor gag reflex from the sight of the war-torn land.

He called to the booth next to them. "Are you seeing this, Jacques?!"

"*Oui,*" Jacques replied laconically, his voice betraying that he was detached, lost in some far away mental state.

Logan kept staring out the window, shocked by the destruction. "What happened here?"

Alistair shook his head, waking himself from the trance. He gulped again, painfully. His throat had become immensely dry. "The Juggernaut happened here." He zoned out for a few seconds. "This is where the Allies got to see the Juggernaut for the first time, in all its dreadful glory." He looked out upon the broken landscape.

"It had to cross here at Panama. No one knew exactly what the Juggernaut looked like before. We knew it was big, but the sight of it still blew our minds. It was so bloody huge!" he remarked, again revealing a slight British accent as he reminisced.

"Now, all the newly assimilated underclass can see how futile it is to fight. This is a great display of the Juggernaut's power, and Geiseric's." Alistair pointed to a nearly two kilometer-wide, zigzagging track of flattened vegetation. Any structures of concrete and metal that were in the path were ground to bits and pressed into the ground as easily as the foliage. The track had huge, squiggled lines embedded into it. "You see," Alistair said, "that was where it made its way across Panama, in its trek from the Atlantic to the Pacific."

Logan looked out towards the sky and saw at least twenty of the strange, centipede-like, flying trains in the air. They were all below the clouds, so that the occupants could see the sorrow below. He looked to the immense pathway that steamrolled through the jungle and cityscape, his mouth agape.

"Jesus," he remarked in disbelief, "was that made by one thing?"

Alistair lifted his eyebrow in an expression of alarm, which quickly turned to resignation.

"Yeah," he sighed. "The Juggernaut's body, not including its limbs, was about six hundred meters long across its axis. It also had huge, tentacle-like arms, dozens of them," he recalled the sight of them with awe, "*each one* bigger than a Sidewinder."

"What the f . . ." Logan breathlessly muttered.

"Exactly," Alistair nodded. "It was *quite* intimidating. Those who saw it in battle were forever humbled. And that damn thing was responsible for a lot of civilian casualties, too. Tens of millions of people," he bowed his head somberly. "The Juggernaut is the single most frightening thing on Earth to the Allied people. It serves Geiseric well to remind us of it."

Logan found it hard to comprehend the dimensions of such a behemoth, man-made creation. "That's incredible," he muttered, almost whispering. He shook his head to reboot his mind, but could not say much else. "Wow."

Alistair breathed in deeply, trying to forget the memories he had of the Apex capital war machine. "There was something so terrifying about that thing," he said, looking down at the flattened track through the forest, images of the mechanized colossus flashing in his mind. "The name 'Juggernaut' comes from the ancient Indian word for a large, unstoppable force." His nostrils flared as he breathed in deeply, a wave of icy terror running through his veins.

"And that's exactly what it felt like," he fell back into the New England dialect that he spoke with more often. Logan could not figure out if Alistair actually had a British accent, or if his East Coast American accent just sounded like it sometimes. But, now was hardly the time to grill him about it. Alistair cleared his throat and stared off, entranced by the recollection of the epic creation.

"The Juggernaut moved deep under the water most of the time, so no one had ever gotten a good look at it up until the Battle of Panama. It had to crawl across here to make it to the Pacific. I was fighting down there that day." The memories of the combat on the beachhead came flooding back to him. Fleeting images of the Juggernaut ripped through his mind.

"It was like a Titan from Greek mythology. It . . ." he stammered in awe, "it seemed to have its own gravity. You felt pulled to it. I imagine it would feel the same if a mountain was moving towards you. That's what the Juggernaut was, a small mountain. Small for a geological formation, but a thousand times larger than anything that has ever walked this Earth," he shook his head in disbelief of the truth. "And, I say walked, because it moved like an animal, like all the other battlemachines. I suppose it more crawled, like a giant octopus, with dozens of unfathomably long tentacles." Alistair swung his arms out in an almost graceful, leviathan manner, trying to replicate the movement.

"See, it would be one thing to see something so huge rolling towards you on wheels or something. But, to see something *that* huge, that looks *alive* . . ." Alistair paused and swallowed hard again. "It was truly a weapon of terror, as much as utility. The Apex knows we'll be haunted by what we see here."

Logan knew he would be. Already, other people in the air-train car could be heard telling their families or friends about the Juggernaut. Most were speaking Chinese, or Russian, or a language that Logan couldn't identify. But he could hear them all say "Juggernaut" in their unique manner, yet still identifiable, over and over again as they told their stories to each other.

"So," Logan looked to Alistair, "was it just meant to crush things and terrify people?"

Alistair chuckled, tickled by Logan's humorous naïveté. It brought him out of his shock, and lightened his mood. "No, the Juggernaut carried something called a particle accelerator, which is a giant, ring-like machine that uses the most powerful magnets in the world to push a *tiny* atomic particle," he pursed his thumb and forefinger together in front of his eye, as if he had something infinitesimally small in between, "to almost the speed of light. Its force comes from its speed. When this particle is shot and dispersed, like a shotgun blast, it blows through and vaporizes pretty much anything. It could blow a three meter-wide tunnel through several kilometers of rock and dirt in a minute."

Alistair zoned out again, hearing in his head the sound of the particle gun firing into the ground from off the coast. "That's how Geiseric got through the Allied Laser Net."

He and Logan mulled over the unbelievable truth.

In the silence, they heard the muted sound of a girl crying in the seat behind theirs. Alistair, Logan and Francesca got up to investigate. Sasha was sobbing with her face pressed into Jacques's chest. She whimpered like a young child, wetting his tunic with her tears. Francesca was jealous to see the attention her father was bestowing on Sasha.

"What a baby," she muttered, loud enough for them all to hear.

"Fuck you, Francesca!" Sasha snapped, releasing a string of curses in Russian.

Jacques was perplexed by his daughter's remark. "Sweetheart," he spoke to her in a low, gentle voice, "why would you say such a thing?"

"Well, we all lost people," Francesca retorted, shrugging.

"You didn't lose everybody at once!" Sasha screeched, bawling with extreme agitation. She was nearly hyperventilating. Francesca just stared at her with cold contempt.

"Francesca," Jacques said softly, "Sasha isn't trying to compete with anyone. She was just expressing her natural feelings. I worry that you don't express your pain enough. Getting angry at Sasha won't help you feel better."

Jacques's defense of Sasha further infuriated Francesca. Alistair interrupted before the situation between the two young ladies became irreparably embittered.

"Alright," he looked to Francesca, "why don't you and me go hang out at the bar." He grabbed her elbow. "Come on."

Tom and Bibi watched with minor disdain, but also with understanding for Francesca. Logan had told them about how she lost her mother. As parents, Tom and Bibi knew that teenagers could be harsh when they were emotionally unsettled. Logan followed Alistair and Francesca, looking back to his parents with an expression that said he would not drift far. They smiled at their respectful boy.

Alistair, Logan and Francesca exited the car, moving through the entrance connecting it with the next car, which held a small bar area. They all sat at the counter on the stools.

"Real nice Francesca," Alistair remarked scornfully.

She shrugged with indifference. "Yeah, whatever."

Alistair raised his hand in the air, motioning for the bartender to come over. The female bartender looked around Alistair's age, and he found her to be quite attractive. She had the gait of a lynx, as her graceful, lean figure sidled over to the group. Resting her elbows on the bar in front of Alistair, she smiled at him enticingly.

"What can I get you, handsome?"

"Three beers please," Alistair replied, looking her in the eyes with subtle evocation. She smiled and left to pour the order.

Francesca sat stiffly between the two guys, staring straight ahead.

Logan nervously licked his teeth. "So . . . what just happened there?"

Alistair shook his head and breathed in deeply. "Sasha lost *nineteen*," he enunciated clearly, "family members, all at once, to a massive tsunami caused by the Juggernaut."

Logan was shocked and speechless. Alistair's eyes went blank for a moment. He shook his head and perked up as the pretty bartender brought over their drinks. He thanked her, but found that he was no longer in a flirtatious mood.

"There's a small island off the northwestern coast of Africa called La Palma," Alistair began, stoically. "A huge part of the island had been cracking for decades. Eventually on its own, maybe in a few thousand years, it was going to break off and fall into the Atlantic. Geiseric decided to help it along. In doing so, he created a tidal wave that ripped across the ocean and destroyed the southeastern coast of Allied North America." Alistair shuddered as he thought about the ramifications.

"There were more than a billion and a half Allied refugees on the North American East Coast, all in relatively flimsy, makeshift shelters. A quarter of these were directly within the path of the tsunami, which pushed as far as thirty kilometers inland at some places." He sullenly muttered the outcome. "Over fifty million people died."

Logan stared vacantly at Alistair. He could not believe it. Alistair took a large gulp of beer and continued with utter solemnity in his tone.

"It was the single most deadly attack that has ever been launched. In that single strike, there were as many people killed as in World War II. That gives you an idea of what World War III was like."

"My God," Logan mumbled to himself. He felt nauseous.

"It was a back and forth terror war at first," Alistair explained. "The tsunami was just the final strike. It all started with the Great Diaspora. Some people called it the Mass Exodus." Alistair tilted his head slightly, thinking about the unbelievable event. "It was the single largest immigration in history by far. Nothing even compares. In fact, it was ten times as large as every other major immigration in history combined."

Alistair sipped on the beer to wet his vocal chords. "As soon as the North American Laser Net was operational, the Allies publicly announced that the whole Allied civilian population was going to be moved to North America. The refugees went on these humungous, plane-like crafts that were officially called some sort of Russian name, I forget. Everyone just called 'em Skimmers. They were big as a cruise ship and had wide wings, but they didn't fly really. They hovered. They were too big to fly. They carried something like 20,000 people at once. So, they hovered close to the surface of the water." He glided his hand just over the surface of the bar counter to demonstrate his words.

"When they achieved a certain velocity, an air pocket was created between the wings and the ocean surface, making for a pretty much frictionless ride. The Skimmers were fast and efficient. They skimmed across the water at about a thousand kilometers per hour." Alistair swiveled in his stool and anxiously tapped his palm on the bar as he spoke. "The technology was created during the Cold War. They were originally designed by the Russians to be used for an overwhelming amphibious assault on the U.S. Amphibious, meaning coming over by water and storming the land. The Allies realized that the Skimmers were just what they needed to transport all their citizens fast. There wasn't enough time to design anything new, so they used the designs of the Russian assault craft and didn't change them much." Alistair laughed at the irony.

"The same transports that were going to be used for a Russian invasion of the United States were eventually used to bring the Allied civilian populations to safety in America. I thought it was a good omen at first . . ."

—— XV ——

RELEASE THE JUGGERNAUT

January 3, 2039

A half-moon lazily tottered on its rounded back in the clear winter sky and, along with the stars, lit the landscape with an extraordinary glow that nearly overpowered the need for any man-made lighting. Although the temperature around the Northern Atlantic hung near freezing, there was no more time to wait. The longer Allied High Command delayed getting the European refugees to safe haven, the more vulnerable they were. The Skimmers arrived in the night at every major port in France, Britain, Portugal, Spain and Norway. People from all of the Allied countries within Europe gathered at the evacuation ports, huddled together to fight against the crisp night air. Altogether, six-hundred-million people cloistered into the ports and makeshift harbors along the Atlantic and North Sea coastlines. They had been waiting for hours, many already secured into their life vests, waiting for the start of the secret mass exodus.

The refugees assigned to the Norwegian ports were extremely anxious. It was unbearably cold and most of the refugees were under-clothed. Even under thick coats and furs, they shivered vigorously, every moment feeling like an eternity.

Suddenly, the alarm bell sounded. It was loud and agitating, meant to bring the refugees to instant alertness, ready to move quickly. Simultaneously, at all the ports, the Skimmers' doors shot upwards. Soldiers helped load the refugees in an organized fashion, barking orders at them and pushing them into lines. They knew there was no time to waste.

When the Skimmers were packed to the brim, the doors came down and soldiers rushed through the aisles, pushing people into seats. They ordered everyone to put on their safety belts. Once they were all was secured, the Skimmers could depart.

The first wave was comprised of one thousand Skimmers, each carrying around twenty thousand refugees. The huge vessels took off like sea planes, floating in the water until the jet engines started up. They began to lift into the air as they gained velocity, but soon halted their climb, never drifting more than six meters above the waterline. Soon they reached their cruising speed of more than nine hundred kilometers per hour.

With their thick metallic hulls that were disproportionately large compared to their wings, the Skimmers resembled giant Zeppelins gliding over the water. They stretched nearly two-hundred meters long, about the length of two football fields. Their hulls were sixteen stories tall, and equally as wide. The turbulence generated in their wake was so tremendous that each Skimmer had to travel at least two kilometers apart from the others to avoid being capsized by the thrashing winds and waves.

The Allied civilians riding within the Skimmers were not alone on their treacherous journey. Their chosen course between Europe and America was well-defended by convoys of battleships, aircraft carriers and submariner fleets placed strategically to ward off a potential attack on the refugee mission.

Much of the Allied submariner contingents were updated models of recently obsolete technology. However, the newer Animalian vessels, called Sharks, were modeled after their namesakes and were the Allied naval counterpart to the Apex Delfin. As they moved through the water, their intimidating bodies and method of travel resembled that of the carnivorous, cartilaginous fish. Their tails swayed from side to side, instead of up and down, giving them greater acceleration and turning ability than their nemesis craft, the Delfin.

German for dolphin, the Delfin had greater speed in a long straight line, but based on what Streicher knew of the designs and according to every strategy he could conceive of, he was sure that the Delfins' mode of travel would prove to be inferior in an all-out sea battle. Streicher never did discover, before he defected, why Geiseric went with the tail and swimming profile of the dolphin, as opposed to the Shark design.

The Allies had ten Shark squadrons prowling the Atlantic for enemy threats. The capital vessels of the Allied fleet were the Great Whites. Weighing in at over twenty-five thousand metric tons, they were 150 meters long, from nose to tail, and thirty meters at their widest point. They were armed to the teeth with a vast array of weaponry, including dozens of the latest, fastest torpedoes. The torpedoes worked by creating air bubbles around themselves in a process known as supercavitation, which kept friction to a minimum. Instead of being encased in water, the weapon was simply surrounded by water vapor, which had less density and resistance, allowing the torpedo to propel at over eight hundred kilometers per hour through the water. The Great Whites could also deploy various submarine-to-surface missiles, which fired off the back of the vessel, propelled up through the water and, upon breaking fully out of the water, fired their rocket boosters and took off. The missiles either arched upwards and came down on an enemy naval or air craft, or cruised across the surface of the water, broad-siding any enemy vessels floating above the waterline.

The Great Whites also each had four half-meter guns — large cannons that fired huge, half-meter wide shells weighing a thousand kilograms, or a metric ton. Most of the cannons' lengths were contained inside the hull, creating the most hydrodynamic exterior possible. They were not very long for such a large shell cannon because they were not meant for precision; they were meant for a close range punch. Not only could they fire through the air, but the shells and cannons were specially designed to be able to fire underwater, albeit, for a much shorter distance.

The Great White was a force to be reckoned with. It only had one drawback. It was slower than the other Shark battlemachines, capable of attaining a top speed of only ninety kilometers per hour, and with terrible acceleration. So, it worked in tandem with the other new Allied naval battlemachines, namely the Mako.

The Mako was sleek and half as long as the Great White. It was not as well-armed, having fewer torpedoes, no missiles, and only two half-meter guns. They also had two quarter-meter guns, meant for a rapid, close-range barrage. The Makos were speedy hunter-killers, capable of going one hundred and forty-five kilometers, or ninety miles, or eighty nautical miles, per hour at top speed. Most importantly, they had excellent acceleration.

There was a subgroup of Mako battlemachines called Hammerheads, named for the wide, flattened and scallop-shaped structure at the head called the cephalofoil, which like a real hammerhead shark, made them much more hydrodynamic. The Hammerhead battlemachines were much smaller and even more agile than the regular Makos, which made it easy for them to help gang up on a tough enemy amongst a crowd of larger Sharks. The Hammerheads were also the outright fastest naval battlemachines in the Allied Fleet, capable of going two hundred and twenty kilometers per hour in a straight line, even faster than the Delfins. But, the cephalofoils that made the small Shark crafts so fast were also weak and vulnerable to collision, especially if placed on larger vessels. That was why the Allies did not attempt to design the other Makos and Great Whites in such a manner. It was also why a relatively small amount of Hammerhead battlemachines were produced. Still, they provided an extremely important role. Altogether, the Allied submariner battlemachines made for a frightening team.

Both the Sharks and Delfins were driven by a single pilot who was also the commander of the vessel. The commander maneuvered the waterborne battlemachines using a Psychiclink connection with their minds. Women were good at piloting the mariner vessels, because navigating and maneuvering the Delfins and Sharks required the ability to multi-task with the Psychiclink technology far more than any other military craft or battlemachine did.

Women had more Corpus Callosum, a tissue that connected the left and right sides of the brain. Because of this, women were able to use more parts of the brain simultaneously than men, and were therefore able to multi-task better than men. Men tended to be more single-minded and focused than women. Both had their advantages.

In general, women were better equipped to navigate the naval battlemachines. Visual reading displays were directly connected into the commanders' brains, giving them the ultimate perspective. The visual display was created using mainly sonar and infrared detection equipment. The pilots actually saw, in their minds, the real-time image of what was occurring outside. By closing their eyes and engaging their mental faculties to the fullest, the pilots watched the display and moved the naval battlemachines accordingly. The crew also monitored the sonar imaging and relayed anything missed by the pilot.

Having been pressured and constrained by time, the Allies feared that mistakes could have been made in the production of the vessels or in the strategy of the mass exodus. The Sharks were still in their adolescent stage of development. They had not been tested for as long as the Delfins, and there could have been some unforeseen glitches.

The overall consensus amongst Allied High Command, though, was that the defense was an impregnable ocean fortress. Besides the naval craft, thousands of Allied jets and other aircraft patrolled the skies, or were ready to be dispatched from carriers and land bases at a moment's notice. For the most part, Allied High Command was confident in their people's security.

Alistair and his family were on the first Skimmers leaving Great Britain. They were strapped securely into their cramped seating arrangements and, as the vessel sped over the water at almost a thousand kilometers per hour, a nervous silence hung in the entire compartment.

Suddenly, sonar readings were picked up by a section of the perimeter defense. Apex naval scouts were spotted in the Sea of Cape Agulhas, near the Cape of Good Hope, coming up around the southern tip of Africa. The scouts were making their way north towards the Diaspora zone, scoping out the route. The Allies were worried because it probably meant that Geiseric was dispatching his mighty Indian fleet — his most powerful armada.

The Allies had estimated from satellite and air surveillance, and through human espionage, that the Apex Empire had about four-hundred and eighty Delfins, the capital battlemachines of the Imperial Navy. Weighing in at about twenty thousand tons, the Delfins measured directly in between their enemies, the Great Whites and Makos, in terms of size, and were capable of going their top speed of 180 kilometers per hour for great distances.

Comprised of about three-hundred Delfins, the Indian fleet was based in the ports of the Indian Ocean. The Germanian fleet was estimated to only have fifty in the Baltic. Eighty Delfins were based in the Greek waters of the Black and Aegean Seas, which were kept from entering into the rest of the Mediterranean by an Allied blockade of one hundred and fifty Sharks. The Japanese Fleet had another fifty Delfins in Japan, which were blockaded by the only Allied Naval Forces in the Pacific.

The Allies, on the other hand, had about four-hundred Great White capital ships and over seven-hundred Makos, which gave them a numerical superiority in naval battlemachines of more than double that of the Apex. The majority of the Allied Naval Forces were defending the convoy zone in the North Atlantic, stretching from the Old World to the New World. The convoy

POTENTIAL LINES OF ATTAC

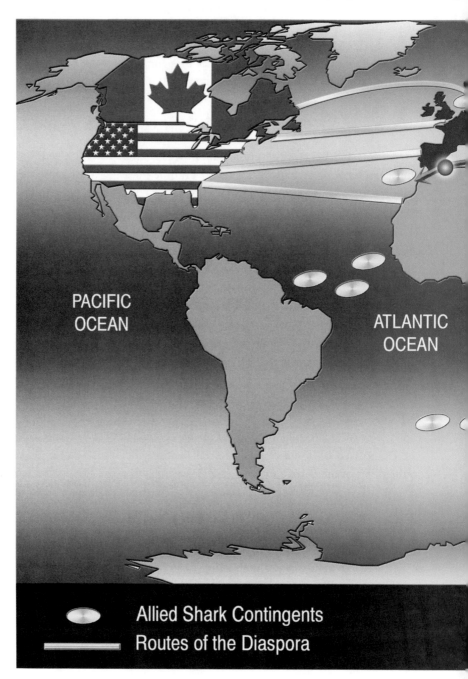

PACIFIC
OCEAN

ATLANTIC
OCEAN

Allied Shark Contingents

Routes of the Diaspora

OR THE APEX INDIAN FLEET

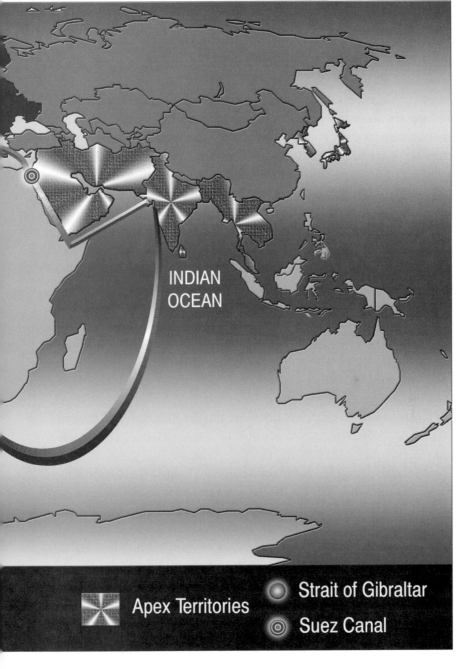

INDIAN
OCEAN

Apex Territories

Strait of Gibraltar

Suez Canal

zone was especially well defended on the southeastern flank, guarding the only possible line of attack that the Allies could imagine, which was the Indian fleet coming around Cape Horn.

Then, just as the Allies expected, a huge formation of submarine vessels was picked up by satellite imaging that tracked the surface of the ocean water using radar. The instrumentation was so sensitive that it could pick up the tiny bulge made on the surface of the water by anything large moving underneath.

Allied Intelligence estimated that around one-hundred Delfins were approaching, in tight formation, traveling at their top speeds. They had departed from underwater ports in the Indian Ocean and were heading southwest from there, towards Cape Horn, following on the tails of their scouts. But to the dismay of Allied High Command, the spy satellites that were tracking the Delfins began cutting out. One after the other, the satellites stopped transmitting, as they were destroyed by Apex spacecraft. The Apex had a greater military presence in space over the eastern hemisphere of Earth, so it was no surprise to the Allied leadership that their satellites were being taken out there. They expected as such, if Geiseric decided to launch an attack on the Allied civilians in the Diaspora.

Now the Allies had to rely completely on air surveillance, which was resulting in the persistent loss of reconnaissance jets. Apex Golden Eagles were ganging up and taking them down with ease over the Indian Ocean, which was within range of Mesopotamia's numerous fighter-jet bases.

For three hours, the Allied leadership, cut off from all communication, had no idea what was going on with the Indian fleet. They braced for the attack. But, the journey around Africa was not short and the Allies believed they had more than a day before the Apex fleet would be within striking distance of the refugees.

The only other possible line of attack would have been for the Apex to somehow bring the Indian fleet through the Suez Canal and into the Mediterranean, but the Allies had prepared for that by protecting the canal with some of their strongest defenses. In late 2034, Britain, the United States, China and France had worked together to keep the canal out of Geiseric's hands, for it was too important to their nations. They secured the canal, along with Egypt, which surrounded the canal, as a mandatory conciliation for allowing Geiseric to take the Middle East. Now, because it was so vital in keeping the Indian fleet away, the Allies had heavily fortified this area. There were numerous defenses along the flanks of the canal. The Allies had blockaded most of it with so much stone and demolished old ships that it would take days to clear. Some strategic sites were even guarded by bunkered Allied Cross Laser defenses.

Then, unexpected news came. A mass communiqué was sent to the Allied battlemachines in the Mediterranean. It was from the Suez defenders. They were under attack by a stunning Apex ground and air strike. Things were getting tricky at the canal, but the Allied commanders claimed they had it under control. They reported the slaughter of hundreds of Kolibri, thousands of Apex ground troops, and even dozens of Panzers. A cheer of joy rang out through the Allied ranks as they learned of their first victory.

Without warning, communications were cut off. The Apex forces had managed to destroy or scramble all outgoing channels from the Suez defenders. The Allies decided to send reinforcements. The one hundred and fifty Sharks already in the Mediterranean, blockading the Greek Navy, could not leave their important posts. So, a contingent of Shark forces was taken off the Allied blockade area in the Atlantic nearby the Strait of Gibraltar. The Strait of Gibraltar was the ocean inlet that fed the Atlantic into the Mediterranean. In total, another one-hundred and fifty Sharks, fifty Great Whites and one-hundred Makos, were siphoned off the convoy zone and dispatched through the strait into the Mediterranean to support the Suez defenders. Their crews' morale was running high, certain they would get their first taste of action by mopping up the failed Apex strike.

However, the Allied leadership was not at all convinced that this was the place through which Geiseric would choose to bring his Indian fleet. Not only were the fortifications dense, but the canal was incredibly thin and shallow, only fifty meters at its deepest. With the demolished ships and other impediments, the Delfins could easily get jammed and have a hard time dodging or turning around. And, if the vessels on the front line were destroyed, their broken hulls would further block the way. The Allied Suez defenders could destroy a contingent of Delfins coming through there like shooting fish in a barrel. The only way the Apex could get through was if they established air superiority over the canal, in which case the Golden Eagles could take out the Allied defenses, allowing the Delfins to pass unabated. But, they would need to destroy the Allied Cross lasers to do so. Those were a hard nut to crack and the Allies could not see how it would be possible for the Apex Forces to take the canal without also taking unacceptable losses.

Therefore, the majority of the Allied political and military leaders were almost positive that it was an attempt at diversion. Kassian, however, did not concur. He knew Geiseric loved to do whatever was least expected, especially

to hit people where they thought they were strongest, so as to humble them. Besides that, he just had a hunch. Prime Minister Dandau tended to trust Kassian's hunches and argued on his behalf, but almost every military officer disagreed with them. So, the Allied leadership dispatched more of their naval forces to the southwest of Africa, waiting for the Delfins to round Cape Horn.

When the Shark reinforcements in the Mediterranean passed by Sardinia, their equipment began picking up numerous explosive vibrations coming from the canal area. Each explosion was equivalent to one hundred tons, more than two-hundred thousand pounds, of TNT. Allied High Command figured that the Apex air forces were probably dropping MOABs — massive ordinance air-burst bombs. They were thermo-baric devices that were the most powerful non-nuclear bombs available to either side. Since Geiseric had an aversion to the environmental impact of nuclear weapons, it was safe to assume he ordered the air-bursters into action, the Golden Eagles dropping them on Allied ground forces outside the range of the Cross lasers. But, High Command still thought the attack was a ploy, because small formations of Delfins had been spotted and engaged nearing the Cape Horn area.

The Allied leaders' hearts sank when another call came in from a reconnaissance jet, just before it was shot down by Golden Eagles. Apparently out of nowhere, the pilot had spotted an armada of at least two hundred Delfins in the Mediterranean, moving west from Egypt. Somehow, the Apex forces had gained air superiority over the canal area and were thus able to protect the aquatic battlemachines as they passed through.

Immediately, the Allies reallocated the majority of their perimeter Shark defenses in the Atlantic, sending them towards the Mediterranean. Another three hundred Makos and one hundred Great Whites converged on the Strait of Gibraltar at top speed.

However, from their distant points on the convoy, it would take ten hours for the Allied reinforcements to completely gather for battle. They did not want to enter in pieces, for that was the best way to be devoured, bit by bit. They needed to attack as a whole. Until that time, the Sharks already battling the enemy in the Mediterranean were on their own.

More than two-thirds of the Indian fleet had already siphoned through the Suez Canal and joined with the smaller but mighty Greek fleet, giving the Apex Naval Forces in the Mediterranean a slight numerical superiority over the Allies. Plus, the Greek fleet was piloted by some of the best captains in the world, second only to those of the Germanian Baltic fleet. Aware of this, the three hundred Sharks in the Mediterranean tried to retreat, but they were encircled and decimated. Whereas, only five of the eighty Greek Fleet Delfins were demolished and six others were damaged. Only fifty of the Indian Fleet were destroyed, with another seventy damaged but still usable. The rest of the Apex Indian Fleet was funneling through the Suez into the Mediterranean to reinforce the Apex forces for the larger battle to come.

There were urgent murmurs in the ranks of the Allied leadership that the Diaspora should be called off. But, it was ultimately deemed necessary to continue on. The people of the world had to reach the safety of the North American Laser Net before Geiseric's forces became even more powerful.

The Apex naval battlemachines rushed towards the Strait of Gibraltar to meet their enemy. The strait was the geologically-formed western passage into the Mediterranean and was far wider and deeper than the man-made Suez Canal, which was located on the opposite side of the large sea. The Strait of Gibraltar ranged from three hundred to nine hundred meters deep and was about thirteen kilometers wide at its narrowest point, which allowed maneuverability, yet was just enough of a bottleneck for the Delfin commanders to use it to their advantage.

Having fully coalesced, the four hundred strong Shark force prepared to enter the Mediterranean. The Apex commanders navigated their vessels to the strait and confronted the Sharks at the bottleneck. By fighting in such a tight space, the Apex minimized the Allied numerical advantage. There was no way for the Allies to attack the flanks of the Delfins, or encircle them.

Fighting erupted within the strait. As the enemy vessels neared each other, the Sharks fired off their torpedoes. Within seconds, the torpedoes were upon their targets.

The Delfin commanders had to time things just right when dodging the torpedoes, which were extremely accurate in finding large, moving objects in the water. The torpedoes were very agile, but a good Delfin commander found that the large Animalian vessels had far more dexterity than the propeller and rudder-driven explosives. Most of the torpedoes missed their mark, going off behind the intended targets. The Delfins easily dodged the waterborne projectiles, because their commanders defensively maneuvered as a cohesive unit, moving together like a giant school of fish. More than three hundred Delfins evaded the torpedoes with only ten Delfins struck directly.

The Apex aquatic battlemachines rushed forward in a wall formation, their beaks shining a brilliant white and red light. They were releasing their dreaded weapons: the drill bolt cannons.

Firing a highly energetic, solid-state laser beam that was a half meter wide and effective at twelve hundred meters underwater, the drill bolt cannon could tear a Mako in half with one well-placed shot. The Delfin designers had sacrificed underwater shell guns and numerous torpedoes for this single annihilative weapon, with its energy generator taking up nearly all space normally allotted to munitions storage.

The Shark commanders found that, as a whole, they were not skillful enough to evade the enemy fire without often times running their battlemachines into their comrades moving parallel to them. Several Makos and Great Whites slammed into each other, their lack of coordination making them easy to strike with the devastating drill bolts, which sounded like lightning as they crackled through the water. The Allied vehicles blew up with the explosive force of the five hundred to a thousand tons of munitions they carried on board. Shockwaves rippled out in all directions, slamming into the hulls of their comrades' vessels.

Before the froth had cleared, the whole of both armadas were upon each other. The Allies used a pack-hunting offensive strategy, breaking off into small, easily manageable groups usually consisting of one Great White working in tandem with three or four of their smaller cohorts. The Great Whites engaged the Delfins one-on-one at first, coming in straight at their enemy, firing their two front-loaded, half-meter guns. While the Delfin commander was occupied and focused on the Great White, three Makos came around fast from the sides and bottom in a wide-arching, triple-pincer movement. When they got in at close range, they fired their front loaded quarter-meter guns and pummeled the Apex battlemachine from all sides. It was a highly effective offensive strategy, at first, destroying twenty Delfins in just two and a half minutes of battle.

As this was reported back to headquarters, the Allied leadership could almost not believe it. They immediately had the report sent to the convoy and read over the intercom speakers on the Skimmers. The Allied civilians on board were not even aware that a large attack was being made on the convoy zone. They just knew that something was making the crews and pilots nervous, causing them to push the Skimmers' engines to full throttle. As they heard about the battle and the Apex losses, loud cheering replaced the anxious silence, and the now hopeful refugees began to talk and speculate with each other.

But the celebration was tragically premature, for the Allied battle tactic was quickly discerned by the enemy and the Delfins began sticking in packs of

five. The Allies could not believe the unmatched skill of the Apex commanders, who could dodge or turn their vessels in unison, as if they were of one
mind. The Allied commanders became quickly overwhelmed by the logistics
of the situation. The strait was too cramped, with so many enormous, fast-
moving vessels battling it out. It was complete chaos and, yet, the Apex Naval
Forces seemed to have their end of the situation under control. The Allies'
confidence and morale was getting shaky.

A weakness in the Apex force was also beginning to show, however. Their
mighty drill bolt cannon had an Achilles heel. Even in the cool water, it could
only fire six shots before over-heating and shutting off, needing to cool for ten
seconds. Ten seconds, in a lethal battle with these machines, was eons.

Suddenly, to the surprise of the Allies, the Delfins began retreating back
into the Mediterranean, trying to use their superior speed to escape. The
overly-enthusiastic Mako captains, using their superior acceleration, gave
instant chase to the fleeing enemy. Most of the Delfins got away, but a few
dozen could not accelerate enough as they were constantly bombarded by the
Makos. The Makos made small strikes and quickly swam off, allowing another
one to strike from a different direction. The Delfin stragglers were thus slowly
devoured. The Admiral in charge of the Allied Shark forces in the strait was
joyous about the unusual turn of events . . . until she realized she had fallen
into a basic trap.

It was the feigned retreat. The fleeing Delfins did a rapid 180 degree turn
and rushed back on their Mako pursuers, who had become separated from
their larger defenders. Without the Great Whites, who were struggling to catch
up, the Makos were severely outgunned.

The wall of Delfins came in at their top speed, firing their drill bolt cannons with terrifying accuracy, eviscerating the Makos at the forefront. The
Sharks blew up with incredible intensity, the resulting storm of metal shrapnel
damaging several other Makos.

This was a downside to using shell guns instead of drill bolt cannons.
While bruised and beaten from the merciless Mako attacks, the Delfins were
often not completely destroyed since their energy generators did not contain
explosive materials. The shells fired from the Sharks could do serious damage,
but it took many direct hits to completely incapacitate a Delfin. And, unlike
the Sharks, when destroyed the Delfins did not act as giant grenades that could
harm other Apex battlemachines.

The Delfins had managed to take out nearly eighty Makos during their
initial counter-strike from their feigned retreat. The Apex forces were cutting

away at the Allied numerical advantage, with about two-hundred and sixty Delfins now facing off against a little over three hundred Sharks.

Watching as the Apex forces charged towards them, the Allied commanders braced for a close-quarters confrontation, but the Delfins merely concentrated their fire to puncture a hole through the Allied barrier. Instead of facing their opponents, the Delfins raced past and continued on out the Atlantic side of the strait, breaking right into the middle of the Diaspora zone. Now there was nothing between the millions of Allied refugees and the Delfins' grisly drill bolt cannons.

The news hit the Allied leadership like a ton of bricks. Though the Allied commanders had not trained as long as their Apex counterparts, Allied High Command had assumed that their military-grade Formula training had brought the Shark commanders up to near par.

But, it appeared that they were wrong.

Just then, the Germanian Baltic Fleet sprang into action, taking on those Sharks blockading them in. The Apex maneuver was clearly meant to keep the Allied North Sea Fleet busy. It worked because the Allies had to shore up their blockade there, which stretched from Denmark across to Norway and Sweden, with numerous fortifications on the Scandinavian islands in between. The Germanian Fleet, while only fifty Delfins strong, had the best commanders and technology in the world. However, with the Scandinavian island fortifications, it was relatively easy to box in the Germanian Fleet in the Baltic. Letting the fleet out, though, would mean serious problems for the Allies. So, pulling away the blockade there was not an option. Allied battlemachines would have to be pulled in from farther areas to take on the Delfins in the Diaspora Zone, but that would take awhile.

Allied High Command decided that they now had to temporarily halt the refugee evacuation. All of the Skimmers still in port waited there until further notice, but those already on the water were in tremendous danger. Prime Minister Dandau had tried to get as many Brits on the outgoing refugee vessels as possible at the beginning of the battle, when the Sharks briefly seemed to have the Delfins on the run. But now that the Delfins had broken into the Diaspora Zone, the enemy was within a few kilometers of hundreds of Skimmers carrying more than three million Brits.

The majority of Skimmers had made it out of range of the incoming Delfin force and were headed off toward America. However, about one-third of them were caught in the path of the enemy battlemachines. Many of these Skimmer pilots chose to turn back to Britain or northern Spain. But those too close to the enemy to turn around decided to push the throttle to the fullest, zooming forward into the looming threat, hoping to fly by. Their hulls shaking profusely, the Skimmers' engines redlined. The people inside began to panic as they bounced violently in their seats.

A group of Delfins lay in wait of the oncoming Skimmers and, once the enormous transports were within range, they opened up with their devastating cannons. The bolts tore through the helpless refugee craft, ripping them in pieces and spewing their passengers into the Atlantic. Bodies living and dead flew out into the cold, dark ocean. Screams echoed across the water, matched only by the terrifying sound of drill bolts slicing relentlessly through the air.

Alistair and his family were among the unfortunate people who were on the Skimmers that had to run the gauntlet. When their craft sped to full throttle, Alistair's stomach clenched up. Although he could not see what was happening outside, he knew the abrupt acceleration meant that the enemy was upon them. He looked at his mother, whose tiny frame was hunched forward in her seat, grey strands of hair falling forward, and put on a brave face. His father, a life-long military man, more easily kept a valiant countenance and, though restrained by harnesses, he reached out and embraced his family the best he could.

Just then, a drill bolt laser grazed the roof of their Skimmer, ripping a long hole across the top. Wind and mist shot in, engulfing the screams of the petrified people. Alistair closed his eyes and waited for the explosion. But nothing happened. As he cautiously opened one eye, he realized that the vessel had not been destroyed. The pilot brought it slowly to a halt and Alistair breathed a deep sigh of relief and smiled half-heartedly at his family. His relief was short-lived, however. The restraints came up and the pilot announced that everyone had to abandon ship immediately. With their life vests on, the passengers slid down inflatable exit ramps into the icy water. As they floated helplessly in the ocean, they looked at their Skimmer, their disappearing promise of escape set ablaze.

The Skimmers that had turned and headed back to Britain were not out of harm's way either. Stopping and turning around took a long time. Before most could accelerate in the opposite direction, a vast amount of Delfins were upon them, ruthlessly firing their laser cannons into the civilian craft, tearing the Skimmers into pieces that tumbled violently across the water for several kilometers, erupting humans in all directions.

Soon, the Allies began to notice a pattern. Not a single Delfin battle-craft went after the African refugee transports, or even most of the European refugee transports. The Apex Naval Forces primarily went after the British vessels, relentlessly, like a pack of ravenous sea predators feeding on an endless amount of easy prey.

Families, friends and strangers clung to shreds of the demolished Skimmers while they shivered in the water, surrounded by dead bodies, floating body parts, and the dying. The Allies had summoned numerous rescue vehicles to the area, but they were under heavy attack themselves.

Finally, the Apex commanders seemed to have quelled their thirst for blood. They abandoned the slaughter and raced back towards the Strait of Gibraltar. The strike had been so rapid that the Allied forces had not yet built up a substantial force of Sharks to stop the retreating Delfins. So, instead of facing certain annihilation, the Sharks moved out of the way and let the Apex battlemachines that had just brutally massacred their citizens withdraw back into the Mediterranean unpunished.

Alistair grabbed a shredded seat floating by in the water amongst the debris. He hoisted his younger sister onto it, while keeping it upright, so she could be mostly out of the water. His whole family had managed to survive the attack, but they were quickly losing strength as their bodies acquiesced to hypothermia. Alistair looked away as tears welled up in his eyes. He knew his small-framed mother, with so little meat on her bones, would not survive long in the penetrating cold.

Suddenly, like a strange, gigantic whale, a Mako surfaced in the water. A porthole opened up on top and a man popped out. He shouted, looking about with spotlights. Others came out of more portholes and joined the search. Alistair's father called out urgently and got the attention of the searchers. They were saved!

Alistair's entire family and several others were pulled aboard. Many other refugees had been in the bitter water for over twenty minutes by now. Yet, they managed to swim through the waves to the Mako and begged to be brought aboard. The Allied craft, however, did not have room for everyone. The crew promised more rescue vessels would be along, but Alistair could tell by their grieved expressions that it was not true. The Allies had simply not been prepared for an attack of this magnitude.

Alistair sadly gazed out of the porthole as it closed upon the people screaming for help outside, begging for the Mako crew to just take their children. He could not help but feel guilty for surviving.

+ + +

Dandau burst through the doors of the War Room with General Ackleworth and one of his top scientists in tow. Hollier, Tierney, Kurtkin, Sinclair, Hung, Streicher and Kassian were already seated around the large table. They hushed as Dandau entered.

The prime minister slammed the door behind him and stood for a moment facing his peers. "Let's nuke them to kingdom come," he stated matter-of-factly.

Streicher shook his head. "Our nuclear weapons won't get through the Net, Charles. The only thing that will get through is radiation, and it won't get far. It won't be of much strategic value and it will only serve to piss Geiseric off. Besides," he shrugged, "Geiseric could just as easily do it to us."

Dandau's eyes widened with indignation. "That's not what I'm talking about," he fumed. "We're not going to **sit here** and do **nothing!** Do you know what the last British casualty count was?!? The numbers are reaching to over *a* **million dead!"**

The Prime Minister was still in shock, but his rage quickly brought him back to reality. "A *million* people dead! In one bloody hour! I've lost two percent of my people!" he roared, slamming his fist down and leaning over the table menacingly.

He inhaled deeply, his nostrils flaring as he did. But he quickly righted himself and fixed his suit a bit, trying to appear rational. "Now . . ." He looked around at all the leaders in the room. They had been quiet out of reverence for the British dead, which had far exceeded all others in the Diaspora. Dandau made sure he had their attention.

"We have a top secret intelligence installation deep underground in what was Poland, in Germania." He paused to let the information sink in. Everyone was stunned by this newly revealed secret.

"It's been there since the Cold War," Dandau continued. "We abandoned it around the turn of the century, but when Geiseric came to power in Germany, MI6 reoccupied it to keep tabs on his move on Poland. When things started looking hot, we placed what is called a Treasure Trove at the installation." Dandau gestured to General Ackleworth. "Please explain."

General Ackleworth solemnly rose, holding a pile of folders. He seemed indecisive and slightly flustered as he walked around the table handing a debriefing folder to each person in the room.

"When Geiseric annexed Poland into Germania," the general started, in a rough, direct tone, "we told our boys in the top secret installation to sit tight. That we might need them." All the leaders hurriedly read the information and studied the diagrams inside. They skimmed ahead of Ackleworth's explanation and gazed in trepidation at what was there. Ackleworth took his seat and looked all the men in the eye, one by one, placing his hands together before him on the table, his fingers interlocked.

"We gave them a Treasure Trove, which allows for a multitude of large-scale, strategic attacks." The general used the end of his tie to wipe his moist brow. "We basically gave them a bit of everything. Chemical, biological, radiological and, yes," he said, looking into the many eyes staring at him, "even a few small nuclear weapons."

The leaders in the room were clearly disturbed by this confession, and they wondered what other things MI6 had done, perhaps in their countries, that they did not know about. However, that paranoia was dwarfed when confronted with the predicament at hand. They were cautiously tantalized by what they saw in their folders. Only the French president outwardly revealed his apprehension by covering his mouth with a clenched hand as he read.

"They have fifteen kilos of VX nerve gas," General Ackleworth continued. "VX has remained the deadliest and most rapidly acting chemical agent in existence, since it was developed in the U.K. eighty years ago. It's also known as phosphonothioic acid, and if a drop of this stuff touches your skin, you will be dead in a minute," he said snapping his fingers. "You breathe it in, you will be dead in fifteen."

"Nerve agents are similar to organophosphates, or insecticides, in that they prohibit the regulation of acetylcholine, a fundamental neurotransmitter that acts as the on and off switch for the central and periphery nervous system. Essentially, a person's glands and muscles are stimulated and cannot shut down, causing convulsions, respiratory failure, paralysis, and a number of other unpleasant things."

Ackleworth rubbed his head with the palm of his hand, nervously disheveling his coarse, black hair. The tension in the room was apparent, and he was wary of the political hostility his report was sure to engender.

"Next," he continued, following the printed list, "they have twenty kilograms of biological weapons, which have been converted into particulate matter, ready for dispersion in an aerosol form. Six kilos," he read down the list, "of the botulinum nerve toxin, the single most toxic substance known to mankind. Theoretically, a single gram of this stuff could kill a million people."

General Ackleworth cleared his throat and his eyes darted over the uneasy expressions of everyone in the room.

"Seven kilos of pneumonic plague, one of the variants caused by the bacterium Yersinia pestis. This is far more lethal than bubonic plague and is also highly contagious." The general rubbed his temples with his fore and middle fingers.

"And there are seven kilos of filoviruses. Mainly the hardier Marburg variant of Ebola, of which parts have been transferred into the composition of Smallpox and other diseases, making it spreadable by aerosol and highly contagious." Under the tension, a vein in Ackleworth's forehead began to slightly bulge. "These are hemorrhagic fever viruses. External symptoms include profuse bleeding through orifices such as the eyes, ears, nose and mouth. Internal bleeding leads to organ disintegration and collapse, giving Marburg a one hundred percent fatality rate."

President Kurtkin laughed mockingly. "Unbelievable! This is what the Soviet Union was developing in the nineteen-eighties and the West was *soooo* up in arms about. Yet, *you* were developing it all yourself." He looked up from the documents in his folder and over to Dandau, who was re-lighting his cigar. Dandau took a puff as he glared back at Kurtkin.

"Indeed." he replied without feeling.

President Sinclair was reading ahead at his own pace, tuning out a lot of what anyone else was saying. When he flipped one of the pages, he gasped at what he read.

"You gave them *cobalt bombs?!*"

Dandau kept puffing away at his large cigar. "Yes, in fact," he retorted unflinchingly, placing a heavily aristocratic inflection in his tone.

Kurtkin quickly flipped ahead to that page. "I thought the test in Australia was a failure."

"That was in the 1950s, President Kurtkin," Dandau condescendingly retorted.

"Yes," Kurtkin shot back, "but the tests were supposed to have stopped!"

Sinclair read the effects of this device aloud, paraphrasing the more detailed parts. "A cobalt bomb is an advanced thermonuclear fusion bomb with an outer core of cobalt-59, which changes to the radioactive isotope, cobalt-60, when the bomb is detonated. The cobalt-60 is ejected into the atmosphere where its particles act to salt the clouds. It is easily taken around vast areas by climactic forces and is rained down onto the environment, where it emits lethal doses of gamma rays."

Sinclair threw his folder onto the table. "*Why* would you *build* such a thing?"

"Because!" Dandau snapped, slamming both his palms down on the table and looking coldly at the French President, "we knew it would really strike Geiseric in the jewels, along with all these Isaianic freaks!" His eyes displayed the wild fury consuming him inside. "We can irradiate all of Bavaria and their beloved environment for *years!*"

"Yes," Sinclair leaned forward in his chair and looked indignantly back at the Prime Minister, "but, if the wrong wind blows, we could contaminate surrounding countries as well. Possibly, France!"

Dandau stared unhaltingly at the French president, cigar smoke slowly ascending in front of his face from out of his nose. "Frankly, President Sinclair, it is a risk I am willing to take."

Sinclair was infuriated. Hollier realized the tension between the leaders was rising exponentially.

"Alright boys," he interrupted, attempting to keep things in check, "let's keep it together here." He shot a look at his British compatriot, signaling him to ease up his rudeness towards Sinclair. Hollier flipped through the pages of his folder. "So, how would we do this, hypothetically?"

Dandau gulped noticeably, but kept up a defiant face. "Well," he began, "there are twenty of our men altogether in Germania, dispersed around the country. Upon hearing the orders, they will deploy their weapons in as many strategic locations as possible." Dandau motioned for General Ackleworth to take it from there.

"They were instructed to first deploy the biological aerosols," Ackleworth explained, "targeting large, crowded buildings, dispersing it through direct means such as air ducts, or if that is too risky, just setting up a small mister in a bathroom or wherever might be fitting. They will also hit mass transportation, of course. Basically, our men will determine where and how to strike in order to cause the most confusion, terror and casualties."

When Ackleworth paused, Hollier scratched his chin thoughtfully. "Alright, the aerosols will be easiest to deploy covertly, but what then? When people get sick, won't they be on to us?"

"We won't wait that long," Ackleworth replied, almost unhappily. "Right before the symptoms of the biological attack begin to show, the VX attacks will commence. The most obvious targets are buildings and mass transportation as well." The general gazed at the instructions for the third phase of the attack.

"Then, they will detonate the three cobalt bombs." The words hung over the somberly quiet table for several seconds before Ackleworth continued. "They were instructed to target the beloved old and new cities of Bavaria, as they are highly prized by Geiseric and the Principles, set among the natural environment and whatnot. With enough wind, the entire state could be contaminated with a layer of radiation. The casualty rate from just this could be in the millions."

Ackleworth took a ragged breath, thinking seriously about all the horrors he had just described. Dandau stood beside him, slowly tapping his foot on the ground while everyone else continued to read over the documents in silence.

Sinclair put his elbow on the table and placed his hands together in front of his mouth in a prayer position as he ruminated.

"You do realize, this is taking the terror war up a notch," he finally stated, looking directly at Dandau.

"What's the difference?" Dandau asked. "Killing is killing. Death is Death."

"Yes," Sinclair acknowledged, "but you know as well as I do that the Apex has restrained from using chemical and biological weapons because of the mutual intimidation that we may do so. We may come to regret upsetting this balance. We all feel slightly contented that the Apex will not use nuclear weapons because of its environmental side effects, but who knows what ghastly things Geiseric will think up and justify in revenge."

"We'll cross that bridge when we come to it," Dandau brusquely replied.

The Allied leaders stared wide-eyed at the British prime minister, whose nonchalant attitude had them more than a little worried.

Ackleworth was the first to break the silence. "Obviously, as a Brit, I'm outraged by the citizens we've lost. But, I wouldn't recommend opening up this can of worms."

"As a Brit, you should demand retribution!" Dandau spat, waving his fist. "If nothing's done, our people will lose all morale! The Apex must bleed! You all want to do *nothing* about this holocaust of my people?"

President Kurtkin stood up abruptly. "Don't forget, Charles, many Russians and French died too."

Dandau glared back at him, his chest heaving. "With all due respect, Ivan, your thousands hardly compare to our million and more."

"With all due respect, Charles," Kurtkin replied coolly, "I don't care."

The two men attempted to stare each other down, Dandau fiercely glowering from the end of the table, and Kurtkin doggedly looking back from his relaxed and seated position.

Sinclair interceded. "The one thing we *can* agree on," he nodded and shrugged, "is that Germania must be punished."

Hollier looked at Kassian and then Streicher, searching their faces for an answer. "Our hand has been forced, gentlemen. What do you guys say we do?"

"This is not a good idea," Streicher answered.

"I agree," affirmed Kassian.

"Not doing anything could destroy the Alliance!" Dandau declared. "We can't allow Geiseric to think he can kill *a million British citizens* with *impunity!*"

"Wrong," President Sinclair asserted, stepping towards Dandau. "We cannot allow Geiseric to think he can get away with acts of terror against the *Allies!*"

It took only three days for all of the Allied civilians to be transported to North America. There were now more than five billion people residing within the borders of primarily the United States. The Allied refugees were from every part of the globe: China, Indochina, Russia, Africa, Europe, the Middle East, South America, Central America and, of course, the United States and Canada. Most were traumatized and grief-stricken by their journey to the New World and they desperately needed a morale boost.

As soon as it was over, Prime Minister Dandau held a press conference about the British refugee massacre. It was the first major address by any Allied leader to the civilian population since they were evacuated en masse from their countries to the coasts of North America. Dandau held the conference in front of the newly-constructed Fountain of the Alliance, located in Washington D.C., near the National Mall. It was an area in the center of the city that featured many monuments honoring American leaders, and was connected to the United States Capitol building. The Fountain of the Alliance was a colossal white marble and stone tribute to the circumstances that had mingled nearly two thirds of the planet's population into North America, now touted as being the last refuge of the free world.

Standing twelve stories tall, the fountain was quite impressive. A series of waterfalls cascaded down from the top of the structure, representing the nations of the Alliance. Every waterfall on the uppermost tier was of equal size, signifying that every Allied nation, even the small third world countries, would contribute an equal part and have an equal voice in the new government. The uppermost falls dropped ten meters down into a large, frothing pool, which in turn spilled over one side into a single giant waterfall, cascading thirty meters down with the mass and force of all the smaller ones put together. The fantastic deluge represented the awesome power of the Alliance, when every country stood united.

The *real* leaders were without question the "Big five," which were the United States, Russia, France, Britain and China. All of the other countries' leaders knew that they were puppets, but the fountain was nonetheless a grand egalitarian gesture and it kept the peace with so many different people packed into such tight quarters.

It was a cold day and everyone was bundled up. They could see their breath in the air, especially the Prime Minister, who was boiling internally from the righteous indignation coursing through his veins. Steam rose from his uncovered head.

Despite the cold, the sky was sunny and cloudless, and the crowd shared a generally hopeful feeling. Dandau stood before the fountain, but at a far enough distance that he was not misted profusely by the falls and his voice was not drowned out by them. He wanted the strong image of the powerful water pummeling down behind him to remind the audience of what the Allies were going do to the Apex.

The press corps, clamoring in the front rows, consisted of the most renowned reporters from the top thirteen Allied nations. They all worked together as a conglomerate now, staffing a single media source that distributed news over the Alliance's government-controlled television and radio stations.

Dandau nodded courteously at the press before starting. He inhaled deeply and stared into the camera with great sadness in his piercing blue eyes.

"I come before you, citizens of Britain and of all the Allied nations, with news of a great tragedy and a great crime, of which many of you may already be aware." He spoke in the melancholy, yet determined way that his mentor Winston Churchill used when beginning his sermons to cajole the British people during World War II.

"Of all the many terrible things that have befallen humans," Dandau continued, "no single act has been so evil, so vile, so wretched, as what has been wrought upon the British refugees and the other poor, defenseless souls attacked by the naval forces of Geiseric's depraved regime."

Dandau sighed, heaving his chest in dismay, and announced, "Nearly one-and-a-half million people were murdered in the cold waters of the Atlantic."

An audible gasp could be heard throughout the crowd, and even the relatively well-informed press corps was horrified at the staggering death toll. Although they had suspected something like this, hearing the actual number drove nails into their guts.

"Yes," the Prime Minister continued, "and out of that horrifying number of casualties, eighty percent were British."

The British reporters groaned in grief and murmured to each other, many in tears. Dandau looked into the crowd and into the cameras, filled with a zeal for vengeance and knowing that his speech was being broadcast to Apex televisions as well. No doubt the enemy leadership and many of the Apex citizens were watching.

"But, let it be known that these acts will not go without retribution," he increased in volume, his bloodshot eyes and the bulging veins in his forehead revealing the fury contained just below the surface.

"The Apex *will pay!* They will suffer in a way that makes our suffering pale in comparison!"

Dandau looked down his nose straight at the cameras before him. "We shall unleash the hounds of hell upon them and, like hunting a fox, we shall wear the enemy down and *rip them limb from limb!*"

When his speech concluded, the reporters hammered Dandau with questions, primarily asking him what Allied High Command intended to do to the Apex and who, precisely, would be targeted. The Prime Minister explained that Germania was at the crux of the recent tragedy, and so they would be the main target. However, he would not say anything more. He ended the questions with a wave and stepped away, leaving to the imagination the details of what would be done and when it would happen.

The majority of the Allied refugees felt solidarity with the Brits, especially those from nations that also lost people in the Diaspora massacre. Other nations had suffered relatively minor casualties, each losing at most a few tens of thousands of their civilians, as opposed to several hundreds of thousands. Regardless, almost everyone wanted to retaliate against the Apex. Though, there were of course those who were frightened. No one wanted to see this cruelty escalate and come back to haunt them.

Dandau's speech was the first time the Allied citizens had seen such an important address since leaving their homes. Their own leaders had only given brief radio announcements when they disembarked in North America. But all the arriving refugees were so emotionally numb then, they could barely comprehend anything.

So, while Dandau's speech was not his best, and while its ambiguities did little to console the British citizens, it had a great psychological impact on the Allied citizenry, in Dandau's favor. Like a newborn animal identifying with the first living creature it sees, smells, touches, or hears, they now saw the British prime minister as their caretaker. Whether they agreed with him or not, they saw him as their source of information, reassurance, and protection.

However, if the speech was meant to frighten the Apex, it failed. Geiseric was constantly feeding his empire propaganda, assuring his people that they were protected and that the death count from the refugee attack was far less than that claimed by the Allies. The Allies, the emperor argued, used their citizens as human shields. The refugee ships were loaded with weapons, which Geiseric touted as an immensely immoral and cowardly move, equating it with what the British did with the Lusitania, the British ocean liner that brought America into World War I.

Geiseric explained the historical pattern to his audience, asserting that in the First World War, the United States government secretly transported armaments to the British on board large civilian ships, something that was deemed against the rules of war. The Germans were aware of this and went to great lengths to warn the American populace, going so far as to post articles in the *New York Times*. Eventually, the Kaiser allowed for the targeting of civilian ships traveling from America to Britain. The Lusitania was struck by a single torpedo fired from a German U-boat. This sparked a second, much larger explosion within the ship. The British claimed that it was coal dust, though it was later confirmed that there was, in fact, a vast storehouse of American munitions on board, including more than four million Remington rifle cartridges.

The truth was, the Allies *were* doing something similar now, but not on the *British* Skimmers. Allied High Command ordered all weaponry destined for America to be shipped on the African refugee ships during their round in the Great Diaspora. None of the European Skimmers were carrying a single war machine or weapon.

It was somewhat baffling to the Allies that Geiseric risked his Delfins against the European route convoy, when he could have taken out a substantial amount of the weapons coming over on the African passage. The intelligence he was receiving must have been excellent, for he was able to target only the British Skimmers, which were not marked any differently than the others. That could not have been mere coincidence. After the Diaspora, Allied High Command put Kassian in charge of a mass sweep of the lower-level military and bureaucratic infrastructures, to purge them of Apex spies as he did for the upper echelons of the Allied political and military administration.

Dandau was not surprised by Geiseric's attack on his people. He understood the depths of the Apex Emperor's hate for Britain that had evolved in the past ten years. Geiseric loathed those in Britain who chose not to move to Germania. He blamed the "nationalist Brits" for the whole antithetical movement against him, and he was right to a degree, for it was they who whole-heartedly supported Dandau, his arch-nemesis, and Geiseric punished them for that.

Dandau had purposely leaked information to Apex spies that had long ago been spotted by Kassian and were allowed to stay, unaware they had been identified. Keeping a few enemy spies in non-vital posts is valuable to feed misinformation to your enemy, or information which is true, but that you don't want your enemy to know you know they know. Such was the convoluted nature of espionage.

The information Dandau leaked made it as plain and obvious as possible that all Allied weaponry would be transported from Africa to the United States. It would have been worth losing the military equipment to save his beloved people, but Dandau now realized that probably made Geiseric only want to kill them more.

What the world did not know was that, in concluding his speech, Dandau had just given the orders for the Treasure Trove squad to execute their long-awaited mission. The final sentence of his speech, "*We shall unleash the hounds of hell upon them and, like hunting a fox, we shall wear the enemy down and rip them limb from limb,*" had been the secret code for his team in Germania to launch the terror strike.

Since it was too risky for the squad to communicate with MI6 when in Germania, they had been ordered to disband and disseminate into Germanian society until their services were needed. That was ten years ago. Some were now in their late forties and gray was just starting to show in small patches along their sideburns. But their skin was not yet wrinkled and they looked just as fit, if not more fit, than when they had left the bunker to become individual sleeper cells. Of course, they had been receiving all the health benefits of the typical Germanian, or any Apex citizen.

All of the British agents had fake identifications. Some knew the language inside and out and assumed a German-born identity, while others pretended to be Isaianic British citizens who had fled to Germania back at the beginning of

Geiseric's rise to power. They had completely immersed themselves in normal Germanian life, appearing average and content with the regime. It certainly was not the worst of missions. The weekly massages stimulated their immune, endocrine and circulatory systems. Their state-sponsored nutritionists discovered their vitamin deficiencies and prescribed remedies for them that the British agents would never have gotten in the U.K.

They had enjoyed the delicious, flavorsome Germanian food, which was regulated by the government and held to the highest standards. The squad had also become quite accustomed to their four day work weeks and regular paid visits to the Austrian hot springs. It was difficult to return to their assignment after a ten year absence from the world of espionage. The complete submergence into normal life had spoiled them.

It was eleven a.m. on the New England coast when Prime Minister Dandau gave his speech, but it was eight at night in Germania. Most of the MI6 agents were off work from the lower-level management and blue-collar jobs they had taken up. One agent was at a bar outside Munich when he saw the speech on the television. He asked the bartender to interrupt the soccer game and switch to the news channel showing the speech, which he had heard would be coming on at this time. Another agent was working the night shift as a mall security guard. He saw the speech on the big-screen, holographic television sets on sale at the electronics store. No matter where the agents were when they heard the code, nearly all of them immediately dropped what they were doing and rushed to their apartments in different cities and towns all across Germania.

None of them knew anything about what had become of the other squad members. The entire unit was designed to be completely untraceable. They never communicated with each other or with headquarters. They just waited, not knowing when the order would come, or if it would ever come. For the first few years, they were on edge, always prepared. But, as time ran on, they fell into their daily routines, nearly forgetting that they were undercover and had girlfriends or wives and kids back home. A few *almost* wished the call would never come. But when it did, it was no surprise. Each one suspected it would come on the heels of an attack upon the British, at the outbreak of World War III. And that time had arrived.

As the agents prepared for their mission, many questions ran through their minds. They wondered what their cohorts had done; if they had taken up the call, or had fallen into blessed obscurity. The agents clandestinely removed their weapons of appointment out of their respective hiding places. Those agents holding biological and chemical weapons simply disguised their vials and aerosol cans. In the middle of the night, they carefully loaded the dangerous goods into their hydrocell-powered Volkswagens, BMWs, or Mercedes and prepared to unleash mass carnage on the people they had been living and working among for a decade.

They waited until the early afternoon of the following day. The plan, made so long ago, had been clear. The agents holding the biological weapons were to act first. Fourteen men altogether were in possession of the aerosol pneumonic plague and genetically modified Ebola virus. Many of the agents had moved within blocks of a Wellenbad, a recreational wave pool, the likes of which were profusely scattered throughout every city and small town in Germania. Seven of these agents had selected the largest and most visited ones; the indoor pools, which would be crowded year round.

The agents drove to their local Wellenbads, their deadly liquids and aerosols disguised as sun tan lotion, drink containers, or deodorant. In spite of, or perhaps because of the tumultuous times, there were people out and about, enjoying themselves in the towns and cities, many seeking escape in recreation. Crowds of Germanians were dining out, going to movies and indulging in various types of entertainment.

As they entered the huge, indoor pool complexes, the agents quickly encountered problems. Things were different from when they had last scoped out the places. The interiors were far better ventilated. There was not the same build-up of humidity as before. The renovations must have happened quite recently. Whether it warranted suspicion was hard to say, but it meant that the diseases would not linger in the air for very long.

Then, when the agents tested the water, they found that it was far warmer and more chlorinated than before. Chlorine was rarely found in recognizable amounts in Germanian pools. Yet, children were rubbing their red eyes and the adults were complaining about its strong odor. The viral liquid plague and Ebola would not last long in that water. And, though there were people out having fun in general, there were disproportionately smaller crowds within the indoor pools than other places, due to the agitating chlorine. Furthermore, the majority of the pool-goers were children. Adults were more indignant over the changes, but children adjusted quickly and wanted to stay and have fun.

An agent at a massive Wellenbad in what was formally the Czech Republic got cold feet when he saw so many children. He was married before he was dispatched to Germania for an indeterminate period, and had children of his own. Although, they would hardly be children anymore, he thought sadly. Whether they had survived the Diaspora or not, he could not know. He realized that he would be no better than Geiseric, if he went through with his mission. He shook his head and came back to the present, deciding to pretend the chlorine bothered him. Rubbing his eyes and holding his nose in feigned disdain, he walked out, returned to his flat, and safely disposed of his biological toxin with equipment that he and the others had in the case a war never happened.

Most of the agents had a bad feeling about the changes at the indoor pools, but five went forth with hitting the primary targets. One of them targeted an indoor Wellenbad in a small town in the Schleswig-Holstein region, right below Denmark. He walked to the side of the pool carrying his towel, and leaned down on one knee, as if to test the water. As he placed the towel down beside the pool, a small piece draped down into the water. It covered his fake bottle of sun tan lotion, which was silently emitting a clear liquid into the pool.

He got up and walked away, carefully but casually holding his contaminated towel and bottle away from him. He strolled into the locker room and used the large wall mirror to see if anyone was watching. When he was satisfied the coast was clear, he quickly threw the towel and bottle in the recycling can (there were no garbage cans in Germania), and returned to the spot where he had left what appeared to be a thermal water bottle. Subtly he took a deep breath, held it, and pressed a hidden button on the side of the water bottle, causing it to spray out aerosolized contagion. Then, he moved nonchalantly toward the exit, trying to act natural while slowly exhaling.

Suddenly, he was slammed up against the wall by two undercover Germanian police officers. They knocked the wind out of him and he had no choice but to gasp for air. Within seconds, dozens of special operations police officers in watertight, full-body suits and masks, stormed into the complex and hastily cleared everyone out of the water, moving them outside where they were quarantined and treated. The four other British agents who attacked the Wellenbads were also caught right after they deployed their particular disease.

The nine other agents with biological weapons focused on other populated public areas, such as malls or *Fussgangerzone*. Every single downtown of every city or town in Germania had a *Fussgangerzone*, which were pedestrian areas where no cars were allowed. The cobblestone streets were often packed with shoppers and diners coming and going, and the *Fussgangerzone* allowed slow biking. Taking advantage of this, two of the agents used bikes with dispersal units on the back that sprayed the plague or Ebola virus into the air as they passed. Others just left a shopping bag unattended in a mall or busy restaurant with a device spewing out the deadly gas. But, the Germanians were prepared for the attacks. All the men were caught either right before or just after they deployed their weapons. Germanian task forces were at the ready to quarantine entire sections of large cities and the people were rapidly tested.

It was obvious that Geiseric's administration had some sort of knowledge of what attacks were going to be launched and possibly by whom. This attracted the attention of the media, but Geiseric's administration tightened its reign on the free Germanian press, asking them to refrain from reporting anything that he did not personally approve, saying that it may endanger society. The leading media groups agreed to run their stories through Geiseric until the end of the war, since it was obvious that the war had just started. And the first thing the media agreed to do was stifle the fact that any biological attacks had occurred. Geiseric did not want to let out that the government knew about any terrorist attacks, because it was better to let the other MI6 agents who had not yet deployed their weapons think that no one was on to them.

Armed with VX nerve gas and botulinum toxin, some of the MI6 agents went after the Volksfesten. Germania was famous for these festivals, held every weekend in the nearest woods. A dirt path led to a large gathering of revelers sitting at picnic tables amongst trees. Beer flowed freely while both old-fashioned and modern music was played.

The agents' original plans were to place botulinum toxin in the beer dispensers, but when they arrived, they found that the areas where the alcohol was loaded into the dispensers was highly guarded. This was curious because, usually, they were not watched and anyone could get behind the dispensers. But, it did not necessarily mean that the terror attack was known. The agents decided to just disperse the aerosolized botulinum and VX. With so many people milling around, they did not notice the undercover Germanian officers who were watching them. The terrorist agents were all caught before much of their poison could be disseminated.

Even though it appeared to the apprehended Brits that the Germanian authorities had been generally well prepared for their terror attacks, this was merely a façade. They were not prepared to respond to an attack at any crowded place in Germania. They could never be ready to respond to everything. However, some unexpected intelligence had prepared them.

One of the British Treasure Trove agents had settled down since leaving the bunker in Poland. He had taken a wife and started a family in Dresden. There, in his happy home, he hid the aerosolized plague dispensers. But, he was seduced by the cushy lifestyle of Apex Germania and, as the years passed, he even began believing in the Isaianic ideology that his wife and neighbors espoused. So, when Dandau spoke the secret code words, he betrayed the mission and his fellow agents.

Of course, he did not know everything. In fact, he did not know much. The cells were designed so that, if one should betray the team, it would not automatically trigger the fall of the mission. The British agent told what he did know to the Germanian authorities: what the attacks would be and, in general, the primary and secondary targets.

The Germanian government did not want to cause mass panic amongst the populace and collapse the system. They also did not want to let the attackers know that they were aware of their plan. It was better for the Germanian authorities to know where the British agents were going to strike and to apprehend them there. If the terror squad was forewarned that they had been betrayed, they could change their plan, attacking a less predictable location.

Geiseric had his own reasons for not revealing that the government had intelligence concerning the terror attack. He wanted to ensure that the cobalt-bombers never detonated their thermonuclear weapons on his prized German landscape. Thus, he could not tell the populace of the first phase of the attacks and allow the terrorists to know they were on to them, even if it meant risking more Germanian lives. He could not bear it if the agents used their environmentally destructive devices to annihilate his beloved Black Forest or Bavarian *Wald*. The British traitor had revealed that there were three bombs altogether and Geiseric suspected that two of these were just in Bavaria. His suspicions were correct.

As two of these MI6 agents drove away from their apartments in Bavaria, they found that the roads had many checkpoints. The soldiers were using numerous weapons-sniffing dogs and radiation-detection devices. The British agents were happy to see them. They figured that the biological and chemical attacks had successfully taken effect and, as a result, there was a general upgrading of security. They had been smart not to pack their weapons, each the size of a large car trunk. Ten years ago they had buried their nuclear devices in the woods around Garmisch-Partenkirchen and Fussen, keeping careful watch over the years on any construction and other development plans in that area. But under Geiseric's forest and historic site preservation policies, the landscape remained unchanged, so the weapons still rested peacefully in their original hiding spots.

Garmisch-Partenkirchen was Germania's largest Alpine resort. It consisted of two towns: the older Partenkirchen and the modern (for its time) Garmisch, which were merged together under Hitler's regime for the 1936 Olympic Winter Games. It had 60,000 residents, but the daytime population reached over one-hundred thousand on busy weekends, which it was today. The surrounding mountain slopes and woods were filled with Apex skiers and *sportif volken.*

One of the agents had his bomb in the forest just off to the side of a ski slope. He skied down to his secret spot and, when no one was looking, moved into the trees. Pulling out a foldable shovel, he extended it and began digging. The device was just where he had left it. He had to come here to arm it, for there were radio frequencies being put out all over Germania by the authorities that were jamming his remote control's ability to arm and detonate it. The jamming frequencies were not specifically singling his remote control out. They were jamming all wavelengths that were not used by the government or identified private sector sources. Of course, there were many legitimate sources using other wavelengths that could not immediately be identified, and so they were hindered. But, such was a small price to pay. The agent was not overly-suspicious of these precautions being taken by the authorities, for it was the expected protocol for any government to go through when being attacked by terrorists using weapons of mass destruction.

The agent looked around for a moment, seeing if anyone was nearby. There wasn't, but he saw the many people in the distance and considered for a second what was about to happen. The blast would generate an intense amount of light in the visible, infrared and ultraviolet spectrum, burning peoples' flesh and eyes, and blinding those farther away when it reflected off the white snow. But, the most devastating part would be the enormous fireball. A super-heated, spherical volume of air generated by the intense energy would set ablaze a large portion of the resort. The blast winds could exceed twelve hundred kilometers per hour, several times greater than the strongest hurricane. The range of the blast would destroy most of the city. Later, a great number of people who survived the day would die from radiation poisoning. It would corrupt one of Geiseric's beloved Alpine regions, leaving utter degradation. The animals would be poisoned and the forests would be completely uninhabitable.

The British agents in charge of detonating the cobalt bombs received more than just their call to task from Dandau's speech. They knew what to listen for and they were also given the arming code to their nukes. Now, the agent in Garmisch-Partenkirchen quickly set about plugging in the code to arm his nuclear weapon. He was just about to start the sequence when, suddenly and just in time, he was shot right between the eyes by a Germanian sniper rifle. He fell sideways into the snow, the pool of blood leaking forth from his forehead quickly freezing and congealing in place.

Another agent had a cobalt bomb in Bavaria and he was living in Fussen. It was located near *Schloss Neuschwanstein,* New Swan Stone Castle, which was a 19th century palace. The castle was built by Ludwig II, Mad King Ludwig, given this name because he frittered the Bavarian taxpayers' money away on extremely expensive building projects. However, their sacrifice was humanity's gain, for *Neuschwanstein* was one of the most visited destinations in the world, and was so whimsical that it provided the inspiration for the Disneyland castle.

This could not be a better place to strike, except for Berchtesgaden, where Geiseric had his mountain retreat. But that area was too well-guarded ever since he rebuilt the Berghof and began to visit there often.

Neuschwanstein was nestled atop a steep bit of mountain at the foot of the alps. Every day, tens of thousands of people from all over the Apex Empire visited the castle and the shops and restaurants at the foot of the mountain.

Most importantly, the castle was a source of tremendous pride to Geiseric. The Apex Emperor had much in common with King Ludwig. They were both fanatical about the operas of Richard Wagner. Wagner was a nineteenth century composer, the king of the Romantic Era. He wrote nationalistic operas such as *Der Ring Des Nibelungen,* the inspiration for Tolkien's *The Lord of the Rings,* with memorable music such as Ride of the Valkyries, the embodiment of Grand Opera. Ludwig built *Neuschwanstein* in commemoration of Wagner's operas and such is why it had such a fanciful appearance. The combination of natural and man-made beauty in this area made it near sacrosanct to Geiseric.

The British agent parked and hiked tirelessly into the woods surrounding the castle, where he unburied his nuclear weapon. It was different than the one used by the other agent. This was a recoilless launcher, which fired a one-hundred and fifty five millimeter nuclear round. The weapon system used a spin-stabilized, unguided rocket. Its ten kilogram nuclear warhead had an explosive yield of .5 kilotons, the equivalent of five-hundred tons of TNT.

He set the device up on a tripod and angled it towards the storybook-style castle. He was about to arm it and press the ignition when, suddenly, multiple large machine guns opened fire on him from every direction, around and above. He only heard the first shot before he was eviscerated by dozens of well-targeted bullets fired by Germanian Federal Police on skis, snow mobiles and in Kolibri chariots.

Geiseric and the entire Principles administration were euphoric. They assumed that the plot to attack Bavaria had been thwarted, and the remaining bomb had been saved for a different area. That notion was reinforced from what they gathered from the British agent who betrayed his team. No one knew for sure, but they were certain enough to disperse their security to other places. They suspected that the Danzig area was the most likely place to be struck, because of the beautiful environment of the whole Tri-city area, and the popular spa-town of Zoppoth. Danzig, located on Danzig Bay in the Baltic, was also the largest ship-building industrial center in Germania. Hitting them there would hit them hard. Detonating a radiation cobalt bomb was especially effective when exploded on ocean water, as it vaporized the salt and sent it up into the clouds. The rain from the salted clouds helped the radioactive fallout disperse over a much wider area.

But Geiseric's intuition was faulty. The MI6 agents with nuclear weapons had *all* been ordered to strike Bavaria. The third was hiking around the *Starnberger See*, Lake Starnberg, which was Germany's fourth largest lake and a popular recreation area for the nearby city of Munich. Mad King Ludwig adored the natural splendor of the lake and the mountains surrounding it. It was here where thousands of swans lived, their elegance enrapturing the king. Such was why he named his castle *Neuschwanstein*. Ironically, in 1886, Ludwig was supiciously found dead in the lake.

The agent diverted off the main trail, slinking low in the brush so as not to be seen. He quickly found and unburied his recoilless launcher. After he set it up, he placed the large, twenty kilogram warhead round on the end of the rifled launcher and aimed it towards the city of Starnberg, which sat on the north of the lake. The round would be fired up and forwards two kilometers, and then burst in the air where it would most effectively spread its cataclysmic radiation.

He checked his watch and programmed his weapon to detonate in twenty minutes. He set the timer and ran away as fast as his legs would go. His car was parked quite a ways down, off to the side of the road at a viewing point where it would look least suspicious. His heart was racing and he was short of breath when he reached his destination, but he held back at the tree line. Germanian police officers were checking out his car and talking on their radios. The British agent softly turned around, trying not to crunch in the snow, but as he took his first step back into the woods two thickly-built Bavarian men sprung out and grabbed his arms. Frost was building in their hardy, light brown mustaches, which covered the whole of their upper lips.

They spun him around and dragged him over to their snowmobiles. One of the officers lifted a rescue stretcher off the back of his vehicle and both of them strapped the MI6 agent's arms and legs down and rapidly secured the stretcher back onto the snowmobile. They drove along the path of the enemy agent's footprints up through the forest, quickly finding the nuclear warhead launcher. In a rage, one of the Bavarian officers fired a shot into the gut of the British agent. He ran over to the launcher. There was only one minute left.

He called over his radio for a Kolibri officer to come up and disarm or move it, but there were none close enough. In frustration, he kicked over the launcher. The British agent just laughed weakly as he bled from his stomach.

"It will still explode you fools!"

The other officer kicked him in the face and stomped heavily on his head. He got on the radio and told everyone to move to cover because they had found an armed bomb. He then ordered his partner to take off, but his fellow officer refused to leave. They both started beating the agent profusely, demanding he give up the deactivation code. They sliced his ears off and viciously stabbed him numerous times. But, the Brit's lips were sealed.

With only ten seconds left, the two Bavarians stood upright and solemnly shook each other's hands. They looked out at the glorious Alpine view. Suddenly, the nuclear round fired off its propellant and rocketed away from the toppled launcher, bouncing off trees and eventually jamming in a large snow bank. The propellant was still going, quickly melting the snow into water, and the warhead was still armed, in the last seconds of the countdown sequence.

As the officers took in their final look at the nature they had grown up in and come to adore, they gave their last respects.

"To *God!*" the ranking officer shouted.

"*Sieg Heil!*" they both roared, giving the salute from their heart forward.

Three seconds.

"To the *Führer!*"

Two seconds.

"*Sieg Heil!*"

"To *Germania!*"

One second.

"*Sieg . . . Heil!*" they belted out with all the passion in their souls.

And they were overtaken by a tremendous light.

It was impossible for Geiseric's administration to keep a lid on the nuclear blast. The initial reports were that there were thirty-thousand casualties, but that number steadily increased as the day faded and night descended. The radioactive fallout spread over one hundred kilometers and was hard to contain, even for the experienced clean-up crews of Germania, who had helped purify the Iraqi sands of uranium.

In the end, over sixty thousand people were killed by the immediate blast, or died later from radiation poisoning and a myriad of other injuries. Another ten thousand were blinded and received fifth and sixth degree burns. The hospitals in Bavaria were overwhelmed and medical staff from all over Germania and the Apex was brought in to facilitate. A disaster of such magnitude could not be stifled. Nor did Geiseric wish to continue the secrecy. For, though he had done all he could to avoid this disaster, he could now use it to his advantage.

Graphic images were broadcast to the Germanian and Apex public, with video of innocent victims, their skin crusted and hanging, their muscles black and blue, melted and charred to the bone.

The news was also released concerning the numerous biological and chemical attacks, which had already killed one thousand people and made thousands more critically ill. It was not released, however, that the government and media had known about these attacks while they were going on. The public was told that Geiseric's administration had been caught off guard by the "despicable terrorism," but the authorities did a superb job in containing the attacks. However, it was released that three people were known to have been exposed to the deadly diseases at an attack site and got away from the sites before quarantine showed up. Thus, they may have unwittingly spread the Ebola virus and the plague in the city of Leipzig. No one knew how many more people were infected or if the infected had left Leipzig. All of Germania and the entire population of the Apex could be at risk.

The entire city of Leipzig was quarantined. No one was allowed in or out until every ailment of every person was accounted for. The symptoms of the pneumonic plague began one to four days after exposure to the aerosolized bacteria and included fever, headache, weakness, and a bloody or watery cough, caused by the infection of the lungs. Without treatment, this led to septic shock, abdominal pain, and bleeding into the skin and internal organs. Unfortunately, there was no vaccine against pneumonic plague and antibiotic treatment only worked when administered in the first twenty-four hours of developing symptoms. In Leipzig, antibiotics cured only fifty percent of the victims.

The symptoms of Marburg Ebola were difficult to distinguish from other common and harmless infections, when it first developed. The infected got headaches, fevers and flu-like symptoms. But it soon turned far worse. Their blood congealed and their capillaries, blocked by dead blood cells, collapsed. The infection then spread to other blood vessels and the organs, which became clogged and began to disintegrate as the surrounding tissue bled uncontrollably. The bruised skin blistered and fell away. In the end, the victims became delirious and vomited their liquefied innards.

The threat of contracting this disease caused a crisis situation throughout Germania. No one could think of a more horrendous way to die, so no one left their homes or, if they absolutely had to, they wore surgical masks. But after two weeks, when no one outside of the city fell ill, it became apparent that the epidemic was contained in Leipzig.

More than five thousand people died from the biological attacks. Most were taken by the plague, but nearly a fifth had suffered the unthinkable Ebola death, most of these being children, due to the predominance of youths at the *Wellenbad* pools. It made the acts seem even more heinous and unforgivable.

Altogether, around seventy-five thousand civilians were killed by the Allied terror attacks on Germania. This would have seemed a devastating blow, if it were not relative to the one-and-a-half-million Allied civilians killed during the Great Diaspora. Also, far from being cowed in fear, Geiseric was filled with livid determination. On top of that, the Allies' foolish maneuver had given him exactly what he needed: fuel for the global fire.

The Allied leadership was not able to gather enough intelligence about the Germanian citizens' political views. If they had better sources, they would have known, for instance, that the average German did not want to go to war, and they were disgusted by the attack on the Allied refugees forced to flee their homelands. Most Germans, the power-base for Geiseric and his administration, truly empathized with the victims of the Diaspora. They were infuriated with their leadership for perpetrating such attacks. But that quickly changed upon seeing Germanian children throwing up their bloody guts, scenes played repeatedly on Geiseric's propaganda television clips. It gave the Germans a taste for blood that, until now, *this* generation had never felt.

Germania, a nation of uniquely individual countries and cultures lumped together under one title, now also felt their first sense of solidarity. Since the attacks were not confined to the former Germany, but happened in places like the former Polish and Czech areas, all of Germania felt threatened. Whether they were Polish, Czech, or German, Principle or non-Principle, it seemed that no one was immune to the Allied wrath and they had only one common protector: Geiseric, the emperor . . . the *Führer*.

Geiseric spoke to the Apex masses, using the grand Olympic coliseum as his forum. More than two hundred thousand citizens of Germania, and many thousands of citizens from other Apex nations, came to watch him give his address, packing the stadium to the brim. The speech was being broadcast all over the empire to an anxious populous.

The Apex emperor mounted his granite podium on the imposing front stage, elevated ten meters high into the air. Many citizens were daring enough to give him the *Sieg Heil* salute, which was not seen much before in the Apex. Military officers and the police had accepted the salute and executed it often and proudly, but the general populace was slow to re-adopt the symbolic gesture. That night, however, it was rampant throughout the audience in the ancient-looking, stone bleachers. Even the non-German Germanians, along with Jews, Indians, Greeks and Japanese, all saluted with the ferocity of their German counterparts.

The audience respectfully quieted as Geiseric raised his hands, signaling he was about to begin.

"*Hallo meine Leute!*" he bellowed in a mighty voice.

"*Hallo mein Führer!*" the crowd shouted back in unison. Geiseric smiled, but quickly became more solemn. The Apex television news cameras, which had been filming the audience's enormous support, focused back on Geiseric.

"I would, first off, like to apologize to all the families of those who were killed by the Allied terror attacks on Germania. I must especially ask forgiveness from the parents of those poor children who died of the Ebola virus. No child, no living being, should have to endure such a horrible disease. I failed to protect them . . . and, for this, I am very sorry."

Almost everyone in the Apex Empire was watching Geiseric's speech, no matter which time zone they resided in. Those at home clutched their families near, thankful for every second of life with their loved ones. They were touched by Geiseric's apology, a grand act of humility.

Geiseric led the audience in a moment of silence, in prayer for everyone who had suffered in the Allied terrorist attacks, and for strength in the inevitable turmoil to come. The whole Olympic amphitheatre fell eerily silent. They prayed for the lost children, for all of the injured and the loved ones left behind. And they prayed, most of all, for God's protection.

As they slowly lifted their bowed heads, someone gave the *Sieg Heil* salute and began chanting. Soon the entire stadium had joined him in solidarity. Finally, their *Führer* motioned again for silence and continued.

"I am so proud of the Germanians, who have endured this attack and only came out stronger. I am proud of the entire Apex Empire, for you have shown your courage by not leaving the empire in this time of great uncertainty. The whole of the Apex stands resolute and united and, thus, we shall not fall. We are the greatest force ever known to history, and the Allies are well-aware of it!" he roared, scowling into the camera. "That is why they stoop to such cowardly levels to discourage us."

Geiseric shook his head. "Of course, it is nothing new for the Allies to behave in a cowardly fashion," he remarked flippantly. "In the first two world wars they committed far more war crimes against Germany than Germany did against them. We treated the Jews and the Soviet Union worse, but the West never really considered them part of the Allies anyway. Besides, Stalin was doing a lot more damage to the Russians than the Germans under Hitler ever did." Many in the audience cheered him on as he spoke exactly what they were thinking.

"But it is truly the *West*, led by the *Anglo-American Front*, that plagued Germany throughout the *entire* twentieth century. It is *they* who are the most ruthless of our enemies!"

The *Führer* looked out at the massive crowd, many of whom were standing in their seats, too anxious to sit, hanging intently on his every word. For a moment, he stood in awe of what he had accomplished.

"Allow me to explain myself," he continued, leaning his right elbow casually on the podium, as if having a conversation with a good friend. "There was a man by the name of Winston Churchill, a greatly lauded man who was boasted as being the champion of freedom, and democracy, and virtue, and everything perfect, warm and fuzzy about the unendingly virtuous Anglo-American Front," he paraphrased mockingly.

"Yet," Geiseric explained, straightening up and holding his wrist behind his back in an upright, military-style posture, "it was this British Prime Minister who wished to gas everything and everyone, way before Hitler even considered the Beer Hall Putsch! One of the finest examples is when Churchill recommended to gas bomb and kill tens, if not hundreds of thousands of Iraqis for misbehaving and not taking to the British leash! This was in the *nineteen-twenties*, long before Saddam Hussein was made to look like a despicable man for doing the same thing!" The audience roared with approval.

He inhaled deeply and paused thoughtfully.

"So," Geiseric continued, "do not be surprised when the Allies behave unjustly, for it is the *great deception* that the Germans are the only war criminals, or that Hitler was the greatest villain in history. Such is the Anglo-American propaganda machine, meant to hide the Native American holocaust," he counted off on his fingers, "meant to hide the British slave trade, meant to hide their empires and their conquering leaders who savaged innocent people and lands *long before* the Germans came into the game. They were the ones who bombed every major city in Germany into dust, and purposefully attacked women and children fleeing as refugees into Dresden!" He slammed his palms down on the podium in anger, and leaned forward.

"The British or Americans *have never*, and *will never*, apologize for that! And, *no doubt*, they would do the same again if they had the chance!

"So," he said, balling his hand into a fist, "the die has been cast and we must stay strong, for we cannot give in to the tyranny of the the Anglo-American Front! Do not be afraid! We are far stronger than they! Together, the Apex is a *Juggernaut!*" he shouted powerfully, thrusting his fist up into the air. "An immense, unstoppable force," he explained with an ominous tone in his voice.

"Now, the people of the Apex are good people and did not ask for this war, nor do we want it. But, it has been brought upon our doorstep, and let it *never* be said that we cower in the face of danger!"

The *Führer* gazed upon the audience and smiled. "The fact is, and it is evident in this crowd before me today, that the Allies have made a grave mistake with their odious behavior. With their crimes, they have brought down upon themselves the wrath of the mightiest empire ever known to mankind!"

Geiseric stood upright, pushed out his chest and absorbed the sights and sounds of more than two-hundred-thousand reverently cheering citizens, all chomping at the bit for vengeance.

"*Woe* to the Allies," the *Führer* roared over them, "for they have awoken a sleeping *giant!*"

Frenetic applause shook the stadium. Geiseric basked in his moment, tirelessly feeding off the emotion, as he stood on the brink of World War III. He once again threw his fist up in the air and ripped it down as if he were pulling a cord.

"Release . . . the Juggernaut!"

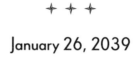

January 26, 2039

Striking towards Russia, the largest country in the world, the Germanian Air Force broke out into Eastern Europe in the middle of the night. The Germanian jets moved out in waves to fly their sorties. In the first wave, six hundred Stealth Eagles tore into Russia. Golden Eagles were, incidentally, designed with a small radar signature, due to their lack of a tail rudder. They maintained stability synthetically, using a powerful onboard computer that made thousands of minute corrections to the engines every second.

The Stealth Eagle bombers had wings twice as wide as the Golden Eagles, but were one third as thick, giving them a far more two-dimensional contour. They were painted black and their engines were nearly silent. They also needed far less wing-rotation capability, because they were not speedy craft, always flying below the speed of sound to avoid forewarning their enemies with a sonic boom. Pouring over the boundaries into the lands of Germania's neighbors, the Stealth Eagles were the spearhead of the war.

Like all stealth craft, they were not completely invisible to radar. Their designs just made them appear much smaller, by bouncing the radio waves away from the receiving radar sites. Although they were twenty-five meters wide and ten meters long, they appeared to be only the size of a sparrow on radar.

At first, the Stealth Eagles moved out individually, for utmost secrecy, headed for the most important radar installations. They made their first strike on the densely packed radar net on the Russian border, which had the strongest and most advanced European defense system to guard the vast resources within the country's tremendous borders. There were two types of installations for the Stealth Eagles to maneuver through. The continuous wave Doppler systems put out a constant radio signal and could only be used for Doppler-effect ranging, to gauge whether an object was moving toward or away from the receiver. Thus, if the jets moved perpendicular to the beam, there would be little Doppler-shift and they would not be detected.

The other type of system, interspersed evenly throughout the entire Russian radar net, was Pulse-Doppler, which could detect an enemy plane no matter what direction it was traveling. Pulse-Doppler radar was quite the opposite of its similar sounding cousin short-pulse radar, in that it showed *everything*, even non-moving objects.

The best way to trick the Pulse-Doppler technician was to charge the beam head-on, making the smallest target possible, which then blends in with the rest of the clutter on the radar screen. The Stealth Eagle cockpits had threat indicator screens that displayed what type of radar was trained on them. The different radar systems were placed in a web to slightly overlap their coverage areas, but the systems could not be placed too close together, for their signals interfered with each other. Thus, the pilots had to deftly weave in between the two, alternating between a perpendicular and head-on approach, adjusting according to whichever their threat indicators displayed as the stronger radar in the vicinity. They called this "threading the needle" and the pilots, even with their specially designed jets, had very little room for error.

Piercing through the radar net, the Stealth Eagles began dropping their payloads. The first three hundred simultaneously dropped twenty-five bombs each. Thousands of half-ton smart bombs careened toward the ground, guided through the air with small tail rudders and onboard computers. The bombs tracked and followed the radar beams down to the transmitters.

All at once, along the entire Russian western border, the ground shook and the night sky lit up from the fire below. Over seven thousand radar sites and mobile Surface-to-Air Missile, "SAM," launchers were instantly destroyed, their operators and crews eviscerated by the explosions. The Apex pilots cheered over their radios as the fireballs took out the Allied defenses and tens of thousands of Allied soldiers and officers.

The next three hundred Stealth Eagles eagerly flew in and dropped payloads of ten two-ton bombs each. The guided munitions swiftly found their marks —the more heavily fortified radar installations and bunkered anti-aircraft mis-sile and gun installations. The explosives carved out large swaths of the first line of defenses, almost completely blinding the Allied forces in those areas.

As the stealth jets retreated back to Germania, three thousand Golden Eagle fighter-bombers flew past at more than seven-thousand kilometers per hour, giving a new meaning to the word Blitzkrieg. They came in low to the ground, attempting to blend into the landscape, to avoid the few radar and missile units left amongst the smoldering remains. Some Allied personnel tried to manually operate the surviving anti-aircraft batteries, but the Golden Eagles' unbelievable speed made it impossible for the gunners to even see them, let alone hit them.

The Golden Eagles came in individually or in formations of five, each carrying four two-ton bombs. As they moved over the front lines, they began dropping their munitions on other tactical military targets of the Russian defensive infrastructure, adroitly pinpointing centers of communication. But the Allied Bald Eagles started coming in fast, racing toward them in a fury. The Apex pilots dropped their payloads as quickly as possible, some settling on earlier or unplanned targets, for they needed to lighten up quickly to engage the enemy.

Behind and over the twelve-hundred kilometer-long Allied front line in Russia, the jets clashed. From St. Petersburg to Rostov, the formations broke and the battle quickly degenerated into a chaotic melee, rumbling low across the blizzard-beaten steppes and high near the upper edge of the stratosphere. The Bald Eagle pilots fighting over Russia were the best the Allies had in Europe and they had a significant numerical superiority to their enemy. Three thousand Golden Eagles faced off to over four thousand Allied Bald Eagles. But the Apex fighters cut into the Allied advantage by being aggressive, taking the initiative and, like their naval counterparts, by working in perfect choreography.

The Golden Eagles fired first, which was a simple but important characteristic to being an aggressive fighter. Sending out the first volley, even if it makes for less accuracy, improved the odds of victory and not only because it was the first strike, but because it placed the shooter in the offensive position right at the beginning. The Golden Eagles aimed and let fly their all-aspect, heat-seeking missiles at the enemy.

In twelve main pockets in the skies over Russia, the Golden Eagles made their stand. They kept a tight sphere in those areas, forcing the Bald Eagles to bunch up around them or get crowded within them. It was a clever tactic, and drastically reduced the Allies' numerical superiority, as it was too cramped for all of them to get in the fight without crashing into each other.

Whenever the Allied Eagles tried to retreat to a distance to fire a dense barrage on a pocket of Golden Eagles, their enemy gave chase and fired on their "six," their tails, and then scattered to the ground to mask themselves in the terrain. And the instant the Allies moved in to overwhelm the Apex in a dogfight, the Golden Eagles would bunch up again. The Germanian pilots

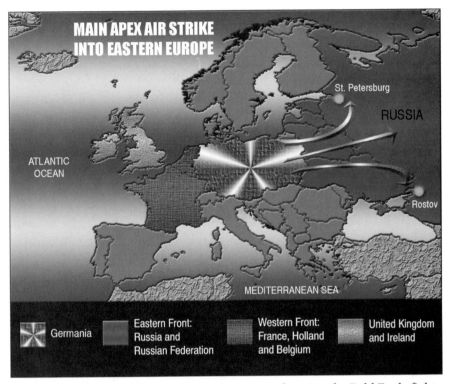

predicted their enemy's next move without error, keeping the Bald Eagle fighters completely off balance in their attempts to form a winning air strategy.

Amidst this tumult, a much smaller Apex jet force set out from Japan and crossed into Russia's eastern end. Russia was now hit on both sides in an immensely wide pincer movement. The Japanese Air Force took a similar strategy, using their Stealth Eagles to take out the radar infrastructure, which was far less dense on Russia's eastern end. They followed up with low-flying incursions by Golden Eagle formations.

The Allies were taking heavy losses and, within three hours, their air defense forces in Russia had dwindled to nearly half their size. The mighty Apex had also lost almost half of their force, more than fourteen hundred Golden Eagles downed. But they had managed to take down close to nineteen hundred Allied jets over Russia, and the Apex pilots knew that they were gaining an ever-greater advantage as they cut into the Allied numerical superiority.

Kassian argued that the Allies should save the Bald Eagles for later battles, so they could analyze Geiseric's tactics and use the planes more effectively. But, the leaders were not in favor of this suggestion, because it would have meant that the land forces fighting on the Russian front would be unacceptably vulnerable to an air assault.

There were twelve million young Russian men in the Allied army ready to fight in the Eastern European theatre. They were, by far, the largest segment of the altogether eighteen million Allied soldiers there. The war had been marketed to them as the third Great Patriotic War, the first of which was the Napoleonic War, and the second being World War II.

Russia was the only nation on the continent of Europe that was not subdued by Napoleon, and when the French emperor made his fateful invasion of the "Motherland," his Revolutionary Army was devastated by the Russian winter and the legendary Cossack warriors.

Hitler's invincible army invaded Russia, looking to kill off all the inhabitants and secure the land, but once again a mighty European military was laid waste in the bitter winters of that land.

Now, another arrogant conqueror of the West was attacking with a mighty army at his disposal, and the Allied propaganda machine promised that Geiseric and the Apex would be dealt with in the same manner as those tyrants who preceded him.

The Allied Forces in Russia believed that they could halt Geiseric and his technologically mighty, Formula-trained military before the war ever really got started. The leaders knew this was a highly improbable scenario, but they needed the Russian front to hold out as long as possible, because of the immense amount of resources that the Apex Empire would gain by taking the gigantic country.

The Allied leadership decided it was worth expending the Bald Eagles in Russia to hold out the enemy's forces. They were presuming that Geiseric would order the full taking and securing of the Russian territory, to build up resources, before he moved on and attacked Western Europe. It would be the more patient and cautious line of attack. In the meantime, the Allies could build up their air force in Western Europe. However, Kassian continued to argue that Geiseric would use the more aggressive tactic of immediately striking West, keeping the Allies off balance so they could not learn and adjust to his tactics.

While the Allied leadership agreed that the more aggressive tactic fit Geiseric's character, they did not assume that his most probable line of attack

on North America was to move west across the Atlantic. It seemed more likely that the Apex forces were going to move east across the Pacific from Japan, where they could island-hop from Midway to Hawaii, and then to California, or move northeast to the Aleutian Islands, which attached to Alaska. Allied intelligence gathered from surveillance and espionage showed the build-up of a massive, amphibious invasion force in Japan. And, at the same time, intelligence showed absolutely no offensive build-up on Germania's western front.

Kassian could only offer that he had another hunch. He tried to argue that he was even channeling Geiseric's thoughts, using the Psychiclink devices created to help him. He admitted that it was difficult to clearly discern most thoughts, what he called "conveyances." However, he said that Geiseric's mind was continually on the invasion and his basic plan was discernible: Western Europe would be invaded first. It was the gateway to the Atlantic and the Apex Forces would use it as a launchpad to the New England coastline.

Dandau argued in favor of Kassian's idea, having taken seriously the ongoing Psychiclink mind-reading experiments that Kassian and a large team of scientists were engaged in. Hollier, Kurtkin, Sinclair and Hung, however, were not convinced. The technology was still too new to trust, especially when the information being attained was completely unfounded by all Allied intelligence and went against what seemed strategically-sound.

Only an hour into the Allied leadership's exasperating meeting, another seven wings of Geiseric's air force struck west over the Germanian borders. Amazingly, Geiseric had managed to keep these three-hundred and fifty Stealth Eagles a complete secret, storing them in underground hangars that quickly ascended out of the ground in order to allow the jets to take off. Using an air strategy nearly identical to the one used to pierce through to the east, the Apex stealth bombers swiftly crushed through the French, Belgian and Dutch radar infrastructures. Thousands of guided bombs also rained down on the Allies' bunkered missile installations and mobile missile launchers, quickly laying this protective weaponry to waste.

With holes punctured in the radar and SAM defenses, the Allies were now blinded on their second front. Two thousand Golden Eagles easily shot out across Germania's western border, cutting low across the terrain in what was known as nap-of-the-earth flying. As they heard of the Apex jets' approach, everyone at Allied High Command was stunned that Geiseric had reserved such a sizeable air armada to attack to the west.

Everyone, that is, except Kassian and Dandau.

To respond to the enemy influx into Western Europe, the Allies quickly sent up every jet they had in France, Belgium and Holland — over three thousand Bald Eagles. But they were still too tentative to send their planes from the eastern front and give up Russia. Nor did Allied High Command wish to deploy their air force waiting across the channel in Britain. Kassian and Dandau were disgusted by the leadership's lack of decisiveness.

If the Allies did not make a commitment of forces to one front, the Germanian forces would destroy them on all fronts. The Germanian pilots were better trained and were utilizing better tactics. The Allies would have to rely on outnumbering the Apex jets, which meant concentrating their forces.

After consulting General Tierney, who was beginning to side with Kassian and Dandau, President Hollier began to see the necessity of this as well. His decision tipped the balance and the rest of the Allied leaders acquiesced to the deployment of all their Bald Eagle forces to Western Europe. One thousand Bald Eagles waiting in Britain were dispatched across the English Channel towards the continent. Those Allied fighters in Russia were ordered to abandon the Eastern European front and were sent to the Western European theatre. The Allied pilots were ordered to halt the Germanian breakout there at all costs — to fight to the last man.

Geiseric then proved how right Kassian's "hunch" was. The Golden Eagles in Russia were immediately deployed to the Western European theatre of battle, instead of being allowed to exploit the vulnerability of the Eastern European land forces.

As if the skies were filled with rain clouds, the ground below darkened with the shadows of hundreds of clusters of dogfighting Eagle jets, and the roars of their engines filled the air like thunder. Their laser cannon fire set the skies ablaze, completing the illusion of a raging storm.

The Allied numerical superiority was even greater now. Five thousand Allied jets faced off against just over three thousand Germanian fighters in the skies over France, Belgium and Holland. The Allies started to form a defensive strategy based on the data the officers were receiving about the battle. As the fighting continued, the Bald Eagles steadily increased their ratio of kills to losses. Hope was rising in the Allied ranks. It appeared that they might actually stall the Germanian air Blitz. This hope was short lived.

As time wore on, another variable began to come into play. The extreme g-forces exerted upon the pilots during the past hours of intense dogfighting strained most of their bodies and minds to the breaking point. However, the Germanian pilots, many of whom had been training since high school, had far

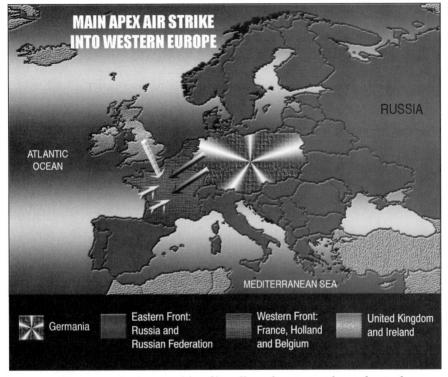

more endurance and were capable of handling the tremendous physical stress. On the other hand, there were a number of Allied pilots who were blacking out, having seizures, and even dying mid-air from the constant lack of blood to their brains caused by the rapid and nearly perpetual acceleration.

The Bald Eagle pilots soon reached their limit and their physical deterioration increased geometrically by the minute. Allied High Command gave the order for retreat, but it was too late for those still in the air, many of whom were by now in a hypoxic delirium. If the Bald Eagles defending Russia had been immediately dispatched to Western Europe when Kassian had suggested doing so, the battle may not have lasted as long. Thus, the Apex pilots' endurance would not have been such a decisive factor.

It became obvious that the Apex would soon have control of the skies. But, for air-superiority to be fully secured, the near-to-ground arena would have to be won.

Moving in like clockwork, the next phase of the Apex assault began. Four thousand Kolibri flyers swarmed into Holland, Belgium and France, coming in at seven hundred kilometers per hour beneath the Golden Eagles, who were mopping up the remnants of the Allied jets. The Apex sky infantry assault was spearheaded by General Gottlieb's creations, heavy sky infantrymen known as Mark II Kolibri Knights. The Knights flew in at between five to fifty meters above the ground, weaving up and down, this way and that, craftily dodging the Allied ground fire.

The Mark II Knights had the strongest attainable armor for a Kolibri flyer and one of the most powerful chariots, second only to the Mark III Knight. The flyers each carried massive steel and ceramic-boride alloy shields, which were longer than they were wide. Like their Medieval predecessors, the Germanian heavy sky infantrymen rushed in, shield at the fore, scattering over a perforated, nine hundred kilometers-long front going into Western Europe.

They raced over the paths torn through the majority of the radar net and heavily fortified defenses, moving in assault groups of one hundred Knights, called centuries. The Knights within each century dispersed over a wide area of about a square kilometer. As they came in low to the ground, they masked themselves against the hills and hedgerows, carefully avoiding the smaller radar sites that operated the automated gun units, which had not been fully destroyed by the Golden Eagle sorties.

The automated gun units were a bane to the Kolibri. They were the only things on the ground fast enough to be highly effective against the hummingbird chariot's dodging ability. The Allied gun units were radar guided and computer controlled, with a Vasculosynth mechanism that rotated and aimed the turret faster than the Kolibri could maneuver out of the way. They fired over seventy-five, forty mm depleted uranium penetrators in one second, which could mercilessly tear the Apex heavy sky infantry apart. Fortunately for the Kolibri Knights, the majority of the gun units had been smashed to bits by the jet assault.

Leading their Knights out of Germania's borders, the commanders of the centuries, called centurions, were some of the most talented fighters to be reckoned with out of the entire Apex military. Von Edeco was in charge of the entire sky infantry operation, having been promoted to field marshal. Like in the times of classical Greece and Rome, this title meant that Von Edeco was the general in the field, with the troops, responding to the moment and able to deliver orders immediately. The bravest of field marshals led their soldiers into the fray, giving courage to those who followed.

Von Edeco was the embodiment of all those character traits and he was the first to cross over into enemy skies. He zoomed along the length of the front, checking in constantly with his centurions.

The centurions expected that a substantial force would be waiting to halt them in their tracks. They led the Mark II Knights in all at once, so they could work together in one giant border-crossing strategy. But when the Apex fighters arrived on the threshold, no Allied sky infantry was there to resist them. Von Edeco ordered the centurions to disperse and find their specified targets. Moving over and behind mainly the the Franco-Belgian lines, the Mark II Knights searched for large concentrations of well-camouflaged troops and battlemachines. They had a general idea of were to look, but they could not be sure.

Most of the Germanian sky infantry punctured the break in the Allied line without losses. However, some centurions found that Allied gun units had already been redistributed along some points of the line that were initially pummeled by Golden Eagles. The automated guns placed in these areas wreaked havoc on the incoming Knights, shredding them and stopping them dead in their tracks. The centurions called in for more Golden Eagles to help clear the way with their smart bombs.

Vaulting high across the sky, faster than the eye could gain a bearing, dozens of objects flashed brightly from horizon to horizon. Seconds later, hundreds of explosions rocked the front, decimating the gun units. The Knights felt the diluted impact waves of MOAB bombs as they were also dropped on the Allied ground forces many kilometers ahead. The Kolibri flyers cheered with euphoric hostility and rushed forth.

Each Kolibri Knight carried a shoulder-launched, shaped-charged missile called a Faust — the German word for fist. The shaped-charge on the tip looked like a suction cup and weighed only ten kilograms, but it packed a mighty explosive punch and could get at the heart of any vulnerable craft. When the missile struck an armored surface, like that of the Lion quadrupedal battlemachine, the French equivalent of the Panzer, the shaped-charge collapsed and funneled all the energy of the blast into a small, acutely hot and pressurized stream. The energy stream pierced a hole no bigger than a pinprick through the Lion's armor, but inside the gun crew would be eviscerated, the bodies left in indistinguishable, burnt mounds.

Rushing over enemy lines, the Apex heavy sky infantrymen searched for something to strike first with their small but deadly missiles. The Lions were hiding all over the surface of France, right behind the front and scattered around the countryside. Like cats in slumber, they lay hidden in ditches dug into the ground with camouflaged tarps thrown over them. But each Kolibri Knight had a device in his chariot that tracked the ground with high-powered metal detectors and sonar devices specifically designed to find the hidden defenders. For this equipment to be effective, though, the Knights had to fly at the most three meters above the ground.

When they found something, they deployed their Fausts quickly and ruthlessly, without waiting for confirmation of their targets. Chances were it was a hidden Lion and, flying that low, the Kolibri flyers were extremely vulnerable. They risked being pounced upon and swatted out of the air by the large, felinesque machines. They had to strike first and ask questions later. As more and more Lions were struck by the shaped-charged missiles, the remaining contingents decided to break their covers early.

The Lions leapt unexpectedly out from their hidden positions, surprising the oncoming Kolibri Knights who swerved and sped awkwardly as they tried to avoid the attacks. The Lions swiped ferociously at the Apex sky infantrymen with their half-meter long, steel-alloy claws and, even if they scored just a glancing blow, they sheared the heavily armored sky infantrymen to pieces.

The powerful Mark II chariots gave the Knights amazing acceleration for their weight, allowing them to avoid most of the counter-attacks. However, the Allied quadrupedal battlemachine drivers, who were called "tamers," also did a good job of ducking and dodging the Kolibri missiles, and most of them ended up coming out unscathed.

After the Kolibri Knights each spent their one missile, they holstered the launchers in their chariots and grabbed their imposing, 30mm Gatling guns. The unique feature of the Gatling gun was its six, meter-and-a-half-long barrels, which were kept parallel together like a bundle of sticks, to form a cylinder. Blasting out five thousand rounds a minute, the Gatling gun created enough heat to melt any metal barrel. So, the Gatling gun rotated its barrels, alleviating the heat of each. The Knights flew holding their large gun in one hand and their sturdy shield in the other, able to heft their battlements because of the strength-enhancing Vasculosynth within their armor.

The Apex heavy sky infantry strafed targets of opportunity, using extricate goggles that allowed them to see the Allied soldiers hidden amongst the landscape. The Allied *ground-based* infantry, simply called the infantry, had tried to position themselves as much as possible behind moving objects, such as vegetation swaying in the wind. This would help to disguise them from extricate goggles, which used short-pulse radar to spot anything that moved. Hiding beneath wind-blown tree branches and leaves, or inside a tussled bush, the defenders had a chance and were able to fire upon the invaders before they themselves were seen. However, for those who were unfortunate to be without the arbitrary grace of the wind, there was no escape from the Kolibri "deathvision" goggles.

Large, dense, tungsten rounds tore through the camouflaged Allied soldiers. The heaviest of the Allied infantry's guns fired large caliber rounds capable of piercing the Mark II Kolibri battle armor, but only at close range and when targeted at a weak spot. So, as the defending troops scattered in confusion, trying to get their bearings and set up to return fire, the Kolibri flyers ran amok slaughtering them.

As more and more blood spilled, the Allied infantry soon realized that, like the Lion divisions, their survival rate would be greater if they broke cover and went on the offense. It gave away their position, but aggression proved to be the better choice.

Thus, the battle quickly degenerated from what was planned to be a timed, coordinated counter-strike, into a giant, chaotic melee across France, Belgium and Holland. The Allied strategy had been to allow the Apex sky infantry to penetrate deep into Western Europe, so that they would be dispersed over a wide area and, therefore, vulnerable. However, things did not go as planned and the Kolibri Knights were having greater success in tracking down the hidden ground forces than was predicted by Allied High Command. So, the leadership went ahead and deployed their sky infantry — the Hornets.

Rushing into the fray, the Hornets wreaked havoc on the enemy invaders. The Allied leadership assembled all of their sky infantry forces that were in Russia to the western theatre. It gave the Allies a two to one numerical superiority over the Germanian forces on the aerial battlefield, and the Dreadnought flyers were nearly equal in skill to the Mark II Kolibri flyers.

The Allies sent in more than eight thousand of their Dreadnoughts, which were as strongly armored as the Kolibri Knights and had similar, but slightly smaller shields. Their name literally meant to "dread not," because the Allied forces had nothing to fear when their heavy sky infantry was there to back them up.

The Dreadnought's chariot was more powerful than the Kolibri Mark II, giving it greater speed and acceleration. The Allied heavy sky infantrymen also carried Gatling guns, but unlike the Kolibri Knights, the Dreadnoughts' guns fired out 30 mm *depleted uranium* penetrators. The Dreadnoughts' rounds could, thus, pierce their enemy's armor, something the Mark II Knights' tungsten rounds could not do.

Suddenly, all across the nine hundred kilometer long western front, the Mark II Knights were showered with pencil-sized, sharpened rods of uranium. The penetrators railed through the Knights' shields, armor and interior vests, blood spurting out of the holes in small geysers. The Germanian heavy sky infantrymen fell like flies hitting a bug zapper, landing burnt and broken upon the enemy ground below.

Most of the Knights did not even bother to fight back when they realized that their tungsten rounds could not pierce the shields and armor of the Dreadnoughts. The uranium was pyrophoric and could maintain a sharpened tip, as opposed to the tungsten, which became misshapen upon impact. Thus, the Mark II Knights began a strategic retreat, most of them having almost run out of ammunition anyway. Those who still had ammunition aimed their guns at the Dreadnoughts' wings in an attempt to damage the most fragile part of the chariot.

The Dreadnoughts gave chase to the fleeing invaders, only to encounter an incoming wave of the most powerful Kolibri flyers in the Germanian sky infantry — the Mark III Knights, aka: the Lancers.

The Lancers got their name from the Lance-22 Drill Bolt gun they carried, capable of firing a twenty-two millimeter wide, solid-state laser beam that could devastate a Dreadnought's shield and armor with one well-placed shot. However, there were some pronounced drawbacks.

Needing a second to cool in between each shot, the Lance-22 could fire less than ten times in ten seconds, while the Dreadnoughts' machine gun could spit out nearly a thousand rounds in that amount of time. Also, the laser only had a range of one hundred yards before the beam lost focus and dissipated. The depleted uranium penetrators, on the other hand, were effective at twenty times the distance. The Dreadnoughts and Lancers were equally matched in terms of armor and chariot horsepower, but in terms of their vastly different weapons, the Apex appeared to be at a distinct disadvantage.

The Mark III Knights did not have a shield, as it was useless against uranium penetrators and would therefore only weigh them down. They held their Lance-22s with both hands most of the time, though for greater mobility they could hold it with one. Needing to get close to the Dreadnought to fire their weapon, the Lancers charged with unbridled bravado towards the numerically-superior Dreadnought force.

Furiously racing at each other, the armored charioteers resembled the medieval warriors who had charged countless times upon the European soil below. However, these modern fighters did not just have the fate of their nation, or even Europe, in their hands. They battled for the fate of the planet.

As the Kolibri Lancers clashed with the Allied Dreadnoughts, many on both sides decided to face each other head on, out of pride. Like the grandest of jousts, the charioteers thundered toward each other. In their perception, they saw and heard the world slow down, as they entered the "zone," a phenomena that occurred when the mind was working at an incredibly fast rate in extreme situations such as this.

Due to the Lancer's shorter range, they had to dodge gunfire at a much longer distance than their opponents, but due to the quick speeds involved, this added up to only a second more. The Lancer flyers were the most highly trained in the Apex *heavy* sky infantry and had far superior reflexes and maneuvering capabilities than the Dreadnoughts. Like their Medieval predecessors, the Lancers had to dodge the enemy's attack while striking theirs home — and strike it home they did.

The Lance-22 was a weapon of devastating authority and they ran the Dreadnoughts through with the powerful laser beams that pierced the air with tearing booms and filled the sky with the pulsing, eerie, red and green light of an atmospheric tempest. The loud cracking of the weapons could be heard all over the western front with near simultaneity, followed by the sound of a sudden deluge of scorched and ragged-edged pieces of metal. Hundreds of armored bodies and obliterated chariots fell to the ground, the overwhelming majority being the smoking pieces of Allied heavy sky infantry. Their larger shields had proven immensely useful against the Mark II Knights' tungsten penetrator guns, but now they just hindered them against the Lancers, weighing them down and making them clumsy.

Throwing down their shields, the remaining Dreadnoughts continued to fight. In the next round of the air joust, they had far greater success against the Germanian Knights. The Allied heavy sky infantry still outnumbered the invading Knights and they were powerfully motivated. This was a pivotal struggle in the first phase of World War III — the battle for Europe. The Dreadnought flyers knew how much hung on their shoulders, now that the Apex Eagles had taken control of the "high skies." If the Knights could be destroyed, it could turn the tide for the Allies, for the Germanian ground invasion would then be decimated by the Hornet forces.

Because of this, the Allies decided to deploy their regular sky infantry into the fray, to help the Dreadnoughts in their fight. The Allied sky regulars were the basic Hornet and, so, had no other name. They were each armed with the two large handguns that Von Edeco had originally designed, which both held two thirty millimeter cartridges in their chambers at a time. The cartridges were packed with a powerful explosive capable of firing the kinetic energy rounds with devastating force. The fundamental difference between the weaponry specifications for the Allied regulars and the Kolibri flyers was, again, that the Allies made their penetrator rounds out of uranium. And so, the Allied sky regulars had a weapon that could pierce the Mark III Knights' armor.

Things looked bleak for the Apex. The Mark III Knights were quickly overwhelmed as they came under fire from all directions. The Hornet regulars were able to move about faster than the more heavily armored sky infantrymen, so the Knights were bombarded with head-on machine gun fire from the Dreadnoughts and shot in the backs by the Hornet regulars.

Von Edeco then deployed the Kolibri regulars into battle. The basic Kolibri flyers were all exact replicas of his original design. It was a desperate move to throw his Mark I Kolibri flyers on the battlefield with the Allied Dreadnoughts, whose armor could not be pierced by the tungsten rounds of the Kolibri regulars. But, the tide of the battle had to be turned. By expending all his resources towards capturing the western front, Geiseric had banked all of Europe on the victory of this single battle.

Three thousand more Germanian sky infantrymen joined the fight. They were vastly outnumbered by their enemy but they were Geiseric's ace in the hole, as they were far more skilled than any other sky infantrymen on either side.

The Mark I Kolibri flyers instantly began lashing at their Allied counterparts. They were Geiseric's most highly-trained Formula fighters; the elite of the elite. Firing their tungsten penetrators, two at a time from each gun, the Kolibri regulars steadily took out the Hornet regulars.

Now, the battle resembled a cowboy gunfight from the days of old. As the opposing regular sky infantry forces engaged, they came within range of one another with their two guns drawn and blazing. Facing their enemy, they fired both guns with astounding accuracy. The Hornet and Kolibri flyers aimed, shot and dodged at speeds greater than the untrained eye could track.

Though they didn't have a greater top speed, the Kolibri and Hornet regulars, because of their smaller size and weight, could accelerate at a far quicker rate than that of their heavy counterparts. Because of this, the regular sky infantrymen had to endure greater g-forces placed on their bodies during the unending dodges and accelerating maneuvers. The Kolibri flyers proved, even much more so than the Golden Eagle pilots, to be far more adapted to the task than their enemy.

The Mark II Knights were also dispatched back into the fight, using their tungsten penetrator Gatling guns to target the lighter armored Allied sky regulars. The entire Apex sky infantry was putting up a remarkable fight, but they were so heavily outnumbered that it looked as though they still might be defeated. They were fighting under an unimaginably dense hail of depleted uranium projectiles and hundreds of Apex flyers dropped from the sky every few minutes. Their hearts were pumping hard from battle and blood spewed profusely from those wounds that were not cauterized by the heat of the lethal rounds. The dead warriors buzzed sporadically to the ground in their chariots, which were still spurred by reaction impulses coming from the flyers' brains.

Geiseric was getting a constant feed of what was happening at the front. When he heard that one thousand of his regular sky infantrymen had been taken down, his most prized fighters, the emperor's heart sank into his stomach. They should have held out for much longer, but the Allied regular sky infantrymen, though not as good as his own, were better than he had imagined. For the first time in a long while, he felt his rock hard faith begin to crack. His entire mission and everything he had been working toward for more than a decade was on precarious ground.

Soon, though, Geiseric's hope soared again as the casualty rate of his Kolibri flyers began dropping and the rate of Hornet casualties began increasing. The tide was turning for two reasons. Yet again, since the Germanian forces were better trained and adapted for the battle, the longer they held out, the better their chances were of winning, for their enemy could not endure the physical strain. The Hornets were faltering, but they still held ground. However, a critical weakness in the Allied heavy sky infantry was beginning to show.

The Kolibri had managed to stand up against the overwhelming onslaught of depleted uranium penetrators just long enough for the mortal flaw of the Dreadnoughts and their devastating Gatling guns to begin taking effect. At such a high rate of fire, the Gatling guns ran out of rounds in just over thirty seconds of continuous shooting. In only thirty seconds of holding the trigger down, altogether, the Allied heavy sky infantrymen had spent their 2500 rounds. Naturally, the Dreadnoughts did not use their guns' ammo all at once. They fired in short bursts, spraying a particular vicinity with a cloud of bullets. All the Kolibri forces had to do was stay alive, ducking and dodging, until the Dreadnoughts had nothing more to fire.

The battle between the two sky infantry forces was an awesome spectacle to behold. The ground forces in Western Europe looked up and watched in amazement. They resisted firing into the melee because there was a better chance of hitting their own guys, since there were more Hornets in the sky than Kolibri. The Allied ground forces had to let the battle run its course. In some areas, the aerial combat was taken much higher into the sky than normal where, to the Allied soldiers on the ground below, the Kolibri and Hornet flyers looked like hordes of gnats buzzing incoherently about. But the steady rain of blood, armor, entrails, and winged chariots was a constant and horrific reminder of the brutality above.

In other areas, the fighting occurred just above the ground, with chariots buzzing right over the heads of the Allied ground forces. The sound of metal wings filled the air with a constant, deafening roar. The ground troops gazed with awe upon the amazing talent of the Formula Elite fighters and realized why they were hailed as being almost superhuman.

Pride was forsaken and most of the fighting devolved into nothing more than quick flybys, where each side would try to come up from behind and shoot their opponents in the back. It was not very chivalric for the most part. But, amidst the incredible rumble, every once in a while a real steady fight ensued between two individuals, or a small group. Some still dared to face their opponents, instead of retreating into the chaos and attacking unseen. These duels truly showcased their skills.

The duels happened primarily between the opposing sky infantry regulars. The typical strategy of a Kolibri regular was to let the Hornet regular attack first. Skirting the rule of shooting first to achieve dominance was something that could only be done by a fighter who was far superior to his opponent. The Allied flyer charged the Kolibri suddenly and rapidly, while firing the four rounds in his two handguns. The Kolibri flyer usually managed to dodge by zipping to the side or downwards. If he darted downwards, he would try to get behind the Hornet while the Allied flyer was reloading. A smart Hornet flyer never spent his four rounds in the first charge, so that he could protect himself on the enemy counter-attack.

Once the Kolibri flyer was in close range to his enemy, he tried to stay adjacent, leaning toward his opponent so that their wings did not clash. As the Apex flyers grappled with their enemy, they usually attempted to hook an arm around the Allied flyers' necks. The Kolibri could then use his other hand to place the gun up to the Hornets' side abdominal armor, one of the weakest spots. A fast pull of the trigger and a tungsten penetrator fired into the Allied sky infantrymen's liver and intestines. The heavy round would either blast out the other side of the armor, or it bounced around inside, ripping apart the flyer's soft flesh. The Kolibri then let their dead enemy fall to the ground below in a crumpled heap.

The superior fighting of the Germanian sky infantry regulars could be entirely attributed to the fact that most had been training for this since they were kids, for eleven years. They grew up in this world, their entire being tailored to it. Some talents could not be honed to a much further degree, whether the soldier trained for ten years or three. However, with the incredibly rapid nature of sky chariot warfare, the fighter was at an advantage the longer he had adapted his body to the combat. Also, a person's reflexes could be honed to ever greater speeds over time, which was overtly necessary for the sky infantry.

As time wore on, more and more of the Allied heavy sky infantry began running low on rounds for their Gatling guns. Von Edeco noticed the weakness and made the pivotal decision to discontinue the strategy of defense and evasion. He ordered the Knights and Kolibri regulars to once more take the offensive.

They mopped up the skies with the Hornets, who had lost nearly all their steam.

The top Allied sky infantry officers quickly recognized the futility of continuing the fight. They ordered a full retreat, but it was to no avail. The remaining Hornets were chased down, encircled and destroyed nearly to the last. The once twelve thousand strong Allied sky infantry force in Europe lay strewn across France, Belgium and Holland, broken and torn asunder.

But the Allied flyers had fought courageously until the end and had mauled the invader quite badly. It truly was a battle to the bitter end for one side, and bitter victory for the other, with few left after to wave the flag.

With the victory of the Kolibri, the Germanian forces now had air superiority over the whole of Europe, and the Japanese forces were coming in from the Far East, securing Asiatic Russia. The Japanese and Indian forces worked together to take China, which was offering only about a tenth of the resistance as Russia.

The Allied leadership knew that, without a substantial air defense, the Allied Army in Europe did not stand a chance. They ordered the evacuation of all ground forces in Western Europe. Because Russia was pinned in on both sides, the troops fighting there would be hard to transport out. Therefore, they were left to fight and die as a diversion. President Kurtkin was deeply dismayed by this decision. However, he was squarely outvoted by the other leaders in the War Room, who reminded him that they had troops who would be sacrificed on the eastern front as well, though not nearly as many.

The Allied troops in Western Europe were boarded onto Skimmers, warships, submarines, and even thousands of private vessels, such as luxury yachts and cruise liners. And so, Geiseric turned all his land and air forces east. His Panzers flooded out of Germania all across the eastern front, spearheading the land invasion. They rushed into the Russian Federation satellite nations of Lithuania, Latvia, Belarus and the Ukraine, splintering all resistance.

The Panzers stampeded across the many different terrains of the region. Eastern Europe was cold this time of year, and in many places it was raining or snowing. But the road to Moscow was by far the bleakest; icy and covered with treacherous drifts of snow. The Apex ground forces were not halted though, for there were many types of Panzers designed for different uses. One model, called the *Schnee Panzer*, had longer legs with feet that spread out wide when they went down in the snow, but curled up when pulled upward. German for "snow tank," these machines easily ran across the endless icy dunes without being slowed down. The entire machine was white, with thin black stripes, which helped it blend in with the frosty terrain. They were lightly armored, so as to not be weighed down. Their scale-type armor showed the sinewy, synthetic muscle that powered the legs underneath. With these four muscular legs, the Schnee Panzer truly looked to be half-animal, half-machine.

A special type of Apex quadruped was designed to be more effective in rain than snow. This Panzer was of the same basic design as the one for the snow, except its feet and legs were rough on the exterior, because smooth surfaces created suction in the mud. There were also many other specialized Panzers. The Tiger was the largest of the Apex quadrupedal battlemachines and so could only be used on solid terrain. There wasn't a hint of the softer, synthetic muscle tissue underneath the thick steel and ceramic-boride alloy plates laid across the body in ways that allowed the Tiger's legs to be flexible.

All along the eastern front, the Panzers ripped the Allied artillery units to shreds, smacking them in between their mighty claws. When attacking any conventional, track-driven tanks, the Apex quadrupeds ran circles around them and broke within the Allied lines. Conventional tanks were destroyed ten to one fighting the Panzers and the Allies in Russia had very few quadruped battlemachines of their own to throw at the invaders. They had the Lion, which put up a good fight, but because they were still in a prototype phase and all of the "kinks" were not worked out, they still perished two to one against the Germanian battlecats.

There were less than five hundred Kolibri flyers left out of the expeditionary force. These were quickly dispatched to the eastern front. Even though they were small in number, they were still a highly effective fighting force, especially being that they were now moving unchallenged throughout the enemy territory. Carrying the double-barreled semi-automatic handguns, machine guns and Fausts, the remainder of the Kolibri pulled more than their weight in the massacre of the Allied ground forces.

When the Apex flyers had used up their ammo, they went to their weapon of last resort — the Kolibri smallsword. Its name was misleading, because it wasn't small. Such was merely the name of the style of the blade. It was a long steel sword designed more for stabbing, rather than cutting. It resembled the rapier, which was often used in fencing, but instead of having a flat blade, the blade of the smallsword was thick and triangular to provide strength.

Tens of thousands of Allied soldiers were impaled through the abdomen, pierced through the throat, eyes or a main artery in the thigh. Such weapons were even more useful in terrorizing the enemy than killing them. It was much like in the wars with early firearms, when spear-like weapons were still widely in use. A furious bayonet-charge would almost always result in the opposing army running terrified in the other direction. As terrifying as being shot was, there was something much more visceral and frightening about being run through by a bayonet or sword.

After the Kolibri and Panzers had taken out the majority of the Allied resistance, the Apex ground infantry, in their full-body armor and wearing gas masks in case the Allies used a chemical or biological weapon, followed in behind to secure all the cities of Europe. Some cities were more heavily defended than others. Most were left completely undefended, becoming ghost towns. From Russia to Spain, Italy to Britain, the Apex forces stormed into beautiful European towns and cities that were completely emptied of their once thriving human populations, something that had not been seen since the Black Plague struck seven hundred years earlier.

The Apex Aegean Fleet had blockaded the Dardanelles, so that the Allied military in Eastern Europe could not evacuate by sea. The Delfins in the Aegean quickly obliterated the small Allied Shark fleet in the Black Sea. All naval rescue craft attempting to transport Allied soldiers on the eastern front to safety were either commandeered by the Apex, or shot, blown up and sunk.

Golden Eagles bombarded all the transports on the ground or in the air that were attempting to shuttle the defenseless Allied troops farther east. Without the Bald Eagles for air support, the transport craft and the unfortunate souls within them fell like lambs to the slaughter. Anti-aircraft battery crews on the ground valiantly stuck to their guns, hoping to provide some defense against the Germanian Eagle force, so that their fellow soldiers could escape. But, they did little to stop the hypersonic jets flying by, scorching and ripping apart everything in their way with their dual laser cannons.

Finally, all hope that the Allied soldiers on the eastern front could possibly escape vanished when the Japanese Eagle force succeeded in fully crushing the Allied Air Force in China and on the eastern end of Russia. Soon after, the Japanese Army launched the largest amphibious assault in history. Six million assault troops crossed the Japan Sea and captured the key cities, fortifications, and bases along five thousand kilometers of East Asian coastline, stretching from Kamchatka to Hong Kong. The Japanese invasion force met little resistance, for most of the Allied defenses in the Old World were concentrated in the European theatre.

The Japanese assault force was far larger than what was actually needed to take China and eastern Russia, but the Allied leadership had little doubt as to why Geiseric chose to launch an expeditionary force of such size. It was a test run for a much larger-scale invasion. The Apex generals were working the kinks out in their strategy, organization and machinery, preparing for the impending invasion of North America.

The Battle of the Old World was over . . .

The battle for the New World was just beginning.

The Apex emperor smugly reveled in his victories. He traveled to Moscow, the capitol of one of Germany's staunchest opponents in all three World Wars. Geiseric went to Versailles like Hitler who, to humiliate the French, had made them sign the peace treaty in the same place where the Versailles Treaty had been signed, which sanctioned Germany after World War I. But the new

German leader especially reveled in the conquering of Britain, the perpetual thorn in Germany's side.

Geiseric had vowed to raze Britain's beloved city of London to the ground, like the British and American bombers did to Berlin during World War II. London was systematically destroyed and the demolition of Big Ben was broadcast live all across the Apex Empire, to the jubilant cheers of its citizens.

The taking of Allied Europe and Asia was a tremendous blow, but even though their defeat had been swift and complete, the Allies were not demoralized. They thought they had seen the full strength of Geiseric's force, and the Allied defenses in Europe were nothing compared to what the Apex would face in North America. Still, the Allied European defenses were no cakewalk. Germania had taken the continent faster than the Allied leadership thought they would. But, confident they had seen the best of what Geiseric could possibly throw at them, the Allied leaders were somewhat relieved.

General Tierney walked briskly into the War Room, his thick frame advancing with a powerful stride. President Hollier, Prime Minister Dandau, President Sinclair, President Kurtkin, Premier Hung and all of their top military officers were sitting or standing around the table. Lieutenant-General Ryan Connor, Chief of Allied Military Intelligence, stood at the head of the room, ready to debrief the leaders. Only Tierney had been missing from the gathering and President Sinclair was perturbed that the Allied Supreme Military Commander was late.

"How good of you to join us, General Tierney," he remarked snidely as Tierney finally sidled into his chair.

Tierney glared back at Sinclair. "Forgive me, President Sinclair," he replied, feigning humility. He then gruffly retorted, "I was taking a shit."

Sinclair was horrified by his crudeness, and was indignant that the general dared speak to an authority in such a manner. The other leaders in the room snickered quietly to themselves.

Lieutenant-General Connor cleared his throat to quiet everyone and get their attention. He then debriefed them on some disturbing intelligence reports. The little intelligence the Allies had inside Japan told them that millions of Germanian, Indian, Japanese, Israeli and other troops, along with tens of thousands of battlemachines were being assembled in the country, from Tokyo to Kyushu.

At first, the Apex conquest of Western Europe seemed to point toward an imminent invasion of Allied North America via a strike on the East Coast. Under this hypothetical strategy, the Apex would use occupied Western Europe, namely Spain and Portugal, as a launchpad for their amphibious invasion force, in much the same way that American forces used England as their launchpad into Normandy during World War II. However, there was no discernible buildup of Apex forces in Western Europe.

The size of the potential invasion force in Japan was what the Allied leaders were expecting — an overwhelming incursion in terms of sheer numbers, attempting to flood through the North American Laser Net. It was the only invasion tactic that the Allies viewed as plausible. They estimated that the enemy would take over ten million casualties before a break in the Laser Net could be made. Then, the battle would just begin.

However, the Apex troops and battlemachines could have all been decoys, much like in the Normandy invasion, when the Americans and British tricked the Germans as to where they were going to invade by having a false force composed of inflatable tanks to fool Nazi surveillance and intelligence.

Connor also explained that something strange was going on in both the Atlantic and Pacific, on the eastern edge of Japan and in the area of the Canary Islands off the coast of northern Africa. Incredibly sensitive devices, which could detect vibrations from across the globe, had been picking up on huge seismic waves emanating from these vicinities. It had been going on for the past two hours in Japan, but stopped an hour ago in the Canaries. The Lieutenant-General could not speculate on what the tremors were or why it was coming from these two areas. No one in the War Room had any idea what could be causing them.

The explosive tremors from the Canaries had been far greater in number and power than the ones coming from Japan, which were slow and steady. They could not figure out what sort of tactic would involve such incredible demolition. There had been the overall equivalent force of ten billion tons of TNT used in these areas. Was it to merely destroy something? Or, possibly, Geiseric was having something built, but needed to demolish something else in order to do so. Or, the whole thing could be a diversion.

Allied High Command had assumed that the Apex expeditionary force was going to try to cross the Atlantic, because it was a hard fought battle to take Western Europe. Now that it was secure in Geiseric's hands, it seemed reasonable that he would choose these ports as his launchpad. Going across the Atlantic was half the distance of crossing the Pacific.

However, Hitler had assumed that the Americans, British and Canadians were going to invade at the *Pas de Calais*. Instead, they chose Normandy, which was much farther away from their ultimate destination — Germany. One of the keys to invasion was to attack where your enemy least expected you.

The taking of Western Europe could have just been the ultimate diversion for an Apex invasion force coming over from Japan.

Allied High Command had been strengthening the North American Laser Net on the Eastern Seaboard since Germanian forces took Western Europe. Immediately, upon hearing that the invasion might be coming from Japan, the Allied leadership had newly-built Cross Lasers deployed to the coasts of Washington, Oregon and California.

Though the Japanese Laser Net was not nearly as fortified as Germania's or North America's, it was still not worth it for the Allies to try to assault the troop concentrations in Japan. Allied High Command decided that the invasion force would be at its most vulnerable when on the water and attempting to storm onto land.

It had only been five weeks since the Great Diaspora brought the entire Allied populous to Fortress North America. Though the Laser Net pretty much encompassed only the United States, "Fortress North America" was the title used by the Allied leadership. It rang of a far more multi-cultural sound than "Fortress United States," or even just "Fortress America." For, although America was actually two continents, "America" almost always referred specifically to the U.S.A.

Altogether, nearly two billion Europeans, Africans and other peoples were brought to the East Coast. On the West Coast, a little over three billion Allied refugees, more than half from China, were cramped into the relatively small amount of space. When the refugees first arrived, they were placed in camps dotting the coasts, anywhere from five kilometers to one hundred kilometers inland, until they could be brought to the more permanent living areas farther inland. They were housed in large halls, each holding a thousand people, with only sheets to separate themselves from others. The areas were cramped inside and the beds were stiff, but most of the refugees at least felt safe behind the fortress walls of the Laser Net.

Eighty percent of the European refugees had already been brought farther inland, but the other twenty percent on the East Coast were still within a few kilometers of shore. On the other hand, almost all of the immigrants on the Pacific Coast were still close to shore. Immediately, Allied High Command stepped up the pace to get more civilians on the western coastline out of the way of the predicted invasion force. Premier Hung demanded that most air transports moving the refugees inland on the Eastern Seaboard be pulled away to help move those in the west out of harm's way.

After much bickering with particularly Dandau, the Chinese premier managed to convince High Command to reassign half of the air transport craft on the East Coast to the West Coast. The Chinese leader was disturbed that he had to lobby so hard to get the Allied leaders to acquiesce to such an obvious move. His people and all those refugees in California, Oregon and Washington were the ones in harm's way. Yet, Premier Hung had begun to realize that, though it was unspoken, to the American and Western European leaders who dominated at the war table, the Chinese people were below the Russians and only a step above the Africans in terms of expendability.

Seven hours passed since the strange explosive, or impact tremors emanating from Japan and the Canary Islands had begun. The powerful tremors had stopped coming from the Canaries five hours ago, but continued coming weakly from Japan non-stop.

The Allies were starting to wonder if Geiseric was considering a two pronged attack, hitting the East and West Coasts at the same time. It seemed highly implausible, for to break through the Net the Apex would need to concentrate their forces as much as possible. Everything about these tremors was disconcerting. The Allied leadership simply could not figure out what was going on.

Allied Naval Forces had kept relatively close to home in the Atlantic, forming a tight ocean wall about a thousand kilometers off shore from the North American coastline. In the Pacific, Sharks were deployed into their battle positions and prepared to meet the Apex invasion forces halfway, as they came from Japan. To avoid a mass panic, none of the Allied citizenry was made aware of the imminent invasion, but the leaders and military braced for it.

A squadron of eighty Shark vessels patrolled the waters off the coast of Florida. Everything seemed quiet, even the current. Vice Admiral Nelson, the officer in charge of this squadron, led the vessels on their rounds in her Great White. She kept the vessels traveling level enough that the crews did not have to be strapped in and could move about to stretch their legs and go to the bathroom.

Taking advantage of the calm waters, Nelson sipped tea, her prevailing blue eyes locked ahead in a meditative trance. She had delegated control of the vessel to her co-pilot. Free from the entanglement of Psychiclink equipment, she stood up from her throne-like captain's chair and walked around the deck. She had a strong yet lithe frame, much like her face, which with her powerful jawline and pronounced cheekbones gave her a warrior countenance, all the while maintaining a graceful femininity. It was topped off with her blazing red hair that she kept shoulder-length. This was against High Command's regulations, but Nelson was too much of a military asset to quibble with over such things.

Without warning, an underwater storm violently churned up the ocean, smashing into the patrolling Sharks at five hundred kilometers per hour. The incredible turbulence tossed the large vessels around like toys in a washing machine. The crews within the submariner battlemachines were thrown into the walls and ceilings as the incredible force of the water whipped their crafts from side to side, or plunged them deep towards the abyss. Several of the Shark vessels were pushed too deeply to recover and their pilots could not take control in time. The pressures of the abyssal waters compressed their hulls. But, instead of being crushed as many non-submariners believed happened, the incredible pressures inside the sinking vessels increased the temperatures to such a degree that the crews were vaporized in an intensely hot ball of fire.

Amidst the tumult, Nelson managed to strap herself in before being injured. Her co-pilot righted their Great White. Most of the squadron managed to regain their bearings after the sudden bombardment from the sea. Then, just as quickly, the water calmed again, leaving what was left of the squadron stunned, injured, and wondering what in the world had just hit them.

There were numerous Allied conventional battleships and hovercraft destroyers that rode along the surface of the water in the vicinity. Up top, there was no sign of a disturbance. Everything was steady and there was no detectable change in water level. Many of the crewmen were bored as they stood on deck, looking over the rails of their vessels down into the water. They tried to spot fish and sea mammals in the places well lit by deeply penetrating rays of sunlight. But instead, they caught a terrifying sight.

Below the placid surface of the water, the ocean had turned into a hurricane. It boiled with white froth as deep as the eye could see. The crewmen standing outside on the ships and hovercrafts caught a short glance of their submariner compatriots' vessels being tossed about underneath.

The men hurried below deck to send warnings out to other Allied naval patrols in the area and back to headquarters. All Shark squadrons were called back up to the surface until the tumult passed. The Allied leaders were paralyzed momentarily, trying to get their bearings and make decisions with no idea what was coming at them. They could only assume that the strange phenomena heading towards the East Coast of the United States was linked to the earlier explosions in the Canary Islands, right across the Atlantic. How large or powerful the phenomenon was, the Allied leadership could only guess.

A team of British and American scientists, a group of men and women that had been studying La Palma, the westernmost island of the Canaries, were immediately summoned to the Allied War Room upon their request. They had been watching the island for decades, for as Allied High Command was about to discover, this island had long shown the potential to cause a disaster of epic proportions.

In 1949, an unstable geological fault running through the island of La Palma caused several cubic kilometers of rock in the western portion to slide a few meters toward the sea. As a result, a two kilometer long fracture opened up, which could be easily seen zigzagging across the terrain. As the scientists explained, if this huge chunk of La Palma, the steepest island in the world, fell off into the sea, the waves would ripple out across the Atlantic towards the United States eastern coastline, causing a tsunami the likes of which had never been seen in recorded history.

The scientists explained that enough nuclear blasts placed in the fracture would cause the western piece of the island to cleave away and fall into the ocean at a far greater speed than what would have occurred naturally. If Geiseric mastered a process of inducing a natural form of lubrication to the slipping rock, it would speed it up even more. This would account for the intensity of the tsunami that appeared to be heading towards Allied North America.

In the open ocean, these waves of mass destruction were nearly invisible and passed by the outer ring of Sharks unnoticed. It was only when the waves reached shallower waters around the coast that they became dangerous. From the tip of Florida to North Carolina, the continental margin on the East Coast had a gentle slope into the abyssal depths. The waves of water began to compress as they came up the slope and that is what bested Vice Admiral Nelson's squadron.

The energy created by the tsunami on the continental slope was nothing compared to what it would turn into when it hit the shelf. In deeper waters, the powerful energy waves rippled underwater without disturbing the surface. As the tsunami hit the shallow continental shelf region, it would build in power and velocity, until it crashed onto shore with twenty times the fury it had exerted upon Nelson's Sharks.

Most of the leaders in the War Room were reticent to believe that Geiseric would use nuclear weapons, because of their harmful environmental side effects. Many thought that the act of destroying an island was also out of Geiseric's character. However, they were convinced that it was a large scale tsunami coming towards their shore and they knew the *Führer* had something to do with it.

The primary target of this artificially-created natural disaster was not the Allied military forces, but the hundreds of millions of refugees on the United States East Coast who were not yet moved inland and were kept only a few kilometers from shore in weak, make-shift shelters . . .

Immediately, all air transports were diverted from the West Coast to help evacuate those on the East Coast to places further inland. If they could not be evacuated from the area, as many refugees as possible were moved into stronger buildings. No one made the citizens aware of what was going on right away. Soon, though, word got out and began to spread like wildfire in the refugee camps. Order rapidly turned into chaos along the entire eastern coastline as the citizens and the military personnel evacuating them ran for higher ground wherever it could be found. Mass stampedes into the hills ensued, and thousands of people were trampled. Older folks, who moved too slowly, were beaten out of the way and left to fend for themselves.

Within a half hour of the underwater storm hitting Nelson's squadron, the Florida shores began receding into the distant horizon . . .

Twenty minutes later, a wall of water more than fifty meters high barreled into Cape Canaveral.

The apocalyptic tsunami pile-drove into the coastlines of Florida, Georgia, South Carolina and North Carolina, carrying with it huge ships, battlemachines and all the weakly constructed refugee shelters in its path. As the raging tide swept in, permeating ever deeper, trees were splintered and all human and animal life in its way was ripped asunder.

All along the low coastal plains of the southern states, the nightmarish wave pummeled in as far as thirty kilometers onto land with demonically treacherous force. Entire cities were swept away in the relentless, behemoth tide. Trains were ripped from their tracks. All types of vehicles were rolled away like tumbleweeds in the rush of water.

Sasha and her family were waiting to be evacuated at a bullet train depot just west of Charleston, South Carolina. Hundreds of thousands of her fellow countrymen were cramped into a few square kilometers. Most Russians, like all the Europeans, had been brought to the northern New England coastline because it was the closest destination on the path from their homelands. But, when it became too cramped at certain intervals in the Diaspora, some of the Skimmers were instead diverted south.

The refugees at the Charleston depot had not yet been informed of the tsunami. They believed that they were being rushed further inland to get them out of the way of a possible Apex invasion coming in a day or so. They had no idea of the immediacy of the threat heading right at them.

Sasha was with her entire family: three sisters, three brothers, her parents, and almost all of her extended relatives. They were in the process of boarding the train when, suddenly, they heard the muffled sounds of thousands of people screaming from a few kilometers off. The screaming intensified and was followed by an ever-increasing, low rumbling. Sasha and her sisters exchanged puzzled and frightened glances.

All the trains in the depot began to take off. Some people were still stepping up into the car when their train lurched forward, sending them tumbling back onto the platform. Others held tightly to the railings as their legs were dragged on the ground. Sasha had just gotten on and two of her brothers were coming through the door when their train suddenly took off at full acceleration. The young men fell out and Sasha and her parents watched in horror as her older brother was caught underneath the train and killed in the most dreadful manner. Her mother screamed in agony, while Sasha could only stare out the door in shock, watching her horrified relatives on the loading platform become smaller as the train shot away.

Suddenly, at the rear of the train station, a towering mass of water came bursting through the windows and doors, bowling over the crowds of people, the barrage of heavy salt water causing the sturdy depot building to collapse. Sasha's aunts, uncles, cousins and grandparents disappeared under the foaming liquid, and the structural materials washed over where they had been standing a moment before. They had survived the Great Diaspora, running the gauntlet across the Atlantic, only to be drowned in its icy waters when they thought they had reached safety in their new land.

Sasha did not have time to mourn the loss of so much of her family, as the tremendous wave was rapidly gaining on the bullet train. She could do nothing but scream as she watched the white, crashing water cascade under the caboose, then the rear car, and the next car, and the next. The rear of the train floated off the tracks and began to jackknife perpendicular to the rails. The front of the train derailed and crashed into the ground, rolling and snapping away from the rear cars. Because the front cars were not floating in water yet, they hit the dirt and were smashed to pieces, along with the poor souls inside.

Flowing relentlessly onward at freeway speeds, the heavy ocean salt water pummeled the rear of the train and broke into segments. Sasha's car broke away from the rest and floated off by itself. The car's length was levered up vertically into the air by the force, and when it slammed back into the water it rolled upside-down. The water flooded in. It was freezing cold, but with her blood and adrenaline pumping so hard, Sasha could not feel it. As the water sloshed around inside the car, she coughed profusely, trying to force the liquid from her lungs. She was panicking and started gasping as air came and then went away. The car wrenched around again and rolled up onto its side, exposing the open door up to the air. It slammed into a small hill and came to a sudden stop. Those inside clamored towards the light, fighting to get out.

Sasha's father fought vigorously to pull his family up to air through the frenzy of suffocating people. He pushed Sasha up out of the train car. She coughed the water out of her lungs and breathed in the wonderful air, practically hyperventilating to get more and more oxygen.

She looked back down through the entrance, watching for her family. Her father took a deep breath and submerged himself again. Sasha sat atop the exterior of the train car, watching the water rise higher and higher around the sides. *Please hurry, Papa*, she thought anxiously.

More people managed to escape and they jumped out as fast as they could, purging the liquid out of their respiratory systems. They all reached in to pull out their loved ones. Then Sasha saw her younger sister, Daniella, struggling towards the doorway. Sasha reached in and grabbed for her. She felt her sister's delicate, small hand in hers and yanked Daniella up, getting her partially out of the water. Her sister coughed severely, attempting to breathe in the air. But she was not given the time. Seven or eight hands came out of the water inside the car and swarmed around Daniella's head and Sasha's arm. Panicked, drowning people grabbed onto the girls, attempting to pull themselves out. A woman's hand, wearing a huge onyx ring, tore at Daniella's arm and yanked her from her older sister's grip. Sasha could only watch in shock and horror as her sister splashed back down into the water. She had held on as long as she could and was very nearly pulled in herself. People were grabbing at her arms and legs, tugging mercilessly on her clothes. She freed herself from the relentless onslaught of strange hands clawing at her body, kicking a woman in the face who was pulling on her leg to get out.

A dozen more people fought their way out of the water-filled train car, not one of them a member of Sasha's family. The rushing deluge finally claimed the car and, yet, she remained perched there looking down until the wave almost dragged her away. Only then did she give up and pull herself further up the hill and out of harm's way. She sat atop the hill crying, as the swell of ocean water rose up and completely swallowed the car with her family inside. Finally, the torrent built up enough force to pry the car off the hill and drag it away.

Filled simultaneously with rage and grief, her entire body shook. The situation was unbearable and Sasha felt like she was wavering in and out of consciousness. The intensity of her raw emotions at a peak, she saw a woman with a familiar face standing nearby. She couldn't remember where she had seen her before, but then she noticed the ring on the lady's hand. Sasha would never forget that ring for the rest of her life. The ring was appropriately as black as night, and there was no mistaking it belonged to the hand she had watched pull Daniella down to her death. Sasha's stomach turned and she gagged back the acid rising from her gut.

A tremendous burst of rage consumed her, like nothing she had ever experienced before. Without a second thought, she slammed ferociously into the woman, pushing her down the hill and into the surging flood Sasha stared coldly, without remorse, as the shrieking lady was carried away and sank beneath the surface.

The Allied leadership was beyond outraged, but they were held in check by their fear. They had no offensive strategy. Terror campaigns were out, for they were proving to be too costly. After La Palma, the Allies were afraid of what else Geiseric might have up his sleeve. No one knew how he had done it, nor did they know what other atrocities he was capable of sending their way. Geiseric had won the terror campaign. What followed was a long, uncomfortable silence.

For a few months, it looked like nothing else would happen. Allied High Command extended the draft to all able-bodied men over the age of eighteen and the Allied Army was built up to five times its original size. Preparations began for the day Geiseric's forces would knock on North America's door. Tensions ran high. Any day the sun came up and went down without an attack was a good day. That was the only benchmark they could use.

Then, one day, after nearly four months of worrying and waiting, the Juggernaut showed up on America's doorstep.

— XVI —

Invasion Of Allied North America

June 5, 2039

The Japanese, Indian, Greek and Germanian Delfins had gathered together and were now working under one title — the Apex Armada — and the Germanian Admiral Von Bismark commanded the impressive fleet. Still, they were vastly outnumbered by the Allies who, even after their beating during the Diaspora, had nearly twice as many Sharks as the Apex.

Geiseric knew, however, that the invaders often had an advantage, for the defenders must scatter their resources trying to protect everything, since they did not know when and where the invasion would commence. And that was precisely the situation Geiseric had placed the Allies in.

A massive invasion force awaited in Japan, seemingly ready to strike the West Coast of Fortress North America at any moment. However, the Allies knew full well that the Apex could have a secret invasion force in Europe ready to pounce on the East Coast. And so, Allied High Command dispersed the Sharks along the eastern *and* western coastlines.

What was Geiseric waiting for? They wondered.

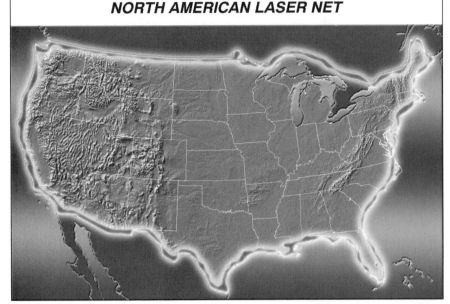

NORTH AMERICAN LASER NET

The Apex Emperor waited on his most powerful and awe-instilling weapon, which slowly lumbered across the abyssal depths like a sea titan of ancient legend.

Finally, the day came when it was in place to begin. Geiseric called Von Bismark and spoke only one word: "Proceed."

Within moments, the Imperial Delfin Fleet overwhelmed the few Allied Shark squadrons in the Atlantic waters off North Carolina. As the Allies had feared, the Delfins then moved into a defensive line to keep the path cleared, no doubt for an overwhelming amphibious assault.

The Allies kept ninety percent of their non-naval forces inside the North American Laser Net, to be used if and when the Apex forces made a break-through. So the Apex air power had no problem overwhelming the few Allied jets defending outside the Net.

Until the Allied Shark Fleet in the Atlantic could be assembled to strike en masse, the Apex Armada was left holding the waters off North Carolina with-out harassment or challenge. The Allies braced for the invasion, which should have come right on the heels of the naval victory. It seemed irrational for the Apex to not send in as many troops as possible to storm the beaches in these first hours, to deal with the Laser Net and land defenses without the added threat of the Allied submariner battlemachines.

Yet, nothing came.

It seemed as if the Delfins had paved the way for nothing. Why had the amphibious assault not been launched? The Allied leaders were, once again, left baffled and disconcerted by Geiseric's stratagem and they nervously speculated about what it meant. Maybe the Apex Army was not synchronized with the naval forces, much like when the Spanish Armada was foiled by their army during Spain's failed invasion of England in 1588. But, most of the Allied leaders and military officers knew that Geiseric was no doubt planning to do something they were not expecting, as always. In fact, the Apex invasion was probably right on schedule.

Suddenly, off the shores of North Carolina, powerful impact tremors began to emanate from a point on the continental slope. Nelson watched the seismogram readouts on the commander's deck of her Shark battlecraft. She saw that the epicenter of the quakes was around Cape Hatteras. Because its shifting sands led to many shipwrecks, Cape Hatteras was once called the graveyard of the sea, a title it would regain once more.

The tremors became more powerful and closer together, until they blended together into a powerful, unending earthquake. Something was pounding into the continental shelf like a colossal jackhammer; each strike creating a force equal to a million tons of TNT.

Inside one of the Laser Net bunkers, where crews waited at the ready to defend the cape coastline, people rushed around trying to steady the vibrating weaponry, praying that nothing exploded from the intense trembling. But, the quake only built in potency, along with an unbearably loud noise that grew ever greater in decibel level. It soon became so overwhelming that almost everyone was knocked off their feet, falling to the ground with their hands clamped tightly over their ringing ears.

Suddenly, the eastward-facing armored wall exploded inward with an incredible blast, tearing straight through the steel-reinforced, ten meter thick cement. Metal shards flew about the room, slicing through skin and puncturing unprotected eyes.

The officer in charge rushed to sound the alarm, covering his head and face from the flames and shrapnel with his coat, as he stumbled over debris and injured people bleeding on the floor. He immediately hit the evacuation siren and got on the line to the nearby control tower.

"Delta 77 is under attack!" he shouted breathlessly, in an utter state of shock. "We're being *completely demolished!* The bunker walls are pierced by unknown projectiles! I repeat! Delta 77 . . ."

But he never finished. The Cross Laser generator was struck and the bunker exploded with the force of a bursting volcano. A Cross Laser generator was different than those of other lasers, in that they used chemicals and processes that were highly volatile. The explosion sent a pyroclastic cloud of rock and ash spewing out, as the bunker and some of the surrounding stone practically vaporized. A smoldering, hundred-meter-wide crater was all that was left in the ground.

Ten kilometers away, Control Tower #79 received the radio message from Delta 77, followed by boulders of cement and rock debris from the exploding bunker, which reached all the way to the tower. Some smaller pieces even careened through the top floor station, slightly rocking the lean structure.

The tower commander shouted into the radio. "This is Alpha 79! Delta 77 has been compromised and destroyed! I repeat! Delta 77 has been destroyed!"

The other bunker containing the Cross Laser that was complimentary to Delta 77 was only a few kilometers away. At this site, operators inside heard the control tower's message and panicked, for the shaking was gaining in intensity here. One of the operators slammed on the sirens and shouted into the intercom.

"Everyone evacuate! Get out of—"

Those in Tower #79 watched in horror as, in the distance, another Laser Net bunker blew up with ferocity.

"Commander!" One of the controllers yelled, as he slammed down his radio receiver. "A Bald Eagle surveillance squadron has just spotted bogies coming in fast, at nearly *twenty thousand* kilometers per hour, sir!"

The commander picked up a phone that immediately connected him to High Command.

"The Laser Net's been compromised! We've got bogies coming in at sector Delta-Bravo!"

In the War Room, the leaders standing and sitting anxiously around the table were stunned to hear the tower commander's words. Hollier, Dandau. Tierney, Sinclair, Kurtkin, Hung, Ackleworth, Streicher and Kassian all could not conceal their utter shock. For a moment, they were speechless with disbelief.

"I repeat," the commander called out once more, "the Laser Net **has been compromised!"**

All over the East Coast of North America, hangar doors ripped open and six thousand Bald Eagles shot out into the sky, headed towards the breach in North Carolina. Most of the Bald Eagles would not be there in time to stop the first wave of incoming Apex aircraft, nor could the Allied jets do much even if they did get to the scene earlier.

Spearheading the Apex aerial assault were the large, yet incredibly fast Condor magneto-thrust planes. The Condor's thrust was produced by utilizing magneto-hydrodynamics. Plasma was fired out of the nose of the plane and sucked back by magnets located in the rear. The plasma spray alleviated drag on the front of the plane by disrupting vortices and other aerodynamic foes. The act of pulling the charged plasma back, over and under the plane, also served to thrust the plane forward at incredible speed. The Condors were the fastest and most efficient aircraft in the world.

They crossed over the breach in the Allied Laser Net without any opposition. Flying at around twenty thousand kilometers per hour, the Condors were nearly untouchable. They carried twenty-five guided bombs, each weighing two tons. The pilots followed general orders to take out any targets of opportunity, because the Apex had gathered very little intelligence on the layout of the Allied military in Fortress North America. All Apex surveillance satellites flying in the Western hemisphere had been shot down. And, of course, no Apex spy planes could puncture through the Allied Laser Net before now.

So, the primary mission of the first wave of Condors was not the bombing run. It was to photograph and record digital footage of the Allied defensive posturing along the East Coast and farther inland.

Along the way, the crew on board the bombers superficially analyzed the footage for any undisguised troops, battlemachine concentrations and heavily fortified areas. It took less than five minutes for the Condors to penetrate a thousand kilometers into Allied American skies. They turned around and made their way back out the way they came in, bombing the obvious targets as they left.

Within another ten minutes, the Condors, which landed on water, glided towards the surface of the ocean hundreds of kilometers off the coast. The landing was one of the most dangerous parts of the mission, because the seas were turbulent and the Condors came in at extremely high speeds. But the pilots were trained for this and the entire squadron landed without injury.

The photographic data was immediately relayed electronically to Germania and, within minutes of being gathered, the surveillance footage and photographs were being examined by thousands of analysts, who scrutinized every detail with the help of shape-recognition computer technology. They were looking for camouflaged fortifications, battlemachines, aircraft and troops. To look for things hidden underground or in mountain ranges, they needed to look for the clues, such as tracks in the ground left by Animalian or conventional vehicles. This is where the technology used by the analysts proved to be astounding. It could identify a small print on the ground from high in the sky, even if that print was somewhat disheveled by someone who quickly tried to cover up their tracks. One had to be quite fastidious in removing all traces of their movements to escape the all-seeing eyes of the Apex analysts and computers.

They quickly pinpointed thousands of targets and dispatched their findings to General Gottlieb, so he could prepare his next attack. He brought together his *Luftwaffe* commanders and they coordinated a massive air-strike using the rest of the Imperial Condors and the Golden Eagles.

The Imperial Condor squadron was based in occupied Portugal, Spain, France, Britain and Ireland. There were another thousand of these magneto-thrust planes that had not yet been sent in. Three hundred were quickly loaded up with a multitude of bombs. The Condors then took off, using jets to ascend from the coastal waters of occupied Europe. Once they reached a certain altitude, they kicked in the magneto-thrust drive, swiftly accelerating into the distance.

Seventeen minutes later, the second wave of Condors had crossed the Atlantic and reached North Carolina. The Apex bombers struck into the breach, but they met far more gun and shell fire than the Condors who preceded them.

By the time the Apex had readied their next wave of planes, the Juggernaut's particle accelerator gun had destroyed more than thirty laser bunkers, slashing a nearly two hundred kilometer long hole in the Allied Laser Net on the North Carolina coast. The Allies were baffled and horrified by the strange Apex weapon that broke through their fortress walls with ease. Then, as quickly as it made its startling and dominating introduction, the mysterious machine disappeared into the ocean abyss.

Allied High Command was stunned. They had not predicted or prepared for an immediate Apex breach through the fortress walls. However, Allied ground forces had managed to redistribute a large amount of anti-aircraft batteries to this gap in the laser defense. Tens of thousands of anti-aircraft guns fired haphazardly into the skies, as the second wave of Condors arrived.

The Allied ground forces did not bother aiming at the Condors, because they knew the planes could traverse from horizon to horizon in less than a blink. So, they simply filled a huge volume of sky with exploding shells to disrupt the Condors' flight patterns, hoping for lucky strikes. The entire two hundred kilometer-long break in the Laser Net was defended by anti-aircraft guns, reaching back in a twenty kilometer radius. The skies throughout the entire area were filled with fire and shrapnel.

As the Condors shot into the deadly patch of airspace, they were blasted full of holes. Planes dropped to the ground with the speed of meteorites, their munitions exploding upon impact. The force of so many Condors hitting the Earth at once shook the ground far into the distance. Anyone in the immediate vicinity behind the front felt the tremendous rumbling and once again their hearts raced with fear. They worried that the strange undersea weapon was again bashing holes through their fortress.

More than one hundred Condors went down as they ran the gauntlet through the breach. Still, many of them managed to drop their payloads on the concentration of anti-aircraft guns before they plunged to the ground in a ball of fire. Dozens more inevitably crash landed with their devastating payloads onto the guns shooting them down. The second wave of Condors and their crews were like kamikazes, blunting the Allied sword by throwing their bodies upon it.

Though dwindled to less than two-thirds their starting number, this second wave of Apex bombers was still able to do a vast amount of damage. Upon crossing the breach, they radiated out to the west, north and south, striking deep into Fortress North America. They found their designated targets and dropped their payloads.

Nearly half of the Condors were carrying two MOAB guided bombs, or Massive Ordinance Air-Bursters. Each bomb weighed ten metric tons, but had the equivalent yield of one hundred tons of TNT, making them the most powerful non-nuclear bombs in the world and, thus, the most powerful in the stock of the *Luftwaffe*. Relying on the information garnered from the analysis of the aerial photographs and digital film, the Condors dropped nearly two hundred guided MOABs on hidden troops and battlemachine concentrations in North Carolina, South Carolina, Virginia, West Virginia, Georgia and Pennsylvania. The bombs created huge pressure waves, which were composed of regions in the air where the air particles were compressed together and other regions where the air particles were spread apart. These regions, respectively known as compressions and rarefactions, crushed all battlemachines within a half-kilometer of the blast radius and effectively evaporated all that lived.

It was a slaughter. Hundreds of thousands of Allied soldiers were massacred where they hid, hunkered down in their well-camouflaged areas. A few of the MOABs had bunker-buster, tungsten tips that allowed them to pierce through dirt and concrete. These were used against large underground targets, such as bases. A special sensor in the bomb could detect when it had punctured through the walls of the facility, for it wasn't encountering any more resistance from moving through solids. It was then that it would detonate, and the MOABs were only amplified when going off inside an enclosure. They not only killed thousands of enemy troops, but shocked and demoralized those who survived.

Discipline broke as many divisions scattered away from their positions, seeking cover. Most of the officers agreed that it was a good idea to leave their highly concentrated locations, but they wanted their soldiers to disperse in an organized fashion, rather than trampling each other and straying from their commanders The Condors were above them too quickly, however, and within seconds the incredible devastation of the MOABs was upon the disparate Allied ground forces stationed farther inland.

Many of the surviving Condors in the second wave carried fifteen smaller guided bunker-buster bombs. The three-ton destroyers crashed through bunkers that were buried fifteen meters deep in the ground and had thick cement walls. Each of these bunkers held six Cougars, the Allied North American equivalent to the Panzer quadruped battlemachines. The confined area in the bunkers once again served to amplify the blasts. Still, many of the battlemachines within were not demolished by the explosions. Instead, as the bunkers collapsed, the vehicles and their crews were buried alive in graves of concrete and dirt.

Some of the Condors carried a revolutionary antimatter-powered "electromagnetic pulse" weapon that was designed to fry the Allied electric power grid and whatever was left of the communications networks. These were highly effective at knocking out the power all over the East Coast, leaving much of the Allied infrastructure in the dark and unable to operate. The battlemachines and Laser Net were left completely unaffected, for they were protected by the highest-grade, and therefore most expensive and limited, anti-radiation shielding. However, nearly all civilian structures lost power, causing panic and chaos. Many lower-level military bases were also shut down, due to their lack of shielding.

A majority of the Allied soldiers and officers who died that day, were killed before they could even attempt to engage the enemy in battle. They were simply bomb fodder. What was even more devastating for the Allies was that so many Animalian vehicles were being obliterated. Still, less than a third of the Apex bombs had struck a good target. The rest exploded into patches of ground with nothing underneath, apparently misidentified by the Apex surveillance analysts.

Regardless, hundreds of Allied ground battlemachines had been destroyed, and the radar showed that seven hundred more Condors were racing high over the Atlantic toward North America. Their options limited, the Allied leadership gave the orders for all the quadruped battlemachines to be evacuated from the bunkers.

Coming in ahead of this third wave of Condors, three thousand Golden Eagle jets raced in low over the ocean and into the breach. They dodged much of the concentrated gunfire at the mouth, zigzagging above trails blazed by the second wave of Condors. A third of them dropped thousands of quarter-ton guided bombs altogether upon Allied anti-aircraft batteries along the way, paving a safer pathway for the largest wave of Condors.

The other two thousand Golden Eagles held four missiles each. Two of these missiles were much larger and were designed to take out quadrupedal battlemachines and other ground forces. The smaller ones traveled fast enough to take out their Allied counterpart — the Bald Eagles.

As the Apex jets pushed deep into enemy territory, they started wreaking havoc on the Allied battlemachines on the ground which, having left their bunkers, were frantically rushing for cover. The Golden Eagle pilots fired their air-to-ground missiles as fast as they could, on any visible targets. They needed to lighten the weight of their jets so they could fly faster and maneuver. They did so not a minute too soon because, just as those missiles fired away, they were met head on by a Bald Eagle force twice their size.

Six thousand Allied swivel-wing fighter-jets raced in to engage the Apex Eagles. Just as in Europe, the Apex fighters kept in relatively tight with each other, confining their flying space to offset the enemy's superior numbers. The immense volume of sky running east from the Appalachian Mountains to the coast, from Georgia to Pennsylvania, may have seemed like plenty of space for a theatre of aerial warfare. However, with nine thousand jets racing anywhere from two to seven thousand kilometers per hour, the combat zone had very little elbow room.

The Apex pilots, whose training was superior in the first place, now had earned experience in the Battle of the Old World, particularly those in the European theatre. The Allied pilots who fought in Europe had been either killed or captured, whereas the Golden Eagle pilots were given the priceless gift of being battle-hardened. There was nothing like the true, life-or-death competition of war to push a pilot's skill up a notch and to calm their nerves in the face of the enemy the next time around. The new Allied pilots fighting to defend Fortress North America were unquestionably better trained than those who died in Europe, and so were reserved for this ultimate battle. However, they had no real battle experience.

The Bald Eagles began to drop like flies all along the United States eastern coast and Allied High Command, having become more cautious since the battle for Europe, made the painful decision to pull their jet fighters back in, to fight another day. The Bald Eagle pilots needed to recoup, to let their combat experience simmer in their minds. Until then, the North American skies were owned by the Apex.

The final and largest wave of the Imperial Condor Armada made its entrance with relatively little opposition compared to those that had preceded them. Seven hundred magneto-thrust bombers fired across the North Carolinian breach. Thanks to the trails blazed through the Allied anti-aircraft guns, almost every Condor survived this time.

Screaming in at more than fifteen times the speed of sound, the Condors dropped their payloads, devastating the Allied ground forces who had stoically adhered to their hidden places, or were still in the process of scattering. Most of the bombers also struck at and crippled the Allied industrial-manufacturing areas and lines of ground transportation east of the Appalachians. It would take weeks to bring up to one hundred percent output again, draining manpower and resources in the meantime.

Having accomplished their mission, the Condors retreated back through the breach, leaving nothing but hell on Earth behind them. All of the magneto-thrust planes were now out of fuel. They landed in the Atlantic, awaited by Delfins there to tow them.

Besieged with trepidation, Allied High Command gazed at the figures. Twenty percent of the infantry had been killed or wounded. Ten percent of the quadrupedal battlemachines were buried or destroyed. On top of that, nearly a sixth of the Bald Eagles had been downed and half of those pilots had been unable to eject. It was an unacceptable loss.

But there was hope. The Allied Shark squadrons were beginning to coalesce and, in just over an hour, they would be in striking range of the Apex Delfin Armada poised off the coast of the Carolinas.

The Sharks were all under the leadership of the once Vice Admiral Nelson, now promoted to admiral, whose strategy was to attack the Apex Armada from both the north and south in a giant pincer movement. Everyone in the Shark Fleet was hyped-up, believing that if they could overwhelm the Apex Naval Forces before the land assault began, the invasion of Allied North America would be impossible.

According to Allied Intelligence, it would be at least another twenty hours before the Condors could be towed back to Europe and loaded up. The Golden Eagles were no longer armed with bombs and large missiles, so they could not do much damage to naval or ground forces anymore. They stayed in the skies over North Carolina only to keep the Bald Eagles at bay. Thus, the Allied Army could make its stand with the Delfins and the capital battlemachines of the land — the Sidewinder moving fortresses.

The Sidewinders' powerful armaments were capable of keeping the Golden Eagles at a safe enough distance that the jets' dual laser cannons were ineffective. The moving fortresses could then defend the beaches without much harassment from the air, which in the minds of the Allied leadership would make an amphibious invasion impossible. In addition, squadrons of rearmed Bald Eagles were being sent out, here and there, to harry the Golden Eagles circling in the skies, slowly nipping away at Apex air supremacy. The Allied jets would strike quickly out of nowhere and then scramble off to the safety of their bases, past the Appalachian mountain range.

Allied High Command could not understand the Apex strategy. How did Geiseric think the ultimate ground invasion was going to come, if the invading forces had little air-to-ground support? The Apex had the Delfins in the area, but most of Allied High Command was sure those were only designed for naval, in particular submarine warfare. After all, they had no indirect fire capability; they could not fire a projectile in an arc that goes up and comes down at an angle. Indirect fire allowed conventional gun battleships to fire shells down onto an enemy that was out of the line of sight, over the horizon, giving their guns far more range. The laser drill cannon on the nose of the Delfin battlecraft could only fire in a straight line, so it had far less range. And the Delfins could not come close enough to shore to fire a shot deep inland, since the coastal waters were too shallow.

Then, the news hit the Allied War Room that the Apex expeditionary force — the amphibious assault army composed of Apex infantry and cavalry — was on its way. Hundreds of transport crafts had been spotted coming across the Atlantic from Western Europe. The transports were similar in design to the Allied Skimmers that had brought over the refugees on the Diaspora. The Apex craft, though, were smaller and sturdier and had a more technical name in German, but most of the Apex troops referred to them as the English word "Skimmer," because they had heard the word so much when they saw the reports of the Allied Diaspora.

The Apex Skimmers were headed towards the United States East Coast at one thousand kilometers per hour. This was the inevitable main invasion force and the first wave was only two hours away.

It was then that Kassian had an epiphany. He saw what none of the other Allied leaders had realized, not even Streicher, with all of his knowledge of the Animalian Projects. Kassian remembered what a dolphin, the real living creature, was capable of doing. A dolphin could stand up in water on its tail, kicking it back and forth to stay upright. Kassian recognized that, if the Apex Delfin battlemachines could do this, they would stand around eight stories high in the water. This would give them the range they needed.

Streicher quibbled with Kassian for a moment, arguing that such maneuvers would be impossible to execute. To stand a massive vessel up in the water was far more difficult than a small animal doing it. Mastering the equilibrium to keep a Delfin battlemachine upright while swaying its tail would require gyroscopic-computer interphase abilities that were years beyond the time — or so he thought.

But Kassian knew how there could be another way. The shape of a Delfin battle machine, like its living counterpart, was not conducive to standing upright. The living mammal performed this feat by making a near infinite amount of tiny corrections to shift its weight, every moment, all over its body, to maintain such an unnatural position. If, somehow, the Delfin pilots were so tuned into their craft, that it was as if their vessels were an extension of their bodies, then the synthetic equilibrium could be created.

The Sidewinders had already been released from their cavernous bunkers, which were two hundred meters under the ground, leaving them completely unharmed by the Condor bombardments. The serpentine behemoths writhed forth from the depths, slithering out of the shadows to face the enemy.

Dozens of them were dispatched to the breach, creating a formidable line for an Apex invasion to cross. The Sidewinder commanders were haughty, confident that, for the moment, nothing could harm them. Exempting the unknown weapon that had carved through the continental shelf offshore, the Sidewinders were the largest battlemachines of either side. Each Sidewinder was nearly five hundred meters long, thirty meters thick and twenty meters

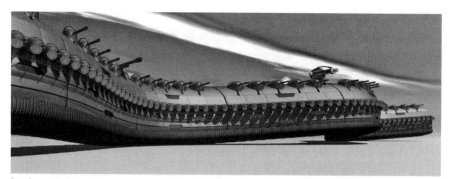

high, weighing in at over two hundred thousand tons. They were truly moving fortress walls, with a tremendous armament that out-classed the big guns of the Allied and Apex naval battlemachines. Thus, the Sidewinder commanders were anxious to meet the invasion forces and quash the Apex assault on the beach.

The moving fortresses arched their guns upward and fired a salvo of two and three-ton shells over the horizon. A deluge of explosives rained into the ocean off the coast, striking several Delfins swimming in the water. The Sidewinder crews relentlessly maintained the barrage and were slightly disappointed that this would possibly be the extent of the fighting—simply firing beyond the line-of-sight and destroying an unseen enemy.

Suddenly, to their disbelief, those on the outer decks of the Sidewinders saw the Delfins protrude up over the horizon, until most of their length could be seen swaying upright. Their laser cannons were powering up, flashing bright red. A split-second later, the immensely destructive, threaded laser beams were let loose, slashing and burning the beachhead.

Not even the exceedingly thick armor of the Sidewinders could stop the drill bolts. The powerful laser beams easily pierced the skin of the Allied capital vessels and, if any shells or other munitions were hit, their ignition would set off a chain reaction that blew up several of the adjoining compartments.

A well-placed shot from the Delfin's drill bolt cannon could slice all the way through a segment of the Sidewinder, cutting the long machine into smaller pieces. However, the Allies had prepared their moving fortresses to be able to move in smaller segments, should one part be torn asunder from another. One of the Sidewinders defending the beachhead was shredded into two big pieces and one smaller piece. The larger segments continued in the battle, while the other was rendered ineffective.

The battle was startlingly larger than life, with the titan enemy battlemachines exchanging fire from their immensely powerful weapons. It was

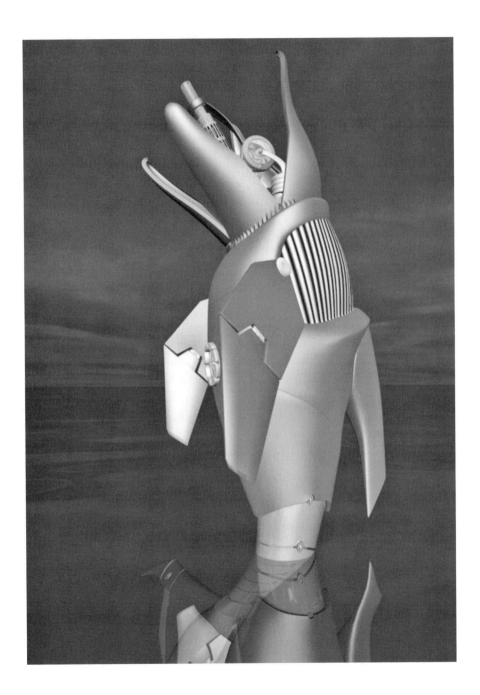

much akin to the battle of Jutland in World War I, when the Germans and British brought their capital vessels to bear upon each other. Their mighty battleships were built up in a naval arms race between the two countries that became the cause of World War I. Years of building up these vessels and their strategies came to a climax in the North Sea off Denmark. All the years, all the manpower, culminated in a battle that lasted only eighteen minutes.

Such was the precarious nature of war, that so much hard work and thought was put into realizing such small moments in time. However, upon these short, pivotal battles, hung the fate of the future.

The Apex Imperial Delfin Armada relentlessly hammered the beachhead, scorching the sand and enemy battlemachines with thousands of laser shots. The Delfins would rise in packs of a few dozen and move through the water in a standing position, either forwards or backwards. They could do this with astonishing swiftness, able to go fifty kilometers per hour back and forth in this upright posture. They were able to maneuver in the shallows nearer to shore when upright, for less of their body was in the water. Moving in slick, coordinated strikes, the Delfins spread the length of the beach with drill bolts, trapping the Sidewinders.

For their part, the Sidewinder pilots were doing an excellent job dodging the laser barrages. The crews of the mighty moving fortresses were also very skillfully aiming their big guns, precisely firing their two and three-ton rounds. The shells struck the Delfins by the hundreds, but not many of the Apex battlemachines went down. That is when the Allies realized something else was going in favor of the Apex forces.

The sheer force of the largest Sidewinder cannons was too powerful when fired straight. These shell guns could be fired either in a straight trajectory, or for greater distance or over-the-horizon strikes the trajectory could be arched. Due to the close-range action and the fact that the Delfins were upright, making them a larger target for direct/horizontal fire than indirect/vertical fire, the Sidewinder crews chose to fire straight at the standing Delfins. But, their range was too close and the potentially devastating explosives were piercing all the way through the Delfins before detonating. Instead of blowing up within the enemy naval craft. the Sidewinders' biggest shells were wasted, detonating in the ocean water behind the Delfins. It seemed as though providence was with the Apex.

However, a glimmer of hope shone through the growing devastation. The tide appeared to slowly turn when the Sidewinder commanders made the strategic decision to halt firing their largest shell guns. They could have been

arched upwards to shower munitions down on the enemy, but the commanders of the serpentine battlemachines quickly realized that direct fire from smaller shells was much more effective. Blasting out the biggest shells at thousands of kilometers per hour generated so much kickback, that the Sidewinders were jolted around, disrupting the maneuverability of the machines and making them more vulnerable to the Delfin onslaught. So, the Sidewinder commanders chose to battle it out with smaller ordinance.

Delfins began falling in the waters, toppling like awkward skyscrapers into the ocean. The water sprayed upwards as the huge Animalian vessels collapsed backwards, sideways or headlong into the sea. The waves caused by the tumult crashed onto shore, slipping past the Sidewinders on the beach. Though the waves were quite large, the heavy Allied capital battlemachines at the front were unfazed.

The Sidewinders had the most success with their skipper missiles, which rocketed low across the water's surface towards the Apex naval vessels. Designed to take out enemy transports and battleships on the ocean surface, the missiles incidentally struck the Delfins at their weakest point — the tail. It was the thinnest portion of the Apex battlecraft and lay right above the waterline when the Delfin was upright. As the skipper missiles struck the enemy in this vulnerable area, the powerful, two-ton warheads splintered the Delfins' tails, separating the kicking fin from the rest of the body.

Only one problem plagued the large missiles. They were not responsive enough to properly target something as agile as the Animalian vessels. The skipper missiles were primarily intended to destroy the oncoming landing craft bringing the Apex ground invasion, which were fast but moved in predictable lines. So only ten percent of the Sidewinder's skipper missiles actually struck their marks, but those that did proved to be devastating to the opponent.

Delfins were falling by the dozens, crippled beyond repair. Crewmen who managed to bail out were left struggling in chaotically tumultuous waters, where they drowned in the waves or were smashed by Delfin tails swishing about in the battle.

The rest of the Sidewinders that were stationed all along the East Coast, were being transported through huge, underground tunnel systems. Soon, another hundred Sidewinders would be deployed at the breach in the Allied Laser Net. The first line of Sidewinders already battling with the Delfins just had to stall out an Apex ground invasion long enough for reinforcements to arrive. This was easier said than done.

The moving fortresses fighting on the North Carolina beachhead made a valiant stand against the Apex naval assault. Much of the outcome of this war rested on the shoulders of these commanders and crews. Unfortunately for the Allies, though, the Sidewinders soon ran out of the highly effective skipper missiles and the tide once again turned in favor of the Apex, as still another variable began to take effect.

When a Delfin was taken out, it fell to the ocean floor, for the most part out of the way of its compatriots still in the fight. When a Sidewinder segment was totaled, it laid on the beach, hindering the rest of the Allied battlemachines.

The Allied leaders quickly realized that they needed to pull the unharmed Sidewinders back away from the beach, farther inland, over the horizon. That way, they could still shell the invading Apex ground forces. Their ability to pummel the invasion forces slightly diminished from what they could do being right up on the beach to meet the assault, but the Sidewinders' indirect fire would still be devastating and could certainly stall out the Apex landing.

Unknown to Allied High Command, there was a forward contingent of Apex Army forces being transported to the North Carolina coast ahead of the main body that was skimming across the water. One of the more daring and ingenious strategies used by the Apex during their invasion was the secreting of their airborne divisions in special planes that could be towed underwater. The planes were water tight and well-armored, allowing them to withstand the pressures of being more than a hundred meters deep in the ocean.

As the large transport planes surfaced off the coast, they fired up their engines and began gliding over the ocean towards the North Carolinian breach. Altogether, they carried four hundred Kolibri Knights, two hundred Panzers, and forty thousand of the Apex Empire's Elite Special Forces commandos, the best armored out of all the Apex ground troops, having the equivalent protection of a regular sky infantry flyer. These heavy *ground* infantrymen were called Hoplites, for they carried with them large shields just as their namesakes in the Ancient Greek heavy infantry had.

At first, the transport planes came in low on the ocean surface to avoid being seen for as long as possible by Allied radar. Then, when they neared the shore, they began a steep and fast incline up to twenty thousand meters, nearly seventy thousand feet, to avoid as much gunfire as possible. Traveling at one thousand kilometers per hour, they prepared to drop their human cargo. It was a feat that would have been impossible in the days of prior paratrooper assaults, because the air was too thin to breathe at such an altitude and the

418

speed was much too fast. However, the Apex Hoplites were nothing like the exposed paratroopers of the past. From head to toe, they were completely sheathed in powerful muscle enhancers helping them hold up the thick, airtight armor, lined with interior regulators and pressurizers.

As the transport planes crossed deep behind enemy lines, they opened their back hatches and the Hoplites poured out into the sky. The Apex paratroopers lay on their shields, like surfers paddling out before they rose to ride the waves. The Hoplites could maneuver through the sky and scatter to far greater distances in this manner. They glided tens of kilometers away from their drop point in the sky. Like the sky infantry, they traveled in one hundred man companies called centuries. The centurions led their centuries to a predetermined landing zone. The shields served to protect the Hoplites from small arms fire coming at them as they fell to the ground, when they like all paratroopers were at their most vulnerable.

Upon nearing within one thousand meters of the ground, they deployed a small parachute that only slightly slowed their descent. Then, within one hundred meters, they each let loose a larger parachute, lurching them back to a greatly reduced speed.

Most of the Hoplites were met by immediate gunfire. They quickly stood their shields up on the ground and ducked behind while they gained their bearings and assembled their weapons, swiftly returning fire.

Panzers were also dropped from the transport planes, each falling with three huge parachutes that decelerated their fall just enough that they wouldn't be harmed upon landing, but brought them to the ground as fast as possible. For the longer they were in the air, the longer they could be shot out of it. The felinesque machines landed feet first and crouched to absorb the impact.

The Kolibri Knights slid off the back of the transport planes and careened towards the earth, their heavy chariots pointed downward, accelerating the flyers to a far greater speed than even the heavy Panzers, due to their aerodynamic shape. Within a split-second from hitting the ground, they fired up their chariots' hummingbird-like wings and raced to help their compatriots.

Rapidly coalescing, the Hoplites, Panzers and Kolibri formed a fearsome strike package. Each of the forty Hoplite battalions was backed up by five Panzers and ten Kolibri Knights. Having been dropped behind the enemy's main lines, these strike packages hit specified targets all over the East Coast, from the Appalachians to the Atlantic. Bearing down on the most protected and heretofore undamaged centers of the enemy's communication, they sent the Allied forces into chaos. They attacked remaining radar and missile installations, gun batteries, and anything else not destroyed by the Condor bombings, moving in quickly to fully secure the sites that had been only minimally damaged.

There was no Allied equivalent to the Hoplite heavy infantryman and the Allied troops were caught off guard by the mighty onslaught. The first who were targeted en masse by the Hoplites were those manning what was left of the concentration of anti-aircraft batteries at the mouth of the North Carolinian breach. Ten thousand Apex paratroopers closed in on the concentration and encircled the Allied ground forces there. There were fifty Panzers in the Apex encirclement; all equipped with disposable, long-range, missile-launching systems. A large box of launch tubes was mounted on the backs of the quadrupedal battlemachines. The Panzers rested on their abdomens as hydraulic mechanisms angled the tubes upward towards the sky. Each box carried twelve missiles, altogether capable of destroying almost anything within a three kilometer radius. The missiles were deployed at strategic intervals along the encirclement, so that they would strike the Allied ground forces simultaneously across hundreds of square kilometers of land.

Coming in on their targets at an angle, the missiles spun like a well-thrown football. At about two hundred meters above the ground, a charge detonated within the missiles, shooting out thousands of sharp metal fragments that were capable of puncturing through a quarter-meter of steel. Hundreds of submunitions, small bomblets, were also dispersed over a vast area as the missile spun. The bomblets hit the ground and fired out more shrapnel, mixed with white phosphorous, which burned extremely hot and blew up the enemy's munitions. Such a colossal and simultaneous bombardment of "steel rain" had not been seen since the Persian Gulf War, when it was dropped on the Iraqi Army. And it did to the Allied soldiers exactly what it had done to the Iraqis . . . made them lose control of their bowels and run for cover.

The tactic of intense bombardment was nothing new. From catapults to cannons, humans have had to endure powerful barrages of fast-moving, often times flammable and explosive material from their military enemies for more than two millennia. However, the tactic passed an important milestone in World War I, when "shell shock" came into the vocabulary. Industrial Age alloys had brought artillery guns and projectiles up a size and scope never approached in history. The essence of Blitzkrieg was to stun an opponent with overwhelming firepower and to roll over them with speed. When the Coalition of the Willing launched their campaign against Iraq in 2003, those in America who constructed the war plan said that they would "shock and awe" the Iraqis.

President George W. Bush touted men like Donald Rumsfeld as creators of the "lightning warfare strategy." This was almost as great a source of hilarity to German military tacticians as when Secretary Rumsfeld declared that the coalition invading Iraq was the grandest ever.

No matter whom the tactic was employed by, or how courageous the soldiers subjected to its wrath, the results of steel rain was always the same. It did not distinguish the brave from the cowardly, the strong from the weak. It tore everyone and everything apart and those who did not run for cover were fools. The Apex Hoplites followed the missile bombardment with an immediate salvo of mortars and small shells fired from self-propelled artillery pieces, which had also been parachuted in from the transport planes.

Once the Allied troops in the breach area had scattered into foxholes and other forms of cover, the Hoplites, along with the Panzers and Kolibri, rushed into the concentration to finish off the job. They charged toward their beleaguered enemy, whose armor was no match. Running in without their shields, the Hoplites fired their formidable assault rifles. Tens of thousands of Allied troops were razed to the ground by the onslaught.

When a Hoplite ran out of bullets, he pulled out a large, stabbing blade that had one sharpened side. It looked like a cross between a samurai's katana and a bayonet. Like the Kolibri flyers had done in Europe, the Hoplites used their blades to finish off the broken Allied soldiers.

They jabbed their steel blades into soft spots in the Allied troops' armor, between the titanium trauma plates. Or, the Hoplites stabbed the long sword into their enemies' necks and faces. Flesh tore loose and hung, and blood spewed forth out of the jugulars of Allied soldiers. The small patch of land at the mouth of the breach in North Carolina, was now only two colors — red and black — the colors of death and destruction. The landscape had been debased to nothing but scorched earth littered with burnt out guns and mutilated bodies.

Already, a battalion of Allied Hornet regulars and three hundred Dreadnoughts were dispatched to the defense of the encircled Allied soldiers. Allied High Command decided not to send more of their Hornets towards the breach, recalling what had happened in the European theatre when they had engaged the Kolibri in open battle. For all they knew, the entire Apex sky infantry was secretly rested offshore, waiting for the Allies to take the bait. The Allied leadership would not risk the total annihilation of their Hornet forces. Instead, High Command decided on a longer term approach, one which allowed the Kolibri in and, when the Apex sky infantry inevitably had to scatter to attack and protect different strategic areas, the Allies would chew away at the invaders piece by piece.

Their strategy was the essence of a guerilla war: allow the enemy forces in and strike at them from hidden places. The Allies decided it was the best tactic for their sky infantry and it was the tactic they had first tried to use on Europe's western front, but had failed to do so because the Allied battlemachines' hidden places were too easily discovered and destroyed. Now, while the hidden battlemachines and troops had taken a beating from the Condors and Golden Eagles, the majority of Allied ground forces were too deeply bunkered to be threatened by the Kolibri's weapons. Thus, endangering them could not be used to draw the Hornets into battle.

For now, only three centuries of Dreadnoughts, along with about five hundred Hornet regulars, were dispatched to harass the Hoplites. The Allied sky infantry strafed the Apex heavy troops on the ground. The Hoplites' armor could not stand up against the uranium penetrators and they were cut down by the hundreds. It was their turn to run for cover now.

The few dozen Kolibri Knights assisting the Hoplite divisions at the Breach were overwhelmed by their enemy's numbers. The Apex field commanders called for sky infantry reinforcements, but the other three hundred and fifty Knights that had been dropped in were dispersed over too wide an area, taking out mobile missile-launchers and making other tactical strikes behind the front. It would take a couple of hours for all of them to gather. The Apex ground forces around the breach were, thus, sitting ducks to be plucked by the Allied sky infantry. It was a fleeting moment of victory for the Allies.

Just then, thirty Delfins that had been patrolling in Raleigh Bay began to siphon into the immense, natural harbor on the North Carolina coast called Pamlico Sound. At one hundred and thirty kilometers long and fifty kilometers wide, it was the largest lagoon along the United States' East Coast. The sound was separated from the Atlantic by the Outer Banks, a row of low, sandy barrier islands, peaked by Cape Hatteras.

The Apex had converted thirty Delfins from submarine battlecraft to transport vessels, saving them for this moment, which was predicted by the Apex strategists. The Delfin transports beached onto the shores all along the North Carolina mainland area inside the Pamlico Sound, under severe bombardment from the Sidewinders over the horizon. The transport Delfins opened up numerous hatches along their upper body and thirty Kolibri flyers buzzed out of each. Several of the Delfins were struck by indirect shell fire, but

most of the Kolibri had poured out quickly and remained unscathed by the Sidewinders' barrage.

The Kolibri flyers rushed to give air cover to the Hoplites around the breach, but the Allied sky infantry flew away in full retreat. The Apex commanders were surprised that the Allies had not sent more of their Hornet forces out to meet them at the breach. There was only one explanation — the Allies were posturing for a guerilla defense. Well, the Apex had prepared for this scenario and immediately launched their contingency plan.

The Kolibri flyers spread out, looking for any target of opportunity, but especially the Allied SADM's, Special Atomic Demolition Munitions. Essentially, the Apex forces were searching for enemy soldiers who had relatively small nuclear weapons, like the ones that had been used in the terror attack on Bavaria. The lightweight bombs could be carried around by one person, a strategy conceived of in the midst of the Cold war.

These ground units were now independently dispersed all over the East Coast. Each SADM carrier was equipped with a recoilless launcher, which fired 200mm nuclear rounds. The weapon system used a spin-stabilized, unguided rocket. Its fifteen-kilogram nuclear warhead had an explosive yield the equivalent of one thousand tons of TNT.

With ruthless efficiency, the invading Kolibri flyers hunted down and exterminated the small, but dangerous SADM groups. From the air, they also scanned for hidden nuclear missile launchers. Many of them had already been taken out by the Condor bombings, but there were a few remaining mobile launchers, which the Kolibri took down by themselves, and when they spotted missiles still intact in fortified silos, they marked them with laser pointers and called in for a targeted air strike.

Two dozen converted Delfin vessels waited in the Atlantic off the coast for just such a call. These were unique in that they had no laser cannons and, therefore, no hefty generators taking up space within their hulls. The volume was instead filled with missiles carrying three ton bunker-buster warheads. They were being held for this particular mission and could not have been wasted earlier. It was vitally important that all of the Allied nuclear missile silos within close range of the breach were taken out before the Apex mounted their ground invasion. Just a few fifty megaton super-warheads could take out the entire invasion force.

Per the request of the Kolibri, the bunker-busters were released. Hundreds of submarine-to-surface missiles poured out of the Delfins, propelling first through and out of the water, and then rocketing off through the air towards their targets. The stationary Allied silos were completely obliterated. It looked like everything was clear for an Apex assault, and it was perfect timing.

Like clockwork, the Apex expeditionary force arrived in their Skimmer transports. The dreaded amphibious ground assault that the Allies had been preparing against was now upon them. Only it was going nothing like the Allied leadership had planned. The Apex ground troops were supposed to be facing off against the Laser Net. But now, even the Sidewinders had pushed back over the horizon, so they could not annihilate the invading ground troops right on the beachhead. Many of the military personnel in the Allied War Room already felt as though the backbone of their defense was broken. But, everything was happening far too quickly for them to even think about conceding defeat. They still had many cards to play . . .

And play them they would.

The first wave of one hundred Apex expeditionary force transports raced into Pamlico Sound. They managed to merge through the narrow inlets in a choreographed, zipper-like maneuver. Going close to full speed, they fired their retro-rocket engines, which abruptly slowed the transports down. Upon entering the sound, a few transports were instantly struck by large shells, sending the massive vessels crashing across the surface of the water, catapulting metal shards and human cargo in all directions, until the bulk of the craft sank, or slammed upon the beachhead. Each Skimmer held ten thousand troops, but those transports that were struck by shells harbored very few survivors.

As is common in war, the invaders were infinitely more vulnerable at the beginning of the invasion. However, only a few of the Apex transports went down; most made it to the mainland beach within Pamlico Sound. Instantly, the hatches to the transports opened and the Apex *Sturm Truppen* poured out.

The *Sturm Truppen* were named after the World War I assault troops who were trained to storm the trenches. After four years of slaughter in that war, both sides of the conflict had adapted new infantry battle tactics. The Germans created Special Forces soldiers called the storm troopers, who would rush towards and infiltrate enemy lines in small groups using rapid assault tactics. The Apex storm troopers, who were now spearheading the amphibious invasion, went forth with the same basic principles as their ancestors had.

All across the mainland shores of Pamlico Sound, the Apex storm troopers ran as fast as they could out of their transports and across the beach. They were met with a soul-splitting bombardment. The Sidewinders, positioned just over the horizon, sent over thousands of tons of shells, along with ATACMS — Army

Tactical Advanced Conventional Munitions Systems — which were missiles that fired out bomblets and steel shrapnel.

Three hundred Mark I Panzers tore loose from the Skimmers, and ran alongside the rushing storm troopers. The Mark I was meant for speed. The quadrupedal battlemachines stampeded across the beachhead at one hundred and sixty kilometers per hour. The shaking of the ground caused by the sixty-ton Panzers went unnoticed, for the beach was incessantly rumbling from the Allied barrage. Dozens of the Apex cavalry vehicles shattered in the percussive blasts of two and three-ton shells exploding on them or nearby. Others were directly hit by the multitude of smaller shells that often blew off a limb or the head of a Panzer, which was the driver's cockpit. The ATACMs were also devastating to the Apex quadrupeds and their drivers, "tamers," inside were sliced to shreds by the metal fragments.

Outside, the steel rain was far more cataclysmic. Apex storm troopers fell dead in the sand by the tens of thousands, their bodies having been infinitely perforated, fluids and entrails seeping from the wounds. The relentless artillery barrage left a pile of identical, unidentifiable corpses, having stewed the bodies and sand together into bloody compost that littered the entire beachhead. Such un-harnessed, relentless gore had never been witnessed on such a scale in all of history, and the Apex soldiers pouring forth from their transports were shocked and sickened by the sight. But, they did not break ranks and with incredible fortitude they ran across the remains of their fallen brethren.

General Gottlieb had a reason for ordering such lightly-armored troops and vehicles into this extreme killing zone. It was simple. The massive shells and other devastating projectiles being fired onto the beachhead were capable of destroying any kind of Panzer, let alone a heavy infantryman. So, armor was clearly useless in such a situation, but speed was valuable. Armor would hinder the invasion forces. It weighed them down.

Besides, Gottlieb figured, there was inevitable expendability in war. Just like the assault troops in the World War II Normandy landing, the first wave of Apex invasion forces were expendable. Of course, only the leaders knew that harsh truth. Those troops served one purpose. They were cannon fodder, meant to draw the enemy's fire, so that the second wave could be successful. And there was no point in spending too much money on protecting dead meat.

Blitzkrieg warfare served to push battles quickly to their end, until one side's forces were completely annihilated. But, when the opponents were so near in strength and power, there were simply rapid battles of attrition, where the leaders of both sides had to reconcile taking huge casualties. This was relatively easy for a politician, who was looking solely at maps and numbers. However, for the Apex forces storming across the North Carolinian beachhead, it was hell incarnate.

The Allied Sidewinders and artillery pieces were running low on ammunition by the time the second wave of Apex expeditionary forces arrived. Two hundred more Apex Skimmers raced into Pamlico Sound and came up on or near shore. This time, two million storm troopers and six hundred Panzers poured out, twice as many as on the first round. Amongst these were even a few dozen of the more powerful Mark II and Mark III Panzers.

As they struck across the beaten and bloodied nightmare laced with sand and saltwater, most of the troops averted their eyes from the ground they stepped upon. They tried not to breathe the putrid stench of death as they rushed forward. They realized they could be seeing, smelling, and running across their own fate. Their predecessors, who only minutes ago were alive and whole, were now smeared across a cratered shoreline.

The Panzers launched themselves from the Apex transports and ran out ahead of the second wave of storm troopers. They caught up with the beleaguered first wave of invasion forces, of which less than twenty percent remained. Seeing the Mark II and Mark III Panzers coming up from behind gave the Apex Sturm Truppen on the front line a boost of morale.

The Mark II Panzer was called the Leopard and it was more heavily-armored than the basic Panzer. Its skin was also able to change colors and texture, enabling it to camouflage into almost any environment in a moment's notice. The Mark III Panzer, called the Tiger, was by far the most powerfully-gunned and armored of all. They could do some serious damage to a Sidewinder. And their tamers planned to.

Reinforcing the shattered first wave forces at the front, those in the second wave of Panzers that managed to survive the initial bombardment combined with the Apex cavalry already there in the fray. Altogether, nearly seven hundred cat-like battlemachines made a formidable pride on the broken mainland coast of Pamlico Sound.

Charging out over the horizon, the Panzers faced the Allied capital battlemachines head on. There were still many of the Sidewinders left from those that had fought the Apex Naval Forces on the beachhead. But, now they were clear of the Delfin's huge and devastating drill bolt cannons. The Sidewinders were busily clearing the land of trees and other vegetation, by steamrolling over everything, making it easier to maneuver and cutting a clear line of

| Pamlico Sound | Laser Net | Sidewinder line |

visibility so that smaller Apex machines could not lay in wait, hidden from view. It was an odd and scary sight. Huge, two hundred thousand ton battlemachines whipped about in propeller-like movements over the surface, like titanic snakes having spasms. As they did, they cleared wide, circular swaths of evergreens, moss-hung cypresses and eye-catching camellias, which were just beginning to bloom.

The mainland coastline of Pamlico Sound was teeming with life. An abundance of plants and animals called the estuaries and marshland home, including the beloved water birds of nature enthusiasts, such as pelicans, herons and egrets. The Sidewinders ripped around the area so fast, that many of the birds never had time to escape. Disgruntled squawking was quickly silenced under the destructive tonnage of the Sidewinders. Within minutes, the Allied battlemachines had ploughed over the once pristine coastal habitat.

The Apex forces were met with the unexpected and disconcerting sight of endless flattened terrain. The Panzers rushed forward, heading straight into the Sidewinders' gunfire. As they fiercely stormed towards their immense opponents, the Panzers were shot like fish in a barrel. They ran the gauntlet, knowing that they only needed to get close enough to deploy their weapons — weapons that General Gottlieb had specially commissioned. The Panzers had a far greater top speed than the Allied capital battlemachines, and even though they were slowed down as their metallic limbs sloshed through the marsh, they quickly closed within striking distance of the Sidewinders. The lighter and faster Leopards and basic Panzers led the attack. They carried one WinderFaust each, which was a giant shaped-charge that worked in much the same way as the Kolibris' smaller, shoulder-launched Faust missile. The WinderFaust was intended to kill the people inside the armored machines and, thus, disable the vehicle.

Nearing within three hundred yards of the Allied capital vessels, the Panzers deployed the WinderFausts, ejecting the conical projectile into a high, forward arc. The heavy, half-ton shaped-charges fell at a steep angle and, when they struck part of a Sidewinder, the charges collapsed and funneled their explosive energy into the interior. The enormous pressure generated within the stricken Sidewinder compartments eviscerated the crewmen and blew off the armored walls of the compartments. Some of the segments struck by the WinderFaust looked, for the most part, completely intact. Only a bit of smoke trickled out of the punctures, suggesting the horrors inflicted upon the crew inside.

Each time a Sidewinder was struck, dozens of crewmen died within. Some of the WinderFausts hit just the right spot, such as a munitions hold. When this happened, an explosion more powerful than a MOAB thermobaric bomb blew the Sidewinder in two and knocked down anything nearby. This was not only devastating, but also served to terrify the crews of nearby Sidewinders, who never imagined that one measly Panzer could demolish a thirty meter span of an Allied moving fortress. Their sense of superiority shattered in a moment. Such lucky hits from the WinderFaust were likewise dangerous to any Panzer that drifted too close to the blast. So, the Panzer commanders had to coordinate intensely disciplined strikes, launching their Fausts and immediately rushing away.

The Sidewinder commanders countered with one of their deadliest tactics; albeit, a tactic as basic as smashing a club over the enemy's head. They drove their machines forward and over their opponents, just as they had done to the landscape. The Sidewinders imitated the snake they were named after. Traveling in a sideways slither, a charging Sidewinder could flatten everything in its way like a giant steamroller. And their charge was deceptively fast. They could move up to sixty kilometers per hour in this peculiar, broadside manner, which caught many of the Panzer commanders off guard.

Dozens of Apex quadruped battlemachines were flattened by the charging Sidewinders. Remarkably, many of the Panzers survived a steamroll attack, because they were pushed down into the soft, moist soil. They quickly burst free from the mud and uprighted themselves for battle once more.

The Allied forces had struck a hard blow to the Apex. In a few minutes of confrontational battle, the Sidewinders had destroyed nearly half of this Apex Panzer force. But, five Sidewinders had been completely demolished and five strained to function through their wounds, with a vastly diminished capacity to maneuver, fire and fight. Another fifteen Sidewinders had been damaged, but were still mostly functional. The mighty WinderFausts had done their job well. What was worse for the Sidewinders was that most of the heavily-armored Tigers were still standing, and they were designed from the ground-up to kill the serpentine titans.

The Tigers pounced up high upon the Allied moving fortresses, digging their powerful, steel claws into the exterior walls of the Sidewinders to hold on. This position gave them a tactical advantage. The Sidewinders could not point their biggest artillery guns back at themselves. The large guns could not angle enough to target something right on top of them, and even if they could, it would have been too dangerous to aim so close to their own armor.

However, there were hundreds of ball turret guns lining the length of the Sidewinders, strung side by side like a pearl necklace. Each ball turret had two, thirty millimeter machine guns, which fired uranium penetrators that could pierce the Tigers' armor.

As they clung to their victims, the Tigers went about swatting at the ball turrets near them with their huge, catlike paws. Having secured their vicinity, the powerful Apex quadrupeds deployed their drill bolt cannons. Though not as powerful as those mounted on the Delfins, the lasers at the head of the Tigers could slice thinly through one side of the Sidewinders' armor. They could then literally crawl along and slowly but surely cut a piece of a Sidewinder off from the rest of its length, like a giant can-opener.

Even though the Sidewinders could function as separate parts, they lost much of their agility. When they were split apart, they were also completely exposed at the sides where the tears occurred. The Apex quadrupeds swiftly leapt inside the openings and wreaked havoc on the interior, slicing the terrified crewmen to ribbons. Sated with their butchery, the Panzers planted timed bombs near artillery shells and jumped off, rushing away at top speed. Seconds later, the explosions finished off the broken Allied battlemachines.

Doing their best to stave off the Tigers, the Sidewinders' ball turret gunners never let their fingers off the trigger. They fought heroically and many of their bullets permeated into Tiger armor and grotesquely slaughtered the Apex tamers inside, blowing their heads and limbs off with large-caliber rounds. However, the Sidewinders, which had all taken wounds and wasted much of their ammunition during their surprising battle with the Delfins, were now being destroyed at a slightly faster rate than the Apex quadrupeds.

Allied High Command concluded that the one hundred Sidewinders they were sending as reinforcements would never make it in time to hold the beachhead. Of the fifty Sidewinders initially sent to defend the shoreline, only seventeen still remained at full battle-functionality and a third wave of Apex troopers and hundreds of additional Panzers were flooding the beachhead.

Again, the Allies were left without a choice. They pulled back the front defensive line to a stretch between where the Neuse River met its estuary, and where the Roanoke River met the Albemarle Sound, about thirty-five to fifty kilometers away from the shore. From this distance, most of the Sidewinders' munitions could not reach all the way to the beachhead. But, the Allied forces had some other tricks up their sleeves

Allied High Command decided to let the Apex ground forces concentrate on the peninsular land regions that went into the sound. Then, the Allies would bombard the landing and invasion forces with everything they had, including nuclear warheads.

Apex High Command was aware that such an attack was not only plausible, but probable. They had eliminated most of the large missile silos within the vicinity and missiles coming from farther away could be easily intercepted by an Apex anti-missile system. However, the Sidewinders also carried nuclear weapons, not as large as those coming from the silos, but certainly large enough to do serious damage. The Apex ground forces took all the precautions they could, including building a vast amount of rapid-drying, cement-walled trenches. The Panzer vehicles could dig in the same manner as dogs, with their forepaws, which speedily created deep channels in the ground

The Apex forces were posted up in the new trenches, preparing for the breakout. The troops had dispersed over the entire secured peninsular area, but it was still quite cramped as over two million storm troopers, nearly five hundred Panzer vehicles and one thousand track or hovercraft transports, hunkered down in the relatively small amount of space. As hard and fast as they worked at it, there was only so much the Apex invasion forces could do to fortify themselves from a nuclear bombardment. After quickly helping to build the trenches, the Panzers rushed forth to see if they could destroy or at least push farther back the Sidewinder line.

Gathered and debriefed, the Allied Naval Forces set out to crush the Apex Delfins guarding the North Carolinian breach area. But, the Delfins did not engage the fully mustered Shark Armada, and instead retreated east towards safety. The Sharks did not give chase. They filtered into Pamlico Sound and began a devastating bombardment on the Apex ground forces.

At the same time, one hundred Sidewinders finally arrived to reinforce the holdouts at the pulled-back line. Each moving fortress was equipped with four missiles that had half-megaton nuclear warheads, giving each missile the equivalent energy yield of a half-million tons of TNT. Altogether, the more than one hundred Sidewinders had enough nuclear artillery to completely destroy the nearly one thousand square kilometers of land that jutted out into Pamlico Sound . . . and destroy it they would.

Locked and loaded, the Sidewinders fired their missiles, aimed to strike everywhere from the beachhead to the Apex front line, timed so that the nuclear warheads would detonate simultaneously.

A brilliant light engulfed the entirety of the peninsular regions in the sound. Powerful gamma radiation and other deadly rays scorched everything they illuminated. Any vegetation or animal life that had survived the battles up until now, were steamed and smoked as they cooked from the outside and inside. Most of the Apex soldiers were in bunkers, vehicles or trenches, all protected with some form of radiation shielding. Even the troops who were not in any form of shelter had radiation shielding in their suits. But suits, makeshift trenches and even armored vehicles could not protect the Apex ground forces from what followed.

The light was immediately chased by tremendous pressure waves. The collective force of the blasts knocked the Earth momentarily off its axis and shortened that day by a few seconds. Such large scale nuclear bombardment had never been seen. The pressure waves were devastating; largely because of the strange way they were interacting at such close range. Like a storm of waves in the ocean, crashing together to form endless whitewater, the blast waves were distorted and, instead of just knocking things down, they crashed around, pummeling and tearing apart everything in their way.

Apex troops and vehicles that were above ground were hit from all sides and ripped into minute pieces. Most of the hundreds of thousands of troops hiding inside the makeshift bunkers and trenches were buried alive as their hasty fortifications crumbled, being no match for the shearing forces.

Altogether, over half a million invasion troops were killed or critically wounded in the nuclear attack. Those who were not burnt by the radiation, or swept away by the blast waves, were consumed by the tremendous fireball of super-heated gas that was the final phase of the explosion. Seventy percent of the Panzer forces in the area were destroyed. This was the major blow to the Apex that the Allies had been looking to strike the entire time, and they were not about to lose momentum.

The Shark Armada, almost nine hundred strong, packed themselves tightly into Pamlico Sound, near the shores of the mainland. They opened up with a tremendous salvo, firing tens of thousands of varied shells and artillery missiles. The Sidewinders opened up from the west and charged east, steam-rolling over their bedraggled opponent.

For a fleeting moment, it looked as though the Allied forces might actually stall out the Apex landing and, thus, the entire invasion. But, once again, the hearts of the Allied leaders sank into their stomachs as they realized they had been tricked by another Apex deception.

From the intelligence gathered through espionage and surveillance, the Allies knew that their enemy had only fifteen hundred Condor magneto-thrust planes. The Allies had kept close track of these incredibly fast bombers, which carried so much destructive power. No matter what it took, they maneuvered planes overhead to survey the Condors being towed across the Atlantic. Allied High Command was confident that they had a good source inside the Apex concerning the planes, so they were sure they knew where the refueling of the planes would occur.

The Allies were led to believe that the Condors could only refuel with plasma at dry-dock stations, which were located in occupied Western Europe. It would take more than a day for the Condors to be towed back, refueled and made ready to attack North America again.

Allied High Command had received this information from a supposed double agent working in Germanian Intelligence and he was their best source for filtering information to the Allies. However, the double agent was, in fact, a triple agent. He had pretended to double-cross his agency, but he had always been working for Germania.

The truth was that the Condor magneto-thrust bombers were capable of refueling and rearming at sea. As they were pretending to be towed home by Delfins, the Condors were being filled up with plasma material and bombs, which could not be seen by the Allied surveillance planes.

Alas, the Condors were already armed and fueled up by the time they were just past the Atlantic Ridge. Waiting for a moment when there were no Allied surveillance planes in sight, the Condors cut their towing lines and turned around. Squadron by squadron, they took off from the sea, their special jet boosters lifting them off the ocean surface.

Thinking they had hours before the mighty Apex bombers were overhead, the Sidewinder and Shark commanders kept their battlemachines in the Pamlico Sound region, out in the open, continuing their relentless pummeling of the enemy's landing forces. The Allied moving fortresses had crushed endless Panzers and storm troopers and were approaching the beachhead again, the territory they had lost only an hour earlier. The Sharks battered the Apex ground forces that were being pushed back toward the shore.

A surge of joy ran through the ranks of the defenders at the front. They felt sure that they were winning the battle and, possibly, the war. They remembered everything they were fighting for: their families who had moved across the world, those who had perished, and those who would perish if the Apex was victorious.

The stakes were extremely high. Only a soldier who has experienced such a battle could understand the wonderful feelings of relief and euphoria that flood the soul when victory is in sight . . .

And only a soldier in such a battle could truly know the physical revulsion that smacked them in their guts and spines, when the battle turned and victory was snatched away . . .

Suddenly, Allied radar stations picked up the incoming Condor force only a few minutes away from the breach. In stunned disbelief, the Sidewinder commanders rushed their machines away from the beachhead, attempting to scatter as much as possible. The Shark fleet in the Pamlico Sound began a chaotic retreat back into the Atlantic, for they were also incredibly vulnerable, cramped in such a small space.

The first wave of Condors was five hundred strong. Half of the bomber force carried torpedo bombs — smart bombs designed for the water. They could rapidly find a mark by tracking heat generated by the synthetic muscles that powered the Sharks' swishing tails. As the Condors flew over Pamlico Sound, they dropped a thousand two-ton torpedo bombs.

There were still hundreds of Sharks in the sound, many trying to filter out of the thin outlets. However, this only further endangered them. The guided bombs came down upon them as they were schooled together, striking their marks with devastating effectiveness. Many of the Allied naval battlemachines had crippling holes blown into their hulls, or their munitions exploded, blowing them into multiple pieces and leaving no hope for the crew's survival.

Even when the Condor bombs missed the Allied vessels, the explosions rocked the sea around the Sharks. The shock waves in the water pounded the naval machines from every direction, twisting their frames and even wrenching them apart. Huge shrapnel bits the size of cannon balls launched from the torpedo bombs and pierced through the Sharks' armor from fifty yards away. Crews inside were ravaged by the gigantic shrapnel.

Half of the Condor bombers had dropped their payloads and, making a sudden arc to the side and up, they turned back towards home. The other half continued on over the front and, within seconds, were upon the retreating Sidewinders. These Condors held a wider array of munitions, such as guided quarter-ton bombs that, while they did little damage on their own, were specifically designed to blow up the explosive shells within the Sidewinders.

Smart munitions, which guided themselves through the air, could not work properly at such incredible speeds as Mach 13. So to aid maneuverability, the guided bombs falling from the Condors had a mechanism to slow themselves down to ten thousand kilometers per hour. The speed of their impact was nonetheless incredible, along with the detonation of their warheads. The two-ton bombs cut straight through the snake-like battlemachines. A number of the smaller bombs found a Sidewinder's shell hold, destroying them with their own munitions.

All that Allied High Command could do was cut their losses and hope to save enough military power to fight another day. They ordered the badly mauled Sidewinders and Sharks into full retreat. In doing this, though, the Allies realized that they were allowing the Apex to gain a secure foothold in Fortress North America.

Day crept into night, as wave after wave of Apex transport crafts brought in storm troopers, Hoplites, Panzers and Kolibri. The invasion forces also brought a substantial workforce of military engineers, who worked quickly under the cover of darkness, building far more solid trenches, bunkers, air-bases and everything else the Apex expeditionary forces needed.

The situation was traumatizing for the Allied leadership. They knew that the Apex military was at its most vulnerable during the invasion, much like the Allies were in the World War II Normandy invasion. The renowned German Field Marshal, Erwin Rommel, was aware of the fact that the Second World War would be won or lost on D-Day. Before the invasion, he was quoted as saying that it would be the longest day . . .

The successful landings in Normandy spelled the end for Nazi Germany. Although the Germans fiercely resisted the Allied forces for almost another year, many military leaders on either side felt that the war was already over at that French beachhead.

Now, World War III had seen its D-Day. Undoubtedly, the Allies would continue to fight, as the Nazi Germans had a century before. But, the longest day was over . . . and it had gone to the Apex.

— XVII —

THE LUNAR MARRIAGE

The Luftzug began its final descent. Alistair, Logan and Francesca walked over to the windows and looked out as they cruised over the peaks of high mountains that cut through the top of the clouds. Flying down the other side parallel with the slope, the Luftzug submerged into the puffy, gray and white clouds. Nothing could be seen outside for a few seconds. Finally, the air transport pierced through the low-hovering, dense layer of mist and everyone inside was able to see the ground.

Below, there was a green jungle that stretched from horizon to horizon in all directions. The Luftzug was no longer flying over the thin isthmus of land that was Panama. It lowered through the shallow-hovering clouds and the unique beauty of the rainforest could be seen clearly.

Flying just above the jungle, there were ever more colors emerging to the eye. Logan gazed upon the many brilliant blooms of pink, white, yellow, purple, orange and blue. Above the treetops, there appeared to be large billows of flower petals scattered through the air by wind. But, in fact, these were gorgeous birds with dazzling, multi-colored jackets.

A man's voice came over the Luftzug's intercom system. He spoke English with a Jamaican accent, in a calm, cordial and jovial manner.

"Hello, I am Jeffrey, your lead steward. I would like to inform you that we are now entering Costa Rica, one of the most beautiful places in the world for the naturalist experience."

The man's voice was so warm, one could almost see his smiling face from just hearing him speak. "Costa Rica is located in the tropical zones of the American continent, also known as the Neotropics. These areas contain a greater diversity of species and ecosystems, as well as a broader range of interactions, than other tropical regions of the world. Obviously, this diversity is also much greater than that of temperate and cold regions.

"This is due to a number of factors," Jeffrey explained, "the most prominent being that the location between North and South America allows living beings from both continents to establish themselves here. The Costa Rican government has also been environmentally conscious for many decades and, so, they preserved more of their land than any other country. Costa Rica has long been home to a rich variety of plants and animals. While the country has less than one-thousandth of the world's land mass, it contains five percent of the world's biodiversity. The government of Costa Rica had no military or navy, but it was said that the leaf cutter ants are the soldiers, the pilots are the macaws and the whales are the navy ships."

Jeffrey's spiel paused momentarily, and they could hear the sound of him covering his microphone with a hand, as he said something muffled to the pilot. As he came back over the speakers, the train slowed a bit.

"If you look out the windows," Jeffrey directed, "you will see Great Scarlet Macaws."

Francesca excitedly slapped Logan's chest with the back of her hand and pointed out the window at the tropical birds perched in the trees.

"What magnificent creatures these birds are!" Jeffrey exclaimed. "Macaws are the largest of the Neotropical parrots. They have no protective coloration. They do not creep about trying to blend in with the countryside. With their long, trailing tail feathers and short wings, they are impossible to confuse with other birds. They are gregarious and rarely seen alone. And like people," Jeffrey paused, and then laughed, "well, like *some* people, they are monogamous for life, and couples are often found sitting side by side, grooming and preening each other, and conversing in rasping loving tones, or flying two by two.

"At the turn of the millennium," he continued in a more serious tone, "the scarlet Macaw population was in danger of disappearing completely, because of deforestation and poaching. But, the Costa Rican government took the necessary measures to ensure that this wonderful bird was saved from extinction."

Again, Jeffrey's narrative paused as he instructed the pilot to fly low over the trees.

"Take notice of the myriad of blossoms displaying their colors in the tree canopy. Most of these are not part of the tree, but are the epiphytes, which are plants that live in the misty upper tiers of tree branches in order to reach the sunlight. This area is known as the cloud forest." Jeffrey allowed some time for the passengers to admire the landscape below. "The epiphytes in the cloud forest are specially adapted to absorb moisture directly from the mist, and they feed off the dust that accumulates around their roots. Many of the blooms you see below are Costa Rica's famous orchids," he elaborated proudly.

"The epiphytes, treetops and vines provide a home for many small animals and insects that live their whole lives in the canopy, never touching the ground. Because of this, the cloud forests comprise some of the world's most complex ecosystems."

As the airtrain flew low over the treetops, Logan squinted and concentrated, trying to spot a monkey or some other strange creature. But the foliage was too thick to catch a glimpse of anything that took refuge in its shade.

"We are presently over the Limon province," Jeffrey continued, "which encompasses Costa Rica's entire two hundred kilometer Caribbean coastline. Limón conjures up images of the coconut-fringed Caribbean beach. It is a wild region with pounding surf and prehistoric jungles, where the inland rainforests converge with the white sandy beaches. Though rain falls periodically year long, it is almost always warm here." Jeffrey momentarily halted once more, as the pilot spoke to him. "Now, if you are not already sitting, I'd advise doing so now," he instructed to the passengers. "We will be coming in for our landing shortly."

There were high winds prevailing in the area, but the Luftzug absorbed the turbulence by gently undulating through the sky. The passengers within felt their cars subtly rise and fall to an even rhythm. Logan remembered when he was twelve and flew from San Francisco to the island in the South Pacific where he lived for the next five years. That flight was incredibly bumpy and his mother, who already had a phobia about flying, screamed uncontrollably every time the small private jet tossed about. But now, cruising on an Apex "air-train," flying was much more tolerable for anyone who was uncomfortable in the skies.

Finally, the Luftzug came to a halt over the shores of Punta Uva, which as Jeffrey explained was considered to be one of the ten best beaches in the world. The serpentine, dragon-like transport hovered slowly down into the water alongside a dock. Logan, Francesca and Alistair rejoined Jacques, Sasha, and Logan's parents. They disembarked the Luftzug with the other passengers and walked along the dock. As they did, speakers along the walkway projected a friendly man's voice, who also spoke in a Caribbean accent similar to Jeffrey's. The man explained that the dock was made completely out of hardwoods from dead and fallen trees, as were all the buildings and bungalows of the Punta Uva resort.

"We did not cut down any trees," the man said. "Before we started building, it took several weeks' work to find, clean and cut the lumber. Some of the Nispero trees we found in the Gandoca Manzanillo Wildlife Refuge have been on the ground for more than 10 years, during which time they underwent a semi-petrifaction process. These woods are hard as iron."

The dock ended at an aesthetically simplistic building. Everyone filtered through single-file into the building. The interior reminded Logan of the lobby of a ski lodge he and his family would visit every winter when they lived in California. That lodge always gave Logan an extreme sense of comfort and security.

Much like a hotel lobby, people waited in lines in front of a long "check-in" counter, where they were helped by friendly "employees," who were in fact fellow underclassmen, clicking away at computer keyboards. Tom, Bibi and Logan arrived to the front of their line and the tops of their hands were scanned. Like everyone else, they were then personally escorted to their living quarters by a bellhop. Jacques, Francesca and Sasha were right behind them in the line, and Alistair behind them. They were all escorted along with Logan and his family out of the building and along a dirt pathway, which meandered into the jungle right on the fringe of the beachhead.

The bellhop leading Tom, Bibi and Logan turned right at a small fork in the road. Logan turned around to see where Francesca was being led. She looked at him and blew him a kiss, mouthing the words, "Don't worry." He reluctantly turned back around and followed his parents, but he was happily surprised to find out that they were already at their place.

It was a small, two-story house conceived in the Caribbean style, which favored living quarters that were in essence an integrated and unobtrusive part of their setting. There were large, covered decks on both floors. This allowed the house to always remain fully open to nature, but as the bellhop explained, the decks could be closed up quickly and efficiently, if one wished.

Inside, the house was simple and rustic in its construction and furnishings. There were some unique appliances and gadgets, to which the bellhop acquainted the family. One of the more interesting devices provided by the Apex resort was the bug vacuum. It was a hand-held, gun-like vacuum, which gently sucked up an insect into a holding container to be freed outside unharmed.

As soon as the bellhop left, Tom grabbed one of the six bottles of champagne that were already in the medium-sized refrigerator when they arrived. He poured three glasses and made a toast.

"To my beloved wife and son being alive and healthy! Thank you God for that! And thank you that I am alive, so I can be with them!"

Bibi and Logan lifted their glasses and clinked them against Tom's, which was held high.

"Amen!" They replied as they had always done when Tom made such toasts/prayers.

Logan took a quick gulp of his champagne. "You guys," he looked at his parents, "can I go find where Francesca's staying?"

Tom smiled. "Of course, just make sure you don't get lost."

"And please check in with us in a couple hours or so," Bibi chimed in, "okay?"

Logan kissed his mom on the cheek. "Okay!" He slapped his dad five and Tom pulled him in for a quick hug.

Logan ran out the door and followed the path where he last saw Francesca vanishing down. He did not have to go far. She, her father and Sasha were staying in the house right around the corner. She was just walking out the door when she saw Logan going by, glancing left and right, trying to figure out where to go.

"Hey!" She ran over and jumped up on him, arms around his neck, kicking her feet up to her bottom. He powerfully lifted her and twirled her around. She was pleased by how easily he could heft her up and hold her. She was not at all overweight, but she was voluptuous and relatively tall for a girl.

"Let's go find Alistair," she said, giving him a kiss on the forehead. "The guy who helped us said anyone who is traveling alone will be staying right down the path in the bungalows."

"Cool!" Logan replied. As they walked away, Francesca wrapped her right arm around Logan's left elbow.

They located Alistair within a few minutes. He was standing on his porch, easy to spot, smoking a cigarette of some kind. As she neared, it became obvious to Francesca that he was smoking marijuana. She laughed with excitement and pulled Logan along faster. Logan did not know what Alistair was smoking, for he had never tried or seen marijuana before. However, he did recognize the smell. He would catch a whiff of it every once in a while on the island, especially when he happened to pass by the Winfield's house at night. They were a radically liberal family who were often adorned in tie-dye outfits.

Francesca did not even greet Alistair. She just leapt up onto his porch, skipping the steps, and took the joint from his lips, placing it between hers. She closed her eyes as she took a long, measured inhalation. When they reopened, Logan could actually see her body language change. Her generally frenetic energy was replaced with a relaxed demeanor. Her pupils were immediately dilated and, moment's later, her brilliant green eyes became slightly glossed over. However, this made them even shinier and their cat-like mystique was enhanced, as she appeared to be peering into a foreign and magical world.

She took a second inhalation off the joint and leaned over to Logan, wrapping her arm around his neck and pulling his face to hers. She placed her lips gently against his and exhaled the smoke as Logan inhaled, taking it in along with her essence. Though laced with the pine scent of the marijuana, her breath was sweet as honey and imbued with the natural perfume of her body's feminine vitality.

The trio walked around the beach, endlessly talking nonsense, which seemed ingenious at the time. Soon, though he did not have a watch, Logan figured that at least a couple hours had passed. He had to check in with his parents . . . but he could barely speak without giggling or stuttering, which would make Francesca crack up, and then they would laugh harder and harder, until Francesca admitted to feeling light-headed and had to sit down for a breather. Alistair was a little more under control. So, he accompanied Logan to check-in with Tom and Bibi.

Fortunately, Alistair had also been provided two pairs of sunglasses in his room, along with the marijuana. At least this helped to cover his and Logan's bloodshot eyes. However, they were doubly fortunate when they arrived to find Tom and Bibi drunk on the second-floor deck of the house. Being that it was so hot and humid, Tom had taken off all his clothes except his beige boxer shorts. Bibi was wearing a tan bikini that she found in the dresser inside and was leaning in Tom's left arm, while he had it draped around her, caressing her thighs.

At first, they did not see Logan and Alistair, for they were caught up by the sight of the sunset on the horizon.

"Dude!" Alistair whispered. "Your mom's hot!"

Logan looked incredulously at his friend, his mouth agape, not knowing what to say and feeling quite indignant for a moment. But, suddenly, he couldn't help but start laughing and Alistair began laughing with him. Tom and Bibi looked over at them.

"What's so funny?" Tom slurred and smiled through his inebriation. Bibi blushed slightly with embarrassment.

"Were you laughing at us?" she asked, slurring her words as well.

"No, no, no," Alistair replied, waving his hand in emphasis. "Francesca did something really funny earlier."

"Yeah!" Logan added, trying to stifle his giggles.

"Well," Tom said, "you guys sound like you're having fun." He could not stop smiling and he looked once again out at the beautiful view. "Isn't this great!"

Logan walked over to the rail and leaned on it, gripping it with his hands. He stared at the awesome splendor of nature, the vibrant colors of the jungle heightened by a dramatic sunset. He took in a long, deep breath of the fresh air. "Yeah," he remarked stoically. "It's such a different jungle than the one on the island. I thought it was beautiful there, but it's nothing compared to this."

Alistair noticed that Tom had small hand impressions that showed red on his chest, along with lightly scratched claw marks from a woman's fingernails — an obvious sign that the two were becoming intimate before their son and his friend arrived.

"Okay!" Alistair said, smirking at Tom and Bibi. "So Logan, there's a movie theatre here."

Logan, Tom and Bibi all looked at him with surprise. "Really?" Tom asked.

"Yep!" Alistair nodded. "I don't know what the hell they show, but I saw it on the television in my room on the main menu. So," he looked to Logan, "I thought we'd go check it out, with Francesca."

"Right on!" Logan exclaimed with enthusiasm "Alright guys," he said, walking over to his parents and giving them both a hug and his mother a kiss. "Is that cool?"

"Of course," Tom replied warmly.

"Stay out of the ocean," Bibi added a bit more soberly. "I was reading that they let the predators in from three to five in the morning and afternoon."

Logan nodded. "Yeah, there's a bunch of signs on the beach saying that."

"Okay," Bibi said, with a subtly worried expression. "But it would ease my mind if you just stayed out altogether, because you never know if they'll make a mistake."

Logan nodded again and smiled. "Okay," he assured her. "You know me. I never really liked going in the ocean anyway. I've always been afraid of sharks."

Logan and Alistair joined back up with Francesca and they all walked to the theatre, which was beyond the bungalow units. On the way there, Alistair lit up another joint and they smoked half of it, before he put it out to save the rest for later.

The theatre building was like all of the architecture in the resort: rustic and made of dead hardwood trees. In contrast though, there were two large signs on the front of the theatre that lit up and displayed the titles and times of the movies playing. They did not display the time in terms of what hour in the day it was. Rather, they had countdown timers next to the titles to show how long until they began. There were only three full-size theatres and no smaller ones. In their altered state, it took a while for Alistair, Logan and Francesca to read the titles and comprehend what exactly they were. Alistair remembered one of the movies.

"*Barbarossa*," he read slowly. "I saw the play version of that."

Francesca's memory was jump-started again. "Oh," she remarked, struck with an epiphany, "these are all Ray Cutlass Productions."

"Yep," Alistair nodded.

Logan knew that name. In fact, Ray Cutlass was a friend of his father. Tom worked with him back when Logan was only five. Though it was some time ago, Logan still had a vague recollection of the man.

"I met him," he said, somewhat nonchalantly.

Alistair and Francesca looked at Logan in disbelief. Alistair was particularly taken aback.

"How?"

Logan shrugged. "My dad worked on a movie with him a long time ago."

"Oh yeah," Francesca looked to Alistair, "remember, I told you Tom was a big movie producer. He produced *The Ark!*"

Alistair recalled the conversation. "That's right! Wow," he remarked contemplatively. "That's pretty interesting. Do you know *who* Ray Cutlass *is?*"

Logan shook his head. "Not really."

"Ray Cutlass," Alistair explained, "is among Geiseric's closest circle of friends."

Logan was astonished. "Really?!"

"Really," Francesca replied, nodding. Suddenly, a bell rang and one of the movie titles began to blink to indicate it was about to begin. The countdown clock next to it was at five minutes. Alistair pointed to the title, called *Parsifal*.

"Let's go see that."

Inside the theatre building, they first encountered a lobby that was quite different than the exterior. It was bright and cheery inside, packed with people, like the average movie theatre that Alistair, Logan, or Francesca had experienced. There was an arcade room and snack counter, and an overwhelming din that was comforting.

The trio rushed to the snack counter and each ordered popcorn, some form of chocolate, and an ambrosia smoothie. They found their theatre and entered right as the movie was starting. Most of the seats were filled, but they managed to find three next to each other in the front-middle portion of the theatre. The screen was twenty meters-wide and Logan noticed that the visual quality of the film was pristine. Such things he had learned to look for when viewing movies in his father's home cinema in California. It was in that home cinema that Logan screened *The Ark* for the first time, with his father to his right and Ray Cutlass on Tom's other side. He could recall Cutlass's angular features, his sharp nose and chin, which showed through even more prominently in profile. Logan could not believe that, in being near this man, he was only one degree separated from Geiseric himself.

Francesca wolfed down her German chocolate bar, devouring it in a few minutes.

"That was so good," she whispered with a satiated voice. Logan wrapped his arm around her and shared his vanilla ice cream sandwich that was made of soft, rich chocolate graham crackers. Francesca ended up having most of it.

"Umm," she moaned happily.

"Shh!" a lady shushed behind them. Francesca turned around and raised a chocolate covered middle finger to the lady, who made an indignant expression. Francesca chuckled and turned back around, lying in Logan's arm as she wiped her hands with the napkins.

Meanwhile, Alistair began to take notice of the buxom young lady sitting by him, opposite of Francesca. He couldn't help but notice her, considering she continuously ate out of his popcorn container. As she did, she cast furtive glances at him, smiling flirtatiously. She reached unnecessarily deep into the container, which was placed on his lap. Alistair wrapped his left arm around her and gladly shared his popcorn.

The rest of the movie was a pleasant blur for Alistair and his new friend, along with Logan and Francesca. Between whispering sweet-nothings in each others' ears and kissing, the two couples caught little of the plot of the movie, which was inspired by a Wagnerian opera and set during World War II. Logan was the most engaged, being very impressed with the cinematography and soundtrack, much of which was the music of the nineteenth century German composer, Richard Wagner. Alistair ended up leaving early with the young lady.

A three-quarter moon illuminated the beach that night, as Logan and Francesca walked together, her lean yet soft physique pressed in his arm against his side. A powerful warmth emanated from where they touched. Logan kissed her ear.

"You know why a girl is supposed to be held under a man's *left* arm?"

"Why?" she asked, her cheeks turning pink.

"Well," he smiled, "so that she can be close to his heart."

"*Aww,*" she purred. Her cheeks flushed and Logan noticed that the delicate capillaries in her eyelids turned a bluish-purple and expanded, giving the appearance of eye shadow. It was as if she had just adorned her face with make-up, but it was all completely natural. She was captivating and Logan did not want to remove his gaze from her, but he felt strange staring at her, so he looked up to the sky for a moment.

"I've never seen so many stars before," he remarked.

"I know. It's amazing. There's so much out there besides us." Francesca commented, looking at Logan. "As big as our problems are to us, they're small compared to the infinite cosmos."

Logan fixed his eyes back on Francesca. Her astute manner made her even more attractive to him.

"What is it?" She asked.

"I don't know. I'm taking it all in."

She smirked and turned her gaze skywards. "Our egos are limited," she observed. "They fight anything that's humbling. Becoming one with the infinite is heaven."

"You have an amazing way of saying things," he remarked.

"Thank you," she replied, smiling sweetly.

"So, how did you get so smart?"

"Hah, I don't know," laughed Francesca. Then, she became more solemn.

"My mom's death and the war helped me understand how fragile life is and how lucky we are to be alive. It put me back into the moment." She closed her eyes, remembering the not-so-distant past, and then blinked and looked back up.

Logan nodded, not knowing exactly what to say. "I'll bet," was all that came out.

Francesca turned around and leaned the back of her body against the front of Logan's, helping to wrap his arms around her torso. He held her in a strong embrace, gently swaying back and forth to console her. They both looked up at the sky, with the great luminescent orb suspended in the blackness along with the infinite amount of twinkling stars.

"The Moon looks surreal tonight," Logan remarked, taking a long deep breath of the refreshing air. Francesca sighed with the contentment of being in his grasp on such a beautiful beach with a warm and clear night.

"You know," she said, "without the Moon, Earth would wobble uncontrollably on its axis. The climate would be completely out of control. The Moon makes our world livable. Without her, life is impossible. She's like a lover who keeps her man stable and, together, they produce life," she glanced back at him with a flirtatious eye.

"How do you know all that?" Logan asked, laughing gently at Francesca's sexy innuendo.

"We were forced to learn a lot, while living in Allied North America," she replied, shrugging. "We were forced to go to school, no matter how old you were. And we learned all sorts of neat things. First of all, everyone was forced to learn English, if they didn't already speak it, like me. I think astronomy was my favorite."

"You know," he smiled, "I can honestly say that I love you for your mind."

Francesca smiled back and turned to face him, pressing the front of her body against his.

"I hope that's not all you love me for."

"Oh, not at all," Logan replied breathlessly, reveling in the warm chills produced inside of him. His voice mildly deepened without affectation, caused by the joy and confidence welling up. "Not . . . at . . . all."

She leaned in, subtly and slowly, toward his lips. Logan's body kicked into auto-pilot. He reached around her thin waist, under her arms, pulling her firmly but gently, pressing her chest against his, and lifting her slightly off her heels. She succumbed gratefully to his kiss. He released her slowly and she opened her eyes, drowsy with endorphins rushing through her bloodstream.

"You're a real good kisser," she said, her voice laced with yearning.

Without speaking a word, they rolled into the sand, removed their one-piece tunics, and made love with the warm tide kissing them every so often, causing their bodies to tingle even more. Logan had never felt so good in his life. The euphoria was heavenly. They moved as one and each knew their time to lead as naturally as night turned to day. When it was over, they stared up at the sky, their naked bodies hidden by bushes that surrounded the spot of beach where they had chosen to lie. No one passed by or saw them, not that the couple would have noticed anyway, they were so immersed in each other.

They lied on their backs, her head on his left shoulder, their hearts pumping in unison, with a strong, even pace.

"So," Logan said, his voice exuding serenity, "you *were* a virgin."

"Um hmm," Francesca answered, smirking and blushing slightly.

Logan just breathed in deeply, satiated beyond his own imagination.

Francesca checked in with Jacques and then spent the night with Logan in his bed. She snuck by Tom and Bibi by deftly climbing the tree outside of their house, declining Logan's offer of help, once again impressing him with her athletic prowess. He said good night to his parents, who had been fighting sleep until he got home. As soon as their son came in, they went upstairs and passed out in their bed.

Logan went up to his room, where he found a beautiful young lady in his bed. They kissed and cuddled all night, going no further, for they needed nothing more. Their intimacy was peaking by simply gazing into each other's eyes and petting each other's hair or arms.

They awoke to the sounds of howler monkeys, exotic songs of rainforest birds, and the sound of the rolling waves of the sea just a few yards away from the house. Francesca crept out of his second floor window and descended the nearby tree as quickly as she had ascended it the night before. She walked the path back to her house to get cleaned up.

Logan found his parents sitting on the upper terrace, having their morning coffee, absorbing the breathtaking view of the turquoise sea and emerald jungle. Radiant blue Morpho butterflies and dashing hummingbirds visited the trees and foliage, providing a whimsical spectacle.

Logan's face was adorned with an uncontrollably large smile, as he walked out onto the terrace.

"Hey guys," he said, stretching. Tom and Bibi turned and it was apparent that they were in a very pleasant mood as well.

"Hey pal!" Tom greeted his son, full of spirit. Bibi reached her arm out for a hug.

"Hey sweetie," she said. Logan walked over and gave her a big hug. Tom noticed a strange, silvery primate on the tree branch hanging near the terrace. It was about a meter tall, with a flat head, a snub nose, and large eyes.

"Look!" He whispered enthusiastically. "That's the two-toed sloth we were reading about in the pamphlet."

They examined the bizarre creature, which moved at an unbelievably slow and measured rate. Tom shook his head in amazement.

"It's like watching a nature film in slow motion."

Just then, they were slightly startled by someone knocking on the front door of the house. Logan ran down to answer it, expecting Francesca. He opened the door and was surprised to see Alistair standing there carrying a backpack on his shoulders.

"What's up!"

"Come on in, dude," Logan replied, standing to the side to let his friend walk in.

"Actually," Alistair said, "I got some plans for you today. Can you take off?"

Logan nodded. "Yeah, let me go tell my parents."

On the way to their destination, they walked past Francesca's house. Logan was anxious to see her, though it had only been a few minutes since he last did.

"Let's wait for Francesca," he said, beginning to divert toward her dwelling. Alistair grabbed his shoulder and kept him on the path.

"Don't trip, mate," Alistair laughed at the young man's earnestness to see his crush. "I saw her when I was on the way to your place. I told her to meet up with us later at my pad. So, what was she doing coming from your house so early anyway? You guys have breakfast together or something?" Alistair feigned naiveté.

Logan chuckled but quickly changed the subject. "So, what are these mystery plans?"

Alistair hooked his arm around Logan's neck in the style of an older brother about to share good news. "Today, you begin your training."

He told Logan to hold his questions for the time being. They walked into the forest about a hundred meters, which felt like much longer because of the dense vegetation they had to move through. Finally, they came to a clearing, where Alistair had already left two thin branches. Cleaned of any smaller appendages and leaves, the branches resembled fencing swords, and that was exactly what they were to be used as.

When they were back at the first detainment facility in South America, Logan had mentioned to Alistair that he had been trained in the martial art of fencing and other types of sword-fighting, such as with the samurai's katana. Alistair took one of the sticks and used it to flip the other up out of the sand toward Logan, who deftly caught the twirling stick and took up the *engarde*, or on-guard position.

"Very good," Alistair remarked, taking the same stance, his feet placed shoulder-width apart at right-angles to each other, knees slightly bent to allow mobility. They both placed their right feet in front, pointed forward, their left feet facing out perpendicularly. Posturing themselves in this way made their bodies' target areas less open to attack. Alistair went about expounding upon the sport he was teaching, while he tested Logan's skill.

"Fighting with swords and other bladed weapons has a face-to-face, man versus opponent quality that nothing else can match. It embodies the essence of the fight," he said, faking a shot. Logan quickly retreated back a few steps.

"Unlike guns," Alistair continued. "Guns are the layman's weapons. Or, more accurately, the *lame*-man's weapons. Guns are for brutes," he said, his speech once again projecting a heavily British inflection. "Anyone can pull a trigger. Sure, it takes some skill to be accurate and the quickest draw, but nothing compares to the skill it takes to be an expert swordsman. Why?" Alistair asked rhetorically, pointing his finger up and smiling like a professor excited about his lecture.

"Because it can be instantly deadly like a gunfight, yet like hand-to-hand combat, fighting with swords involves true physical exertion. It involves moving through time and space!"

He lunged forward and thrust the stick at Logan's abdomen. Logan parried the stab away with his stick. Alistair struck quickly twice more, but Logan was able to block both attacks. Alistair's eyebrows shot up. He nodded his head, impressed with Logan's reflexes.

"Very good! You see, sword-fighting entails everything necessary to be a great warrior. That's why the Apex had such an advantage in battle."

"What do you mean?" Logan asked, keeping the mock-sword up in the fighting position.

"The Apex Formula training system focused on fighting with bladed weapons and a dozen other types of martial arts. Whereas, the Allies mainly focused on teaching their soldiers and officers how to use guns." Alistair engaged Logan in several overhand and underhand clashes, the wood pieces projecting a hollow sound when they hit together.

"The Allied leadership thought it was pointless to learn all the different methods of fighting in warfare," Alistair explained, his breathing only slightly heavier, though he had been carrying on a conversation while moving around so quickly. "But that was stupid for a number of reasons. The Allies never fully understood the Formula. They never got the fact that when you learn one thing it helps you accomplish something completely different."

Alistair stopped to take a breath, poking the end of his stick into the soft ground, and leaning on it slightly for support. "If you learn piano, you'll be a better fighter. If you learn math, you'll be a better fighter. If you learn anything, you can be better at everything. That's just the way the brain works. It's strange that way."

"The thing is," he plucked his stick back out of the ground, "even the Apex leadership didn't predict swords being used en masse like they were."

"Well," Logan offered an explanation, "it sounds like all they were really used for is to finish people off. It doesn't seem like that needs much training."

"Oh yeah, that's right. I haven't told you about all that." Alistair absent-mindedly twirled his stick as he explained. "Sure, they were a secondary weapon like a bayonet at the beginning. But, swords were the main weapons used by the Kolibri in one of the most pivotal battles of the war. One of the most interesting things about this war was its blending of old and new."

Alistair unexpectedly thrust his stick once more towards Logan's abdomen, but again Logan was ready and he parried the attack away. Alistair quickly struck overhead, as if to slice into his skull, but Logan blocked it.

"Wow," Alistair lowered the stick and tilted back a bit with an astonished expression, "you've got real talent!"

"My mom just taught me the same basic moves and made me do them over and over again," Logan explained, smiling slightly with pride.

"Well, she did the right thing. You need to learn certain basic concepts in order to develop your highest potential. There are no secret shots that win the day. It's practice," he waved his hand out horizontally, "plain and simple."

Alistair held his pointer finger up, counting off his points. "You must practice simple moves over and over again." He raised his middle finger as well. "You must train yourself to breathe correctly, which I see you are also very good at." He raised his ring finger. "And you must be as physically fit as possible, in every way. Experts make it look easy, because they're performing relatively simple moves that they've mastered. The experienced fighter always seems to throw his shot at just the right time." To demonstrate his point, he jabbed at Logan, who, listening intently to Alistair, failed to react and received a minor poke to the chest.

Alistair raised his eyebrows and smiled. "That's because great fighters have a solid grounding in the basics. Their actions flow without effort, because their effort was put into the training. When they enter into battle, they have already reached a sort of auto-pilot level with the basics. In that clear state of mind, a fighter's instincts can be better engaged. You want to fight at an intuitive level. React without consciously attending to each action. If you have to stop and think, a more skilled opponent will use that split second to kill you." Alistair jabbed his stick at Logan's neck to exemplify his point, but this time Logan was ready and diverted the lunge.

"One of the most important aspects of learning to fight with a sword is finding a good teacher, and it appears that your mother was one," Alistair nodded with approval. "The most subtle aspects of a game are often its most important. A good teacher can help you understand the difference between timing that is good, and timing which is near perfect," Alistair explained, taking a playful bow as if he were offering his services.

"Now, a good *student* is engaged and listening to what the teacher says." He tossed his stick from his right to left hand and back again. "The immature and arrogant learner will not truly grasp what his teacher is trying to convey." Alistair slapped Logan on the shoulder and looked him straight in the eye. "You are a good student, Logan. I can tell already. You don't bullshit. You're paying attention to what I'm saying," he observed, stepping back, "*and* doing. That takes humility."

Alistair jabbed left and right and then at Logan's ribs. Logan carefully responded to each strike, barely needing to move his feet at all. Once again, Alistair was astounded with the skill of his young opponent. He let the end of his stick drop to the ground again, and he leaned on it as he looked Logan straight in the eye.

"Be confident Logan, but not overly confident to the point of letting your guard down. Don't form preconceived notions about who will win and who will not. Just observe and react. That's what's interesting about you, Logan. You are tough and savvy, yet unassuming. A very dangerous combination. Now, don't let that go to your head!" He laughed.

After only about an hour of training, Logan was already tired. Alistair made him switch off wielding the stick with his right and left hands. Naturally, since Logan was right-handed, he was less coordinated with his left. However, he caught on quickly to this ambidextrous method of fighting. Still, an hour of the intense workout left his entire body exhausted.

Alistair led them out of the jungle and back to the houses, where Logan finally was able to see his beloved Francesca again. The two embraced and kissed as if they had not seen each other in months. Alistair instructed Logan to go take a cold shower in Francesca's house for about ten minutes, to halt any inflammation to his muscles and joints caused by the workout. Then, they would all hop in her spa.

Logan used her shower, turning the knob to cool. He breathed in deeply, making sure oxygen was being supplied to his burning muscles. When he was done, he wrapped his lower half in a towel and walked over to the Jacuzzi room. It had a fantasy ambience to it, with a shape that gave the feeling of being inside an oyster, lit by sunlight shining through amorphous windows decorated with colored glass.

Alistair had rolled a marijuana cigarette while Logan was in the shower and the three smoked it together, sitting in the warm, frothing water, lost in a drug-enhanced reverie. Logan stared at the beautiful young woman leaning on his chest and shoulder and felt euphoric, much like the night prior, without the full physical engagement.

"Where did you get the weed anyway?" he asked Alistair. Alistair took a light puff off of the cigarette and held in the smoke for a moment, passing it to Francesca.

"I found it on my nightstand when I first got in the bungalow," he replied, slowly blowing out the pungent cloud of marijuana particles. "I used to smoke pot all the time before the war, and I managed to do it plenty during as well. I don't know exactly how our supervisors knew that, but it might have something to do with why we were all knocked out for a day or so when the takeover happened. You know, when that darkness, or whatever, took over our minds." He imitated the entranced look of a zombie.

Logan nodded and chills ran up his spine as he was reminded of the horrible, invasive force that took control of his mind and body, knocking him unconscious. Alistair dipped down in the water a bit, putting his shoulders into the way of the Jacuzzi bubble jets.

"They may have been studying our bodies to see what we were used to," he said, his voice quaking a bit from the pounding massage of the jets on his back and shoulders. "Or what we needed."

The marijuana seemed to give Logan greater clarity in terms of being able to conjure up the feeling he experienced when he was possessed by the ominous force. He had forgotten how absolutely traumatic the sensation was . . . until now.

"What was that terrible," he paused, not knowing how to express himself, "that terrible blackness?"

Alistair shook his head, taking a drag off of the joint. "I don't know. I'm guessing it was some sort of Psychiclink device." He thought about it for a while. "Yeah, I mean, it must be the next stage of Psychiclink's potential. First, it was used to allow the mind to control computers and machinery. Now, it seems that it can be switched in reverse, so that it controls our minds."

Logan's eyes widened. "That's kinda freaky," he remarked, sarcastically subdued.

Alistair nodded vigorously. "It's very freaky. But I don't think they're near close to doing this continuously, on a mass-scale."

This did not placate Logan much. He gulped with trepidation. For the first time in a while, he felt truly terrified of the regime he was under. Francesca reached her arm around the back his neck, rubbing his hair and forehead with her hand.

"Don't trip, Logan," she cajoled. "They have no need to use that on us."

"Yeah," Alistair added assuredly, "don't worry man. We really don't even know to what extent it was used before. For all we know, this method of taking us over was only used on some Allied citizens, who maybe didn't seem as threatening. I mean, after all, it was a relatively non-violent way to capture us."

Logan nodded, feeling slightly better. Alistair deftly changed the subject to the tours available to the underclassmen in Costa Rica. There were smaller Luftzugs which departed the resort area every hour, bound for the north, south and west. The whole of Costa Rica was available for sight-seeing.

Closing his eyes, Logan let himself become lost in his own thoughts, tuning out everything around him. He drifted into the past, reminiscing about his youth. Memories of fencing with his mother kept popping up. His mother, Bibi, introduced him to martial arts when he was in kindergarten. She focused on wrestling, teaching her son how to defend himself from future bullies, without harming his opponent. Bibi also taught Logan how to be aware of his breathing and to breathe constantly, at an even pace. While other kids joined little league and football teams, Logan spent his after school hours learning many yogic methods. He noticed that during class his fellow students would often breathe irregularly while listening to lectures and taking exams. Many of them would yawn and Logan knew that it was not because they were tired so much as that their brains were deprived of vital oxygen when they needed it most. His mother taught him that, unfortunately, humans often reacted to stressful situations by breathing less, or by taking shallow inhalations from the upper chest.

Bibi began to teach her son how to fight with a rapier when he was thirteen, right after they moved to the island. It was the first weapon he ever used. He donned a full body guard and face-mask and began his induction into the art of mortal combat.

It was then that he realized how important it was to breathe well. In the fast sport of fencing with a rapier, there is much need for quick reflexes and speedy decision making. Logan could really feel when he was not taking in enough air. A lack of oxygen produced rigid movements — a vast detriment when fighting at such speeds. He noticed the oxygen-deprivation most in his eyes. His vision would blur, which was particularly problematic being that the rapidly whipping blade already appeared blurred at times.

Logan took to the sport quickly and, within two years, he was a worthy dueling opponent for his mother. Bibi was the master swordsman on the island, and Logan was her apprentice. He aided her when she instructed the other youths. The students were all in excellent shape, which was useful in keeping proper oxygen levels in their bodies. All of the parents on the island, including Tom and Bibi, put an emphasis on their children learning sports and doing other cardiovascular activity.

Bibi and Logan showed the fencing students on the island how to breathe in synchronicity with their movements. They were to strongly exhale, Bibi instructed, when striking at the opponent. Just like feeling thirst means that the body is already dehydrated, when someone feels the effects of oxygen deprivation, the body has already begun weakening. In a true swordfight, those seconds, even split-seconds, could give the opponent the fatal advantage. The kids effectively retrained their autonomic nervous systems so that they could breathe in a new and better way without thinking about it, a skill necessary in stressful situations.

Another basic necessity for almost any sport and for everyday life was to have a good sense of balance. The students on the island all had an edge concerning their balance. They played soccer in the beach sand, a difficult field that required giving close attention to their feet. The students began respecting the effort it took for bipedal animals, such as humans, to stand and move about. Walking and running were forms of controlled falling. With only one point contacting the ground at times, humans pushed their limits of balance on every step, nearly falling as one foot came up, and then catching themselves as the other foot came down. Bibi constantly reiterated that people tended to underestimate the importance of balance and overestimate their sense of it.

Good timing was emphasized as the most critical factor in the attack. Timing was what made the good shot "great." Timing was also one of the least conscious factors in sword fighting. The upside was that it was one of the few variables that could improve infinitely with practice. Some people had naturally faster reaction times, but to a great extent, the more someone practiced fighting with a sword, the better their timing would become, for the brain became better at programming their muscles to respond correctly. Timing also depended on one's ability to predict the other fighter's next move. The conscious and subconscious brain could learn, based on probabilities calculated from previous experiences, what the opponent intended to do.

As Logan dueled with his peers on the island, he came to understand their personal styles and when they were in different moods that would make them stronger or weaker. He also learned their many telegraphing signals, the barely perceptible movements that people made before they attacked. Some shifted their weight, or dropped their shoulders; others were not so obvious. These signals gave away their intentions and the more Logan fought, the more he came to sense his opponent's line of attack before it happened. While his opponent was only thinking about his or her own shot, Logan had already blocked it in his mind and planned his counter shot.

Logan was particularly adept at not projecting his telegraphing signals. The biggest giveaways were usually the eyes. Most people would show that they were about to strike by squinting slightly, or blinking, or looking in a particular direction. Bibi was amazed at her son's ability to keep a poker face right up until the moment he attacked. He was an excellent fighter for a number of reasons, naturally quick reflexes being one of them. His greatest gift, though, was his instinctive ability to keep his opponent guessing until it was too late.

Only Bibi knew that Logan almost never made telegraphing signals. She told Logan to keep it a secret and instead, to use contrived attack signals. That way, he maintained the pretense that he had no control over his subtle indicators. In this, he could fake out anyone he engaged, by giving them a false sense of security. They felt they could read him, when in fact they were falling right into his trap.

The next month brought Logan and Francesca even closer, as they explored the island together. In fact, everyone had more fun than they could remember having in a long time.

Logan hardly ever saw his parents after the first day, except to say goodnight to them just before hitting the sheets. The tennis courts at the underclass resorts were lit and open for late-night recreation out of the heat of the mid-day sun. Tennis being their favorite sport, Tom and Bibi took full advantage of the amenities. They played day and night, both bronzing to a nice dark tan from their time spent in the sun, either lobbing balls back and forth for practice, or pounding the courts in a competitive game. Every night before bed, they swore up and down that their games had improved dramatically, and credited the sleep and relaxation they were getting on this unique vacation.

Logan and Francesca, and occasionally Alistair, spent much of their time exploring the fascinating natural environment of the island. The three of them took several tours on relatively small Luftzugs, viewing their tropical destination from the air. There were so many national parks in the region, but by the end of the first week, Francesca was bored with sitting in the Luftzugs and hearing about the attractions second-hand.

"Look what I have," she sing-songed to Logan as they met for another day of touring. She waved a thin pamphlet under his nose.

"See the forests by horseback," Logan read the cover. "Hey, that's a good idea."

"Yeah, I think we'll have a much better chance of seeing some of the plants and animals they keep telling us about if we can do it from under the trees instead of over them!"

Logan flipped open the pamphlet and skimmed the inside, which included a brief history of horses in Costa Rica and, of course, the Apex's involvement. Apparently, the Apex had banned the use of all vehicles in Costa Rica's parks in order to maintain the pristine forests, so tours were lead exclusively on foot, by horse, or from the air.

"Well, let's go wrangle us some horses, ma'am!" Logan said in a badly mocked cowboy accent.

Within the hour, the couple was astride two young, but very sedate trail horses. The guide, a petite young woman with shortly cropped blonde hair and a red riding helmet, told them she was a former jockey from Great Britain. She introduced herself as Amelia and then lovingly introduced the animals. Francesca was told she was atop "Gigi" and Logan was mounted on "George." After brief instructions on trail safety and how to turn and stop the horses, Amelia led the couple onto the fragrant forested trail behind the resort.

The horses followed each other automatically in a single-file line, and from behind Francesca's horse, Logan noticed how strong his sweetheart's long legs looked hung over Gigi's sides, stretching down into the stirrups. His own feet kept slipping awkwardly out of the stirrups. On top of that, George seemed more interested in snapping at flies and grazing on passing plants than staying in line. But Logan made do, so as not to interrupt the tour.

There were an infinite amount of fascinating sights and sounds; everything from a lone toucan perched on a tree branch eyeing the passing horses and people suspiciously, to a group of howler monkeys screeching as they passed through the park from branch to branch. Amelia stopped to ask how far away Logan and Francesca thought the monkeys were. After several guesses that they were only a few meters away, she told them that this particular species of monkey was the loudest land animal on the planet and their voices carried for many kilometers.

There was one sighting in particular that truly floored Francesca. After the horseback expedition, some fellow underclassmen told the couple about the canals just north of Limon — the *Canales de Tortuguero*. They highly recommended the scenic gondola that carried passengers from Limon to the northeast. Taking their advice, Logan and Francesca took a gondola ride the next day and it was there that Francesca spotted a basilisk, sitting on a rock just beyond a natural lagoon.

"Wow!" she exclaimed, completely intrigued. "Look at that giant lizard!"

Logan looked toward where she pointed and his eyebrows shot up in surprise.

"That is a basilisk," stated the gondolier, their sole companion through the canal. He was a short, pleasant man from a tribe that had lived in the Costa Rican rain forests for thousands of years.

"Some call it the Jesus Lizard," their guide elaborated. "Look now! He is about to meet trouble." As Logan and Francesca focused their attention on the strange reptile, a monstrous snake slithered down from an overhanging branch. But the basilisk sensed trouble and, rearing up on its back legs, it jumped into the lagoon and ran across the surface with incredible speed.

"It walks on water!" Francesca cried out in awe. She could not stop talking about the lizard for days, telling everyone they met about the fantastic creature.

In the evenings, Logan, Francesca and Alistair usually hit the hot spots: bars, pool halls, dance clubs. Logan noticed that Alistair was having no trouble with the ladies. Since he had been on vacation, he was projecting some incredible energy, a relaxed and inviting vibe. As a result, he was at no loss for dance partners . . . partners that Logan sometimes noticed leaving Alistair's room in the morning. Logan was happy his friend was having fun, but at the same time he was relieved that he had Francesca. He did not miss the flirting, seducing and head games that Alistair seemed to thrive on.

In between sightseeing and the seemingly endless nighttime parties, Alistair practically forced Logan to train in swordfighting. He said it was because Logan was so talented, it was a travesty not to nurture it further. Though Logan enjoyed the activity, he did not see why it was so vitally necessary, especially when he could be spending his time with Francesca.

Alistair had gone scouting and found a better spot to practice. Less than a kilometer beyond their resort lay what used to be a lush sugarcane field. However, this field appeared to have been unworked for many seasons. Birds had long since picked the stalks clean, which then keeled over and disintegrated into the earth, leaving a wide open stretch of field.

Every other morning, very early before the humidity and heat of midday cloaked the region with its thick veil, Alistair and Logan jogged the kilometer to the field to warm-up. At the beginning of each session, Alistair led them in meditation. Both of them knew that meditation had physical, mental and, of course, spiritual healing benefits. However, Alistair prioritized the specific art of concentration; how to go inside one's own head and relax, focus, and sharpen cognitive skills. By implementing these exercises, Logan was on top of his game every time they sparred.

The two men would arrive at the field and sit cross-legged in the grass facing each other from about three meters away, their eyes closed. The first few times, Alistair narrated the meditative and breathing exercises that were new to Logan, but within a week Logan had easily mastered the routine and the two could simply prepare their minds in silence.

As the weeks passed, Alistair was more than impressed with Logan's advancement. The tools he had given Logan quickly played out during their swordfighting practice, as they weaved and jabbed with their makeshift weapons. By the end of the month, Alistair had no doubt that Logan was the best swordfighter he had ever met.

— XVIII —

It's A Dog Eat Dog World

Having been summoned to a new counselor, Tom, Bibi and Logan sat in the office of Herr Hardt, who was a far more authoritarian figure than Frau Dorner was.

Herr Hardt wasted no time in enlightening the family. "Today, as you know, is your last day at this resort. All of you are being sent to the Great Lakes region of North America, where you will work the soybean fields. We in the Apex believe that hard work is necessary in order to gain relativity. So, we send you all there first to pay your dues. If you work hard, when it comes time for your review, you will be given a choice of other jobs."

Tom, Bibi and Logan nodded their heads and, knowing better than to ask a bunch of questions, they simply thanked the counselor. Herr Hardt then tersely excused them from his office, telling them that they were to immediately board a Luftzug that was going to take them to North America.

As the family walked down the long hallway with a crowd of other people, Logan was struck with a familiar feeling. Once more, a tremendous anxiety overwhelmed him at the thought of not seeing Francesca again. It took every ounce of strength available to him to avoid running in the opposite direction to go find her. He crammed negative thoughts back in his mind. He and his family reached a large lobby area, where people were standing or seated, waiting to be let out of the sliding glass exit doors on the opposite wall of the hallway entrance. Outside was the boarding area for the Luftzugs.

There were thousands of underclassmen mulling about in the lobby area.

"I'll be right back," Logan said to his parents. Tom caught him by the shoulder.

"Be *right* back, son," he said, looking Logan in the eye. Logan nodded and ran off through the lobby. He recognized many of the underclassmen from his stay at the Costa Rican resort, however, many of them he recognized from as far back as the language school in Colombia. Now, it seemed that they were all heading for the same place once more. It was a source of comfort to see so many familiar faces, though most he had never spoken to and only a few he had become acquainted with. But, those who Logan had become close friends with, and the one who Logan now loved, were nowhere to be found.

His heart wrenched in agony with every passing minute that that he couldn't find her. He fell into an extremely dark mood. And, finally, feeling that he had looked over the entire waiting area, he sulked back to his parents . . . only to be thrown into a state of ecstasy by the sight of Francesca sitting by Tom and Bibi, along with her father, Sasha and Alistair.

They all sat together on a Luftzug in a large booth, as they departed Costa Rica and headed for North America. The Luftzug settled at a cruising altitude of about two and a half kilometers in the air. Francesca turned to Jacques, who was staring out at the endless light blue sky along the horizon.

"What are you thinking about, Papa?"

Jacques took a long, deep breath. "Nothing, really."

"Are you thinking about flying the Eagle?" she asked.

Jacques simply nodded.

"Is it a good memory?" Her eyes glinted in the sunlight streaming through her window.

"It was dangerous . . . and frightening."

"I know, but from what you've told me," she inquired, her face displaying her enthusiastic admiration, "it must've been exciting."

"Yeah," Logan smacked the back of his hand on Jacques's arm in emphasis, "tell us one of your war stories. Francesca's always bragging about you. I wanna know what it's like to fly an Eagle."

Jacques looked down for a second and smirked, then focused his attention out the window again. He was unable to hold back a smile. "It's beyond what humans can normally feel. War isn't something to glorify. But, somehow, between the screams of people being burned alive and the mind-numbing roar of battle, there were moments of pure exhilaration . . ."

The Bald Eagle pilots of the 23rd Fighter Group were in charge of protecting Allied ground forces moving from the United States to Panama, on a course to defend the canal, which linked the Atlantic and Pacific. The Allied foot soldiers and quadruped battlemachines were vulnerable to air strikes on their long trek outside of the Laser Net, as they traveled through the wide-open deserts and plains of Mexico.

Through his earpiece, Jacques could hear the carnage of the hot zone. He was the squadron commander, in the lead of a dozen Bald Eagles. The 23rd Fighter Group was comprised of many of the most talented pilots flying for the Allied side. They were all chomping at the bit to get in there and light the Apex air forces on fire. A steam catapult akin to those used on aircraft carriers, except far larger and more powerful, fired the Bald Eagles off of their Sierra Madres mountain base, accelerating the jets from zero to fifteen hundred kilometers per hour in three seconds. Flying up into the sky and west over the range, the squadron climbed to an altitude of twenty-thousand meters.

Jacques spoke to his team via their two-way radio system.

"We're heading over to sector Sierra Zulu, boys. That's right in the thick of it. So, keep sharp and get in the zone."

Anti-aircraft shells began exploding all around them.

"Split up!" Jacques commanded, and his squadron broke up into groups of three Bald Eagles. The fighter pilot flying on Jacques's left wing was the first targeted by Apex fighters using long range, air-to-air missiles.

"Eagle One!" he shouted to Jacques. "I've got Adler-120s locked on me!"

"Kick in your vector nullifier, Eagle Four!" Jacques shouted. His cockpit now lit up, blinking with red warning lights, telling him that missiles were homing in on him as well. Jacques flipped a switch and a specially designed, non-destructive laser was emitted from the underside of his jet to the nose of one of the missiles, confusing the missile's tracking and guidance system. The missile veered off sharply, allowing Jacques to evade it. Eagle Four was still being tracked. The pilot of Eagle Four was Jacques's best friend Roy.

"Merde!" Jacques roared. "Drop the flares!"

"Roger, Eagle One!" Roy shouted back. He dropped dozens of incredibly bright and hot plasma flares to attract the missile, but his timing was a split-second off and the missile didn't go for the flares. Time slowed down for Jacques, as he watched the missile gaining on his friend's jet.

"Dump the shells Roy!"

The infrared seeker missile targeted Roy's jet and collided with it, blowing up the right side of the craft and sending the Bald Eagle spinning to Earth, shattered and flaming. It was tumbling so fast that Roy could not move, due to the g-forces pressing on him. He began to black out.

"Roy!" Jacques shouted. *"Eject! Eject! Damn it—!"*

Eagle Four careened into the desert below at seven thousand kilometers per hour, vaporizing the jet plane in a cloud of fire and ash.

Jacques tilted his head back against the seat and looked up. Everything was happening so fast. He couldn't think about Roy right now. He and his other wingman, Eagle Two, joined up with the other group of three.

"This is Eagle One," he called out to them. "There's more coming in, boys! Time to play Chicken!"

The jets turned around and arched down toward the oncoming missiles. They flew at the missiles until the last moment, when the Bald Eagle pilots turned their jets sharply, letting the Adler-120s fly past.

"That's what I like to see!" Jacques cheered his fighter team on. "Gorgeous and graceful!"

One of the missiles turned around, targeting Jacques. His cockpit warning lights began blinking rapidly.

"Merde!"

The missile moved in. Jacques used his vector nullifier, but the missile was coming at him at a particular angle that hindered the laser's capabilities. He fired out flares, but the missile didn't explode. It redirected, targeting Jacques again.

"God damn it!"

"Alright Eagle One," his wingman called out, "just . . ."

"Got it!" Jacques shouted back. He nose-dived the jet towards the ground, suddenly pulling up and arching parallel to the slope of a mountainside. The missile, unable to follow Jacques's path, slammed into the mountain and exploded. But, Jacques immediately found himself in a hail of gunfire and shell explosions coming from Panzers and Kolibri vehicles on the mountain. Seeing a patch of Panzers, he fired three missiles, striking two of the Apex quadrupeds.

Jacques pulled high into the air and turned back to dive-bomb. He brought up an electronic display screen on the cockpit windshield that showed what was in front of him in telescopic vision. He could see the armored vehicles on the ground from ten kilometers high. He dropped guided bombs and, when he neared, let loose a drill bolt barrage on the enemy. Some of the Panzers had automated anti-aircraft guns, capable of targeting fast-moving, flying objects. The guns fired at the incoming Bald Eagle, but Jacques deftly maneuvered his plane and evaded the enemy barrage. He fired his lasers and hit a Panzer Mark III twice, destroying its right side. Jacques arced up above the Panzers and dropped four smart bombs from two kilometers up. One tracked and fell onto the downed Panzer and the others took out a large cluster of Apex Hoplites.

Suddenly, two Apex Eagles appeared on Jacques's radar coming straight for him.

Jacques tried to evade and drop shells on the pursuers, but the Golden Eagles dodged the shells, moved into position and fired their drill bolt cannons on him. Jacques couldn't shake his attackers and his jet was hit repeatedly. His right afterburner melted shut and his wing engine exploded, but the jet kept aloft.

One of Jacques's wingmen flew to his aid, taking out one of the Golden Eagles with a laser salvo. But, soon, he too was being tailed.

"Fire her into overdrive, Eagle One!"

"Roger that, Eagle Three!" Jacques called back. "Let's kiss the ground!"

They dove toward the Earth, dodging their pursuers' fire, then pulled up and flew parallel to the ground, with scarcely a few meters between them.

"Get ready to dump and duck under these guys!" Jacques directed.

"Roger, Eagle One!"

On Jacques's command, they rose and dropped their shells, setting a trap for the Golden Eagles. Reacting as predicted, the Golden Eagles rose high up over the shells and after Jacques and his wingman. Suddenly, the two Bald Eagles arched their wings, causing the jets to decelerate quickly and fall below and behind their pursuers.

"Sweet Jesus, it worked!" Eagle Three exclaimed. *"Let's fuck 'em up!"*

Jacques caught one of the Apex jet fighters in his sights. "Roger that, Eagle Three!"

They tore into those who once pursued them. Injured but intact, the Golden Eagles parted and forced Jacques and his wingman to split in pursuit. Jacques pushed his jet to full throttle to keep up with the rapidly accelerating Apex Eagle. They flew up into the upper levels of the stratosphere, and then careened back down. Jacques fired three missiles, but the Golden Eagle averted them all. He fired proximity shells, but quickly exhausted his supply. Next, Jacques barraged the Golden Eagle with his laser cannons.

The Apex jet dove toward the mountain valleys below and, for a moment, Jacques lost sight of him behind a peak. The Golden Eagle decelerated, pulling up and over, letting Jacques move under him. Suddenly, the Apex jet came in on top of Jacques, firing its lasers.

For the first time in his career as a fighter pilot, Jacques thought he was done for. Then, thinking of his friend who had just perished, he became enraged.

He slammed on his air brakes and retro-boosters. The Golden Eagle was forced to pull up or run into Jacques's jet. Jacques quickly exploited the advantage, getting behind the enemy and shredding the Apex fighter plane into pieces with a drill bolt laser salvo . . .

Jacques came back from his reverie, looking intently out of the Luftzug window at the skies where he had fought. "You shouldn't fly too close to some-one who has nothing to lose."

Logan and his parents were speechless and just stared at Jacques in awe. Francesca hugged her father's arm, completely captivated by her hero.

Alistair slapped him on the back. "Good show, Jacques!"

A waiter came around to their booth and took food and drink orders. Minutes later, everyone was eating gourmet vegetarian meals, swallowing it down with beer and wine.

Suddenly, after a few hours of relaxing amusement, an explosion was heard coming from the ground. Everyone within looked out the nearest window. Below, there was a familiar sight — a war torn setting, charred and annihilated. It was apparent that the area was probably once a gorgeous marshland, but no longer.

Alistair breathed in slowly, realizing what he was looking at. "We've crossed into what was Fortress North America." The carnage only increased as the Luftzug continued on over the horizon.

"Once again," he remarked coolly, looking down at the source of the explo-sion, which was yet another building demolition, "they are showing us how futile it is to fight them."

Jacques recognized the land below through the devastation. "Alabama certainly looks different from how I remember."

"This is Alabama?" Logan asked, taking everything in.

Alistair nodded. "The site of one of the hardest fought battles of the Third World War . . . "

— XIX —

The Last Stand

Summer 2039

The Apex forces fully exploited the breach created in Fortress North America. Within six days of the successful invasion, the Apex military had secured and occupied North Carolina, South Carolina, and most of Georgia. They now held a third of the United States' East Coast.

In that time, though, the Allies managed to move nearly one billion refugees out of the area and into the permanent encampments west of the Appalachians. The commanders and crews of three-dozen Sidewinders held the rear guard and fought the invading forces tenaciously to the end, giving the Allied refugees time to escape.

Fortunately for the Allied forces, Geiseric prohibited the Apex military from defoliant-bombing, so the invaders could not resort to destroying entire forested areas by using napalm and defoliant chemicals. This gave the Allies a badly needed advantage. With vast areas of trees and other vegetation to hide in, the defending forces could wage a bitter guerilla war with the Apex expeditionary forces.

Allied High Command was well aware of their enemy's probable line of attack. Every army throughout history, no matter how powerful or cunning, has looked with trepidation at crossing a mountain range. The logistics involved, when moving and supplying a large army over mountainous terrain, were extremely difficult to manage. It was not as if it could not be done. In fact, it *had* been done before. The great Carthaginian general, Hannibal, marched his army over the Alps and successfully attacked the Romans on their own turf. It was Hannibal's use of this unexpected route that proved that sometimes it was best to go through the very place the enemy did not think was feasible. However, such daring was not needed, for the Apex forces were winning the war and their commanders, no doubt, did not want to risk their lead.

Clearly, the best way to puncture into the core of Fortress North America was to circumvent the Appalachians around their southernmost point, through Alabama.

The Apex forces had already been heading south from the North Carolinian breach. They were, to no surprise, attempting to swing beneath the Appalachians, where they would launch a final assault into the heart of their enemy. If they made it around, billions of Allied civilians would be in danger. Indeed, it could force an end to the war.

Two-thirds of Alabama was covered by forest, mainly pines and hardwoods, but also a myriad of other blooming shrubs and trees. The Allies could hide well in this thick, gorgeous foliage. It was perfect. Allied troops could not only wage a guerilla war on the Apex ground forces pushing through, but they could also launch surprise attacks on Apex bases and supply lines in Georgia and the Carolinas.

The Apex thrust began in the middle of the night. The expeditionary forces crossed the Chattahoochee River, which formed the border between Georgia and Alabama. There was very little moon or star-light coming through the clouds. The air was warm and humid, and in the gentle breeze the soldiers caught the light, sweet scent of magnolias.

As the Allies had predicted, the main body of the Apex assault was coming through the Black Belt, a strip of rolling prairie wedged between the southern section of the Appalachians and Alabama's coastal plain. It was the only non-forested land that the Apex forces could come through. While most of the ground forces moved through the Black Belt, a quarter of the Apex expeditionary force made their way through the forested regions surrounding the belt, attempting to route out the guerilla defenders. Among those moving through the forests were the heavily armored Hoplite commandos.

From the very beginning, they were met with bitter resistance from the guerillas. The Allied defensive strategy was simple; it was a number's game.

They had more than thirty-five million soldiers spread out over the twenty thousand square kilometers of forest lining the north and south of the Black Belt. Basically, they had nearly two thousand Allied infantrymen hidden in every square kilometer of forest, a daunting number for the invaders to face.

As the Apex contingent pressed through the thick Alabama woods, they were relentlessly cut down by an oppressive hail of gunfire, bursting forth from every direction. Allied snipers fired from treetops hidden in the branches, and from the dense shrubbery. They popped out of small holes in the ground that were connected by a vast network of tunnels. Camouflaged gunmen were seemingly everywhere . . . yet nowhere.

There was so much shooting, it was impossible to identify any one source of it. And any patch of land not defended by an Allied soldier on, above, or below, was strewn with mines. As the Apex military engineer teams worked to clear the mine-fields, the Allied guerilla fighters harassed them incessantly, bleeding them for every square kilometer they took.

The main body of Apex ground forces was not making headway any faster. It rained frequently during most Alabama summers; the atmosphere cooling itself from sweltering 100-degree-days. The skies sent down violent thunderstorms that crackled across the land, relieving the evening air, and the minds of the worried defenders. The day after the Apex launched its assault through the Black Belt, rain came down uninterrupted for three days. Often, the storms brought down sudden torrents of water, cleansing the land with flash floods and nearly grinding the Apex thrust to a halt.

The belt of prairie land they were moving through was named after the black clay soil in the area, and it was incredibly sticky when moist. It pulled downward and sucked in anything trudging through it. The mud proved especially debilitating to the quadruped battlemachines, even those designed for marsh-like conditions. As their weight sank them deeply into the sticky mush, the Panzers had to exert extreme strength and energy with every step they took, pulling their legs and paws out of the mud with a hefty yanking motion. However, the real problems for the Apex expeditionary forces came when the Allies launched their numerous surprise attacks on their column.

The invasion forces made their way towards Montgomery, the capital and one of the largest cities in Alabama. It sat on the northern edge of the Black Belt, next to the Tallapoosa River. But the city was now deserted of civilians, transformed into a major supply base and shelter for the Allied guerilla fighters.

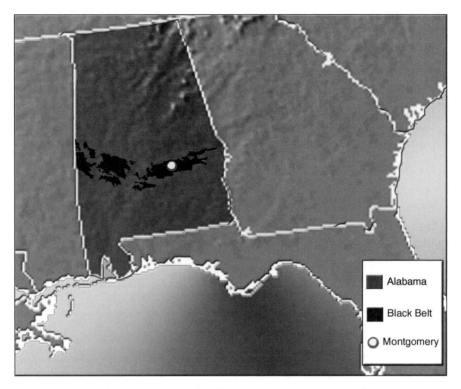

Alabama

Black Belt

Montgomery

Condors and Golden Eagles had bombed Montgomery with over ten million tons of explosives, yet the city endured. In fact, the Allied manufacturing centers in and around Montgomery still operated at sixty percent. As in any war, bombs could not do everything. They could never supplant the infantry. No matter how intensely Stalingrad and Berlin were bombed during World War II, there still needed to be feet on the ground to take those cities.

In fact, the Second World War proved how effective military forces could still be within what appeared to be completely devastated cities. The Nazi German forces were never able to take the razed city of Stalingrad, and this was the turning point in World War II, where the Germans received their first major defeat. The Soviet forces pushed the invaders back to the city of Berlin, which had been laid waste by the Anglo-American bombing raids. The Soviets met staunch resistance from within the apocalyptic landscape they entered, the German defenders extracting two million deaths from the Soviets before the city was taken.

Allied High Command felt that the battle for Montgomery could be their Stalingrad. They planned to launch endless stealth raids and surprise assaults on the Apex ground forces, especially the slightly over-extended Apex supply lines. In modern warfare, the biggest weakness of a powerful army was their supply lines. Blitzkrieg-style warfare focused on the continuous advancement of the ground forces. As the front pushed forward, it became ever harder to supply the advancing troops and war machines. Fuel, water, food, ammunition and every other type of supply convoy became incredibly vulnerable as the rear guard, which was in charge of protecting the army's back, became dispersed over a greater area.

The Allies withheld their counter-strike until the Apex expeditionary forces were within twenty kilometers of Montgomery. Converging on the city in a massive pincer movement, the main Apex column moved up north from the Black Belt and the contingent moving through the forest proceeded south. There they came up against a series of fortifications and defenses surrounding the perimeter of the city. The Allied defenses were crude, but effective. Thousands of anti-Panzer structures encircled the city in two kilometer-thick lines. The primary anti-Panzer defense was called a Briar Patch, and it was similar to the anti-tank defenses of World War II, only taken to a far greater level.

The Briar Patches were vast swaths of land covered with tens of thousands of sharp spikes made of steel girders taken from destroyed buildings in Montgomery. The spikes ranged from one meter to several meters long and were pointed diagonally upwards at forty-five degree angles, toward the oncoming forces.

Estimating that it would take at least a day before the Apex could blow a path with bombs and artillery through the Briar Patch encircling the city, the Allies figured they had time to prepare for the ground assault. But, the Apex infantry decided to push ahead without blazing a trail into the forest of spikes, for the ground troops were small enough to weave through. However, interspersed in the ground amongst the steel spikes were a myriad of different types of mines. The mines were powerful enough to debilitate a soldier, but did not harm the Briar Patch.

As the mines exploded, many of the Apex infantrymen were blown upwards and landed on the spikes, skewered, the steel entering their backs and piercing through their stomachs. Thousands of storm troopers hung impaled from the taller spikes, convulsing as they slowly died. Thousands more had their legs blown off and their lower torsos shredded. They fell shrieking and writhing upon the ground, pleading for their fellow soldiers to help them, or put a bullet in their heads. Even some of the more heavily armored Hoplites were taken out. As their compatriots came to their aid, hidden Allied guerilla fighters popped out of the ground and fired on them. Cramped together in a sophisticated underground tunnel system were nearly two million Allied soldiers, ready to surprise the enemy anywhere in the vicinity.

It was a slaughterhouse, as the guerillas sprang up from beneath the ground, ambushing the Hoplites and storm troopers, killing many as they kneeled down tending to the injured. Within minutes, hundreds of thousands of dead or mortally wounded Apex infantrymen littered the Briar Patch. The Hoplites and storm troopers broke into a hasty retreat from the deadly steel forest. But they were met with a second, larger wave of Allied guerillas, which sprang from out of the underground tunnel system behind the Apex soldiers. The Allies had a large chunk of the Apex infantry surrounded, and they took no mercy.

The light-armored storm troopers fell like wheat to the scythe. The field marshal in charge of the Hoplites, Alois Battenburg, made the clever and brave decision to turn around and press forward. He knew the Allies would not be expecting it, for it was risky to separate from the rest of the Apex forces outside of the Briar Patch.

Battenburg personally led the charge forward, turning his demoralized and confused Hoplites around. Inspired by his courage, the Apex heavy infantrymen immediately followed their commander, rushing up against the Allied guerillas who had chased them into retreat seconds before.

In the chaos, the Hoplites could not recklessly spray their machine guns, or plasma-throwers, because there were fleeing storm troopers everywhere. So, Battenburg commanded his Hoplites to engage the enemy in close-quarters fighting, meaning they could only fire on an enemy within five meters and with short, accurate bursts from their weapons. As the Hoplites got in closer, they pulled out their long, bayonet-like blades and went to work on the guerillas.

The guerillas wore barely any armor. Like the Russian soldiers in the battle of Stalingrad, these Allied fighters were nothing more than disposable, moving gun platforms.

With the Hoplites in so close, the guerillas found it near impossible to fire their guns effectively. They certainly could not use their larger caliber guns that were too big to wield about in close-quarters fighting. And most of the smaller gunfire could not pierce the Apex heavy infantryman's armor.

The tide had turned and the massacre was now one-sided in favor of the Apex. The Hoplites were actually breaking their steel blades off in the bodies of their enemies from overuse. When that happened, the Hoplites used their incredible strength, derived from the Vasculosynth lining their armor, to pick up the Allied fighters and impale them on the anti-Panzer spikes. After watching thousands of their fellow soldiers brutalized in this fashion, many of the Allied guerillas on the interior line ran away.

Thus, a hole was punctured in the forward line of Allied defenders in the Briar Patch. The Hoplites fully exploited the break and made haste guiding the storm troopers through it. As fast as they could, they rushed forward out of the deadly field of spikes, breaking free on the interior side. Though they were temporarily relieved, they now found themselves to be cut off from the majority of the Apex expeditionary forces on the exterior of the anti-Panzer defenses.

Altogether, only three hundred thousand storm troopers and Hoplites, less than half of the force that entered the Briar Patch, emerged from the carnage within. As they poured out on the interior side, they immediately came under attack from Allied snipers, once again popping out of the underground tunnel system. When the Hoplites and storm troopers rushed at their attackers, they found that the ground was even more full of mines than within the patch. All of the mines were shaped-charges, which focused the energy of the blast upwards, so as not to destroy the Allies' well-utilized subterranean system.

As Apex infantrymen were blown up left and right, their legs and lower bodies ruptured and shredded, Allied guerillas jumped out of their holes and attacked. The Apex found most of the mines the hard way, but the defenders knew where the mines were buried and easily dodged around the ones that remained intact. The guerillas weaved throughout the mine-fields, picking off Apex soldiers who were paralyzed where they stood, not knowing where to step. Every single one of the Apex engineers was immediately picked off by guerillas as they tried to determine the locations of and remove or destroy the remaining mines.

Allied High Command was pleased by the way things were transpiring. There were still eight more defensive rings encircling Montgomery that the Apex ground forces needed to pass through. The Allied fortifications and guerillas fighters were making the trespassers pay dearly for every bit of territory they gained.

However, what was extremely worrisome to the Allied leadership was the fact that they could not find the Juggernaut. Since the Shark Fleet had taken such a beating from the Condor bombings during the Carolinian invasion, the Allies could not challenge the Delfin Fleet in waters far off the coast of North America. Although they still held numerical superiority over the Delfins, the Allies did not want to risk losing the rest of their naval forces, yet. Furthermore, the navy had been demoralized by the destruction of so many of their Sharks in the Pamlico Sound. Allied High Command worried that their naval forces were not in the right frame of mind to fight another battle.

Without support from the Sharks, the Allied conventional surface ships and submarine crafts patrolling the Atlantic and the Gulf of Mexico were taken out by Apex Delfins. If the Allies had let their Sharks venture out a bit further, they may have found the Juggernaut, for it was nearer than they imagined. As it turned out, the titanic Apex battlemachine was hidden and being refueled in the Puerto Rican Trench, the deepest part of the Atlantic Ocean.

In the Allied War Room, the leaders sat around the circular table, brainstorming over the Juggernaut. Admiral Nelson was summoned to the War Room to address the leadership once more. She had already done so three weeks earlier, right after the Apex invaded. At the Battle of the Breach, Nelson led her Shark battalion in a valiant counter-strike against the Delfins. While in the hot zone, she happened to catch a glimpse of the titanic Apex battlemachine.

"Admiral Nelson, do you remember anything new of what you saw of this *Juggernaut*?" Dandau pronounced the word with disdain.

"No, Sir," the Admiral shook her head. "Just what I already told you all before. There were long, metal tentacles," she explained, in her aristocratic British accent, "each, I'd guess, more than a kilometer long. They were attached to a giant, elliptical body." She stared off blankly for a moment. "I must tell you, it was quite unnerving."

Streicher had his eyes closed as he listened, mentally processing the information. "That's it!" he thought aloud. "I've been so busy with everything else that I didn't see it until now. It's so obvious! That must be what the tentacles are for. It has to be extraordinarily heavy. So, it needs all those long limbs to displace all that weight over a large amount of surface area. It's probably so huge, because of this weapon it carries . . ." he paused and contemplated what the Allies were up against, "this weapon that can blow holes through many kilometers of rock and dirt in minutes."

Nelson was struck with an epiphany. "It would seem then that the Juggernaut's most effective line of attack is from the ocean. I'm guessing that its weight would make it quite slow on the land. The buoyancy of the water, especially on the ocean floor, makes it many times lighter."

Streicher nodded, becoming ever more intrigued by this mysterious battlemachine. "And there may be another reason the Juggernaut did not come onto land. From the coast, it can hang on the continental shelf and fire holes diagonally up through the ground at our bunkers. It would not be nearly as easy if the Juggernaut had to attack from the land."

President Hollier took in what he was hearing, while leaning back in his chair, his feet up on the table. "So you're saying, if we can finish building up the interior wall of laser defenses, like we've already started doing on the western side of the Appalachians," he looked at Streicher with almost pleading eyes, begging for something to give him hope for the Allies, "if we can build up this interior Laser Net," he restated, making absolutely sure he had it right, "we can possibly debilitate that giant machine?"

Streicher thought long and hard before responding. "Something that large would weigh too much to cross such distances overland. Doing so would expend an inconceivable amount of energy. Plus, firing from the continental shelf allowed the Juggernaut to stay out of the line-of-sight of our Kreuz Lasers, which could probably do some serious damage to it. If the Juggernaut is forced to attack from the land, it will have to start tunneling from over the horizon, which will multiply the amount of land to be tunneled through ten-fold. Altogether, these variables should sum up to the Juggernaut being desperately handicapped."

Hollier slammed his palms down on the table and stood up suddenly. "OK, then. We need to establish a line of Cross Lasers at least a thousand kilometers inland. How fast can we do that?"

Sinclair was, as usual, perturbed. "Since when have you become *the* voice of *our* war policy?"

Hollier shook his head with contempt and his eyes narrowed, as he began to lose his cool for the first time. "Now's not the time Sinclair," he spoke through his gritted teeth. "I'm not gonna sit here and play games with you anymore. The whole fuckin' world is at stake here!"

The two presidents stared at each other from across the table, silence hanging in the air for moments that felt like an eternity.

General Tierney, realizing that the situation in the War Room was more precarious than it had ever been, decided to interject, hoping that because of his position as a military man, he would come across as neutral.

"Here's the thing. I already came to the same conclusion," he lied. "And it had nothing to do with any of you talking heads," he pointed to all the leaders, trying to diffuse Sinclair's anger by putting down everyone equally.

Sinclair broke a slight smile. "You believe this is the right course, General Tierney?"

The general nodded. "I do."

Sinclair paused to contemplate this. "OK, then, what do we do?"

Tierney thought fast and created some impromptu plans, bent on both keeping the peace in the War Room and helping his commander-in-chief, President Hollier, get his way. Besides, he knew that Streicher's assertions were right. As he spoke, Tierney glanced at Streicher now and then for guidance on what to say next. Streicher played along, filling in the blanks in a deferential way that made it seem that Tierney was in control of the conversation. The charade worked and Sinclair was effectively appeased.

Allied High Command agreed to completely pull back the Laser Net from off the North American coastline and redistribute it to an interior defensive wall that encompassed the American Midwest, from the Appalachians to the Rockies.

Kassian and his personal team of scientists were pushing the envelope in the field of cybernetics, specifically having to do with brain-computer interface, or Psychiclink. Kassian was the perfect test-subject for the engineers and medical doctors who were designing the equipment. In his younger years, he pursued the meditative and transcendent arts, traveling to places such as India seeking spiritual enlightenment. This was when he was friends with Geiseric, when they were two bandmates in one of the most successful rock bands of all time. They were young, healthy, and the world was at their fingertips. In between the relentless partying, touring and womanizing, Kassian and Geiseric managed to study and learn many different and fascinating arts and sciences. They even took a year off from everything and studied with the Dalai Lama in Tibet. The two young men made a powerful impression on the Buddhist holy man. He was astounded at how quickly they understood and applied the ancient wisdom and techniques of his teachings.

As incredible an experience as that was, nothing compared to the time Kassian and Geiseric spent with the Gikata tribe in the Amazonian jungle. The two young men were initiated into the warrior-witch doctor elite of the tribe, the Siongi. It was the Siongi who most enlightened Kassian and Geiseric in how to galvanize and activate their "sixth sense."

These memories crept into Kassian's mind every once in a while and he had become deft at pushing them out quickly. That was a lifetime ago. Geiseric was no longer his friend . . .

He was his greatest enemy.

The Allied scientists, doctors and other staff working on the Psychiclink projects examined Kassian's brain structure and how each part of his brain worked. They were particularly interested in his ability to achieve a mental trance state, enabling him to tap into psychic abilities once thought to be mythical. He was one of very few people who seemed capable of actually reading minds. Psychiclink technology apparently allowed him to expand his range to be able to pick up on anyone's brainwaves on the entire planet.

Of the Allied leadership, Prime Minister Dandau was the most ardent supporter of the project. President Hollier was highly skeptical, at first, but was slowly but surely being won over by the facts. Hollier personally partook in an experiment in which Kassian attempted to read his mind. Kassian did not know every little thing that the president was thinking, but he could pick up on very important thoughts that spun over and over again in Hollier's mind. He could pick up on them broadly, especially if he had a context. For instance, Kassian knew that the main issues in Hollier's head concerned the war. So, within this context, he would patch together the blurbs of thoughts and images he picked up on. The president was impressed at how well Kassian did in perceiving things that he had not yet told to the rest of the Allied leadership.

However, Hollier was still not completely convinced that Kassian was actually monitoring his thoughts, and not just particularly astute at gauging people by psychological analysis. These points of skepticism aside, there was a strong divide growing in the War Room, as Dandau and Hollier began to side increasingly with Kassian's input. President Sinclair blindly refused to look further into the Psychiclink projects, out of spite for Kassian. Though Kurtkin believed very much in the possibilities of Kassian's research, he and Premier Hung sided with Sinclair, for they strongly believed that the Anglo-American clique considered the Russian and Chinese people to be little more than decoys and human shields to protect their own people.

General Tierney, being the Supreme Commander of the Allied Forces, was becoming much like his predecessor of World War II, Dwight Eisenhower. Eisenhower had to be the consummate diplomat, while also being a military man, for he had to keep the bickering Allied leadership together. Such was no different in this war and the reasons for the quarreling were just as inane as in the second and first world wars.

Kassian became ever more omnipresent at the top Allied war meetings, much to the dismay of his opponents in High Command. However, over time, President Kurtkin began to realize that he could not ignore the research going on with Psychiclink. Though he was a bit skeptical, he often acquiesced to Dandau and Hollier's insistence that Kassian's findings be heard. This provided just enough of a bridge in the rift in the Allied leadership.

Most of the intelligence reports the Psychiclink team had gathered concerned attempts to read the minds of Geiseric and all top political and military leaders within the Apex, namely, Germania. As he had known Geiseric for so long and helped him create what became known as the Formula, Kassian had been able to develop a detailed psychological profile, which allowed him to further contextualize and, therefore, conceptualize the Apex emperor's next move.

Nearly a month had passed since the Juggernaut had pounded into the East Coast shoreline and breached the walls of Fortress North America. With every day the titan war machine remained missing, the Allied leaders grew increasingly nervous and agitated, and they quarreled incessantly over its next probable line of attack.

Kassian leaned forward in his chair and shouted, "He won't waste time trying to get around South America! Going north around Canada and Alaska is too difficult! He'll try to cross through Panama," he said, pointing to a map of the Americas on the table. "We have to prepare for an attack from the Juggernaut there!"

Sinclair looked down his nose at Kassian and shook his head. "I do not think Geiseric would do this."

Kassian's eyebrows furled with consternation. "What do *you know* about Geiseric?!" He threw up his hands. "You haven't once been able to predict his strategy!"

Sinclair glared back at Kassian. "The Panama Canal is the most heavily-fortified place in the Allied defense!"

Kassian rubbed his eyes in frustration. "Why are you telling me this? You don't think I know that?!" He snapped, slamming his palms onto the table. "It's all fucking irrelevant! The Juggernaut *must* get to the West Coast before we can pull the Laser Net back," he explained, as he angrily pointed out everything on the map. "The Apex will open up a second front and come at us from both sides, crushing us in between!"

Sinclair launched himself upright from his seat. "We do not even know if Geiseric will use the Juggernaut again! For all we know, it is already back in Germania!"

"Right," Kassian remarked sarcastically.

"Right!" The French president vehemently nodded, staring bitterly at Kassian through squinted eyes. "We have not fully halted the Apex forces in Alabama! Maybe Geiseric will just continue pushing through there! He does not need a second front!"

"He does if he wants to *ensure* his victory!" Kassian slammed his fist onto the table again, as if it would help Sinclair understand. "Geiseric did not go through all the trouble of building such a large and expensive machine just to *use it like a pussy!*"

Sinclair looked up and gesticulated to the ceiling, as if calling out to God. "He wants us to divert forces all the way to Panama because he thinks Geiseric does not want to be a pussy!"

The other leaders just sat quietly, waiting for yet another one of Sinclair's and Kassian's arguments to cool off and smooth over. President Hollier shook his head. He was bewildered at how Allied High Command was in constant deadlock, fighting as much with each other in the War Room as they were with the enemy on the battlefield.

Another shouting match and a headache later, a compromise between the leadership was finally reached. Allied High Command authorized the deployment of a large contingent of naval and ground forces to Panama, but not nearly as large as Kassian had demanded. Hollier and Dandau wished to send more, but they acquiesced to the complaints of their three colleagues.

Kassian was furious that Hollier and Dandau went along with the compromise just to appease Sinclair, Kurtkin and Hung. He believed they were making a fatal mistake by not concentrating all of their expeditionary forces in Panama.

Alistair was dispatched to Panama, along with his entire Sabretooth battalion. The Sabretooths were the most powerful quadruped battlemachines created during the war. They were mass-producible by the Allies soon after the North Carolinian invasion, and they outclassed all of the Apex Panzers, including the Mark III Tigers. The Allied Sabretooths had slightly stronger armor protection and weaponry than the Tigers, and far greater agility.

The gap in technology was not insignificant. It was one of the main reasons that the Allies were able to hold their enemy in Alabama. The reason that the Apex did not have as good a quadruped was simple. Geiseric had invested a vast amount of human and material resources into the creation of the Juggernaut. In the meantime, other technological advancements were put on the back burner. But, the Juggernaut was the only way the Apex could crack through the Allied Laser Net without taking unacceptable loss of life, so Geiseric saw it as a necessary sacrifice.

The 10th armored division, consisting of a battalion of one thousand Sabretooths supported by nine battalions of mechanized infantry and artillery, was sent down to Panama. They had to move overland, because the Apex's naval superiority in the waters along the trek made it too risky for the Allies to transport their expensive and indispensable quadrupeds by sea. But, the trip from Fortress North America through Mexico and Central America was also fraught with peril.

The 10th armored division left the safety of the Allied Laser Net, where it bordered the Rio Grande. They crossed over from the United States to Mexico, making their way as quickly as possible, along with six Allied Cougar divisions, two million heavy and regular infantrymen, and a handful of Hornets and Dreadnoughts that could be spared from the Alabama front. On their journey, they were perpetually harassed by Golden Eagles and other Apex aircraft, which strafed and bombarded the Allied ground forces every step of the way.

Yet, the Allied land convoy made it to Panama faster than expected, with ninety percent of their forces still intact. They found shelter in the largest military base in the world — Louisburg — named after the massive French fortress in eighteenth century Canada, in order to further appease President Sinclair. King Louis XV jokingly boasted that "he could see the fortress from Paris!" The new Louisburg in Panama was as large as New York City and was protected by the only Laser Net defense system outside of North America and the Apex Empire. Cross lasers surrounded the base and kept those inside safe from assault, for the time being.

The soldiers, pilots, commanders and other Allied officers patrolled in and around the base, studying the Panamanian environment, getting to know the layout. For eight hours a day, the Allied fighters trained, each arm of the ground forces rehearsing their part of the grand defensive strategy. But, the Allied soldiers and officers still built in enough free time to let loose for a few hours every day. Dozens of different bars had been set up at the base, to quench the fighters' thirst for brew and help them relax. Most of them chose to drink a few beers before nodding off to sleep, to ease their anxiety-ridden nightmares.

Alistair visited a cabana bar one night, and he happened to run into an old friend.

Jacques had been a fellow trainee in the Parisian Formula Institute's class of 2038. The Parisian school was the best place to receive Formula training outside of Germania, for a couple of reasons. Geiseric was fervently inspired by the physical discipline of Parkour, the art of physical displacement, which originated in Paris. The founders of Parkour started out in a group named the Yamakasi, which was taken from a Zairian word meaning "strong spirit, strong body, strong man."

Parkour was a sport and an art, which involved simply the movement of one's own body through space, over, under and around all obstacles in one's way. It was a basic concept, but it involved using every form of acrobatics and maneuvering that a human body could achieve, all gelled together in a graceful, rhythmic movement.

The Parkour artists speedily maneuvered through the modern city of Paris. They would run with an explosive energy and, without pausing, surmount a small building by jumping off the corners of walls and rapidly pulling themselves up, holding on to anything that stuck out of the buildings. Within a second, they could climb a two to three-story structure in a way that seemed superhuman. Then they would run across the roof and jump off the other side, flipping down five to ten meters, yet landing softly on their feet with bent knees on the concrete below. They could also absorb the impact more by rolling on the ground, which allowed them to jump up and be off and running again without a halt. The Parkour artist was like water flowing in a constant stream. It was a sport designed for the individual to fully experience the human body — that machine which allowed the human spirit to interact with and travel through reality.

Parkour, Geiseric quickly came to realize, was also an invaluable skill for any warrior to learn. It was mandatory for all Apex soldiers and officers to learn the physical art during their Formula training, no matter whether they were infantry or pilots. Thus, Paris already had an edge in Formula training, due to their people's affinity with one of the primary aspects of the program.

Many of those who taught at the Parisian Institution had worked for Cirque du Soleil as showmen who, like the Parkour artists, seemed to perform almost superhuman acrobatics.

There was another reason why Paris had an edge on Formula training, and why the rest of the West, such as Britain and the United States, came there to train. The French government, like Russia, had not fully sided against Geiseric until only a couple years before the Great Diaspora. France and Russia had been somewhat of Allies to Germania and, later, to the Apex Empire. Because of their collaboration with Germania, France and Russia had gained much to fight the Apex with. Not the least of which was some of the top-secret Formula training techniques they had required Geiseric to share during his dealings with them. France had the best-trained military personnel in the world, outside of Germania.

Alistair, like thousands of other military officers from soon-to-be Allied countries like Britain and America, attended the Parisian Formula Institution in August 2036. While there he met Jacques, who was required to go to the school in order to become a fighter pilot in the French Air Force. Alistair enjoyed hanging out with Jacques after classes to grab a drink because, for whatever reason, the Parisian girls just loved the two of them and would hit on them in hordes. There always seemed to be certain duos that worked magic on the girls, the sum being greater than the parts. Quite probably, it had something to do with how different they were from each other.

Alistair was an attractive, young, black man in his late twenties. Jacques was a rugged, blue-eyed French man in his early forties. And, despite his age, Jacques projected some sort of invisible animal magnetism that drove the younger ladies wild. Girls in their early twenties went mad for them both. Being well aware of the strange effect they had on the opposite sex when together, Alistair took full advantage of it. Jacques, on the other hand, was never looking for anyone in that sense. He would usually end up boring the many women who took an interest in him, by ceaselessly bragging about how smart, caring and beautiful his daughter was.

He had not been deeply intimate with a woman since his wife died. Of course, he had kissed a few lovely ladies and never objected, but it also never went any further.

Upon coming to Fortress North America, Alistair and Jacques were coincidentally both stationed at the same base on the New England coastline. There they awaited the imminent Apex invasion for five months. During that time of such heightened stress, they became like family to each

other. Alistair had never been very close to his own father and he came to see
Jacques almost as a surrogate parent. And so it was to their great dismay that,
after the North Carolinian invasion, the two were sent to different battle
zones.

When they were reunited at the bar at Fort Louisburg in Panama, they
were exuberant to see the other alive and healthy. But, Alistair noticed that
Jacques was exhibiting nervousness and something he had never seen in his
friend . . . fear.

Jacques explained that he had been worried sick since his daughter had
been drafted into the war. Two weeks prior, all Allied citizens over the age
of eighteen and of able body were subjected to mandatory recruitment into
the military. Most of them would receive the most basic training and, so,
would perform relatively simple tasks, such as manning the light artillery
and anti-aircraft guns. However, manning these weapons was no less hazard-
ous, for though they were not targeted by the enemy bombings as often, they
did not have the ability to move out of the way that the Allied quadrupeds or
Sidewinders did. Jacques was very disturbed that his daughter might be performing one of these dangerous tasks.

After a few days of catching up with Alistair over drinks, Jacques seemed
to be cheering up. One night, though, Jacques didn't show up to hang out.
Thinking that he might be depressed again, Alistair decided to rally his French
comrade out of the dormitory and into the fresh air.

There were many transports, most running on tracks, carrying the people
inside the base to all its corners, which were several kilometers apart. Alistair
took a small tram across to the opposite side of Fort Louisburg, where the
pilots' living quarters were. There, he happened to catch a glimpse of Jacques
hurriedly running out of his dorm building. Jacques jumped in a tram before
Alistair caught up to him, but Alistair saw where he was going and managed
to follow on another tram.

After disembarking, Alistair saw Jacques on the platform, holding his
daughter in a bear hug with tears in his eyes. Alistair watched the two walk
toward one of the lesser gates, where troops entered or left the base for their
patrols. The guards at the exit recognized Jacques, for he had gained a reputation as one of the best fighter pilots in the world. Almost everyone around the
base knew and respected him. Usually anyone who wished to leave the base,
even to go on patrol, needed to show clearance paperwork. But Jacques simply
explained that he wanted to show his daughter a gorgeous jungle area he had
come across, and the guards just waved them by.

Alistair tailed them. He also walked out of the base with ease, for he too was well-known, not least of all for his military exploits . . . and other exploits. Similar to Jacques's excuse, Alistair had many times left these gates with a pretty young woman in tow, wishing to go look at a beautiful patch of rainforest, only for far different reasons. Figuring that he was scoping out another spot to take his ladies, the guards smirked when they saw him and just waved him through.

Outside of Fort Louisburg, there was endless untamed rainforest. Alistair nearly lost Jacques and Francesca, and in fact almost lost his own way in the thick jungle. After nearly an hour of tailing them, Alistair found what he had suspected. Jacques had secreted away a small, four-man craft called a Skipper, which could fly across the surface of the water like a diminutive Skimmer. It was floating on the shore of a wide river and he and Francesca were about to board. Alistair broke into a sprint, but neglecting to pay attention to where he was going, he tripped over a fallen tree, thudding loudly in the dirt. Startled, Jacques turned around and saw his friend sprawled out on the ground.

"Alistair!" Jacques was confused, but obviously relieved it was his friend.

Alistair was solemn as he stood up and brushed off his uniform. "What are you doing?"

Jacques inhaled deeply and sighed, looking his friend in the eyes. "You know what I'm doing. Please, do not judge me."

Alistair was infuriated for a moment, but he quickly calmed down enough to reason with his friend. "Jacques! The Allies need you! Do you know how much it's going to hurt morale to hear that *you* deserted?!"

Jacques was unfettered. "I will be frank. I do not care."

Alistair was stunned and offended. "You don't care?!"

Jacques approached his friend and put his hands on Alistair's shoulders. "Listen." he said sternly. "They have drafted my daughter and I will not tolerate it. I have already lost my wife and, now," he paused as he thought about what could happen if he stayed, "now, they want to take my daughter!" He shook his head emphatically. "No! She was the only reason I was still fighting. If they wish to endanger her, then *they* are now my enemies."

Alistair gulped, processing what he just heard. He sat down on the severed tree and nodded to show Jacques that he understood, but he did not have the energy to say anything. He felt like he had been punched in the stomach for a number of reasons, not least of which was that he was coming to really see how vile this war was. There were a few minutes of silence as Jacques respectfully let his friend gain his mental bearings. Reluctantly, Alistair finally summoned enough fortitude to send his friend off.

"Well, go with God, Jacques. I know you aren't doing this out of cowardice," he stood up, slapped his friend five with his right hand and hugged him with the other arm, "for you are the bravest person I know." He gave a quick punch on Jacques's back and Jacques did the same.

Tears welled up in the Frenchman's eyes and a pang of regret and guilt turned his stomach. He had not known if he could fully trust Alistair before, and that was why he had not told his comrade about his plans. Now he realized that Alistair was, truly, his friend — a friend who guarded his safety like family. Jacques walked over to the transport and leaned inside, pressing some buttons on the dashboard to begin warming up the engines. He walked back over to Alistair.

"You know, if I may be straightforward with you again," Jacques began, half-heartedly saying something he did not wish to, but felt he needed to tell his friend.

"The truth is, I don't think this war can be won any longer. If you ask me, we lost when the Apex punctured through the Net in the east. I think you feel the same."

Alistair just stared back at Jacques, unable to admit that he was right. Jacques looked down, filled with frustration. "I hate to think that I'm leaving the Allies in this time, but it hurts me more to think of a good friend staying here while I leave. You should come with us. There is room in the skipper."

Alistair's eyes widened, and for a moment he sincerely considered the offer. But, he shook his head. "You know I can't."

Jacques just nodded. The two slapped each other five again with their right hands and hugged with the left.

Before he took off, Jacques quickly explained where he was going, just in case. He knew Alistair would keep it a secret.

General Tierney called all of the leaders to a meeting in the War Room.

"Apex aircraft are penetrating deeper than ever into North America," Tierney said, pointing to the digital map on the table and looking everyone soberly in the eyes. "They're flying cross-country all the way to the West Coast, trying to hinder our attempts to peel back the Net."

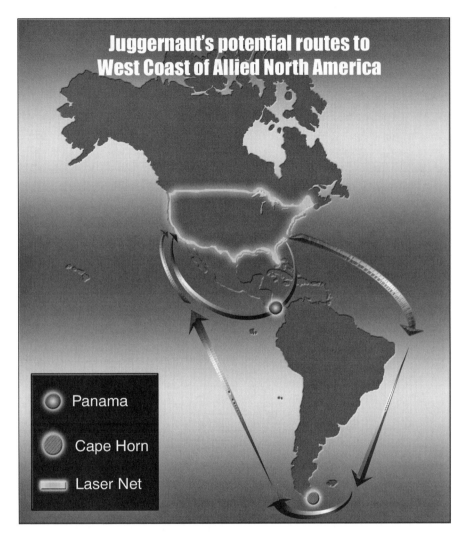

Juggernaut's potential routes to
West Coast of Allied North America

Panama

Cape Horn

Laser Net

Tierney pressed a button and the map on the screen changed, displaying a thinning outer Net boundary bordering the United States. The exterior Laser Net was noticeably thinner on the eastern border and visibly thicker on the West Coast. Tierney tapped on the screen and it focused in on the interior Laser Net boundary surrounding the Midwest, bordering on the Appalachians in the east and the Rocky Mountains in the west. The interior Net was far more developed on the east side than on the west.

"Right now," explained Tierney, "Apex forces are traveling between our inner and outer Net barriers. We have to shore up areas in between so they can't travel across."

Tierney pointed as the screen switched to a map of Panama. "Panama is being attacked by Apex air and naval craft as we try to build up heavier defenses there. But, we're ahead of schedule. Reports are good, so far. We're blowing their aircraft out of the sky left and right, and our underwater defense is making scrap metal out of the Delfins. The Shark schools have been tracking Delfin packs more accurately since we installed our new J3 sonar systems. The bad news is that the action in the water has been relatively quiet, compared to the amount of air-sorties being flown. I don't have a good feeling about that."

Hollier looked puzzled. "Why?"

"Because," Kassian interjected, "it seems the Apex is saving their Delfins for a major offensive."

"Or," President Sinclair remarked snidely, "maybe they are not going to attack Panama. Maybe everything they are doing there is a diversion."

Kassian's nostrils flared with rage, but he kept his reply relatively contained. "You will soon be proven wrong . . . and, then, you will feel like quite an ass."

Once again, the tension in the War Room remained thick enough to cut. General Tierney asked Kassian to apologize to Sinclair. Kassian simply laughed, for he knew he would be vindicated. However, not even he realized just how soon that would be.

Only hours after Kassian and Sinclair sparred over the issue, the Allied leaders received the news that the Juggernaut had been spotted by a small contingent of Sharks. The behemoth machine was treading across the floor of the deep Colombian Basin, heading towards the coast of Panama. It was defended by nearly the entire Apex Imperial Delfin Fleet.

In the Allied War Room, the leadership sat around the table listening intently as a military commander's voice came over surround-sound speakers in the room. Admiral Nelson updated High Command from her frontline position in a Great White battlemachine off the eastern coast of Panama.

"It looks like it's heading for the lock, Sir!"

"Is it in range of striking the Cross Lasers?" Tierney asked.

"Not yet, Sir!"

Everyone in the War Room looked relieved.

"How long?" Tierney asked.

"At present speed, it will be within range in thirty minutes."

Tierney looked around at the shocked expressions of the men around the table, and then roared over the intercom, "Send out the Sharks, Admiral! All of them!"

The rest of the Shark Fleet surged out from the docks that had been built into the coastal walls of Panama and Colombia. They swiftly converged on the Juggernaut and the Delfin Fleet. As they moved in closer, they began to take on heavy laser fire.

Admiral Nelson, who was leading from the front, was the first in range to fire and she shouted for all of her Shark commanders to follow her lead.

"All torpedoes away!" she blared in her thick British accent.

The Sharks turned on their high beams to get a visual on the situation. Surrounding the submarine Apex force in a giant sphere, they let loose their torpedoes towards the center. Their high beams lit up what looked like a giant, wriggling school of fish. It was the Delfin battlemachines in the distance.

The torpedoes raced forward, moving with tremendous agility as they sought their marks.

Dozens of Delfins were fatally struck by the torpedoes, which were shaped so that all their power was funneled forward into the target. The effect of a direct strike on a Delfin was devastating. Their hulls were blown out and their crews poured into the salty water. Some of the people tried uselessly to swim upwards, but they were too far down and the pressure crushed their bodies within seconds, their cold bodies littering the ocean floor.

The Shark commanders could not see whether any of the torpedoes made it through the barrier of Delfins to strike the Juggernaut. Having spent most of their torpedoes, the Sharks moved in to fire their shell guns. As the Sharks came in closer to engage their enemy, the Delfins immediately began a counterstrike, firing the powerful laser cannons that were mounted on their heads.

A portion of the Delfins pushed forward ahead of the Juggernaut and the rest of the pack. They approached the first series of the Allies' underwater armament and fortifications, which began about a hundred kilometers off the Panamanian coastal wall. On the ocean floor, the Allies had placed the most imposing drill bolt cannons yet created, the Big Reds. Named after the particularly reddish beam they emitted, these cannons were seven times larger than those mounted on the heads of the Delfins, and were powerful enough to do some serious damage to the Juggernaut. The behemoth war machine, on the other hand, could not strike them by way of burrowing through the ground, for they were mounted on moving platforms.

Having far greater range, the Big Red guns obliterated many of the Delfins before the Apex battlemachines could get near enough to fire off their own lasers. The powerful Allied cannons sounded like thunder when fired, terrorizing underwater life for many kilometers. The blasts and crackles of this man-made, submarine tempest could be heard through the hulls of the Delfins, by the crews and commanders inside, testing their nerve.

The eternally dark abyss was alight with the neon radiance of the energy beams. Still, there were many regions of pitch blackness. To avoid drawing attention, the Sharks turned off their search-lights. Each side now relied primarily on sonar technology to read what was going on around them. Thus, the two forces often battled in darkness, with only the lasers providing momentary visuals on the three-dimensional, underwater battle arena.

At a huge cost to the Apex Naval Forces, a path was cleared through the Big Reds. The Delfins then set forth getting rid of all the mines in the vicinity. The mines were like none ever used in warfare. Hidden underneath the ocean floor, each mine had a thirty-kiloton, nuclear bomb inside, which was more powerful than the bombs used on Hiroshima and Nagasaki combined. The bombs were placed inside thick, metal-alloy bowls, specially curved so that the force of the explosion was concentrated upwards. The Delfins fired their laser cannons incessantly into the ground, destroying any nuclear mines they could locate. This did not detonate the bombs, in the sense that it did not start the chain reaction that typically causes a nuclear explosion. This chain reaction occurred when extremely dense elements, such as uranium and plutonium, were brought to a critical mass. A plutonium bomb worked by essentially compacting the element to even greater density. This was done by completely surrounding a sphere of plutonium with shaped charges. The shaped charges were all pointed inwards and timed to fire off at exactly the same time. They could not be off by even milliseconds. Firing all at once, from all directions, squeezed the metal ball into such a small sphere, that the atomic particles within began to collide and — Voila! — man imitated the sun's power by setting off a nuclear chain reaction.

Demolishing a nuclear bomb was relatively safe, for it was nearly impossible, statistically, to set off every shaped charge in the device at exactly the same time by merely firing upon it. But, while they focused on locating and destroying the mines, the Delfins were thrashed by their Allied counterparts. Never before had the Sharks inflicted such casualties upon the Apex Naval Forces. There was no way for the attacker to avoid these losses, for the underwater defenses provided too strong a hindrance. However, they were not as strong as Kassian had recommended, and eventually the Delfins carved their way through.

Charging up from behind, the Juggernaut raced toward the path cleared by the frontal assault of Delfins. The main body of Delfins provided a shield against the Shark Fleet, keeping the Allies at a safe distance from the capital war machine, like a football team defending the runner heading toward the end zone. To the surprise of the Allies, after cutting through the torn first line of fortifications, the Juggernaut diverted from its assumed course, the Panama Canal. Instead, it moved across lightly-fortified territory, aiming for a patch of the coastal wall nearly eighty kilometers northeast of the canal.

Here, where the Allies had placed very few defenses, the Juggernaut began to climb out of the abyss.

Admiral Nelson was stupefied over this deviation.

"The Juggernaut!" she shouted into the radio. "It's not going through the lock! It's going across the land! It's bloody well going over the land!"

The Allied Bald Eagles immediately headed east to where the Juggernaut was surmounting the Panamanian coastal wall. Meanwhile, Admiral Nelson attempted to decisively break through the Delfin barricade to take a clean shot at the Juggernaut. Nelson commanded three-dozen of the Great Whites to launch a massive salvo of torpedoes at a concentrated area, to blow a hole through the protective sphere of Delfins. She led the group of Great Whites and twice as many Makos into the defensive sphere of enemy naval machines and straight towards the great colossus itself.

The Sharks took fire from all sides, as they had willfully caused themselves to be surrounded. Amazingly, Admiral Nelson's Shark was barely scratched as she took it on a straight course for the titan war machine. The same could not be said for the rest of the Sharks following her in. They were demolished all around her, yet she seemed invincible as she charged towards the target.

Nearing the Juggernaut, Nelson could see it clearly for the first time, through the video-feed coming from the cameras mounted on the exterior of the Shark. She was awestruck by the vastness of the creation, which loomed up like a gigantic octopus. Her emotional disarmament almost prevented her from reacting fast enough, when she suddenly came under attack from the Juggernaut itself. Three of its huge tentacles swiped at and grabbed for Nelson's Shark. Jolted into defense mode, Nelson deftly maneuvered her vessel through the gauntlet and immediately found a suitable target on the Juggernaut.

When she was near enough, she let fly all the torpedoes that were left in her Shark and immediately followed up with a bombardment of shells at close range, precisely aiming the entire salvo at part of one of the huge tentacles that was not moving. Nelson turned for a fast retreat as the massive explosions consumed the area with froth. The Admiral watched through a rear-mounted camera and saw that her strike was successful. The Juggernaut's arm was badly

damaged and the end of it was hanging from the rest of its length by a relative strand.

"Now we're getting somewhere!" Nelson shouted with euphoric madness, astounded that she was able to injure the goliath.

Her jubilation was short-lived, for Nelson's Shark was abruptly snatched up by one of the Juggernaut's tentacles. The limbs of the Juggernaut, like those of a squid, had thousands of smaller hooks lining the underside. They were made of steel, but they served the same purpose as the squid's — to grab and tear at the enemy. More tentacles latched on and the Great White battlemachine was torn asunder by the amazing power of the enormous Apex creation.

Water poured in, rushing over the main deck, knocking the Admiral out of her seat and bowling her over. The cold water came in at a high pressure and quickly filled the room. Nelson and three crewmen managed to swim to an emergency escape pod and jettison out of the demolished vessel.

The pod rose to the ocean surface and the Admiral wasted no time opening the hatch. She emerged halfway and looked around. They had popped up right in the middle of a battle, in the Delfin's zone. The Apex naval battlemachines were popping up out of the water and standing upright, several stories above the ocean surface. They thrashed about, engaging Allied defenders on the beachhead in much the same way they did in North Carolina. Cannon fire and explosions filled the air, as the battle raged above and around Nelson.

At one point, one of the Delfins moving upright on the surface of the water, swishing its tail back and forth, came within a few dozen yards of Nelson's escape pod. The large wave generated by the Delfin's kick slammed into the escape pod and filled it with water before Nelson could refasten the hatch. Fortunately, the pod was designed to float even in such a case, as were most life-craft. Nelson and her crewmen clamored for the opening to get air, tightly mashing together to fit through the hatchway.

They looked toward shore about two kilometers away, just as the Juggernaut began to surface. Giant metal tentacles emerged from the water and crashed down onto the Panamanian beachhead with a tremendous roar. The Admiral stared in astonished disbelief. It looked much larger than before, now that she saw it with her own eyes, instead of through a camera feed. She could almost feel the incredible mass and gravity of the Juggernaut pulling upon her.

An Allied Mako surfaced next to the pod and a side door opened up. A plank fell from the door onto the pod and two of its crewmen came out to assist Nelson and the three other survivors as they scampered inside to safety. Nelson took one final look at the Juggernaut as it pulled itself up onto the beachhead. The sight of the war machine had a potent effect on her psyche. It instilled the fear of God into her soul like nothing had ever done before. This titanic creation was more than a machine; it was the embodiment of power . . . and terror.

Admiral Nelson always had a respect and, even, an admiration for the Apex military. Now, for the first time . . . she had a fear of it.

In that moment of apprehension, Nelson saw the arm that she had bombarded. The end of the limb, nearly a hundred meters of the length, had fully broken off. That gave Nelson the boost of morale she desperately needed. Seizing control of her anxiety, she resolved to face the goliath once more. She commandeered the Mako and again piloted straight towards the Juggernaut.

"To the guns, men!" She rallied the crew, speaking with all the gusto of a Shakespearian actor, instilling courage into those on board.

"We shall devour this elephant one bite at a time!"

The Admiral skillfully weaved through the defensive barricade of enemy battlemachines and laser cannon fire. Two Delfins rushed up to defend the Juggernaut and Nelson could not shake them. She pulled her pursuers through the fray of the hot zone, managing to evade most of their fire. The glancing strikes began to take a toll on her Shark, but she was near enough to once more bombard one of the Juggernaut's arms. She ordered that every gun and torpedo available on the Mako be unleashed and the resulting explosions churned up the waters into white froth.

In a flash, dozens of Delfins targeted Nelson's Mako. Seeing that she had no chance of escaping back from where she came, the admiral piloted her naval craft upwards, the Delfins following in hot pursuit, tearing the Mako apart with their relentless laser fire. The Apex commanders could not figure out what in the world their opponent was doing. Nelson charged the Mako up to top speed.

"All hands, strap in!" she shouted over the intercom.

Going nearly a hundred and fifty km/h, the fifteen-thousand ton animalian vehicle broke the surface of the water and fired out into the air. It skipped across the ocean surface and crashed clumsily onto the beachhead, rolling and thudding over sand and debris until it came to a complete stop.

Once again, Nelson gave evacuation orders, only minutes since the evacuation from the first vessel. She helped some of the crew climb out of the main hatch, and then jumped down to the ground herself. They ran from the beached battlemachine as fast as they could, seeing the Delfins standing upright in the water, preparing to fire on the Mako. Nelson managed to run just out of harm's way, when the Mako was struck by a well-placed drill bolt, exploding in a ball of fire and metal. The admiral was knocked over by the blast, but not injured.

She got up and looked around to get a bearing on where she was. Just down the beach, the Juggernaut pulled itself up out of the ocean, causing tremendous swellings of water to pour onto the land. Its body was elliptical and its layered armor resembled an ancient shelled creature from the primordial seas. It moved with its long side heading forward. Just the body at the center of the many arms took up the same volume as two of the largest sporting stadiums in the world. Dozens of arms branched out from the sides and bottom of the Juggernaut's body, radiating out a kilometer away from the center, pulling its colossal frame up onto the land. Nelson stood on the beach, momentarily lost in amazement by this spectacle, completely oblivious to the artillery and laser fire going off around her.

Standing right in the path of the Juggernaut, Alistair was similarly paralyzed with awe. He watched from the cockpit of his Sabretooth quadruped battlemachine as the Juggernaut headed straight for him with remarkable speed for its size.

Alistair was entranced by the unimaginable size of this sea titan that seemed to be a mythological monster brought to life. He could feel its gravity beckoning him. Suddenly, he was ripped from his trance as a giant, metal tentacle slammed down right next to him. The shock wave caused by the impact of the Juggernaut's arm upon the ground shook his Sabretooth off its feet. Alistair quickly righted his vehicle and, having reconciled with his own inevitable death, he raced his Sabretooth with suicidal fury towards the arm.

He flung his quadruped battlemachine onto it, the Sabretooth jumping nearly three stories high, digging its powerful claws into the steel skin of the tentacle. The four paws clenched firmly onto the arm, giving Alistair a stable platform to fire the 120 millimeter cannons mounted on the chest and shoulders of his Sabretooth. He relentlessly fired the large uranium penetrators into the steel armor, tearing into the Vasculosynth beneath.

Alistair did not let his finger off the trigger until he had run out of rounds, which only took thirty seconds, but in that time he had fired twenty-five hundred depleted uranium penetrators into this segment of the Juggernaut's arm. To his relief, his efforts seemed to produce a slight effect in the massive tentacle. A spasm undulated from where he was shooting into the arm, all the way down to the tip about fifty meters away.

Suddenly, the entire arm jerked rapidly up into the sky. Alistair could not release his Sabretooth in time and suddenly found himself in the low clouds. The tentacle began furiously whipping about, attempting to shake loose its attacker. Unable to hold on, the Sabretooth reeled into the air.

Flying even higher into the sky, the Sabretooth spun and rolled in a long arc. Alistair noticed that everything seemed to slow down. His mind raced so fast that the world around him appeared to be crawling in slow motion. As his vehicle tumbled through the air, he caught glimpses of the Earth below. He drifted farther away from it, for what seemed like forever. Then, he began his rapid descent back toward the ground, gaining velocity as he did. Though he thought he may die, Alistair felt no fear and was filled with a sense of complete inner peace.

The Sabretooth drifted over the ocean and, with a powerful crash, it slammed into the water.

Alistair was knocked out by the force of the impact. His battlemachine fell into deep water and was spared from destruction. The Sabretooth was airtight and, though it was large and had heavy metal armor, it was buoyant enough to float back up to the surface, where it drifted for a moment. Alistair regained consciousness and looked out his cockpit window. He was a few kilometers out to sea, amidst a turbulent hot zone of battling Delfins and Sharks.

Fortunately, his quadruped vehicle was capable of swimming. It moved quickly through the water in the same manner that four-legged animals did, with a dog-paddle, walking motion, and Alistair was soon on the beachhead again. He looked all around the vicinity, checking out his new situation. He was now quite a ways from the Juggernaut, yet it still looked gigantic. Then, Alistair saw something that slaughtered his morale. Three of the Juggernaut's arms picked up a Sidewinder — the Allies' mightiest battlemachine. The tentacles brought the Sidewinder up into the air with ease. The moving fortress was completely incapacitated, unable to aim a shot on the Juggernaut or its arms. Alistair gazed with trepidation as the three tentacles began shredding the Allied capital battlemachine to pieces. Hundreds of crewmen fell out and plunged to their deaths.

Out of nowhere, a Sabretooth emerged from the jungle racing towards Alistair, coming from the direction of the battle zone around the Juggernaut. Alistair realized it was General Foss's vehicle. The Commander of the Allied Quadruped Forces in Panama came up beside Alistair and immediately recognized him.

"What are *you* doing here?!" Foss hollered over the short-wave radio links between their Sabretooths. "I ordered a retreat!"

"What?!" Alistair shouted with surprise. "Why?!"

"We're getting wrecked out there!" Foss shouted back. "Three Panzer divisions just stormed the beach! We didn't have enough quads to hold them off. I couldn't send my men to the slaughter anymore!"

Alistair noticed that Foss's Sabretooth was badly damaged in several places. In fact, it was surprising that it was still functional.

"Come on!" Foss shouted. "We're going back to base!"

With that, he took off in his cat-like battlemachine, Alistair following closely behind. Alistair beheld all the destruction wrought on the beachhead by Apex Delfin and Golden Eagle strikes. The bodies of tens of thousands of Allied artillery crewmen, gunners and the like, lay dead and burning on the ground.

To his astonishment, Alistair spotted an acquaintance, Sasha, moving slightly in the dust and ash. He detoured from the general's lead without telling him and rushed his Sabretooth towards Sasha. He got out of his battlemachine and checked her out. To his relief, she appeared to be relatively uninjured. Suddenly, her eyes opened.

"Hey," she said groggily.

Alistair smiled. "Are you okay?"

She gulped a bit and winced. "I think so."

Alistair looked around at the carnage and saw that the battle seemed to be moving closer to them.

"Good," he said. "Then we gotta get you out of here."

He carefully picked her up and carried her to his Sabretooth, which was lying on its haunches in the same manner as a cat, in order to be low enough for the occupants to board. Her small frame easily fit with Alistair inside the cockpit in the head of the vehicle.

Alistair raced his battlemachine off in the opposite direction of the Juggernaut and the battle, but not in the same direction the general went. He headed into the jungle to disappear.

"Where are we going?" Sasha drowsily asked, trying to keep her eyes open.

"Shhh," he gently soothed her, "leave it to me."

With that, she passed out from exhaustion, breathing powerfully, which let Alistair know she was probably not critically injured in any way.

He raced on without stopping, deeper into the Panamanian rainforest, hidden from the world outside. He traversed the tropical terrain until it became sparser. He reached the Pacific coast, just south of the canal. He then plunged his Sabretooth into the ocean and swam out until he could not see the coast, maneuvering around the Allied defenses, going unnoticed by the Shark contingents.

As night set in and they drifted out on the open ocean, a calm settled over Alistair. The moon was coming up on the horizon, full and luminescent in the clear night sky. A tremendous peace overwhelmed him and tears streamed down his cheeks. He had gone from hell into heaven, and he was not going back.

He paddled the quadruped for five hundred kilometers across the open Pacific, and landed on a gorgeous stretch of South American beach, far away from both the Apex and the Allies.

Dawn was breaking and before him there was nothing but luscious, green rainforest and a gorgeous, soft, white sand as far as the eye could see. Alistair fired a low flare into the sky and began running his Sabretooth a great distance up and down the beachhead. After a few hours, he spotted a welcome sight.

Jacques stood on the beach, alone, waving frantically to Alistair as he rode up in his battlemachine.

Over the next few weeks, Jacques helped nurse Sasha back to health. At first, she was bitter with him, Alistair and Francesca, who she thought were all traitors. It was hard for them to take care of a person who constantly said hateful things to them, even while she ate the soup they made. But they had all briefly gotten to know Sasha before, when she was training with Francesca and many other young ladies who had been drafted. Francesca, Jacques and Alistair knew that Sasha had lost her entire family and their sympathy for her was, at first, enough to deal with her anger towards them.

They stayed in a beautiful colonial estate in Ecuador. The mansion itself was sixty thousand square feet and the lot was hundreds of acres, but the well-kept gardens and lawns had been grown over by vines and other wild vegetation. The surrounding jungle even crept over the house itself and blanketed half of the white pillars and rooftops in greenery. The owner did not want the estate to look like it was still inhabited. He was an old friend of Jacques's and a former leading peace activist in France. Of course, he would cynically laugh about how he failed miserably at his task.

Jacques, Francesca and Alistair settled comfortably and thankfully into the new situation. They did not have to do much to help the host. The estate was entirely self-sufficient. It derived its energy from solar panels, which could be quickly hidden with the flip of a switch if needed. There was plenty of water, taken from a nearby river and filtered free of parasites and pathogens. There was enough good food stocked to last ten people for fifty years. The threat of the war began to seem distant. For the first time in ages, everyone felt at ease. Even Sasha, though she did not want to admit it, was very happy to be somewhere safe. She had not slept so well in nearly a year.

One night, Jacques came to her room to bring her soup. He was the only one that Sasha did not verbally decimate when bringing her food. She had a sharp tongue that was starting to grind on the others' nerves and it was not good for Sasha to become so riled. Jacques became her designated nurse, for everyone's sake. As he came near her door, he heard her crying.

"Sasha," he said quietly through the door, "are you OK?"

She just continued to cry. Jacques did not know what to do.

"Are you decent?" He asked, but again, she did not answer. He decided to open the door, and as he did, he turned the other way. He heard no reaction, just her crying more clearly now. He slowly turned around.

She was covered, for the most part. She slept in the nude and had not put on any clothes yet. The sheets were not fully covering her. Although very little of her was showing, he looked down as he walked in. He placed her soup by her bed, on the nightstand. He then turned around and began to walk out again, not wishing to intrude on her mourning.

"Wait!" she cried out, sobbing profusely. Jacques stopped and, keeping his head down, he walked back and sat on her bed, placing the sheets on her exposed areas so that he could look back up. He put his hand on her shoulder.

"What's the matter, my dear?"

She could not answer him. She shook her head, her tears becoming evermore abundant.

"Shhh," he consoled. "You will be alright, sweetheart."

She suddenly hugged him and clung to him as she bawled. The sheet fell from her upper body. He sighed and just hugged the poor girl. "That's okay, just cry," he soothed. "It's a good thing to cry. It's a way to heal."

Sasha's hysteria lessened as she leaned in Jacques's arms, while he rocked gently back and forth. He looked up to the ceiling, so as not to catch a glimpse of her nakedness. She finally spoke.

"You know, I haven't cried since my family died. Even then, I didn't cry much. It was strange. I just went . . . numb."

Jacques sighed and shook his head, as he contemplated this poor girl's tragedy. She still clung to him powerfully, her hands tenaciously digging into his side and back. Though it hurt, Jacques did not complain. Then, her hands slowly began to loosen and moved across his shirt. She rubbed the area where she had been clawing into him. She lifted his shirt a bit and saw her nail marks in his side.

"I'm sorry," she whispered softly.

"It's okay," he replied nervously. Sasha leaned forward and kissed the five small wounds.

"There," she smiled. "All better."

Jacques stared at her classically beautiful face. He knew he should get up and walk out, but he felt paralyzed. She put her hands under his shirt and rubbed his back. Slowly, she lifted his shirt completely off and pressed her warm, bare torso against him. He had not been this intimate with a woman since his wife had been killed more than two years prior. It felt wrong, not only because of his wife's memory, but because he was more than ten years her senior. But he could not summon up the self-control to stop Sasha, as he had done so many times before with other women.

She gazed into his eyes and he was helplessly drawn into hers. A powerful surge of pleasure and passion fired into his brain and he felt his body responding against his will. He swept her up and all the stress built up in both of them was suddenly released in a storm of ecstasy, consuming them in the physical and spiritual worlds. Afterwards, as Sasha lay naked and satiated in his arms, Jacques felt guilty, because that experience had never felt so good.

It took the Juggernaut twenty-eight hours to cross the tiny strip of land that was Panama. Yet, Allied ground reinforcements could not arrive in time to halt the incredible battlemachine, because of perpetual harassment from Golden Eagles overhead. The Bald Eagles had some success in injuring the great beast. They broke through the Golden Eagle defense enough to nearly completely destroy five of the Juggernaut's tentacles. Though the behemoth machine had many more, this attritional loss of its limbs was slowing it down.

However, it was too little too late. The Juggernaut made its way across Panama and crawled into the Pacific Ocean on the western coast. Part of the

Imperial Delfin Fleet had been dispatched to the Pacific before the attack on Panama, in order to protect the submerging Juggernaut. These squadrons valiantly engaged the Allied naval battlemachines attempting to funnel through the Panama Canal to the Pacific side. Though they were hopelessly outnumbered, the Delfins fought to the bitter end, until all met their demise. Their courage, however, provided enough time for the Juggernaut to enter back into the relative safety of the sea, and disappear into the abyss.

Once again, the Allies could not locate the gargantuan machine in the vast ocean depths. They had expected the Juggernaut to head north right away, towards the western coastline of the United States. Instead, it turned south and hid in the Atacama Trench, one of the deepest parts of the Earth's surface. Running along the length of Chile's and Peru's Pacific coastlines, the trench was a tremendous valley that stretched eight kilometers deep into the ocean floor.

A bucket-line of Delfins stealthily toted the hundreds of thousands of tons of fuel needed to power the Juggernaut's immense arms and weaponry. The enormous, man-made beast had consumed most of its energy in its relatively short trek across the land. It took longer than Apex High Command had foreseen to get the supplies to the waiting giant. Shark patrols incessantly searched for it, forcing delays in the Delfin supply line.

Things were going well for the Allies in Alabama. They still held Montgomery, even though the city had been subjected to three carpet-bombing strikes by Condors. Ninety percent of the buildings in the city were demolished, leaving only some of their steel-reinforced skeletons. Yet, amazingly, within the city there still existed an Allied military infrastructure, much of which resided in basements, underground systems such as storm drains and sewers, bomb shelters, and a handful of above ground structures that were still standing. The city's rubble was infested with Allied guerillas, who found shelter in every small pocket or makeshift cave in the concrete ruins. Here, they slept, ate and lived for days, turning into weeks. Many were underfed and near starvation. If they died, there were always more poorly trained draftees to throw into the fray.

The Apex ground forces had cracked through the eight fortified lines encircling the city, but they could not take Montgomery. Whenever they entered the city, they were barraged with relentless fire. The Allied guerillas drew the storm troopers, Hoplites and Panzers in and then ambushed them, firing large-caliber guns and shoulder-launched missiles that were, if aimed properly, highly effective at killing the tamers inside the Panzer cockpits. The pressurized energy funneled in and reduced those inside to a mush scattered on the walls and interior windshield.

A single machine gun was distributed to groups of three Allied guerillas. They were also given a few grenades and small sidearms. But, they were ordered to focus on utilizing the machine guns. One person fired it, until he was killed. Another man in the group would then pick up the gun and fire. When he died, the last man would take the gun back to base. At this point, the guns were worth far more than human lives to Allied High Command.

The guerilla tactics also worked against the Apex sky infantry, but the Kolibri appeared to be having more success than their comrades on the ground. The Apex flyers had proven to be a more effective force than the Allied Hornets, when they battled in Europe. Since the Apex invasion of Fortress North America, the Allies had attempted to launch some large strikes on the invading sky infantry in Georgia and Alabama. Though they were often outnumbered, the Kolibri flyers either emerged victorious, or escaped without taking excessive losses.

Because of this, Allied High Command used their Hornets primarily for guerilla strikes, mainly on the Apex expeditionary forces around Montgomery. The Hornets hid in the thick forests of Alabama and waited for the right time to hit their opponent, launching lightning assaults from all sides. Most of the Kolibri charioteers, altogether nine thousand around Montgomery, guarded the perimeter of the Apex ground forces against the attacks.

Hidden amongst the trees and other vegetation, the Allies had a trained sky infantry force in Alabama that was nearly three times larger than the invaders'. Still, Allied High Command did not want to risk an all out assault on the Kolibri around Montgomery. They needed an ace in the hole.

Field Marshal Von Edeco was the commander of the entire Apex Sky Infantry, but he personally led the light-armored battalions when in battle, distributing authority of the Apex heavy sky infantry to his trusted friend, General Roscher. The Kolibri regulars fought with the chariot and weaponry that Von Edeco had personally designed years earlier and they were the only force on either side to go undefeated in every battle. They never lost, for in every battle the Allies had underestimated the power of what were known in the Apex as *The* Kolibri.

The Germanians especially adored the field marshal and his Kolibri. He was still known as "the Captain," his original rank from when he first attained glory as a German fighter pilot in the 2020s. To his enemies, Von Edeco was known as the Flying Fox. It was a title he happily wore, for it was a tribute to his military likeness to the German commanders, Hermann Von Francois and Erwin Rommel.

Von Francois became a hero to his people and a terror to his enemies in World War I, when he outwitted the Russian Army and was pivotal in its destruction at Tannenberg. He often disobeyed orders, but because it resulted in victory, he was forgiven. Because of his craftiness, the Allied soldiers and officers nicknamed him "the Fox."

In World War II, Erwin Rommel pummeled the British Imperial Forces in North Africa. Though outnumbered and undersupplied, Rommel was able to consistently defeat the British, until the weight of the American Army joined in the fight. Rommel was a general who led from the front and, because of this, he was able to see exactly what was going on, right when it was happening. Thus, he outsmarted the British at every turn. He became known as the "Desert Fox" to his enemies, a legend that was hard to break in the minds of the average British and, eventually, American soldier.

Like his predecessors, Von Edeco, the Flying Fox, was highly respected by his enemies. In many ways, the Allied sky infantry had a reverence for him, which was only curbed by their terror. He was undefeated and many thought he was undefeatable.

However, Von Edeco's reputation was about to betray him, for he had come to believe his own legend.

On the night of August 28, 2039, nearly three months after the Apex had invaded North America, the Allies launched a massive attack on the Apex sky infantry. Twenty-four thousand Hornet flyers sprang from their hidden bases in the forests around the Black Belt. They quickly encircled the Kolibri regulars and heavies. On both sides, the regulars made up two-thirds of the fighting forces, with only one third consisting of the Dreadnoughts on the Allied side and the Knights on the Apex side.

Von Edeco immediately seized control of the situation. His subordinate, Roscher, was given much freedom to make decisions on the battlefield. This was often necessary due to the sheer speed of the fighting.

The Field Marshal raced along the perimeter of the expeditionary forces around Montgomery, gathering his Kolibri where the enemy forces were attacking. As usual, Von Edeco exposed himself to the peril of the most intense fighting, in order to fully assess the battle and gauge his strategic capabilities.

Like the many other great military leaders who had done the same throughout history, such as George Washington, Napoleon and Alexander the Great, Von Edeco went unscathed, while others fell around him from the hail of gunfire. This amazing but true aspect of Von Edeco lent itself to his myth of immortality.

The Allies had never sent so many Hornets at once at the Apex sky infantry. This was the epic battle that Von Edeco had been preparing for. Apex Intelligence had been pointing towards the Allies launching a huge sky infantry assault. Von Edeco was ready. In the past week, the Apex had poured much of their industrial resources into creating thousands of anti-sky infantry weapons. They had been installed around the perimeter of the invasion forces to protect them from the Hornets. These automated guns and missile launchers had radar-controlled, computerized targeting systems. The weapons represented the cutting edge of computerized-targeting technology and were almost as effective as the Formula-trained sky infantry flyers . . . but not quite.

The guns that encircled the Apex expeditionary force were primarily enormous Gatling guns, which fired 120 millimeter penetrator rounds. Though the rounds were made of tungsten, they were four times larger than the uranium penetrators used by the Allied Dreadnoughts. Thus, the 120 millimeter guns could easily devastate the Allied heavies. Although the anti-sky infantry guns were five meters long and weighed three tons each, they could swivel and aim with blurring speed. They stood mounted on the ground and boasted a range of up to five kilometers.

Coming in at just above the guns' range, the Hornets pushed their crafts to the limit to reach the necessary altitude. The sky infantry chariot functioned in much the same way as a helicopter or propeller plane; it pushed through the air like an oar through water. However, at over five thousand meters high, the air was so thin that the Hornet flyers had to buzz their wings to full throttle and, even then, they could only reach a little more than half of their top speed on the ground.

Slowed by the lack of air, the Hornets made easy targets for the anti-sky infantry missiles on the ground. The missiles worked much like the "steel rain" artillery missiles, but instead of arching towards a forward vicinity on the ground, they poured the deadly shrapnel into a spherical volume of air. The shrapnel could puncture through heavy and certainly regular sky infantry armor, when blasted out with such explosive force. Every salvo filled tens of cubic kilometers of sky over Montgomery with "steel fireworks," as these weapons were appropriately nicknamed. For, when the missiles exploded, the giant sphere of steel particles that emanated from the center of the blast reflected off the fire and other light, giving it the semblance of a brilliant firework display.

The Apex sky infantry and ground forces in the area found shelter in underground bunkers, away from the dangerous fragments that inevitably rained to the ground. The Allied sky infantrymen caught in this deadly onslaught had no chance. Nearly a third of the Hornets crossed over into the trap and, as they fell to the ground, their armored bodies resembled metal cheese graters, full of an infinite amount of punctured-through holes.

About eighteen thousand Allied sky infantrymen were left, outside of striking range. They had stopped before being pulled into the trap themselves. Seeing that they had lost a third of their force, the attack was called off and the Hornets went into immediate retreat. Von Edeco and the Kolibri flyers had several times before beaten the Hornets in battle, when outnumbered two to one. Now that the Hornet flyers appeared to be in a chaotic retreat, they would be even more vulnerable. Seeing his chance to annihilate the opponent, Von Edeco ordered the anti-sky infantry guns and missile systems turned off. He then led all the Kolibri forces out to give chase to the fleeing Hornets.

The Apex Field Marshal commanded General Roscher to attack a mob of fleeing Dreadnoughts. Roscher led his three thousand Knights after the Allied heavy sky infantry and overwhelmed the fleeing battalions one by one. Meanwhile, Von Edeco led his Kolibri regulars after the Hornet regulars, using the same tactic as he had commanded General Roscher to use. The Allied sky infantry had dispersed as they retreated, and they were no longer in large enough concentrations to have a chance against Von Edeco's and Roscher's Kolibri forces. The two Apex commanders reveled in what seemed like their inevitable victory. It appeared that the Allied sky infantry would soon be eradicated.

However, looks could be deceiving. Field Marshal Von Edeco had just led the Apex sky infantry into an elaborate Allied trap.

The Allied plan had been relatively simple. While the Apex for the past week had poured much of the empire's resources into the manufacture of the anti-sky infantry weapons around Montgomery, the Allies had put everything they had into building another ten thousand Hornet chariots with body-armor. However, there were no available flyers to fill them. The Allies had thirty-five-thousand chariots, but only twenty-five thousand trained flyers capable of facing the Kolibri. The Allies had filled the new chariots with poorly trained soldiers who barely knew how to fly the strange mechanisms, let alone fight in one.

The Allied commanders kept their new flyers naïve as to how unprepared they were for battle against the enemy. In fact, the entire division was kept secret from the rest of the Hornet flyers until right before they attacked the Kolibri forces around Montgomery, in order to keep their lack of readiness classified. What these ten-thousand Allied flyers did not know was that they were mere cannon fodder — the sacrificial lambs of an elaborate deception.

It was they who led the attack and had been slaughtered by the barrage of steel shrapnel. When Von Edeco led his counter-strike, the elite Hornet flyers purposefully retreated without informing what was left of the rookies. Thus, the Kolibri Forces had only been destroying the new, untrained contingents.

What was perhaps the most important part of the deception was Von Edeco himself. He had become his own worst enemy and Allied High Command knew it. He believed in his own mystique that, with him at the lead, the Kolibri Forces were unbeatable. Because of this, he never questioned how poorly his opponents were fighting in this battle. Roscher radioed Von Edeco to report that the Allied flyers he had encountered so far were surprisingly inept. Von Edeco simply disregarded this, believing their enemy's weakness to be a result of their being caught off guard by the well-timed counter-strike.

By the time Von Edeco began to suspect the truth, it was too late. The trap had sprung. Suddenly, in one grand, choreographed maneuver, all of the professional Hornet flyers turned around and charged toward the Kolibri. Simultaneously, another ten thousand Hornets emerged from hidden bunkers in the ground. The true, Formula-Elite Hornet flyers were ready to turn the tables on their enemy.

Von Edeco was suddenly overcome with a sense of his own doom. He had been too arrogant, as he chased the enemy down, so positive he was about to crush the Hornets and once again be the war hero. The Allies knew he had become used to seeing his enemy retreat, and they had exploited his bravado.

With the Kolibri regulars separated from the Knights, the Allies not only sent more than ten thousand Hornet regulars, but a third of their Dreadnought force at Von Edeco, knowing that no matter how skillful they were, the Kolibri regulars would be at a severe disadvantage taking on a large force of Allied heavy sky infantry. Their tungsten rounds could not pierce through the Dreadnoughts' armor and Von Edeco was consumed with a tremendous rage at the fact that his government would not commission uranium rounds. But, he summoned up his center, prayed to God for a split-second, and took charge of the situation.

He did the exact opposite of what his enemy expected. When facing a massive force of heavy sky infantrymen, the Allies would have expected him to retreat. However, Von Edeco knew that if he retreated, the Hornet regulars and Dreadnoughts would gang up on the Knights and annihilate them. That would leave the Kolibri regulars completely vulnerable to a future attack by the Allied sky infantry. The stand had to be made here.

Von Edeco led his Kolibri flyers in a charge against the Dreadnoughts. Amazingly, he once again went unscathed as he struck toward the enemy far ahead of his force. It was as if he had an invisible shield, some holy aura protecting him from harm's way. The Kolibri regulars followed immediately after their fearless leader and they received the miracle they needed . . . a window of time.

The speed of the sky infantry battles made every second count. When the Kolibri regulars charged at their enemy, the Dreadnoughts were not only caught off guard, they were completely startled. Everything about the trap had been going like clockwork, and this was the one part of the strategy where they definitely expected a specific outcome. Von Edeco was supposed to flee. Or, he was at least supposed to go after the Hornet regulars. Had the Dreadnoughts not been so confident, they would have braced for a possible charge and laid waste to the Kolibri regulars with their thirty-millimeter Gatling guns. But, they had fallen into the same confidence trap as Von Edeco. His stratagem shocked them into momentary inaction and this gave Von Edeco and his Kolibri the time they needed to rush in on their opponent. The fight deteriorated into an all out, hand-to-hand rumble. And Von Edeco's men were well-prepared for such combat. It was the Hail Mary and they knew exactly what to do.

The Kolibri regulars ganged up on the Dreadnoughts, three on one. Two Kolibri held a Dreadnought flyer's powerful, strength-enhanced arms, while the other inflicted damage on the heavy infantryman's weakest point — the head. If a Kolibri regular could fire the tungsten rounds at point blank range at a Dreadnought's helmet, which was hard to do unless he was being held back by other flyers, the impact of the round upon the helmet shook around the flyer's head within so violently that often his cranium cracked and his brain liquefied.

The Hail Mary tactics served to be more effective than Von Edeco ever imagined. If a Dreadnought wanted to help a fellow fighter who was being ganged up on, he could not simply fire his Gatling gun at the Kolibri, for fear of killing his comrade. So, the Dreadnoughts had to go in and grapple with them, which was far easier said than done.

The Kolibri regulars' agility made them highly elusive. However, most of them were grappling with the enemy heavies and, so, could not watch their backs closely enough. The Dreadnoughts' most efficient method of killing the enemy was to smash an Apex regular's face in with a hard cross punch, leaving a crushed piece of steel where, a moment before, there had been a Kolibri flyer's helmeted head. And so, the battle somewhat resembled an immense bar-brawl, with thousands of enemy flyers chaotically tussling and waling on each other.

Overall, the Kolibri regulars proved to be more effective at close range. As the Dreadnoughts, coming to the aid of their comrades, tried to kill one of the Kolibri regulars, the Kolibri ducked out of sight. Before the Dreadnought could mentally assess whether to help his friend or look for the Kolibri first, he was knocked unconscious or worse by a blast to the back of his helmet from a double-barreled, tungsten penetrator gun.

All of this happened so fast that the Hornet regulars in the vicinity did not have time to formulate an effective counter-strike to this new strategy of Von Edeco's. Thus, their defense of their heavy compatriots was poor to say the least. The original plan was to encircle the Kolibri regulars and keep them from escaping while the Allied heavy sky infantrymen went to work on them. Being thrown off balance now, the Hornet regulars were unable to establish a cohesive tactic. The Allied sky infantry force battling with Von Edeco's Kolibri had no other choice but to temporarily retreat, so that they could regroup and attack their enemy again. This provided Von Edeco and the Kolibri regulars with another badly needed window of time.

Most of the Dreadnoughts and many of the Hornet regulars were attacking the Kolibri Knights. For their part, the three thousand Knights had been holding up remarkably well against four thousand Dreadnoughts and nearly twice as many Hornet regulars. General Roscher had made the strategic decision to enact the Hail Mary plan, for reasons that were much the same. Roscher knew that, if he went after the Dreadnought battalions, the enemy regulars would come up from behind and blast the Knights with precise shots to the back. The Hornet regulars did not have to get close to fire on the Knights, which the Kolibri had to do with the Dreadnoughts, because the Allies' depleted uranium penetrators easily pierced a heavy infantryman's armor.

Roscher saw that his only chance for holding out was to throw his Knights into the swarm of eight thousand Hornet regulars. He led his men into the fray, startling his enemy just as much as Von Edeco's maneuver had. Once again, the Dreadnoughts could not fire on the Knights, this time for fear of killing their lightly-armored comrades, who enshrouded the Apex heavy infantrymen like a cloud of locusts.

The Knights, however, had only managed to jump from the fire into the frying pan, their situation being not much better. They were under attack from all sides by Hornet regulars firing their double-barreled guns. Roscher knew that the Lance-22 laser drill bolt cannons, which the Knights carried, were not an efficient weapon in this type of situation. The Lance-22 was designed for battle against heavy sky infantrymen. The laser cannon was too slow in battle with a swarm of Hornet regulars. The general realized that it was time to try out the swords that all the Kolibri Knights carried.

Not a single Apex heavy sky infantryman had ever unsheathed his sword in true battle. Their steel broadswords were as long as an average man was tall, and seventeen centimeters wide at the fattest part, near the hilt, where the blade was nearly six centimeters thick. The sword was seven times heavier than its average Medieval predecessor, and the steel-alloy had been brought up to near ideal strength using supercomputers in the alloying process. These mighty swords, when wielded about with the power of the strength-enhancers in the Kolibri Knights' armor, were capable of hacking through the light sky infantryman's armor like butter . . . and so they did.

As the Hornet regulars harried them, the Knights whipped their swords about, sending torsos of Allied flyers raining to the ground. They were often severed right above the rim of their chariots. Just the sight of the large Kolibri Knights bearing down at nearly seven hundred kilometers per hour, wielding about the huge swords, was tremendously unnerving, another psychological ploy that was a powerful weapon in and of itself.

These Hornet regulars now broke into retreat. With their backs turned to the Knights, the light-armored Hornets were mercilessly chased down and cut to pieces with even greater ferocity. Roscher's Hail Mary tactic had worked even better than Von Edeco's.

Field Marshal Von Edeco had pioneered the tactical use of hand-to-hand combat, grappling and sword-fighting in the Apex sky infantry. Before this battle, most of the tactics had not actually been used against the Allies. The Allies had not even bothered equipping their sky infantry with bladed weapons. Allied High Command thought it was ridiculous—crazy and suicidal. Even the Apex leadership, as radical and revolutionary as it was, did not want to risk fighting an entire battle with bladed weaponry. It seemed insane. Yet, the proof was on the field. General Roscher's crew slaughtered thousands of Hornet regulars and had the rest on the run.

Von Edeco and his flyers arrived on the scene just in time to see the Knights chase the Hornet regulars from the field, hacking the lightly-armored Allied flyers to bits. The field marshal's heart burst with pride as he saw the Knights effectively engaging the enemy with their broadswords. It was absolutely poetic; truly, a medieval battle, airborne, as if the warriors were mounted on winged horses.

Von Edeco took control of his Kolibri regulars, preventing them from giving chase to the fleeing Hornet regulars. Instead, he redirected them to help Roscher destroy the four thousand strong Dreadnought force. General Roscher's two thousand remaining Knights coupled with Von Edeco's five thousand enduring Kolibri regulars to face the Dreadnoughts.

These Dreadnought flyers were fresh, having not been engaged in the first part of the battle. However, though the Knights and Kolibri regulars had already fought intense battles, they were invigorated, having turned the tide from inevitable defeat to possible victory. The Apex sky infantry had already felt the icy grip of imminent demise and had overcome all odds. Having their faith in victory revitalized and lacking any fear of death they may have held before, the Kolibri flyers audaciously tore into their enemy.

Von Edeco rallied his regulars behind the Knights. Roscher led the Knights forward and pounded into the concentration of Dreadnoughts. During the battle, the Apex flyers proved that when an opponent was near evenly matched technologically, the vital aspects distinguishing one fighting force from the next were the psychological factors. The Allies had greater numbers, but the Apex had superior leadership and training. This evened the score and would have left two evenly matched militaries, if it were not for one thing—the mindset of the fighters.

The Kolibri flyers were unmatched by anyone in the Apex or Allied forces, largely because of their die-hard belief in Isaiism and their loyalty to the Principles regime. A majority of the Kolibri regulars had just become adults. They were almost entirely young men ranging from eighteen to twenty-five years old; the first generation to go through Geiseric's education system, some for its entirety, from kindergarten through to graduating from Germania's high schools. Many in this generation had gone on to the new Apex universities, which while providing the youths with the best educations in the world, also pushed the Isaianic Creed and had great success in converting most of the students.

Waging war for ideological purposes was a relatively new concept to humans. It began in the Bronze Age and reached its zenith in the Iron Age.

Even in the beginnings of historical civilization, five thousand years ago, wars were fought primarily over resources, such as water. To be prepared to fight and die for an ideal was foreign to humans, at first. Why it came into existence was not completely explicable, but when the ideological wars came into being, they set the world ablaze like never before and the fires never stopped burning. Generation after generation risked life and limb, and the welfare of their loved ones, for nothing more than their beliefs. Through the epochs it was proved that, as counterintuitive as it may have seemed, those who were empowered by their beliefs were far better fighters, on the whole, than those who fought just for their welfare. The reason for this was that those who fought for an ideology believed that it was far more important than their own welfare. They were thus imbued with an even greater courage and willingness to sacrifice for victory.

It was a correlation that the Allies either did not make or did not believe . . . and that was why their sky infantry was about to be annihilated.

With General Roscher at the lead, the Apex heavy sky infantry ripped into their opponents, Von Edeco and the Kolibri regulars right behind. The Knights' blades were now useless against their heavily-armored enemy, so they grabbed their Lance-22's and ruthlessly unloaded on the Dreadnoughts.

It was a massacre, as the loud crack of endless drill bolts tearing through the air marked the end for evermore Dreadnoughts. The Kolibri forces broke through into the concentration of Hornet heavies and all hell broke loose. Being so heavily outnumbered, the Allied heavies were quickly routed and destroyed, the ashes and incinerated bodies of nearly four thousand Dreadnoughts scattering to the ground.

Having consolidated their surviving forces, the Allied sky infantry that had retreated earlier now arrived back on the scene. However, even though they still outnumbered the Apex two to one, with the Kolibri forces bursting with morale, the numerical odds boded ill for the Allies.

The Apex overwhelmed their enemy both tactically and psychologically, although great losses were taken on both sides. Amidst the most harrowing tumult, General Roscher, who like Von Edeco could always be found at the charge, fighting side by side with his soldiers, was struck down, his luck or blessings having run out.

A stray DU penetrator round from a Dreadnought's Gatling gun, aimed at another Kolibri flyer off in the distance, struck General Roscher right through the face. Von Edeco saw the hit and immediately knew in his mind and gut that Roscher was dead. A Knight caught the general as he fell to the Earth,

and Von Edeco rushed over to see for himself. Hardly anything was left of Roscher's head inside the blown out helmet and face-mask.

It was more than Von Edeco could take. For a moment he clutched his gut and a piercing pain shot through his temples. But, he pushed his sickening sorrow back. He turned away, determined not to think about the trauma of losing his old friend, or of seeing Roscher reduced to organic sludge. At least, not right then in battle.

Von Edeco ordered the Knight to drop Roscher and get back into the fight. As the general drifted to the Earth below, Edeco looked down to catch one last glimpse of his friend in flight and, as he did, became filled with an incomparable rage.

Storming headlong into the melee, Von Edeco unleashed his fury upon his unfortunate opponents. At this point, as if possessed by their commander's incensed spirit, the Apex sky infantry entered the "zone." Time slowed and, even more, they felt they were of one mind, all working in perfect harmony. When the plan had to adjust, they uncannily all knew and acted together simultaneously. Von Edeco and the Kolibri flyers were like a single, enraged beast taking on a swarm of pesky insects.

Acting in such synchronicity, the Apex beast devoured the Allied sky infantry, large chunks at a time. If an Apex flyer was struck down, his death was immediately vindicated as his comrades shot the killer down, along with

a number of other Hornets nearby. Von Edeco and his Kolibri regulars ran out of ammunition for their double-barreled guns, but they did not break a step. They immediately seized their blades, a European smallsword, which they all carried in their chariots.

The smallswords were made for stabbing. The blades had a sturdy, triangular width that was six centimeters thick at the fattest point, making it extremely sturdy. Its entire meter and a half of length was made of steel alloy brought up to near ideal strength. With the power of the Kolibri regulars' strength-enhancers, the smallswords could easily pierce weak points on a Hornet regulars' armor.

Allied sky infantrymen fell left and right, stabbed through the neck or eye visor, or debilitated with a wound to the armpit. Most of the wounds punctured major arteries, sending profuse geysers of blood into the air. As thousands of Hornets were run through with the swords, blood poured from the sky in a deluge, like some bizarre Biblical phenomenon.

Once again, the Knights holstered their laser cannons, unsheathed their broadswords and set about hacking apart the Allied regulars. The Hornets fell like wheat to the scythe.

Then, the impossible happened . . .

To the horror of the Kolibri forces . . . the Flying Fox was shot down.

Von Edeco engaged a Hornet and struck with his smallsword which, weakened by so much use, broke on the Allied flyer's armor. The Hornet flyer laughed and fired on the Apex field marshal, striking him through the upper torso area. The fighting had moved to just a few meters above the treetops and the invincible Von Edeco plunged down into the dense vegetation, out of sight.

Before the Hornet could attack Von Edeco again, the Allied flyer was cut cleanly in half by a Kolibri Knight. The Knight ducked into the trees in search of Von Edeco, but was ganged up on by two Hornets and blasted four times with depleted uranium slugs. Then, like a row of dominos collapsing, those two Hornets were taken out by two Kolibri flyers. It went on this way for what seemed like an eternity, both sides fighting to find Von Edeco, though both sides somewhat expecting him to be dead already.

The Kolibri forces began to lose their edge, as word spread and a slow wave of panic ran through their ranks. The loss of their beloved leader froze their priceless momentum and, as their spirits waned, the iron beast began cracking into pieces. It seemed that the battle would turn in favor of the Allies.

Suddenly, the Apex sky infantry received its third miracle of the day . . . and it was the greatest one. Von Edeco rocketed out of the foliage and flew back into the battle, seemingly uninjured by the blast he took. His flyers were stunned for a brief moment, overtaken by the mythological character they called the Flying Fox. Now, the Kolibri flyers were certain that they were being led by someone half-divine, who was truly immortal in battle.

Together, the Kolibri forces let out a tremendous cheer, coalescing once more into an iron hammer. The sight of Von Edeco alive and well rallied the Apex flyers more than anything else could have. It was time to crush their opponent, once and for all.

They savagely reduced the Hornets to near equal numbers as themselves. And without significant numerical superiority, the Allied flyers were doomed.

In a panic, the last tatters of the Allied sky infantry chaotically scampered away in a final retreat. Now that the battle was over, Von Edeco's top officers rushed to his aid, checking his wound more closely. They hovered around him and were amazed by what they saw. Von Edeco had appeared to be barely injured when he came back into the battle, as if he had only been grazed by the DU round. In fact, he had been shot squarely through the top of his chest, near his right shoulder. The penetrator round had gone through Von Edeco and out the back of his armor, leaving a hole in the corner of his chest that was as wide as the length of a forefinger.

The Kolibri officers could look through the wound and out the other side. They were astounded by their leader's strength of mind and body.

Suddenly, Von Edeco collapsed from exhaustion and shock. He fell through the sky, but was quickly caught by his officers. They disengaged his Kolibri chariot, sending it hurdling to the ground below. The officers rushed their beloved field marshal to the medical facilities within the Apex lines around Montgomery.

Von Edeco was incredibly lucky. Or blessed, which was how the Apex chose to look at it. More often than not, a penetrator would not blow out the other side of armor. Usually, the round would not have enough kinetic energy to blast through the armor again. This made the round far deadlier, as it instead diffused its kinetic energy by ricocheting around within the armor, shredding the flyer's soft flesh and innards. The DU round that struck Von Edeco was fired at such close range that it blasted out of the armor without inflicting greater injury to the field marshal's body. Von Edeco was doubly fortunate because he was struck through a non-vital area.

Von Edeco's injury was completely contained to the area of the wound. But, because of his delay in seeking medical attention, his right arm had been deprived of blood and oxygen and, thus, began to die. The doctors were near entirely sure that the limb could not be saved, but Von Edeco insisted they try. So, though his arm looked black and blue and drained of live blood like the appendage of a corpse, the Apex field surgeons decided not to amputate . . . yet.

Deep beneath the ocean's surface, on the northwestern coast of South America, the Juggernaut roared to life once more . . .

The dust of the ocean floor kicked up and clouded the water as the titan's arms writhed about. It began its ominous ascent out of the Atacama Trench's deep abyss.

The Allied lines were crumbling in the east of North America. With the Hornet forces annihilated, the Apex had complete near-to-ground air superiority. Yet, the Allied ground forces were still holding out in Alabama, partially due to the technological superiority of the Sabretooth battlemachine over the Panzer Mark III. However, the Allies were pouring most of their strength onto the eastern front. There was no way the Allies could defend two fronts, but the Apex had to strike soon, for the interior Laser Net was nearing completion.

It was time for the Apex to strike the final, crushing blow to the Allies. It was time to once again . . . release the Juggernaut.

—— XX ——

THE GOD OF WAR

As the air-train began its descent, Logan saw hundreds of farm fields below, interspersed with trees and other wild vegetation. Connected in a loose, broken-up, grid pattern, the fields stretched past the horizon to the north, south, east and west. As the Luftzug neared the ground, Logan could discern people working in individual field patches, which were each a few acres wide. Next, the air-train flew over a small, lush, green pine forest and, finally, all those gazing outside the windows were able to see their living quarters.

Placed in long rows parallel to each other, were hundreds of single story, rectangular buildings with light grey roofs. At least half of the buildings were conjoined, sharing their walls with those on either side, or connected two-by-two, as a duplex. The rest were sitting independently.

The Luftzug touched down on a humongous, raised landing platform perched more than fifty meters off the ground, far above the tree line. The platform was relatively slender, only a meter thick and supported by surprisingly few metal columns, which as Logan noticed reflected a muted, polarized glare, as if those who gazed upon them were wearing sunglasses. It was bright, but didn't hurt his eyes.

Lowering its landing struts, the Luftzug hovered down to a soft, still landing. Logan watched as dozens of other airships touched down and took off from the huge platform. His car's doors opened and a mobile staircase was wheeled to the exit, driven by an underclass man wearing a loose-fitting, beige tunic. The guards directed everyone to exit the air-train.

Logan and Francesca disembarked together, down the steps to the landing deck, where they walked twenty paces to a staircase leading down from the platform. Tom and Bibi were right behind them, with Jacques, Sasha and Alistair heading up the rear. From the lower deck, Francesca and Logan stared out at the beautiful sunset and she affectionately wrapped her arm around his waist. Bibi, wracked with a mother's hidden contempt, looked away. When Tom saw Bibi's contorted face, he laughed to himself and put his arm around his wife's shoulders.

"Our boy has gotta grow up some time," he whispered in her ear.

"I know, I know," Bibi replied. "Just not yet."

Kolibri guards soared close overhead.

"*Shritt hin zu den Fluren!*" they snapped gruffly in German, telling the underclassmen to move towards the corridors. The masses of people were ushered through a dozen large, open corridors leading into a colossal, oddly-shaped building. It had a flowing, surreal form, and was tinted a metallic green color, which blended somewhat with the surroundings.

Logan, his family and his friends gathered into cordoned-off lines separated by wooden handrails that appeared to be made of dead oak. The aisles led to small booths with underclass workers inside stamping people through and giving them numbers. The turnstiles at the end of the line reminded Logan of the entrance to an amusement park, all of which was quite surreal considering the current circumstances.

Tom received a number for his family and Jacques got a number for himself, Francesca and Sasha. Alistair was given a number only for himself.

"I feel lonely," he joked.

"Ahh, poor Alistair," Jacques whined in an exaggerated, sympathetic voice, hugging him and petting his head. Alistair smirked.

Francesca and Sasha got in on the fun and both hugged Alistair, one on each side. "Poor baby," they consoled.

"Ahh, that's nice," Alistair smiled, putting his arms around them.

They exited the corridor into a spacious lobby with high ceilings and good ventilation. The walls and ceilings were a metal, geodesic skeleton of titanium with many large triangles of a transparent, glass-like material in between. Sun shone brilliantly through the panes, illuminating the lobby and showcasing the forest outside. The peripheral trees held nesting boxes where colorful birds made their homes.

Waiting on long, comfortable benches for their numbers to be called, the underclass arrivals were calmed by the serene music that played gently through speakers hidden under the floor's white marble tiles. Underclass waiters brought snacks and ambrosia shakes. Francesca leaned lazily on Logan's shoulder, soon falling further to rest her head in his lap. As Alistair finished his glazed pastry, Sasha wiped the sugar from his face with a napkin, because it disgusted her too much to look at it.

After waiting for half an hour, Tom's number was announced. Francesca sat up and kissed Logan quickly on the cheek, making his body come alive.

"Come looking for me," she whispered.

"Oh, I will," Logan said.

"You look for us and we'll look for you," Alistair said.

Logan gave a thumb's up. "Cool," he said, slapping him five.

Tom waved to everybody. "We'll see you all soon I'm sure."

Logan and his family made their way to the front of the lobby where dozens of underclassmen worked behind the counters. Their suits were a bit more formal and tighter than the people who had checked everyone in at the docking platform, and these workers all wore caps. Tom and his family walked up to a young woman who was not helping anyone else and showed her their number. She directed them to a room across the building.

Tom turned the French-style knob and opened the door to see their counselor sitting across the desk from them. Like all of the other female counselors, she dressed somewhat akin to a nineteen-thirtie's school teacher, except with a modern flare. She also spoke in the elite Prussian-German dialect typical of all the counselors. The woman stood and smiled.

"Macht die tür zu, bitteschön," she said, and Tom closed the door as she had asked. "Please, sit." She motioned to the chairs in her bright, spacious office. On her desk, she pressed some buttons on her holographic monitor, accessing the family's record on the database.

"Ich bin Frau Nüsslein," she introduced herself. "And you must be Tom, Bibi and Logan."

"Jawohl, Frau Nüsslein," they answered properly, as they had been trained.

"Gut, gut," she muttered, placing her finger to another of the hologram buttons, reading what came up.

"Okay," she spoke in English, so they were absolutely clear. "You will be going to Arbeitskamp Delta to help on the soy fields. Most likely, your jobs will be to keep the dead leaves and such off the ground, which helps keep bugs and parasites away from the harvest. It's all fairly simple. Your living quarters will be in Delta Sector, in room five hundred and fifty. Do not worry about remembering that. It will be written on the pass I give you. Your particular suite is not sharing a wall with any others. I'm sure you'll find the interior to be acceptable. The suites are nicely-furnished with good amenities." The counselor smiled. "You have four rooms because, and I'm happy to inform you of this, we have found your parents," she looked at Tom and Bibi, "and they should already be waiting there for you."

"Oh, thank God!" Bibi exclaimed, crying joyously into Tom's shoulder.

"Thank you so much," Tom replied with passionate gratitude. Frau Nüsslein gazed sympathetically at them.

"I'm sorry it took so long," she said. "And we will also be uniting you with your brother and his family, Tom. And that was all you had as part of your core family unit, correct?" Frau Nüsslein confirmed.

"Jawohl, Frau Nüsslein," Tom answered.

"OK," she said, "then that is all we can do for now. We cannot move around everyone's friends and extended family to be with each other, yet. I can only tell you that the people who you listed upon arrival in Colombia have all been accounted for and they are fine. In fact, they are all working the soy fields in this general vicinity. I will arrange for you to speak to each other via videophone sometime in the near future."

Logan and his parents walked out of the office and followed throngs of people down the hallway opposite from the way they had come in. They passed through a spacious corridor, much like others Logan had seen during his time under Apex dominion. Though, these were much higher and had many levels of walkways crossing back and forth above the underclassmen. Here was where the counselors and other Apex citizen staff walked hurriedly back and forth. Below them, on the ground floor of the corridor, Logan moved with the crowds of Allied prisoners in their beige tunics and identical haircuts and could not help feeling an incredible kinship with his fellow underclassmen.

The corridor ended at a three-story station where magnetically-levitated trains came in every minute. The counselors rode the top rail, while the underclass was relegated to the bottom rails. The bottom-most train was the largest, yet it was nearly silent as it moved. Tom and his family moved through a checkpoint and handed their papers to a worker at the booth. The worker told them they were to board the red line, which would be arriving momentarily.

Tom, Bibi and Logan rushed to the loading platform just as the train pulled up. They boarded quickly, with one hundred other people. Unlike the commuter lines of Logan's youth, a glass tunnel surrounded the tracks. He watched as the line moved over the trees, noticing that the thin metal beams supporting the tracks from the ground barely took up any space in the forest. As they came over a crest, Logan could see far into the distance in every direction. In front of him were the flat-roofed suites, lined up a few dozen rows deep. The orange-pink color of their walls was extremely pleasant to look upon and reminded Logan of a tropical sunset.

The houses were set amongst the trees and natural pools that glittered in the sun. Beyond the houses, Logan could make out endless fields separated by grids of trees. The train sped down the hill and stopped abruptly at the first unloading station, which was for Sector Omega. A few dozen people disembarked. It then moved south for another ten minutes and stopped at the unloading station for Delta Sector. The workers at the station directed people to their abodes and siphoned them through the turnstiles in an orderly fashion.

With Tom leading the way, his family exited onto a pebble walkway that cut through grass and bushes growing high over everyone's head. Bibi was wringing her hands in nervous excitement, ready for the long-awaited family reunion. Seeing their suite, they picked up their pace. As they entered, Tom's and Bibi's parents accosted them all in a big group hug. The confirmation of everybody's livelihood caused the entire family to burst into tears. They held each other for what felt like a blessed eternity.

That night, they all sat around the wooden card table in the small dining area beside the kitchen. Tom parked himself happily by his mother, opposite his father. Tom's father was a man of good humor, yet had an air of calmness and humility. He held himself upright and, for a man in his seventies, was in excellent shape. Tom's mother cast a similar aura. She was vivacious in her winter years and had a youthful physique. Logan affectionately called them Grandpa and Grammy, and was always eager to hear their childhood stories.

Bibi only had her father left, and everyone called him Papa. He was also a spry seventy-something, but shorter and sturdier than Grandpa. His bronze skin tone nicely complimented a full head of silver hair. He pulled the blinds up on the large window by his chair to admire the sunset, streaking purple and red on the horizon. Outside, people were congregating in the trimmed-grass courtyards amongst the longhouse suites, drinking ambrosia and beer, munching on all sorts of delectable confections.

While Grammy served up tea and cake to everyone gathered at the table, Papa decided to open the window and take some fresh air into his lungs. The breeze's crisp and natural fragrance wafted pleasantly into the suite, dissipating any lingering stuffiness. He could hear at least four other languages besides English and German being spoken outside. Papa watched a group of African people singing quietly. They smiled and danced playfully to their chanting rhythm. Their song sounded optimistic and they looked so carefree, Papa couldn't help smiling too. He looked around some more and saw a large group of Swedes, drinking beer and having a good time. Someone must have told a funny story or joke, because the group suddenly broke into intense laughter, several of them holding their stomachs and hunching over with gleeful hysteria.

Although he could not see them, Papa overheard a woman yelling at her children from a neighboring suite. Her Spanish was not that of Spain or Mexico. Possibly, it's South American, he thought. A Chinese family passed by under the window, apparently on their way to the communal grills, where tantalizing shish-kabobs consisting of the imitation meat and smoked vegetables were being served. Everyone in their family, from the youthful to the elderly, seemed upbeat as they sipped their ambrosia.

Papa closed his eyes. He thought to himself that it was nice to be here. It was nice to be surrounded by his family, in an interesting setting. He was fully aware of the gravity of the Allied situation; the lives that were lost and the fact that he was a hostage. But the present situation, at least so far, was gratifying. And so, with a tinge of guilt, he was happy.

"Papa, you're not falling asleep on us, are you?" asked Tom, gently nudging his shoulder.

Papa opened his eyes and chuckled. "No, no, just enjoying my time here with you all."

Logan and his family made their way out to the fields with several dozen underclassmen. There they gathered on the edges, on the grassy area surrounding the longhouse quadrant. The family clustered next to each other, simultaneously trying to position themselves so they could see the rather petite lady standing on the stage in front. She had short, wavy, red hair and looked in her forties, but had the youthful vigor of someone in her late teens or early twenties. She stood next to a large chalkboard, the top of which she had to stand on her tip-toes to reach with her piece of chalk. She wrote out in German, "How to Be an Organic Farmer." Logan's family collectively deciphered the words, each pitching in scattered knowledge of German to make out the sentence.

The next thing the lady wrote was, *"Um Biologisch Anzubauen, musst man Bioligisch Denken."* Once again, Logan's family worked to translate the sentence. Logan noted, semi-amused, that most of the underclassmen similarly muttered in their native tongues with their family members, looks of concentration scrunched on their faces.

"To . . . organically farm . . ." Logan struggled to remember what he had learned. His mom filled in.

"Denken is think, I think." Bibi giggled.

"To organically farm . . ." Tom tried to piece it together.

Tom's mother whispered excitedly. "Wait, I know! To organically farm, one must think organically," she finished proudly.

The lady on the stage put her chalk down, spun around, and spoke to the crowd in English in a perky German accent.

"Raise your hand if you understand English well," she commanded the audience cordially. Everyone in the crowd raised their hand. "Okay," the lady said, "now you all should know the basics of German. But, how many of you understand it well enough for me to conduct an entire session in German."

A few raised their hands at first, but others tentatively followed suit so as not to anger her. No one wanted to be punished or set out as an example for being a slow learner. Eventually, almost everyone in the field raised their hands. Tom's parents raised theirs and urged the rest of the family to do so.

The lady on the stage just smiled. "Well, I guess I will conduct this lesson in English." Many in the crowd laughed, releasing nervous energy.

"OK," she began, "I am Frau Hartwig."

"Hallo, Frau Hartwig," the group replied in unison.

"Very good," the Frau said, pleased with their discipline. "Today, you will be learning about organic farming. All of the Apex's agricultural products are produced organically, including produce, grains, eggs, fibers such as cotton, and even our flowers." She stepped closer to the end of the stage, so everyone could hear her better as she spoke.

"Organic farming relies on developing biological diversity in the field to disrupt habitats for pest organisms. In addition, we use natural methods such as crop rotations and cover crops to purposefully maintain and replenish soil fertility. Organic farmers are not allowed to use synthetic pesticides or fertilizers. The methods can seem very complex and sophisticated, and scientific knowledge is required. However, for the most part, organic farming is a simple matter of good instinct and common sense. So, who knows what this says?" she asked, stepping back again and slapping her pointer stick onto the chalk board. A young man's hand shot up and the Instructor called on him.

"To farm organically," he spoke in a thick Indian dialect, "a person must think organically."

Frau Hartwig smiled warmly at him, "Very good." She walked around, holding both ends of her pointer stick. "Organic farming cannot be reduced to a singular, easy to understand concept. It is a way of *being* that reflects a wish to be in harmony with our natural surroundings." She released her left hand from the stick and waved it around in one continuous motion, to indicate the field and surrounding forest land. "One of the most obvious differences from conventional farming practices is that wild land is considered vital to the crop land. Integrating and maintaining wild land protects the crops against infestations of crop-destroying bugs, so we do not have to use pesticides, which destroy nature and poison our food and water," she squished up her face in distaste at the thought.

"Wild vegetation, especially trees and their roots, prevent soil erosion. And we do not use machine tillers, which destroy and loosen the soil. We do not till much in general, in keeping with a more natural approach. For those of you who do not know what tilling is, it is the stirring up of the topsoil. This rips up the residue, which is whatever was left of a crop that was harvested and the roots of that old crop as well. Doing this makes homogenous topsoil with an even consistency. However, this is very destructive to the land. Overtilling was one of the many inorganic practices that resulted in the American Dust Bowl. So," she held up her palm in emphasis, "we do a little hand tilling to prevent too much clumping of soil and air pockets, but we leave the residue. The residue falls and we help flatten it into the ground a bit," she stomped her feet gently in demonstration. "What this does is help to conserve water, because it acts as a groundcover and slows evaporation. This groundcover also helps prevent soil erosion.

"Organic farming requires a more hands-on approach," she said, kneading her fingers in the air as if through dirt, "because it prevents the use of machines in the field for the most part. Large machines like seeders and harvesters are destructive to the ground life. They inevitably crush the soil and ruin the small ecosystems within. Worms, which help to fertilize dirt, are killed by heavy machinery. So, organic farming requires a little more human labor. But, do not fret," she smiled, "you will work five to six hours daily at the most. Those over fifty need only work two or three. Those over sixty-five are, as many of you already know, not required to do this type of labor. We are no slave-drivers," she remarked, waggling her pointer finger to give emphasis.

That night, Logan awoke to the sound of knocking upon his window. Before he even opened his eyes, he smiled.

He had wished to go search for her immediately, but had been guilt-tripped by his parents into spending the rest of their day with the grandparents, about which he ended up being happy. He opened the window and held out a hand to help her in, but as usual she pulled herself up and jumped in.

The next morning, as the sun began shining through everyone's windows, a bell went off, chiming twice, alerting the masses that it was time for breakfast. The underclassmen walked out of their suites and headed slowly and groggily to the cafeteria. Logan and his parents stood in line, heaping their trays with food. As they moved down the buffet, they grabbed ambrosia, a fruit cup and a hot meal plate of scrambled eggs, steamed spinach and baked potatoes. For a sweet snack, they were given a cup of bread pudding.

Tom, Bibi and Logan placed their trays down at one of the cafeteria tables. Logan ravenously feasted upon the food on the hot plate. The eggs were delicious, as was the imitation turkey cooked within them.

"What do you suppose this stuff is made of?" he asked, holding up the fake meat and jiggling it.

"I don't know? Soy probably?" Bibi guessed. She tilted her eyes up as she thought further. "Although I hear sometimes it's made of wheat."

"Wheat!" Logan's eyebrows shot up.

Bibi nodded. "Yep, wheat. Weird, huh?"

Logan made a frown of intrigue, nodding his head. "Yeah."

Tom devoured his meal and took a large sip of ambrosia to wash it down. "Mmm," he groaned with delight. "Tastes like turkey to me!"

They finished their breakfast and walked back to their place. On the way out of the cafeteria, Logan read a sign that he also saw going in. *You are responsible for cleaning up your own mess.* It was a phrase posted all over the Arbeitskamp, work camp, including within the suites. That was one thing he would miss about Costa Rica: maid service! Well, that and the beach, the rainforest, the perpetual free time . . .

Back in the suite, the grandparents could be heard snoring loudly in their rooms, each in his or her own unique way. Tom, Bibi and Logan relaxed, waiting for their summons. After being acquainted with the organic farming process by Frau Hartwig the previous day, the underclassmen were given their work schedule for that week. On their first day of labor duty, they were to work for only two hours starting in the morning. The underclassmen did not have access to any clocks; there were none in their rooms, or the cafeteria, or any other place where they gathered. Their schedules ran by the many different tonal bells that rang out across the complex. Therefore, they only had a general idea of what time had passed between the bells. However, there was plenty of time to eat and relax before they were summoned to work.

The work bell rang and, following the simple instructions provided them, Logan and his parents walked along one of the main paths, marked by yellow arrows. They made their way to a wide open, trimmed-grass field, where a few thousand underclassmen had already coalesced. There was plenty of room on the large field for everyone to move around, sit, or even lie down and catch a little more sleep before work, as some were doing.

Suddenly, a loud, irritating buzzer rang out, startling everyone to alertness. The whirring sound of Kolibri wings was heard overhead and everyone looked up. They saw a man in a Kolibri chariot, wearing all of the body armor, but without a mask, so that everyone could see his face.

He had long, silver hair, braided tightly at the nape of his neck and hanging halfway down his back in a straight line, over his spine. The braid lifted and trailed behind his head whenever he accelerated in his chariot. He had sharp features and an angular facial structure that was enhanced by his hawkish, grey-blue eyes.

His chariot and armor were unique, a glossy, blood-red color, with black stripes painted over the entirety much like a tiger's markings. He spoke into a cordless microphone headset that was transmitting to a speaker system surrounding the field.

"Guten Morgen!" he greeted them semi-warmly, yet with a strong, authoritarian undertone.

Everyone replied by saying "good morning" in German, as much as possible in unison.

"Ich bin Marshal Speer," he introduced himself.

"Hallo, Marshal Speer," the underclassmen replied together.

"Sehr gut," he remarked with approval.

He set about explaining their specific labor-duty for that day. The underclassmen were informed that they were going to be seeding the fields. The workers would be separated in groups according to their age. So, parents were separated from their children. However, Marshal Speer assured everyone that the work duties were quite safe and everyone was going to be fine.

Logan was put on a hovercraft called a helioron. Riding in the open-air vehicle, he and twelve other youths from seventeen to twenty-two were whisked over the soy fields. He looked down at the underclass workers toiling below. Within minutes, the helioron arrived at an area that needed more hands. It hovered down to the ground and the underclass youths disembarked onto the residue-covered ground. The residue was made of the leftovers of plants that had already been harvested, plus added groundcover planted to help the soybeans grow.

Today his group's job was to plant soybeans, which they did using a device that reminded Logan of a pogo stick. Each worker was given one of the devices, merely called a "seeder." It stood a little over hip-height, with a metal, cylindrical body. Atop, it had two handlebars and near the bottom there were two foot bars. The very bottom of the device tapered to a blunt point. The workers picked up the device by the handlebars and jammed the point into the ground, using one of the foot bars to add pressure if needed. Then, a grip switch was pressed and the seeder fired a few soybean seeds into the ground. Using the device enabled the workers to do their job without hunching over all day, which would harm their backs.

Logan found the work to be easy. He barely broke a sweat. The laborers were offered small, portable music players, which clipped onto their work tunics. The headphones provided good sound quality. There was a limitless choice of songs, from classical to electronica. It was easy to get lost in the music and time passed quickly.

After an hour or so passed, Logan took the headphones off and listened to the sounds around him. There were birds chirping in the nearby strip of woods that zigzagged through the soybean fields. A group of Italian boys sang a cheerful and repetitive melody.

Logan's seeder became clogged with mud. He was taught how to clean it out and did so relatively quickly. However, his seeder had gotten clogged more than others and he was beginning to fall behind the line of workers on either side of him. The young man working the row next to him gave him some advice.

"Lift the seedah up a bit when you pull the switch," he said in a southern United States dialect. "That'll clear it."

Logan nodded. "Thanks."

Over the next hour, Logan got to know the young man, whose name was Randy. His younger brother Marty was working right beside him. Randy was twenty years old and Marty was nineteen.

The work went fast as they kept up a good, light conversation. However, the exchange led Logan to bring up family, and he casually asked about their parents. Both brothers immediately clammed up and Logan just looked down at the work, sorry he had obviously touched on a painful subject for them. He just kept on seeding, looking intently at what his hands were doing. Finally, Randy mustered up his strength and pushed the words out through clenched teeth.

"They're dead," he said quickly.

Logan assumed that their parents' deaths had something to do with the war, but he wouldn't pry. He felt a tremendous surge of appreciation to still have his parents.

"I'm sorry to hear that," he said with sincerity, uncomfortable that he could not think of something better to say.

Randy started taking his anger out by furiously stabbing the dirt with the seeder. His younger brother wiped a bit of moisture gathering at the bottom of his eyes.

"I swear, if I could git in fronta Geiseric . . ." Marty sniffled. He bit his lip to stop it from quivering and started again. "If I could git in front of that son-a-bitch," he held out his fist and squeezed the air in front of him, "I'd kill 'im with my bare hands! I'd rip his fuckin' throat out!" he shouted. People nearby in the field looked over at them uneasily.

"I don't care what they would do!" He shook his fist at a Kolibri guard flying past about a hundred yards off. The guard could not hear Marty, but Randy quickly jumped on his sibling to shut him up.

"Are you fuckin' crazy?!" Randy howled, looking incredulously into his brother's reddened face. Marty just gulped and, slowly, the tears held back for too long began to well up in his eyes. Randy hugged his brother and patted his back.

"Come on man," he said to Marty, "let's git back to work."

Little by little, as they continued to plant the soybeans, somewhat on autopilot now, Randy told Logan about what had happened to their parents during the war. They were slayed during what was to be dubbed "The Midwest Massacre."

By late fall of 2039, the Allied citizens had been relocated and were living predominantly on the vast strip of land between the Appalachians and the Rocky Mountains known as the United States Midwest. The Allied leadership had been preparing for a grand Thanksgiving Holiday, a celebration they thought would boost the morale of their citizenry. The celebration was seen as strategically important for a number of reasons. It was a holiday about the arrival to America, the New World, where the five billion Allied citizens now resided. It was about hospitality and friendship and unity. And, it was about giving thanks for what they did have, instead of brooding over what they had to give up, at a time when so much had been sacrificed.

Allied High Command needed a celebration that everyone, no matter their background, could partake in and get their minds off the war raging around them. Thanksgiving was not heavily associated with any particular religion, which was key to uniting a heterogeneous population of secularists, Christians, Muslims and many others. Equally important was that Thanksgiving reinforced meat as a deeply embedded part of most human rituals. The Allied leadership wanted the populous to remember all the great feasts, banquets, barbecues, and other gatherings that filled people with warmth and security. They wanted their citizens to associate these feelings with the meat they ate and, therefore, rile the people with indignation that some foreign government was attempting to take their sacred, embedded rights away.

However, a large minority of the Allied citizenry was sick of and terrified by the war, and nothing could shake that. They were no longer interested in fighting to preserve their right to be non-Isaianics. Allied High Command informed them that it was well beyond that now; Geiseric no longer wished to just convert the world, but to own it and subjugate anyone who had refused to come into his fold earlier. Still, many of the Allied citizens simply did not believe this, or just wanted to end the war at any price. They felt that subjugation was better than death.

Regardless, about sixty percent of the Allied populace was still squarely in the fight, and they worked hard to convince their wavering brethren about its importance. This majority was filled with righteous fury at Geiseric, who wished to control the world and form the populace in his image. Did he think he was God?!

The celebrations would last four days, beginning Monday and coming to a climax on Thanksgiving Day. The festival got off to a powerful start. Tens of thousands of handmade floats, adorned with papier-mâché and flowers, paraded down the main streets of all the major cities and towns in the Midwest. The streets were clamoring with people, already drunk before noon, laughing, shouting and having a raucous good time.

Tuesday began much the same, except it was even wilder. Many likened it to Mardi Gras, only with far more people and drunken debauchery than the southern festival had ever seen. Many people had not even slept, preferring to drink and eat the night away. They made voodoo dolls of the Apex leaders and burned effigies. All the stress, rage and frustration that had been building up during the war, was released through intoxicated abandon. It was akin to the Dionysian festivals of Ancient Greece and Rome, where the people would celebrate and let loose all their inhibitions.

People streaked and exposed themselves. They made love in public with those they knew and those they had never met, the young and single, along with the middle-aged and the married. When the citizens tired, they ate from buffets prepared for them and always at the ready; their plates piled high with flesh and little else. The entire Midwest was an orgy of feasting and sex. Allied High Command was very pleased at how things were transpiring.

To keep their citizens safe during this relatively vulnerable time, the leadership poured all their resources into creating a surface-to-air defense system. The missiles were fast enough to take out the Apex Golden Eagle jets and even the Condor magneto-thrust bombers. The Midwest was, for the most part, safe from aerial bombardment. The Allied missile defense, however, was built to destroy planes, which flew mostly at high altitudes in predictable arcs and lines when they maneuvered. It was not designed to take down small, erratically moving objects like the Kolibri.

The Allies did not delegate resources for the creation of a strong anti-sky infantry defense system, because they assumed that, with the Hornet forces destroyed, all Kolibri flyers left would be concentrated on the battlefront in Alabama, specifically Montgomery. In the triage of war-planning, Montgomery would be sacrificed to the Apex for the greater good of the Allies. Allied High Command knew that it was more important to keep their civilian population motivated than to defend Montgomery, even though the city was of incredible strategic value to mount a defense on the eastern front. But, without the backing of the citizens, the Allies were already lost.

By mid-afternoon on Wednesday, the festival was still going on without a hitch. Afternoon found the streets of the cities and large towns in the Midwest packed with hundreds of millions of people in various degrees of drunkenness.

They watched the floats that paraded down the streets from early in the morning until late into the night. Those riding atop the floats taunted the spectators with words and trinkets to shirk off their clothing. The revelers danced incessantly, almost hysterically, purging themselves of all their anxiety.

With the people in elated stupors and the Allied leadership patting themselves on the back, no one realized that the Kolibri forces were heading straight for them. Allied High Command had devoted a myriad of resources in an attempt to deceive the enemy. They utilized all the known Apex spies in their midst and fed false intelligence to the enemy through them, hoping to trick them into believing the entire Allied citizenry still firmly backed the war.

However, Geiseric saw right through the lies. He already had a hunch that his enemies' populations were faltering. They had been dragged across the world, endured the loss of tens of millions of civilians and soldiers, and they were losing every major battle. The Allied intelligence's deception was overzealous. It only confirmed Geiseric's suspicions.

It was in the dark of the previous night that the remaining twelve hundred Kolibri flyers in the Apex expeditionary force stealthily penetrated into the Allied Midwest, keeping low over the treetops to avoid detection by radar. They dispersed into their typical one hundred man centuries, with about ten Knights in each. Flying out in different directions, the twelve centuries found clever places to hide and wait for the right time to strike. Most hid in densely wooded regions on the western side of the Appalachians, where they refueled their chariots with the synthetic glucose they had carried in large canisters. As afternoon rolled around, the invading flyers buried their fuel canisters and took off in their fully energized chariots.

Further breaking up into groups of five to twenty called fireteams, which were the smallest military units in the ground and sky infantry and cavalry of either side, the smallest teams headed for some of the most crowded towns in the Midwest, while the larger teams headed for the cities.

The first major strike was on St. Louis, Missouri. A band of twenty Kolibri flyers, including five Knights, entered the city together from the southwest. As they crossed over the Mississippi River, the few Allied anti-sky infantry weapons surrounding the city opened up, but the weapons were placed too far apart to be effective against a small force. The Kolibri were able to weave around the holes in the defense, and not a single invading flyer was struck down.

The sound of the defensive guns alerted the people celebrating in the city. Before the music even turned off, the Kolibri were upon them. The Apex flyers split up as they entered St. Louis, half heading north up Grand Boulevard, and the other half zipping down Kingshighway Boulevard. These streets, and the smaller ones connected to them, were packed with civilians watching the parades and enjoying the celebration — hundreds of thousands of people crammed into a few blocks, like Times Square on New Year's Eve.

The first phase of the Kolibri's attack was innovative and terrifyingly effective. The Kolibri deployed a weapon of mass destruction that had never been used before. Each flyer carried one anti-matter grenade that harnessed the most powerful energy source known to mankind — an energy source even more potent than that unleashed by nuclear weapons.

Anti-matter and matter are the yin and yang of reality. Every type of sub-atomic particle has its antimatter counterpart. When matter and antimatter collide, they annihilate each other in an immense burst of energy. The hand-held grenades contained only one gram of anti-matter, but it was enough to unleash an amount of energy equal to the bombs dropped on Japan in World War II.

The Allies never suspected that the Apex was so far ahead on this research. Besides the creation of the Juggernaut, the anti-matter research was the most highly classified military project in the Apex. Anti-matter particles were incredibly hard to contain. Special containers known as Penning traps used magnetic fields to prevent the anti-particles, such as an anti-electron, or posi-tron, from contacting the wall of the container. If that happened, the positrons would be annihilated on contact with the material. The positrons were very hard to keep in place, for they had the same charge and, therefore, constantly repelled each other. The Apex had managed to efficiently store the positrons in a more stable form called positronium. Still, each grenade cost the Apex five billion Imperial Marks, or twice as many American dollars.

Beyond its power, there was a particular reason Geiseric supported the use of anti-matter weaponry. Unlike nuclear bombs, positron bombs did not eject plumes of radioactive *debris*, which were elementary particles that con-taminated huge swaths of the environment for years. When positrons and electrons collided, there were no massive explosions. The primary product was an extremely lethal burst of gamma radiation. Gamma rays formed the highest-energy end of the electromagnetic spectrum. While destructive, the rays would not endure for years contaminating the environment like fallout, which anti-matter weapons did not produce. So, the positron grenade was a clean bomb that killed its targets without ruining the countryside for an extended period of time. The gamma radiation could not permeate far into the tall, steel and concrete buildings lining the streets, so the blast of a grenade was confined to the street it was dropped on. But, almost every living thing within the immediate vicinity would be scorched beyond recognition.

On Grand Boulevard, three of the Kolibri flyers set and dropped their grenades on the populace below. Before the people knew what was happening, a bright light blinded them. For a second, the flash overwhelmed a kilometer of the street and it burned the eyes of anyone looking in that direction. Blood poured from their sockets and their flesh peeled from the intense heat. Three other Kolibri flyers followed suit, dropping their grenades on the Allied civilians on Kingshighway Boulevard. Those people also suffered unimaginable and fatal burns. Within seconds, hundreds of thousands of people lay baked and writhing along the two major streets of St. Louis.

Hundreds of thousands more tried to run away, into the smaller alleys. It was impossible for the running mass not to trample the victims lying on the ground. Those who had been debilitated and fell were crushed by the stampede of their panicked peers. As the people tried to hide in the alleyways, they were pushed together tightly and many were squished to death, meeting the same fate as those they had callously trampled over seconds earlier.

The Kolibri flyers then unsheathed their blades and set about hacking apart everyone who was trying to escape. They easily shredded dozens of people with every pass.

The rest of the Kolibri attacking St. Louis converged on Forest Park, a large 1,400-acre park located west of downtown. The Thanksgiving party was concentrated there, with nearly two million people filling the park to the brim, and packed into every building, field, path and forested area around it.

They were having a wonderful time, until they heard the city's perimeter guns go off. Panic struck their hearts. They heard the distant screaming of thousands of people, getting ever nearer. Every muscle in their bodies tensed, and their veins ran cold. No one knew what to do and, before anyone took charge, the Kolibri were upon them.

It would have made for bad public relations back at the homefront for the Apex to decimate such a beautiful setting like Forest Park. It would have seemed hypocritical, considering the Isaianic stance on environmentalism. Granted, the Apex had destroyed far more of the natural world in this war from indirect means, such as when the Juggernaut crossed Panama and crushed a huge swath of forest, and the animals living there, beneath it.

But, politics was often not about the truth. It was about perception. The Apex emperor had often said, "I will not lose the war for environmentalism by being an environmentalist. Nor will I lose this war for animal rights because of my love for animals." He reasoned that what he needed to do in order to win was infinitesimally small compared to what was already being done en masse to the Earth and its inhabitants before the war.

Regardless, burning the one and only piece of beautifully landscaped nature in St. Louis, during a targeted terror strike, simply would not look good to the Isaianics. Geiseric knew better.

Thus, the anti-matter grenades were out. But, the Kolibri flyers did not need such weapons to be effective in Forest Park. Their blades would suffice. In fact, the Knights were equipped with a special edged weapon today, created for just such an occasion. They each carried a huge, dual-grip scythe, which had a two meter-long, steel alloy blade. Scythes were originally intended to cut down wheat, but these were made to cut down people. The Knights made passes into the crowd, hacking at the people left and right, as if they were the harvest.

Not knowing where to go, the Allied civilians scrambled in every direction. The "Scythians," as the Knights on this mission dubbed themselves, focused in on the perfect spot for their attack. The hub of the celebrations in Forest Park was around the Emerson Grand Basin, which had an enormous, shallow, square pool that hundreds of thousands of people were gathered in and around.

The people did not have time to react to what they had heard in the distance before they were under attack themselves. The Scythians flew too fast to get a good look at them and, when anyone did get a good look, they were dead in a split-second. The Knights held out their scythes and zipped by low to the ground, making mincemeat out of everyone on the wide bike path that went around the perimeter of the water. Many of the screaming people jumped into the pool, as if crouching in the water would save them. Hundreds were mortally slashed with each quick flyby made by the Scythians. The screeching of the mass of terrorized humans was deafening.

Within minutes, nearly all lay dead, in pieces, floating in a giant pool of blood.

Altogether, the same strategy was used on nearly one hundred Allied North American cities and towns. The Kolibri flyers continued to slaughter people throughout the night. When the dawn sun rose, its gentle rays illuminated a gruesome sight.

Hundreds of kilometers of streets and roads were strewn with the remains of those who had breathed and celebrated, full of life, only hours before. In every major city, the Kolibri flyers had left behind towering piles of slaughtered and roasted bodies. The stench was sickening, and it seemed to permeate the entire Midwest.

Tens of millions of survivors were injured, suffering from acute radiation exposure. Their skin hung from the bones. They were pale white and their hair fell out in clumps. Sores covered their bodies and their throats swelled shut. They would be dead within weeks, if not days. Others were destined to develop cancer from the gamma-rays emitted by the anti-matter grenades. Their bodies were damaged on a cellular and molecular level by the radiation. Although they could not see it, the rays ravaged their DNA. Those that managed to go on with their lives would unwittingly pass down untold numbers of birth defects to their progeny.

The Allies hastened to create gigantic crematoriums, in order to dispose of the bodies before disease and pests set in. Many cadavers were burned in outdoor pits, as far away from civilians as possible, but given that there were nearly five billion people living in the Midwest, that was hard to manage. There was no time to haul the bodies elsewhere. For two weeks, the fires raged, consuming the millions of corpses. The civilian death rate slowed dramatically after that, but it was a lottery as to who was going to suffer the long-term illnesses.

The streets and buildings were cleaned until they were spotless. Swarms of vultures, rats and other animals that fed on decaying flesh had done the first round of cleaning. They were cleared out and the cities and towns were polished to a shine, made to look better than ever. Fragrant flowers and blossoming trees were planted, ones that emitted pleasant scents to make the people feel alive . . .

Yet, the smell of death remained in the air.

Over the next few days in Logan's first work week, he came to befriend Randy and Marty, who were consistently placed next to him in the labor order on the fields. Logan noticed that everybody's placement was the same everyday. He figured it had something to do with helping to keep track of the underclassmen.

Randy and Marty were an amazingly resilient duo and Logan was impressed with how they managed to cope with so much loss. Like Sasha, Randy and Marty had lost their entire family to the war, yet unlike Sasha, they did not appear to harbor perpetual rage and frustration, which would then bubble over onto whoever was near. The two brothers often laughed, finding humor in themselves and everything around them. Randy was a particularly strong soul and Logan could see that he was always keeping up a tough exterior for his younger brother. Though only slightly older than Marty, Randy had taken on the father role. He deftly led the conversation to light-hearted joking, whenever he noticed his younger brother falling into the grip of depression or fear.

Though Randy did a good job of keeping off the subject of what *specifically* happened to his parents and relatives, Logan did manage to gather that it was unbelievably heinous. Randy and Marty's parents worked in one of the factory farms producing meat for the Allies in the Midwest. When the Kolibri flyers struck into the interior of Fortress North America to terrorize the citizenry, they perpetrated their most horrendous atrocities upon the workers of the Allied livestock farms.

Many slaughterhouse workers were put onto the very machinery they used to butcher the animals. Tens of thousands of humans were sent along the factory farm slaughter line, as trillions of animals had before. They were hung upside down and their throats were slit, but before they could bleed to death, they were sent down the conveyor to be dunked in scalding water. They were then flayed alive by special machines meant to peel flesh. Like a large percentage of those animals forced to endure the factory slaughterhouse, the workers were conscious as they were sent down the line, which finally ended in them being disemboweled and their limbs torn asunder.

While Logan digested this appalling image, a question was brought to his mind.

"Is that how they normally kill the animals?" he asked, realizing that he had never put much thought into it. "By cutting their throats?"

"Well," Randy answered casually, "you could do that, or my favorite is when you string 'em up and put the knife in their gut and pull down," he smiled, mimicking the action. "Their guts fall right out," he laughed, shrugging matter-of-factly.

Logan was stunned. He just stared at Randy for a moment.

"Are you fuckin' kiddin' me?" He asked.

Randy was surprised that Logan did not partake in his revelry, and resented the accusatory tone. He squinted his eyes with suspicion and instinctively looked around, checking to see if anyone else was listening.

"Never mind," Randy retorted tersely, shaking his head and going back to his work.

Logan continued planting the soybeans, but he could not shake the gruesome image of the disemboweled animal.

"So, you really think that's cool?" he remarked in disbelief.

Randy controlled his anger. "Just forget about it. Damn, I'm sorry I even told you."

Marty, on the other hand, could not hold back his indignation with Logan. He walked over and haughtily poked his seeder towards Logan's chest. "Fuck animals!" he shouted. "*What are you*, some fuckin' *Isaianic?!*"

Logan was startled at his harsh reaction. "No," he shook his head, taking a step back, "but, I don't think you have to be an Isaianic to know that's cruel."

Marty laughed, bitterly. "You know what me and Randy used ta do fo' fun?"

Logan's eyes drooped, and he clenched his fists with growing anger, as Marty persisted in testing him further. Randy's eyes widened with fear.

"Shut up!" He muttered to his younger brother, but Marty ignored him.

"We used ta tie any animal we could find to the train tracks!" He laughed hysterically.

Randy was getting nervous. "Shut the fuck up, man!"

Marty dismissed Randy with a wave of his hand and continued. "Usually little things," he remarked, purposefully nonchalant, "like squirrels and hares. They ain't as hard ta catch as you'd think. Sometimes we'd go out and get a deer by shootin' it with our twenty-twos! That wouldn't kill 'em. Just disable 'em." His eyes thinned into malevolent slits. "Animals were put here fo' man to do wit' as he sees fit!"

Completely taken aback, Logan's mouth hung slightly agape. Marty was titillated by the shocked reaction. He smiled as he stared at Logan.

"Hey Randy, rememba' when we put that firecracka' in that hound's ass . . ."

Randy suddenly pushed his brother down. "You fuckin' idiot!" he roared. He hushed his voice and looked around, filled with paranoia. "You're gonna get us fuckin' killed!" he spewed through gritted teeth.

Marty's evil expression left, and a blank stare replaced it. Suddenly, he dropped his face in his hands and began crying. Randy felt bad for his poor brother, who had lost everyone but him. And now he was beating down on him too.

"I'm sorry bro," he said, helping Marty up and giving him a hug. Randy looked to Logan.

"Ya know," he said, smiling, "he wasn't being serious. He was just tryin' to get unda yo' skin."

Logan didn't look up from his work. "Whatever."

Logan and Francesca sprawled on the cool grass together and stared up at the nearly full moon. Her head rested against his shoulder and his arm was around her. A wonderful ambience permeated the night air, filled with the fresh, invigorating scent of pine and all the other delicious aromas of nature. Some were light, like perfume, while others were pungent, yet strangely pleasant too. Often these unfamiliar scents conjured up an incredible energy in Logan's and Francesca's bodies and souls. A tremendous peace came over them and, as they cuddled together in the cool night, they felt warm and safe, their hearts beating in tandem.

Suddenly, a wretched noise pierced the still air. At first, it sounded like a child screaming, but it was different and bizarre. Logan knew what it was, for he had lived in the midst of tropical nature for years. He was familiar with the unnerving sounds made by small prey animals as they were attacked and eaten by predators.

Logan and Francesca ran toward the noise. As they got near, they tentatively made their way closer, unsure what they would be faced with. They hid behind some bushes and parted them slightly to look out.

A predator was, in fact, attacking a small animal, but this predator was not the type of animal that Logan expected to see. It was Marty, and he was brutalizing an infant deer, which had already been mauled by coyotes. The mother deer was attempting to save her child, but to no avail. Marty had a large stick, a piece of a branch that had fallen to the ground, which he swung around at the doe when she came near. Then, he picked the fawn up by its neck and swung its body around, breaking the fragile bones inside. Marty laughed as he threw the baby animal at its mother.

The mother leaned her head down to lick the wounds of her child. Marty suddenly jumped forward and slammed the heavy length of wood upon the head of the doe. She trembled and her legs buckled. Marty laughed intensely as he beat the mother deer, over and over again, across her entire body.

Logan was sickened. He ran out of the bushes shouting with rage at Marty.

"What the fuck are you doing?!"

Marty held up the bloodied stick at Logan.

"Don't come near me!" he began to cry.

Logan could not pity Marty, but he did fear him in this insane state. He looked at the dead fawn and the dying mother, who was convulsing on the ground near her child.

A feeling took over Logan that he had experienced very few times before. It was an inexplicable darkness; anger so deep, so powerful, that it took control of his body before he could think.

He deftly grabbed the branch and ripped it from Marty's hands. A guttural yell escaped Marty's throat as his palms were filled with wood slivers. But, he did not have time to fully comprehend the pain. Before he even looked up from his hands, he was struck in the abdomen with the point of the bloody club. He keeled over, unable to catch his breath. Logan raised the stick up, looking over Marty's body and thinking about where to bring it down. He wanted to club Marty's head, but he reconsidered. He looked at less critical, but extremely sensitive parts of the body. Marty sucked enough air into his lungs to begin screaming for help.

Before Logan could exact another strike upon Marty, Randy ran up from behind and tackled Logan. He looked at his bruised and beaten brother lying helplessly on the ground and was infuriated.

"You bastard!" he shrieked and punched at Logan. Francesca ran out of the bushes and kicked Randy in the side. Logan jumped up and tried to explain what happened, but Randy would not hear it.

"Fuck the deer you animal-lovin' faggot!" He picked up a rock and threw it at Logan's head, but Logan ducked and it whizzed over. Logan flew into another rage. He charged Randy and, with one precise right-fisted blow across the chin, knocked him to the ground, temporarily unconscious.

With the two brothers subdued, Logan and Francesca quickly ran over to the mother and baby deer. Francesca broke into tears as she gazed down at the battered fawn. At least the mother had finally died too and the two creatures were no longer suffering. Logan just shook his head as he stared at the heartbreaking sight.

"What kind of person could do such a thing?"

Suddenly, they heard a familiar sound that sent a bolt of fear through their spines. It was the hum of Kolibri chariots, just overhead.

"I'll tell you who can do such things," they heard a recognizable voice say.

Logan and Francesca looked up and saw Marshal Speer lowering his chariot towards the ground. As usual, he was not wearing his helmet and everyone could see his face, which was adorned with a look of gentle pity. With this tender expression smoothing out his rugged exterior, Francesca found him to be quite handsome. He came down in front of them and hovered only a few meters above the ground, the whirring wings lightly kicking up the leaves and dust below.

"Monsters like these young men on the ground here," Speer answered with cold sobriety, as he looked down upon Marty and Randy. "*They* do these things. And men like this used to rule the world." He looked to Logan and Francesca, who were still visibly frightened.

"Do not worry," Speer assured. "I am not going to harm you. I saw the end of what happened, when you tried to save the doe."

Looming over them menacingly, the marshal turned his gaze once more to the two brothers who were beginning to regain their senses. Marty looked up and was paralyzed with fear to see Speer above him, seething with rage.

"Yes," Speer said, looking down on Marty, "now it is time for you to tremble."

Randy looked around for ways for him and his brother to run away, but he knew it would be useless. They could never outrun a Kolibri.

Suddenly, the marshal's torso armor began to remove itself from his body. The synthetic muscles within unfastened the bindings and rolled the armor up, down and to the side, ultimately curling up behind his back. Now, adorned only with the protective flight suit worn by all flyers under their armor, Speer jumped out of his chariot and landed nimbly upon the ground.

He could still operate the chariot via a remote Psychiclink connection. The chariot tilted, pointing two compartments down towards Speer. Reaching into the compartments, the marshal quickly withdrew the two blades within. These were not the heavy weapons used by the sky infantry, but rather his personal katanas, which were the slightly curved, one-edged swords most often associated with the samurai. Speer flipped them and caught them by the end of their blades, holding the katanas out with the handles facing Randy and Marty. His lean, strong frame was intimidating, and Marty and Randy both took a step backward as he approached them. He seemed to tower over the brothers, who gulped with apprehension as they took the swords.

The marshal spoke quietly into a small microphone in an electronic wristband on his left hand. Immediately, six Kolibri guardsmen showed up, hovering overhead. Speer commanded that one of his subordinates supply him with a katana. One of the guards lowered his chariot to the ground and unsheathed a katana, handing it to his superior officer. Marshal Speer unhitched the protective flight undersuit and threw it to the ground. Underneath, he wore only a beige full-body outfit that served as the undergarments. He looked as humble and plain as any person in the underclass. Suddenly, he began slicing his katana rapidly through the air, warming up for battle.

Marty began to quiver and tears streamed from his eyes. Randy held out the blade he was given. Logan could not just stand by and watch as Randy was punished equally along with his sadistic brother.

"Marshal Speer!" Logan shouted. "Please! Randy did not do anything to the deer!"

Speer laughed. "Yes, *now*!" he shouted, staring into Randy's frightened eyes. "But, I have a talent for seeing people's souls, my boy. And, believe me, Randy is of the same ilk as his brother. He is simply smarter."

Speer stared at Marty, who was incapacitated with terror. He could barely hold the katana. The marshal shook his head slowly, clicking his tongue.

"Do not be a coward now. You were so courageous and mighty before, when you were beating those fearsome animals," he pointed to the dead deer.

Randy stepped forward and lowered his sword. "Please! We will never do it again!" he pleaded, starting to cry.

Speer was unmoved. Moving into a fighting position, pointing his katana at them, he replied with a cold and vacant stare. "You're right."

Logan and Francesca watched with foreboding as the marshal began circling, slowly, giving the brothers a chance to gain their bearings. The moonlight glistened off Speer's blade as he intimidatingly swiped it through the air, snickering at the startled jumps of his opponents. The Kolibri guards watched from above, talking and laughing with each other.

Randy finally submitted to the circumstances and decided to attack. He jumped forward and, showing tremendous skill, he sliced at the marshal's neck. When Speer dodged it, Randy spun and lowered himself, slicing at the marshal's legs. Speer flipped backwards, just in time.

Marty gathered his growing courage and raced at the marshal, slicing relentlessly at him. Randy jumped in and attempted to attack Speer from the opposite side. Speer held them at bay with ease. He seemed to be on a different plain of reality, never appearing to exert much force as he blocked the blade attacks coming from either side. At times, Speer seemed to have eyes in the back of his head, as he dodged or blocked attacks from directions he was not looking.

Then, first blood was drawn. The sight traumatized Logan and Francesca, and they momentarily closed their eyes. Speer had sliced into Marty's shoulder. A large gash, ripped through his deltoid muscle, was bleeding profusely and had completely incapacitated his left arm. Marty hollered out with pain and his knees buckled.

Randy was horrified by the wound inflicted upon his brother. Instantly filled with rage, he boldly attacked the marshal, swinging at him furiously. Speer looked almost caught off guard. Marty summoned up his strength and charged back into the fight. The marshal, though, was not shaken. He was just toying with his opponents.

Having grown bored of the deadly match, Speer took control. He sliced Marty's hands off clean, from the wrists. Marty fell to the ground in shock, as blood spewed forth in long streams from the ends of his arms. Now that the tables had turned, Logan felt nothing but pity for Marty. Francesca buried her head in Logan's chest, sobbing. Logan couldn't avert his eyes.

Randy went mad at the sight of his younger brother so brutalized. He sliced and stabbed at the marshal with reckless abandon. Speer spun and sliced Randy diagonally across the chest, upwards from the bottom of the ribs to the opposite shoulder. Randy fell backwards onto the ground, completely disabled. He writhed about in pain, sobbing out what sounded like the Lord's Prayer.

Unable to stop his own blood loss, Marty was quickly fading He shivered from lack of the warm, vital fluid. Within a minute, he was unconscious. His brother soon followed. Shortly after, they had both passed away.

Speer summoned Logan to his office in the Arbeitskamp administrative building.

"I know your father," Speer said. "He made that movie, *The Ark*."

"Yes," Logan nodded, sitting across from the marshal at a massive, imposing oak desk. He was nervous and his voice was unsteady.

Speer chuckled. "Do not be afraid of me, young man. I will not hurt you. Listen, I saw you last night, how you defended that poor deer. A person like you has *no* need to fear the Apex. In fact, even though you are in the underclass now, you have just as much chance as any citizen to rise through the ranks of the Apex hierarchy. If you are a good person, you will be very happy, and so will your family."

He paused, thinking, and then nodded his head. "You know, *The Ark* had very Isaianic overtones. I know what your parents were about. They understood, hell, probably even agreed with the Isaianic movement. They were just afraid of Geiseric." Speer laughed softly. "Hey, that's not unusual. Even I was a little afraid of Geiseric at first. But, he's a good man and that's why there's always room in this new world order for those who are good."

Speer opened up to Logan, telling him all about his own rise to power. As he listened, Logan became more relaxed. He leaned back in the faux leather swivel chair and listened with interest to the marshal's story.

Speer was a dedicated follower of Isaiism. He was a unique man long before Geiseric came to power: a vegetarian since his youth and the only high-ranking officer in the German military that had been a passionate animal rights activist before the Isaianic movement. His moral stance distinguished him even from General Gottlieb who, though eventually becoming one of Geiseric's top advisors in the Germanian Cabinet, was not yet a full vegetarian when Geiseric became chancellor. Speer was, therefore, highly trusted by the Apex Emperor, and that was why he was given charge over the largest underclass complex in the world—known as Citadel 1.

The marshal informed Logan that there were thousands of underclass work camps all over the world. The largest ones were in North America, because the United States was the Apex's center for agricultural production. Much of the land was perfect for farming almost all of the products most important to the Apex, especially soybeans. Not to mention that a farming center in North America kept much of the underclass, hundreds of millions of potential rebels, far away from the Apex imperial core and its citizens.

Though he tried at first to fight it, Logan came to enjoy the marshal's company. The man was genuine and exceedingly intelligent. As time wore on and a friendship began to build, Speer told Logan about his family life. The camp marshal who sternly ruled the Allied civilians held in Citadel 1 was a loving family man. Speer had thirteen children, conceived both out of desire and out of will. Because of his devout religious beliefs, he made a conscious decision to have as many kids as possible. Isaiism preached obsession with Eros, the creative and loving spirit represented by the Greek god of love and sexual desire, as opposed to Thanatos, the destructive and deadly instinct represented by the Greek god of death. Thus, Isaiism preached that the good, especially, should be fruitful and multiply.

To that end, Isaiism permitted polygamy. Naturally, only the most radical followers engaged in this practice, but those who did so, woman or man, did so of their own free will. The Apex long had the toughest laws in the world when it came to domestic abuse. Their judicial system tended to favor the woman in divorce proceedings, in terms of fiduciary obligations and custody issues.

Speer had three wives, and they were all pregnant again. The saying went that, "A woman would be far happier to be one of three wives to an Isaianic than the only wife to an evil and boring man."

Speer then laughed as he said to Logan, "Or so we Isaianic men would like to believe!"

Logan felt that the marshal's views were chauvinistic; however, he could tell Speer was being sincere. He did not sense that the marshal was trying to brag, or that he thought himself a playboy. Logan could see in Speer's eyes, and the way he spoke about his family, that he truly loved his three wives and, at least to his knowledge, they loved him, as peculiar as it all was to Logan.

One day, Speer brought Logan up to what he called "the ring." It was a circular platform made from a thin sheet of modified steel about fifty meters wide, raised fifty meters high into the air, supported by a single, thick pole in the middle. There were no ladders or anything around the platform and support except for a wide, open, grassy field. The general hopped in his chariot, grabbed Logan, and hauled him up.

The ring was a place where the marshal practiced his martial arts, especially the art of the sword. Speer had a number of different bladed weapons to choose from, none of which were sharpened. The first time he brought Logan up to the ring, they sparred with rapiers, a long, narrow sword typically used in fencing matches. The marshal was impressed with Logan's capabilities and, more importantly, with Logan's willingness and ability to learn.

It seemed that the marshal had taken Logan under his wing. For what reasons, Logan could not completely understand. However, it became their near daily ritual to practice or learn for at least an hour almost every combat style known to man, all of which Speer was well-acquainted with.

Logan's parents and grandparents were nervous. They did not know what Speer's intentions were. In such situations, where people felt relatively little control over their lives, it was easy to let one's mind drift to the paranoid. There was much to ruminate on, such as the fact that this man had recently butchered two young men not much older than Logan. While they knew Logan would never do something as stupid as Marty, nor had the character of the two brothers, it was still unnerving. They felt their boy was venturing too far into the snake's den. Logan never mentioned any of this to the marshal, nor did he ask any questions. He patiently held his tongue, keeping his mind in the moment, forgetting all doubts and conveying no suspicion. One day, after weeks of training, Speer decided to teach Logan something new.

The marshal had a humungous storage shed on the edge of the ring. He disappeared into the shed and reemerged moments later in a Kolibri chariot, his upper body encased in the typical teal-blue armor of the Kolibri, as opposed to his flashy red marshals' armor. Another chariot came whirring out, but there was no one riding in it, apparent by the fact that the body armor hung drooping flat atop of it like the molted skin of a reptile. Speer was also controlling this one via a Psychiclink device in the armor he presently wore, which was part of the chariot that he used for combat training. While these chariots he kept in the storage shed were not as unique and powerful as his red one, the marshal informed Logan that they were of the caliber used by many frontline Kolibri regulars in the war.

Logan was in awe of the machine, as Marshal Speer taught him how to don the armor. Climbing up the chariot using the foot and hand grips that protruded from it, Logan hopped in, sliding his legs down through the hole atop. Inside, there was a silky material enveloping his limbs and waist that compressed around him for a tight fit that held him in, but never was too constrictive or chafing.

Speer told Logan to hold his back and head completely upright and to hold his arms out directly to the side, like a crucifix. Doing as he was told, Logan suddenly felt the armor creeping onto him, the synthetic muscle within it seeming to bring it to life. It curled up his back and around his abdomen, neck and arms, smoothly fitting itself together and latching shut. Finally, Speer handed Logan a helmet and face mask. Putting them on, Logan felt them shape around his facial structure so that, once again, it clung to him well and would not fly off, but there were no annoying straps pulling tight under his chin or anywhere else, as was often the case.

Surprised by how flexible the suit of armor was and how natural it felt being in the chariot, Logan took to it as if he was already familiar with the machine. So much so that the marshal found it somewhat dubious that his apprentice had not flown a hummingbird chariot before, or at least had some experience using Psychiclink interface. Logan reasoned that it must have been from watching and studying the Kolibri flyers ever since he was captured. Or maybe, it was from hearing people describe the sensation of flying in a sky infantry chariot. Speer eventually judged that Logan was telling the truth, in terms of having no prior experience. Like with everything else, the young man was just an amazingly quick study.

They flew about over the woods and grassy prairie regions that surrounded the farming fields of Citadel 1. They fought with fake guns, which fired harmless lasers out of the tips. When the lasers struck the other's chariot or armor, a buzzer would go off inside the helmet of the person who got hit, which was annoying but, like a game of laser tag, non-injurious. Speer taught Logan much of what he knew about sky infantry warfare. Logan caught on quickly and, after a month of Kolibri training in the practice suits, Speer declared that Logan was the most innately talented student out of the many he had taught over the past decade, many of whom were top officers in the Apex military.

At the end of each day, the marshal led Logan back to the ring so that they could return the practice chariots and armor. Sometimes, they would fence for an hour or so after the flying lesson, before Speer took Logan back to his family.

At the end of one particularly grueling day of training, the two sat beside each other in meditative positions on the ring, watching the pastel colors of the sunset drift across the sky in the distance. They sipped ambrosia, which nourished and revitalized the drained athletes.

"I am going to be straightforward with you," Speer determined, his tone filled with gravity. "I think you have a gift. I think you have the gift of the Formula Elite. You learn so much faster than the average person. And you know why? It's because you are humble, and so you listen and carefully study. You have not arrogantly preconceived your own notions of the truth. And, I believe your humility comes from your compassion."

Speer paused as he deliberated for a moment. "Logan, compassionate people are able to transcend themselves, because they are empathetic. Empathy not only allows you to feel and understand someone's or something's pain. Empathy also allows you to see exactly what someone, or life itself, what everything is communicating to you. It is very hard to explain. Geiseric explains it best. But, I'm sure you understand vaguely what I am saying."

Logan just nodded. He did not know how to react to such accolades. Speer chuckled.

"You see," he pointed out. "I have already disarmed you by showering you so much with compliments. I'm telling you Logan, you have a gift and you are, obviously, compassionate. I knew you were special the first time I came across you working in the fields. I have the gift to truly see people. I can read auras, and yours is powerful and good. And think on this," he stood and extended a hand to help pull Logan up from his sitting position, preparing to leave, "I have charge over more than one hundred million Allied underclassmen and, out of all of them, you stand out. I foresee that you will have a bright future in the Apex new world order."

"Logan," Alistair began solemnly, "it's time you knew the truth."

The two sat down on a grass field at the perimeter of the suites, staring up at the stars while having a beer.

"The truth is, far more people are doomed to die. The reason you have not seen your Uncle Doug," Alistair paused and sighed, "is because he has been indicted by the crimes against life tribunal."

Logan stared at Alistair in disbelief. Although he had no idea what exactly this indictment would mean for his uncle, he knew it was going to be bad.

"All people in the underclass," Alistair continued solemnly, "found by the tribunal to have been linked to things like factory farming, or animal testing, or any other major industry which killed or tortured animals, will be put on trial. If found guilty, they could be given a number of punishments." He swallowed hard. He hated to upset Logan, but he had to say it.

"The most serious crimes will be dealt with in an 'eye for an eye' fashion. Geiseric wants to turn the tables, to show them what it was like to be one of those animals. Logan, it's going to be really bad. Those who worked at slaughterhouses will be slaughtered just like the animals. Vivisectionists will be dissected alive purely for punishment."

Logan felt woozy, light headed. The world around him started to spin and for a moment he thought he was going to pass out. "So!" he snapped, not wanting to see what this had to do with his uncle.

Alistair grimaced with frustration, not wishing to explain the truth in detail. "You know what your uncle was, professionally, right?"

Logan shook his head. "He was . . . uh . . . he owned a clothing store! What does that have to do with animal cruelty?!"

Alistair grimly stared into Logan's eyes. "That store chain he owned was one of the largest distributors of fur clothing in the world. They bought their furs from Chinese companies that skinned the animals alive."

Shock again set in on Logan as he realized what this meant for his Uncle Doug. The blood drained from his face, and he looked pleadingly at Alistair, hoping he heard wrong. "What are you saying?" he demanded feebly.

Alistair looked down. "I think you know what I'm saying."

"Are you saying that they're going to skin my uncle alive?!" he shouted upwards into the air, at nobody. He keeled over, feeling like he was going to throw up.

Alistair placed his hand on Logan's shoulder. "There is a way to free him."

Logan, his face red and wet with tears, looked up at Alistair. "How do you know so much?"

Alistair helped Logan upright himself. "What I'm about to tell you, you have to swear not to tell anyone. Not even your parents. You swear?"

Logan nodded, his eyes squinting with curiosity. "Yeah, I swear."

Assured as much as he could be, the young man who had been Logan's friend throughout the entirety of this strange experience in the underclass took a deep breath and dove in.

"My name is not Alistair," he said, his voice changing slightly as his words took on an upper-crust British inflection. "My name is Rodney Ackleworth," he asserted. "My father is the AQVC, the Allied Quadruped Vehicles Commander."

Logan's eyes widened, his mind absorbing this startling information, as the young man that he once knew as Alistair continued.

"The Apex thinks I'm dead and that's why I have not been found out, yet. *But,* if they knew I was here, I would be held as a hostage to be used against my father and the Allies. So, you must understand how important it is that you tell *no one* of this."

Logan nodded again. "Of course ... but, I thought the Allies were destroyed!" he said with emphatic confusion. "I mean, I thought everyone's been captured! Isn't the war over?!"

Rodney shook his head. "No, Logan. The war is not over." He inhaled deeply again, looking around nervously. "That's all I can tell you, right now." He tilted down his head a bit and looked up at Logan with a tinge of vulnerability, holding out his open palm for Logan to slap him five. "So I can trust you, right bro? You're not going to rat me out?"

Logan fell silent, lost in thought, just thinking about what all of this new information meant. He shook himself out of the trance and slapped his palm into Rodney's, gripping it strongly for a moment. "You know I got your back man."

"I know it," Rodney smiled. "I know it."

When Logan went back to his suite, he felt as though he were in another world, gazing through a window upon this one. He was disassociated from his body. His parents and grandparents noticed that something was wrong with him, but he just kept telling them that he was tired.

Everything seemed to have a red tint, a crimson aura, which corresponded with the fear, rage and general inundation of hyper-stimulating emotions that Logan was experiencing. Fortunately, he recalled a praying tactic that his friend formerly known as Alistair had taught him. Instead of asking God to bless one's self, the prayer blessed God. Rodney said it went back to pagan ritual magic, which taught that whatever blessings a person prayed unto the great creative spirit came back to that person many times fold.

After praying for an hour, Logan went to sleep in an utterly tranquil mind-set, unlike anything he had ever felt before. His faith had been completely shored up by some potent spiritual force. Never before had Logan been so sure that there was a higher power.

Over the next week, Logan behaved as if nothing had changed. He never once mistakenly referred to Rodney as Rodney. Of course, Logan had known him as Alistair for far longer, and so it wasn't hard to keep that name in the forefront of his mind. Francesca, Jacques and Sasha all knew that their friend was not who he claimed to be. He had only come up with his alias upon capture by the Apex. Naturally, Rodney had told his friends that the Allies were still up and running. But, no one talked more on any of this, always keeping the conversation light, patiently waiting for when Rodney felt it was the right time to discuss it any further.

Finally, one night, Rodney led Logan out to the lake, swimming into the middle of the water. They weaved carefully through the people who were standing in shallower areas or were keeping themselves afloat by treading water. Rodney found a spot where the roar of the crowd around gave cover to his conversation. He and Logan tread water for a moment to catch their breath, and then Alistair began in a hushed tone.

"Like before, you cannot repeat this to anyone," he asserted sternly. "You got that?"

Logan nodded and zipped his fingers across his lips to show his solemn pledge.

"Good," Rodney said, taking a deep breath. "Alright, so here's the deal. So, as I said, the Allies are still in action."

"Where are they?!" Logan whispered impatiently.

Rodney simply pointed up to the night sky. Logan gazed to where he aimed his finger and saw a red dot glowing brighter than most of the stars.

"There were many evacuated to Mars," Rodney said. "More than a billion Allied civilians and military personnel are there now."

Logan was so stunned he almost forgot to keep his legs paddling. He blinked the water from his eyes and gestured for Rodney to continue.

"Allied High Command is preparing a rescue operation to save another billion of us in the underclass and bring us back to their bases on the Moon and then to Mars."

"And you all of a sudden want to get back into the fight?" Logan asked.

Rodney stared off into the distance for a moment, profoundly vexed. "I was a fool and a coward to think I could run away from this war. Geiseric is not the man I portrayed to you when we first met. You know that now. I did not tell you everything I knew, because you were a scared kid then. As much as I could help it, I didn't want to freak you out. But, even *I* didn't know the half of it. I have recently found out much more." He gulped and made a face of disgust. "Beyond setting up crimes against life trials, Geiseric has a plan to depopulate the underclass."

"What?!" Logan practically shouted. "You mean kill them?!"

Rodney pressed a finger up to his own lips, in a gesture to silence Logan. "Exactly," he said quietly. "He doesn't trust the underclass. The trials are just to satiate his thirst for vengeance right now. Later, he plans to launch a Stalinist purge of unfathomable proportions. He wants to wipe out anyone in the underclass who is even remotely suspected of being rebellious. What that means, though, is that *most* of the underclass will be dead, because Geiseric is suspicious of anyone who did not have Isaianic inclinations *before* the war."

Logan's face and eyes went blank, as his mind rebooted. "So," he finally asked, "why doesn't he just do it now?"

"He would," Rodney asserted. "But he still needs us. The war is far from over. Why throw away all this free labor, when he can use us to feed and build up his military machine? So long as the Allies hold out, we are relatively safe."

Logan was in a state of shock, but he managed to keep his mind on an even keel. "Where did you hear all of this?"

Rodney explained that a spy operating covertly in the underclass had identified him as the son of the Allied General Rod Ackleworth. The spy communicated the information back to General Ackleworth, who then told the spy to relay his son a message — "the cavalry is on the way."

Rodney placed his hand strongly on Logan's shoulder, his expression rife with gravity. "You are in a position to help the rescue operation."

"How?" Logan asked, surprised.

"At present, it is nearly impossible for the Allies to smuggle weapons to Earth," Rodney explained. "But, *you* have access to three battle-worthy Kolibri fighting vehicles!"

Logan was perplexed. "What's *that* gonna do?"

Rodney smiled. "That's all we need."

The following day started out ominously. The skies were blackened by rain clouds. Logan awoke at around seven without the help of the alarm system, being that his body's circadian rhythm had been trained by being woken up at the same time for weeks now. He gazed outside his room window at the turbulent wind driving the watery deluges, which were accompanied by claps of thunder and bolts of lightning. There was something oddly invigorating about the powerful weather raging out on the fields and above the underclass residential complexes.

As Logan stared at the energetic forces, he felt as though he was absorbing some of the strength of the storm, into his psyche. Amazingly, thinking about everything he had been told by Rodney concerning Geiseric's Armageddon-like "final solution," Logan felt little fear. Strangely enough, he was imbued with an intense faith.

The alarms never went off. Instead, a message came over all the televisions in the suites saying that everyone had the day off. Tom and Bibi slept in, along with Tom's parents. Papa was already awake when Logan walked out of his room to grab some orange ambrosia out of the dispenser in the kitchen.

"Hey Papa," Logan greeted warmly, giving his grandfather a strong hug. Papa smiled and hugged him back.

"Hey Logan, my boy!" he replied, full of zest.

The two decided to walk over to the cafeteria to grab some breakfast. Today, there was far more variety in food selection. Because everyone had the day off, those in control of the work facility decided to give the underclassmen food that was intended more for good taste, rather than for health. Usually, for work days, the underclassmen were given high-protein breakfasts to balance their internal hormones, such as insulin, to give them strength and to help them heal from the day's labor. On weekends and on days such as these, the cafeteria was overflowing with dessert breakfasts, such as Belgian waffles with whipped organic butter and fresh maple syrup. These happened to be Logan's and Papa's favorite and they each had two of the giant, grid-like batter cakes, smothered in cream and powdered sugar.

Papa had always been a relatively vital elderly man, but since the capture he seemed even younger and stronger. When Papa was on the island, he had many aches and pains, particularly from old war injuries to his lower back that he sustained in his youth. However, in the four months or so that he was captured by the Apex, Papa had healed. He no longer complained of his soreness and he exuded the youthful energy of a man in his thirties. For instance, he could never have gone out in a storm before without getting a horrible pain in the back of his neck, from the cold. However, he was so warm-blooded today that Logan could see the rainwater steaming off of his head.

After gorging themselves, they both brought trays full of food back to the suite, where they found Bibi and Tom's mother, Lia, already awake. The ladies were sitting at the dining table in their robes, having a morning cup of ambrosia and gabbing to each other. There was no coffee or coffee-maker in the suite and rarely was coffee served at the cafeteria. However, today there were many types available, from French Roast to Mocha Java. Bibi and Lia clapped for joy when they saw that Papa had brought them back a pot of their favorite morning brew.

But, the joy was short-lived and the two ladies looked anxiously at Logan.

"What's the matter?" Logan asked.

"Well," Bibi said, looking at Lia, and then back to him, "Marshal Speer sent a message to you on the TV."

"Yeah," Logan used the same emotional game face he utilized when sparring, so as not to betray the fact that his heart started to pound rapidly in his chest. "So . . ."

Bibi nervously squeezed her fingers into her palms. "Well, he just wanted to see if you were ready to train today."

Logan impatiently gestured for her to continue. "Yeah, and . . ."

Bibi shrugged, looking to Lia with an expression of mild confusion, and then back to her son. "That's it. You know how that just makes us a little nervous every time you go out there, flying around in those dangerous vehicles, especially in weather like this." She cocked her head and squinted her eyes. "Why, is there something else that should worry us?"

"Not at all," Logan dropped his shoulders a bit with relief. "I better go."

An hour later, Logan was hovering above the ring in a Kolibri chariot, wearing the full body armor and helmet. He was opposite Marshal Speer, who was levitating in his Kolibri chariot above the raised platform. Reaching its zenith, the storm cast down water in torrents, carried by near hurricane force winds. Bolts of electricity tore across the sky, illuminating the area and reflecting off of the two fighters' chariots and armor.

Speer assured Logan that the lightning would not touch them. He explained that the ring was specially designed with non-conductive materials at the base, so that it was not grounded and, therefore, would not act as a lightning rod. Speer then added that, even in the off-chance a bolt was to strike them, the armor and chariots had special linings within to insulate against electrocution. However, the marshal grinned and advised Logan to stay away from trees.

Fighting in the chaotic skies that day was a mind-expanding experience for the young apprentice. Logan experienced what it meant to be in "the zone." Something about the powerful and ominous atmosphere was acutely inspiring. The size and intensity of the storm appeared almost supernatural. As lightning bolts sizzled around the fighters, Logan could understand how ancient people envisioned a god, or just God, to have a hand in this. Flying through the air, zipping up to the lower strata of the dark, viscous clouds, Logan could almost perceive a sentience within the storm.

Speer explained that the conditions were ideal for training, because the unpredictable crashing of thunder and the flashing light simulated the distractions in a real battle and tested one's concentration. The marshal brought his apprentice through the entire regimen of fighting exercises, including live-fire training with the massive handguns that shot thirty-millimeter tungsten penetrator rounds used by the Kolibri during the war. He had only let Logan try these weapons once before in a highly controlled setting. But, in these heightened circumstances, Logan could tell that the marshal was a bit uneasy, for these guns could easily blast through Speer's armor.

However, the marshal trusted Logan and he showed this by not keeping behind the trainee during this live-fire exercise. Instead, Speer joined Logan in destroying the targets on the "demolition grounds," an area set up with obsolete American tanks and other armored vehicles from the late 2020s, which the Apex found when they conquered Fortress North America. One well-placed shot by the powerful handguns could take out one of the large tanks. The penetrator round blasted through the armor, into the fuel tank or shell hold and the vehicle went up in flames, often exploding with a mighty roar.

Even though the Kolibri armor absorbed much of the force from the kickback of the guns, Logan was still usually jarred within the armor each time he fired. But, as he entered "the zone," everything appeared to slow down, including the firing action of his handguns. He was thus able to adjust to the rapid motion of the kickback.

Gazing around him, Logan was able to see clearly for the whole length of the demolition area, which was many kilometers wide. The lightning also slowed according to his perception. He could hear their individual crackling and booms, as they sliced through the atmosphere. The seething force of the environment and the energy of the weaponry he was brandishing about was enough to charge the veins of any young man, who by his very nature was prone to love untamed speed and power.

After a few hours, the storm faded away and Speer decided to end the training session. Through all the excitement and majestic grandiosity of the day, Logan nearly forgot his mission. Much of this was subconsciously intentional, for he had come to have a great respect for the marshal and it hurt him on some level to be abusing Speer's trust. But, as his armor came off and he jumped out of the chariot, Logan remembered what his motivations were. He remembered the thought of his uncle being tortured, skinned alive, along with millions more.

Rodney had given Logan a miniature device capable of monitoring the coded radio frequencies emanating from a transponder. Speer's armor on his upper forearm had a transponder within that opened the locked storage area on the ring containing the Kolibri chariots and other weaponry used for training.

The device Logan carried was only one centimeter wide and was as flat as a piece of paper. It was irregularly-shaped and colored a reddish-purple in order to blend in and be hidden underneath his tongue. It was as soft and flexible as plastic wrapping, so that it did not affect Logan's speech, which was of the utmost importance to not give it away.

All Logan needed to do was be within ten meters of the marshal when Speer opened the storage area. However, Logan had no way of knowing if the device worked, or if he had done his job right until later, when it was analyzed. For now, he carefully and respectfully dried off the chariot and armor in the storage area and the marshal gave him a lift back to his suite.

That night, Rodney confirmed to Logan that the device had successfully intercepted the marshal's transponder signal. Rodney debriefed his protégé on the next mission, which Logan accepted whole-heartedly. He wondered where he derived this mighty courage, but he more and more came to believe it was coming from some force greater than himself.

Carefully timing their escape, Logan and Jacques slipped away during afternoon free time. They made their way toward the forested area at the northern end of the residential complex. When there were no Kolibri guards-men around, Jacques and Logan ran across the half-kilometer of open, grassy terrain that separated the suites and the trees. They made it to the forest with-out being noticed. There they met up with Rodney, who was waiting with equipment provided to him by the Allied infiltrator.

There were three specially-designed suits, one for each of them, made out of an incredibly thin material. They had been folded to such a small size that all three could by held in Rodney's right hand. The suits were designed for two things: to change color in order to camouflage into the surroundings, and to keep heat in, in case a Kolibri guardsman was scouting the area with thermal-vision binoculars. They did not have to wear the suits in the dense forest. They planned to put them on when they reached the open field around the ring, where they were exposed and the guards made their rounds frequently.

Rodney quickly showed them the device that was going to help them get up to the top of the platform. It was in three pieces, making it hard to discern its purpose, but he explained what it could do. It was called a ricochet dart gun and it fired out a steel bolt attached to a steel cable. He also showed them pieces of a relatively small nuclear bomb, which nonetheless had the power of five hundred tons of TNT. It was divided in three pieces so that the three motley commandos could carry them later.

But they did not need the bomb, yet. Taking their suits and the pieces of the dart gun, they ran through the thick forest, keeping a steady pace. They ran almost five kilometers, up and down hills and small slopes, all within twenty minutes, arriving at their destination ahead of time.

At the end of the forested area, they quickly slipped into their special suits and exited out onto the wide grassy field encircling Speer's fighting platform. The field was easy terrain compared to what the three had just run through. So as not to be out on the open field for too long, they sprinted across, constantly looking about to make sure they weren't spotted. Their suits changed color automatically to camouflage into the grass. Just as they made it to the ring, the sound of Kolibri flyers could be heard approaching from over the treetop horizon. Jacques, Rodney and Logan rapidly fell to the ground and laid as flat as they could in the grass, shaded by the platform high above.

Two Kolibri guardsmen, on their usual patrol, slowed down as they entered the field. They lowered their chariots closer to the ground and flew back and forth overhead. Logan tried to flatten himself more and more, dig-ging his fingers into the dirt, as if to pull himself farther down. His body was so tense that he felt as if his back would snap. He heard the guardsmen hovering around nearby, their loud buzzing wings kicking up dust and small rocks onto him. Logan thought for sure that he and his comrades had been discovered. He felt nauseated and incredibly dizzy — the temperature quickly rising within his suit — the Reaper breathing right over his shoulder.

Then, just as suddenly as they had shown up, the Kolibri guardsmen zipped away at top speed, heading in the opposite direction from whence they came.

Rodney stood up slowly.

"Shit!" he whispered loudly. "I'm fucking boiling alive in here!"

Jacques ripped off the mask of his suit. "Alright," he panted heavily, "let's do this."

The three of them took out the different pieces of the ricochet dart gun and rapidly snapped everything in place. Once it was assembled, Rodney punched in the settings on the keypad, programming it for the desired height and other options. He propped the device on his shoulder and fired it upwards.

What emerged was a small, rocket-propelled cylindrical projectile with a thin steel cable trailing behind it, uncoiling from within the launcher. The rocket propulsion was incredibly silent as it shot upwards. When the missile's altimeter registered that it had reached seventy meters up, which was twenty meters above the platform, the rocket shut off and it began to fall. The weight in the head of the missile caused it to arc downwards. The missile then fired a steel dart out of its head, which also trailed steel cord behind, and its pointed tip plunged deeply into the top of the platform, giving a secure hold for the three hopeful commandos below.

Rodney was first to try it out. He pressed a button on the launcher and held on as a strong winch inside the mechanism quickly pulled him up. Within seconds, he had reached the top of the ring. With another press of the button, he lowered it back down to Logan and Jacques. Rodney checked to see if the dart was still secure. Seeing that it was, he made his way over to the storage holds atop the ring.

When Jacques reached the top, he could not find Rodney. He was startled when his friend suddenly appeared behind him in a Kolibri chariot and armor, carrying Logan. Jacques and Logan happily threw off their dreadfully hot camo-suits and jumped into the two other chariots that were in the ring's storage area. When they placed their helmets on, the armor came to life, clasping around their bodies.

Hurriedly, they flew back into the woods and retrieved the pieces of the nuclear bomb. Each taking a part, they placed them in the carrying holds within their chariots. Jacques then led the way to finish their mission. His chariot swiveled to make its length parallel to the ground, so that he was in a horizontal position, lying on his stomach and looking up and forward like a hummingbird in full flight. The wings sped up and he was off in a flash.

"Come on," Rodney waved at Logan to do the same and they both sped off.

As they raced over the heads of underclass field hands in far off quadrants, Logan was overcome by a bizarre feeling, looking down from his keepers' vantage point. Jacques led Rodney and Logan low over the fields, trying to avoid being seen by Kolibri guards. Though they were disguised, they could still be questioned as to what they were doing and where they were going.

Over the horizon, the tip of the Rose poked up three hundred meters into the sky. Soon, Logan could see the whole of the unique spire. It was beautiful, just as he had remembered, reflecting a multitude of different, bright colors like a prism. It mostly cast a silver and white light, but the reflection of sunlight off the Rose was not blinding. The materials it was comprised of diminished glare. It was fascinating to Logan, this awesome structure with so many Kolibri flying to and fro, refueling at the hundreds of small pumps winding around and all the way up the length of the spire.

Jacques beckoned the other two towards a pump station about halfway up the Rose. Rodney and Logan pretended to refuel at the pumps next to the one Jacques had chosen. Although they checked around to see if anyone was watching, they knew it was still risky. At the speed with which the Kolibri flew, they could pop up within a split-second.

They subtly opened the storage compartments in their chariots and carefully took out the different bomb parts to assemble. As Logan was about to hand off his part to Jacques, a Kolibri flyer zipped nearby and startled him. The three watched in horror as Logan fumbled with and dropped the piece of the bomb. Jacques, showing tremendous reflexes, shot downwards and caught it. They all sighed with relief, but were far from relaxed. Logan's heart beat so hard that he could hear its throbbing in his ears, overwhelming nearly all exterior sounds.

Carefully assembling the bomb as fast as he could, Jacques checked over his work to make sure that he had done everything correctly. He then fastened the bomb next to the pump and pressed the button to start the detonation sequence. He gave the thumbs up to his comrades and they were off at top speed.

As they raced from the spire, Logan became ever more conscious of what he was doing. He was partaking in a major Special Forces operation for the

Allies. It all seemed completely surreal, like he would wake up at any moment. But, as they raced away from mortal danger, he knew this was no dream.

The three of them stopped at a safe distance and turned around to confirm their work was not in vain. As the time counted down, Logan looked around at the hundreds of Kolibri flyers, zooming this way and that, unaware of what was about to happen. His mind and metabolism were running at such a heightened level that the outside world seemed to be moving slower than he had ever experienced, bringing him deeper into the "zone" than he had ever been.

An overwhelmingly bright flash and a tremendous rumble broke the serenity.

Logan, Jacques and Rodney watched as the nuclear blast wave slammed into the Kolibri flyers around and nearing the Rose. The brightness of the explosion dimmed and the three makeshift commandos witnessed the successful completion of their mission. The great spire toppled onto the ground, smashing into several pieces. Only the bottom quarter of the colossal structure was still standing, rooted firmly into the earth. Hundreds of Kolibri lay dead or disabled on the ground, many trapped under the heavy ruins of the spire.

Jacques and Rodney quickly surveyed the scene, noting how badly they had wounded the enemy's sky infantry forces. From the looks of it, nearly half of the Kolibri flyer garrison at Citadel 1 was taken out of commission. The Rose, the Kolibri's main refueling structure, was completely destroyed, lying prostrate on the ground like a fallen titan.

Somewhat stunned by what they had accomplished, the three commandos flew back to the fields and residential complexes.

Fifty thousand kilometers away from the Earth, a battle erupted in space. The Allies, though far outnumbered now in manpower, managed to build up their space armada to a strength that could temporarily contest that of the Apex. If all went well, this window of time would allow for a successful rescue operation. The billion and more citizens of the Allied Nations that had been evacuated to Mars had been forced to work day and night in the mines, refineries and factories, and it was on their blood, sweat and tears that this vast Allied space fleet was created.

Nearly five hundred-thousand transport crafts rocketed through the vacuum. They were guarded by a convoy of ten Allied Triton Class space battleships. The space fleet had been secreted to the Moon, which was used as a launchpad for the invasion. Since then, the powerful engines created for the transports and battleships had perpetually accelerated them towards Earth.

Because space had no air to slow down a propelling object, the Allied fleet continued to gain velocity until by the end of their journey they had reached a top speed of 130,000 kilometers per hour. At this speed, the Apex had little chance to organize their defenses.

Each Triton battleship carried three of the largest laser cannons ever produced. The cannons had a range of over one thousand kilometers and the battleships were designed completely around the huge guns. Before the Apex commanders could form a strategy to cope with the devastating onslaught, seven of their capital battleships were destroyed and six others were badly damaged. The Allies had managed to break through the Apex space defenses without any losses to their own crafts.

Immediately, the Allied convoy slammed on the retro-rockets and began an intense deceleration. The abrupt change wreaked havoc on some of the less adjusted pilots and crewmen. As their bodies withstood the incredible G-forces, many of them passed out, but this was expected and their craft had been set to auto-pilot. However, they had little time before they had to reawaken or die.

As the Triton battleships came to a full halt and formed their defensive wall against the inevitable attack from Apex reinforcements, the smaller transport craft continued on. Upon entering the far exterior atmosphere of the Earth, the transports were still speeding down faster than a rifle bullet. The pilots had to guide their crafts at a gentle slope through the Earth's atmosphere to avoid burning up. Those who had not yet regained consciousness were quickly incinerated with their spacecraft.

Far below, Logan, Jacques and Rodney spotted the man-made meteorites showering through the air, leaving long streams of flame and smoke in the sky. Moments later, they heard the sound of thousands of the transports flying overhead, the rumbling of their retro-boosters shaking the ground below.

Within a half hour of the nuclear strike on the Apex Rose, day had turned to night and Logan's family had been gathered together, with the help of Rodney. It turned out that Uncle Doug and his wife and kids had been nearby since the first day Logan and his parents had arrived to the work facility. Tom had not been reunited with his brother, for Doug and his family were placed in Sector Omega. Omega Sector, as Rodney explained to Logan, was where those who were charged with "crimes against life" were held, along with their spouses and children.

Allied Intelligence had provided Rodney with the location of Doug, his wife Mary, and their five children. When three Kolibri suddenly appeared above them, Doug and his family were frightened that they had done something wrong. They were that much more astonished when one of the Kolibri flyers removed his helmet, and they saw Logan's face. They were whisked away to a small field of grass concealed by surrounding trees, where there was a tearful reunion for the whole family.

Jacques grabbed Francesca and Sasha and brought them to the secret gathering place. In an attempt to remain as hidden as possible, the families crouched next to the trees. Logan, Rodney and Jacques kept lookout while also trying not to draw attention.

Riveted, Logan gazed upon the first of the transports making their way down towards the Sector Delta residential complex, exactly as planned. The rectangular rescue craft swiveled their jet nozzles from a horizontal to a vertical position, enabling them to hover down to the ground for a soft landing in the grassy areas between the suite rows. They were about one hundred meters long and had running lights along their sides. Bright flashing arrows pointed towards the entrance doors, which opened up like gaping jaws. A voice blared over the craft's loudspeakers.

"We are the Allies! Everyone into the ships now! Move! Move! Hurry!"

People were hollering and crying with a mixture of shock, trepidation, joy and relief as they ran from their rooms toward their rescuers. Hundreds of Hornets swarmed out of the transports to protect the underclassmen from the Kolibri. Even from a good distance away, Logan could see the tiny figures being herded onto the transports under the protective umbrella of the Allied Hornets. They looked like chaotic little ants scurrying ever so quickly into their nest.

Within minutes, most of the first wave of transports were filled and were firing up their jet engines, the outtake nozzles swiveling to push the transports on a swift, diagonally upward trajectory.

Moments later, a transport appeared overhead of Logan, Rodney, Jacques, and their loved ones, and set itself down in the hidden field. Immediately, the doors lifted and out came a dozen Hornet flyers. The lead flyer's chariot was unique, both in its design and gold coloring. Rodney immediately recognized who it was.

"Dad!" he shouted joyfully, taking off his helmet. Rodney raced his chariot toward his father. General Ackleworth took off his helmet and smiled wide, overjoyed at seeing his son alive, having once believed him to be dead.

"Rodney!" he shouted back. But, he wasted no time with further greetings. "Get everyone in! Now!"

The thunder of Eagle jets loomed overhead, their sonic booms vibrating through the air. Once again, Logan witnessed the contrails made by their engines when darting across the sky, now accompanied by laser blasts. He stared in horror as the Apex Golden Eagles ravaged the Allied transports at high altitude.

A multitude of transports were struck and plunged to the ground, leaving trails of fire and burnt material in their wake like a comet. But, the vast number of transports was overwhelming and most made it through the gauntlet. A loud, deep buzzing neared the residential complex — the distinct sound of hummingbird chariots. A battalion of almost five hundred Kolibri, what was left of the garrison at Citadel 1, moved in swarm phalanx formation over the suites of Delta Sector.

Logan could hear a harsh voice blaring in German and English over the facility's loudspeakers in the distance.

"Everyone stay in the suites or you will be killed!"

The Kolibri flyers descended upon anyone trying to escape, slaughtering them with blades and firepower. The Hornets valiantly defended the underclassmen boarding the second wave of transports. Logan turned his gaze back to his family as they started to board the craft in the hidden field. Before hardly anyone got on, though, the transport suddenly exploded and erupted into flames.

Most of Logan's family, along with Francesca and Sasha, were blown backwards from the force. They appeared to be relatively uninjured, but as Logan raced towards them in his chariot to check out what happened, he could not find Tom's parents, Grandpa and Grammy. They had already gotten on.

A horrible sensation slammed Logan in the gut and branched over his entire body. He could feel the blood throbbing in his veins as he looked frantically around. His chariot's buzzing wings helped clear the smoke emanating from the transport, and he saw what he had feared. The craft was demolished. There was no way anyone could have survived within. Somehow, a Golden Eagle flying overhead had spotted the craft in the field and targeted it with a smart bomb. The middle of the transport was gone and fire boiled out of the front, rear and sides.

Logan felt his soul recoil in horror. But, he did not have time to think for long, for the enemy was soon upon him.

A squad of Kolibri flyers had been alerted by the blast of the smart bomb and saw the smoke rising from the hidden field amongst the trees. They moved in quickly to investigate and saw what looked to them like three Kolibri flyers dealing with a dozen Hornets. Jacques and Rodney surprised the Kolibri squad by turning and attacking them, assisted by General Ackleworth and the Hornets. The general's specialized Hornet chariot was far faster and more agile than that of the Kolibri he faced. The fight was swift and within seconds, the Kolibri squad was defeated. However, only one of the Hornet flyers survived, besides Ackleworth.

The general gloomily surveyed the situation. "We have to get out of here Rodney."

Rodney looked around at Francesca and Sasha, along with what was left of Logan's family, hiding in the bushes, trembling and terrified. "I won't leave my friends," he answered his father.

"Don't be a fool!" Ackleworth barked at his son. We have to get to another transport before it's too late! Pretty soon, they'll be shooting half of them down!"

Something came over Rodney, and he clenched his hands into fists, in disgust of his father's indifference to the human statistics. For the first time in any battle, he was completely unafraid. "We will save my friends," he asserted to the general, "or you can leave me."

His father took little time to think it over. "We can't bring a transport over here, because it will call too much attention," he muttered aloud, more to himself than his son. "Everyone! Grab someone and follow me!"

Ackleworth raced down, grabbed Logan's Aunt Mary by both arms and hauled her off through the air. The other Hornet flyer grabbed Logan's cousin, Sandy. Logan carefully grabbed his cousin Lucy by the arms.

"We'll be right back!" he shouted to his family, and then quickly gave an assuring wink to Francesca.

Rodney picked up Sasha and followed after Logan. Jacques stayed to stand guard over those left behind. He did not wish to take his daughter right away, for he felt that the longer she was on the transport, the greater danger she was exposed to. The general flew toward the suites and patched through to a transport that was just landing. The craft paused in its descent and the entrance doors opened. Ackleworth tossed Logan's aunt into the cabin and she was caught by the crewmen inside. The other Hornet flyer did the same with Sandy, but more gently. Logan and Rodney moved much more slowly than the others while letting Lucy and Sasha off, trying not to hurt them.

"Hurry!" the general hollered at them. He again patched through to the pilots of the transport and asked them to wait.

On the second run, Logan's three older cousins and Uncle Doug were whisked to the rescue craft. But, when they were dropped off inside the transport, the general noticed that the hovering ship was beginning to attract attention.

"Get out of here!" He commanded the pilot.

The pilot was stunned. "But we have much more room!"

"I said get out of here!" Ackleworth bellowed with authority. The pilot didn't question him twice. The doors to the transport snapped closed and it took off into the sky at full speed.

Logan felt guilty that a whole transport was used up on just eight people, but it was worth it to watch some of his family rising high into the sky, out of harm's way from the ground guns and, soon, out of range of the Golden Eagles, as the craft disappeared into space. However, his thoughts immediately returned to his parents, Papa and Francesca, who still needed a transport out of there.

Suddenly, a loud shot rang out and the Hornet flyer that was helping transport the family was struck down on his way back to the hidden field, his continued momentum propelling him forward at a downward angle. He spun rapidly as he descended and finally careened into the ground, awkwardly bouncing across the dirt.

Rodney was next to come under attack. Penetrator rounds zipped by him, grazing past his armor. Bravely turning and facing his opponents, he saw three Kolibri flyers headed straight for him. He grabbed the double-barreled guns in his chariot, holding one in each hand, and unloaded on his enemy.

His courage startled his opponents and one of the Kolibri flyers was shot through the chest. The flyer plummeted and hit the ground with an explosive impact. His two comrades divided up and attacked Rodney from either side, their guns blazing. General Ackleworth came to his son's aid and blasted a hole through each of the enemy flyers. Before the Kolibri charioteers even hit the ground, though, Rodney and his father were under bombardment by a hail of penetrator rounds. They turned and saw five more Kolibri flyers charging them.

Jacques raced up from the field to help his friends. With a well-aimed sniping, he took down one of the Kolibri flyers on his ascent. The general and his son opened up in unison and took down another two flyers. The other two Kolibri then broke into retreat and Rodney slapped his father five. But suddenly, to his horror, he saw Jacques careening toward the ground, shot through the face.

Rodney watched in disbelief as his friend's lifeless body slammed into the dirt.

"Jacques!" he called out, his voice cracking with emotion. He tried to head down to help him, but immediately came under attack again by another group of Kolibri.

Logan glimpsed at Jacques's armored body lying limp and prostrate on the ground. Jacques's helmet had massive holes in the front and back, where the round entered and exited, leaving little to the imagination of what happened to him. Turning away with abhorrence from Jacques's headless corpse, something finally snapped in Logan's mind and spirit. It was as if all his fear, frustration and rage were channeled into an intense, inexplicable power that carried him toward his enemy free of any apprehension in his heart.

His inner clock working at lightning speed, Logan charged at the enemy flyers, pulling his two mammoth guns from their holsters and carefully aiming them. Squeezing the triggers, he felt the kickback of the deadly hand cannons jolt his frame. He pulled back again and the rounds pierced his opponents. Two Kolibri flyers fell by his hand, to the amazement of General Ackleworth and Rodney. They didn't waste time in wonder, though.

"Split up!" Ackleworth called out, and Logan bolted into action like a seasoned warrior. Three Kolibri went after General Ackleworth, recognizing him from his chariot as a highly-ranked Allied officer. Among the three was a flyer that Logan recognized. It was Marshal Speer. His crimson red armor and chariot were strongly distinguishable even in the late dusk light.

Logan and Rodney flew in the opposite direction of the general, firing back at the three Kolibri flyers that were chasing them. Logan followed Rodney's lead. They both flew as if they were swimming through the water on their backs. They crunched their abdomens and necks up slightly in order to see and fire on their enemy. Their new position made a far smaller target for the Kolibri flyers to strike.

Rodney blasted out a continuous stream of bullets at his and Logan's pursuers. He fired one gun at a time, placing the other in the chariot holster to be automatically reloaded and used again when his current gun was out. There was no pause in the barrage of rounds he sent at his enemies. Firing both guns simultaneously would have given the enemy a small window of complete freedom while the guns were both reloading. Logan followed suit and the two kept their pursuers at bay.

Rodney deftly aimed and took down one of their pursuers. Things had evened out; it was two against two, a fair battle. But, it lasted only a moment.

There was one major disadvantage to the defensive retreat. To fly and fire backwards required that the fighters' eyes avert from where they were headed. At such intense speeds, while looking in the other direction for even just a second, the flyers could find themselves in a completely different situation. And Rodney had spent too long looking back when he took down the last Kolibri. He didn't see what was charging right towards him from over the horizon.

He turned forward just in time to see a Kolibri Knight heading straight at him. They collided at the collective speed of one thousand km/h, the Knight's heavily armored shoulder plowing into Rodney. Logan looked over just in time to see the force of the impact crush into his friend's face plate and torso armor. The heavy sky infantryman was barely even fazed, his armor and the powerful synthetic muscle layer beneath having absorbed the shock of the hit.

Blood seeped out from behind Rodney's armor as he and his vehicle crashed to the ground, skipping across the grass and dirt. He had made only a very small grunt when he was hit by the Knight, which could be heard by his father and Logan over their radio com-link. But somehow, his father knew Rodney was in dire straights.

"Rodney!" he shouted over the com-link, hoping against hope that his son was alright. "Rodney!"

Logan summoned up the inner strength to tell General Ackleworth what he had seen.

"Rodney's down, Sir!"

Ackleworth made a strange choking noise and could not reply. He immediately turned around and headed for his son, straight through his attackers. The general carried specially-designed, three-barreled guns. He fired his six rounds with amazing accuracy, taking down two of his pursuers. Quickly holstering his guns, he pulled out his broadsword, which was also specially made for him and was strong enough to take down a heavy sky infantryman. He flew straight at Speer and swung at him. Speer evaded the blow and Ackleworth flew past him.

The general saw his son lying face down in the dirt where he had been thrown from the chariot on impact. He flew to his son and picked up his limp body. He carefully took off Rodney's helmet and saw that his face was smashed, blood pouring out of his nose and crushed cheeks. Ackleworth's eyes filled with tears and he howled with fury.

"Noooooooo!"

The general raced off, bearing his broken son to a nearby transport. He communicated to the pilot of the craft and the doors opened. Ackleworth gently handed Rodney off to the crew inside. He ordered the transport to take off and he flew beside it to give any protection he could. As he followed it into the sky, he looked up to space and saw a remarkable sight. One of the massive Triton battleships was falling through the atmosphere, plunging towards Earth in flames.

It thundered past about thirty kilometers to the west of Ackleworth. The gigantic size of the craft made it seem much nearer, especially when it blotted out the sun for a split-second. Moments later, the Allied battleship careened into the ground and exploded with the force of a multi-megaton nuclear bomb. The blast wave smacked into Ackleworth and the transport craft with tremendous force, considering how far away it was. But, both the craft and the general were able to get back on course.

Down below, the Triton battleship had crashed much closer to Logan and his pursuers. Logan saw the impact and, in his sped-up mental state, he saw the blast wave coming towards him, knocking down and shattering the trees like toothpicks. The blast wave smacked into Logan and the force instantly knocked him unconscious. He hurtled down from the air and hit the ground. His pursuers lay unconscious in the dirt nearby.

In the far distance, two more Triton battleships fell from space, burning through the atmosphere. They were not shot down. Their commanders had piloted them and their crews to their doom on purpose. The huge lasers and most of the smaller guns on the three battleships had been taken out during the intense fighting in space. They had been incapacitated to the point that they were no longer viable for battle and could only wait to be taken by an Apex boarding party, for they did not have enough fuel to retreat.

Ninety percent of their fuel capacity was used up on the journey from the Moon to the Earth. There were Allied space stations along the route, which held fuel, but they were meant to supply the convoy of transports carrying the refugees. That fact was not known to the altogether two hundred thousand crewmen of the Triton armada. It was known only to the top officers on board each battleship. They had all been specially chosen for this suicide mission to rescue more than a billion captured civilians. The commanders' orders were to sink their ships into the Earth's atmosphere and let them plummet to their destruction, so that the Apex could not use them in the future. A heroic — and necessary — sacrifice.

The Admirals in charge of each battleship had a special overriding mechanism in their cabins to take over the controls and steer the Tritons. The thousands of men on board each battleship began to panic when they realized what was happening. As the ships were caught by Earth's gravity and began to fall with greater velocity, the men and women on board were tossed about mercilessly and pressed up against the interior walls. For most, the agony was temporary, because the acceleration of the huge craft soon caused the people inside to black out.

The commanders on board made sure they were on a course that would not crash them into the Allied civilians' rescue area. Before they became unconscious, the Admirals also did their best to aim their ships onto an Apex military target, such as a base, which was what the first Triton had careened into. Thus, like kamikazes, their deaths were accompanied by that of their enemies.

On the ground, about ten kilometers away from Delta Sector, Logan was lying where he had been struck down by the tremendous blast. His armor and chariot were both still intact and attached to him. He awoke just as Marshal Speer and another Kolibri flyer neared. The blast had fortuitously knocked one of Logan's pursuers to the ground closer to him. The other unconscious Kolibri flyer was separated, lying amongst the toppled trees a good distance away, giving the appearance that he was the imposter. Thus, the marshal and the flyer next to him kept their guard on the wrong man.

Suddenly, Logan fired up his chariot and charged them, firing both of his guns. One round went straight through the stomach of the flyer with Speer. Speer adroitly dodged the salvo, immediately drew his guns and fired, striking Logan down.

Logan fell onto a tumbled grouping of trees that had been flattened into the ground. Speer advanced toward him, holding his guns drawn and aimed, but he did not fire. He flew over to Logan and holstered one of his guns, putting the other's barrels right up to Logan's chest armor. Speer then took the helmet off the flyer he had shot down and saw what he had been wishing he would not.

He breathed in deeply and frowned with disappointment and sadness. Then, he noticed that Logan had not been hit anywhere serious. The round apparently struck his chariot's right wing, causing him to go down quickly. Once more, Logan awoke from unconsciousness, shaking his head groggily. Realizing his situation, his heart clenched with terror. He saw Marshal Speer above him, also no longer wearing a helmet, holding a gun to his face now.

"You are a very good learner," Speer said to him. Logan was too frightened to speak. Speer sighed.

"Why, Logan?" he asked, with sincerely pleading eyes. But this fleeting gaze was quickly replaced by anger. **"Why?!"** he roared in Logan's face.

Logan's lips slightly quivered, along with most of his face. He summoned all the strength within him and replied matter-of-factly. "I did it for my family."

Speer winced upon hearing this. "You fool! I had big plans for you! Do you think I would have allowed your family to be harmed?!"

Logan could not answer.

"No matter," Speer sighed. "Now, what to do with you? If I take you in, they will no doubt interrogate you," he remarked coldly, "try to find out what you may know. Unfortunately, that will probably entail torture." The marshal sighed again. "And, I know you don't know anything. You are just a pawn. Let me guess. An Allied spy contacted you when we became friends?"

Logan nodded.

"And when were you contacted?"

"Two weeks ago . . . about."

Speer shook his head, frustrated over the false reasons that caused Logan to betray him.

"And how many contacted you?"

"A guy," Logan replied. "Just one guy."

The marshal looked down his gun barrels at Logan. "I do not imagine that he gave his name."

Logan just shook his head. Then, a look more terrifying than any other dawned on Speer's face. Logan no longer saw sadness, rage, or any other emotion in his former teacher's expression. In his blank stare, the only thing Speer conveyed was complete disassociation. His eyes were cold and vacant.

"Well, my boy. You have acted as a spy and used my kindness and faith in you to harm my government and those under my command." He sighed once more, gazing at Logan from an executioner's stance.

"I saw an amazing future for you in the Apex hierarchy. But, maybe this is good. It is better that I found out that you were not trustworthy now, than to find it out later, when you could have been in a place to do serious damage." He gulped and, for a very brief moment, he seemed sad and plaintive again. But, it was once more fleeting and he quickly became expressionless.

"Take off the armor and get out of the chariot," Speer commanded. Logan did as the marshal instructed and stood there in the full body undergarment worn beneath the Kolibri flyer armor.

"You cannot be allowed to live," the marshal brusquely asserted. "However, I will not simply execute you."

Speer's armor peeled off of him, curling down behind his back. He leapt out of his chariot with his characteristic flip in the air. In a display of tremendous speed and dexterity, he unsheathed the two katanas held within his chariot as he flipped, making the steel blades ring. Landing gracefully, he tossed one of the swords. Logan winced as it stabbed into the ground right in front of him.

Speer's eyes were fixated on Logan's in an icy glare. "Draw your weapon."

Logan gazed at the sword propped upright in the dirt before him. Grabbing the handle, he plucked it from the ground and held it up in a defensive posture. He knew by the look in his eyes that Speer's mind was made up. It was the same look Speer had when he gave the swords to Randy and Marty. Logan did not bother trying to bargain his way out. He just silently gathered all the spiritual, mental, and physical strength he had.

They circled each other a few times. Speer struck the first blow, stepping forward rapidly and slicing downward at Logan. Logan blocked upward and sliced across Speer's chest, but the marshal jumped out of the way with ease. Speer broke a slight smile.

"Very good counter."

They circled each other three more times. Logan decided to strike first this time. He began by moving in closer to the marshal, slowly, getting within distance to where the swords almost touched. Speer had admiration for his young opponent's courage. They both swiped at the other's blade a few times and made quick strikes, meant only to keep the other at bay. Suddenly, Logan struck at the marshal with full force, but Speer had seen the attack coming a long time before. After the weeks of sparring, Speer had come to notice that Logan nearly always tightened his lips, very slightly, before attacking. It was almost imperceptible and would have gone unseen by someone lacking such keen vision and skills for observation.

The marshal dodged and sliced across Logan's left arm. Logan pulled his arm away just in time to avoid having it lopped off. He looked at the large gash hewn across his forearm. The pain seared through his body, emanating from his injured appendage. Blood rolled down to his elbow and dripped to the ground. Logan did not grab for the gash, though. He kept both hands on the sword's handle and maintained a fighting position.

Speer shook his head. "I did not want it to be this way, Logan. You could have been a tremendous asset to the Apex. But, what's done is done. And," the marshal took in a deep breath, summoning up the strength to deal his death blow, "I am sorry to say that, until now, I never fought at my best level with you."

Suddenly, the marshal noticed that Logan was about to attack. Logan tightened his lips slightly and Speer prepared his block and counter-attack. Logan struck in the exact manner that Speer predicted. The marshal blocked the attack and struck back, swiping across at Logan's abdomen, but amazingly, Logan was prepared for this. He blocked the attack, to the marshal's surprise. This was because Logan's first strike was not his true strike. It was to bait Speer to attack.

Logan thrust his blade forward and pierced through the marshal's stomach, driving the point through until it went out of Speer's back.

"You assumed that *I* had," Logan replied, as he too had saved his best fighting for just such a moment. Logan had purposefully conveyed the subtle telegraphing signal of tightening his lips when fighting, and had always done so as he trained with Speer.

Logan pulled his blade from Speer's body, his eyes wide with disbelief that he was able to defeat the marshal. Even with his tricks, Logan knew he would have been no match if Speer had not been so sure of himself. Speer assumed he was going to win, and that was the one thing Logan had going for him. Logan was also fighting for his life, while the marshal was simply putting someone to death with nobility. Inevitably, Speer did not even now unleash his strongest fight against Logan. Had he taken Logan seriously, the marshal would have no doubt won. Instead, he was now dying at Logan's feet.

Speer kneeled down and gazed up at the stars. Logan watched as a totally new expression took over the marshal. It was yet another look he had never seen on Speer's face — pure ease and contentment. It was peace itself. Logan had never seen it before in anyone else for that matter; not in such totality. He was paralyzed with awe as the marshal died before him. With his mind's eye, he caught a glimpse of Speer's aura — his soul. Logan had never seen this intangible thing which others had spoken of before. He could now see it clear as anything else. It was white and yellow; it was light. It radiated out of the marshal like a vapor, moving through everything, including Logan. This energy, this ethereal mist, brought Logan's mind to a more clear and focused state than he had ever attained. He felt everything within himself and around him. He knew who he was and he knew everything relevant: to the moment and to life. That which he did not know he had faith in. He felt nothing but courage and power and, in this, he knew exactly what he needed to do.

Logan jumped back into his Kolibri. He flew over to Speer, picked him up and placed the marshal in his unique chariot and armor. For a moment, Logan felt anguished at seeing all the vitality drained from his former mentor, as he placed him in the bright red Kolibri. But, his sympathy quickly dwindled. Logan drew his guns on the marshal and unloaded a dozen rounds at the body, trying to cover up how Speer had truly died. He grabbed the two katanas and, using the enhanced strength provided by his Kolibri armor, he ripped and crumpled the blades and scattered the unidentifiable pieces over a wide area. Logan took three conventional grenades from the marshal's chariot, and then quickly flew to find his parents, Papa and Francesca.

To his relief, they were fine, patiently hiding where he had left them. He looked up to the sky and saw the Allied transports being shot down in ever greater numbers. He saw that some enormous Apex drill bolt and plasma cannons had been moved out onto the fields. Their massive barrels could be seen in the flickering light of their deadly fire.

Each gun was the size of one of the suites. The plasma cannons fired quickly, like a machine gun, emitting orbs of the hot substance that grew to be three meters in diameter as they flew through the air. The sound these cannons made was like the low thumping produced by a helicopter. Logan could make out humanoid figures being hit by the plasma fire. It was the Allied Hornets coming from all directions, taking a heavy beating by the plasma orbs.

One precise laser strike from the drill bolt cannons caused a transport craft to explode powerfully, each spewing out thousands of refugees into the air, many charred and aflame. Those who were conscious shrieked as they plunged to their deaths. The air was filled with fire and the cries of thousands of terrified human beings. Bodies rained to the ground, often bouncing slightly upon impact.

Assessing the situation, Logan determined that it was too risky to put his family aboard one of the transports. He flew high enough to see far into the distance and spotted a large area of suites that appeared to be more or less safe from the battle. After quickly explaining his plans to his loved ones, Logan grabbed his mother and hauled her to the safe zone. The area was almost completely abandoned of underclassmen. Most had run off to find a transport, although, some were too frightened to leave their suites. Logan found an empty one and left his mother there. He whisked back and forth, bringing Francesca, his grandfather and his father back to this suite.

Content that his family was safe, at least for now, Logan flew out to an area of collapsed trees. He ripped open the shell hold to his chariot and nearly two hundred of the large cartridges fell out. Logan set about breaking off the explosive charges of a few dozen of the cartridges. He took the putty-like explosive and used it to bind together the rest of the cartridges into a large, amorphous block.

He unfurled his armor and jumped out of his chariot, letting it fall onto the makeshift bomb. Taking the three conventional grenades he pilfered out of Speer's chariot, he pulled all the pins and threw them onto the pile, running away with all the strength he had.

An inner power overcame him and he sprinted faster than he could have ever imagined. Without even touching the bark, he hurtled the nearly meter and a half thick trees that lay all around. Six seconds later, the grenades went off and detonated the cartridges, blowing the chariot and armor into an infinite amount of pieces. Logan hid behind a large tree to protect himself from the blast. Amazed at everything he had just done, he stood and laughed almost hysterically.

As he ran across the tall grassy field back to the suites, Logan heard a pair of powerful sonic booms coming from high overhead. It was the Allied Bald Eagles. A split-second later, the plasma cannon near Logan blew up in a spectacular orange explosion. Large chunks of the cannon flew all around for hundreds of meters. Ten other guided bombs struck the anti-aircraft installations around the perimeter. Shrapnel of the destroyed armament cut through the nearby residential complex and a huge mass of molten and flaming metal careened through an entire row of suites. Logan could hear the screams of those still inside the demolished houses. Several people came running out, their clothing and bodies set ablaze.

Without warning, a Hornet flyer crashed to the ground right in front of Logan. Somehow, whether it was by being hacked apart by a Knight's broadsword, or being sawed in half by a Gatling gun, the flyer's legs were taken off from just below the waist. He rolled on the ground, blood ejecting out of his waist in long streams. Mercifully, he went unconscious, his body twitching in spasms. Logan stared wide-eyed at the sight, breathing heavily. It seemed like the end of the world, as mutilated people and machines rained from the sky. He continued running toward where he had left his loved ones.

The next day, everything bizarrely went back to normal. The administration of the Apex work facility played down the dramatic battle that had ensued the previous night. People were summoned to the cafeteria to report any loved ones missing. Tom used his heartache over losing his parents to give credibility to his pretense that he did not know where they were. The Frau did not question him concerning his brother, for to her knowledge, he did not even know where Doug and his family were before the rescue. Francesca also pretended not to know where her father was and her tremendous grief was enough to convince her counselor that she was not lying. This lie, Francesca intensely craved to be true. She wished Jacques was just missing, potentially alive. But, knowing her father's fate, her gut wrenched with an agony she had not even felt when she lost her mother.

She now only had Logan.

The rest of the day was spent relocating the underclassmen still left at the facility into livable houses. For the time being, the counselors allowed Francesca to live with Logan, his parents and Papa. She lived in his room and slept in his bed.

The day after, the morning bell sounded. Today, the underclassmen were made to do only two hours of work, which involved cleaning the fields of debris. Much of the dead matter had been cleaned by Apex professional crews. However, the underclass workers were often horrified by stumbling across a piece of burnt flesh here, a limb there.

Afterwards, Logan walked alone through the field, lost in a trance, reliving everything that had happened, as he had every waking and dreaming moment for the past two days. He wondered how his family who escaped was doing and prayed that they made it to Mars unharmed. He prayed for the souls of his grandparents who had been killed, And for Jacques as well. He also prayed for his friend Rodney, who was so critically injured in the battle. He prayed for his parents, Papa, Francesca and himself. He had never prayed so much in his life. Even as he walked, he muttered prayers to God, never forgetting to bestow blessings as well.

The only thing that kept Logan sane was Francesca. He was meeting her out in the field in a little bit. She was showering and freshening up back at the suite.

Suddenly, Logan had a cloth bag pulled over his head. He was wrestled down by four large, strong hands and arms. The bag was pulled tight across his mouth, so he could not speak or shout. But, there was a hole that let his nose through to breathe. As he struggled, his hands and feet were quickly bound by plastic wire and the two assailants carried him off.

They ran at top speed while carrying him with ease. He heard them running over grass, then shrubs and dirt. They were taking him into the forest. He was certain that this was it. Somehow, Speer had conveyed his part in the Allied rescue operation to the Apex administration. Logan went into shock, assuming he was being taken to his death.

A few minutes later, he was put down and his captors spoke to him. They were wearing electronic devices across their mouths that changed their voices to an unidentifiable robotic sound. But, Logan could clearly understand their words.

"We are not going to hurt you," one said. "We have a message for you from General Ackleworth."

Logan was flooded with relief. The other man placed earpieces through holes in the bag into Logan's ears. He played a sound into the earpieces.

"Nod if you heard that alright," he said to Logan. Logan nodded. "Good," the man said in his monstrous, electronically-garbled voice. "Then just listen up."

Logan sat there on the dirt, hands bound, his eyes closed and in darkness, while the general's voice streamed into his ears.

"Logan, this is General Ackleworth. I want you to first know that your family is fine and well taken care of. Here is your uncle."

"Hey Logan," Doug said. "Buddy, you are an amazing kid. Ha! What am I saying? You're not a kid anymore. You saved me, my wife, my children . . ." he choked up a bit. "General Ackleworth explained to me how I was going to be tried for crimes against life. I can never thank you enough. Stay strong, buddy. Everyone got here okay. You and your parents and Papa just stay strong and we'll get you here soon."

General Ackleworth came back on. "Logan," the general said, "my son told me that you were someone who could be of tremendous value to the Allies. That was proven when Speer made you his apprentice. I was amazed at how well you fought in your first real battle. And, if I had not witnessed it with my own eyes, I would never have believed that you killed Speer in a one-on-one swordfight. I watched from space. I was able to zero in on you with an electronic telescope when you were fighting with him. I saw the whole thing. There was nothing I could do to help you at that point in time. I dispatched some Hornets, but they were all too far away. But, you beat him! I couldn't believe it! Well done, young man.

"And you have no need to fear. You did an excellent job destroying the evidence. Our intelligence shows that there is no suspicion in the Apex hierarchy of your involvement with the mission. Speer's electronic journal was destroyed, along with everything else in the Citadel 1 administrative facility, when a Triton battleship landed on it.

"I can't tell you how, but I can tell you that you and your parents will be rescued soon. Until that time, you will be treated the same as ever under Apex dominion. I am aware that my son told you about Geiseric's final solution. Don't worry. Things will not get any worse because of the other night's operation. We are keeping Geiseric at bay. I can't tell you how this is all happening. What I can say is that Allied High Command has given a sufficient threat to Geiseric, to stall his final solution for mankind." He paused, obviously wanting to give his words a chance to imprint onto Logan's mind.

"I'm sure you are wondering how Rodney is doing," the general sighed and went quiet for a moment. Suppressing his anguish, he cleared his throat and continued. "Well, he is in a coma right now. The doctors don't know if, or when, he will come out of it. But, we obviously have our best people working on him. I must tell you, Logan, he had a lot of good things to say about you. I trust his instincts. He told me not to leave you behind, if he was harmed. But, of course, I could not do that. When I saw him wounded like he was, I felt there was no time to help anyone else. I thought I had lost my son, before. I couldn't lose him again. I'm sorry for not ensuring your safe evacuation. I will do the next best thing, though. I shall make sure that we have intelligence agents looking out for you and your family. We will keep in contact. I can't tell you when or how, but just know that some of the top people in Allied High Command are keeping a watch out for you. Goodbye, Logan . . . and God be with you."

The recording ended and Logan's captors took the earphones out of his ears.

"Nod if you understood everything," said one of the electronically-altered voices.

Logan nodded.

"Alright," the man said, "we are going to take off the bindings on your hands and feet. You leave the hood on your head and stay seated for thirty seconds. Count silently. You then take the hood off and run in the direction you are facing. That is the way back to the suites. You leave the hood where you are seated now. Do you understand?"

Logan nodded again. He heard the men run and began counting in his head. His mind was reeling from information overload. He finished counting and did everything just as he was instructed. He ran out of the forest and into the grassy fields, making his way toward the residential complex. He spotted Francesca, who was worriedly looking around, calling out for him. She saw him and jumped for joy, having become ridden with anxiety thinking that his part in the rescue operation had been discovered by the Apex administration. He ran to her and swept her up in his arms. They shared a long, deep kiss. As he brought her back down to her feet, he just held her.

"Where were you?" she asked.

He laughed, just slightly. "You're not gonna believe it."

Sneak Preview!

The Keepers, Part Two: Tribulation
by Richard Friar

Futurist writer Richard Friar once again dazzles readers with big battles and saucy science in *The Keepers: Part II: Tribulation*. Like the first installment of the trilogy, Friar skillfully blends history and human motivation with his larger-than-life science fiction fare. From invisible commandos whose suits are based on present light-redistribution (cloaking) research being conducted at UC Berkeley, to the new Animalian battle machines modeled after everything from insects to dinosaurs, the readers are shown that not only will this technology be available in the far distant future, but in fact within a few decades. All that would be needed is the catalyst of a man that is Geiseric, the leader of the Apex Empire, who manages to coalesce and utilize the human and natural resources necessary to spark an arms race and war the likes of which humanity has never seen. In *Tribulation*, it is 2040 and the Allies are still up and running at their refuge on Mars, with the readers coming to see how the Apex lost its territories on the Red Planet. The Battle of Olympus Mons takes place atop the largest mountain in the solar system, preceded by a continent-wide, Martian dust and electrical storm. In their fight, the Allies encounter an unforeseen and bizarre enemy, ending in a signature plot reversal that will leave readers stunned. Geiseric's formative days are explored, bringing greater depth and texture to a character that has already enraptured so many fans of the first book. The war technology is once again lavishly illustrated in a high sci-fi style that will appeal to the science fiction fan in everyone, combined with a dramatic writing prose better than one often finds in books of this kind.

The Columbia PARTNERSHIP LEADERSHIP SERIES The Columbia Partnership Leadership : inspiration- and wisdom-sharing vehicle of The Columbia Partnership, a community of Christian leaders seeking to transform the capacity of the North American Protestant church to pursue and sustain vital Christ-centered ministry.

"Those who read this book and follow Hammett and Pierce's coaching will find a win-win approach to reaching both of the cultures present in today's world."

> Bill Easum, of Easum, Bandy & Associates

Many church leaders are asking how to keep people over sixty years of age, who often hold church culture values, while at the same time reach people under forty, who often hold postmodern values. Does satisfying the needs of one group necessarily create a barrier to working with the other? *Reaching People under 40 while Keeping People over 60* looks at the church as it seeks to function in a postmodern world, a global change that encompasses more than generational differences.

"It is sensitive to the current culture, relevant to church today, easy to read and understand."

> Ruby Fulbright, executive director/treasurer, Woman's Missionary Union of North Carolina

"Regardless of your generation, there are truths to be gleaned and put into practice."

> Bo Prosser, coordinator for congregational life, Cooperative Baptist Fellowship

"His dissatisfaction with the status quo in the church world and his vision for transformation is so refreshing."

> Raymond Hoggard, Faith Assembly of God, Winterville, North Carolina

EDWARD H. HAMMETT is senior leadership/discipleship consultant for Baptist State Convention of North Carolina, senior coach and coach trainer for Valwood Christian Leadership Coaching, and a founding partner for The Columbia Partnership. He is the author of many books, including *Spiritual Leadership in a Secular Age* (Chalice Press), and his Web site (www.transformingsolutions.org) contains information for people upgrading ministries to ensure they are more effective and fulfilling in the twenty-first century.

JAMES R. PIERCE is a certified life coach with more than fifteen years of experience in business development and organizational behavior. He has great passion and insight for helping individuals and organizations dealing with change management and has established a Web site (www.thespiritualbandit.com) focused on transitions.

CHALICE PRESS

ISBN 978-0-827232-54-9

9 780827 232549